THE DUFFY OMNIBUS

Dan Kavanagh was [b]orn in Co. Sligo in 1946. After an uncompromising adolescence [h]e came to England, where he has enjoyed a range of employment [at v]arious points on the social spectrum. For a while he was an assis[tant m]arshal at Romford Greyhound Stadium, but a spell in the dom[estic an]d service side of a leading catering firm has also enabled him to s[ample the] high life. He is currently working in London, at jobs he dec[lines to s]pecify, and lives in north Islington.

DAN KAVANAGH

THE DUFFY OMNIBUS

DUFFY
FIDDLE CITY
PUTTING THE BOOT IN
GOING TO THE DOGS

PENGUIN BOOKS

PENGUIN BOOKS

Published by the Penguin Group
Penguin Books Ltd, 27 Wrights Lane, London w8 5TZ, England
Penguin Books USA Inc., 375 Hudson Street, New York, New York 10014, USA
Penguin Books Australia Ltd, Ringwood, Victoria, Australia
Penguin Books Canada Ltd, 10 Alcorn Avenue, Toronto, Ontario, Canada M4V 3B2
Penguin Books (NZ) Ltd, 182–190 Wairau Road, Auckland 10, New Zealand

Penguin Books Ltd, Registered Offices: Harmondsworth, Middlesex, England

Duffy first published by Jonathan Cape 1980
Published in Penguin Books 1988
Fiddle City first published by Jonathan Cape 1981
Published in Penguin Books 1988
Putting the Boot In first published by Jonathan Cape 1985
Published in Penguin Books 1987
Going to the Dogs first published by Viking 1987
Published in Penguin Books 1988
This omnibus edition first published in Penguin Books 1991
1 3 5 7 9 10 8 6 4 2

Copyright © Dan Kavanagh, 1980, 1981, 1985, 1987, 1991
All rights reserved

Printed in England by Clays Ltd, St Ives plc

CONTENTS

DUFFY

To Pat Kavanagh

1

The day they cut Mrs McKechnie, not much else happened in West Byfleet. Not much happened in Pyrford either, or even in the whole of Guildford. It took a week's hard work to fill the crime page of the *Guildford Advertiser*, and even then it was mainly soft-collar, middle-class stuff: company frauds, menopausal shoplifting, dog licence evasion; occasionally there was a disco scuffle, though most of the kids were too scared of forfeiting their Y.C. membership for that. So when they cut Mrs McKechnie, you'd expect the *Advertiser's* story on Page Seven to have led with this fact; but it didn't. It led with the other thing the men did, the afterthought, the nasty, sick thing which even Big Eddy, with his sense of humour, didn't really approve of. That tells you something about journalists.

When Rosie McKechnie opened the front door of 'The Pines' in the middle of an August afternoon, she thought it was the gasman. Anyone else would have thought the same. When you get to the front door, see a shortish figure through the stained-glass panelling, undo the catch, and immediately hear the word 'Gas', you naturally think it's the gasman. You don't think about how long it was since you last had your meter read.

The little man came through the door fast, with his head down, and butted Mrs McKechnie hard in the left breast. Then he pinioned her arms to her sides and simply stood there holding on to her. She felt a sharp, continuing pain in her breast; she looked wildly down at the top of the little man's head and saw that his hair was covered in gauze; she looked up towards the open door and was

3

nerving herself to scream when the second man arrived. He sidled in, closed the door gently behind him, put his finger to the flat, fleshy area which was all that the stocking mask showed of his lips, and went,

'Shhhh.'

She felt calmer when he did this; then, suddenly, she felt very frightened indeed. She opened her mouth to scream, and at once the second man was by her side, his hand clamped over her face.

'Now, no mouth, Rosie,' he whispered, 'no mouth. We don't want mouth. We don't need mouth. Understand?'

She understood. She had little choice. One man was cracking two armfuls of ribs; the other was nearly suffocating her. She swivelled her eyes downwards and could only see a stockinged head against her pearls (oh God, my jewels); sideways, and she could only see a powerful forearm and a blur of brown pullover. She was alone. Mrs Brenan, the char, had left at twelve after dropping her weekly bottle of scent; the only other living thing in the house apart from the three of them was Godfrey, the cat.

The tall one was speaking again, straight into her ear.

'Now listen, Rosie, an' I'll tell you what we're doing. Or rather, I'll tell you what we're not doing. We ain't gonna kill you. We ain't gonna prong you. We ain't gonna hurt you. We ain't gonna steal nothing – well, not unless we see something we *really* fancy. Understand?'

He loosened his grip on her face; she began to open her mouth, changed her mind, and simply nodded.

'Good, Rosie, and no mouth, like I said. Now, we've only come to do one thing, and when we've done, we'll go. A'right?'

She nodded again.

'But we don't want you interfering with us, so I'm afraid we're going to have to tie you up a bit. A'right?'

She nodded. Her jaw hurt from the tall man's hand. The

4

little one hadn't spoken at all, merely held on with a sort of silent frenzy which reminded her of her courting days.

'What I'm going to do first is let go of your mouth, take this fucking mask off, and tie it round your eyes so we won't have to bother about you identifying us. Now, you could scream' (he always seemed to be just ahead of her thoughts) 'but if you do, I'll make sure your dentist gets a good month's work, darling. So – no – fucking – mouth,' he repeated slowly.

Then he softly let go of her face, moved behind her, ripped the stocking off his head, and quickly bound it round her eyes.

'Well done, darling. Now, the little fellow's going to take off his mask now, and put it round your mouth, 'cos we may have to go round the house a bit, and we wouldn't want to have to run back and shut you up.'

She felt her arms being released, and then just stood there, blindfold, as the two men bound her mouth. The stocking pulled her lips back harshly at the corners, then pressed her tongue back and seemed to fill up her entire mouth. It tasted nasty. One of the men knotted it firmly at the base of her skull.

'Sorry about the Brylcreem, darling,' said the tall man. He seemed to be the only one who spoke. 'It was Brylcreem or dandruff. We should of offered you the choice. Not too tight, is it?'

It was; it hurt at the edges of her mouth; it felt as if her lips were being split open. She nodded her head up and down.

'Oh, a bit tight, is it? Sorry about that, Rosie, but you must appreciate our problem. It just wouldn't do its job if it was any looser. Tell you what, this'll make you feel better. Other blokes who are in our line of work, what they do is, they fill your mouth up with cotton wool first. Not nice. Tickles the back of your froat. Makes some of

5

them frow up their stomachs. Heard of one case, some old geezer frowed up his stomach and choked to death on it. Nasty. Not nice, was it?'

He was clearly addressing the little man, who gave a grunt. Then she heard a soft tapping noise. From the tall man's reply, she worked out that the little one must have been tapping the face of his watch.

'O.K., mustn't let the grass grow under our feet. Hang about a sec, Rosie, don't go away.'

They left her for a couple of minutes, then came back and propelled her into what she worked out was her lounge. They sat her down in a wheel-backed dining chair which one of them must have brought from the kitchen. Then she felt her ankles being tied together with something that wasn't rope. Finally, they bound her hands.

'Now, that's two pairs of best nylons, Rosie. Best Marks and Sparks. Autumn Beige we picked for you. Thought that was the sort of shade someone like you might wear.' It wasn't, but why this familiarity anyway? If they'd come to steal something why didn't they just get on with it? But they couldn't just have come to steal, else why would they have bothered to find out her name? How did they manage to come on one of the two afternoons when she didn't regularly have friends round, or go out to bridge? Had they been watching the house? They must have been. And what the hell did they want? How long would it be before Brian came home? Maybe they were after Brian for some reason? No, they couldn't be – they wouldn't have come so early if they'd wanted Brian.

The tall man with the quiet voice with bits of London rough in it was still going on about the stockings.

'Two pairs of frees, Rosie. Better than having the Fuller's brush man round, isn't it? I mean, if you don't like the shade, you can always give them away, can't you? I should look on the nylons as the silver lining to this little business, Rosie, I really would. An' as I say, if they don't

6

fit you, they might fit Barbara, mightn't they? Yes, I think they might fit Barbara.'

Rosie McKechnie didn't know anyone called Barbara. She might have known a Barbara or two in her teens or twenties, but she didn't know anyone called Barbara now. She was in her late forties, and couldn't remember meeting a Barbara for twenty years. So why had the man repeated the name? It sounded so deliberate.

There was a pause. When the tall man started speaking again, his tone was almost apologetic.

'I'm afraid we come to the hard bit now, Rosie. You see, we had to tell you a little lie to begin with, just to get you to co-operate. Well, two lies, actually, I suppose. I mean, we aren't from the gas, either.'

He paused again. Rosie was suddenly very frightened indeed. Her body told her she was frightened. She felt a trickle of pee come from her, then stop.

'It's a'right, we ain't gonna kill you, we don't deal in that. We ain't gonna prong you, neither, though, if you'll allow me to say so, Mr McKechnie's a very lucky man. But I'm afraid we're gonna have to cut you just a little. It'll hurt a bit – there's no way we can avoid that, but we'll try and make it hurt as little as possible. I mean, we're not sadists, you know. And the boss did make his instructions very clear. So it won't be as bad as it could be.'

Rosie McKechnie began to cry into her blindfold. She was sure they were going to cut her face. The face that Brian had picked out from the chorus line of *Ahoy There!* on a foggy evening in November 1952. He'd picked it out from the sixth row of the stalls, despite the fact that she was wearing a matelot suit and had a silly cap on her head with a red bobble on the top of it. In France, Brian had explained to her, girls go up to sailors and ask if they can touch their bobbles for luck; the price is a kiss. When Brian had arrived backstage with a bunch of Michaelmas daisies and asked if he could touch her bobble, she hadn't

7

understood; or rather, she thought she'd understood all too clearly. But he hadn't meant that, as he'd explained to her over dinner. And that was when he first called her 'My little chorus girl'. Now his little chorus girl, the one he'd picked out from the sixth row, was going to have her face cut. She knew it.

'Time for Stanley, I'm afraid,' said the tall man softly. Stanley: that must be the little fellow's name; she'd better remember it. 'Now, Mrs McKechnie,' (he had suddenly become formal) 'what we're going to do is make a little cut, just a nick really, round about your shoulder.' Thank God – they weren't going for her face. 'Now it'll hurt a bit, but you ain't going to bleed too hard, few stitches, eight to ten I'd say, and, well, no backless dresses for a while, but you'll be surprised how quickly you'll get over it.'

She waited. There was nothing else she could do but wait and see what happened next.

What happened next was that the little man dug in his pocket and pulled out a thick, heavy lino-cutting knife with a retractable blade. It was gunmetal blue, and had a little serrated catch on the top which, when you slid it forward, brought the blade into view. At a sign from the tall man, he walked out of the lounge, down a corridor past a few framed theatre bills, and into the kitchen. He didn't notice Godfrey sitting on the dresser; but Godfrey certainly noticed him.

Godfrey was the McKechnies' large, paunchy, grey-haired tom cat. A big, swaggery, macho cat with firm ideas about territoriality. The sort of cat who would pin females up against the wall and accuse them of being frigid if they wouldn't submit. Even in the feline world, where selfishness and cunning are cardinal virtues, Godfrey was an outstandingly mean cat. Other cats fought shy of him; some of the smaller local dogs had been seen crossing the road to avoid him; not even his owners really liked him.

They gave him everything he needed and stayed out of his way as much as possible.

As the little man passed the dresser, he heard a sharp, sibilant hiss. He turned and saw Godfrey. The little man thought he knew his way round cats, and he reached out a hand to tickle Godfrey's chin. Godfrey didn't like his chin being tickled; he didn't really like humans coming near him. As the hand approached, he slashed at it with his right paw.

Godfrey kept his claws in good trim. Three white lines appeared on the back of the man's hand; after a few seconds they seemed to pop, and beads of blood appeared. The man looked at his hand disbelievingly. He stood there and glanced slowly round the kitchen. When his eye fell on the fridge-freezer, he suddenly shot out a hand and grabbed Godfrey by the neck before he could move, walked quickly across the kitchen, pulled open the door of the freezer section, threw the cat in, and slammed the door. He turned, and looked round the kitchen again: bar area, concealed ceiling lighting, stainless steel surfaces, gadgets everywhere; a cooker with an eye-level spit-roaster. He nodded to himself.

Then he walked over to the sink and ran the cold tap. First he washed the blood off his hand, and held it there for a couple of minutes to try and stop the bleeding. After that he filled a kettle and set it to boil. When the steam began to rise from the spout, he took his blue knife, unsheathed the blade, and held it in the steam for about a minute.

When he got back to the lounge the tall man was looking impatient for the first time that afternoon. The back of the woman's dress was now open.

'Took yer time.'

The little man held out his right hand and spoke the only two words Rosie McKechnie ever heard him say.

'Focking caht.' It was a lighter voice than the other

man's with a strong flavour of Irish in it. A few fresh beads of blood were beginning to pop on his hand as he took the knife in his right hand, laid his left flat on the middle of the woman's back, bent her forwards, and made a sudden but careful vertical incision in her right shoulder a couple of inches away from the strap of her bra. The pressure on the knife made the blood run again from the little man's hand; automatically, he brushed it off on the back of the woman's dress.

The tall man was speaking again.

'Three inches. The boss said three inches.' Rosie was bent right forward now, hunched with pain. 'And three inches it seems to be.' He crouched down beside the gagged woman and spoke to her almost gently. 'Lean back, love, you're only making yourself bleed more like that.' She sat up, trying not to pull on the wound. 'Eight to ten, you'll need, I reckon. Maybe twelve. You'll be O.K. We could give you some drink if you like.'

She shook her head. She didn't drink spirits; never had. A glass of brandy now was more likely to make her throw up than the taste of hair cream from the little man's mask.

'We'll be off soon,' said the tall man.

The little man took the knife back to the kitchen to wash it off. He turned on the cold tap, held the blade under it for a minute or so, dried it on a J-cloth, and returned the knife to his pocket. Then he put his hand under the tap again, though the blood by now had almost stopped coming. With his handkerchief he dabbed dry the three parallel red weals on the back of his hand, and walked across to the cooker with the eye-level spit-roaster. He turned one of the switches to Full, and then wandered thoughtfully across towards the fridge-freezer.

Back in the lounge, the tall man was loosening the stocking over Mrs McKechnie's eyes.

'Now, if you shake your head a lot, this should work itself off in a bit,' he said. 'Sorry we can't do more for you, but you must understand our position. We gotta do what the boss says. It isn't worth anyone's while not doing what the boss says.'

She heard the sound of the little man returning from the kitchen.

'All cleared up in there?' the tall man asked, and got a grunt in reply. 'Yeah, I've wiped here as well,' he went on, and then turned towards Rosie McKechnie for the last time.

'Well, so long, Rosie, we'll be off now. Oh, and, er, hope the stockings fit. Fit someone, anyway.'

A few seconds later the front door closed quietly. Mrs McKechnie felt her dress wet to the waist with her own blood. She scarcely had the strength to shake the gag free from her eyes. Eventually it fell off, and she found herself staring out of the window at her back garden. At least, she thought, they haven't cut my face. At least they haven't taken anything. At least they haven't smashed things out of malice, like burglars are supposed to do. But then, were they burglars anyway? Brian would be home in a few hours; he would be able to tell her what had happened; to tell her why.

When Brian got back from London he thought his wife had burnt the dinner again. A heavy, slow, red-faced man, he stood in the hall puffing from his walk from the station, uncertain whether to go into the kitchen or the lounge first. From the kitchen came a pungent smell of burning, though somehow it wasn't the charred-dinner smell he'd had to get used to over the years; it was something odder, sharper. It smelt as if mattresses were being singed. From the lounge he could hear muffled sobs: Rosie blubbing again about having spoiled his dinner. Her tears always disarmed whatever irritation he felt on these occasions.

Brian was a considerate husband, and he headed for the lounge rather than the kitchen. A few more minutes' charring wouldn't make much difference. Then he saw Rosie tied to the chair. He rushed across to her and was about to put his heavy arms around her when he saw the blood. He untied her mouth gag, then freed her wrists and feet. As he held her head between his palms and kissed her on the cheeks and forehead, she looked at him with the eyes of a lost child and couldn't manage a word. After a minute or so of this traumatised silence he went to the phone and called his private doctor; then he called the police. As he put the phone down and walked back towards her, Rosie suddenly spoke.

'Who's Barbara?'

'Barbara? I don't know. Why?'

But she merely replied, 'Who's Barbara?' in a distant voice.

McKechnie frowned and hurried off to try and rescue what was left of the dinner. Barbara was the name of his current mistress. But she was a mistress of only a few weeks – how could anyone have found out? And why bother? What had it got to do with his wife being assaulted? Why were the Georgian candlesticks still safely on the lounge table? Why had nothing been touched?

When he reached the kitchen, he discovered there was something in the house which had been touched. What was revolving slowly on the eye-level spit-roaster was definitely not Brian McKechnie's dinner.

2

The doctor came, inserted thirteen stitches, sedated Mrs McKechnie, and put her to bed. An hour later two police-men arrived, apologising for the delay and blaming it on undermanning; they discovered that the victim was heavily drugged, asked Mr McKechnie a few questions without getting anywhere, told him not to touch any-thing – 'What do you mean, *anything*?' he replied – took a cursory look at doors and windows, and said they would be back the next day.

Mr McKechnie sat over a bowl of Heinz oxtail soup wondering why anyone should want to attack his wife and tell her the name of his mistress at the same time. He wasn't aware of having any particular enemies. His mis-tress, who doubled as his secretary, wasn't married; and though she wore her hair prettily coiled up on the top of her head, smiled at strangers and waggled her bottom more than she needed to when she walked, he wasn't aware of having any rivals for her affections. Besides, if a rival did come along, Brian wasn't that attached to her: if she wanted to go, she could. His days of fighting to keep a woman were over. Not, for that matter, that he was in any state to fight. The only exercise he ever took was with a knife and fork; he panted after climbing stairs, sweated a great deal, was moderately overweight, and only the previous year had had a minor, admonitory heart attack.

The next day a detective-sergeant from the Guildford C.I.D. sat on Rosie McKechnie's bed with a colleague. Gradually they pieced together what she knew; though mostly it was what she didn't know. A tall man with a roughish Cockney accent and a brown pullover; a short

13

man with a possibly Irish accent who had 'passed a re-mark', as Rosie delicately put it, about Godfrey. The short man might have been called Stanley. There had been two – almost three – deliberate mentions of someone called Barbara. There had been mentions of someone called the Boss.

'Had any quarrels, Mrs McKechnie?'

'No – I don't quarrel. Except with the char. What sort of quarrels?'

'Oh, arguments, disagreements, you know, *words*, that sort of thing.'

'No.'

'Know anyone called Stanley?'

'Well, there's Brian's uncle, but . . .'

'We understand, madam. What about Barbara?'

'I've been trying to think. No, no one, absolutely no one.'

'Well, looks like we'll have to rely on forensics. Unless your husband can give us any assistance, of course.'

The two policemen walked slowly downstairs with Mr McKechnie.

'Problems, sir,' said Bayliss, the detective-sergeant, a sandy-haired, slightly truculent man in a blue suit. 'Problems. No identification; or none that doesn't leave us with most of the population of England under suspicion. No dabs, according to my colleague. No theft. No obvious motive, you'll agree?'

'None that I can see.'

'And a particularly vicious crime. Not forgetting the cat, of course. Now the problem is, work of a maniac, pair of maniacs, or not? If it were just the cat, I'd say yes. There are some pretty sick people about. I've known maniacs toss cats off high buildings, just for kicks. But spitting and roasting, that's something new to me. What about you, Willett?'

His colleague thought for a bit about the crimes against

14

felines that he'd come across. 'I've had drownings, and I've had, you know, mutilations,' he replied. 'I've heard about a jerry-can job, but that was some time ago. Nothing like this.'

'But then you see, sir,' went on Bayliss, 'the injury to your wife seemed planned, didn't it? I mean, they knew her name, they seemed to know when she'd be in, and, if you'll excuse me, they knew exactly what they intended to do to her. Didn't they?'

'You're the experts.'

'Yes, I suppose we are. Kind of you to say so, sir. So what I'm driving at, sir, is motive. Now, Willett, what did Mrs McKechnie say they said about this Stanley fellow?'

Willett opened his notebook and turned back a few pages. 'Something like, "Time for Stanley", she said she thought the tall one said.'

'"Time for Stanley". Almost sounds as if he was letting the other one loose. Sort of letting him off the leash, almost. Know any Stanleys, sir?'

'My uncle, but . . .'

'No, quite. No one else?'

'Afraid not.'

'All right. Now, let's turn to the easy one. Who's Barbara?'

'I've no idea.'

'You a bit of a ladies' man, are you, sir?'

'What do you mean? Certainly not.'

'Never played around at all, sir? You must have had your chances, if you don't mind the phrase. Never stepped out of line?'

'Certainly not. I'm fifty-five. I had a heart attack last year. I should think the exercise would kill me.' (It was true, Barbara and he did have to take it a bit easy every so often; it would be a great way to go, he used to think, if only he were able to face the embarrassment. Though of course, he probably wouldn't be there to face it.)

'So you and Mrs McKechnie . . . ?' Bayliss was doubtless referring to the fact that Rosie had her own bedroom.

'Since you seem to get a kick out of knowing that sort of thing, the answer's no, actually, we don't any more. We're still great friends, though.'

'I don't doubt it sir, not for a minute. Now what about your wife? Does she . . . have any callers?'

'What the hell makes you think you've got the right to ask that sort of question? My wife's been knifed, she hasn't been raped. Why don't you look for the weapon or something? What on earth is the point of this sort of questioning?'

'Well, you don't always know that till you get the answers. So, no Stanley, no Barbara; no fannying about; and what about this person called the Boss?'

'Could be anyone. Everyone's got a boss.'

'I suppose that's true, Mr McKechnie. It's a funny tale though, isn't it? I mean, here are these two people who break into your house, assault your wife, kill your cat, and mention three people's names, and nobody seems to know anything about any of them. Who's *your* boss, Mr McKechnie?' Bayliss didn't seem particularly friendly.

'I'm my own boss.'

'Tell us about what you're boss of, Mr McKechnie.'

McKechnie and Co Ltd. Registered company. Trading head office Rupert Street, W.1. Importers and distributors of toys, jokes, novelties, disguises, indoor fireworks, magic kits and funny masks. Policemen's helmets for sale, though strictly in junior sizes. Trade a bit seasonal, low in summer, high towards Christmas, naturally. No business difficulties. Turnover in six figures. Stock in trade held in two small warehouses, one in Lexington Street and one in a little courtyard off Greek Street. A small, profitable, honest business. That was McKechnie's story.

'Sounds almost too good to be true, sir. You wouldn't

mind if we came up one day and talked to you at your office?'

'Of course not. I'm going to stay at home and look after my wife for the rest of the week. You can come and see me, if there's any point in it, early next week.'

'That's very co-operative of you, sir. Now about this end of things. I'll be sending the police surgeon round tomorrow to have a look at your wife's wound – see if he's got any sort of an idea what the weapon was. We'll take away the cat, if that's all right with you; and we'd like the dress your wife was wearing too. And if you do remember about any of those names, you'll let us know, won't you, sir?'

'Of course.'

As soon as the police had left, McKechnie called his office. Barbara answered the phone; she was bound to – she was the only person there. He asked her if he hadn't always been nice to her, and she said he had. He asked her if she'd do him a favour and she said she hoped it was the same one as usual because she enjoyed it. He said no, not this time, you little temptress, it was a bit different. He'd had a few problems which he'd explain to her some other time. He wanted her to close down the office and take three weeks' paid holiday. No, she could still have her annual three weeks as well, at a later date. No, he wasn't trying to tell her she was being sacked. Yes, he was still very fond of her. Yes, they'd do that again soon too. Soon, soon. And he'd send a cheque for a month's salary to her home address.

He made a second phone call, to a temp agency in Shaftesbury Avenue, and asked for a secretary for a couple of weeks, starting the following Monday. Then he sat down and wondered whether he was doing the right thing.

This was on a Tuesday. On the Wednesday the police surgeon came, examined Mrs McKechnie, offered his condolences about Godfrey, and left, muttering about Islamic methods of punishment.

On the Thursday two things happened. The *Guildford Advertiser* came out, with a headline halfway down Page Seven reading: BIZARRE PET DEATH IN MYSTERY BREAK-IN: MANIACS HUNTED. And Det-Sgt Bayliss turned up again with Willett in tow.

'We've had the surgeon's report,' said Bayliss, 'and I think we can rule out your Uncle Stanley.' McKechnie looked puzzled. Bayliss pulled out a short, typed document from his briefcase and read from it: '"Victim . . . Wound . . . Surrounding Area . . ." Ah, here we are, "Possible Instrument: medium to heavy knife with fine blade. Small area of blade used, so probably not flick-knife type of instrument, or sharpened domestic knife. Some sort of modelling knife, perhaps, or specialist wood-cutting instrument. No evidence of previous usage of the instrument was obtainable, since the wound had already been thoroughly cleansed by time of police examination; but possibly some specialist instrument, like a Stanley knife."'

Bayliss looked up and smiled in a self-satisfied way; then he nodded to Willett, who dug in his notebook and quoted back Mrs McKechnie's words: '"Something like 'Time for Stanley'".'

Bayliss still looked pleased with himself. McKechnie couldn't imagine why the neutralisation of one of the very few clues Bayliss had should afford him any pleasure. Bayliss explained,

'Well, before we were looking for everyone called Stanley. Now we're only looking for people with Stanley knives. It must increase our chances a little.'

McKechnie didn't know if he was being flippant or simply foolish.

The following week Bayliss and Willett came up to McKechnie's Rupert Street office. They were shown in by his new secretary, Belinda. He'd deliberately told the agency that he wanted a really efficient girl because he was fed up with tarts in short skirts who doubled the size of his Tipp-Ex bill and tried to make up for it by flashing their panties at him when they were filing. The agency understood what he was saying, wrote 'Religious' on the back of his card in their private shorthand, and sent him Belinda, a girl with a slight limp who wore a huge silver cross between her breasts as if to ward off sweaty male hands. McKechnie was happy with her, even though she wasn't noticeably more efficient than the girls who cutely pointed their gussets at him on their first afternoon.

As Bayliss arrived, he asked casually how long Belinda had worked there; but McKechnie was already prepared for that. He always had temps, he said, because he found them more reliable, and it wasn't hard to master the work, and he sometimes closed down the office for a few weeks, and anyway, the office was too small to risk getting stuck with a secretary you didn't get along with. Oh, he got them from all sorts of temp agencies – sometimes one, sometimes another; he couldn't even remember where he'd got Belinda from – they could ask her if they wanted to. His previous secretary's name? Oh, Sheila, and before that, Tracy, and before that, oh, Millie or something.

When Bayliss and Willett left, McKechnie felt as if he had just pulled off a deal. He walked up to Bianchi's and treated himself to the best the kitchen could offer, just to show how pleased he was with himself.

The next week he got the first phone call. Belinda told him that there was a Mr Salvatore on the line.

'Mr McKechnie?'

'Yes.'

'And how are you today?'

'Fine.'

'Quite sure you're all right?'

'Yes, quite. What can I do for you?' These immigrants

did go on a bit – thought it was all part of British civility. McKechnie knew one Greek retailer who, by the time he got to the end of all his preliminary bowing and scraping, had usually forgotten what he was ringing about. Then he had to ring back with his order later.

'And your wife, Mr McKechnie, is she well?'

McKechnie bridled, though the man's tone hadn't changed. 'She's fine. What can I do for you?'

'Because where I come from, we have a saying – a man's wife is the centrepiece of his table. Don't you think that is a pretty phrase, a gallant phrase?'

McKechnie hung up. Whoever the man was, he could either come to the point or bugger off. Besides, McKechnie wanted a little time to think what might be going on.

He didn't get it. The phone went again almost at once, and Belinda said apologetically,

'You're reconnected, Mr McKechnie. Sorry you got cut off, one of my fingers must have slipped.' That was the sort of secretary you got nowadays – the old sort, and even some of the gusset-flashers, at least knew when they'd cut you off. This lot didn't know whether they had or not; they merely assumed – and it was a correct assumption – that they had.

'Terrible, this telephone system of yours, Mr McKechnie,' said the voice. 'They tell me it all went wrong with nationalisation, but of course I do not remember that myself.'

'Are you calling me on business, Mr . . .'

'Salvatore. Well, yes and no, as you say. I am not in the business of ringing up strangers simply to reduce the Post Office's deficit, anyway. So, I tell you why I am ringing. I am ringing to say that I am sorry about the cat.'

'The . . .'

'Yes, Mr McKechnie, it was, how shall I say, you understand French, Mr McKechnie, it showed *un peu trop d'enthousiasme.* In simple language, the lads got carried away.'

'You . . . fucker.' McKechnie didn't really know what to say; he didn't in fact care much about the cat; it had always been, as she herself put it, Rosie's baby.

'Well, I accept your rebuke. Now, the second thing I have to say is, I hope very much that your lady wife is recovering from her unpleasant ordeal. And I suggest that you do not hang up.' The tone had hardened. McKechnie did not reply. The voice went on. 'Well, I take the liberty of inferring from your silence that she is, as you put it, on the mend.'

Again, McKechnie did not reply.

'And the third thing I have to say to you is this. Don't you think it is extraordinary that the police have no idea what might have happened, or why, or who would have done such a thing? By the way, I assume you did not tell them about your pretty secretary who seems not to be working for you any more?'

McKechnie still did not reply. He was trying to write down on his telephone pad as much as possible of the conversation.

'No, you did not. I think I can tell that. So, if I may sum up, Mr McKechnie, what I am saying to you is this. Isn't it extraordinary, and isn't it a little frightening, that two such unpleasant things could happen in your very own home, and that the police, after full investigation, have found no clues that are of any use to them? Is it not ironic that the one clue which might have been of use was denied to them by you? It is not a pretty situation, is it, Mr McKechnie, at least not for you? I mean, the point is, isn't it, that something similar, or even, though I do hesitate to say so, something quite a lot worse, could happen, and you would be fairly certain that once again the police would not be able to be of any assistance? What do you say to that, Mr McKechnie?'

'I say, you never can tell.'

'And I say to you, Mr McKechnie, that some of us can, some of us can tell. I mean, take the present case. Say you go back to your police. Say you tell them you're sorry, you lied, you didn't tell them about Barbara. Do you think that would make them redouble their energies, if you went and told them you had been lying to them? They are only human, after all, Mr McKechnie, they would merely think you had been telling more lies, they would probably say to each other, as you put it, "Stuff him". And then, if they did take you seriously, where has this new piece of information taken them? How much nearer are they to their quarry? There are other crimes every day, even in your neck of the woods.'

'What do you want?'

'Ah, I am happy that you asked me that, Mr McKechnie. It shows at least that you are not a stupid man. What I want you to do is to *think*. What I want you to think about is what people call the angles. That is all that I want you to do, for the moment. And now I will get off this line and let you go about your lawful business.'

The phone was put down.

McKechnie dutifully started to think about the angles. Was he being preshed? Not yet, anyway. Was he being softened up for being preshed? If so, they were going about it in a pretty extreme manner. Was his wife safe at home? Was he safe? Should he go back to the Guildford police? Should he go along to the station here, West Central, up in Broadwick Street? Should he perhaps try and get the investigation transferred to West Central, and hope that the bit about Barbara would get dropped on the way? But what did he really have to tell them here? One thing he could do was go and have a chat to Shaw, the detective-sergeant at West Central he'd had a few drinks with now and then. Maybe he'd do that.

He rang West Central, and was told that Shaw was on

22

holiday for a week. Did he want to talk to anyone else? No, he didn't.

Two days later Belinda buzzed him and said she had Mr Salvatore on the line again.

'Mr McKechnie, still well? Good. I won't take up all that much of your time. I take it you've had your think. You haven't been back and made your little confession, of course.'

McKechnie was silent.

'No, of course you haven't. Now, I'll tell you what you're going to do for me. You're going to give me some money. Not very much money. Very little money, really. Twenty pounds. No, let's say twenty-five. Now, you go to your bank in the morning – or you take it from your float, I really don't mind which – and you wait for me to ring again and tell you what I want you to do with it. It's quite straightforward, Mr McKechnie. Oh, and you can be assured that even if you haven't done this before, I have.'

The phone went dead. McKechnie took a deep breath, put on his jacket, told Belinda he was going out for a few minutes, and walked round to West Central police station.

West Central was one of those stations which they kept on not getting around to modernising. Ten years ago they took away the blue lamp mounted on its wall bracket, and five years after that they put up a new sign, a long thin white one, lit by a neon tube, which said WEST CENTRAL POLICE STATION. But then things slowed down considerably: the grey paint inside got blacker; the canteen plates got more chipped by the year; tempers got shorter.

Shaw was still on holiday, and instead McKechnie was shown in to see Superintendent Ernest Sullivan, twenty-five years in the force, ten on this patch, a surly, fleshy man unimpressed by all forms of crime and by most forms of complainant. McKechnie told his story – the assault on his wife, the spitting of his cat, the phone calls, the demand for money – while Sullivan shuffled some papers round his desk and occasionally picked his ears with a matchstick.

When he'd finished, Sullivan merely said,

'Never heard the cat thing before. Heard the rest before. Must take quite a bit of strength to push a spit through a cat. Probably get scratched, wouldn't you?'

McKechnie was impatient with the amount of interest shown by the police in the death of his cat.

'What about the wounding of my wife and the blackmail?'

'How do you know it is blackmail?'

'Well of course it's blackmail.'

'Did the man say what he'd do if you didn't pay?'

'No.'

'Then maybe he's just trying it on. Maybe the two things aren't connected. Maybe he just read your local paper and thought he'd try his luck.'

That couldn't be the case, McKechnie thought, as the Salvatore fellow had known about Barbara, and nothing of that had been in the paper. But all he said was, 'Not very likely, is it?'

'It's possible.' Sullivan seemed keen for the case to give him the minimum trouble. McKechnie waited. Eventually, Sullivan shifted in his seat, picked his ear again, and said, 'I suppose I could get the case transferred up here.' He showed little sign of enthusiasm. 'Shall I do that?'

'If you think that's best. Whatever's happening, it's obviously got nothing to do with where I live.'

Sullivan nodded, got slowly to his feet, and disappeared. When he came back, he seemed, if possible, even less keen on McKechnie's presence in his office. If only McKechnie would go away, his look implied, he could get on and give his ears a real cleaning out.

'Well, they're sending me the file,' he said. 'Chap named Bayliss. Said that forensics reported the cat had been on the spit for about three hours. Nasty smell, was there?'

'I don't remember.'

'Come, come, Mr McKechnie, I'm sure you do. And, er, while we're on the subject of nasty smells, there's a bit of a one in here, isn't there?'

McKechnie looked round.

'No, you don't need to look round. I mean, there's a bit of a nasty smell coming from your chair, isn't there, Mr McKechnie? Not always kept our own nose exactly clean, have we? Bit of a fiddler, really, aren't you, Mr McKechnie? It is going to be McKechnie for a bit longer, isn't it? Because if you're thinking of changing again, I'd better nip out and update our file.'

'That was all years ago.'

It had also been two hundred miles away. A bit of bad company, temptation, it could happen to anybody. You can't run a business without being tempted occasionally. But how had Sullivan got hold of his record?

'It's all years ago,' he repeated. 'I thought there was a Rehabilitation of Offenders Act or something.'

'There is, Mr McKechnie, there is.' Sullivan was livening up. He seemed to be enjoying this part of the conversation. 'But it doesn't apply to us, now, does it? Or not the way they meant it to. And when someone moves into our patch, in however small a way, we like to know just a little about him.'

'Well, you know, Superintendent, you can't run a business without being tempted occasionally.'

'Yes, I'm sure, Mr McKechnie. I'm just surprised, reading our little file on you, that there weren't more road accidents up in Leeds.' He chuckled. 'What with all this stuff falling off the backs of lorries.'

McKechnie was silent.

'Still, I suppose we'd better let bygones be bygones.' Sullivan sounded as if he didn't hope to convince even himself of this principle, let alone anyone else.

'Turning to my current problem, Superintendent.'

'Of course, of course.'

'What should I do about the twenty-five quid?'

'Pay it and write it off against tax as a bad debt.'

'Are you serious?'

'Completely. Isn't that what your natural instinct would be to do? Isn't that what any self-respecting fiddler would do?'

'You're telling me to piss off, aren't you?'

'No, I'm not, I'm merely saying Business is business. Your business involves writing off small amounts of money every so often. My business involves not wasting the time of my men if some local villain reads a Guildford newspaper and squeezes a pony out of another local fiddler. Funny how private enterprise springs up, isn't it, Mr McKechnie? We had a villain once, he used to read the deaths column in the *Telegraph*, and send out small bills for tailoring alterations addressed to the dead man. The deceased's family used to get the bill – it was only four or five quid, he wasn't greedy – and most of the time they paid up. Natural instinct, really. Mean not to pay your dearly beloved's bills, isn't it?'

'What went wrong?'

'Ah, yes, something always goes wrong, doesn't it? Except that sometimes nothing goes wrong, and then there's no story at all. What went wrong was as simple as what went right: he made the mistake of sending in a bill to a deceased member of a family tailoring business. Everyone was quite amused really. No one was hurt, I suppose. He only did a couple of years.'

'Have you heard of this man called Salvatore?'

'Oh yes, I've heard of Salvatore. Big local villain. Girls, smokes, bit of smack, mossing, tweedling; a very democratic villain, Mr Salvatore.'

McKechnie was surprised; and cross. 'Why didn't you

26

tell me earlier? Now you can tap his phone when he calls me tomorrow.'

'Patience, Mr McKechnie.' Sullivan seemed to be enjoying himself again; he'd even forgotten about his ears. 'We can't tap phones like that, you know. All sorts of red tape involved. Have to get Home Office permission; Home Secretary's signature. Now he wouldn't give his signature for a pony's worth of squeeze, would he?'

'Why not?'

'Well, I'll tell you why not, Mr McKechnie. Because Mr Salvatore no speaka da English, only speaka da Eyetalian. Tutto his life. And in the second place, he isn't with us any more. He died about five years ago. Nice old fellow. All the boys here chipped in for a wreath.'

'So who did I talk to?'

'Well, there aren't any other Salvatores around. So I reckon you've got yourself a joker, Mr McKechnie, that's what I reckon you've got.'

'So what do I do?'

'You do what you like, Mr McKechnie. You pay up if you want to, you tell him to fuck off if you want to.'

'And if he doesn't fuck off?'

'Well, put it this way. If he carries on and gets up to a ton, you come back and see me. Under a ton, it's just not worth our while.' There was a meaningful look in Sullivan's eye as he said this. Was he giving McKechnie a price?

The next morning, Brian took Rosie breakfast in bed, as he had done every morning since the attack, and sat downstairs with his paper and the letters. They had always opened each other's letters; it seemed a sign of how close they were. There were a couple of business letters for Brian, some circulars, and a small brown envelope addressed to Mrs B. McKechnie. It felt fatter in one corner than elsewhere, and the envelope seemed a little stained. He opened it carefully, looked inside, and then glanced quickly towards the stairs in case Rosie might be coming down.

The first thing he withdrew from the envelope was a photo of Barbara. It wasn't one he'd seen before. She was walking down a street, somewhere in London by the looks of it; to judge from the angle of the photograph, it might have been taken from a passing car. It was a good likeness, but he couldn't tell quite how pretty she was looking because the photograph was stained. Half her face had been smudged where the emulsion had run. He looked in the envelope again and saw why: a used condom was slowly leaking its contents. He screwed the envelope up and pushed it into his pocket. Then he turned over the photograph. Typed on the back, in capitals, he read:

DEAR MRS MCKECHNIE WE THOUGHT YOU MIGHT LIKE TO
SEE A SNAP OF BARBARA

McKechnie looked back at the photo. He gradually made out one or two of the out-of-focus street signs – a clothes shop, a bank, a theatre. It had been taken in Shaftesbury Avenue, just round the corner from his office.

On his way to work he threw away the envelope with the condom in it. At his desk, he tried to think about that morning's orders, but instead found himself waiting all the time for the phone to go. Eventually, of course, it did.

'Mr McKechnie, and how are you today? As well as always, I trust?'

'Fine.'

'Your wife well?'

'Yes, why shouldn't she be?'

'Why indeed. Unless, of course, she didn't enjoy opening her letters this morning.'

'I wouldn't know – I left before the post came.' He wasn't quite sure why he lied; he was just fed up with being outguessed all the time.

'Anyway, to business. We're a little displeased with

you, Mr McKechnie. You'll understand why, of course.'

'No.'

'Come, come, it really was very silly of you to go to the police. What makes you think that one branch of the police force is likely to be any more efficient than another? I'm sure they can't have been much help to you.' (He didn't know how right he was) 'Anyway, since you seem interested in raising the risk, I'm afraid I'm going to have to raise the stakes. The twenty-five goes up to fifty because of your little indiscretion. But, just to show you that you're dealing with businessmen, you can have another day to pay. Fifty by tomorrow, and I'll ring you in the morning about delivery.'

'How do I know you're serious?'

'Suck it and see, Mr McKechnie, suck it and see.' The phone went dead.

He rang Sullivan and explained what had happened; Sullivan didn't seem at all pleased to be hearing from him so soon. He grunted once, said 'Pay it', and put the phone down.

After a night's reflection, McKechnie went to the bank early the next day and withdrew fifty pounds. It was just possible that Sullivan was right; that it was a one-off job. But the more he thought about it, the less likely it seemed. He had a very unpleasant feeling that this was the start of something which could go on a long time. But he thought he'd take it gently to start with. At eleven o'clock the phone went again. This time the voice was brusquer.

'Brown envelope, please, Mr McKechnie. Two rubber bands round it, one in each direction. If by any foolish plan you asked the bank for new notes, go back and change them. Drop the envelope in the middle dustbin by the back entrance to the Columbia cinema at one o'clock.

McKechnie did exactly as he was told. He got to the middle dustbin on time, lifted the lid, dropped the envelope into the half-filled bin, turned, squinted round a bit to see if he could catch anyone spying on him, then marched off purposefully. He walked west along Shaftesbury Avenue, turned down the lower stub of Wardour Street, doubled back along Gerrard Street and stopped by an advertising hoarding. From here he could just make out, when traffic and pedestrians allowed, the three dustbins by the back entrance to the cinema. He'd been there twenty minutes or so, worrying each time a bus blocked his line of sight, when he gradually became conscious of a man watching him from a distance of about ten feet. A broad-faced, gingery, fleshy man with glasses and a slightly wild look in his eye. When he saw that McKechnie's attention was on him, he walked slowly towards him, then round behind him, then laid his chubby chin on McKechnie's shoulder so that they were now both looking across towards the dustbins, then turned sideways and grinned straight into McKechnie's face, then came round the front again, then took a big freckled thumb and forefinger and playfully grabbed a stretch of McKechnie's cheek, then said, with a friendly, slightly mad smile,

'Scram.'

McKechnie scrammed back to his office, his heart beating too fast for its own good.

Two weeks later 'Salvatore' called again.

'My dear Mr McKechnie, how nice to be talking to you again. It was so kind of you to help me out the other week when I was short. I'm sure the Revenue will understand when you put it through your books. Now, I do seem to be having a bit of a cash-flow problem again. I wonder if you could possibly help me out. I'm afraid I need just a little more this time, though. I think we'd better settle for a hundred.'

'I don't do that sort of business.'

'Well, Mr McKechnie, I don't happen to believe you. I'm sure a man with two warehouses and an office, however meagre they are, can find a hundred pounds to help out a friend.' McKechnie paused. He was wondering why Salvatore, who had had a fairly strong foreign accent during his first call, now seemed to be speaking almost standard English. He answered,

'All right.'

Secretly McKechnie was pleased. Now the police would have to act. He rang Sullivan and told him the demand had gone up to the level which justified his interest. The next day he did as instructed, made the drop at one o'clock in a litter bin strapped to a lamp-post in Frith Street, went back to his office and waited for Sullivan to call. When he did, the news wasn't good.

'Lost them, I'm afraid.'

'What do you mean, lost them?'

'Well, we covered the place with a couple of men, watched you make the drop, but by the end of a couple of hours when nothing had happened they checked out the litter bin. The cupboard was bare.'

'Your men must have been incompetent.'

'Now, now, Mr McKechnie, that's a very slanderous thing to say. The streets were very busy – that's why the fellow chooses one o'clock – and my men can't exactly stand around in blue uniforms, you know. And I can't put my most experienced men on the job – their faces are too well known. That's the trouble with this patch.'

'So what do we do now?'

'We try again.'

'What about my hundred quid?'

'Oh, I'm sure you'll find a way to write that off, Mr McKechnie.' Why did everyone seem so certain that his losses were tax deductible? Were they trying to make it easier for him – or for themselves?

A fortnight later Salvatore called again; another drop was made, and another hundred lost as Sullivan's men failed to spot the pick-up, or were distracted for a few vital seconds, or, as McKechnie suggested down the phone, fell asleep.

'Now these slanderous suggestions won't help anyone, you know,' Sullivan said. He sounded formally apologetic about his men's failure, but not deeply unhappy.

McKechnie *was* deeply unhappy. He'd agreed to let Sullivan take over the case in the hope of getting some action. Since then, the file on the cutting of his wife had been moved from Guildford to West Central, and that was about all the action he'd had. He'd lost £250 in four weeks, no one knew who had attacked his wife, and Sullivan didn't seem to care. He couldn't even go and visit Sullivan because Salvatore or his mates were obviously following him, or had a spy somewhere; so all he could do was sit in his office by the telephone and wait for Sullivan to report the bad news to him.

It was when Sullivan lost him the third hundred that McKechnie decided on a new initiative. He called West Central and asked for Det-Sgt Shaw. He explained that he needed to see him urgently and privately; could they meet for a drink in the next day or two, but well away from their normal stamping ground? Shaw agreed.

They met at a drinkers' pub near Baker Street Station, a large, cheerless place where they never bothered to get rid of the fog of cigarette smoke between shifts; the drinkers relished it mainly because it was so murkily different from what they were going home to. They were going home to wives and children and cleanliness and their favourite dinner, so they valued the pub for its dirt and its smell and its maleness and its churlish refusal to go in for peanuts or crisps or new types of mixers or anything which might attract gaggles of typists after work and disturb their serious masculine drinking. Shaw often stopped off on his way home up the Metropolitan Line; McKechnie had never been here before.

'I want advice,' said McKechnie. 'I want you to listen to

me while I talk. I'll tell you everything that's happened to me, and if at the end you think you can't say anything without compromising yourself or your job, then I'll quite understand if you just down your drink and head for the door. All I ask is that you don't pass on what I tell you. Is that a deal?'

Shaw nodded. He was a small, foxy man, always too worried to smile. McKechnie told his story. When the name of Sullivan first cropped up, he thought he saw a slight twitch of a muscle on Shaw's face, but no more. When he had finished, Shaw lit a cigarette to add to the general fug, drew on it a few times, and then spoke without looking at McKechnie. It was as if he were avoiding responsibility for his words, as if McKechnie were simply overhearing him in a pub.

'Let's say that I appreciate your problem. Let's say that it could have happened before. Let's say that once a case is with an officer of a certain rank, it's not easy to get that case transferred except at the officer's own request. As a general rule. I'm naturally speaking in very general terms,' Shaw drew in another lungful, 'and it would be more than my job is worth to speculate on motives in individual cases.'

'Of course.'

'And nothing I say must be read as criticism of any officer.'

'Of course.' There was a long silence.

'If we were in America,' said McKechnie, 'I suppose I would go to a private detective.'

'You could do that here,' said Shaw, 'if you fancy hiring an active pensioner who once used to be good at catching couples on the job. They don't exist any more, and if they do, you might as well give your money straight to Oxfam as use them.'

'So what do I do if I don't want to go on paying out a hundred quid a fortnight for the rest of my life?'

'That's what I'm thinking about,' said Shaw. He tilted his empty glass towards his companion.

McKechnie got up and fetched them some more drinks. The pub was such a bastion of maleness that it didn't even have barmaids. A fat man in a striped shirt with beer stains down it served him with a convincing display of surliness. A few commuters were resignedly gathering up their raincoats and briefcases before heading off dejectedly towards sun and light and domestic bliss. McKechnie thought how, in comparison, he was quite happy with Rosie. Despite his occasional mistress, he was really fond of her. Her wouldn't want anything to happen to her. As he set down their drinks, Shaw said,

'You could try Duffy.'

'Who's that?'

'Duffy. Nick Duffy. Used to be a sort of buddy of mine. Did a couple of years in vice. Left the force, oh, about four years ago.'

'What does he do now?'

'He set up as a security adviser. Tells companies how to vet their staff, how to put their money in the safe, that sort of thing. Does the odd bit of freelancing; and he certainly knows the patch. He might do a job if he was free.'

'Why did he leave the police? Was he kicked out?'

'Let's say he left under a bit of a cloud.'

'Is he a criminal?'

Shaw looked up and smiled a wan, ironic smile.

'Well, we all have our own definitions of criminality, don't we? It's rather a big subject. But if you're asking me is he honest, then I'd say to you that Nick Duffy has got to be honest.'

'How do I get in touch with him?'

'He's in the book.'

'Well, thank you.'

'No, don't thank me. You don't thank me because you haven't seen me. O.K.? And two things. I didn't put you

34

on to Duffy: you've never heard of me, O.K.? And the other thing: it's probably not a good idea to ask Duffy why he left the force. He's a bit touchy on that score.'

Shaw left quickly, before McKechnie even had time to finish his drink.

3

The sunlight streaming in through the high window of the Paddington mews flat twinkled on the gold stud in Duffy's left ear. He'd sometimes dreamed of trying to invent a miniaturised alarm system, so that when the stud heated up a degree or two with the sun, a tiny bell went off in his ear. He'd given up the idea for two reasons: half the time he slept on his left side; and in any case, only a fool would rely on the sun.

Duffy had toyed with the idea in the first place because he hated clocks. He couldn't sleep if there were clocks in the place. He could hear a wrist watch from the other side of the room. An alarm clock always worked for him because its tick prevented him from getting to sleep in the first place. As he lived in a one-room flat ('open plan' was how the house agents dignified it), there was nowhere for clocks to go. The only timepieces allowed in had to be wrapped up. There was a Tupperware box in the bathroom marked 'Watches' for those who stayed the night. His kitchen clock was hung outside the kitchen window, in a polythene bag, its face pressing up against the glass. Sometimes, in the winters, birds would alight on it, thinking it was some sort of feeding apparatus, and peck inquisitively at the polythene. Then the bag would leak and Duffy would have to buy a new clock.

Duffy hated alarm clocks even more because they made him sweat when they went off; their tone seemed panicky, and this always got through to him before he was properly awake, so that he came into consciousness feeling anxious. It was never the right way to start the day. For the same reason, he hated alarm calls in the morning, and tried instead to train himself to wake up at a pre-determined time. Sometimes it worked, sometimes it didn't. It worked often enough to persuade him once to try leaving the telephone off the hook, so that he wouldn't be made anxious by some early morning call. But when he did, he found that all night the dialling tone roared at him across the room like a cageful of lions. Then he thought of buying a big soundproof box to put the telephone in at nights, but decided that if he started doing that he would end up crazy, living in a flat where everything that made a noise – telephone, radio, refrigerator, front door bell – was neatly boxed in. You just had to live with a certain level of anxiety, he reckoned.

So when the telephone went that morning he reacted normally – that is, he jumped as if the bailiffs had just booted in his front door. The girl beside him stirred and started shaking herself awake. Duffy was already across the room and standing naked at the telephone. He was a short, stockily built man with powerful forearms and haunches; he wore his hair in a longish brushcut which added perhaps an inch to his height. As he turned while talking on the phone, the girl ran her eyes over his slightly bowed legs, his cock, his pubic bush which was just catching the light, his chest with its concentration of dark hair round the nipples, his broad, strong face with a slightly small, tight mouth; she noticed a sudden flash from the stud in his left ear.

The girl sat up in bed and listened to Duffy's side of the conversation. It mainly consisted of pauses, grunts, 'nos' and 'all rights'. Duffy never said Yes. If he was with you and meant Yes, he'd nod his head. If he was on the phone, he'd say 'All right'. If you asked Duffy to marry you and he wanted to, he'd still only say 'All right'. She couldn't be completely sure, of course, but that was her guess. She'd once asked Duffy to marry her, and he'd said 'No'.

As Duffy put down the phone and walked back towards

the bed, she slightly turned towards him. She had a pretty, circular Irish face, and cute, high breasts with small dark brown nipples. She looked at Duffy's cock nostalgically.

'Duffy,' she said, 'do you still remember what it was like to fuck me?'

Duffy frowned.

'We've been into that,' he said, and walked away to the bathroom. There he opened the Tupperware box marked 'Watches', saw from Carol's Timex that it was after ten, washed, and started to lather his chin. From behind he heard Carol's voice from the bed,

'I know we've been into it. I just wanted to know if you used to like it.'

Duffy paused in his lathering, cleared his lips of soap with the back of the little finger of his right hand, and grunted back,

'All right.'

By the time he had finished in the bathroom, Carol had already laid the breakfast at the round table at the other end of the room. She sat wearing his blue towelling dressing gown. He had put on the light, short kimono which she always kept at the flat. It finished just below his rump. He wore it quite a lot.

'Work?' she asked.

He nodded. 'Maybe.'

'Telling me about it?'

'No. Not until I've taken it or not taken it.'

'You need the money, Duffy.'

'I know.'

Duffy Security had had a pretty up-and-down three years. Duffy had started up at a time when security was already a booming business. Prospective clients could look in the Yellow Pages and get a choice of any number of firms; even with a display box round your name, you were still competing with lots of better-known organisations offering every sort of service – mobile patrols, cash transit, dog patrols, keyholders, static guards, personnel screening. Duffy didn't have a dog, though he did have a van; he also didn't have any staff apart from an answerphone and a friend who came in once a month to help with the accounts.

What Duffy did have was lots of expert knowledge and a highly practical mind. But you can't put that in an ad. People who want security naturally assume that the bigger the firm is, the better its operation. In fact, as Duffy knew only too well from his days in the force, the large firms were always being infiltrated by ex-cons and stoolies; a hundred quid in the right place could buy you a lot of information if you were in the business of knocking off cash transfers.

The only way to get successful in this field, Duffy knew, was to work at being really efficient and then hope for word-of-mouth to back you up. You couldn't advertise in any effective way. Or rather, there might be ways, but they just weren't feasible. One would be to have a variety of crooks who'd been nabbed as a result of one of your systems quoted saying things like, 'I'd still be out there nicking if it hadn't been for DUFFY SECURITY'. But even old lags have their pride. The other way would be to get firms you had advised to endorse you: 'We've never had a break-in since we called in DUFFY SECURITY'. But anything like that would just seem an open challenge to every operator in town.

So Duffy checked out his answerphone every day, took most of the jobs that were offered, and just about kept going. He wasn't sure about the job this fellow McKechnie was offering; but he'd meet the guy at least. He said,

'What time's your shift?'

'Three. Three to eleven.' It was the shift Carol disliked the most. Nothing much happened all through the afternoon and early evening, and then, as soon as you were really tired, you were likely to get a bit of trouble on your hands.

'Ah, the old shit shift.'

Duffy got up from the table and walked to his fitted wardrobe at the other end of the room. A stranger would have thought his flat a bit empty. Duffy thought his flat a bit empty too. It had been like that since the second robbery.

The first time he was robbed they only took the television set and his electric razor. It had been more of an embarrassment than anything else, especially the one-inch para in the *Evening Standard* headed 'SECURITY MAN ROBBED'. He'd been wanting to get a new T.V. anyway; and, just to prove to the thieves that he didn't really miss anything, he went back to wet shaving.

The second time he was robbed they had come back for everything else: they arrived in a van marked Handimoves, took his furniture, his electric cooker, his fireside rug, his radio, his new television, his electric kettle, his pile of sixpences and even a pot plant. All they left were his fitted carpet, the ashtrays, and his bed. Why hadn't they taken the bed?

The first thing Duffy had done on this occasion was ring the news desk on the *Standard* and speak to an old mate of his. He bartered the story of the break-in – which was bound to reach them sooner or later – for a small case of drunken driving by a judge which he'd heard about a couple of days earlier and which was being quietly hushed. Only then did he call the police and get ready for their cracks when he told them what he did for a living.

In fact, Duffy didn't really mind the robberies. He quite liked buying new furniture, and the insurance company had paid up on both occasions without any quibbles. Moreover, Duffy always maintained that insurance was the best form of security. When he first started advising people about how to protect their homes and offices, he used to tell them that there were four systems to choose from. The best was total, comprehensive, wall-to-wall insurance. The second was a complex network of electronic beams and scanners so sensitive that it triggered when the night watchman farted. The third was your average burglar alarm, of the sort which thieves practise dismantling with their eyes closed just to keep in trim. And the fourth was a white plywood box; painted on it in red were the words DUFFY SECURITY, a miniature skull and a ragged flash of lightning. You attached a few fake wires to it and stuck it high up on the front of your house. In terms of cost-effectiveness Duffy used to recommend the fourth system: until, that is, the funny look in clients' eyes began to make him realise that they didn't want to hear the truth: they wanted to be told what they wanted to be told. From then on, that was what he told them.

'Will I see you tonight?' He asked the question in a deliberately casual way.

'Oh, I don't think so, Duffy. Not two nights on the trot. That would be just a bit too much like old times, wouldn't it?'

'All right. See you then.'

'See you.'

Duffy pulled on a green suede blouson with a big plastic zip up the front, and left Carol to finish breakfast by herself.

He reached McKechnie's Rupert Street office by half past eleven. Between a shuttered dirty bookshop and a twenty-four-hour minicab service he found a doorway; a couple of grubby plastic strips screwed to the side wall announced WORLDWIDE PRODUCTIONS (LONDON) INC. and MCKECHNIE IMPORTS. He walked up to the first floor, pushed open a door and saw a plain secretary wearing a long skirt and a big silver cross; she was reading a magazine. She did the full secretarial college number on him, but her face said that his arrival in the office was a high point in the day. Visitors were clearly as rare and fascinating as white men at the source of the Limpopo.

'Mr McKechnie is just a little bit tied up at the moment, but I'll see when he'll be free,' she said.

'He said eleven thirty,' said Duffy. 'It's eleven thirty. If he's busy then I'm buggering off.'

'Oh, I'm sure he'll be able to fit you in,' she smiled, and buzzed the telephone. 'Mr McKechnie, we have a Mr Duffy to see you in reception. Thank you, Mr McKechnie. Mr Duffy, would you go through, please, it's that door there.'

Duffy looked round the secretary's office. It was about the size of a broom cupboard, filled with box files and steel cabinets. There were only two doors – the one he had come in through and another opposite. Maybe there were a few customers who thought McKechnie had his office out on the stairs or something. As he put his hand on the knob he looked round the secretary's room again.

'Is this reception?'

She smiled and nodded.

'Just checking.'

McKechnie rose to shake hands with Duffy. He was a bit surprised how short the security man was, but he looked quite strong. He also looked a bit of a faggot to McKechnie's eye. He wondered about that gold stud in his ear. Was it just fashion, or was it some sort of sexual signal? McKechnie didn't know any more. In the old days, you knew precisely where you were: all the codes were worked out, you could tell who did and who didn't, who was and who wasn't. Even a few years ago you could still not go wildly wrong; but nowadays the only way of being quite sure who was what and who did what was when you asked your secretary to clean your glasses and she took off her knickers to do it with.

Duffy reserved judgment on McKechnie. So far he was

just another client – just another red-faced middle-aged man who might or might not be honest, might or might not be just after some free advice, might or might not be wasting his at the moment not very valuable time. He listened while McKechnie told him the first part of the story, the part to do with the break-in; McKechnie was relieved that Duffy didn't smirk when he told him about the cat. Actually, Duffy thought it was quite funny – he'd seen so many nasty things happen to humans that he didn't have much space left over for animals – but he refrained from laughing because at the moment he needed almost every customer he could get. Then McKechnie told him about Sullivan and West Central and the three hundred and fifty quid. He waited for comments.

'So why did you come to me?'

'I asked around.'

At least he hadn't said he'd picked Duffy's name out of the Yellow Pages with a pin.

'And what do you expect me to do?'

'I don't know yet. I want to hear what you say first.'

'Well, I'd say you've got two problems, maybe separate, possibly connected. First, what happened at your house and the phone calls. I must say I hadn't thought of doing the presh that way round before. It's quite clever.'

'What do you mean?'

'Well, normally what happens with presh is that they send a heavy man round who tells you the fee and the delivery date, and then tells you what they'll do to you if you don't deliver – set fire to your house, kill your dog, kidnap your kid, or whatever. You think about it and then usually you do what they ask. And then maybe, after a while, after a few deliveries, you don't pay, and they decide to sort you out, except that you're expecting them to do that and so you might just have the blues there or *something*. But this way round, they do the rough stuff

43

first, when no one can possibly be expecting it, let the customer stew, and then put in for the fee. It's a different system, it's not so predictable, and it throws in an extra element of craziness. The customer – you in this case – thinks, Christ, well, if they cut my wife before I hadn't even not done something they asked, what the hell would they be like to mess with if I *had* done something they didn't like; for instance, if I hadn't paid up. So their first bit of heavy takes them coasting a long way, you see.'

'I do. And who do you think this Salvatore is?'

'No idea. I knew the old Salvatore a bit. You used to see him in Italian restaurants trying to look like a mafioso. Used to walk in, sit down, not say a word, eat his food, drink his wine, get up, walk out. Very dignified, slightly sinister, dressed in black, had a pepper-and-salt moustache. All the other diners thought he must be a big protection man. Well, he was a medium-sized protection man; did a few smokes and tarts as well, I think. Some of the restaurants he really did have the screw on; but the others, well, he just had a slate there and they used to send him the bill at the end of the month. And he always paid. He was a humorous old bugger, that's for sure; quite a character. It sounds as if this bloke knew him, or maybe inherited a bit of his patch; or maybe he just liked his style. He sounds as if he's got a bit of a sense of humour from what you say.'

'Well, it's the sort of humour which appeals to him more than me. So what about the second part of it?'

'Hard to say. Could be anywhere on the scale from straight incompetence up to a lot of bent. I can't imagine the blues losing three drops in a row. Not unless standards have fallen since I was there. But quite what it means is another matter. This guy at West Central might simply be telling you he doesn't need the business: hasn't got the time, hasn't got the men, doesn't care enough about your problems.'

'I didn't know the police could do that.'

'Not in theory they can't. They've got a duty to investigate. But they've also got practical problems. They naturally spend most of the time going for the big stuff and only go for the little stuff when there's a good chance of an arrest.'

'So this is little? My wife has thirteen stitches and I'm paying out a hundred quid a fortnight?'

'Well, Mr McKechnie, there's big and big. And there are a couple of other possibilities.'

'Which are?'

'That the bloke at West Central is keeping tabs on what's going on but thinks it's too early to come in. He's waiting for it all to blow up like a great boil full of pus, and then he'll come in and burst it. Some people call this the romantic approach to police work. Some people call it the lazy approach. And then of course . . .' Duffy paused.

'Yes?'

'There's another possibility. This guy . . .'

'Sullivan?'

'Yes, Sullivan – he may be thinking that it's all a private business anyway; that it's just a little squabble about a patch. What about that, Mr McKechnie?'

'What do you mean?'

'Well, I don't know anything about you. As far as I know, you're a perfectly normal trader who deals in funny hats or whatever. But, of course, if you had form, that might be different . . .'

'Form?'

'You haven't got a criminal record, I hope, Mr McKechnie?'

'I hope so too. No, of course I don't.'

'Good. Well, then, there's only the last possibility, which wouldn't be the easiest one for either of us. That this guy Sullivan is in direct collusion with whoever is using Salvatore's name.'

45

'And what would you do if that were the case?'

'I'd advise you to sell up as fast as you can and get your tail out of the area, Mr McKechnie. An expanding operator and a sleeping policeman are a very unpleasant combination to come across.'

'But we don't by any means know that, do we, Mr Duffy?'

'No, fortunately, we don't.'

'And in the meantime?'

'In the meantime I can do some scouting about for you. I don't think I – or you for that matter – want to get too near the second area of concern. If you're dealing with a bent copper, the only rule I know is, stay away.'

'And what about the first area?'

'Well, we haven't got much to start on. We've got a short man and a tall one at your home, one of them with a Stanley knife. No prints. One of them a bit sick by the sound of it. We've got a fat bloke with glasses and ginger hair just off Shaftesbury Avenue. And we've got a voice down the phone. What sort of a voice, Mr McKechnie?'

'Quite deep. He started off a bit Italian; now he's got more English, but possibly not quite English. Sometimes has what sounds like a slight accent, sometimes puts his words in a funny order. No, that's not quite right, but he did start off saying lots of things like "As you say" or "How do you put it?".'

'Doesn't tell us much. If he gets a kick out of pretending to be Salvatore, maybe he likes putting on a bit of an Italian accent as well. I'll fix a tape on your phone as soon as I can.'

'So what do we do next, Mr Duffy?'

'We wait for you to get your next orders. And then we see what they are. And then we decide what to do. In the meanwhile I'll mooch around and see what I can pick up. I'll come back tomorrow and fix your phone; but after that we'd better not meet here again, just in case you're being watched. We'll keep in touch by phone.'

They bargained briefly about money. Duffy asked for thirty a day, and settled for twenty (however long the day was), or three quid an hour for part of a day, plus tube fares and any goods he bought for which he could produce a receipt. Then he asked for a silly hat and a mask.

'I don't think our sort of masks will make you a master of disguise, Mr Duffy.'

'It's just to have in my hand as I leave, in case you're being watched. Makes me look more like a potential customer who's been given some samples.'

'Very true, Mr Duffy. Shall I invoice you for them?'

'Yes, please.'

McKechnie wrote out an invoice. With a smile, Duffy handed it straight back to him. 'Expenses receipt,' he said, and left. He walked out into Rupert Street with a cone-shaped clown's hat in one hand and a King Kong mask with plastic hair in the other. Two Cypriot youths were loitering at the entrance to the minicab office and an unhealthily pale man was taking down the wire shutters on the window of the dirty bookshop. It was beginning to cloud over.

McKechnie had lied to Duffy about his bit of trouble with the law. Duffy, on the other hand, had lied to McKechnie by pretending not to register Sullivan's name. He knew Sullivan. He knew Sullivan from way back. And the memory of him tugged with it all those other memories which he normally kept locked away at the back of his skull, and which only escaped by chance, or when Carol said something to him like she'd said that morning.

Duffy knew more than just Sullivan. He knew West Central like the back of his hand. He'd been a detective-sergeant there for three years before the thing happened which finished his career. He'd done a year's general there, and two years' vice. He'd loved the work; he'd had a good giggle with the rest of the lads at the Xmas blue film shows; he'd got to know the patch and the whores, and made friends with a few of them; he'd known who handled smokes, who handled snort and who handled smack; he'd got an inkling of how the tight, impenetrable Chinese community ran itself – of when they ceremoniously deferred to white law, and when they didn't give a wine waiter's cork about it – and he'd learnt all about presh. He was on his way to becoming one of the best officers on the patch. Not just that, but one of the happiest too: when a pretty, round-faced, dark-haired, Irish-looking W.P.C. had joined them, there'd been the usual stampede from his colleagues. He'd hung back a bit, waited for the dust to die down, and then got talking to her. She got talking back, and they were away. Things couldn't have been working out better.

What wrecked it all were two things: honesty and sex. Duffy, like most coppers, had a slightly flexible approach to the truth. You had to if you wanted to survive: not survive as a copper, but survive within yourself. The zealots who saw truth as indivisible ended up in either A10 or the cuckoo farm. Most of the time you stuck to the truth as closely as you could, but were prepared to bend with the breeze if necessary. Sometimes, for instance, it might be necessary to tell a little lie, fiddle your notebook just a bit, in order to make sure that a much bigger lie didn't get to pass itself off as the truth. On those occasions you felt bad for a bit, though you knew you didn't have any choice in the matter.

But Duffy, like most coppers, knew that you always drew a line somewhere. You might tidy up your verbals a bit, fiddle your evidence slightly, forget a little something, but you always knew why you were doing it: you were fixing the record in favour of justice. You weren't doing it to get promotion, you weren't doing it to get your own back on a villain for personal reasons, and you weren't doing it because you were on the take.

That was the way it normally was, the way it was for most coppers. But not for all. Some coppers were bent as corkscrews, and they didn't last long. The tricky ones were the half-and-halfers. Sullivan, for instance. You could never be quite sure about the Super. He always kept his own company, always seemed a bit lazy, a bit bored; he turned in a good enough arrest record, yet always seemed to be keeping some of himself in reserve. Partly it was that he'd been at the station longer than anyone else. He'd say things like 'My experience tells me, lad . . . ' and 'When you've been around West Central as long as I have . . . ' and 'Listen, my boy, I was charging Jasmine when you still didn't know what your middle leg was for . . . ' Most of the younger men tried to look on him as an avuncular figure, but none quite succeeded.

One summer a couple of new whores had started operating from a gaff on the corner of Bateman Street and Frith. One was a black kid, the other white, and they worked as a pair when they street-hustled. There wasn't that much street-work going on – at least not in broad daylight; but these two were new to the patch, and they either had a brash approach to the market or else were run by a very grabby pimp, so they often hustled the street. One would keep a lookout and the other would proposition a prick. If he didn't walk off at once, but couldn't quite make up his mind, she'd point to her lookout and say, 'Maybe you like my friend?' The hesitating punter felt flattered at being given a choice, and thinking it almost impolite to refuse both of them, would make his selection. Duffy saw them work this trick lots of times.

They had looked like a couple of tough-faced twenty-year-olds who could take care of themselves. But they cut just as easily as anybody else. One evening in Bateman Street someone stuck a knife into the black girl, first into her shoulder and then, as she was falling, into her rump, as near to her cunt as he could. The girl lay in the gutter and bled a lot; and then she was taken to hospital where she was stitched up. She told Duffy she'd cut herself opening a tin of baked beans.

Stabbing at the cunt is the way pimps warn other pimps off their patch. You don't cut the pimp, who might fight back, you cut one of his girls. Duffy wasn't sentimental about whores, but he didn't much like that sort of crime, and on this occasion he got a bit tough. He leaned on Polly, as the black girl called herself, for the name of her pimp. Then he went to the pimp and leaned a bit harder on him. Then he got a lead on someone called Savella who'd tried to warn off the pimp a few times in the weeks before the attack.

He started to lean on Savella, which was a lot harder than leaning on the pimp because Savella was a whole deal smarter and had a bright villain's grounding in the law. Duffy went to see him a few times and made a nuisance of himself. He played it like one enthusiastic copper. He asked who Savella worked for. Savella wouldn't tell him – 'Amma self-ampaloyed' he kept repeating – but Duffy went on asking around. Finally, he came up with a name: Big Eddy. No other name, no description. He carried on asking. He was keen on his case.

Eventually, Sullivan called him in.

'Not getting very far with this stabbing, Duffy.'

Duffy begged to disagree. He'd got to the pimp, he'd got to Savella, he'd got to the name of Big Eddy. He'd made a few new contacts. The girls might talk more. He thought he'd got hold of someone who might have something he could use to put pressure on Savella.

'My experience tells me the case is folding,' said Sullivan.

Again, Duffy begged to differ. Anyway, he'd carried on in the past with much less to go on than he had now.

'I repeat,' said Sullivan, fixing Duffy with a couple of

small toad-like eyes, the only live portions of his flabby, inanimate face, 'that my experience tells me the case is folding.'

Duffy knew at the time that this was one occasion when he should bend with the breeze, one of those times when you shrug and say, 'It's only a whore' – and, in this case, not a particularly nice one either. Foolishly, he didn't. He went on with the case. He wasn't exactly in breach of police regulations because Sullivan hadn't officially closed the case, or taken it over, or handed it to someone else. It was just that in every other respect Sullivan had told him to lay off.

He'd just got a fresh line on Big Eddy when the rug was pulled. Quite how it happened and who was the stool he never knew, but there must have been a tip from someone inside the station. Everyone there knew he'd been going through a sticky time with Carol. They'd had one of those spells everyone gets after a year or so of knowing each other, when the freshness has worn off a bit and everyone starts treating you as an established couple and whistling the Wedding March at you and doing cradling gestures and you suddenly wonder whether you're doing the right thing after all. You want to stand back, think about it a bit, make sure you're on the right path. Duffy had tried to explain this to Carol, who'd assumed he was trying to drop her in as painless a way as possible. She wasn't going to be dropped like that by anyone. She yelled and she cried and he told her she was jumping to the wrong conclusions but that her acting like this was anyway proving that she was assuming things which they hadn't ever discussed, and that of course he still loved her, but she really ought to try and see the relationship from another angle. Like his, for instance, she said.

Eventually they agreed on a couple of months apart, no strings, no bed, no conditions; then they'd see how they felt.

After about three weeks Duffy started getting pretty itchy. They'd agreed not to impose anything on each other for the two months: they could be as free as they liked. Duffy debated with himself about what to do, and then gave in.

The point about Duffy was, as McKechnie surmised, that he plugged in both ways. He didn't need a transformer. He'd had a very gay phase when he was eighteen, then sobered up a lot when he joined the force, and since then pretty well divided his favours equally between the two sexes. His mates at work saw he was keen enough on women for them not to suspect him; the other half of his preference he kept more or less to himself. He told Carol, who merely said she'd always thought that she had a rather boyish body, and asked if he'd like her to dress up as a bloke from time to time. He said it wasn't exactly like that; but he was pleased at the way she reacted.

When they took their two months' separation from each other and Duffy got itchy, he thought a lot about which way to go. If he went for a girl, Carol would be bound to be jealous, despite the agreement. If he went for a guy, then maybe she'd feel he was – what would she say? – slipping backwards; but maybe she wouldn't feel so threatened when he told her. In terms of sexual pleasure, it didn't make much difference to him; he wasn't picky when it came to orgasm.

The first time he went trawling at the Caramel Club and took a chubby journalist back to the flat he was then living in off Westbourne Grove. A couple of nights later he went to the Alligator and landed himself a polite undergraduate hot off the Oxford train. The third time he went back to the Caramel again, drank a bit more than usual, and was half-helped home by a nice black kid of about his own age.

Ten minutes after that his flat door was kicked in by two full-sized policemen, the black kid started yelling, 'He bought me drinks, he bought me drinks,' and the larger of the two policemen seized him by the bare shoulder, twisted him round on the bed and said, with heavy irony, 'Excuse me, sir, but how old is your friend?' The whisky fumes were clearing from his head as if someone had switched on an Xpelair, and he knew he'd been set up.

The kid was a plant; he said he was nineteen. The police took an address and told him to scram. They took Duffy down to the station and charged him. When he told them his profession, one of the two policemen turned his back while the other punched Duffy in the kidneys. 'Fucking bent queer copper,' he said; then 'Fucking *queer*,' and punched him again.

Duffy knew it was curtains. He was suspended from duty and sat around gloomily at home. Eventually he was called to West Central. And who should give him the good news but Sullivan?

'When you've been around as long as I have, nothing much surprises you, Duffy. But this does. This does. I've argued for you, though personally my instinct would be to throw everything at you. I've talked to the investigating officer in the case and I've got you the best deal I can; a sight better than you deserve. And I've done it not for your sake but for the sake of the station, I don't mind telling you. Westbourne Grove have agreed not to prosecute; they'll say it might cause the kid too much psychological harm to give evidence and they're writing the case off. Now go away and come back in five minutes with your resignation.'

It was a perfect fit-up. It destroyed his career, and it wrecked his relationship with Carol. Moreover, Duffy failed to appreciate Sullivan's avuncular touch when he called Carol into his office to explain what had happened. She had stayed away from Duffy for two months, trying to understand what had happened. When she came to see him, he did his best to explain, but there were too many scars. They tried going to bed together to see what that

53

would do, but she was tense and nervy and he couldn't get a hard-on. Sleeping was all right, though, and waking up together was usually nice. Gradually they got back together a bit, but only as wary friends. Sometimes Carol stayed the night, but they never made advances to each other in bed. He never got a hard-on when she was in bed with him, not even a sleepy, unintended one.

'Brother and sister?' she'd once said to him as they were falling asleep. Brother and sister, but with a suspicious loitering past. Brother and sister with a lot of previous.

Duffy had good reason to remember Sullivan.

4

Duffy woke up out of a bad dream. It was a bad dream because for Duffy life within it was all fivers and éclairs. In his dream he was a Chief Super in whose presence villains shrank to the size of earwigs; he snapped his fingers and cases on which the brightest blues had broken their teeth simply fell open in his hands. After a triumphant day at the office like this he was driven home to a large detached house deep in some beech woods where Carol and the kids were waiting for him. As he drove through the gates his eldest son, a flaxen-haired rascal, fired his bow and arrow at the car; the rubber sucker on the end of the arrow glued itself to the hub-cap and the car rolled along like Boadicea's chariot, slicing the heads off bluebells all the way up the drive. No matter, Duffy thought in his dream, the bluebells will never run out. Then they got to the house and Carol was waiting on the steps. As they stepped inside the door, she gently tugged on his sleeve and took him upstairs. She slipped off her dress and was wearing nothing underneath. Duffy threw his suit over a chair, climbed out of the rest of his clothes, and as he approached the bed where she lay on top of the candlewick cover she exclaimed, as if surprised by joy, 'Duffy, you're so big, you're so big.'

'AAAAAAaaaaaaaaaaaaaaaaaaaaaahhhhhhhhhhh . . . ' He screamed himself awake. It was one of those dreams when you know all the time you're dreaming. Usually they're bad dreams, and you comfort yourself with the knowledge that your brain is just having a mean time with you. But when you're in a good dream and know that it's only a dream, then you feel an undercurrent of bitterness all the way through and you wake with ashes in your mouth and strange pains and an unconquerable sense of loss. You feel as if America has slipped through your fingers.

Duffy lay on his back shaking a little. Out of curiosity, he lifted the bedclothes to see if he had a hard-on. No dice. Even if he dreamed he had a hard-on with Carol, even if he was fucking her in his dream, he awoke to a peeled prawn and a walnut. No dice.

Duffy wasn't impotent. He couldn't lay that at the door of whoever fitted him up. He was just impotent with Carol. At first he'd thought it was the shock of what had happened. Then he began to realise that he might get over the shock and still not recover his powers with her. Perhaps never. He'd tried lying in bed with her and ordering his cock to obey, silently shouting and cursing it. He'd tried closing his eyes and thinking of other women he'd fucked, and other men he'd fucked, and the most exciting pornography he'd ever clapped eyes on. No dice. Desperate, he'd even tried wanking himself to erection and then turning towards Carol; but his cock, unruly to the bitter end, wilted like a flower at dusk. No dice.

And the end *was* bitter. If you can't fuck the one person you want to fuck, then pleasure got from fucking other people is even more lined with irony. After a while, at Carol's insistence, he went off and tried fucking other people. To his distress, there was no problem; to his further distress, he always found himself enjoying it just enough to want to do it again. He fucked men and women indiscriminately, but found that, without realising he was doing it, he was setting himself a rule: never twice. The sweetest girl, the randiest guy, both would leave in the morning. However much they asked to see him again, and however nice he thought they were, he would never say 'All right'. Never. It was, perhaps, a sort of fidelity to Carol, even if a fidelity wrung from the most fevered promiscuity.

What Carol did he never asked. He didn't ask because all the answers she could give were bad. If she was sleeping with lots of guys, he knew he'd hate it; if she was sleeping with just one guy, he'd hate it more; if she was sleeping with no one, he'd hate it less but feel the pressure on him even more intolerable. Duffy, in short, was in a state of pain.

It's a state for which the only cure is work. Duffy had mixed feelings about McKechnie's job. It might increase the pain inside him to go back prowling round his old patch; maybe it would just stir everything up and never give him the chance to come to terms with it. On the other hand, maybe there would be some opportunity of making a settlement with his past. But what if there were, and he muffed it?

Still, it was work, it would get him out of his flat some mornings. It was twenty quid a day plus tube fares. Duffy could do with that. The bars he cruised had suddenly put up their prices a lot. People said it was the one pleasure that was free, but it wasn't. You had to pay one way or the other: either with your feelings, or else in buying drinks as you tested the company, weighed it up, went through the social rituals which were essential if you wanted to end up not feeling a complete whore.

Duffy dug out his basic electrician's kit from a cupboard and set off for Rupert Street. He'd already told McKechnie to bring in a small tape recorder and a number of tapes. At the office they sent Belinda out for a couple of take-away coffees and Duffy pressed a rubber sucker on to the body of the telephone on McKechnie's desk. A short length of wiring connected it to the portable Sony in the top drawer.

'Secret Service stuff, eh?' said McKechnie, who was getting quite excited.

'This is Cubs' stuff,' replied Duffy. 'Put me up to thirty a day and I'll get you free calls to Australia.'

'We're not quite *that* big yet. What about Barnsley?'

'It's harder to fix than Australia, funnily enough. Cost you forty.'

'You're a hard man, Duffy.' Duffy winced. McKechnie must have heard that line somewhere and thought it was the thing to say.

'Now, it's quite simple. When Salvatore comes on the line, you just press the Record button in the normal way. And don't forget to talk natural.'

'What do I do with the tape?'

'Call me afterwards and I'll tell you what to do. I won't come and collect it. Maybe I'll work out a drop. Or you could always post it.' The last suggestion sounded rather limp, even if it probably was the most efficient. Duffy constantly found that clients expected all sorts of secret tricks for their money. They wanted you to use a walkie-talkie when it was easier to use a public callbox; they wanted the windows of your car to be all blacked out although this made you the most conspicuous vehicle on the road; they wanted to leave things for you behind lavatory cisterns and wear false moustaches and buy complicated telephoto lenses which they couldn't work. The last thing they wanted to see you doing was sitting on your butt, applying your brain to their particular problem, and coming up with a one-word solution. And the last thing of all they ever wanted to be told was, 'I should go to the police if I were you.' They hated that. Clients, Duffy reflected, were dumb.

Duffy turned down the offer of a second King Kong mask (he couldn't be bothered to take one, but what he actually said, to boost customer morale, was, 'No, it's a better disguise *not* to have one this time'), and stepped out into Rupert Street. The pale man who ran the dirty book-shop had just taken down his shutters and was fiddling with the neon sign in the window. So far it only read BOO.

Duffy took a breath, headed up to Shaftesbury Avenue, crossed it, and found himself back on the patch he'd worked for three years. He'd been back a few times, to a restaurant or something, but always in the evening, under cover of dark. Now he felt more unprotected, more recognisable. He dived into a coffee bar. Sitting over a *cappuccino*, he gave himself bottle. Four years was a long time: whores change, villains change, the blues change. If that was bad in terms of finding things out, it was good in terms of not being recognised. Besides, he looked different now. Before, it had been two-piece suits from Burton's and Hepworth's, with a sports jacket for when he was trying to look casual. Now it was Jean Junction, street markets, suede and leather, faded denim; his hair was quite a bit longer at the sides, and brush-cut on top; sometimes he wore shades with pale yellow glass in them.

And on top of that, the answer was to walk like a punter. Punters had two ways of walking – very fast, as if they had a couple of minutes to catch a train and couldn't get out of the Golden Mile quick enough, and very slow, as if they were killing time before an appointment, and that was the only reason they were loitering through the place. And whichever method they adopted, they always walked with their heads a bit down; they didn't look people in the face, and they believed, if they kept their eyes lowered, that no one could see if they were squinting sideways into the windows of dirty bookshops. The people who walked at a normal pace with their heads up, and who looked other people in the eye as they passed them, were the people who owned the place: the shopkeepers, the whores, the pimps, the restaurateurs, the villains, and the blues.

As a copper, Duffy had been street-wise. He knew the way the place worked, how to get around in it, where the skeins of power ran. You picked it up slowly, partly from other coppers, but just as importantly by finding out for yourself; by getting to know the patch not just physically, but somehow emotionally as well. You sensed it pulsing away. This wasn't the main part of being a copper: you didn't stand in the middle of Soho, mystically sniffing the air like Maigret, and then head off and run a villain to ground. It was just background; it was knowing where you were. But to Duffy it was a vital preliminary to the job.

He finished his coffee and went out to get the feel again of his old patch. He walked along Old Compton Street, up Greek, down Frith, up Dean, across little courts and alleys into D'Arblay, down into Broadwick (past West Central on the other side of the street), down into Brewer, along to where it nearly joins up with Berwick in a fetid knot of street markets and escort agencies and cinemas, past Raymond's Revuebar and back across into Dean. He ate a lasagne and green salad in a corner café, and reflected that he still had almost eighteen quid left for the day (McKechnie, after some protest, had paid him seventy-five pounds in advance).

In four years it had changed a bit to his eyes. There were more bookshops than before, and more sex shops with rubber cucumbers in the window. Massage parlours seemed to be holding steady. Strip clubs were a bit on the decline, and had largely given way to porno cinemas. A few years ago Soho simply had normal cinemas, but showing naughtier films from the regular distributors: *Danish Dentist on the Job, Nurse Call, Catch 69, Vixens Behind Barbed Wire*, those sort of films. If you wanted something a couple of degrees hotter, the only place to go was the Compton Cinema Club in Old Compton Street; and if after that you were still unsatisfied, as you came out there might, if you were lucky, be a tout or two on the pavement offering you a really blue film. Now, though, there were whole series of cinema clubs, called Triple-X and X-Citing and Double Blue and Eros Eyrie and Taboo, with gaudy signs outside offering XXX-rated movies to those over eighteen.

The heat of the early afternoon made Duffy feel, not exactly randy, but definitely a bit interested. Head down, he turned into a dirty bookshop on the corner of Greek Street. At the desk a Mediterranean youth was reading the racing news and watching over the small shelf of dirty movies. On two sides of the shop were racks of mags, arranged by customer interest. The largest section was the Hetero one; then came Homo; then Leather and S & M and Bondage and Big Tits and Schoolgirls; finally a few shelves of paperbacks. The sales technique of the shops hadn't changed: you left English mags open for browsers to see – let them get turned on by *Rustler* and *Rapier* and *Playbirds* and *Lovebirds* and *New Directions* and *QT* – but sealed up the more expensive American imports so that they looked as if they must be a lot hornier. Duffy smiled at the hopeless self-deceiving gamble which the punters continued to go in for, still trusting in a hot cover, an inflated price and a polythene bag. He glanced at the rack of Big Tit mags, whose publishers had always seemed to work harder at the titles of their mags. *D-Cup* was still going strong, he noted, and so was *42-Plus*; *Bazooms* was there too, making tits sound like ballistic missiles; and a new one called *Milkmaids*. Duffy remembered one that had started up a few years ago called *Charlies' Aunts*, which had tickled him at the time; it had folded after a couple of issues – the punters probably thought it contained beaver-shots of old ladies. Maybe the invention had gone out of the industry, he reflected.

Next to the Bondage section – a few copies of *Hogtie* and one or two of *All Roped Up* – was a doorway leading to some cubicles. 10p X-RATED PORNO MINI-MOVIES CHANGE AT DESK read the sign. This was something new since he'd been around. He got some change at the desk and went into one of the cubicles; pinned to the door was a torn-off box lid advertising the film he could see there: 'LESBO LOVERS – Two girls all alone and left to their own vices go horse riding and find lots going on underneath!!!'

Duffy sat down on the bench and fumbled with his change. There was no lock on the door, which you kept shut with an extended foot while you watched the film being projected on to a white board on the back of the door. Duffy kicked the door to, and then couldn't see where to put his money in. He opened the door again and found a metal box near his right hand. 10p and the film began. A large black girl sat in a bath and soaped herself, concentrating on her pubes and her tits. The film stopped. 10p and the girl took the shower attachment and hosed off her tits, then hosed off her pubes, rolling her eyes back as she did so. The film was a bit out of focus, but it might get more interesting as it went on, Duffy thought. Where were the other girl and the horse? 10p and the girl was in the bath still, soaping her tits and pubes again. Whether the film was being long-winded, or whether it had come to an end with his second 10p and was starting again, Duffy couldn't quite make out. His concentration began to wander. The light from the projector showed up the comments which previous punters had scrawled on the 'screen': NO FUCKING GOOD one of them had written, and another, ALLIE'S ARMY.

As he came out of the booth, Duffy's heel slipped a bit on the floor. With a pile of change still in his hand, he tried another cubicle. This time there were two girls, kissing each other rather demurely. 10p and they started rubbing each other's tits as if they were polishing silver. Duffy wondered – was it worth risking another 10p? Well, it's on McKechnie, he thought. 10p and the girls started stroking one another's pubes and acted opening their mouths in delight and surprise. The focus was better in this booth, and Duffy found his cock was quite enjoying the show. 10p and one of the girls was lying on top of the other. That wasn't so much fun. 10p and a skinny bloke with a moustache jumped out of the shower and the girls acted 'Eeeek!' 10p and the skinny bloke started smacking their bottoms. There was no fun at all now; his cock told him it had had enough.

As he came out of the bookshop a girl jumped towards him. She was a plump, clean-looking girl with round, gold-rimmed glasses. She stood in front of him and pinned a badge onto his lapel. He squinted down and saw that it read 'Have a Happy Day'. She chirruped,

'We're trying to help poor children all over the world. I'm sure you'd like to make us a donation.'

She was bright in manner, polite, and firm. You couldn't take objection to her. Duffy could. Fucking Moonies, he thought, can't even leave the poor old guilt-ridden punters alone. He unpinned the badge and offered it back to her; she was already pulling out a record from her shoulder-bag,

'We're trying to help poor children. I'm sure you want to make a donation,' she repeated.

Duffy couldn't help saying what he thought. 'Fucking Moonie,' he said, dropped the badge and turned away. As he went she hit him over the head with the record.

That was new too, then, he reflected. He walked on down the street past a few Triple-X porno-blue clubs (he'd save them for another day), and came across something else that was new. PEEP SHOW, it said, LIVE GIRLS DANCE NUDE WHILE YOU WATCH. As he approached the place, head slightly down, he squinted sideways: 50p, the sign said, and DIFFERENT GIRLS. He walked on, then did a classic punter's double-back, putting on speed and suddenly jumping through the door. He changed a couple of quid at the desk and went into a tiny cell. The lock just about stopped the door from swinging open. At eye-level in the opposite wall there was an opening about the size of a letter box. On the floor were Kleenex tissues; some of them were damp. Disco music was being played on a powerful sound system.

Duffy dropped a 50p into the slot and a metal shutter at the level of his face jerked up, revealing a glass slit window. He pressed his nose against the glass and saw a girl dancing. The booths formed an almost complete circle round her, with a gap for her to come on and off stage. She was naked, thinnish, with a noticeable appendix scar and breasts which had probably been siliconed. She played with her tits and rubbed her pubes while dancing, and kept an eye on the row of slits, moving to face each new one that opened for a few seconds. Duffy laid out another 50p on her, though some of the time he spent looking round at the other letter boxes, at the anonymous pairs of eyes.

He'd had about 40p worth of the girl when the music suddenly stopped and she ran off stage. At once the next girl ran on, shedding her track suit as she came. Quick, quick, don't make the punters angry. She was a black girl, and she seemed vaguely familiar to Duffy. She was thinnish like the first girl, with a hard-looking, impassive face. She danced a lot better than her predecessor, and was a lot more athletic. She was also a lot dirtier. She played with tits and pubes while she danced, as the other girl had done. But she also leaned right over, stuck her bum in the air, and pulled her cheeks apart so that you could see her cunt and her bum-hole. Then she would bounce over towards a letter box and put her leg right up in the air, resting her foot against the wall of the booth while she dabbled at her cunt with her fingers. After a few seconds she would dance away again, then attract in turn the attention of all the punters with their visors raised and appear to pick out one of them. The lucky man, provided his 50p didn't run out, then had his window squeegeed by the girl's cunt. This happened to Duffy after he had spent about £1.30. It wasn't exactly a turn-on (though it certainly wasn't a turn-off), but it was a bit odd: rather like sitting in your car at a garage while they chammy your windscreen.

Duffy wasn't quite sure why he dropped the fourth 50p into the slot – after all, he knew he'd seen the best part of the show. With other men the action would have sprung from the generosity of the satisfied punter who's been ripped off so many times that he likes to show his appreciation for once. With Duffy it sprang from a still lurking curiosity. He somehow felt he'd seen the black girl before. On his final 50p, he didn't watch her tits or her cunt; he watched her face. There was something familiar about it. Then he switched his gaze and saw it – a thin white scar on the right shoulder. It was the girl who'd been stabbed four years ago, the girl he'd visited in hospital and leaned on a bit.

Duffy waited around outside the Peep Show for a while. He couldn't do too much of this, he realised. Standing around on street corners in Soho was all right as far as the public went: they just thought you were a pimp. But the other pimps and the blues tended to come by for a closer squint at you. After a bit Duffy looked around for a café and saw one forty yards down the street. Not the best location, but he might be able to get a clear view from there. He sat over a coffee – the boredom of it brought back to him his days with the force – and waited for about half an hour. Then the black girl came out of the Peep Show and started walking down the street in his direction. He abandoned his coffee and stepped outside. She was twenty yards short of the café when she suddenly jumped into a taxi and disappeared.

Duffy went home thinking that there were parts of his job he quite enjoyed. What he really needed to discover was how the new power structure of the Golden Mile worked: who owned what, who dealt in what, who fixed and ran what. He could ask Carol, of course; though he didn't like to involve her, especially if the case was going to get anywhere near Sullivan. He could try chasing down a few old contacts; he could see if the black girl – what was she called? – would help. Not that he'd been very nice to her apart from taking her some flowers at the hospital when she'd cut her bum on the baked bean tin. There was another possibility – calling on Renée, that is, if she was still working. Renée was a whore he'd always got on well with, a sharp, businesslike whore with a sense of humour; she'd been around the streets for about twenty years now, and must be pushing forty. But she knew most things that were going on, and was willing to sell most of the things that she knew. If McKechnie wanted an invoice, though, he'd have to whistle for it. Renée didn't exactly fill out V.A.T. forms.

Next morning McKechnie called.

'It's gone up,' was the first thing he said.

Duffy was not surprised. 'How much?'

'Hundred and fifty. But I've got four days to pay. Salvatore said he was feeling generous.'

'That's standard,' said Duffy. 'Did you record it all right?'

'Yes.'

'Then this is what I want you to do. Turn the tape over and start on side two. Phone Sullivan and record your conversation. Take a tough line with him, say you've already lost three hundred and fifty quid thanks to him, tell him the fee's gone up again and you want some action this time. Tell him that when you make the drop you want to be certain that there's an officer watching. Tell him you want a description of that officer and his name and where he'll be, so that you can check that Sullivan is doing what he says he is. Try not to put his back up too much, but pull an outraged-citizen act . . .'

'I *am* outraged,' said McKechnie.

'Of course; sorry. But act like someone who is getting towards the end of his tether and might do something Sullivan wouldn't like. Give the impression you might go to his superiors or to the newspapers or something. I'm sure he'll be hell-bent on calming you down. Do you think you can manage that?'

McKechnie said he thought so.

'When you've made the call, take the tape out, put it in an envelope and give it to your secretary. Tell her' (Duffy quickly thought up some gumshoe ploy which would make McKechnie feel he was getting his money's worth) 'to go to the snack bar at the west end of Paddington Station at three o'clock. I'll be sitting with my back to the counter with a large brown parcel on the seat next to me. She's to ask if the seat is free and when I say it is she's to slip the envelope on to the counter between us. Do you think she can do that?'

'She's proved more or less capable in all I've given her to do so far.'

'Good. Oh, and there's another thing. I'll need some cash for some information. I'm going to talk to a whore, and as you probably know, whores don't give receipts.'

'How much?'

'Not sure. Maybe fifty or so.'

'Mr Duffy, I wouldn't want to find you proving as big a drain on my resources as Mr Salvatore is. Do you follow me?'

'All right. So can you put the fifty in with the tape.'

'No. Take it out of your advance. She may not talk, after all.' That was true enough.

'O.K. And remind me what your secretary's called.'

'Belinda.'

At three o'clock Duffy was at Paddington Station, his back turned to the snack bar counter. Suddenly there was a tap on his shoulder, and a high-pitched voice trilled,

'Oh, Mr Duffy.'

He spun round. It was the secretary. He winced.

'Mr McKechnie asked me to give you this.' She handed him a brown envelope. 'I don't like to be nosy, but I think it's got a tape recording in it.' Then she leaned over to him, smiled, and whispered, 'I say, Mr Duffy, isn't all this *exciting*?'

If Duffy had had them with him, he would have walked out of the snack bar wearing his King Kong mask and his clown's hat, just to make sure that nobody noticed him.

Back at the flat, he found that the first side of the tape didn't have anything unexpected on it. Duffy played it through, mainly just listening to Salvatore's voice. It didn't seem as foreign as McKechnie had described, but it had the authentic tang of a man who's calling all the shots and enjoying it. Towards the end of the conversation, McKechnie said,

'You're squeezing me too hard, don't you know that?'

'Squeezing you, Mr McKechnie? *Squeezing* you? I can promise you that you'd be feeling it if I were. No, no. You're just helping me out with my little cash-flow crisis, that's what you're doing.'

'Where am I going to find a hundred and fifty in four days?'

A little chuckle from the other end of the phone.

'Oh, I'm sure the shareholders will accept a reduced dividend just for this one year.'

'You mean you're going to lay off me?' He sounded whingeingly hopeful.

'No, I don't exactly mean *that*, Mr McKechnie. Indeed, I can't see my cash-flow crisis being solved in the immediate future. I might even have to call on you for some increased sums.'

'I can't find the amount you're asking for.'

'Well, Mr McKechnie, all I can say to that is that you might find yourself called upon to liquefy some of your capital assets.'

'What do you mean?'

'Well, I'm sure you don't need all that storage space you've got. *Two* warehouses – I would have thought with a better storekeeping policy you could probably manage with just the one. Wouldn't you?'

'I couldn't get rid of one of my warehouses.' There was almost a note of panic in McKechnie's voice. 'I couldn't.'

'Suck it and see, Mr McKechnie. Suck it and see.'

On the second side of the tape McKechnie was displaying a lot more bottle. Maybe he'd caught it from Salvatore; maybe he suddenly realised that Duffy would be listening and wanted to put on a less craven performance. After hearing it straight through, Duffy rewound and picked it up again in the middle.

'. . . the last time.'

'Well, we'll do our best, McKechnie, I won't promise you anything more than that.'

'I haven't been too impressed with your best so far, Sullivan. I'm just suggesting to you that now might be the time to get your finger out. I'm suggesting that what I want this time is some assurance.'

'Like what?'

'I want to know that one of your men is at the scene when I make my drop.'

'O.K., you have my assurance.'

'I want more than that, Sullivan. I want to know who's going to be there; I want a description of him so that I can check he's there; I want his name and rank so that if necessary I can get in touch with him later.'

'You trying to teach me how to run my department, McKechnie? I'm not having some . . . . coming on to my patch and telling me how to run my shop. I'm not having you interfering with my boys.'

'I hope you won't be too unco-operative, Sullivan.'

'What do you mean?'

'Just what I say.' McKechnie played it cool. 'I think it would be in everyone's best interests if the police afforded a local trader the normal degree of co-operation.'

'Hmmm.' If Duffy had been Sullivan, he would have

called McKechnie's bluff and told him to bugger off. Sullivan was more cautious. 'Well, I'll see what I can do. I'm not telling you any officer's name or rank, but I'll give you a description of one of the officers covering the drop. Ring me when you know where it's going to be.'

Duffy stopped the tape. Then he ran it back for a few seconds and got Sullivan speaking: '. . . run my department, McKechnie? I'm not having some . . . . coming on to my patch and telling me how to run my shop.' There was a gap in the tape about two and a half seconds long. Duffy rang McKechnie.

'There's a gap in the tape.'

'What?'

'There's a gap in the tape. What was Sullivan saying?'

'Oh, that, Mr Duffy, yes there is, you're quite right. It's quite all right, it wasn't anything of relevance to the case.'

'What was it and why did you wipe it?'

'Well . . . you see, it struck me that if this tape ever . . . well, ever became part of an investigation for instance, if it ever became part of a case, you know what I mean, Mr Duffy?'

'All right.'

'Then I wouldn't want to be thought of by those listening to the case in the terms in which the Superintendent chose to describe me. You may think I'm being over-sensitive, but that's how I reacted anyway.'

'And what did he call you?'

'I'd need your assurance that you wouldn't repeat it.'

'All right.'

'Well, he called me . . . a syphilitic sheep-fucker.'

Duffy smiled into the telephone.

'Your secret is safe with me, Mr McKechnie.'

This was on a Tuesday. The drop was on the Friday. At eleven McKechnie phoned Duffy at his flat.

'Same time. One o'clock. Dustbins again. Brewer Street. Dustbins by the garage entrance next to Gino's

Delicatessen. The one farthest away from the shop. Sullivan said he'd have a man in the window of the café opposite Gino's. Said I should come down Brewer Street on the wrong side, pretending not to see Gino's, check that his man was there, and then cross the road and make the drop.'

'What did he say his man looked like?'

'He said he'd be wearing a scarlet tie so that I'd see him easily through the window. He wouldn't tell me anything more about what he looked like.'

'O.K. You do exactly as both of them told you. I'll be in touch later.'

Duffy wanted to be in place early, to see Sullivan's man arrive. But Sullivan's man would have to get there early to make sure he got a window seat in a café at one o'clock. So Duffy would have to be there even earlier. He took a cab. McKechnie would have to pay for this necessary luxury.

He got to Brewer Street around eleven thirty and walked slowly down its length in punter style. He spotted Gino's quickly, and then the café on the other side of the road. The dustbins could be seen easily from the café. But the trouble was, there wasn't anywhere obvious for Duffy to place himself and be able to observe both the drop and the café. There was a pub fifteen yards down from the café: he could see the drop from there, but then he wouldn't be able to see Sullivan's man. Or there was a dirty bookshop from where he could see the café but not the drop; perhaps he could buy something, so that he wouldn't get thrown out, and then just browse for a bit. No, that was no good; he had to see the drop. Then why not sit in the café as well? It might get a bit awkward when both he and Sullivan's man got up to tail the pick-up at exactly the same time, but he'd just have to cross that bridge when he came to it.

Duffy decided on the café. He went in at about twelve and sat at a side table away from the window. He ordered a

71

meal he didn't in the least need, and began his wait. Twelve fifteen and a few early lunchers arrived. Twelve thirty and the place was really starting to fill up. There were only two free tables left in the window. Twelve forty-five and there was only one. At least the other customers would give Duffy cover, but where was Sullivan's man? Then he noticed that the one free table had a plastic Reserved sign on it. That was getting a bit lordly. Twelve fifty and the man in the scarlet tie sauntered in. Duffy took a quick look and put his head down.

Shaw. Christ, he hadn't reckoned for that. Old Rick Shaw, as he'd been nicknamed at West Central. He hadn't allowed for that; he'd thought it would be some wet-ear he'd never set eyes on before. That changed everything. He didn't at all fancy trying to tail the pick-up man and stay out of Shaw's way at the same time.

At twelve fifty-five Duffy carefully left the café, turning his head away as he walked past the window occupied by Shaw. He got to the pub and saw to his relief that there was a knot of drinkers on the pavement. With a half of bitter in his hand he stood around as if he could almost be part of their group. At twelve fifty-nine McKechnie went past the pub, walking as if looking out for something, peering rather shortsightedly into shops. He was doing it well, Duffy thought. He saw him reach the café, go past it for ten yards, stop, turn, then suddenly pretend to spot Gino's on the other side of the road. At a minute past one he reached the dustbin and made the drop. Then he headed off back the way he'd come, turned down Great Windmill Street and disappeared.

At four minutes past one Shaw came out of the café, turned sharp right, didn't give the dustbin a glance, and hurried off. That was not part of the plan at all, as far as Duffy had imagined it. Was Shaw merely there to keep McKechnie happy, and was Sullivan in effect simply handing the money over to Salvatore? Or was Shaw just part of a two-man team, and Sullivan had wisely pulled him out in case someone watching had seen McKechnie look in at the restaurant window? Still, at least it meant that Duffy wouldn't have to worry about mixing his tail with Shaw's.

At one fifteen a scruffy youth in denims came hurrying down the street. He stopped by the dustbins, rooted about in the right-hand one, then the middle one, finally landed on the one where the envelope was, picked it out and stuffed it in his pocket. Whether he'd gone through all three dustbins because he wanted to look like an authentic rag-picker or whether he'd done so because he was all fucked up and couldn't remember which bin to look in, Duffy didn't know or care.

Duffy had guessed that the youth would head east along Brewer Street. This wasn't a difficult gamble, as west would take him out into Regent Street, and he didn't see this kid losing a tail by mingling indistinguishably with the clientèle in Jaeger's. As the scruff was making up the hundred yards to get level with him, Duffy squinted round looking for likely police tails. Part of being taught how to tail is being taught how to recognise tails and lose them. The kid was almost level with him and nothing likely had presented itself. He let the kid go thirty, forty yards before deciding he couldn't let him get any farther away; not in Soho. He'd just have to risk it about Sullivan's tail.

Duffy closed down the gap quickly: you could lose someone in ten yards at that end of Brewer Street. Shit, he was cutting through to Berwick Street market. Duffy should have predicted that. Past the Revuebar, and then in among the stalls. One person pushing a bit in a street market didn't show. Another person pushing to keep up with the first person showed a lot. The youth dodged about a bit among the stalls. Fortunately he wasn't very competent; or maybe he hadn't been trained very well, or

73

maybe he thought he didn't need to try. After a bit of hide-and-seek he dodged down St Anne's Court, into Dean Street, across Bateman, and into Frith. Duffy turned the corner into Frith in time to see him disappearing up the steps of the Double Blue Cinema Club.

Duffy paused. He was sure of two things. One was that Sullivan hadn't had the kid tailed: Shaw had simply walked off and that had been the end of the surveillance. The other was that if he rushed up the steps into the cinema straight away he might as well be wearing a tin badge and whistling the theme from *High Noon*. He stood around for a bit, waited for a couple of punters to go into the club, prayed for another celluloid lecher to turn up quickly, and when he did, followed him quickly up the steps.

5

The grey-suited punter Duffy followed up the steps of the
Double Blue looked round nervously at him, as if Duffy
were a private detective hired by his wife. At the plywood
box office he bought a subscription for ten pounds and
paid a fiver to go in. He disappeared ahead of Duffy.

'Member?' asked the cashier, who looked like a soiled
hippy.

'No. But I'll have the normal rates, not the ones you
charge shits in suits.' Duffy knew there was no real
'normal' rate; it fluctuated according to the punter, and
often the cashier's wages at the end of the day depended
on how much he took. It was up to the man in the box
office to find out how much the market could bear.

'All right. Fiver for membership, three-fifty to go in.'

Duffy looked at him quizzically. 'Sure it isn't two-fifty?'

'Nah. Never has been, chief. More than my job's worf to
drop it that far.'

Duffy nodded. Hell, it was only McKechnie's money.

'Name?' The cashier had pulled out a grubby white
membership card on which he had inscribed a number
and a date.

'Daniel Drough.' The hippy wrote it out in capitals,
clearly finding it a change from the long run of J. Smiths
and H. Wilsons that he was used to. Duffy took the card
and went into the cinema.

There were two dozen people inside a large corridor of a
room, with a screen about ten feet by six at the end of it.
While waiting for his eyes to acclimatise, Duffy watched
the film. It was like a larger version of the 10p Mini-Movies
he'd watched, but a bit dirtier. It also had very bad sound.

There were two girls, supposedly lying on a beach, who had taken their bikinis off and were dabbing palmfuls of sun-oil on each other; it made a slapping noise, like the sea against a harbour wall. Then one of them produced a vibrator from out of nowhere, and switched it on. It sounded as if someone had started to Hoover the beach. She applied this to the other girl's tits; the other girl smiled. Then she applied it to the girl's pubes, whereupon the second girl immediately flung her legs apart as if for gynaecological examination, threw her head back, and began to pant. In order to be heard over the sound of the vibrator she had to pant very loudly. It sounded as if a large sheepdog had been harnessed to a Hoover, was pulling it up and down the beach, and getting very tired. Duffy's cock informed him that this wasn't a very good film.

He looked round the punters, searching for his man. He covered half of them, then moved his seat. Movement isn't very popular in these cinemas. It disturbs the entranced communion between the man in his seat and the image on the screen; it makes the punters shifty and guilty about their hard-ons. Some managements send a patrolling heavy round every so often to make sure the punters aren't jerking off over the seats; others decide this is bad for business as it disturbs the customers, install washable plastic seats, and pay the cleaners a bit extra.

Duffy couldn't see his man among the second half of the audience either. He looked around the cinema, while careful not to catch any punter's eye for fear of enraging him. Down at the end, next to the screen, there was a toilet (the clubs are wisely punctilious about G.L.C. regulations on membership procedures and toilets). The side walls of the cinema were solid. The box office had just been a plywood insert into the front six feet of the building.

Duffy got up again and went to the toilet. A narrow

corridor ran past it for another fifteen feet or so. Duffy went along to the end and saw some stairs doubling back up to the left. At the foot of the stairs on the right was an emergency exit. The two horizontal push-bars, one on each door, had been chained together; the padlock which held them looked rusty. Duffy slowly walked up the stairs, trying not to make any noise. When he was about halfway up he heard a door open, and footsteps at about the level of his head. Immediately he started walking up at a normal pace, whistling quietly as he did so. When he got to the top of the stairs he saw a large, ginger-haired man with glasses closing a door on the right.

'Where's the pisser, mate?' he asked in a no-trouble voice.

'You walked right past it,' the man replied. 'First bloke to walk past our pisser,' he added genially, 'yer nose must be all blocked up.'

Duffy pulled out a handkerchief and blew hard, then sniffed, and acted being knocked out by the stink. 'Think I can find it now, mate,' he said, and headed off downstairs. There'd been three rooms at the top of the stairs, and he could hear voices coming from the one on the right. He walked back to the toilet, waited a few seconds, and pulled the chain; nothing happened; he pulled again and smiled at the wasted subterfuge.

He sat in the cinema for a bit longer while a girl with big tits who ran a sex shop invited customers into her back room for a bit of mild fladge (Duffy caught himself wondering who was minding the shop in the meantime). She pulled up her skirt, took down her knickers and leaned over a desk. The men pretended to beat her with a riding crop while she made a whimpering noise which the sound system turned into the cry of an eviscerated goose.

As Duffy left he had a bantering word with the hippy cashier, who confessed he found the films 'really boring', that he'd 'been through that scene'. Duffy recommended that he try again, and mentioned the sex shop number. 'I mean, maybe tits aren't your scene, but if they are, man, then that's the film for you, I'd say.'

'Nah, I think they're all really boring.'

Meanwhile, Duffy had completed his casual examination of the locks on the cinema doors; he said goodbye and wandered off.

When he got back home he phoned McKechnie.

'What did Sullivan say?'

'He said he couldn't understand it. He'd put two of his best men on the job, and the bloke had got clean away again.'

'Did he say how?'

'Yes, he ran into Regent Street and jumped into a cab. Sullivan's men waited on the pavement but there wasn't another cab for a while.'

'Did you believe him?'

'No. Should I have?'

'No. Did you tell him you didn't?'

'No. What really happened?'

'The red-tie merchant in the café when you made the drop got up and left almost at once, just scarpered. Whether there was another guy or not I can't be sure; but if there was, he couldn't tail a man in a wheelchair. He was nowhere when I got to the end of my run.'

'Where was that.'

'A place called the Double Blue. It's a cinema club in Frith Street. The bloke vanished inside. Somewhere upstairs. I couldn't follow him.'

'So what do we do now?'

'Dunno for the moment. I'll nose around for a bit. By the way, the cinema cost me eight-fifty.'

'Got a receipt?'

'I've got a membership card.'

'I said receipts, Duffy.'

'I'll tell you about the films in incredible detail if you like.'

'It wouldn't be the same.'

'No – it'd probably be better.' McKechnie laughed.

Duffy wasn't sure what line to follow. He sat down to review what had happened so far. Some things were certain, some things were hopelessly ambiguous. Someone had cut McKechnie's wife for a start. Someone was now trying to presh him, though how far was anyone's guess. Someone with a sense of humour was using a dead racketeer's name. Then there was Sullivan – what was he up to? Was he simply taking the easy way out by missing the pick-ups, or was he taking a cut? What was Shaw doing – old Rick? Was he just doing what Sullivan told him, or was he being cut in? He'd always remembered Shaw as a copper who didn't go in for accepting too many Christmas turkeys. Still, every year around the Golden Mile brought different temptations. He knew how it happened: you didn't take the free booze even if everyone else did; you didn't take the first girl you got offered; you turned down the smokes and the snort; and then something quite trivial happened, like you asked for a couple of days to pay at the bookie's. Quite suddenly, the place had got you. It wasn't necessarily that there was a particular gang always on the look-out to bend coppers (though sometimes there was); it was somehow the place that got you. It was one square mile of pressure, and everyone had a weak point.

Duffy felt he had to know some more background. He really needed to talk to someone like Shaw, but that was out of the question. Maybe Carol; or maybe that wasn't fair; well, maybe he could ask her about the place without letting her know what he was up to. Apart from Carol, there was Renée: he ought to go and have a chat with her, if only for old times' sake. That was a dangerous phrase, 'old times' sake' – if he started thinking like that he'd be sentimentalising about Sullivan before he knew where he was. And then there was the black girl at the Peep Show. What was she called? Something with a B or a P. Belinda? No, that was McKechnie's dumb secretary. That was it – Polly. Not that she owed him any favours.

And then there were a few other things which Duffy wondered about. One was that McKechnie didn't seem as worried by everything as Duffy thought he ought to be; he even seemed to find parts of it almost exciting. No, maybe he was just phlegmatic; and he had seemed genuinely upset when he'd told Duffy about what had happened to his wife. Perhaps McKechnie was really much richer than he thought, and could soak up a lot more presh; though you'd never guess, to look at the shack he operated from. It wasn't exactly buzzing with clients, either. Still, maybe that sort of business was mainly mail order. But then – there were so many buts in the case – what about the gap on the tape? McKechnie had been completely plausible about it; but was it Sullivan's style to call a member of the public a 'syphilitic sheep-fucker'? Well, that again was possible; actually, quite probable. And finally there was the little incident at Paddington Station that nagged at Duffy: if the secretary had managed to remember about getting there, arriving at the right time and the right place, and recognising him, could she be so thick that she didn't carry out the rest of the instructions he had given McKechnie? Or what if McKechnie had changed those instructions, what if she'd actually been doing exactly as she'd been told? That was an undermining thought; but Duffy decided to shrug it off. McKechnie probably wasn't an entirely straight-up-and-down guy, but which of his clients ever had been? And did you expect a guy who sold King Kong masks in Soho to behave like a clergyman? There was one rule you tried to stick to in this business: you believed the client was dealing straight with you until you had strong evidence to the contrary.

He rang Carol and asked her if she'd like to come round that evening. She said she couldn't, she was going to the pictures (who with? But the rules said you weren't allowed to ask). She could come the next night, though. Duffy said Yes please, and he'd make her the best toasted cheese she'd had since the last time she'd had toasted cheese.

He contemplated another evening alone in his flat. Maybe he'd better go out and find someone. Soho made you randy, there was no doubt about that. Not the films he'd seen – the Hoover, the sheepdog and the goose – or the memory of having his windscreen squeegeed in the Peep Show; it was just being there. The air over mill towns used to be heavy with a precipitate of soot; you breathed it into your lungs and body; over Soho, the air seemed filled with a precipitate of sex.

Duffy's mind idled over the choice between trawling for a man and trawling for a woman. To Duffy it was like choosing between bacon and egg and bacon and tomato. Whichever you decided on you had a good time; it was just what your taste-buds felt like that evening. Women were usually less likely to leave you needing a visit to the clinic. On the other hand they were a bit more expensive; they tended not to stand their round if they were going to go to bed with you later; and some of them made the sentimental mistake of believing that because Duffy was nice to them it meant that he wanted to see them again. Then he had to be firm, and tell them no, and that often added a sour note to breakfast.

The other thing was that, in practical terms, men could be more relied upon if you wanted to get laid. You spent longer chatting up women than you did men; and even if you were in a singles bar where it was generally assumed that everyone was on the prowl, it was still part of the accepted convention that a girl had every right to dump you with a final No, even if all evening she'd been giving off signals which said Yes. Whereas if you went to a gay club, you never left disappointed. Not everyone went there determined to get laid, of course; there was a certain amount of 'Well, I'll see', and 'Try me later'; but as long as you were clean and neat, you were bound to end up with someone. There was rarely any of that breakfast trouble, either. Indeed, what some of the guys you brought back wanted to do was just get up and leave before the sheets were dry. Well, that was O.K. by Duffy too.

It looked as if it was heading for another evening down at the Alligator. Besides, if he were seeing Carol to-morrow, it always gave him a jolt if he'd spent the previous night with a girl. And that spoiled the previous night as well; it had him making all sorts of comparisons which weren't a good idea. No, Duffy decided, it would definitely have to be a guy tonight. He headed off to the bathroom to smarten himself up.

A few hours later, he finished his evening at the Alligator with Jack, a gentle, blond American from the Mid-West who was hitch-hiking round Europe with a copy of the *Spartacus Gay Guide to Europe* and a reverent determination to visit every major club and bar listed in it. The tourism side of the venture almost outweighed the gayness side of it: Jack had been sipping a Campari at the Alligator in the manner of a camera-laden tripper lighting a candle at Chartres. He almost had to be reminded about wanting to get laid. Over breakfast, Jack confessed a shy desire to start up his own *Good Gay Guide* along the lines of the *Good Food Guide*, relying on reports from members and occasionally sending out inspectors to make spot checks on establishments which seemed to be slipping. Duffy said he'd get in touch if ever he needed a job.

After Jack had left, Duffy tidied up, changed the sheets for when Carol came (and for if Carol stayed, which weren't at all the same thing) and went off to track down

Renée. She'd always operated from a little flat in an alley off Wardour Street; it was a two-girl gaff, partly for mutual protection and partly in case clients wanted a sandwich job or an exhibition. She'd always worked for the same pimp, called Ronnie, who owned the flat, gave her what protection she needed, and took the usual cut. Renée was a lot smarter than Ronnie, though, and after she hit thirty she persuaded him to adopt a system whereby each year – as she got older and the competition got tougher and her earning potential got a bit less – she would pay him a slightly smaller percentage of what she earned. She pointed out what a good name this would get Ronnie among the other whores, and how this would make it easier for him to get new girls.

Ronnie had bought the scheme, perhaps imagining that Renée would give up at thirty-three or so. But she'd soldiered on, and, as she had planned, the scheme had worked to her advantage. Ronnie had moaned a bit, but kept to his promise after Renée had threatened to bad-mouth him all the way from Soho Square to Piccadilly Circus. That had brought him to heel; and then, to keep him sweet, Renée had upped the rent of the girls she shared the flat with.

As Duffy turned into Wardour Street, he remembered his visits to Renée. Money had occasionally changed hands, though strictly for information received. She had from time to time offered him a Christmas box (she'd smiled as she pronounced the phrase), but he'd thought it best to refuse. Still, he carried on calling on her, often just for chats; and he always followed the cardinal rule of scarpering when a client arrived.

Duffy saw the two lighted bell-pushes labelled RENÉE and SUZIE, pressed the top one, and walked up. He remembered the landing: one door straight ahead, with a card on the outside saying SUZIE; the other, to the right, saying RENÉE. It looked as if the gaff was two separate flats, but in fact they connected up and had an alarm system from one to the other. You knocked on the door and either it opened or you got a shout of 'Five minutes, love', like an A.S.M. giving an actor his call.

Duffy knocked on the door on the right. It opened, and there was Renée in a long dressing gown, her dark hair half piled up on top of her head and half tumbling down one side in long curls to make an elaborately confected coiffure. She looked a bit older, a bit plumper, as she briefly cast an eye over him in the way that whores do, to see if he was either copper or someone from the whores' blacklist; it was a dispassionate gaze, like that of a shop manager checking a credit card.

'Come in, love,' she said, and backed into the room. As she did so she let the dressing gown fall back so that he could see a black garter belt and stockings and a black bra.

'Nothing dirty,' she announced, before he had time to close the door. 'I don't do nothing dirty. I don't do it up the bum and I keep me mouth to meself. It's ten if you want it straight, eight for the hands, an extra two if you want to see me tits; and there're a few other things I might do but you've gotta ask for them.'

'Renée,' he said, 'I'm Duffy.'

'Sorry, love, never remember a face in my business.'

'No, I'm Duffy, I'm not a client . . .'

Renée looked up, very cross.

'What d'yer mean, you're not a fucking client? Whatcher doing here if yer not a client?' She looked at him again, then suddenly she recognised him.

'Duffy. Of course. Duffy.' She looked embarrassed. 'Why didn't you stop me in the sales spiel, you bastard?'

'Didn't have time. You never let a fellow get in edgeways, Renée, did you?'

'I'd let him in edgeways; just wouldn't let him in from the back. Hey, Duffy, what've you come to see me for?' She pulled her dressing gown across her body. '*And* I let

84

you see what's become of me. I oughta charge you for that, Duffy. What've you come to see me for?'

'Well . . .'

'Oh, Christ, I've just remembered. I've just remembered why you stopped coming to see me. I didn't know you were bent, Duffy. I mean, I don't judge, but I didn't know you were bent. Bent and little boys, it was, wasn't it, Duffy, that's what they said. I don't judge, but little boys I don't approve of, I'd better tell you that straight out.'

'It wasn't little boys.' Duffy was furious. Is that what the whisper was? 'Who said it was little boys?'

'Oh, you know, that's what they said. People. You don't remember who.'

'It was a fit-up, Renée. I was fitted up by someone to have me thrown out. The kid said he was nineteen when the coppers kicked the door in, but he could have been twenty-five. I thought he was, but he told the blues he was nineteen. It was a fit-up, Renée.'

'Sorry to hear it, Duffy.' Renée was sceptical about coppers who were flung out of the force; they always said they'd been fitted up. Still, Duffy had always seemed to be fairly honest.

'Is that why you never took Renée's Christmas box, Duffy? 'Cos you were bent?'

'I was only a bit bent, Renée. I like fish as well as meat. It's no problem to me. But it wasn't little boys; it's *never* been little boys.' Duffy was still cross. Who did he have to thank for that: fucking Sullivan? Another of his little avuncular acts?

'O.K., Duffy, calm down.'

'And I didn't take the Christmas box because, well, for one thing I knew you were much too smart not to find a use for it later. I knew that I'd be after someone, or a mate of mine might be, and then there'd be a phone call from our Renée and she'd say, "Duffy, remember that Christmas box? Well, now I've got a little something to ask you in return." I knew you were much too sharp not to use that sooner or later.'

'You're no fool, Duffy.'

Duffy nodded agreement; with someone like Renée you always had to work out exactly where you stood.

'Now, what have you come back for if it's not to add to poor old Renée's pension fund?'

'Well, I might be able to make a contribution. It's information I need, Renée.'

'Not back in the force, are you?'

'No. I'm – well, let's say I'm acting in a freelance capacity for a certain party who's being preshed locally.'

'What's wrong with the wonderful boys in blue?'

'Well, it looks as if all their blind eyes are pointing in the same direction at the moment if you can imagine.'

'I might have heard of it happening before. And so this particular fellow called for Duffy?'

'All right.'

'Why you?'

'I'd been recommended.'

That was another thing which Duffy was puzzling over: who'd recommended him to McKechnie. What had he said? 'I asked around'? Where had he asked, Duffy wondered. Certainly nowhere near his last two jobs – advising on a burglar-alarm system for a factory in Hounslow, and telling a slice of posh trash where to hide her jewels. (She'd been too mean to insure them or buy a safe and too lazy to put them in the bank and take them out when she needed them: she just wanted Duffy to go round the house with her and tell her the last place a thief would think of looking. She'd been reading some story, she said, where something had been cleverly hidden in the most obvious place and no one had ever found it: wasn't that *such* a good idea? Duffy told her that the most obvious place for her jewels was in her jewel box, and what chance did she think there was of burglars looking there? She'd looked a bit put down, and Duffy went on to rubbish the whole theory of keeping things in obvious places: lots of burglars are so thick they only look in obvious places. So what about somewhere that isn't *terribly* obvious and isn't *terribly* difficult, she asked? Then the medium-grade burglars find your jewels, Duffy said. So they settled for the hardest place after all. Then it turned out that what she'd *actually* been thinking about was the elephant's-foot waste-paper basket that grandpa had brought back from India and which had a false bottom. Duffy said that this was ideal, wrote out a bill for fifty pounds, tore it up, wrote out a new one for fifty guineas, sent it off and swore to himself that if the posh trash didn't pay he'd make sure a little leak went in the right direction. To someone, for instance, who collected waste-paper baskets.)

'But the Mile's changed a bit, I expect, since I was here. I thought you might be able to fill me in. You know, who runs what, who's new, what sort of presh is on, that sort of thing.'

'Funny you should ask me that, Duffy, I was only talking to Ronnie about it the other day. I'm not a moaner, you know that, and it's not just an old tart talking who's getting elbowed off the street by young scrubbers . . .'

'You're looking younger than ever,' Duffy responded automatically.

'Don't shit me, Duffy, I know I'm getting to a difficult age for a tart. You get past a certain age and you've got a choice: either you're content with your regulars – and I am on the whole, I've got a nice bunch, quite clean most of 'em – though you gradually see them dropping off a bit; you know, trying someone a bit younger or a black tart, or someone who does something different. Or you do . . . oh, what's the word for it, Duffy, you do that thing what big companies are always doing . . .'

'Diversify?'

'That's right. You have to diversify. And that, believe you me, is a U-fer-mism. Diversify means you have to take anyone who comes up those stairs, diversify means taking mean shits who want to hurt you. It means you have to let punters fuck you up the bum, and I'm *never* going to do that. It means you have to let them give you a bashing with whips and stuff. Some of them . . . well, I'm not easily shocked, you know that, Duffy, some of them, soon as they see I'm not fifteen, they want to do things I won't even tell Suzie next door, corrupt her poor mind. Personally, I blame all this pornography the Labour Government let in, that's what I blame.'

Duffy smiled, though he wasn't sure if he was meant to; Renée often laughed when she was serious. But one thing was clear: she wouldn't be diversifying.

'When I started in this gaff it was a nice trade, being on the streets. Sure, there were a few nasties now and then, but it was a nice, friendly trade. You set yourself up, you built up your custom, you got known for what you did best, and you turned an honest penny. You saw some things which you probably shouldn't have seen, but you kept your trap shut. I remember when I used to have a cabinet minister from Harold Macmillan's Government in here regular as clockwork; every Friday after adjournment, before he caught the train back to his constituency. Well, he was only a junior minister actually, but I wouldn't tell anyone his name. That's what the business was all about. And I wouldn't tell *you* his name, neither.' Renée looked at him belligerently.

'I'm not asking.'

'That was nearly twenty years ago, anyway. I liked the work then. You had nice holidays, the streets were friendlier, almost everyone asked for it straight, and if they didn't they were very apologetic about it. You'd say, "Come on love, out with it, you can't shock Renée," and then they'd babble on about boots or whips or school uniforms or something and you'd say, "Sorry, love, I'd really like to, I just don't have the equipment with me, but I tell you who you ought to see and that's Annie," and they look terribly grateful and go off and you quickly ring up Annie and tell her you've sent someone round and she either does the same back or sends you a few quid for the introduction.

'We weren't cut-throats because we knew there was enough punter to go round. But that's changed a lot since then. You've no idea the way the average tart's living's been attacked in the last twenty years, Duffy, no idea. There was that Permissiveness for a start, when all the girls who didn't use to suddenly started putting out. *That* didn't do us any good, as you can imagine. And then there was that Women's Liberation which amounted to exactly the same thing. Then all the films started getting dirtier and dirtier, and the books did too. You could go to the theatre and see girls waggling their twats on stage and everyone was calling it art so that they didn't have to put a newspaper over their head when they came out. Art – fart, if you ask me.' Renée was really getting launched. Duffy just sat back and listened.

'So what happened to us was that a bit of good old-fashioned straight with tarts got the squeeze. Sure, there's enough of it to keep you going still, but when fellows could get it at home or from their secretaries or from any old pub scrubber for nothing, why should they lay out good money on us? So two things happened. One was that we started noticing we were getting a bigger percentage of oddballs than before – you know, crips and hunchies and things. Not that I really mind them, they're quite sweet really; it's just that, you know, given the choice . . .

'And the second thing was that the punters weren't wanting so much straight as before. All of a sudden lots of punters wanted you to wank them off. I mean, you'd think that was the one thing they could do for themselves, wouldn't you? I don't mind doing it, as long as you've got something to catch the drips, but I do find it's hard on the wrists. I mean, five or six punters in a row and none of them want to put it in, it takes it out of you. You feel you've been lifting boxes of apples all day. I *did* think of charging more for that than for straight, I don't mind telling you.

'And it wasn't just wanking. Suddenly, they were all wanting mouth stuff. Well, I don't do that, I really don't, I think it's disgusting really. But I always make sure the girl I share with will do it, then they can pop across the landing if they really want that. The other things, too, well, as I say, I blame all that Labour pornography. And all those film clubs and massage parlours – have you seen them, Duffy?'

Duffy nodded.

'They've been a terrible blow, too. All the punters just go and sit in the dark and watch films of people fucking. What good is that to trade? And as for the parlours, you know I sometimes wonder why they haven't run us girls out of business. I suppose the only thing that keeps people coming to us is the thought that they might go into a parlour and find out they had to have a real massage – have some great fat German woman hitting them in the back like she was beating steak, and then push them in an ice-cold plunge shower, and all for fifteen nicker or something.'

Renée laughed. She liked the idea of it. She didn't take her business too seriously, even when she was complaining about it. Duffy laughed as well.

'Still, I suppose that isn't quite what you wanted to ask me.'

'Not quite. I was thinking a bit more about who runs what, and that sort of thing.'

'Well, that's changed a lot too, and if you ask me it's not

got any nicer neither. And it all happens so quickly you can't keep up with it. Now, the old days, it was all the Maltese boys. They got a really bad press, the Malties did, but I always thought that was, you know, racial prejudice. They'd stick a knife in you soon as look at you if they thought you were shitting them, but I never had no trouble. They used to buy up houses and set them up real regular. Strip club in the basement, dirty bookshop on the ground floor, escort agency on the middle floor, tarts on the top. It was like a layer cake, that's what it was like. And the runner would come round every Friday evening and collect a tenner from every floor. Forty quid the building. Sounds peanuts now, doesn't it? But I suppose the rates were much cheaper then, and these Maltese boys, you know, they had a sense of what they wanted out of their investments, and if they got forty quid a house, they were happy. Mind you, you had to pay, even if business was bad, otherwise you'd be sitting at home and suddenly a paraffin heater might come flying through the window. Not nice, they weren't, when they were riled, the Malties; but they were fair, I'll say that.

'Then there was a big clean-up and lots of the Malties got put in pris or kicked out; some of them just ran away and got given a stretch in their absence. And I suppose everyone thought, Oh well, that's cleaned out the Malties, now we'll be able to take the children walking up and down Old Compton Street with ice cream cones in their mitts. Silly buggers. What they should have known was that the Malties were the best we've ever had. Just because they put the Malties in pris, it doesn't mean the tarts are going to go away, does it? Stands to reason. It just means someone new's going to come in and take their slice.

'Well, that's what happened of course. You know that as well as I do, Duffy. Ever since, there's been absolutely no stability. No stability at all. A few local pimps got bigger, some fellows from up north muscled in; we've had a few Paddies, only they didn't last long; there's the blacks there now, and even some of the Chinkies have tried expanding a bit. I mean, it stands to reason, doesn't it? And then, after the Malties went, all your wonderful boys in blue started getting bent as hairpins. With the Malties, it was just a little bit here, a little bit there, either side step over the mark and they go down for a bit. But when the Malties went, didn't the blues get grabby? The tarts were paying the pimps, the pimps were paying the blues, the tarts were paying the blues. It was a real free-for-all, I can tell you, and the coppers were getting way over the top.

'Then the coppers got sorted out, or rather they didn't really get sorted out, just packed off for an early retirement and all their winnings stacked safely away in their wives' names. It's disgusting, it really is. Coppers' cows sitting on all that money.'

'Who took over from Salvatore?' Duffy thought it was time to be specific.

Renée looked quite nostalgic.

'Dear old Emilio. I had him, you know. Only once or twice, but I had him. He had a funny habit. After he'd finished, he'd get dressed, wouldn't say a word, put on his hat, went to the door, raised his hat, and went off. Not a word, and no money. I mean, the first time it happened I told him the price before, and when he didn't put it straight in the dish I assumed he'd give it me later. But he didn't. Just walked off. Then a couple of days later your money arrives in the post. Always happened that way. I suppose he liked to think he was the big boss getting everything for free at the time. But he never didn't pay.'

'And when he died?'

'I think he had a nephew or something, but he wasn't up to much and got chased out. The Chinkies took a bit, took the smokes and whatnot. The restaurants and things went to Big Eddy, I'm fairly sure of that. The whores went to a black guy, name of O'Reilly.'

'Who runs smokes and the rest?'

'Chinkies. Old Max a bit, but not very seriously. Mad Keith. Finlay.'

'Whores?'

'Big Eddy. O'Reilly. Mad Keith. There's a batch of bents – pardon – run by Fat Eric. Remember him?'

'The one who used to boast about how hairy he was – "From the tip of my nose to the tip of my dick" – that Eric?'

'Yes. And Henderson. He's quite big in tarts at the moment.'

'What about the bookshops and the clubs?'

'Same as the whores, mainly. Mad Keith owns the Peep Shows. And I think there's a new bloke called Johnny Grease who's got a few.'

'Protection?'

'Well, bit of everyone, as you know. Depends who's biggest in any particular area, doesn't it?'

'Who's big round Rupert Street?'

'Which end? South or north of the Avenue? It makes a difference.'

'South.'

'Ah, pity. North, I'd definitely have said Big Eddy. But south, well, it's a fairly quiet patch, usually. Maybe O'Reilly. He's the black guy.'

'Hmm. What about the coppers?'

Renée looked at him sharply.

'You sure you're not with them?'

'Cross my heart.'

'You're not one of them clean-up coppers are you? A copper for coppers?'

'I wish I was.'

'Say me no.'

'No.'

'Good. Now tell me how much you're paying me for what I'm telling you.'

'Twenty-five . . . ?'

Renée laughed.

'Ha, Duffy, it's all coming back to me now. You never were any good at that sort of haggling, were you? Now, let me remember. You're offering twenty-five. That means you've got fifty to spend, so I'll ask for seventy-five and then in a few minutes we'll fix on sixty and you'll be wondering if you'll have to find the extra ten out of your own pocket.'

Duffy grinned.

'Sixty it is, and probably ten from me. What about the coppers?'

'Problems with the coppers. They're in a very jumpy mood at the moment. Ronnie and me were talking about it the other day. They're being very unpredictable. Some of the time they let everything go, you'd almost think they weren't there. And then again they might jump on you with everything because one of your seams isn't straight. It's almost as if they don't know who's running them themselves.'

'Anyone particularly bent at the moment?'

'Hard to say. One or two of the younger ones go visiting a tart or two, but that's standard. From what I know, it's no worse than usual. It's just that, well, the coppers are giving off a very nasty smell at the moment.'

'Anyone in particular? Stanton? Wetherby? Sullivan? Shaw?'

'Stanton's left. Didn't you know?'

'No. The others?'

'Nothing I can lay my finger on. Maybe they're just a bit jumpy about things. Something's going on somewhere, I'm sure.'

'Do you know who's moving, Renée? Who's on the grab? Who's upsetting all your stability?'

'You know what happens to tarts that talk?'

Duffy nodded. He'd had to identify a couple of them in his time – on the slab.

'I'm not gabby, you see. I'm just a tart that speaks her mind, everyone knows that. But I'm not a tart that squeals to coppers. Never have been.' It wasn't true, but she had her own picture of herself to protect.

'I understand, Renée, and I'm not a copper. I'm not in the force. I've never been near West Central for four years. I'm just an old friend come to call.'

Renée looked at him, raised an eyebrow, and continued.

'Well, it's got to be Big Eddy. And it's not because he tried to put the squeeze on Ronnie the other day. Rang up about how the books in one of Ronnie's shops might go up if someone threw a firelighter through the door. But he's on the move, no doubt about that. It's bad news when someone gets as hungry as Big Eddy.'

'Big Eddy who?'

'Martoff. Big Eddy Martoff. His dad was one of the Malties that got rounded up. Married a nice tart, the dad did. Sad thing was, he died in pris. Eddy was a teenager at the time. Very cut up, from what I hear.'

'What happened to the old man's patch?'

'It got split up. His widow moved away, and we all thought that was the last of the big Malties. Then, about five years ago, Eddy turned up. He'd bought himself a slice of the north end. He was quiet at first, and, you know, just seemed to concentrate on buying out some of the old men. A bit of presh, but not much. Some of it was completely legit, I expect. It was funny having a Malty back – though I suppose he's only half Malty. His mum was pure East End, as far as I remember.'

'Ever seen him?'

'No. You hear much more than you see around here.'

'And what do you hear?'

95

'Well, first we heard he was a quiet kid. Big and strong but quiet. Then we heard that he was a bit of a joker. Keen on taking pictures. I heard once, a few years ago, he had a false mirror put in one of his tart's flats – she didn't know anything about it. Eddy would let himself in, and while she was earning, he'd take a reel of Polaroids of the punter on the job. Then he'd slip out into the street and when the punter came down the steps he'd stop him and offer him some snaps. The punter usually bought them, as you can imagine. Only trouble was, it didn't do the tart's trade any good.'

'What else do they say?'

'Well, they say he's very grabby. They also say he plans a long way ahead.'

'Has he done any time?'

'Wouldn't know.'

'Got any particular coppers house-trained?'

'Wouldn't know.'

'And what makes you think he's on the move?'

'It's just what you hear. Sometimes you hear wrong. But I don't think so this time.'

'Maybe that's why the coppers are jumpy – they think something's going to break.'

'Maybe. That usually makes coppers excited, though, doesn't it? Nothing coppers like better than villains carving each other up, is there? But the coppers don't seem that sort of excited at the moment. They're just smelling bad.'

'Anything happened so far?'

'Well, bits you can't connect. The thing with Ronnie.'

'How did Ronnie know who it was?'

'Process of elimination. Couldn't have been anyone else. Then there've been one or two bits of nasty lately. A tart got cut up a bit.'

'Sorry,' said Duffy automatically.

'No, no one I knew, but it makes you edgy. And a club

got burnt out – you know, accident, the usual thing. Just happened Big Eddy was interested in the property. Just happened he bought what was left of the building for a little nothing. You see, it's all a bit like that; but you know that if you've heard one or two little things, then you can be bloody sure that other people have heard others, and that they're likely to add up to a move.'

'Who works for Eddy?'

'Lots of people.'

'Anyone in particular?'

'There's Georgiou – remember him? Nick Georgiou?'

'No.'

'Fat guy – ginger hair, glasses, a bit crazy; everyone says don't cross Georgiou. He's a bit sick, they say; likes to make you think he's friendly, then you've got a billiard cue across the kneecaps before you know where you are.'

'Who else? Who does Eddy's dirty?'

'Well, Georgiou likes doing some. Puts in for it. Then there's Kyle. Thin guy, full of mouth. About six feet or so. Very bad teeth. Talks out of the side of his mouth. Very gabby.'

'Anyone else?'

'One or two. Paddick – he's a sort of tough, blond guy. They say he's bent, but everyone's bent nowadays I reckon. Pardon, love. Oh, and Hogan – little Irish guy. Nasty fellow. Grew up throwing paraffin heaters at old ladies.'

'Charming. Where does Eddy hang out?'

'People like that don't hang out, Duffy, you know that. You don't stand around in billiard halls waiting for the Eddies of this world to turn up. He doesn't sit in bars and wait for his runners to deliver. The bars go to him. People like him don't hang out, Duffy, they don't hang out.'

Duffy smiled.

'Well, it's been a good twenty-five quid's worth, Renée.'

97

'Sixty, love, or I'll be after you with a parry heater.'

'Thanks, Renée, you've been very useful. And to think, I haven't even been here.'

'O.K., Duffy. Just make sure you leave like a punter.'

He left the flat as if in a flurry of guilt, and walked down the alley trying to look like a man who had been tied to a bed for an hour while three tarts in school uniform poured golden syrup all over him and then licked it off. He kept his chin tucked into his neck and didn't look round. If anybody had seen him leaving Renée's flat, he wouldn't have known.

At home that evening, he brought all his artistry and ingenuity to bear on Carol's Cheddar on toast.

'Not bad, Duffy, you're really coming along with your cooking. I don't think I could have bettered this Cheddar.'

Duffy looked pleased. He'd decided to learn to cook after he'd stopped being able to eat cheap copper grub; after he'd got impotent with Carol; after she'd suggested they might still get married and he'd turned away and said 'No'. But cooking didn't come easily to Duffy. Carol kept telling him he ought to develop the right instincts – 'How do you develop instincts?' he asked, puzzled – and his approach was methodical and painstaking. He reweighed flour time and time again to get exactly the specified amount; he scrubbed vegetables as if they had to be clean enough to take part in a moon shot; he regarded every egg and every tin of luncheon meat as if they were explosive devices which had to be defused with the tenderest care.

'It's the mess I don't like,' he had said.

'There isn't any mess,' Carol had answered, looking around.

'That's because I made sure there wasn't.'

Duffy devoted as much time to getting rid of wrappers and packaging the leftover food as he did to cooking. If you opened his refrigerator door, you wouldn't see anything to eat: you'd see shelvesful of opaque Tupperware

98

boxes; polythene bags with neurotically doubled knots in their necks; even, occasionally, Tupperware boxes *inside* polythene bags. The first time Carol took a look, she called out,

'Hey, Duffy, is the food trying to escape or something?' and ever afterwards referred to his fridge as Colditz.

When they had finished supper Duffy washed up at once, in case any germs escaped from the decomposing food and started tunnelling their way into Colditz. Over coffee he asked casually,

'What's going on down at the patch, Carol?'

'What do you mean?'

'Well, you know, what's it like down the station? They jumpy or anything? Anyone getting ready for a move in the patch or anything?'

'Duffy,' she said sternly, 'you don't want to know about that. You're not a copper any more.' Her dark eyes looked at him severely from out of her pretty Irish face.

'I'm interested.'

'Duffy, it's four years. You haven't asked me in four years. We agreed you shouldn't ask. We agreed it wouldn't be good for you.'

'What's going on, Carol?'

'No.'

'I need to know now.'

'No unless you tell me why. And even then probably no.'

'If I tell you some things it might make it harder for you at work.'

'If it looks like getting that way I'll stop you.'

Duffy told her everything he'd learned since that first phone call of McKechnie's which had got him leaping out of bed away from her. He told her the lines along which he was guessing, told her his flickering doubts about McKechnie, told her everything he'd been told by Renée. He didn't disguise the fact that he was as much fired by his interest in Sullivan as he was by earning his money helping McKechnie. At the end, Carol said,

'I don't think I should, Duffy, I don't think I should.'

'Why not?'

'I've lost a lot because of you, Duffy. I've lost four years of maybe being happy.'

'That wasn't because of me, that was because of who-ever fitted me up.'

'Same four years, Duffy, same four years. And the black kid may have been a plant, but' – she looked at him re-proachfully, for the first time in years – 'you chose him, didn't you?'

'But that was all part of our deal.'

'Well, there's deals you hope will go one way, and deals you hope will go another, aren't there?' Carol sounded almost bitter; she had every right to. She didn't look at him as she continued. 'So now what you're asking me to do is spy on the people I work with, all so that you can earn twenty quid a day from someone who for all you know is a crook. *And* so that you can get your revenge on Sullivan or whoever it was at the station who helped fit you up. Revenge isn't a good idea, Duffy.'

'They say revenge gets better the longer you leave it.'

'Bollocks,' said Carol fiercely. 'Revenge screws you up. You've got to go on living if you don't want to be screwed up. And *I've* got to go on living,' she said with sudden emphasis. 'I haven't had all that much fun for the last four years. There've been some good bits, but I've mainly just been ticking over. And why I keep ticking over is because of my work. I like my work, Duffy, you must remember that, even if we don't talk about it. I may not be keen on everyone at West Central, and I may even have my private sus about some of them, but I'm going to go on working there, Duffy. You screwed up some of my life four years ago, but you're not having another bite at what's left of the cherry.'

'Will you tell me what it's like at the station nowadays?'

'No.'

'Is anyone preparing a move?'

'No. Duffy.'

'Will you tell me how Sullivan's behaving?'

'No.'

'Will you look out the file on Big Eddy for me?'

'No.'

'Then will you do this? Will you – wait for it – will you look out the file on McKechnie for me, because if it turns out you've got reason to know him at West Central then I might just have to pull out of this job, mightn't I?'

'Don't take it as a promise, Duffy, in case it gets broken. All I'll say is if I'm near his file anyway, and there's no one about, and there's no chance of it ever, *ever* getting out that I looked at it, then I might.'

'One last question.'

Carol looked weary.

'Will you stay the night, please?'

Carol nodded, smiled, went off into the bathroom and unsnapped the plastic box labelled 'Watches'.

6

The next morning Duffy made a phone call to an old friend, a specialist at the sharper, technological end of surveillance. Geoff Bell could bug a phone just by scowling at it; could lift a voice-print out of thin air; could lay down a surveillance system which would tell him three miles away if a police dog was taking a leak. He wasn't entirely honest – his moral sophistication lagged a little behind his technological sophistication; though the only time the coppers had tried it on and raided him they got a nasty shock: Bell had so completely bugged and monitored his own flat that three days later he sent them a one-hundred-page dossier detailing what each of the three coppers had done for every second they were in his flat. He even knew that the big, burly copper with the black moustache had approved of the girl's photo that was pinned above the desk. And the day after the dossier arrived, Bell filed suits for trespass, criminal damage and wrongful seizure of property. Somehow the police seemed to lose interest in his case after that.

'Geoff, it's Duffy. I've been in touch with Control and he says could you drop the package behind the cistern in the middle bog as you're leaving Lenin's tomb. The plane tickets will be arriving in the morning.'

'All right, Duffy, I won't record you for once.'

'But you were recording that bit?'

'Of course.' With Bell, documentation was as much a mania as a job.

'And you'll wipe that first sentence of mine?'

'Yes.'

'And then it won't be there?'

'No. Because I'll have wiped it. You slowing down, Duffy?'

'It really won't be there?'

'What's on your mind, Duffy?'

'I've got a tape with a gap on it. Two and a half, maybe three seconds.'

'Nixon's secretary put her foot on the autowipe again?'

'That sort of thing. What I wondered was, do you think you could get anything out of it?'

'Depends. Depends on quite a lot of things. How loud the original recording was. How determined the guy was to wipe it: if he went over it lots of times there probably wouldn't be anything left. Depends if he wiped it on the same machine he recorded it on. Depends how good the tape and the machine were in the first place. Depends how much of a hurry you're in for it as well.'

'Couple of days, would that be enough?'

'I'll do what I can. Most of the time, wipe means wipe, though.'

'Sure.'

Duffy rang off and went and rooted in his tool chest. He found a pair of powerful, short-handled, snub-nosed metal-clippers, and slipped them into his pocket. Then he collected McKechnie's tape, scribbled a note, and put the tape in an envelope to drop through Bell's door. As he ruffled Carol's hair by way of goodbye, she said,

'I haven't seen a thing, Duffy, and I'm sure I wouldn't have liked it if I had.'

'Just a new tin opener, darlin'. Made in Switzerland.'

'Where the nuts come from,' was all she said.

Duffy dropped the tape off at Bell's and took the tube in to Piccadilly Circus. It was beginning to feel like going to work.

He walked up the Avenue, turned left, and approached the Peep Show with his punter's gait. He changed a couple of quid with the cashier, and settled in to a cubicle.

It was early in the day: the Kleenex on the floor was quite dry. He reckoned that the Peep Show probably ran on eight or ten girls. Each girl had about a ten-minute turn, so that they'd have to wait maybe an hour and a half before their next routine. They wouldn't be sitting around in a dressing room with their feet up talking about skin conditioner, that was for sure. Soho was one of those places where time translated directly into money. The old-style whores used to operate like taxi-cabs. You'd have to finish in ten minutes, otherwise they'd start an 'I can't hang about all day' routine; if you wanted another go after you'd finished the first time, the same rate applied, only they gave a discount if you could finish in five minutes.

At a guess, the girls in the Peep Show did a circuit to other such places, or maybe to strip clubs – Duffy wondered if the skin clubs would cease to exist in a year or two – or maybe they popped home and did an hour's trade. Duffy inserted his first 50p piece and the metal shutter slid up. A skinny, underfed girl with tiny tits was dancing as hard as she could, except that it didn't seem like dancing, not compared to some of the others, it seemed more like running on the spot. Round her neck she wore a velvet choker in what seemed a pathetic attempt to distract attention from her waif-like body. Even her pubic hair, Duffy noted dispassionately, seemed lacking in vigour, and grew patchily, with no enthusiasm. When it came to straddling the glass letter boxes, she did it in a wooden, automatic routine, glancing round anxiously to see if she was missing anyone out. Duffy wondered if any of the anonymous circle of eyes found it exciting. He just wanted to throw a Red Cross blanket round the girl's shoulders and feed her some hot soup.

He left his letter box closed for the rest of her act, then dropped in another 50p. Two minutes with his slot open, watching and partly watching; then five minutes or so with it shut. He wondered if punters had to keep up a certain percentage of time with their windows open before they got their doors kicked by the management. Maybe no one minded any more, they made so much money. It was like in the dirty bookshops. In the old days there would be cardboard signs up above the racks of mags saying NO BROWSING. Large men came up to you and said things like 'Two minutes more' and then, with a heavy parody of civility, 'Can I help you?'. Now nobody seemed to care that punters stood in shops for hours on end and then left without buying; the turnover was obviously quite lucrative enough and harassing the customer didn't particularly improve your trade.

Duffy changed some more money, and after he'd got through three quid his slot clanged up to reveal the black girl, Polly. He watched her more closely than the previous girls, checked out the white scar on her shoulder, and then, when she bent right forwards to give the punters a double-barrelled shot, he looked at the top of her thigh: there, right where the thigh joined the buttock, was the pimp's cut: a white scar running down into her groin.

Duffy left at the end of that 50p's worth and waited across the street for the black girl to emerge. When she did, he crossed quickly and caught up with her before she had the chance to disappear like the last time.

'Excuse me,' he said as he came level with her.

'Yeah?'

Duffy didn't know quite how to begin.

'Er, excuse me,' he said again. He felt almost embarrassed; he certainly must have looked embarrassed, because she suddenly gave a hard, professional smile.

'Okay, love, I was going to do some shopping, but I'll fit you in.' She turned round and started walking back in the direction she'd come. Duffy followed, having to catch her up again. She was already rattling off her price list.

'Ten for straight. You wan' it straight? Do you Greek if

you like. Greek's twenty. Blow's fifteen. Hands? Well, hands is ten too, I know it sounds a lot love, but honestly, it's as much trouble as the other. Made up your mind?'

It was only half past twelve. He didn't feel particularly randy. But having got this far he didn't think stopping, explaining who he was, and asking a few questions would produce a helpful response. At her gaff he dropped ten pounds into a little woven basket on a dresser and got on with it. She made a great show of being excited to hurry him along. He made a similar show to fool himself and hurry himself along. Their thoughts were miles away from their bodies.

'There, that's better now, love, isn't it?' For a tart, she was chatty.

'You're Polly, aren't you?'

'If you like.'

'I brought you flowers once.'

She looked at him strangely.

'Listen, love, none of my punters bring *me* flowers. Not even my regulars.'

'No, I brought you flowers in hospital. Four years ago.'

She stopped pulling up her skirt and looked at him again. Then she said,

'Fucking copper, aren't you?'

'Not any more.' He finished dressing and zipped up his blouson.

'I don't take coppers. I never take coppers.'

'I'm not a copper. I'm private now. Can I talk to you?'

'No you fucking can't.' She seemed frightened, even though she was acting angry.

'It wouldn't take very long. I just want to ask you about four years ago.'

'No way. Fucking get out. Get out, copper. FUCKING GET OUT.' She ran to the side of her bed and pressed a bell.

Duffy got out. He got out very fast indeed.

He bought himself lunch at the Casa Alpina, a little

Italian café where he sat next to the hatch and listened to the waiters bawling down the intercom. As he sat over the menu a youngish waiter with a bald head and a black moustache rushed at the hatch and deposited a pile of sticky pudding plates in the pulley lift, at the same time bending his head to the intercom and shouting, 'Piccolo hors-d'oeuvre twice!' Duffy liked places like this: the noise, the friendliness, the cheapness. He ordered himself bacon, sausage, eggs, tomato, baked beans, double chips and a half carafe of wine.

He hadn't been counting on Polly, so it wasn't too much of a blow that she wouldn't talk. You just have to try every avenue and hope that some of them lead somewhere. Most of them don't, of course. In any case, he reflected, Polly didn't exactly owe him anything. The flowers had come off police expenses; and he had leaned on her more than a little at the time.

After lunch it was back to the Double Blue. He hoped this bit of the day would go better. He dug out his membership card in the name of Daniel Drough and presented it to the soiled hippy in the box office, who shook his head.

'Sorry, mate, your membership's expired.'

'Don't be stupid, I only joined a few days ago.'

'Sorry, mate, that's not what your card says.' He handed him back the card: Membership for one year from . . . ' it said at the bottom, and on his previous visit the hippy had filled in '10 June 1978'. He'd written '1978' instead of '1979' so that the card appeared to expire the day he had sold it. One of the oldest tricks in the book. Duffy kicked himself.

'Look, you sold me that card a couple of days ago.'

'Me? Not me, mate. I only came back from holiday today.'

'Where did you go?' Duffy was pissed off, especially with himself. The hippy looked mystified. What was this punter doing getting all uppity?

'And besides,' the hippy went on triumphantly, 'this isn't my writing.'

Duffy handed over another fiver.

'Same name again this time is it, guv? Or do you fancy a change?'

'Heath,' said Duffy, 'E. Heath.'

Inside, there were about the same number of punters as before. Twenty or so diligent E. Heaths who might never have moved since Duffy had left the last time. On the screen the beach movie was showing again. Now a fat man had joined the two oily girls, who were toying with a beachball. For some obscure reason – perhaps as a punishment for their lesbian activities on a public strand – he kicked away their beachball, turned them over on their fronts, and began slapping their bottoms. With the amplifying system at the Double Blue, it sounded as if someone were beating carpets: a loud, extended, reverberating crump.

After ten minutes or so of this, Duffy decided to move. He got up from his seat and made his way to the toilet. He walked slowly past it and stopped by the emergency exit opposite the foot of the stairs. He looked up the stairs, listened for a bit, then took out his metal-clippers. He could go for the padlock or he could go for the chain. Both of them were a bit rusty, and almost certainly never used, but Duffy thought it possible that the padlock got a few glances occasionally. He started work on one of the links in the chain. Then he stopped, looked for a rustier one, and started again. After several silent heaving bursts on the clippers, he severed the link at a point where one of its straight sides began to go into a curve. Then he moved the clippers along about an inch and started work again close to the other curve. Soon a short, straight piece of link just under an inch long tinkled on to the stone floor. He picked it up and put it in his pocket.

Next he slowly slid the bolts at the top and bottom of the left-hand door. The door could now be pushed open from the outside until it came up against the chain, which would still hold tight despite the missing piece of link. The exit was in a dark part of the corridor, getting a little faint light from the top of the stairs, and Duffy hoped that no one would take a look at it. It would be just his luck if the G.L.C. decided to send round someone from their licensing department for a spot check.

Duffy walked softly back to the toilet, went inside and shut the door. The cistern had lost its lid at some stage, and Duffy climbed on the seat and peered in. He took the metal-clippers out of his pocket and gently lowered them into the water. The inch-long piece of chain followed. Then he climbed down, satisfied. That was the mechanical side done. The human side was always much more likely to go wrong.

He went back to the stairs and started to climb them. When he got to the top he saw three closed doors. He walked quickly across to the one on his right, the one from which the voices had come before, and knocked. Nothing happened. Instead, there was a voice from behind him.

'Not still looking for the pisser, are we, mate?' It was the big gingery man he'd seen before. 'Because if you are, then all I can say is you can hold it for quite a lot longer than I can.'

He had come out of the left-hand door, and beckoned Duffy across towards him.

'Now, what can we do for you, mate? Not happy with the fillum or something?'

'The film's fine,' Duffy said, 'absolutely terrific. The punters are loving it. They're climbing up their seats with happiness. You're Georgiou.' He hoped to God his guess was right.

'I might be.'

'Going to invite me in?'

'Pardon my manners, squire,' said Georgiou, 'but I'm a bit picky about who I have in my parlour.'

'You don't seem too picky about who you get to collect your drops.'

'Meaning?'

'Meaning the bloke in the denims who did the run from Brewer Street the other day. You must have to tie a ball of string to his ankle or something to make sure he doesn't get lost.'

Georgiou looked at him and grinned.

'I think I might invite you in after all, Mr . . .'

'Wright.'

'Mr Wright? Sounds like it's my lucky day.'

He pushed open the left-hand door and politely let Duffy precede him. Or he could have been making sure Duffy didn't scarper. Duffy went in. It was a small office with a few box files and a girlie calendar on the wall and a little kitchen off to one side. It was reminiscent of McKechnie's office. The main difference was that the pick-up man was lounging on a tangerine settee. Same denims as before; just as scruffy; a half-hearted moustache.

'Take a seat, Mr Wright. I think you'd better have my chair, and I'll sit on the sofa just in case one of the two of you wants to kill the other. By the way, this is Mr Jeggo.' He continued the introduction in formal style. 'Mr Jeggo, I don't think you've met Mr Wright. Mr Wright, I think you *have* had the pleasure of seeing Mr Jeggo.'

Jeggo had clearly heard the conversation on the landing and stared impassively at Duffy. It was the sort of gaze you might run into in an abattoir.

'Mr Wright was just saying, Jeggo, that he thought you could brush up your technique a bit. Weren't you, Mr Wright?'

Duffy judged that there was little to be got from ingratiating himself with Jeggo; it was probably too late anyway.

'Yeah. First thing I'd say' (Duffy took on the tone of a subaltern running through the mistakes of a squad of new recruits: firm but understanding) 'is that you ought to try and remember which dustbin the drop is being made in. There's no point in Georgiou or Eddy or anyone *asking* for the drop to be made in a precise place and then have the pick-up man acting hunt-the-thimble in broad daylight.'

'You a copper, asshole?'

'No. Second, don't walk along the street to the drop, pick it up, turn round, and walk back from the direction you've come: no one walks down Brewer Street, looks in a dustbin, picks something out and then retraces their steps unless they're a pick-up man. Approach the drop, make the pick-up, and then carry on in the same direction.'

'Asshole,' said Jeggo quietly.

'Third, you did quite right to go up Berwick Street.' (Duffy made it sound as patronising as possible) 'A nun with a wooden leg playing the mouth-organ could lose a tail in that market. But you've got to try: you can't just hope that the market will do the job for you. You've got to *use* it – use the stalls and the people and the way it all works. And the fourth point' (Duffy noticed that Georgiou was smiling to himself) 'is that you'll never spot a tail if you don't look for one. Simple as that. You didn't know if you were being tailed or not; you didn't bother to find out. You just picked up the drop and buggered off home with it.' He turned to Georgiou. 'Oh, I hope you didn't train him, Georgiou. I don't like to seem rude.'

'Not at all rude, Mr Wright. I'm sure Mr Jeggo will do a great deal better next time, eh, Mr Jeggo?'

'I think I'll kill this asshole,' said Jeggo in a toneless voice. Duffy decided to bait him some more.

'Then let's hope you're better at being a killer than you

are at being a messenger boy. I wouldn't let you lick the stamps for my letters at the moment.'

'He's a copper,' said Jeggo, 'he reeks of copper.'

'No,' said Georgiou, 'he's too smart to be copper. He reeks of smart, that's all.'

'I wanna kill him,' Jeggo repeated petulantly.

'I don't think that's a good idea, Jeggo. I do think we ought to ask him what he wants first. But we'll bear the idea in mind. Now, Mr Wright, we've had a few laughs, and you haven't come for the pisser, so what's it all about?'

'What's it about is, I don't tell you in front of messenger boys.'

'Very well. Jeggo, go and kill someone in the other room, will you?'

Jeggo got up and left.

'I want to see Eddy.'

'Of course you do.'

'Well?'

'Oh, Mr Wright, I'm merely waiting for you to state your business.'

'I'm from McKechnie. I want to deal.'

'Ah. Well, that's interesting. Would you like to tell me what you have in mind?'

'No. I want to talk to Eddy.' Duffy didn't sound to himself as if he had much of a leg to stand on.

'Well, Mr Wright, Mr Eddy prides himself on the vertical structure of his business. He likes to think that everyone should have access right to the top. I'll go and see what he says.' He disappeared, then put his head back round the door. 'Oh, I shouldn't worry, I don't really think Mr Jeggo means to kill you. It's just one of his exaggerations.'

Three minutes later Georgiou returned.

'Mr Eddy will see you now.'

They went out on to the landing and Georgiou opened the middle door. They were in a short passage, and Duffy immediately felt a change of atmosphere: there was carpet on the floor, and fresh green paint, and a couple of prints on the wall. At the end of the passage was a cream-painted door. It was opened and Duffy stepped through into another world. He found himself in a high, elegant, Georgian double-cube sitting room, painted pale green. There were pier-glasses between the windows and old prints round the walls. The room must be almost twice as wide as the Double Blue below, Duffy reflected; it must run through into the next building, and perhaps the one on the other side too. There were chintz-covered sofas and in one corner a large executive's desk with several telephones on it and a bronze statuette of a swan. The windows were double-glazed, and the pale green carpet was thick beneath Duffy's feet.

Big Eddy Martoff came through a door in the left-hand corner of the room holding a manila file in his hand. He laid it on his desk and walked over to the two of them. He was taller than Duffy; but then, most men were. Still, he was no taller than six foot, and not especially broad. 'Big' was doubtless a street name which had most effect on those who had never met him. He was a good-looking man in his middle-thirties, dark crinkly hair, sallow complexion, brown eyes, high cheek bones above a long expanse of cheek. He was dressed like a man who ran the sort of modern art gallery whose paintings you couldn't afford. A lightweight medium blue suit, soft cream button-down shirt, French tie, expensive mocassin shoes.

'Mr Wright. You like the room?'

'All right.'

'I'm very fond of it. And I'm especially pleased with the Morland prints. I think they suit so well.' He talked like he looked: soft, smooth and expensive. Old Martoff must have left a nice little educational trust for him, Duffy reflected. 'The window seats are very pleasant too,

Mr Wright. Not common in this part of London, as you can imagine. You can sit on one of those window seats and feel the sun on your face and simply forget all about the pressures of business.'

'Hope the floor's soundproofed.' Duffy thought of all the amplified sheepdogs and carpet-beating raging on below. He also thought that, even allowing for a bad tape, there was no question but that Martoff was 'Salvatore'.

Martoff smiled.

'Ah, of course, you came up the back way like a trades-man. I hear you gave a sparkling piece of instruction to one of our trainees on the way in.'

'I think I'll leave by the front entrance when I go, if that's all right by you.'

'Well, let's talk our business first, Mr Wright.' He went and sat behind his desk, beckoning Duffy to a sofa. The sofa felt quite a bit lower than the desk. That corny old executive's trick, thought Duffy; ah well, if he needed it. Georgiou went and parked a fat ham on a window seat.

'Now, Mr Wright.'

'McKechnie says you're squeezing too hard. McKechnie says he's too pressed for funds, business is bad at the moment. McKechnie says will you lay off for a while. McKechnie says what sort of deal do you want from him?'

Martoff laughed lightly. 'Mr Wright, do you realise you started every sentence with the words "McKechnie says . . ." It's like that old game we used to play as children, O'Grady Says. I do hope the same rules apply and that I don't have to do everything that McKechnie says. That would be a severe disappointment to me. What do *you* say, anyway, Mr Wright?'

'I say the same – you're squeezing too hard. After a while you can't get blood out of a stone.'

'Correct me if I'm wrong, Mr Wright, but you haven't come here on a charitable impulse? That is to say, I take it you are not just an old friend of McKechnie's who happened to be passing and was moved by the sight of his distress to come and plead on his behalf? That, I take it, is not exactly the case. You are, are you not, receiving an emolument from McKechnie? Indeed, you are being paid for coming here and pleading McKechnie's poverty, are you not?'

'Not so's you'd notice.'

Martoff smiled.

'Well, let's not quibble. My point is that *you* seem to be getting a bit of blood out of the old stone at the moment. So, for instance, McKechnie could easily give me your blood, couldn't he?' Martoff sighed a little, and stroked the bronze swan. 'It always saddens me, Mr Wright, how much people lie about money. With peasants, well, one expects it; but in business . . . I suppose I'm just a bit too idealistic for my work. You'd be surprised how people squeal that their pips are squeaking when all I have done is gently pinch the peel of the orange between thumb and forefinger, like a housewife at market.'

Duffy waited. With men like this, men used to power, you always let them talk on. Martoff seemed to be coming out of a reverie.

'But then I suppose I am a bit too idealistic anyway. Take the question of you, for instance.' Duffy held his breath. 'I agreed to see you because of what Georgiou said to me. He told me that you had said to him that you wanted to deal. I believed it. So I invite you in, and wait for you to say your piece, and what do I discover? No deal. Nothing like a deal. I mean, what I understand by a *deal* is that one party says, "If I give you x, will you give me y?" and that the second party thinks it over and says either "Yes", or "No", or tries to haggle about the terms. Correct me if I'm wrong, Mr Wright, but as far as I can see from examining your "deal", your "deal" consists of saying to me, in simple terms, "Lay off". Now, isn't that what it amounts to?'

'McKechnie says what to you want from him?' Duffy doggedly repeated his only line.

'Oh dear, Mr Wright, I don't seem to be getting through to you, do I? My point is that it's all very well for McKechnie to say his stone is exhausted and has no more blood in it, but what has he got to offer me as a disincentive from having occasional modest stabs at this famous stone of his? That's what I understand by a "deal", anyway. I'm sorry if I'm a little old-fashioned, but I simply see no "deal" at all.'

'Well, I'd better be off then,' said Duffy. He began to rise from the sofa.

'Let me detain you a little longer, if I may, Mr Wright, because there are a few things which it might be in both our interests, not to mention that of your paymaster, to get clear. There are three areas in which I think I could probably help clarify your thinking. I hope you'll bear with me.' He was clearly a man used to being borne with.

'The first is that you didn't come here to "deal". Let's get that straight. You don't have a "deal". I doubt if you even talked about it with McKechnie first, because if you had, then you might have come up with something a little less feeble. So, perhaps you should admit to yourself the real reason for coming. You came in order to see me. I quite understand. I am a local businessman of some standing. A lot of people want to see me. Maybe you thought that unless you invented some "deal", I would not judge you important enough to receive. Well, you may have a point there. But I think we should all remain as clear about our own motives as possible, don't you?

'This leads on to my second point. You were asking, in a rather confused way, about my own motives and intentions in regard to the man whose stone writes so many of your cheques. I think I can be quite open with you, Mr Wright, because if you haven't worked out my intentions by now then you must be as fuddled as poor Mr Jeggo out there. In simple terms – and there are no complicated terms – I am taking over Mr McKechnie's business. That is my intention. If you ask my motive, that is not very shadowy: my motive is that I want to own his business. So, I am dispossessing him of his two warehouses and his office. It is as simple as that. I am sorry if there has been any ambiguity, but I'm afraid my style of business has always been to take things slowly. I like people to get used to the idea of losing their possessions. It sometimes takes them a while to adjust, to make new arrangements. But I'm sure Mr McKechnie will adjust.'

'What if he doesn't want to hand over?'

'Oh, come, come, Mr Wright. Or is that question designed to make me utter some quotable quote? You wouldn't have a tape recorder strapped to your body, or anything foolish like that, would you? We shall be forced to have a look before you go, you understand?'

Duffy grunted. Quite right to dump the metal-clippers.

'Well, the short answer is, that if he doesn't hand over his property to me I shall do various unpleasant and quite possibly violent things which will persuade him to do so; but it would be pushing my current candour too far to tell you precisely what.

'And the third thing is this, Mr *Duffy*.' Duffy looked up, startled at the sound of his real name. He felt his shoulders move and his sphincter contract in a sudden wave of fear. Georgiou chuckled. 'Ah, I'm glad that worked. I do so enjoy surprises. The third thing is this.' Martoff flipped open the file and read from it. '"Duffy. Nicholas, usually Nick. West Central, 1972–5. Average to good arrest record – took in Leverty for a bit, also Spiro, though didn't get a conviction, and Docherty as well. Known to refuse Christmas presents, various kinds tried. Last case – stabbing incident in Bateman Street. Pushy on that one. Dealt with, May 1975. Homosexual, though known to go with women as well. Engaged to W.P.C. Carol Lucas, broken off." My condolences.' Martoff fished in the file and threw a photograph at Duffy. 'Not a very good likeness, is it?' The photo fell to the floor. Duffy bent down and glanced at it as he picked it up. When he looked back at Martoff he found himself staring into a Polaroid camera with a flash attachment. A bulb went off in his face.

'This one, I think, will make our file much more up to date.'

Martoff put the camera down on his desk and came round to the front of it. He sat with one buttock on the edge and looked long at Duffy.

'Two final points. The first is that, though I am not a philosopher, I am sometimes tempted by philosophical formulations. And the one which seems to me most suitable for the current situation I would formulate like this: Knowledge is Power. Remember that, Mr Duffy.' He leaned back over his desk and tapped Duffy's file.

'And the second point, which really follows on from the first point, is this. I am not given to making threats, so you must not interpret my next remark as a threat: it is simply an instruction, a clear, unequivocal instruction, and to make it clearer still I will put it in coppers' slang for you. Get off my patch. Do you understand? You will not return to my area of business operations ever again. You will not upset my employees or trespass on my property or walk the pavements which *I* own ever again.'

'What if I do?' asked Duffy.

Martoff leaned closer to him; the brown eyes stared expressionlessly out of the sallow face.

'Suck it and see, Mr Duffy, suck it and see.'

7

Duffy was thoroughly frisked by Georgiou and sent off back through the Double Blue. They wouldn't let him go down the front steps, wherever they were. As he said goodbye to Martoff, Duffy took a quick, final look round the large green room. In particular, he noticed the wiring high up on the wall above the door from which Martoff had emerged: wiring which led to a little square box painted cream to melt into the background. In the carpeted passage, Duffy stopped to look at a print, and glanced back at the door leading to the green room: nothing there, as far as he could see.

As he headed off down the stairs, Georgiou said to him, 'Hope Jeggo isn't waiting in the pisser for you,' and chuckled.

Duffy rather hoped so too. He had far too much on his mind to have to bother with clobbering Jeggo as well. Not that it'd be much trouble. If you gave Jeggo a knife and told him to kill an old lady, he'd probably grip the cutter by the blade and beat her to death with the handle.

He made his way home oblivious of the light crush of mid-afternoon tube passengers. He was thinking about Big Eddy Martoff. What an inappropriate name it now seemed to him. It was the name of some lunkhead whose hairline came down to his eyebrows and whose hands brushed his shoelaces. Whereas the reality was a person who talked like a member of an Any Questions panel. 'Our team tonight,' Duffy murmured to himself, 'consists of Norman St John Stevas, Richard Marsh, Isobel Barnett, and a newcomer, the London businessman, Big Eddy Martoff.' The name was all wrong: but then maybe it was one of his jokes. He clearly prided himself on his sense of humour.

What Martoff had revealed of himself to Duffy was more than a bit scary. A second-generation Malty, street-wise from his cradle, then sent to some minor English public school to be taught the robber-baron ethics of the British businessman: it wasn't a pretty combination. He was naturally smart, enjoyed his power, and looked forward to enjoying it for a long time more. And he wanted his power to continue so that he could enjoy other things as well: the clothes, the room, both spoke of a man who enjoyed his wealth. That again was the sign of a second-generation villain. The first generation, they're often stuck with the memory of having nothing, so they stay very tight-arsed, very mean: they're the sort of villains who never give donations on flag days and probably keep their money under the bed because they don't trust banks. The second generation always know more about the potentialities of money, are much keener on using the institutions of the legit world to their own advantage. First-generation villains think of themselves as outlaws, outsiders, sometimes even suffer guilt about their social status. Second-generation villains think of themselves as businessmen, protecting and building up inherited capital. Some of them have accountants.

Building up: that was what Duffy was worrying about now. How far did Eddy's ambitions go? He'd appeared to be completely candid with Duffy, and yet he hadn't really told him anything. He was obviously intending to take out McKechnie completely: not just squeeze, but take out completely. Duffy could have guessed that, probably: you didn't open up with a high level of violence unless you were interested in going all the way.

But what about a bigger move? Eddy certainly had the ambition for it, and he certainly had the nerve. He probably had the resources too, in case he had to hire a few out-of-town mercenaries. He'd said that his style of business was to take things slowly; but maybe that was just sales-talk. The most important thing about making a move is being sure of the exact strength of the opposition, and calculating how likely it is that getting active will make that opposition gang up against you.

But hadn't Eddy answered this point? 'Knowledge is power,' he'd said. It was the sort of phoney generalisation Duffy had heard often enough before from villains who fancied themselves, but maybe this time it had a more specific application. Maybe Martoff really did know things. When he'd opened the manila folder and started to read, Duffy had thought it was just a flash trick. One call to a friendly copper or a medium-sized Christmas box to a station filing-clerk and he could have had all that. The folder was just to make it look professional, to make Duffy report back to McKechnie that Eddy knew everything about everybody and that he should just give in, pay up, and move out.

But what if that wasn't the object? What if it had all been an ordinary part of what Eddy constantly referred to as 'business'. After all, he'd known that Duffy was Duffy, so he must have had him spotted at some time. And whose file did it read like – a copper's or a villain's? When it came to the bit about the stabbing incident, Martoff had read out something like 'Pushy on this', and then shortly afterwards 'Dealt with'. That didn't sound like a copper's file. And if it were Martoff's own file, when had it been compiled? At the time of the stabbing? Presumably so, because the photograph was an old one. So how up to date did the file come? Did Martoff know, for instance, that Duffy was Duffy of Duffy Security? Not that he'd need a complex intelligence system to work it out: a glance at the Yellow Pages would do.

And another thing which the file – and the comment 'Dealt with' – meant was that Martoff was admitting that it was he who had fitted Duffy up. 'Pushy on this', 'Dealt with' and 'Homosexual' all added up in Duffy's mind to the Caramel Club and the door being booted in and 'Excuse me, sir, but how old is your friend?' and the fist in the kidneys and the whispered hatred of 'Fucking bent *queer* copper'. So Eddy didn't care if Duffy knew he'd framed him. And having told him in so many words that he'd fitted him up, he then told him to keep off his streets. That showed a lot of confidence. And it left only one question in Duffy's mind about how the Caramel Club incident came to happen: who'd talked on him at West Central? Who'd been the link telling Martoff how to work the frame?

When Duffy got home he telephoned McKechnie.

'Not good news, I'm afraid'.

'What?'

'I've been talking to our friend Salvatore.'

'*Talking* to him? Who is he?'

'He's called Martoff. Big Eddy Martoff. An important member of the local business community, at least if we take his word for it. Has a finger in just about everything by the looks of it.'

'And?'

'And, Mr McKechnie, I'm afraid that what he wants is quite simply everything you've got. It's not just protec. It's the whole way, I'm afraid. He wants your office, your two warehouses, in fact everything you've got.'

'And I suppose he thinks I'm just going to hand it all over, does he?'

'I'm afraid that's exactly what he thinks, Mr McKechnie.'

'And if I don't?'

'Well, from what he says, he will impose a rather severe penalty on you.' It was odd how Duffy found himself almost talking like Martoff.

'So what do we do?'

'What do *we* do, Mr McKechnie? I think it's more a question of what do you do? I'm only an employee of yours.' Duffy had decided to stonewall the conversation as much as possible; he'd let McKechnie stew for a bit.

'Well then, what would you advise?'

'There seem to be only three possibilities. You can hand over, you can try the police again, or you can look around for some powerful friends. Those are the normal courses of action. Of course . . .'

'Yes?' said McKechnie hopefully.

'You could always hire somebody to kill Martoff. People in your situation have done that before. But I should advise you it's strictly against the law.'

'I'll get back to you, Duffy.'

'Any time, Mr McKechnie.'

That evening, as Duffy was finishing up a tin of cannelloni, he had an unexpected visitor. A face from the past gave him an uneasy wink from the doorstep.

'Long time no see, Duffy.'

'Well, well, well, this is a surprise. Not the television licence again, is it? It just keeps slipping my mind, officer, I'm afraid. I'll do it tomorrow, I promise.'

'Inviting me in?'

Duffy paused, considered, looked Shaw up and down, wondered what he'd do if he simply shut the door in his face.

'Of course.' Duffy watched him as he came in. Same small, worried, foxy face; the hair a bit greyer now, the suit a little shinier at the elbows, but essentially the same Shaw. He'd never worked directly with him, but knew his reputation: diligent, tended to fret away at a case, largely honest. They always said he was a bit of a puritan. He'd been at West Central almost as long as Sullivan, and yet he was supposed to be still quite shocked by some of the more routine trades of the Golden Mile. Duffy fixed them both some Nescafé and asked,

123

'How's business?'

'Oh, mustn't grumble, you know. Always a lively turn-over. Try to keep on top of it.'

'I'm sure you do. How's the old patch?'

'Oh, much the same, much the same.'

'Good.' Or bad, for that matter. Shaw was acting as if he'd come for a mortgage or something. Duffy eased him along.

'West Central needing an alarm system?'

'What? Oh, no, haha.'

'So what can I do for you?'

'Well, it's a bit awkward, Duffy, but I'll come to the point. Er, I'm here in a strictly unofficial capacity, you understand.'

'No, I don't as a matter of fact. I never understood it when I used to say it. Now I'm an ordinary member of the public, maybe I can ask you to explain.'

'Look, Duffy, there's no point in getting clever. I know you're clever, you know you're clever, so let's leave it at that.' He paused. He looked worried. Eventually he spoke. 'I can say it in two words, Duffy, Lay off.'

'Will you repeat them?'

'Lay off.'

'Who's paying you, Shaw? I ask it in a purely unofficial capacity, of course. Who's got your pisser in his pocket?'

'I'll ignore that remark. Lay off, Duffy, and go back to your burglar alarms. You're in over your head and you don't even know it. Just collect your week's wages and stay away. Trip over something and hurt your foot. Plead industrial injury. You don't want to work for McKechnie. You don't want to go nosing about after Martoff.'

'Leave it to the professionals, eh?'

'And you don't want to start treading on corns at West Central, either.'

'You know, Shaw, I didn't like that red tie much. I really didn't think it suited you. A bit too flash. Not your style at all.'

'What do you mean?'

'The red tie for the café window. I mean, it's gangster stuff, isn't it? All that turning up only two minutes before the drop and having a table reserved for you – it's really not your style, Shaw, not your style at all.'

'We're not talking about style.'

'O.K., let's talk about something else. It wasn't a very conscientious job on your part, I didn't think. I mean, correct me if I'm wrong, but I don't think you managed to hang around long enough for the pick-up, did you, Shaw? Another engagement, no doubt. Pressing business, I'll bet. Skipping off down the street almost before my client's back was turned. Where were you off to – collect your ten per cent?'

'Watch it, Duffy.' Shaw's trouble was, he wasn't good at sounding menacing. He just sounded worried.

'I'm making a strictly unofficial suggestion, of couse. But I'm afraid my client wasn't very happy about your performance, Mr Shaw. And he wasn't very happy either about the lies he got told when he phoned Sullivan for a report. "Ran off into Regent Street and caught a cab", or something like that. If you'd stayed around for a couple of minutes longer, you'd have set eyes on the pick-up merchant and realised that the only way *he* could get a cab to stop for him would be by lying down in the road in front of it. So how much of the three-fifty has come your way and Sullivan's?'

'Duffy,' said Shaw quietly, almost sadly, 'you don't know the half of it.'

'I've used that line before as well and I never understood what it meant. I just used it when I didn't know what to say next.'

'Well, I'll give you just a tiny idea, just a glimmer. Why did McKechnie hire you?'

''Cos he thought I was good, I suppose.'

125

'But how did he find you?'

'Oh, he said he asked about.'

'And what did you make of that?'

'That my reputation is spreading faster than you think.'
It was true, though, Duffy had wondered how McKechnie
had got hold of him.

'*I* told him about you, Duffy, *I* recommended you. He
came to see me and *I* said *you*. You ask him.'

'I will. Why?'

'It seemed like a good idea then. From what I knew. But
I didn't know then what I know now.'

'Well, that's very clearly put. Care to explain?'

'No.'

'What's going on, Shaw?' Shaw didn't reply. 'Is Martoff
making a move?'

'I can't tell you, Duffy. I don't know everything, and
what I do know keeps changing. What I will say is this.
You know as well as I do that in a place like our patch
there's always a delicate balance between us and the
villains. It's not a great war like the public seems to
imagine and it's not a lazy heap of coppers on the take like
you seem to imagine. The villains and us carry on side by
side and there's a sort of what you call osmosis between
us. You understand what I mean by osmosis, Duffy?'

'I understand what other people mean by it as well.'

'Well, you're upsetting this delicate balance, you see,
Duffy. That's about as clearly as I can put it to you.'

'You can't put it any more clearly?'

'No I can't. So lay off.'

'What about a deal, Shaw? Everyone's quite keen on
deals around the patch, it seems to me.'

'What sort of deal, Duffy?'

'Well, what about this? I'll lay off, as you put it, if you
tell me who it was at West Central who fitted me up.'

'Not still worrying about that, are you? It's all dead and
past, Duffy.'

'Well, if it's dead and past, it won't matter you telling me, will it? Who helped Martoff set me up?'

'I never really knew, Duffy. I had my sus, same as anyone else, but you can't just operate on sus, as you know. Though I can't think who else it could have been.'

'Is it a deal? I'll lay off if you tell me who helped fit me up?'

Shaw paused for a bit.

'O.K., Duffy, it's a deal. But I'd rather you guessed and I nodded my head.'

What difference did that make? So that Shaw could deny having told Duffy? So that he could say Duffy must just have guessed? Still, if it made it easier for his sodding conscience.

'Sullivan.'

Shaw nodded immediately. Duffy picked up their cups and took them to the sink. Then he walked wordlessly to the door and held it open for Shaw to leave.

It was funny. He hadn't minded in the very least lying to Shaw.

He sat and reflected on the odd coincidence of being warned off twice within hours, once by Martoff and once by Shaw. Was there some connection? Had Martoff told Sullivan to send a messenger boy round? What were they afraid he might find out? What was all that stuff about 'delicate balance'? Usually, all it meant was 'Stop interfering with my slice of the take.'

At nine o'clock the telephone went. When the pips finished he recognised Carol's voice, but she didn't say hello.

'I'm not ringing you, you haven't heard from me, you haven't seen me for a week.' She sounded quite calm, as if setting out her terms.

'All right.'

'Your client's warehouse in Lexington Street is burning.'

The telephone went dead. No goodbye, nothing.

Duffy took a taxi, left it in Shaftesbury Avenue, and dodged up Windmill Street through the crowds of punters gawping at the cinema stills. The south end of Lexington Street was cordoned off by police. Half way up he saw a couple of fire engines parked. One had run up a ladder and a fireman at the top was playing a hose on the small one-and-a-half storey warehouse from above. Two more hoses were being aimed on the building from ground level. Duffy wondered if the firemen knew what was inside. There must be quite a danger of an explosion if you had a hangar full of the sort of things kids liked for Christmas: cheap masks painted with cheap, flammable paint; indoor fireworks; paper hats.

Duffy wondered if the coppers had bothered to inform McKechnie. Then he had a thought. He walked along Brewer Street for a few yards and turned up Great Pulteney Street, which ran parallel to Lexington. Half way down it he came to a short alley which went along the side of a pub and was only used by draymen delivering their loads. At the end of the alley there was a fence. Duffy shinned up it and took a look round. He found himself about three houses up from McKechnie's warehouse. The two streets were close together, with only tiny back courtyards between them. Almost all the houses had long since been turned into shops and offices. There were no lights in the windows; everyone had gone home.

The warehouse was still burning brightly as Duffy worked his way gradually across the courtyards. When he got almost opposite he stopped and looked. The flames were stabbing through the roof, despite all the water being poured in by the fire brigade. It was clear that McKechnie's stock would be entirely destroyed. Duffy wondered why Martoff had ordered it: the stock wouldn't be any use to him now; neither would the building. At best, he'd be able to buy up the site cheaply. Maybe that was all he wanted. Or maybe it was simply a move which, like the cutting of Rosie McKechnie, had no obvious motive at the time. Maybe there were payoffs in several directions; maybe people in similar positions to McKechnie were being shown what could easily happen to them.

Suddenly the warehouse caved in. With a long, rumbling roar, the roof gave way. Everything seemed to move in opposite directions at the same time. The roof fell in, the flames shot up, sparks flew in every direction, the rear wall half collapsed backwards and out, and burning bales of McKechnie's goods came hurtling out of the warehouse into the courtyard.

Duffy ran back as the collapse occurred, and waited while the fire took new life with the influx of air. Then, gradually, the hoses began to get it under control again. Duffy walked across to the fence belonging to the office which backed immediately on to the warehouse, and, out of curiosity as much as anything, hauled himself up it. He peered over the top at the burning bundles of McKechnie's goods which had been hurled out by the explosion of heat; the flames were beginning to die down. He looked again. Then he quickly threw a leg over the fence and dropped quietly down into the yard. The only person who might spot him was the fireman on the ladder high above the wrecked warehouse; but even so, Duffy kept in the shadows. A roped cube of McKechnie's goods lay in front of him, about three feet away: it was a charred bundle of magazines. They were not the sort of magazines you gave to a kid in a King Kong mask and a clown's hat.

Duffy reached out a foot and kicked the bundle apart. A few of the blackened magazines on the outside burst briefly into flame again; the rest sprayed out. He read the familiar titles: *Private, Colour Climax, Selecta, Animal No 9, Sex Bizarre, Ero*. Standard imported hardcore, the secret currency of dirty bookshops. In Duffy's time on the patch, they went for five or six quid a time. He didn't know what to allow for inflation, but he reckoned that he'd just kicked a bundle of five hundred quid or so, in street terms. Big Eddy was right: there was a bit more blood in McKechnie's stone than Duffy had thought.

He climbed back out into Great Pulteney Street and walked down to Brewer. He strolled along to the end of Lexington Street and took another look up it. There were only two hoses on the fire now; it seemed to be coming under control. He wandered on along Brewer Street, fairly certain that neither Martoff's nor Sullivan's men would be giving him a thought. When he reached the end of Brewer he spotted a little knot of gawpers gathered on a corner staring into a dirty bookshop. Not the usual sort of behaviour for punters, he thought. Then he noticed that the shop window had a hole in it and the interior had been damaged by fire. Not gutted – just blackened a bit here and there. Through the window a man in a brown coat could be seen sweeping up.

Duffy chased a memory of five years ago. Hadn't this been one of Ronnie's bookshops? Ronnie, who was Renée's pimp? He checked again in his mind, and was pretty sure it had been. Ronnie in those days had had four shops. This one, one near by in Old Compton Street, one in Frith and one in Greek. Sticking to his punter's gait, Duffy ambled his way along Old Compton Street. Outside the bookshop there he found a shabby fat man taping a newspaper over a hole in the window.

'Get a brick, mate?' he enquired chummily of the man.

'Brick? Fucking paraffin 'eater.'

'Why'd anyone want to do a thing like that?' asked Duffy in a naïve voice.

'Well, it wasn't that Mrs Whitehouse, I can bleeding tell you,' came the indirect reply.

Duffy walked round to Greek Street; as he approached the third of Ronnie's shops the cluster of gawpers round it told him all he needed to know. He went into a pub and dialled Renée.

'It's Duffy,' he said. 'What's happened?'

'What's happened? You've fucking ruined Ronnie, that's all that's happened. Why the bleedin' did I ever let you in? What've you ever done for me, copper? And now you go and lose my Ronnie all his shops.'

'When did it happen?'

'About an hour ago. Heaters through every shop. Frightened the wits out of the punters. All your fault, copper.'

'I'm not one any more, Renée. And how do you know it's got anything to do with me? You said yourself that our friend had already threatened Ronnie.'

'Yeah, well he was going to do only one shop, see? Only you came sniffing to see me. So he rang up Ronnie special, just half an hour ago, to tell him how he had been going to do only one shop, but seeing as I'd been so helpful to you, he'd decided to do all four. So what do you say to that, copper?'

Duffy couldn't think of anything to say, but it didn't matter; Renée put the phone down on him.

He sat in the pub for a bit, wondering about what had happened. It was like a blitz. Was Eddy declaring war in every direction at the same time? And why the old parry heater method? It didn't really work in terms of setting the shop on fire, though it was very sudden and very frightening. It was an old-fashioned technique, used by the generation of, well, Salvatore. Maybe Eddy was being nostalgic, like when he imitated Salvatore's voice; more likely, he found the lapse into barbarism a nice contrast with his green office, his chintz, his window seats, his soft suits.

After a couple of drinks Duffy wasn't closer to any answers, but he had begun to relax. The pub was full; he felt safe. He also felt a bit randy. Maybe he should have pocketed a few of the uncharred mags from McKechnie's Christmas stock. As he sat and thought about it, he definitely did feel randy. It was now almost a week since the future author of the *Good Gay Guide* had dropped his watch into the Tupperware box. Jack had protested that the watch was completely noiseless, the very latest in digital-display quartz technology. Duffy had looked at him sceptically and pointed firmly to the box.

It struck Duffy that one aspect of local life that he hadn't yet checked out was the massage parlours. If McKechnie were as flourishing a businessman as his fire suggested, he could surely afford to treat Duffy to a little body-rub. Every business allows for a percentage of its turnover going in expenses fiddles. Duffy could always claim that he'd spotted Jeggo diving in for a much-needed sauna and had followed him.

He left the pub and looked up and down Greek Street. No time for a consumer survey; besides, he was only a couple of hundred yards away from Martoff's head-quarters. He put on his punter's walk, crossed the street, and pushed open the door of Aladdin's Lamp ('Executive Massage'). In the little front office sat a middle-aged woman in a white nylon housecoat; she smiled at him in a friendly fashion. It seemed to Duffy like going into a ladies' hairdresser's.

'Um, I'd like a massage please,' he mumbled. He hadn't ever used the line before.

'Of course, dear. Do you want sauna too?'

'Er, I don't think so.'

'Well, you can have single girl for eight pounds; single girl topless for ten; two-girl for twelve, two-girl topless for fourteen.' Duffy wondered what the rates included; probably not much.

'How long's that for?'

'Twenty minutes.'

Oh well, in for a penny.

'I'll have the two-girl topless please.'

'Very good sir, Number Three, you'll find a towel in there.'

Duffy handed over fourteen quid (almost a quid a minute, he suddenly thought), and went past the woman's desk into a narrow corridor. There were a row of cubicles constructed of stripped pine. They didn't seem very soundproof to him. The lighting was subdued.

He opened Number Three. In the middle was a sort of high narrow bed: mattress, blankets and a top covering of plastic sheeting. A chair for his clothes, with a towel hung over it; a cupboard or two; and a dresser with some oils and powders laid out. He undressed and put the towel round his waist, noticing that it was too small either to go round his waist properly or to cover his pubic region properly. Then he lay down on the bed.

The two girls bubbled cheerfully into the room. They wore cut-off denim shorts and Dr Scholl sandals. One of the girls had small, tight, high breasts; the other larger, more dangly ones; perhaps that was how the pairs went, hedging the clients' bets.

'Oil or powder, sir?' One of the girls was setting a kitchen pinger for twenty minutes.

Duffy couldn't decide. Wouldn't oil take a long time to get off? But powder didn't sound much fun. Oil sounded much sexier.

'Oil, please.'

They turned him over on his front and began to massage him. One concentrated on his shoulders and back, rubbing oil into him and dipping her tits down every so often and rubbing them against his back; this was the girl with the larger tits, and he certainly knew it. The other girl worked on his legs, getting ever and ever closer to his groin. He felt his erection getting squashed between his thigh and the bed.

Then they turned him over on his back. As they did so,

the towel seemed to fall half off him and his erection lurched sideways into view.

'Oh, what a naughty boy,' commented the girl down that end. 'What have we here?'

Duffy didn't feel he needed to answer that one. The girls continued working on him with their oil and their breasts. The way the oil got wiped off his body on to their breasts seemed very nice indeed to Duffy. Everything, in fact, seemed very nice to Duffy, especially the way the girl down the bottom end was getting nearer and nearer his cock. Every so often her forearm seemed to brush it, nudging it into ever harder erection. She didn't actually touch his cock, though. He remembered vaguely that there was some legal nicety to be performed before they would actually wank him off. Yes, that was it: the client had to propose the idea. Duffy wondered at the form of words. Eventually he tried,

'I'd like you to go on doing that.'

Quick as a flash the lower girl replied, without stopping her handiwork,

'You want relief?'

Of course, that was the phrase, Do you want relief? He nodded.

'Relief's ten.'

He pointed at his pile of clothes, and the girl at his head went over, rummaged for his wallet, and showed him the two five-pound notes she was taking. Meanwhile the lower girl took a dollop of oil and started smoothing it into his cock and balls. Ah, that was bringing him some relief already, he felt. The girl at the top end started rubbing her tits enthusiastically over his chest.

'I think it's time for a nice surprise,' said the girl at the bottom end, 'so close your eyes.' The girl with the big tits helped him by holding her breasts over his face, running them up and down a bit and then settling the nipples softly on his eyelids. Even when the girl at the other end momentarily stopped rubbing him, his cock still pulsed and soared. He heard a cupboard door click open, then shut, and wondered what she was doing. Maybe she was getting out a box of tissues.

The larger girl's nipples were pressed tight against his eyes. The girl at the end pulled a couple of times more on his oiled cock; then he felt something being gently slid round the base of his balls. Maybe some oriental device to make coming more exciting, he thought.

'You can look now,' said the girl at the bottom end. The nipples were removed from his eyes and he looked down the length of his body. What Duffy saw then was the most frightening thing he had seen in his whole life.

Looped around the base of his cock and his balls was a thin copper wire. The wire met and crossed over itself where his cock joined his stomach. At each end of the wire were wooden handles; the slimmer girl was holding one in each hand. It was a garrotte. She said to him very quietly,

'Don't move, copper.'

The other girl went across and pushed open the door. In walked Big Eddy Martoff. He was smiling.

8

Eddy gently took over the wooden handles of the garrotte from the massage girl. He nodded his head towards the door and the two girls went out. Eddy went on smiling.

'What about my ten quid?' asked Duffy. 'My ten quid for relief?'

'Oh, this could give you relief from everything,' said Eddy softly, 'from absolutely everything.' He tugged very gently on the garrotte.

'And another thing,' said Duffy, acting anxious in an attempt to stay cool. 'Why does everybody keep calling me "Copper"? I'm not a copper, you know that. Why did you tell them I was a copper?'

'Such semantic niceties, Mr Wright. At a time like this, too. I don't think the girls would have enjoyed having you on so much if I'd told them that you were only an ex-copper. I don't think they would have put their hearts into their jobs quite as much. I trust, by the way, that there was nothing wrong with the service you received up to the moment I came along?'

'Absolutely no complaints,' said Duffy. 'I'll always come here again.'

'I'm so glad.'

Eddy looked down at Duffy's groin. Depleted by fear, his rig now lay like a large snail, its head flopping sideways across his thigh.

'Well, we do seem to have lost our enthusiasm, don't we?'

'What about my ten quid?' said Duffy. It was the only way he could keep his mind off horrifying possibilities.

'I think that's the least of your worries.' Eddy, equally,

was determined that Duffy should keep his mind on horrifying possibilities; he tugged gently on the handles; the thin copper wire bit slightly into the base of Duffy's cock, and gathered his balls up tighter together.

'Now, Mr Duffy, you have bought cheese in your time, I expect?'

Duffy had.

'Then I expect you will remember how they cut cheeses. Not the soft cheeses, but the hard cheeses. Cheddar, Cheshire, that sort of cheese.'

Duffy did.

'Well the wire they use for that is the same wire which is currently threatening to do you a serious injury.'

Duffy thought about foot-high barrels of Cheddar being sliced vertically in half. Even enfeebled old ladies on the cheese counter didn't break sweat. The wire just slipped through the Cheddar as if there were no obstacle at all. Duffy wasn't sure that he would ever be able to face cheese on toast again.

'Now, Mr Duffy, I admit that meat offers rather more serious resistance than cheese. All those sinews and bits of muscle and veins to sever. But I'm sure we'll discover that roughly the same principle applies. What's the betting I could tug your tassel right off with one pull?'

Duffy had run out of complaints to take his mind off what was happening. He lay there silently, staring at Eddy's powerful wrists, at his fingers on the handles.

'You do realise, Mr Duffy, I hope, that if I pull these handles it will be curtains for you? I don't just mean that you will be kissing your dubious masculinity goodbye. You will be doing that, of course, without question. But you will probably die as well. Did you realise that?'

Duffy croaked a quiet no.

'Oh, yes indeed. You see, the area I am, what shall I say, hovering over, is one of the major nerve centres of your body. Normally the body is quite unable to cope with the severing of the genitalia. Quite unable. The shock is simply too enormous. Very few people have ever survived such an event. Of course, it's possible that by warning you in this way, your body will have the opportunity to build up some resistance to the forthcoming shock. But I'm not an expert on the nervous system, so I'm afraid that I can only hazard this opinion.'

Duffy wanted to vomit; he wanted to shout Sadist, Murderer, Shit, Bastard, Fuckpig, and anything else that came into his head. But he was unable to utter a word; his eyes simply remained fixed on the backs of Eddy's hands.

'I suppose the general public would probably approve of my action if they saw it as removing a homosexual from the community.' Eddie was in a musing vein. 'After all, I don't really believe that a lot of the legislation Parliament gives us is a reflection of popular demand. For instance, the people have never been in favour of the abolition of hanging. Yet Parliament decided that hanging should be done away with. I call that fundamentally undemocratic, don't you, Mr Duffy? Oh dear, we have gone quiet, haven't we? So what about homosexuals, Mr Duffy? I mean, do you really think that most people in this country *approve* of homosexuality? I don't. I think most people in this country think it's disgusting. But does our Parliament understand this? No. And why? Because, of course, our Parliament is stuffed with bents who are frightened for their jobs.'

'In the same way as Parliament is stuffed with murderers who are frightened for their necks?'

'Very good, Mr Duffy. I was beginning to be afraid that this was turning into a monologue. Yes, you're quite right, my comparison does not extend all the way. But I'm sure I'm right about the homosexuals in Parliament. I remember one I was at school with. Frightful fellow. Always off behind the cricket pavilion. He's an M.P.

now – completely safe Tory seat somewhere up in hunting country. Now if his constituents knew, I bet there'd be an awful scandal.' He paused, and seemed to ponder. 'You see, what chaps like you don't understand, Duffy, is that the British people hate bents. They really do. Think of all the nasty names they have for them. There aren't any nice names, are there? Give me a nice name, Mr Duffy.'

'Gay.'

'*Gay?*' Eddie chuckled. 'You don't look very gay to me, Mr Duffy. You've never looked very gay to me. I shouldn't think you looked very gay when the coppers had to come and kick your door in to rescue that poor unfortunate youth from your clutches. I understand he was a black kid as well. That does seem to me to be taking a very unfair advantage, Mr Duffy.'

'Was he working for you, Martoff? Or did you sub-contract?'

'I couldn't possibly tell you a thing like that. Anyway, I don't employ queers.'

Not even twenty-five year old black ones who look younger and can act like the Royal Shakespeare Company, thought Duffy.

'Still, I don't want to get drawn into discussing the wider social questions which might be raised by you being bent. We could go on all night once we embarked on such subjects. One issue simply leads on to another.'

'Has anyone ever told you you ought to go on Any Questions?'

'What a charming thought. I wonder how you get on to the panel?'

'I think the normal way is to blackmail a few radio producers and stab their wives.'

'Duffy, you are a witty fellow. You know, I'm rather enjoying our conversation.' Eddy smiled again. He was a keen smiler. 'But anyway, I suppose, since I seem to have you currently rather at a disadvantage, that I'd better ask why you are still soiling my pavement with your presence? I thought I told you, quite plainly and clearly, to avoid walking on *my* streets.' Eddy wasn't smiling any more. 'I seem to remember instructing you in copper language, so that even you would be able to understand, to get off my patch.'

'You burnt down my client's warehouse,' said Duffy.

'Ah,' said Eddy. 'I think that's rather jumping to conclusions, don't you? I should imagine that if there were a third person here, I could probably sue you for slander. Yes, I'm sure I could. Not that I'd get much money out of you, I suppose. You haven't got private means by any chance, Duffy?'

'You must be joking.'

'Well, I am really. So there wouldn't be much point in suing you. I'd merely end up with my own legal costs to pay. Suing you really would be like trying to get blood out of a stone.'

'What did you want to burn McKechnie's warehouse down for? You won't get any money out of him that way. All those King Kong masks and novelties and hats going up in smoke. I can't understand you, Eddy. What sort of money do you think McKechnie can get for a load of charred kids' toys?'

It was the only way Duffy could think of to play it. Not exactly play the innocent, that never fooled anybody. But play the smartass who doesn't really know as much as his opponent. People enjoyed outwitting smartasses.

'Duffy, I repeat, I did not "burn McKechnie's warehouse down". Unless you want to get into trouble we had better adopt the formula "McKechnie's warehouse burnt down". The intransitive mood, please, it's much less contentious.'

'Well, now that his warehouse has burnt down, he's going to have even less money to pay you off with. I can't understand why you did it – sorry, I'll rephrase that – I can't see that the sad loss of one of my client's warehouses will produce any immediate benefit for you.'

'Very well done, Mr Duffy. I'm talking of your language, of course, not your thinking.'

'What's he got now? Just another warehouse packed with toys and novelties. That's all his capital assets. Plus a rented office. You might make him, I mean, he might decide to scram and, er, sell out to you. But what good is a burnt-out warehouse to anyone?'

Suddenly Duffy saw what he should have seen earlier. Insurance. Of course, that was it. When he first set up business he used to tell clients that the best security they could buy themselves was insurance. Naturally, McKechnie's stock would be insured. So, instead of pushing for a hundred quid a fortnight or whatever, Eddy helps McKechnie liquidise half his assets in one go by burning down his warehouse. McKechnie gets the insurance money, and Eddy demands it all, presumably under threat of something very nasty happening. Eddy also agrees to take over the lease of the warehouse, or what is left of it, on terms not too disfavourable to himself.

The only trouble with this idea was that the warehouse was full of porn. Insurance companies would hardly pay for the replacement of *that* stock-in-trade. So McKechnie wouldn't get any money. No: more likely, Duffy realised, was that only parts of the warehouse were full of porn. McKechnie probably ran a legit business as well for the sake of cover. Most of them did. So what happened if his warehouse burnt down was that he got compensated by the insurance company for the loss of his legitimate stock, and – with a little encouragement from Eddy – he got prosecuted by the coppers for his cache of *Colour Climax*. McKechnie ended up with cash to hand over to Eddy and got the push from the coppers at the same time. And all for the price of a box of Swan Vestas. If that was how he'd worked it, it was bloody clever. But would Eddy have known what was in the warehouse beforehand? Well, his slogan was 'Knowledge is Power'; Duffy wouldn't have put it past him.

The last thing Duffy wanted to do, though, was let on to Eddy what his guesses were. His best hope was to carry on playing the dimwit smartass to the end.

'Or maybe you want to build on the site of the warehouse?'

It was the sort of idiot's suggestion which appealed to Eddy. He chuckled to himself.

'I'm afraid you simply don't understand business, Mr Duffy.' And then, indulgently, 'I might want to build on it at some future date, yes, that could be a possibility.'

Eddy appeared to be thinking. His grip on the garrotte slackened a little. The wires round Duffy's rig relaxed a bit.

'I think I must consider what to do with you,' he finally said. 'My father always told me as a boy that a rushed decision was usually a wrong decision. I shall have to think about you for a bit, Duffy. You'll bear with me, of course. Georgiou,' he shouted.

The door opened and the plump ginger head of Eddy's Number Two appeared. He smiled at Duffy.

'Still looking for the pisser, mate?'

Duffy shook his head.

'Go through his clothes.'

Georgiou searched Duffy's clothes and pronounced them clean. The garrotte was carefully unwound and he was ordered to dress. Duffy vaguely thought of rushing them, but the possibilities of success seemed slim. They seemed even slimmer when the door opened again and Jeggo came in.

'Ah, Mr Jeggo,' said Eddy, 'been out practising our pick-ups, have we?'

Jeggo scowled. He produced a pair of handcuffs.

'Yes, Mr Duffy,' said Eddy, 'I'm afraid we're going to have to handcuff you to take you to, well, to somewhere else. Would you put your hands behind your back, please?'

Duffy did as he was told. Jeggo clipped the handcuffs on and racked them up tightly. As he did so he whispered into Duffy's ear,

'Kill you, asshole.'

'Jeggo,' said Georgiou, 'you're not threatening Mr Duffy, are you?'

Jeggo turned round.

'Copper in cuffs,' he said, and laughed.

They led Duffy along the passage past the other massage cubicles, and out through a back door. Duffy looked around him – it was a change to discard his punter's droop – and worked out where they were going. Across a courtyard, through a garden, past the back yard of a pub – that must be the Duke of Hamilton – left through a gate, and out into another garden, flagged this time. They walked him across to a back door, through a kitchen, up some stairs, and pushed him ahead of them into a side room. There were three beaten-up armchairs in it, plus a table; a calendar with a view of the Lake District hung at an angle on one wall.

'I really must do something about the furniture in here,' Eddy commented. 'It's just too depressing. And the lighting. We must stop all this central lighting we've got everywhere, Georgiou.'

Georgiou nodded in agreement. He waved Duffy across to an armchair. He and Jeggo took the other two, while Martoff closed the door and went away. Jeggo was in the armchair immediately opposite him, staring at him with a sort of contented hostility. Duffy felt he just wanted a rest after his ordeal in the parlour. He didn't feel like baiting Jeggo. In any case, it hardly seemed fair to bait Jeggo. In two meetings he'd revealed a vocabulary of barely a dozen words, at least five of which were the same word: 'asshole'. While he was thinking about this, Jeggo suddenly revealed a new corner of his vocabulary.

'You a Norman?'

Duffy hadn't been looking at him and didn't pay any attention to the remark. Jeggo got up slowly and kicked him on the ankle. Then he sat down again and repeated,

'You a Norman?'

Duffy looked across at Georgiou for elucidation. Georgiou smiled. It must have been a trick he had caught from his boss.

'I think you'll have to explain,' Georgiou said.

'You a Norman?' Jeggo repeated again. 'A Norman Scott? You queer, copper? You are queer, aren't you? Whatcher wearing that earring for if you aren't queer?'

Duffy didn't reply. None of the standard replies seemed appropriate, and with his hands manacled behind his back he didn't feel much like provoking Jeggo into taking free kicks at his ankles.

'Hey, Georgiou, the copper's a Norman. We've caught ourselves a Norman. Haw, haw.' For the first time in their brief acquaintance, Duffy noticed Jeggo showing signs of pleasure. He was becoming positively lively. Almost companionable. 'I wouldn't be in your boots, copper. Mr Eddy doesn't like Normans. He doesn't like coppers much either, but he *hates* Normans. I bet he's thinking up something really special for you. Haw, haw.'

Duffy didn't reply. He also tried to keep his mind off the garrotte.

'Shall I tell him, Georgiou? Shall I tell him some of the things Mr Eddy's thought up?'

'If you like, Jeggo, we've got time to kill.'

'We've got assholes to kill as well.' Jeggo seemed to be reverting to his more usual theme. Duffy waited. There wasn't any alternative to waiting.

'I remember we had a Norman once. We let him run a

little restaurant. Our mistake, really. What did he do? Hired a load of queers as waiters. Proper lowered the tone of the neighbourhood, it did.' Duffy wondered where Jeggo himself had to go in order to raise the tone of any neighbourhood. 'Still, for a bit we said it takes all sorts. Bit soft he was on Normans in those days, Mr Eddy. So what happens? He falls behind with his payments. Well, we did put them up a bit on account of him bringing all these queers into the district. So, anyway, he doesn't pay. Asks for a bit of time. So we go in and we do a little damage. Not much, you know, but I suppose we did put the wind up a few of the customers. They all ran out into the street shouting about how to get soup out of their lace frillies.

'So anyway, this Norman decides he's had enough, and he asks Eddy to buy the lease back off him. Well, Eddy gives him a fair price, though it's not very much, because well, the place was a bit broke up, and anyway, he didn't exactly have much goodwill to sell, did he? So Eddy's a bit disappointed, you know, I mean he's a bit sour at the way this particular piece of business has gone. So he finds this geezer, very pretty guy, Norwegian I think he was, off a ship, and he slips him a few notes and sends him off to the restaurant. Well, the Norman who runs the place, you should see his mouth water, he really thinks it's his lucky day. The pools have come up, he says to himself.

'What he doesn't know is what Eddy knows. So he gives this Norwegian fellow a slap-up meal on the house, and then they flap wrists at each other, and then he takes him home. Three weeks later he starts getting a bit itchy. Then he starts pissing razor blades. Then he goes down to the clinic for Normans and finds out he's got the worst case of syph they've seen in years. In three places, too.'

Jeggo seemed really happy. He chortled, looking pleased that Duffy had dropped in. In case anyone had missed the point, he summed up, 'He doesn't like Normans, Mr Eddy doesn't.'

'Oh, really?' replied Duffy.

They sat in silence for a while, until Eddy put his head round the door and summoned Georgiou.

'Keep Mr Duffy entertained, will you, Jeggo?'

There was another silence. Duffy hoped that Jeggo's idea of entertaining him was to leave him alone with his own thoughts. It wasn't.

'I can't remember any other Norman stories offhand,' he said, 'but I remember a very funny thing Mr Eddy did to a squealer once.'

'I'm not a squealer,' said Duffy, hoping to head off the story with logic.

Jeggo looked cross; he'd been interrupted before he could get into his full narrative flow.

'You're a copper, though.' Why couldn't they learn around this place, Duffy wondered. 'Coppers and squealers are about as bad as each other.'

Duffy let that one go.

'We had this squealer once,' Jeggo began again. 'Now, if there's one thing we hate in our business it's squealers. We hate Normans a lot, but not as much as squealers. Now, if we could find a squealer what was *also* a Norman . . . ' Jeggo seemed to come over all dreamy.

'Anyway, we had this squealer once. He was an Irish fellow. Nice boy, but a squealer. He tipped off a rival firm about a nice big lorryload of books someone was bringing us. Don't know why he did it. Must of been the money I suppose. Anyway, a couple of the lads picked him up and they brought him back to see Mr Eddy. Mr Eddy was pretty cheesed, I don't mind telling you. I mean, nobody squeals on Mr Eddy, and that's a rule.

'But Mr Eddy didn't do anything on the spur. He likes to think a lot before he does things. A big thinker, Mr Eddy. So after he's been thinking for a while, he comes in and he sends me out for a tube of that super-glue. You know what I mean? Bonds in seconds. Says on the packet you've got to keep it on a high shelf, 'cos otherwise kids get hold of it and stick all their fingers together. And then you have to take them down the hospital.

'So I gets this glue and bring it back to Mr Eddy and we go in to see this Irish boy. He was shitting himself, you can imagine. Mr Eddy was quite careful really. Course he struggled a bit, once he saw what was coming. Mr Eddy puts the glue all over his lips. So he pulls his lips right back. So Mr Eddy puts some glue on his front teef as well. Then we pushes his mouf together.'

Duffy winced. It was presumably Eddy's way of making the punishment fit the crime.

'And now we come to the good bit. You see, Mr Eddy wanted to make the Irish lad understand what he'd done. I mean, he'd lost us a lot of books. It wasn't just the squeal-ing, it was the loss of business Mr Eddy minded. There was a lot of books in that lorry.

'Now the Irish boy was, how shall I put it, well, he wasn't a Jew, understand what I mean? We took him into a room, and he was holding his face in a funny sort of way, but otherwise he was all right, and one or two of us held him down a bit, and then Mr Eddy, well he believes in the personal touch, pulled down this Mick's trousers. Then he got his little bit of flesh and pulled it down a bit and glued it all together. Like they say, bonds in seconds, takes two elephants to pull it apart. It all looked so neat, we just had to have a giggle. And the Mick, he just looked down at himself. He was really beginning to sweat, I can tell you.

'What he didn't know was that it wasn't going to get any better. We cuffed his hands behind his back – I fink they may be the same bracelets you're wearing – and took his trousers off altogether, and then took him into another room. Big Eddy had really thought about it. The room had nothing in it except for books – you know, magazines. All spread out and opened up, they were. Just the sort of stuff he'd lost us. And we locked him in there. Think of that – wherever he turned there was nothing but tit and beaver and cum-shots. And you can't keep your eyes closed for ever. And even when you do you can't stop where your mind's going.

'I don't fink he liked it much. I fink if he'd stayed there longer than he did he'd of gone crazy. But after a day or so, Eddy decided to let him go. Put him in a car and dropped him outside a hospital. I don't fink the Mick squealed again.'

For the second time that evening Duffy felt like vomiting. It wasn't the violence and the craziness which made him feel bad. It was the awful strand of logic which ran through what these people did. The sort of logic whereby the victim is persuaded that there's some sense in the violence that is being inflicted on him. There was another reason why Duffy felt like vomiting. He didn't think that the evening was over for him yet.

'Mr Duffy, are you feeling all right?' Eddy had come back into the room and was leaning over him. 'You haven't been abusing him, have you, Jeggo?'

'I been telling him what we did to that squealer Mick.'

'Oh dear, yes. Well, let me put your mind at rest, Mr Duffy. I don't think it's going to be an evening for the glue. I hope your strength will keep up, though, because I think we might have a bit of a night still ahead of us.'

They took him out of the room and along a corridor. As they went through each door, Duffy scanned the doorframes. At the end of the corridor they hit carpet. Carpet and sporting prints. Duffy flicked his eyes over one as they passed. A country gentleman was sitting beneath an oak tree after a hard morning's shooting; he cradled a long-barrelled musket in the crook of his left elbow and knee; one dog lay sleeping at his feet, another was bounding on to his right knee, eager for more killing; on the ground beside him was a careless pile of dead rabbits, made bloodless and picturesque by the artist. Duffy read the caption: 'Rabbit Shooting – La Chasse aux Lapins'. Printed with the export market in mind, he reflected – just like today's porn mags, whose brief texts came in four languages.

Through another door and they reached the Georgian double-cube room. Duffy was led, still handcuffed, to the sofa. As he was about to sit down, Eddy suddenly stopped him.

'No, no, that must be very uncomfortable, sitting like that. We'll put them on you again from the front. You won't, of course, struggle, or do anything silly.'

'Can I rub my wrists a bit?'

'Of course. But I think we'll sit you on the sofa first. It's very hard to surprise people when you're sitting on a sofa.'

They sat him down and crowded round him while they undid the cuffs. He rubbed his wrists for a couple of minutes, then held them out forwards.

'Perhaps not quite so tight, this time,' Eddy instructed. Jeggo looked disappointed. 'After all, we're not dealing with Houdini.'

Then he dismissed Jeggo and told Georgiou to stay. Duffy looked round the room again, ostensibly to admire, really to check the doors and windows. The latter were hidden by full-length chintz curtains which matched the sofa and chairs. Brass standard lamps supplied the sort of light Eddy was presumably hoping to install in his other rooms. Duffy wondered, not for the first time, at the way in which this graceful, genteel room, the prints, and Eddy's elegant clothes were subsidised and maintained by punters peering through glass letter boxes, by the amplified wailings of sheepdogs and Hoovers, by thousands of copies of *Hogtie* and *42-Plus*. He kept such thoughts to himself.

'Very pretty,' he simply murmured.

'Yes, indeed. Now, Mr Duffy, it's already midnight, but I'm afraid we're going to have to detain you for quite a bit longer. An hour or two, probably. I hope no one is expecting you back?'

Duffy didn't reply. Eddy watched him from across the top of his desk.

'Of course, your private life is no business of mine. Still, I should think that most of the late-evening customers of the Aladdin's Lamp would, on balance, probably not be going home to bed-partners, if I can use as neutral an expression as possible. Georgiou and I occasionally have to work as late as this, though we always try and let our wives know in advance. We certainly let them know we would be working late tonight, though of course until you turned up we didn't know quite how late we might have to stay. But then, that's business. By the way, Mr Duffy, did you register the appropriateness of the name I chose for the Aladdin's Lamp? I hope you found it as witty as I do.'

Duffy hadn't actually thought about it. He doubted if many of its other patrons had either.

'Now, Mr Duffy, I propose to be fairly frank with you. I trust that you will be equally frank in return. I am, of course, more than a little displeased that you took my instruction to stay away from my pavements so cavalierly. But now that I have you here I would like to take the opportunity for a little exchange of information. We like to keep our files up to date. Now, you left the force some four years ago, as we have already discussed. What have you been doing since?'

Duffy didn't know how much Eddy might have on his file that he hadn't revealed in their previous meeting, so he played it reasonably straight.

'I set up a security firm. Advising businesses about how to vet personnel, that sort of thing.'

'Oh, I see. Quite an appropriate profession. What other sort of things?'

'Well, I tell them how to set up scanning equipment to stop pilfering, that sort of thing.'

'Ah, we may have to come to you for advice one day. At the moment the punters in the shops are much too timid to try running off without paying. That is one advantage we have over other businesses. And how is your firm doing?'

'So-so. It's a bit seasonal. A big rush of crime always helps.'

'How ironic. You depend on crime for your job. I depend on silly laws and public prudery to keep my business ticking over. But Mr McKechnie, when he came to you, didn't come for a scanning system.'

'No. He wanted me to find out who was preshing him.'

'And why did he come to you?'

'He knew I did a bit of freelance work on the side when trade was slack. I was recommended to him.'

'And you found out who was preshing him?'

'Yes. You.'

'And you told him who it was?'

'Of course.'

'And what did you tell him he should do?'

'I said he had three choices: give you what you want, have another go to see if there was a straight cop at West Central, or look for some powerful friends.'

'Perfectly sound piece of thinking. And what did he say in reply?'

'He said he'd ring me back.'

'And did he?'

'No.'

'And did you suggest any other alternatives to him?'

Duffy considered. A sudden suspicion came to him.

Maybe their conversations hadn't been entirely private. He said lightly,

'I told him he could always try and kill you. But I warned him it was against the law.'

'So it is, Mr Duffy. I'm glad you pointed that out to him. I wouldn't want him running away with any wrong ideas. You didn't suggest yourself for this project?'

'No, I didn't suggest it seriously.'

'And did McKechnie indicate to you whether or not he might go looking for some powerful friends?'

'No.'

'Do you think he has any?'

'I wouldn't know. I shouldn't think powerful people would be interested in the friendship of a bankrupt importer of King Kong masks.'

'Well put, Mr Duffy. So, in short, would you say that the task for which McKechnie hired you is complete?'

'I suppose so.'

'No lingering reservations? No pricking conscience?'

'No.'

'Good, Mr Duffy. I think you've been very frank with me. Franker, if anything, than I expected. Now I'll tell you a thing or two. You have, if I may say so without sounding patronising, done very well in your investigation. You seem to me to have worked diligently and efficiently. Since we first became aware of your presence you haven't done anything to draw attention to yourself unnecessarily. Indeed, the first time you were pointed out to me in the street by Georgiou, I said that you looked just like an ordinary punter. As a businessman, I admire that professionalism.

'You've found out various things, and you've reported back the knowledge you have obtained. You understand in a small way what I practise in a big way. I think I explained the previous time we met my philosophy that knowledge is the basis for power. And the corollary of that is that your small piece of knowledge can be easily neutralised by my much larger amount of knowledge. Your small piece of power obtained through your investigations can be rendered entirely harmless by the considerably greater power I obtain from my considerably more thorough researches. Why do you think great men have always established great libraries? Because they understand the secret of power.

'Don't look at me like that, Mr Duffy. Just because I talk of great men it doesn't mean that I have delusions of grandeur. You'd like that, of course, it would make it all much neater for your copper's mind, wouldn't it? On the contrary, I have no claims or ambitions to be a great man of any sort. I am a successful businessman with very precise business aims. I obtain the knowledge I need for the implementation of those aims.'

It all sounded so reasonable in this easy, sanitised language. Duffy had difficulty reminding himself that the 'business aims' involved things like paraffin heaters through Ronnie's windows and a Stanley knife on Rosie McKechnie. He also couldn't work out whether or not Eddy was telling him any secrets: whether he was giving away a lot, or giving away nothing.

'You see, let's take the present case. Yourself. Now, many businessmen in my position would react extremely unfavourably to your presence, even to your existence. I should think your average local businessman, put in my position, might react rather sharply. Wouldn't you agree?'

'Depends how smart they were,' said Duffy.

'Oh, come come, there's no need to try and flatter me. What I am going to do with you has been entirely decided, anyway, and you couldn't possibly change my mind about it. No, we are talking in general practical terms. Now, the average local businessman, having already warned you off his patch as I did only the other day, would undoubtedly take it as a severe affront to his sense of machismo that you returned. He would also – rightly or wrongly – feel that what you had found out was a threat to him. So he would naturally be extremely unpleasant towards you. This unpleasantness would doubtless express itself in violence. In some cases, the scale of the violence might be such as would result in your death.

'Now, I am not necessarily against such drastic measures in business terms. And if I made such a business decision about you, there wouldn't be much trouble implementing it; I'm sure you'll agree, if you think of Jeggo's quite severe hostility towards you, that there wouldn't be any problem of implementation. Well, this particular course has been urged in your own case, but I have been inclined to take a different line. Why eliminate, I always say, when you can neutralise? Why be so proud of your knowledge and not use it to the full?'

Eddy suddenly got up from behind his desk and disappeared into his side room, the one with the tiny cream-coloured box perched just above the door. He came back with several manila files under his arm and sat down next to Duffy on the sofa. He tapped the first file.

'Now, this one will be familiar to you already.' He opened it and Duffy saw it was his own file. 'Updated, you see,' said Eddy, and pointed to the latest Polaroid of Duffy. It showed him sitting exactly where he sat now, holding in his hand the earlier photograph from the file.

'Quite an ironic picture, don't you think? I suppose we could take another now of you sitting looking at a photo of yourself looking at a photo of yourself. Like those mirrors set in parallel where your image recedes for ever.'

He put Duffy's file down and tapped the others. 'It wouldn't be a good idea to let you see all of these, but I'll show you enough to tantalise you.' He flipped open the first and Duffy saw a bundle of photos of Ronnie; Eddy quickly flipped through the papers beneath: reports, transcripts of telephone conversations, Xerox copies of

Ronnie's letters, a sketch map, photos of Renée and several other tarts. It looked at least as full as the sort of dossier West Central would have on Ronnie.

Eddy opened the second file and chuckled. Duffy looked at the first photo; after a while he said, 'My God,' and Eddy chuckled again. It was McKechnie's secretary. She wasn't wearing her silver cross and she wasn't wearing her long skirt. She wasn't wearing any skirt. Or knickers. Or anything. She had her hair done in a different style and looked as if she was about to bounce on stage at the Peep Show.

'One of yours?' asked Duffy.

'Trade secret,' said Eddy. 'Not that it matters. I think she might well have a bad case of 'flu by the time it comes for work tomorrow.' He opened the third, thickest file, and said, 'I think it might be a mistake to let you see more than the photos in this one.'

Duffy looked.

Sullivan! Sullivan blurred, walking down a street. Sullivan in beach shorts on some possibly foreign beach, surrounded by businessmen, also in beach shorts, none of whom Duffy recognised from his days at West Central; they were all raising their glasses to the camera. Sullivan in a restaurant with Eddy, and looking round very crossly at a candid cameraman's sudden flashgun. Sullivan looking much younger – maybe twenty years younger; that was interesting. Sullivan with someone who just possibly might not be a tart on his arm. Eddy closed the file, and moved on to the next.

'And the next I probably shouldn't show you at all.' He merely turned the file sideways and showed Duffy the name down the spine: McKechnie.

Eddy gathered up the files and took them back into the side room. Then he walked to his desk, picked up one of the phones and pressed a button.

'You ready? . . . Yes . . . Good . . . Two minutes.' He

looked up at Duffy. 'And now, Mr Duffy, while you think over the implications of what you have just seen, you're going to find out the difference between being eliminated and being neutralised.'

This time they blindfolded him, took him along the corridor they had come in by, and down some steps; they turned him round on the spot so many times he was giddy, then walked him a bit, took him up some steps, out into the open, back indoors, along a corridor, past somewhere hot, and eventually got him to lie down on what felt like a high bed. Then they pulled his manacled hands up over his head and tucked them behind his neck. (Was that why they had handcuffed him more comfortably in the green room?) He heard a faint clink and discovered he couldn't move his hands. Then his shoes and socks were removed, his trousers and pants taken down. He lay quietly; there was little point in kicking out if you were blindfolded and had your hands manacled behind your head. Two people took him one by each foot, pulled his legs apart a little, and tied some sort of straps round his ankles. He felt helpless, exposed, felt that he was going to be castrated.

Then they simply cut the clothes off the top half of his body. He felt a large pair of shears snipping up the arms of his blouson, then up to the neck, and the garment fell of him in three pieces. His shirt was sheared away from him. Now he was completely naked and strapped down. Someone laid a couple of cloths – perhaps towels – over the straps restraining his ankles. His thoughts chased their own tails round his head. And all this time no one had uttered a word. It made the isolation worse.

And it made what happened next feel odder. He smelt something sweet quite close at hand. Then he felt something damp being poured on to his stomach. Then a hand began to massage oil gently into his stomach. Then another hand joined it and began to spread the oil up to his chest. Shortly afterwards another pair of hands began to work on his legs. Every so often he felt tits brush gently against him. Then something different from the previous time in the Aladdin's Lamp happened: a mouth lowered itself softly on to his cock and began to lick.

If the body could obey orders of the mind, his cock would have stayed the shrunken, tiny, timorous object it had been all the way up to this point. But the body is fractious, temperamental, disobedient. Duffy knew this from his night with Carol: how many times had he sworn at his recalcitrant flesh? And this time, though his mind was tense with fear, his body relaxed. As oil was rubbed smoothly into his cock, it grew and prospered. Tits grazed softly over his chest, then went away. His cock was being wanked with the gentle firmness of a professional. He felt flesh ease itself between his knees – perhaps the girl who had been at his chest was now kneeling between his legs. The silence continued, broken only by the soft swish of oiled flesh. He felt a fresh touch on his cock, and then, from darkness and silence, the world suddenly, horribly roared into light and sound.

It took Duffy perhaps five seconds from the blindfold being withdrawn for his eyes to get used to the light, and to see what they had done to him. And in five seconds a Polaroid fitted with a Powerwind can take maybe half a dozen pictures. The ones which Eddy took after the first six were probably not of much value to him, for Duffy let out a roar of pain and anger, his face contorted, and Jeggo had to punch him very hard in the ear to shut him up. But the first half dozen, with the angelic, flaxen-haired, seven-year-old boy grasping Duffy's erection, and Duffy himself, his arms crossed behind his head in the posture of a sybarite, looking up with a puzzled stare of pleasure – those six would do for Eddy's purposes.

They untied Duffy and told him to collect his clothes. He put on his trousers, shoes and ripped shirt, and folded up the three bits of his blouson. They kicked him out of a side door and he stood on the pavement in Frith Street with tears trickling down his face. A cruising taxi passed but refused to stop for this weeping scarecrow who was probably just another Soho drunk. Sick to his stomach, Duffy set off to walk home.

9

Duffy got home as light was breaking and the first milk-
men were clinking their way on their rounds. He looked
through his kitchen window at the clock wrapped in
polythene. It said two minutes past six. He fell on his bed
and slept without a murmur, without a dream. It was
when he woke that he had the dreams, and found his
present flicker-lit with jagged flashes of the night before.
Of the whirr and splut of the Powerwind Polaroid dis-
gorging its prints. Of Eddy, Georgiou and Jeggo hanging
over them while they developed, giggling like school-
boys at their first X-film. Of Eddy turning and saying to
him, 'Don't go away, we may need another set.' Of the
child between his legs, looking as if he had just been set
down in a grand sort of playpen. Of the two girls who had
wanked him suddenly coming over all maternal with the
child, who had started crying when Duffy began roaring.
Of Eddy's smile of triumph, knowing that he didn't even
need to explain the angles to Duffy. And of Eddy's final
gesture before they booted him into the street – reaching
across and tucking into Duffy's shirt pocket the least
useful of the prints.

Duffy suddenly had a thought. Maybe the picture
showed him being hit by Jeggo. Maybe it showed handcuffs. Maybe he could take it to the police, to some police
somewhere, and show that it had all been a put-up job? He
dug out the photo, looked at it, choked, and despaired.
There was no ambiguity about what the picture showed: a
masochist paedophile who liked being chained up and
beaten while a young boy held his cock. Given the
context, Duffy's open-mouthed roar of pain translated as
the expression of a deviant reaching climax.

Duffy screwed up the photo and threw it in the waste-paper basket. Then he dug it out, took it over to the stainless steel draining board and put a match to the edge. The white cardboard caught slowly, then burned towards the edge of the print. Duffy half expected it to go out when it reached the chemicals, but it caught more fiercely, with enthusiastic flame and gouts of black smoke. Bubbles ran across the surface of the print ahead of the flames; the photograph curled and bent as they started to die. Duffy sniffed the deep black smoke; the fumes smelt of burning oil refineries in a distant land.

All day Duffy sat with his body roaring hotly for revenge, and a cool, wise voice inside his head telling him that there was nothing he could do. Big Eddy had neutralised him, as Big Eddy had neutralised Sullivan and Ronnie and even that secretary of McKechnie's who looked like a religious maniac but had a Peep Show body. Duffy wondered about Sullivan, about how they had ensnared him. A long, slow business, no doubt, a gradual putting-together of evidence, a deliberate recording of what would seem to the outside world like little favours but which to Sullivan may have seemed innocuous, and may even have been innocuous at the time. Take the photo of him eating with Eddy. Perhaps Sullivan had been invited to lunch by a third party: an informer, say, or someone with whom he dealt. They sit down to lunch – maybe they're going Dutch, or maybe Sullivan's paying – have a few drinks, and after a bit Eddy arrives and greets the stooge in a chummy way. What do you do if you are Sullivan? Get up and walk away? So Eddy sits down, you set a glass in front of him, perhaps he has a snack to keep you company, and suddenly the flashgun of a passing restaurant photographer goes off in your face. Do you get up and arrest him? Eddy seems as upset as you are, chases the man out, comes back saying how bad for his business the photo could be. And so you forget about it. Except that the photo ends up in Eddy's file, and what does it show now? A West Central Super having a friendly lunch – all wine and camaraderie – with one of his patch's top villains. Somehow, the stooge is obscured by Eddy's body in the picture, and it looks as if Sullivan and Eddy are lunching tête-à-tête.

And after that it gets easier. Easier for Eddy, and, in a way, easier for Sullivan. Soon you stop being certain where your world ends and the villains' world begins. You even begin to meet Eddy socially: you think you might be able to get something out of him. He might get drunk and let something drop. Of course you have to get drunk in order to encourage him to do the same. And what does a cigarette lighter matter: you needed one anyway; it's hardly a bribe, is it? Of course it's not a bribe – it stands to reason. What copper would risk his job for a cigarette lighter – *therefore*, it cannot be a bribe. Even if it is inscribed. And then, maybe, you take a holiday with one or two fellows you've met drinking. A bit of abroad, shake the dust off your feet, look at the pretty girls on the beach, have a few jars, well, maybe we won't take the wife, say it's an Interpol conference or something. And Eddy turns up; had business in the area, thought he'd drop in. Joins in the fun, good company Eddy is, life and soul, have a few drinks, a few photos, and then maybe, well all the other chaps are doing it, Eddy's doing it, it seems churlish not to, you have yourself a bit of local girl. The girl's very nice to you, doesn't seem to mind that you don't parliamo the old italiano, doesn't seem to mind that you're a bit fat and a bit drunk and that you don't do it all that well. And then Eddy bids you all goodbye, wouldn't like to embarrass the Super by arriving at Heathrow with him, pop off now, byeee. And he goes. But it all ends up on Eddy's file, and however it was, however Sullivan knew it really was, it can only look the way it looks on Eddy's file.

And after the meal, and the holiday, and the girl, and the cigarette lighter, it all gets easier and easier. The favours come: maybe Eddy feeds Sullivan the odd villain or two; after all it's in *his* interest to see that Sullivan remains a successful local copper. Not *too* successful, of course, in case he gets transferred, so Eddy feeds him mainly minnows; but he helps keep him in business. And then, gradually, comes the payoff, or rather the beginning of the payoff, because it goes on and on and on, and will keep going on, until there's no more paying to be done. It's none of my business, Ernest (they'd be on Ernest and Eddy terms by now), but from what I hear I think you've got the wrong chap in that little case where the pimp got cut: I've been asking around and this is what I've come up with – and then evidence so good any copper would buy it, release his suspect, and arrest the man Eddy decided to fit up. And Eddy would keep your telephone calls on record as well.

And so it goes on. Oh Ernest, I'm having a little local trouble with some new fellow called McKechnie. I don't know what you've got on him, but I'll send you round what I know; he's a bit of a trouble-maker from what I hear. I shouldn't think he'd be a good influence on the patch. And then a bit later, Ernest, funny thing happened, you know, I had a little chap come to see me today, quite a bright little fellow. Face from the past, I expect you'll remember him, name of Duffy. Yes, that's right, yes, queer. Bright fellow, but, well, I think he's getting into the wrong company, Ernest. He seems to be doing some sort of job for McKechnie; no, I'm not sure exactly what, and I'm pretty sure he doesn't really know what McKechnie's up to. I mean, I don't like to see a fellow like that get into any trouble, even if he is a queer copper we had to get rid of; I was just thinking maybe you might send someone round to have a word with him? Straight away? Oh, no need to hurry, Ernest, but, well, now you come to mention it, that would be quite useful. You've got his address, have you? Good.

Duffy didn't find corruption hard to understand, and it didn't make him priggish either. Anyone could go the way of Sullivan, and then live for twenty, thirty years making little payoffs here and there, bending things just a bit, justifying it to yourself by keeping up your arrest record – and all the time there would be a sort of tapeworm inside you, feeding away in your guts. It wasn't guilt, and it was too imprecise to be fear; it was a sort of hideous worry, a nagging certainty that one day you'd be called on to deliver too much, one day it would all be put in black-and-white terms instead of these comforting neutral greys, one day Eddy would be there flourishing all he knew about you and saying, 'Fucking do this or I'll break you.' And you knew that if you didn't do it, he'd break you; and if you did do it, you might get broken by someone else, but there was just a chance that you might get away with it and that it wouldn't show, and it was always the better chance to do what Eddy suggested. So you did it, and this time it went wrong, and you were busted, broken, chewed up and spat out, sent down for a few years while your wife had to handle the shame and the loneliness and the sudden loss of your pension; what she'd married wasn't after all a successful Soho gangbuster but a fat convict who'd never really been very nice to her, who'd lied and gone off on holidays with criminals and slept with foreign whores and now, at the end of his career, wasn't even going to bring her home a pension. And how are you going to face the neighbours with *that* in the papers, Mrs Sullivan, without a trip to the doctor's and talk of stress and the change and a bottleful of little pills and then, well, Ernest isn't going to start seeing how fast the sherry's going down now that he's in the Scrubs, is he?

That was one of the points about corruption: you never

thought of the side-effects at the time. As you clinked glasses and climbed into your beach shorts, you didn't really think about a Stanley knife tracing a three-inch cut down the right shoulder blade of Rosie McKechnie, who may have been married to a pretty shady fellow, but being married even to a murderer isn't a crime yet, is it? That's the sort of connection you don't make, you don't think cause-and-effect operates in that way; and yet it does, it's exactly that sort of equation which in the end is presented to you, maybe in court or in your head, though usually by this time you're head's so muddled it can't even follow simple equations like that. No, your head says, it wasn't *me* that cut Rosie McKechnie, you can't blame that on *me*, I was miles away, I was at my desk, no, I was even arresting someone at the time. You may have been, but that was only cover.

Duffy understood Sullivan perfectly; and understanding him didn't make him feel morally superior; but it did make him feel free to hate Sullivan with all the rage at his disposal. Because one of the little cause-and-effect links Sullivan might or might not understand any more was that it was he who had destroyed Duffy's career. Sure, Eddy set it up, set the black kid up for Duffy; sure, it was because Duffy was after Eddy that Eddy did this; but without Sullivan as informant, as tip-off man, as maker perhaps of that final phone call to the Paddington police – without Sullivan, all you had was a villain trying to frame a copper. Not much headway usually made there. Sullivan it was who made it work.

And now Duffy had gone back to his old patch and got caught in Eddy's net all over again. And Eddy, like a great big spider, had neatly trussed him up, injected him with something which made him quite harmless, and let him go. Eddy knew that the scraps of information Duffy had gathered were valueless compared to one corner of a single snap that Eddy had taken last night. As he was booted out into the night from the side door into Frith Street, Duffy, the tears welling in his eyes, had mumbled to Eddy that he'd come back and break his cock off. Eddy had chortled back at him,

'Suck it and see, Mr Duffy, suck it and see.'

And the three men had giggled, as they'd giggled when they'd watched the Polaroids gradually developing.

Duffy wanted to ring Carol, but he wasn't sure he dared. He wasn't even sure she'd believe what he told her. He wasn't sure he ought to sleep the night with her ever again after what had happened. The last time Eddy had fucked him up he'd been left unable to make it with Carol; he'd been left a compulsive one-night-stander, a user of whores and casual trade, bruised and wary when it came to emotional contact. What would be the result of Eddy fucking him up again this time? He didn't like to think.

He tried not to think of lots of other things during the rest of that day. He roamed around his flat, fed casually, walked the streets, dropped over to his office to see if there was anything on the answerphone, went home, watched five solid hours of television and collapsed into another dreamless sleep. Not surprisingly, since all the horrors came to the surface naturally enough during the daytime.

The following morning he tried to kick himself into working. He pulled out some plans of offices and tried to give himself tests, asking how he would fit the cheapest and most efficient scanner network, or alarm system, given the particular area and its problems. The trouble was, he didn't really care. All he cared about was what was going on underground in his mind.

In the course of the day he got three phone calls, all of which helped him come to a decision. The first was the briefest.

'Oh, Duffy, it's Brian McKechnie here.'

'Fuck off, McKechnie.'

'I beg your pardon?'

'I said, Fuck off McKechnie.'

There was a vague, spluttering noise at the other end.

'Oh, McKechnie, don't ring off. There is one thing. Is your secretary in today, by any chance?'

'My secretary? Why? No, she isn't as a matter of fact. She's got 'flu. Some sort of summer 'flu, I suppose.'

'Thank you. Now fuck off, McKechnie.'

Duffy put the phone down. The second call came in about lunchtime. Duffy had almost forgotten about it. As he picked up the phone, he heard a thick Russian accent.

'Meester Daffy, ees yor controll. You weesh to yoin Keem in Moskva thees week orr nechst?'

'Geoff, hi. What is it?'

'What is it? Only the little job you gave me. Nixon's secretary with her foot on the autowipe – remember?'

'Sorry. Of course. No, I had a bad night's sleep last night.'

'Are you sitting comfortably?'

'Yes.'

'Then I'll begin. I take it the tape you sent was recorded on a Sony portable SK 6500?'

'I don't know; well, I know it was a Sony.'

'Well, it must have been an SK 6500 then. Fortunately they don't rub out that well – the manufacturers often assume that on these little portables you'll never just want to rub out so that you get absolute silence, you'll only want to rub out when you re-record over the top. And the guy who wiped it – who I presume is the same guy who is speaking in the bit that's erased . . . '

'Can't tell you, Geoff. You never know who might be listening.' Duffy always liked teasing Bell about his paranoia. Bell never noticed.

'Quite right. Anyway, the guy who wiped it used the same machine that he recorded it on, which wasn't the thing to do if he was really keen to lose it. And it doesn't

look as if he knew about these machines because he only
went over it once, I'd say.'

Bell stopped. It was the techniques of finding things
out that fascinated him much more than what could
actually be found out by using such techniques. Duffy
prodded.

'That's terrific. And what did you find?'

'Ah, that took a little while. The traces weren't perfect,
I had to re-record, blow it up, break it down – shall I tell
you exactly what I did?'

'I'd rather hear what was in the gap.'

'Ah.' He sounded disappointed. 'Shall I tell you over
the phone?'

'Let's risk it.'

'I don't like that word "risk". Never use it myself. Well,
the sentence, let me get my transcript, the sentence read,
"I'm not having some GAP GAP GAP coming on to my patch
and telling me how to run my shop." That was before I
filled it in.'

'Yes, Geoff, and after you filled it in?'

'Ah, let me get my other transcript . . . "I'm not having
some grubby ex-fiddler from up north coming on to my
patch and telling me how to run my shop." I had a bit of
difficulty getting "grubby" out of the tape, but I'm pretty
sure that's what it is.'

'No doubt about the rest?'

'None at all.'

'Thanks very much, Geoff.'

'What shall I do with the tape?'

'Could you possibly deliver it with the transcripts to an
address I'll give you? Today.'

'Well . . . ' Geoff sounded doubtful.

'I can't tell you why, I'm afraid.' That clinched it.

'Of course.'

The third phone call came late in the afternoon, when
Duffy was already rooting in his work cupboard for

supplies. As he picked the phone up, he carried on checking the set of screwdrivers, the plastic-handled pliers, and the cutting knives he might need. He heard the pips panicking, then Carol's voice came on. Like last time, she didn't identify herself.

'I'm not going to repeat it. Born Brian Kelly, 1929, Newcastle. '49 London, '52 back north, Leeds, Manchester, Newcastle, '73 London. '51 receiving London. '53 receiving Leeds. '54 receiving Leeds. '61 indecent material through the post Manchester. '65 Obscene Publications Act Manchester. '70 receiving Newcastle. Probation, six months, six months, fine, three months, one year. Released '71, clean since, and don't ask me ever to do this again Duffy are you all right?'

'I've got to see you tonight, Carol.'

'Sorry, Duffy, I've got a date.'

'No, I mean got to, Carol. Got to. Please cancel it.'

There was a silence.

'I've never asked you to cancel before. It's always been part of the agreement, that I'd never ask you to cancel. I'm asking now. I'm serious, Carol.'

'O.K.'

'Your place, please. I'll be late. Probably very late.'

'I don't want to hear why, Duffy. Just don't tell me why.'

'I won't. And thanks.'

Carol hung up. Duffy went on with his quiet, methodical preparations. He laid everything he might possibly need out on the table, and then selected in order of probability of need. There was no point setting off festooned with equipment like a fucking Sherpa. He might as well carry a large sack over his shoulder labelled Swag.

He wondered about the best time. Everyone said two in the morning was the best time. Duffy thought it was a rubbish time. Two in the morning is when sounds travel for ever, when a sticky window makes a soft squeak and three Panda cars hear it from miles away. Two o'clock is when insomniacs look out of their windows and long for an excuse to phone the police, just to talk to somebody, anybody. 'Oh, officer, there's a rather suspicious cat on the roof next door. It's got four legs, a ginger coat and is carrying a jemmy.' Two o'clock is when the burglars who get caught go burgling.

Duffy settled for ten thirty. Lots of punters still on the streets, the pubs still going strong, lots of stray noises drifting about. The tarts getting into double figures for the day.

He wore an anorak with pockets all over it, jeans and soft-soled shoes. He went in by tube as usual to Piccadilly Circus, strolled slowly along the Avenue and put on his punter's walk as he turned up a side street. He worked his way across to Greek Street, crossed to the east side of the street to avoid walking past the front window of the Aladdin's Lamp, crossed back, and went into the Duke of Hamilton. He bought a half of lager and went out into the tiny garden at the back. It was a cool night, and the only people there were a couple sitting at a table holding hands. They didn't pay any attention as Duffy walked to the farthest table and sat down. They didn't pay any attention as Duffy sipped his drink slowly and watched them out of the corner of his eye. When the barman called Time and they dragged themselves out of each other's eyes, they didn't even notice that there was no one else in the garden with them.

As he sat in the shadows of the courtyard behind the Double Blue he realised that he had miscalculated. There were no lights at all in the upstairs windows; but downstairs the cinema was still going strong. Easing their way out of a back window and floating towards him came the noises of amplified pleasure: the sounds of wailing sheep, and of bats being bludgeoned to death.

At eleven the noises stopped. At eleven ten the lights were turned out. At eleven thirty Duffy thought it was time to move. He pulled on a pair of very thin, transparent rubber gloves, got up out of the shadows and walked quickly to the cinema's emergency exit. He listened for a moment with his ear to the door, found himself uttering not exactly a prayer but a profound wish, and pushed gently on the right-hand door. It opened an inch, two inches, then the retaining chain was pulled taut. Duffy paused, fished in a pocket, took out a pencil-thin piece of metal about three inches long, and tugged on the end. Three sections telescoped outwards, until he had an instrument about a foot long. He poked this through the gap in the doors, pulled the right-hand door almost shut on the metal rod, and moved it slowly upwards until it touched the chain.

By closing the door Duffy had relaxed the chain as much as it was possible. He pressed upwards on the chain, his eye squashed against the eighth-of-an-inch gap between the doors. Nothing happened. He pressed again, then started jiggling the chain up and down with his rod. Suddenly the cut link freed itself, and the two ends of the chain swung down, the one on the left striking the metal door with a clang.

Duffy listened, then pushed very gently on the door. He squinted through again. The padlock was clearly attached to the right-hand bit of chain, the bit he couldn't see; but its weight meant that as he pushed, the section of the chain that was gradually freeing itself, clinking slightly as each link ran over the rail of the push-bar, was the part he could see, the left-hand end. What he wanted to avoid was the whole end of the chain swinging free and falling away to hit the other door. Duffy pushed until the door was about six inches open, then decided on another course of action. He pushed his rod through one of the links of the left-hand chain, and simply began to lift. This freed the chain and at the same time eliminated the danger of part or all of it falling loose.

When the chain came free of the push-bar on the left-hand door, Duffy pressed on the door until it was wide enough open to let him through, then slipped inside. Quietly he replaced the chain as it had been before, fitting the cut link back into place. Then, being doubly – maybe unnecessarily – careful, he slipped the bolts on the open door back into their slots.

After the lager and the nervous wait until the Double Blue closed, what Duffy needed most was a piss. He knew it would only be on his mind if he didn't have one, so he walked down the corridor towards the cinema and found the toilet. He debated whether to leave the door open for more light, or close it for better sound-proofing. Eventually he pushed the door to, lit his tiny pen-torch and pissed carefully against the side of the bowl. Then he climbed up on to the bowl, fished in the cistern, and collected his heavy, snub-nosed metal-clippers. No point in leaving more evidence on the scene that you had to.

He dabbed the cutters dry on the thigh of his jeans and walked quietly up the stairs. He got to the landing and was about to open the middle of the three doors when he suddenly noticed a light coming from beneath the door of the room on the right. Then he heard a slight banging and shuffling noise, followed by a distinct cough. Fuck it. Damn. He wondered if someone was sleeping the night there. Or perhaps they were just locking away the takings from the Double Blue. All the doors opened into the rooms from the landing, which didn't help Duffy. Eventually he decided to wait pressed against the wall by the side of the right-hand door. He waited there for five minutes or so, then heard footsteps approaching.

As Jeggo put his head out to look for the light switch on the landing, Duffy hit him as hard as he could on the side of the head with the metal-clippers. Even the shortest fights are noisy. Jeggo roared with pain, and Duffy hit him again nearer the temple with the cutters, grunting loudly with the effort as he did so. Jeggo fell to the floor about as quietly as an entire sack of coal being emptied down a metal chute into a coal cellar.

Duffy had knocked enough people unconscious to know that they didn't necessarily stay that way for as long as you wanted them to. He took Jeggo by the back of the collar, and carefully avoiding the blood which was staining the right side of his face, dragged him through the middle door and along the carpeted passage. He flicked a light switch, climbed on a chair, and examined all the surrounds of the door-frame at the end of the passage. It was clean. He turned the handle and found it was locked.

First he squinted through the keyhole to find out whether there was a key left in the lock. There was. Then he extracted a little probe with a magnet on the end which snapped on to the snub end of the key and allowed him to manipulate it. The magnet wasn't strong enough to unlock the door with the key; but strong enough to turn the key itself to a vertical position, so that he could push it gently backwards until it fell out on to the carpet on the other side. Duffy then took out his set of skeleton keys and had the door open in a minute.

He dragged Jeggo through into the green room and dumped him on the floor. He bled quietly on to the carpet. The curtains were closed, so Duffy turned on one of the lights, the brass standard lamp nearest to the side room. Then he pulled a chair over to the door and climbed up on it. With his pen-torch pressed close to the cream-painted box, he examined every edge of it, found some screws which had been crudely painted over, and with a short screwdriver chipped away at the hardened paint. Then he slowly undid the screws. As they loosened, he pressed against the cover of the box. The screws fell to the floor, and the lid was held in place simply by his hand. He laid his face close to the left-hand side of it and very slightly pulled the cover away on that side. Then he did the same on the right-hand side. He couldn't get at the top, so he ran a thin blade between the top edge and the wall. Again, nothing. He couldn't get at the bottom edge because it was tight against the top of the door-frame. This was the big one you simply had to risk. Duffy looked round to make sure he'd worked out the quickest way to the door in case there was a trigger on the bottom edge. Then he gently began to lift the cover away.

Nothing happened. Nothing happened except that, when Duffy looked at the alarm he nearly giggled. Then he did giggle. Jackson and Horwill had started making these in 1952, and for some reason had kept them in production until the mid-1960s. They weren't bad – that's to say, they went off reliably, they made a loud noise, they didn't need servicing – it was just that, well, burglars practised on these when they were still at primary school. They were the sort of alarms which villains taught their wives how to defuse, just so they could get a feeling of what hubby's job was like. There were hoary burglar's stories which turned on getting to a job with the very latest equipment and finding yourself faced with a Jackson and Horwill '52.

Two minutes and a few keys later, Duffy had opened the door to the side room. As he did so, he heard a sound from the floor. Jeggo was moving a bit, making a little noise. Duffy walked quickly across and kicked him on the side of the head that was nearest him – the side that didn't have blood on it. If that fucked up the inside of Jeggo's head, he thought, it could only be an improvement.

The room was very neatly arranged. On the far wall were the manila files, covering about three shelves. A to Z. He reached up to the top shelf and pulled out 'Duffy'. In a pocket on the inside of the left-hand cover were the

Polaroids from the night before last. He put the file on one side. Then he looked for one or two names in particular. Then, on an impulse, a sudden, slightly sick impulse, he looked for Carol. Thank God, she wasn't there. He looked for Shaw. There was a very thin file, a photo or two, nothing much, a few notes, as if either they hadn't tried to get anything on him, or else he was one dourly honest copper.

Duffy pulled out the rest of the files and tipped them on to the floor. Tightly packed papers burn poorly, so he scattered them loosely. Then he looked around the room and noticed two metal filing cabinets. Locked, but Duffy could open them blindfold. One was full of cassette tapes, again filed in alphabetical order. He went through them slowly. The other had a number of 8 mm. cine-films in it. He broke one open, went back into the green room, and held a strip up to the light. Then he piled the films and the tapes on top of the manila files.

He took his own file, opened it up and placed it flat on the carpet. He took out the Polaroids and built them into a house of cards. Then he took a box of matches and lit the edge of one of them. It caught, the edge burned, and then with a sudden flare the chemicals on the print surface lit. Soon all the prints were alight, and papers round the edge were beginning to catch as well. He watched unblinkingly while the Polaroids bubbled and flamed, and started giving off smoke and the smell of burning oil. He watched them curl and bend, and then the house of cards he had made collapsed. More papers caught, the fire was well alight; Duffy fed on some tapes and films, then some folders, and decided it was time to leave.

He propped open the door into the side room to help ventilate the fire. Then, as he left, dragging Jeggo with him, he propped open each door in turn. Already as he left the green room he could feel the heat of the fire. He dragged Jeggo bumping down the stairs, pulled the chain out of the emergency exit door, slipped the catches, and propped both the doors open. That should help the draught.

Still careful not to collect a dab of blood, he dragged Jeggo to the end of the courtyard and left him there. If he wanted to rush in and try to put out the fire when he came round, he was welcome to. Duffy hopped over a few fences until he came to an alley leading back out into Greek Street. There were still a few cruising taxis, looking for drunken foreign punters whom they could drive to hotels a mile away and charge them ten quid. They're a greedy bunch, cabmen, that late at night, but Duffy didn't care. When the first taxi didn't stop, he simply waved a five-pound note at the driver of the second and told him to take him to Carol's.

Eddy certainly wouldn't think that it was Duffy who had done him. Not straight away, at least. Duffy was sure Jeggo hadn't had time to see him. But Eddy might work it out by process of elimination. He might connect Duffy's security business with the fact that someone had bypassed the burglar alarm on his side room. And he might come up with a name at the same time as he realised what he had lost. What had he said that time? Great men have their libraries. Eddy had his files and tapes and films and Polaroids. Only Eddy didn't have them any more. Knowledge is Power; and without that room Big Eddy Martoff was going to be no more than just another pushy Soho villain.

Duffy didn't want to be around when Martoff realised that. He didn't like to think of Martoff running his finger down the telephone directory for Duffy's home address. So Duffy wouldn't go back to his Paddington flat, not for anything. In any case, after two burglaries there wasn't much left there that he valued. Everything was replaceable: clothes, tools, television set.

There were a few last things to do, of course, before

Duffy disappeared into another part of London. As he sat in the taxi he felt the front of his anorak. The files made him look pregnant. He'd taken two: Sullivan's and McKechnie's. In the morning, after he'd slept with them under his pillow, he'd pop round the corner and have Sullivan's Xeroxed. Five copies. He didn't worry so much about McKechnie; but Sullivan wasn't getting away.

Then he'd pack the files up, enclose the tape and transcripts Bell would have delivered to Carol's by now, and send them off to A10. He didn't know what A10 would do about McKechnie – probably pass the file on – but he knew what they'd do about Sullivan. And just to make sure that they knew what they were going to do about Sullivan, he'd send off four of the Xerox copies to crime desks in Fleet Street. The fifth he'd keep for himself. It should see Sullivan good for five years at least, depending on which judge he drew.

When Duffy got to Carol's, she was still up. The package from Bell was on the kitchen table. She hadn't seen Duffy so cheerful for months. He grinned at her, pressed his file-stuffed anorak against her and gave her a kiss. Then he looked at her oddly, shook his head an inch or two, and said, 'Sorry'. Sorry, she supposed he meant, in case you misinterpreted that. But she didn't ask. She didn't ask either what he had been doing, or why he wanted to stay the night tonight, or why she had had to put off her date. She didn't ask, because she really didn't want to know. All she said to him was,

'Duffy, I thought you might be hungry, so I've got us some bread and cheese.'

He looked up, then suddenly seemed lost in memory. He was thinking about the last few days, about the fears and the anger; he was thinking about the cubicle at the Aladdin's Lamp, and the thin copper wire wrapped threateningly around him. But all that he said to Carol by way of explanation about Martoff and Jeggo and

Georgiou, about Sullivan and Shaw, about McKechnie and Bell – all he said about what had happened to him in the past weeks, and what he had done, was,

'I really don't think I could face cheese, love.'

And then he gave her an enigmatic smile.

FIDDLE CITY

To Craig and Li

The day they crashed McKay, not much else happened on the M4. At least, not on the stretch between Heathrow and Chiswick; further west, that was somebody else's patch, so who cared? Especially as it was one of those warm, hazy August mornings when the police cars bask like lizards on their special roadside ramps; when those few extra feet above the tarmac permit a careless, unobserved, cap-tilted snooze. And then, perhaps, towards 11.30, the quiet phut and crackle of the FM radio would be eased a bit lower, and finally drowned out by the tiny portable in the blue pocket, tuned to the ball-by-ball.

And the cars weren't giving any trouble either. By ten, the last commuters had vanished east in a swirl of nicotine and bad temper; they wouldn't be back for at least six hours. The commercials, the heavies, the twenty-tonners were un-characteristically well-behaved: something to do with the sun, no doubt. And the civvies: well, on the way to the airport they were too scared of wrecking their holiday to do more than forty; while on the way back, they were so baffled by driving on the left that they often stayed in third gear all the way to the Cromwell Road.

So the blues weren't too pleased when McKay got crashed, when a taxi driver who had seen – well, hadn't really seen anything, just a wreck and a paint smear on the crash barrier – radioed in to his office, who called the local police, who called Heathrow, who transferred it to Uxbridge, who at the third time of asking (England 8 for 1, Boycott bowled Chappell 2: even that bit of the day was going well) managed to raise a drowsily laconic panda crew. Who weren't too pleased with McKay for fucking up their morning. It was almost as if he'd done it deliberately.

What was left on the crash barrier might have been paint, but it wasn't. McKay's car had bits of red on it, but not that much. It was a customised Cortina with a tiger motif. At the front, a trompe-l'œil radiator grille whose vertical bars formed the tiger's teeth; along the side, the massed lightning of gold and black jagged stripes; at the back, a tail painted across the bumper, and (McKay's own suggestion, of which he was in-continently proud) a pair of tiger buttocks which met at the point where the special central exhaust protruded. At work, to his face, they called him, as he planned, 'Tiger'; when he wasn't there, they tended to refer to his as The Farting Cat. Sometimes they would watch him drive off, and laugh together at the first gust of blue-grey smoke from between the tiger's buttocks.

McKay left the Western International Cargo Market and headed east towards London. But he didn't drive like a tiger. After a flash bit of foot-down and tyre-squeal as he left work (someone was usually watching, if only a cleaner and his broom), he settled back on the motorway to a steady forty-five. No point burning out the engine before its time. Besides, he liked being in his car – the longer it lasted, the better. Proper little maharajah's palace in here, he used to say. The sound system; the row of miniatures in the 'cocktail cabinet', as he loftily described his glove compartment; the small, padded steering wheel, all black leather and studs; the full Cyril Lord underfoot; sheepskin seats ('The wife makes 'em from the sheep Tiger runs over,' he would explain); even a sheepskin rear-window shelf. On this shelf – another of McKay's favour-ite touches – lolled a large soft toy. A tiger, of course. McKay was vaguely irritated that its colours didn't match the body-work, and he'd nearly punched the soft-toy salesman who tried to assure him that the colours were definitely authentic (as if the colours of his Cortina weren't). Still, McKay was able to make a virtue of this whenever anyone mentioned it. 'Tigers come in all colours,' he'd quip, modestly referring to himself as well.

McKay looked up past the too-pale toy and checked the traffic behind him. Just a coach, some twenty yards back. He moved his head a bit and studied his own reflection. The broad, slightly sweaty face, the cupid's-bow mouth, the impassive eyes – they all pleased McKay as much as ever. Vroom, vroom, he thought to himself. Idly, he tugged on the chain around his neck until a thin silver swastika, about two inches square, appeared from beneath his shirt. The leading edges of the emblem had been filed to sharpness: for no particular reason at the time, except that it felt like a good idea. And later, it had proved useful now and then. When he was in the caff, for instance, and that Pakki had started looking at him. Not doing anything, of course – they never dared; they just looked. McKay had dug out a match, reeled in his swastika, and started sharpening the match to a point right in front of the Pakki's face. Then he let the badge dangle and picked slowly at his teeth, all the time staring at this guy. That was one Pakki who didn't bother to finish his sweet.

McKay shifted the swastika in his right hand, selected one of the legs, and began to pick inquisitively at his left nostril with it. That was another reason for keeping to a steady forty-five; though of course, with a racing wheel like this you could drive at seventy with just one little pinkie if you felt like it. As he told people.

He worked methodically at his nostril, occasionally flicking a bogy on to his jeans. A lorry began to overtake him. For a few seconds it was alongside, thumping and shuddering; then it fell back. McKay glanced in the mirror to see where it had gone, but all he saw was the same coach as before; it was a bit closer than last time, maybe ten yards behind.

Typical of fucking lorries, McKay thought. They bang past you going down a hill, swerve in front as soon as they can see six inches of daylight, and then you have to overtake them all over again on the next uphill stretch. Ridiculous; they ought to be made to stay in the slow lane where they belong. Always half-overtaking you and then changing their minds just because there's a one-in-fifty gradient.

McKay didn't check on whether it had been a one-in-fifty gradient that had made the lorry fall back. He just assumed it, as anyone else might; and he just happened to assume wrong. Instead, he shifted the swastika in his hand, selected a new leg – he wasn't a dirty bugger, he knew about clean sheets – and began to pick up gently at his right nostril. As he did so, the thump and shudder repeated itself at his shoulder. If McKay hadn't been otherwise occupied, he might have been tempted to have a little game with the lorry, accelerating just enough to keep ahead of it, slowing as the lorry slowed, really getting on its tits. He liked doing that to lorries. But it was a nice morning; McKay was feeling unusually good-humoured; he was on a routine delivery run; and besides, he was picking his nose. So instead, he merely looked ahead (there was a bridge coming up) and then in his mirror – that coach was still there; funny, it was right up his exhaust – and settled back to let the lorry pass.

It was well planned; but then the men hadn't been cheap: they only did one-offs, and they never took rubbish jobs. They were proud of their work; proud, that is, of the way they carried it out. They knew where to steal what they needed; they weren't afraid of wasting a few days on research; and they didn't keep telltale cuttings books on what they did – even though they had, in their own quiet way, made the papers a few times.

The lorry, an articulated eighteen-wheeler, all swaddled in canvas and ropes, drew level with McKay about three hundred yards before the bridge. Gradually it began to inch past, until the back of the trailer was level with the rear offside door of the Cortina; then it seemed just to sit there, straining and burping, unable to get past. Fucking run out of puff again, thought McKay.

The coach, meanwhile, took up even closer order. Anyone following the three vehicles would have concluded that there were only two – a lorry unwisely trying to overtake a coach; the Cortina was completely hidden. And from the front – well, the lorry would hide the car from those directly across from them; and the bridge, they assumed, would take care of the rest. That was what the men had planned; and they were men who weren't cheap.

As the cab of the lorry emerged into the sunlight on the other side of the bridge, the driver twisted the wheel and stamped on the brake at the same time, putting the vehicle into a controlled snake. The back part of the trailer slewed suddenly left and rammed the Cortina in the midriff. 'Just a little boomps-a-daisy,' was how the driver had described it when accepting the first half of the money; but then he was always prone to understatement.

The first effect of just a little boomps-a-daisy was to make the sharpened edge of the swastika rip through the fleshy outside of McKay's right nostril. McKay intended to swear at that point, but events rather got the better of him. Besides, if he had sworn, he might have used up all his best words before something much more unpleasant than a torn nose happened to him; and that would have been a waste.

As the lorry struck the Cortina, the coach pulled out into the middle lane to get clear of whatever might happen. The car was batted diagonally across the hard shoulder. The nearside rear indicator light was the first thing to break against the crash barrier: but then that, compared to the final toll, was about as grave an injury to the Cortina as was McKay's nose to the rest of his body.

Crash barriers work in the way they are intended to, as long as the angle of approach is within a certain range. The Cortina's wasn't. It hit the barrier, stood up on its boot for a second – at which point the doors burst open and McKay was shrugged out – then skipped over the barrier and cartwheeled down an escarpment. McKay himself made a long red trail on the metal barrier in a way that no one could quite understand. It looked, to those who could first be bothered to stop, as if he had been exaggerating terribly: if you were thrown out of your car, why didn't you just land on the barrier and stay there, canted over it like a carpet ready for spring beating? Why did it look as if someone or something had *smeared* the poor fellow all along the barrier? 'Darling, *no* darling . . . *don't* look.' Of course he probably wasn't wearing a seat belt, but even so, it did look a bit much. 'Darling, I *told* you not to look. Darling, are you . . . well, quickly, use that patch of grass over there . . . Oh *Christ*.' Why did one stop for accidents; why didn't one do as all the other fellows did?

No one had seen what had happened. Or rather, no one came forward to say that they had seen what had happened. There was a muted discussion, about an hour later, as an Alitalia DC-8 took off for Palermo, about what exactly had occurred, and those big lorries shouldn't be allowed on the road, I always say, and do you think we should have stopped, and I hope no one took our number, and they couldn't have, they couldn't have known we were watching; but after ten days of a Thomson package, of sun and drink and not too many ruins, the whole incident was more or less forgotten. It was just a bump in the memory, no bigger than the bump in the crash barrier a few yards beyond the bridge.

The police resigned themselves to not getting back to the cricket until it was 63 for 4; it was always 63 for 4 when England batted first against the Australians, so they supposed they could take the rest of the morning as read. The few motorists who had bothered to stop were routinely quizzed, but none of them had seen anything. The drivers of the lorry and the coach turned off at the next junction, and left their vehicles in a lorry park close to the Gunnersbury tube station: they both wanted the District Line, and didn't see why they should have to change, especially after doing a job. They soon forgot the details of their morning's work, and were never required to reflect any further on the crash.

The only people who reflected on it – apart from McKay, of course, as he wheeled himself around in later years – were the two policemen in the panda car and the surgeons at Uxbridge Hospital. As the constables were driving back to their lizard's ramp, one of them switched off the two-way radio and said,

'You know, we could do some business.'

'. . . ?'

'Someone's got to pick up that car, haven't they? I mean, some garage. I mean, it's business, isn't it? It wouldn't be far out of our way to pop round to a garage and tip them off when there's a crash. They'd be bound to be grateful.'

His colleague grunted.

'Been done.'

'Has it? What . . . locally?'

'Not here. Up on the M1, couple of years ago. Big stink. Few early retirements. Didn't work out.'

'Hmm. Well, maybe they were too grabby or something; maybe they got too sure of themselves. I bet we could work it. Just pick the right garage. Not do it too often. Not ask them to be too grateful.'

His colleague merely grunted again, and turned on the two-way radio. It might be worth a think.

Meanwhile, at Uxbridge Hospital, the surgeons were having a more serious think. Should they start on the legs first, or the pelvis? One of the legs looked really messy; it might have to go altogether. On the other hand, with a pelvis you never knew what else you might find until you started digging around. It looked as if there were problems with the back as well. Oh God, that was the trouble with crashes – you never knew where to start. The chief surgeon looked up at McKay's broad, tanned face. Why did they drive so *fast*, for Christ's sake? Oh well, better get on with it. The anaesthetist caught his glance and eased the oxygen mask off McKay's face. The side of the right nostril was slit open to a depth of about half an inch. The bleeding had stopped. Well, at least *that* could wait.

1

Three months earlier Duffy had been sitting over a drink at the bar in the Alligator, trying to decide which of two alarm systems to recommend to a customer: the one which worked better, but on which he got a smaller cut; or the one which worked less well (that electronic eye could be bypassed by a Scotty dog, let alone the fellows with A-levels who were joining the business nowadays), but on which he got a larger cut. Really, he supposed, there was no conflict: he'd disliked the customer so much – the way the fellow had automatically given him a beer while he had sherry (not that Duffy liked sherry), the hoity way he had put Duffy down about the most likely method a burglar would use to break in. Now what he'd do . . .

'Mine's a virgin on the rocks.'

Duffy looked up. A chubby-faced man with pronounced five o'clock shadow was easing himself on to the next stool. He had a pasty complexion and didn't look very fit. Duffy turned back to his whisky. What he'd do was draw up one of his specially complex-looking wiring plans for the old fart's house, recommend the system on which he got a larger cut, shove in a slightly bigger bill than normal, and then hope for the best. It was all luck with burglary, really: if you landed a smart pair of gloved hands in the night, you couldn't stop him; if you landed a trainee, or a shitter, or someone who was only really doing it to get away from the wife, then all you needed was a big white box with a few wires sticking out and they buggered off to the next house.

'I said, mine's a virgin on the rocks, old chum.'

Duffy didn't look back. He wasn't in the mood to be picked up; he certainly wasn't in the mood to spread the drink around. He'd got his bank statement that morning. So he merely raised his glass in the direction of the barman and said, when he came across,

'I think the gentleman on my right wants to buy himself a drink.'

He heard a chuckle, then:

'Virgin on the rocks, same again for my friend here, whatever it is he's got his fist wrapped around, the name's Leonardo.'

Duffy continued to gaze into his whisky. If chubby-chops wanted to buy him a drink, that was up to chubby-chops. He turned, and caught a look of scurrying anticipation from the next stool.

'Leonardo . . . virgin . . . oh, forget it. Barman, put a vodka in that, will you. Large one.' Then he turned back to Duffy. 'Pity, that would have been an easy round for you. I'm not a cheap date after the first.'

'You're not a date,' said Duffy.

'Eric Leonard,' said the newcomer.

'Duffy,' said Duffy.

'Anything else? *Sir* Duffy.'

'There's a Nick.'

'There usually is. My dear Nick,' Leonard repeated the name needlessly, in a mildly ingratiating way. Duffy almost didn't recognise himself. At work he was Duffy; to his close friends he was Duffy; the only people who called him Nick were acquaintances who didn't know – or weren't allowed – better. So that was all right for the moment.

'And you shall call me Eric.'

'I'll think it over.' Duffy was always suspicious of people without proper surnames. Two Christian names: it wasn't right; it wasn't . . . neat.

Duffy wondered what Leonard wanted. Apart from going to bed with him of course. Which was a long way from being a certainty. Mostly you went down to the Alligator so as not to go home alone – that stood to reason; but sometimes you just went for the atmosphere, a bit of drinking company, and then, with a 'some other time, perhaps', you were on your way. That was one of the things Duffy liked about the Alligator. It wasn't a hard raunch club; it wasn't a place where people came Concording out of the closet in a splatter of supersonic bangs; it wasn't a place for clones – the lumberjack shirt, the little tache, the logger's jeans; it wasn't a place for leather and chains and 'Hang on, I'll just go to the toilet and grease my fist'. It was a quiet, neat place for quiet, neat people like Duffy. It was even, he supposed, a bit middle-class.

Which was why Eric struck Duffy as a slice of rough. The pushy manner, the double entendres – that was so out of date, all that stuff; as out of date as bottom-pinching. You may be gay, Duffy thought to himself, but that's where you start from, not where you end up. Duffy wasn't a prude, but he might have been a bit of a puritan. He wondered what sort of job Eric did; but he didn't wonder hard enough to ask.

Eric, for his part, had put Duffy in the same category. He hadn't been to the Alligator before, and found it depressingly conventional. You might as well be in a singles bar in midtown Manhattan, he thought. All those blue blazers, and striped shirts, and *ties* for God's sake. And in the middle of them, this shortish fellow in a blouson with a big plastic zip up the front, and a polo-neck sweater and a longish brushcut. As he slid on to the barstool, Eric had noted the broad, strong face with a slightly small, tight mouth; the hands too were strong, with stubby, square-ended fingers. The first time Duffy turned towards him, Eric noted the gold stud in the left ear lobe. You'll do me, he thought, you'll do me, my nice little slice of rough.

Except that he didn't. When Eric finished what had turned into a bloody Mary he leaned across and said,

'Well, Sir Duffy, shall we mount up?' the fellow had simply put down his glass, shaken his head and replied, 'No.'

And Duffy had wandered home, depressed by the thought of his bank statement, and depressed by the way he'd very nearly not said No.

Eric, meanwhile, was regretting the drink he'd had to pay for. He had a rule about drinks: Leonard's Law, he called it to himself. Always buy more drinks than are your due for those richer than yourself; but sponge off those poorer than you. That way, both lots respected you.

The funny thing was, it hadn't worked with this Duffy fellow. He hadn't seemed to need to be sponged off. Some psychological hangup, no doubt. Maybe, Eric thought, he ought to have asked the fellow more questions about himself. They always liked that.

A fortnight later, Leonard called in at the Alligator again. This time, when he spotted Duffy, he altered his act a bit, played it more ordinary, even went so far as to ask him what he did.

'I run a firm.'

'Ah, what line of business?'

'Security.'

'Would I have heard of the firm?'

'You heard of Duffy Security?'

'No.'

'Then you wouldn't have heard of it.'

Eric was suddenly a bit keener than before to get off with Duffy. He'd fucked a policeman once, but never anyone in the security business. He had a vague, half-formed ambition to sleep with someone from every trade and profession (there were exceptions, of course, like bankers and stockbrokers and barristers; but then you weren't a left-wing journalist for nothing: sometimes you simply couldn't help running up against your principles). Fucking a security man; that was something new. Though of course he didn't tell Duffy.

And in reply, Duffy didn't let on that he was only a one-man

firm; that his office was an answerphone; that his van was 'F'
registration; that he didn't even have a dog. Not that he ever
needed a dog; it was just that some people thought they
gave status. But Eric didn't cross-question him on the details;
his curiosity was more or less exhausted by now. Instead he
asked:

'Can you give me a lift home?'

And Duffy replied,

'All right.'

In the event, they went to Duffy's flat, the bottom half of a
semi in Goldsmith Avenue, Acton. At first the flat struck Eric
as very neat; then he realised that it was less neat than empty.
What there was by way of furniture and decoration was tidily
enough arranged; but the effect bordered on the monkish.

'You been burgled or something?' he asked, thinking that
this was the sort of remark a security man might be amused by.
But Duffy didn't reply. Instead he pointed at the bathroom and
said,

'Watch in there.'

'I beg your pardon?' What was he meant to watch?

'*Put* your watch in there.'

Ah. Well, if that was how he ran things. Eric wandered into
the bathroom and saw a square Tupperware box with a label on
it. The label said 'Watches'. He unpeeled his strap and dropped
the watch in; then, puzzled but feeling distantly indulgent, he
unsnapped his silver name-bracelet with the 'EL' almost
camouflaged by engraved curlicues, and he dropped that in
afterwards. Maybe it was like giving up your valuables to the
groundsman. He'd have to ask Duffy about that.

If he had, Duffy might have told him about his ticking
phobia. But Eric didn't ask. When he got to the bedroom his
host was already between the sheets. Eric vaguely looked
around to see where to put his clothes. Duffy's own were
nowhere to be seen. Tidy again. Oh well, he thought, it was all
part of meeting the people.

The next morning Eric left in a normally ambiguous frame

of mind. He'd added a security man to his list, that was something. On the other hand, fucking Duffy was much like fucking someone who wasn't a security man: if you closed your eyes, you wouldn't find yourself thinking, I am clearly in the hands of a man skilled in cash transfers, alarm systems and personnel screening. You wouldn't think that. So, while in one way it made every difference to Eric that Duffy was a security man, it also made none at all. Well, that bit of wrong-footing was nothing new about sex, he thought.

He'd sort of quite liked Duffy – as far as one did on such occasions (and liking was often alloyed with relief that it had all passed off O.K. and hope that there wouldn't be any bacterial after-effects). He'd even gone so far, on leaving, as to say,

'See you around.'

'No,' Duffy had replied politely, and Eric found himself thinking, I didn't know I was *that* bad. But Duffy's negative had no connection with the night before; it only had connection with Carol, and events of four years ago, and a lot of past history that he certainly wasn't going to spill to one-nighters.

And there were only one-nighters in Duffy's life at the moment. One-nighters of both sexes, as it happened; but however erotically competent they were, or clean, or interesting, or even good old-fashioned nice, they only got to drop their watches into his box once. Carol, ex-colleague from West Central police station, ex-girlfriend (no, still girlfriend, sort of), and also ex-fiancée (no, not quite: she'd asked him, and he'd said No) – she was the only exception; and a bitter, wry exception at that. The one person Duffy wanted to succeed with in bed; the one person with whom he automatically failed – had failed so often now that he no longer tried. Potency with Carol, Duffy had long decided, was an idiot's mirage. You might as well believe in Heaven.

'Mine's still a virgin on the rocks,' a familiar voice whispered in his ear at the Alligator three months later. 'Where've you been, Sir Duffy?'

Duffy signed at the waiter, and interpreted.

'Tomato juice, lots of ice.'

'Oh well, old thing, if you're buying . . . ' Eric retained the waiter with a flick of the eyebrow. 'Dunk a couple of vodkas in it while you're about it.'

'No, you're paying,' said Duffy, stubborn about being taken in by that sort of trick.

'God, you don't guard cash transfers for nothing, do you?' Eric gave a theatrical groan. 'Anyway, I'll come straight to the point.'

'No,' said Duffy. 'I said not again, didn't I?' Why did people always think No meant Yes, soon?

'Wait. Waity-wait. Job. Want a job?'

'Maybe.'

'That's why I've been looking for you.'

'I'm in the book.'

'Yes, but it's much more fun sitting here being bought a drink than talking to your secretary down the phone, isn't it?'

Duffy let one of the two remarks pass, but picked up on the other.

'You're still buying.'

'A friend of a friend . . . is having a little trouble.'

'That doesn't surprise me.' There was something about the pallid face and the buoyant manner which irritated Duffy. Be one or the other, he thought.

'Always a little tart, eh?' (Duffy let that one pass too.) 'A little thieving seems to be going on at his establishment.'

'There's this quite useful branch of the civil service they've set up, you know. It's called the police.'

'Well, obviously he has his reasons.'

'What are they?'

'It's a small establishment – half a dozen or so employees. Good relationship all round, just happens to be one rotten apple. Now if he went to the police they'd come clumping in with their great boots, stir everything up, put everyone under suspicion, wouldn't they?'

'They might stop the stealing.'

'So he thought, get someone private in, let him sniff around. Can't do any harm, can it?'

'No. It can only cost money. Why did you suggest me?'

'Well, you run a security firm, don't you?'

'That's not how you know me.'

'No, but we must stick together, mustn't we?'

Ah, thought Duffy: gays as the new masons – is that what's happening? Would he have to learn a new handshake soon? He was irritated. Once you didn't need solidarity, you resented its offer.

'Tell me more.'

'His name's Hendrick. He runs a transport and storage business out of Heathrow. He's been losing rather more stuff than he cares for lately.'

'How would he explain me? I'm not much good leaning on a mop.'

'One of his men just had a car crash. He'll be off for some time.'

'Convenient. What do I do?'

'He'll tell you.'

'I charge . . . '

'Duffy,' Eric cut in, 'I'm not a fucking broker. You fix that up with him. I don't care what you earn. You want the job, go and see him.' Eric was annoyed. First Duffy acted as if he expected to be raped; then he got all uppity. Eric scribbled on the top of a newspaper. 'This is his London office. Ring up, say you've called about the papaws.'

'The what?'

'The papaws. As in fruit. Tropical. It's a code, Duffy. It's not a good idea, we thought, for you to ring up and say you're calling about sorting out the thefts.'

'I get.'

'I hope so.' Eric began to slide off his barstool. He felt he'd been misjudged. He certainly hadn't taken Duffy's No to mean Yes, soon. He'd only taken it to mean Perhaps, in a bit.

'Oh, two things.'

'Yes?'

'Who's your friend?'

'. . .?'

'The friend who's the friend in "a friend of a friend".'

'Oh, it's not relevant.'

'How do you know?'

'Because *he* hasn't been stealing from his friend's firm, that's why. And what's the second thing?'

'Oh – don't go without paying for the drinks.'

Duffy sat opposite Roy Hendrick in an office the size of a bus shelter just off the Euston Road. His secretary had a room the size of a large refrigerator. Hendrick didn't seem very comfortable. Perhaps he wasn't that familiar with his office – perhaps it was only here for tax reasons, or to impress customers by appearing to show a London end to the business. Or perhaps Hendrick was uncomfortable for some other reason; maybe he was lying to Duffy. Clients often did.

Hendrick, a fleshy, saturnine man with dirty blond hair and a flapping suit which might just have been handed on from someone else, explained the problem.

'I'm not an angel, Mr Duffy, and I don't expect other people to behave like angels. It's just that there are limits.'

'Uh-huh.'

'If you get the removers in, when you shift house, you expect to lose a bit, don't you? I mean, if you're sensible, you pack up the stuff you really care for and take it yourself, and then don't get too surprised if you suffer a small attack of removers' perks in the course of the job. That's the way it is, isn't it?'

'If you say so.' The only removers Duffy had ever come across had been burglars. At his last flat he'd been burgled twice: the second time, they'd taken everything, his pile of sixpences and his electric kettle included; they'd even taken his pot plant. He'd been left with a few ashtrays, a bed and a carpet. That scarcely warranted hiring a pantechnicon when he moved flats.

'Well, the freight business is rather the same. You expect to lose a bit if you ship by air. It goes through so many hands, has to be opened by customs – well, there are more temptations than Adam ever had, if you follow the expression.' (Duffy didn't look a bookish fellow to Hendrick.) 'And you know what they say about Heathrow?' Hendrick paused. It was clear from Duffy's expression that he didn't know what they said about Heathrow. 'No one who works there ever needs to buy fresh fruit and veg. They tell me there's scarcely a greengrocer within miles. Anyone around there who catches his wife trying to *buy* a pound of apples or whatever practically has her committed on the spot.'

Hendrick stared at Duffy, inviting vague complicity towards the opposite sex. Duffy looked blank. Hendrick stared briefly at the gold stud in Duffy's left ear. He felt like giving it a tweak, if only to make the man say something. Eventually Duffy did speak, if reticently.

'Uh-huh.'

'What do you mean by *uh-huh*?'

'You've been losing apples, is that what you're saying?'

'No. Well, yes, sort of, but that's beside the point. I've been running the business for five years. Always accepted a certain percentage of pilfering. There's almost an unspoken agreement at times: it helps them bump up their wages, I charge it to the insurance and turn a blind eye. Not worth going into.'

'But recently . . . '

'But recently, about once a month or so, it's got out of hand: a really big dip. Something I can't go along with.'

'Like?'

'Caseload of calculators. Half a dozen furs. Two crates of smoked salmon.'

'You carry only luxuries?'

'Not really. We freight a pretty mixed bag; bit of everything. But you don't shift stuff by air unless it's valuable, or perishable, or has to be shipped quickly because of the state of the market. We don't get many crates of garden furniture or dried pigfeed, if that's what you're asking, no.'

'So how do you get me in?'

'You can take McKay's place. Poor old McKay,' Hendrick added, as if confirming compassion; but the repetition made it seem artificial (and perhaps it had never been very sincere in the first place). 'Nearly wrote himself off. Did write his car off. Very nice car.' In the last comment at least Hendrick was indubitably sincere.

'What do I do?'

'Bit of everything: we're a small firm. Everyone mucks in. Bit of driving, bit of humping things about, bit of helping Mrs Boseley.'

'. . . ?'

'Oh, she runs the shed for me. First-class woman, keep you on your toes.'

'Wears furs a lot, does she?'

Hendrick looked up, the saturnine face pulling itself lethargically into an expression of shock. Before it got there, Duffy flashed an uncommon smile. 'Just a little joke, Mr Hendrick. Have to ask, don't we?'

'You report to her as soon as you can start. Tomorrow?'

'The day after. I charge twenty-five a day.'

'Yes, well that's about what McKay was getting, so that'll be all right.'

'No, that's on top of McKay's salary. If I'm doing two jobs I want two paypackets.'

They haggled. As usual, Duffy opened firmly, then lost a bit of interest and ended up conceding enough to make him feel cross with himself afterwards. Still, he was getting one and a half times his going rate, and he wouldn't mind shifting a few sacks now and then. Especially if that included not going to the greengrocer's for a few weeks.

2

'Up the bum?' repeated Duffy incredulously.

'Up the bum.'

Duffy's sphincter tightened involuntarily. Willett kept his smile within himself; funny how that always got to them. He went on,

'Four up the back, three up the front. Or it may have been the other way round. Not that it makes much difference. Nice girl, too. Well, niceish – you know, posh as usual. Time was, of course, when any bit of posh would go straight through, or give you the sharp edge if you dared to ask her if you could possibly examine that tiny *valise*' (he pronounced it in a mimsy, fake-upper-class way) 'which just happened to have fifteen furs poking out of the side. Nowadays, a bit of posh, travelling alone, bit unsteady on her feet, and we know the full story before she's even started telling us. These girls, think they're so grown-up, go off round the world, meet this *ebselutely sweeeet* Persian, or Arab, or something, fall for him – sometimes he's fed her a bit of coke, but often not, they do it for love nearly all the time – and before they know where they are they're teetering off the plane with half a dozen condoms of heroin up them. Well if you've had *that* up you for, what, say, twelve hours, you know about it, don't you? And some of these poor girls – these foreign gents they fall for aren't stupid, I mean they know we watch planes from the obvious places, so they make them do great detours round the world before fetching up here – some of these girls have had half a dozen up them for thirty-six hours. I mean, they look as if they've just got off a horse. Silly stuffers.'

'That what they're called?'

'Stuffers – yes. Silly girls. Lots of them are quite sweet. "What will *Memmy* say . . . And Abdul – I did *so* adore him." Silly stuffers. And of course we never do get the Abduls. Sometimes they send someone to ride shotgun with the girls – make sure they don't have a bright idea and dump it all down the toilets on the plane.'

'So who gets it out?'

'Eh?'

'Who searches them – the stuffers?'

'Up there? No, it's not on. You have to wait for it to come out. I mean – it's an assault against the person or whatever. We can strip-search them, but we can't probe. Thou shalt not probe.' Willett let his smile come out this time.

'So what do you do?'

'Whip them down the special stuffers' toilet.'

'. . .?'

'It's a room we put them in when we think they're stuffing. Bed, couple of chairs, and at one end this toilet on a sort of throne. Raised up, looks quite posh. The bowl has a plastic lining, like what the wife puts in the pedal bin. I mean, it's obvious what we're there for: the toilet's the sort of central feature of the room, and anyway we usually tell them what we suspect. And then one of us just sits there and waits for them to get on with it. After all, if they want to prove they're *not* stuffers, there's an easy way, isn't there? Bit smelly, but easy.'

'How long do you have to wait?'

'Oh, days, sometimes. The trouble is, you can't take your eyes off them either. If you nod off you know what they'll do.' Duffy didn't. 'They shit it out and then swallow it again.'

Duffy gulped, and gazed queasily at his chocolate éclair.

'They do *that*?'

'If it's that or seven years, I reckon you might bite the bullet.'

Duffy reckoned so too, though he didn't care to give the choice very much thought.

'It must be boring, all that waiting.'

'Well, it is. If we were in Hong Kong or somewhere like that, we could give them Ex-Lax in their coffee and then Bob's yer uncle. But not here – that'd be another assault, giving them the Ex-Lax. So we just have to wait, and we hold them as long as it takes. And then when they finally see they can't leave without first being excused, it's on with the rubber gloves, clothes-peg on the nose, and think of England.'

'You sure there's nothing in this coffee?'

'Just a little persuader or two. You see, I want you to take these packages of fruit-gums out to Baghdad.' Willett grinned. He rather fancied finishing off Duffy's éclair for him. 'Oh, and in case you're wondering, the record for a stuffer is fifty-five. Includes back and front, of course. And the record for a swallower is 150. That's one thing you won't find in the *Guinness Book*.'

Duffy grinned back at him. Willett was a nice old boy; well, not that old – fiftyish. His hair was thinner now than when they had first met, but he was still the same stocky, crease-faced, garrulous old bugger Duffy remembered. He had the face of your best friend's favourite uncle – which was perhaps why he was such a good customs officer. You couldn't lie to your friend's favourite uncle: or if you did, you felt so guilty that it showed. Willett had been a senior officer since Duffy had first come across him in the line of business; and he'd been in the service long enough to still think of himself by the abandoned but cherished title of Waterguard.

They were sitting over coffee in Terminal One's Apple Tree Buffet. Behind Duffy's back was the excuse for the name: a dead tree, fifteen feet high, decorated all over with red and green fairy balls. Above his head the main departure board occasionally rattled out the summonses of the afternoon; the same information was repeated here and there on pairs of television screens. Every thirty seconds or so an instruction boomed calmly over the public address, and teas were abandoned half-drunk. 'Final call' was a popular phrase in these parts: it rang in Duffy's ears like a *memento mori*. He bet there were retired pilots who named their sunset bungalows 'Final Call'.

Only Willett's presence prevented Duffy giving way to medium-grade paranoia. He hated airports. He hated planes too. Both, doubtless, because he hated Abroad. He didn't hate foreigners – at least, not more than most people – but he did hate where they came from. Duffy had never been abroad, of course, but he knew without going that some form of craziness would be bound to strike over there. And so he hated everything that reminded him of the ease with which this dreadful fantasy could be made real. The sight of planes in the sky made him duck; a British Airways bus cruising harmlessly along the Cromwell Road filled him with anxiety. He didn't even like meeting stewardesses – he felt in some obscure way that they might kidnap him, and he'd wake up gagged and bound in the cargo hold of a nose-diving DC-10. And that was another thing about planes: they crashed; they killed you. If Duffy were king, all aircraft would have painted along the side of the fuselage: 'THIS PLANE CARRIES A GOVERNMENT HEALTH WARNING'.

There was another thing about this place, this Heathrow. It was like being in a foreign city. People stopped being English here – even if they were English. They banged into you with cases and didn't apologise. They pushed in front of you in queues. They shouted. They unashamedly expressed emotion at the departure gate. They were already competing with foreigners at being foreign. And all around there were these tiny Asian women in brown smocks: carrying trays, pushing mops, clearing ashtrays, walking gracefully in and out of the toilets. Most of them were so small they made Duffy feel full-sized; many of them struck him as quite old; they never spoke, except to each other, and then in a tongue from Abroad. The only thing that made you think it wasn't Abroad were the signs everywhere and the unnervingly calm-voiced announcements on the public address. But even that didn't mean you had to be in England. As a tiny Asian woman removed Duffy's tray he realised what the place felt like: a thriving outpost of Empire, with an efficient local slave population.

'What's it about, Duffy?' Willett was doing his avuncular look. That was O.K. by Duffy. He liked Willett. And in any case, customs officers didn't count the same as stewardesses: after all, they were there – or so it felt to Duffy – to discourage people from going abroad, to make things nasty for them, vaguely to represent the disapproval of authority. Not at all like stewardesses.

'I don't know yet. I'm just sort of on the scout. I've got a job starting tomorrow in the cargo market. Bit of thieving. Don't really know any more. Just thought I'd remind myself a bit of the place – and keep up with you, of course. I don't have much call to come here normally.'

Willett creased his face again; he knew about Duffy's phobias.

'Thieving's not much of a surprise. After all, this is Fiddle City, Duffy.'

'Uh-huh.'

'I mean, the papers, and the judges, they call it Thiefrow, don't they? But the thieving – that's only a small part of it. It's Fiddle City, Duffy, this place – Fiddle City.'

'Uh-huh.'

'It's true. What does Joe Public think? Joe Public thinks it's all about smuggling, doesn't he? He thinks this place is all about sneaking the extra bottle of duty free, or asking to see the receipt for your camera; and then occasionally there's this great boogie comes hoofing it through the door, and there's something about him that makes us think, bingo, he's the one, and he has this big leather cap on his head, and we take it apart, and in the little button on the top we find a diamond, or a tab of L.S.D., or a microdot with the secrets of the atom bomb. That's what Joe Public thinks, isn't it? Joe Public's a bloody muggins.'

'Uh-huh.'

'It's a city, Duffy, it's a city.' Willett was settling back and getting launched. 'It's as big as Newcastle, and the population changes every day. Think of it like that. So of course you get your smuggling, but that's only the speciality of the place. You get all your other city crimes as well, and you get your sharper operators because they're smart enough to see why it's different from a normal city. It's different because it's very rich, because it's open twenty-four hours of the day, and because lots of the people who are here are only thinking of getting home, and as long as they get home without losing *too* much, then that's O.K.

'There's the smuggling, sure. Then there's the thieving. Then there's the armed robbery. Then there's the pickpockets, and the forgers, and the pushers, and most of all the fiddlers. There's so many fiddles, Duffy, you wouldn't believe. You know what they say . . . '

'About the fresh fruit and veg? I heard it.'

'Well, that's one you've heard. You've probably heard about the cowboys at the cab rank too – three hundred quid to Birmingham and then drop you at the first motorway sign to Brum and let you walk.'

'Uh-huh.'

'Do you know the car park one?' Willett felt competitive, needing to impress Duffy with a really good fiddle.

'No.'

'Ah. Car park.' Willett waved a vague hand in the right direction. 'Short-stay car parks, long-stay car parks. O.K.?'

'O.K.'

'Long-stay park much cheaper, but it's a bit further away. You have to take the bus to the terminal. Dump your car, leave the keys, fill in a form saying when you'll be back to collect it, fly off to the sunshine and the señoritas. What happens? Little car-hire firm springs up. No questions asked, and a lot cheaper than your Hertz or your Avis. Who's going to remember the mileage on his car all the way through a lovely holiday? And if they do, well, you can always turn the clock back, can't you?'

'Sounds foolproof. Is it still working?'

'No, silly cowboys had too many crashes. Got themselves closed down. As far as anyone can tell, of course.'

'It's a good fiddle,' Duffy said admiringly.

'First-class while it lasted. Pity they made a Horlicks of it.'

Duffy nodded. He knew the feeling; it was common to all branches of law enforcement. After an initial period when you wanted to arrest everyone for everything – when every Troops-Out badge or half-flicked V-sign appeared to be Conduct Liable to Cause a Breach of the Peace – you settled into a realisation that you'd never catch everyone, you'd never clear up every-thing. You caught quite a lot of people because they were stupid, and you came to despise them for taking up a trade they were so ill-equipped for; you caught quite a lot of people because you were lucky; and you caught quite a lot of people because you worked very hard and wanted very much to catch them. Murderers, child molesters, that sort of thing – you hated them. But there were some crimes and some criminals you couldn't help admiring, even liking. Crimes which had a lot of thought put into them, which were very well executed, and which hurt nobody – or virtually hurt nobody. You almost didn't want to catch whoever was doing it because it gave you something close to pleasure: and if they then went and made a Horlicks of it, you felt irritated with them; as if, by letting you catch them, they'd somehow let you down.

'How do you know who to search?' It was a question everyone asked Willett sooner or later.

'Trade secret. No, I'll tell you. Mixture of science and nose, that's what it is. And I mean literally nose sometimes. We've got one officer here, got a better nose than his dog. True, I swear it. We'll be going over a cargo with a dog – the dog's meant to sniff the cannabis, but this mate of mine often gets there first. Tells the dog where to sniff. Dog jumps up and down, wags his tail and gets another steak dinner. Amazing nose.'

'But would you search me, for instance?'

'Depends. Sometimes we get tip-offs, of course. Sometimes we take a little peek at the suitcases before they come up on the carousel – that helps us a bit. And we'll watch you, often from the moment you get off the plane. Not *you*, necessarily, but some people. And don't trust any mirror, by the way, don't trust any mirror.'

'Doesn't sound as if you'd stop me.'

'No, maybe we wouldn't. But then every officer's different. If you don't have any information, then you're down to your nose. There are two sorts of nose – what I call scientific nose, and what I call random nose. Scientific nose is when you look for guys who are nervous, or haven't got what feels the right amount of luggage. Sometimes their case might come up first on the carousel – we can arrange these things – but they pretend not to notice it, and then only grab it when about half the other passengers have already taken theirs. Well, you'd turn *him* over. That's what I call scientific nose.

'Now random nose is different for everyone. For instance, I stop everyone with a raincoat slung over their left shoulder. Sounds silly, doesn't it? But you need some sort of random factor to operate on, if only to keep you on your toes yourself. I know officers who stop people wearing white suits; if you ask them to explain, they say it's for really deep psychological reasons – they reckon the guy puts on the white suit to make other people think he's pure and innocent and not trying to get away with something. Of course, often the guy's got his white suit on because he doesn't want to get it creased in his suitcase, or thinks it might get nicked, or wants to try and pick up a stewardess. But the officer thinks there's more to it, or persuades himself that way, when really he's just using random nose. It varies: some officers stop people who aren't smiling, or who are smiling, or blond men, or bald men, or men who are with girls the officers fancy. That's often just to get a longer look at the girl, or it may be jealousy after a hard night on the feet and getting the pip at seeing these swankies jetting in from L.A. I can't say I blame them.'

'Do you search the crews?'

'Of course. That's rummage – that's what we call it. I was on rummage last week. We turned them upside down as usual. Didn't find much – though it's done to deter as much as to find stuff.'

'Anyone you can't search?'

'Diplomatic bag. Though there are always ways.'

'Such as?'

Willett smiled.

'Send in a ferret, of course.' Duffy should have known better than to expect a straight answer. 'No, but the short one is, Duffy, like I said before, this is Fiddle City. No one's above the law, and a hell of a lot of people are below it.'

Duffy didn't like to speak his next thought, so instead he merely cocked an eyebrow towards his friend.

'Cheeky sod.'

Duffy recocked his eye.

'Well since you ask, no, not in my experience. Not here. There was a bit of a rumble down at Gatwick a few years ago – the odd backhander was finding its way through from pilots of an airline we won't mention. But here? Half of them are Scottish, which is a good start, and I say that as an Arsenal supporter. No. It's much more than their job's worth, you'd get a hell of a sentence, and it'd be very hard to pull off. Though sometimes I can see it happening: the haul of a lifetime – you might just be tempted. And if anyone was tempted, I'd blame Mrs Thatcher. No, really, I would.'

'I always thought you were a Tory.'

'Am. Voted for the lady. Don't tell the wife,' Willett looked conspiratorial, 'but I fancy her a bit. All those nicely tailored suits. I'd let her through any day: she could come up my green channel and no questions asked. *But* – the lady did a terrible thing: she stopped the reward system. I'm sure it wasn't Mrs T.

herself, *personally*; but the next time the little civil servant who thought it was a good idea comes through here, he's going to get the linings taken out of his suits and no mistake.'

'You voting Tory again next time?'

'Take more than that, Duffy. But you know, they talk about incentives – what incentive have we got now? Why do they stop anything that works, Duffy?'

'That's not my sort of question.' They stood up together, and Duffy shook Willett's hand. 'I'll maybe come and see you again in a week or two.'

'Any time. Who knows, I may be round your shed for a rummage before you can say Jack Robinson.'

'Well, you don't know me if you do.'

'Sure. Watch out for illegal golf clubs, Duffy. They're sort of long and thin and made of metal and come in bags.'

'I'll keep my eyes skinned.'

'Keep them skinned for the cowboys as well. I mean that. The cowboys round here aren't any nicer than the cowboys anywhere else. Very short on morals, some of them.'

'Got you.'

And Duffy headed off through the raucous bazaar of this strange imperial city.

Next day, before leaving for work, he rang Carol and asked her round that evening. She said she couldn't make it; as always, the news gave him a stab. He didn't ask; she didn't explain; that was the deal. At one time she used to tell him when she was going to do things she knew he wouldn't mind about – go to the pictures with a fellow-W.P.C.; or visit her aunt – but this only made him think that when she didn't explain she must be going to the Ritz with Paul Newman, or making half a dozen pornographic films that evening. So they went back to the original system of her not saying, and his not asking. She'd come the following night instead.

He guessed his clothes for Hendrick Freight: a denim jacket

which looked as if it were made from separate patches but wasn't (Duffy felt cheated when Carol had pointed out that it was done with false seaming); his oldest jeans, with authentic patches on the knees; desert boots. That should do it.

As he climbed into his van he reflected yet again how smart he'd been not to have it plastered with business slogans saying DUFFY SECURITY and pictures of red skulls and crossbones or whatever. Some firms worked like that: high visibility, they called it. He did, actually, have a board with DUFFY SECURITY painted on it: there were rubber suckers on the back and it could be stuck to the side of the van if he was going anywhere on official business. He'd originally had two such signs, one for each side of the van, but he lost one on a trip to Barking. He must have been producing a poor quality of spit that day.

So: his clothes were O.K., the van was O.K. (that's to say, it had started), the interview was rigged and so presumably would be O.K. (Hendrick had said the best story for Mrs Boseley would be that Duffy had done a lot of odd jobs around his house for him and was now looking for something permanent). He was driving along the M4 in the opposite direction to most of the commuter traffic, so *that* was O.K. The only thing which wasn't O.K. was that he was going to have to keep tracking back to Heathrow every day and listen to the aircraft whining in pain, and watch them taking off at a ludicrously untenable angle, and it would be just his luck if one of them decided to stall into the freight area during the next few days.

His was a rational unease. If you worked around airports and *didn't* fret, you were the odd one, Duffy had long ago decided. Across to his left, a long slow morning line of jumbos was queuing up to land, sticking parallel to the M4. (It was obviously the only way they knew how to navigate. 'Well, personally, I take the A205 through Mortlake . . . ' 'Oh, I'm much more of a North Circular man myself . . . ' That was all the pilots ever talked about.) The planes kept a mile astern of one another, which was a criminally inadequate distance, as even Duffy could see. And they were flying so slowly – barely overtaking him. It was probably some competition to see who could go the slowest without stalling.

Look at it this way, Duffy told himself. The sooner you find out who's nicking Hendrick's stuff, the sooner you can stop worrying about a DC-10 turning into a Stuka, or about a cubic yard of frozen pee landing on your head from 20,000 feet. Fair enough. He turned off the M4 at Junction Three, ducked his head automatically as he cut across the flight path of the jumbos, and skirted the perimeter of the airport.

Freight was handled on the south side of Heathrow. Inside the fence was the bonded area: there, the sheds belonged to individual airlines, who were responsible for cargo until it had cleared customs. Then they handed it either direct to the importer, or to one of the gaggle of freight agents just outside the fence.

Hendrick Freight stood in one of the less fashionable areas of this subsidiary cargo market. Smarter forwarding agents were clustered under one roof in a modern shed close to the road. The security man on the gate let Duffy through after a brief phone call, and directed him to Hendrick Freight. It was a high, airy shed – Duffy hoped the job didn't drag on until the winter – with side walls of yellow-painted breeze-block and an arching, corrugated tin roof. Bundles of goods lay on rust-coloured, triple-tiered racks. Large red numbers hung above each storage bay.

As he stood there a yellow fork-lift truck suddenly whined past and nearly ankle-tapped him with one of its two flat metal prongs. Better watch out, thought Duffy. Collect one of those in the leg and you'll be catching up on a lot of reading before you know where you are. He began to walk slowly up the length of the shed. Neolithic strip lighting lurked in the roof, and had to be helped out by the occasional bare, hanging bulb. Weighing machines, old from age rather than use, stood here and there. Though it was a warm, dry day, the shed felt damp.

He passed the fork-lift truck, which was now fussing with some hessian-wrapped bundles, and reached a raised glass office at the far end of the shed. Mrs Boseley sat here. She didn't really need the office to be raised: she seemed to be looking down on everyone already. She was about forty, with the sort of face people call handsome. This might have been expected to appeal to Duffy, but it very much didn't: he liked women small and dark and friendly, like Carol, not high-boned and aloof and eight-ninths hidden beneath the surface. Her blonde hair was scraped back off her face and pinned at the nape of her neck with an ivory comb. She examined Duffy's cards as if he had offered her an expired Libyan passport. Duffy determined to be as polite to her as he could possibly manage. He didn't find it easy.

'Worked for Mr Hendrick long, have you?' she began.

'A bit. Off and on.'

'Enjoyed it, did you?'

'All right.'

'Nice wife Mr Hendrick has.'

Duffy didn't know whether that was a question or a statement. He didn't even know if Hendrick had a wife. He decided to treat it as a statement and let it go.

'And he tells me you've done all sorts of odd jobs for him.'

'Uh-huh.'

'What sort of things?'

'This and that . . . Lifting things.' Duffy vaguely thought this must be a qualification for working here. At the same time, he felt pissed off that he was being cross-examined: Hendrick had assured him the interview would be a formality. Maybe the woman was only keeping him in here so that the others wouldn't get suspicious of him.

'Mow the lawn?'

'I beg your pardon?'

'You've mowed the lawn for Mr Hendrick, for instance?'

'Sometimes.'

Why, Mrs Boseley thought, didn't the fellow ever say yes? But Duffy never said Yes; he either nodded, or went Uh-huh, or said All right. Carol thought that you could ask Duffy to marry you and he'd half look away, nod and say, All right. This was only a guess. She had asked once, and he'd half looked away, gone quiet, and then said, 'No'.

'Well, I can't say we've exactly established your qualifications for the job, but we do want someone in a hurry, and if Mr Hendrick recommends you then I suppose that's the end of the matter.' She looked up and gazed at Duffy expressionlessly for a few seconds. He thought it was his turn to speak.

'Thank you very much, Mrs Boseley.'

'Hmm. I should say one thing to you though. The manner of your appointment is – how shall I put it – just a trifle irregular.'

'Uh-huh.' (She didn't know the half of it.)

'Normally what happens in such circumstances is that the men who work here might be expected to suggest someone: one of their friends, for instance. These are hard times, you know, and everyone knows someone who's out of a job.'

'I see.'

'I'm glad you do. Then you won't be surprised if you encounter a little, how shall I put it, a little hostility at first?'

'It doesn't bother me.'

'I hope it doesn't.' She put her head outside her glass cage and shouted at someone Duffy couldn't see.

'Tan. Tan, ask Gleeson to come up, will you?'

They sat in silence until the door opened and a muscularly plump man in a dark blue boiler suit came in; he had dark hair and mutton-chop whiskers. He looked without acknowledgement at Duffy before turning to the desk.

'Mrs Boseley?'

'Gleeson, this is Duffy, who as I told you is joining us. Make him comfortable, show him around, tell him what to do, will you?'

Gleeson nodded and left the room. Duffy glanced at Mrs Boseley but only met the top of her head as it bent over some invoices. He followed Gleeson out into the body of the cargo shed. As soon as he had caught up, Gleeson marched him across to a row of lockers and tapped the only one with a key in the door.

'Yours. Overalls. In you get.'

'I'm not that small,' said Duffy, but Gleeson declined to smile. Duffy opened the locker and saw a pair of overalls. He also saw a Page Three girl pasted inside the door and a miniature tiger dangling on a string.

'McKay's,' said Gleeson by way of explanation. The same name probably also explained why Duffy's overalls were over-generously cut.

'There's room for another in here,' he said. But Gleeson was already moving on.

'You drive a forkie?' he said suddenly.

'What?'

'You drive a forkie?' Ah, a fork-lift truck.

'I'm sure I'll pick it up.'

'Well, you can start with a trolley, or a barrer. McKay could drive a forkie. Very neat. We reckoned he could pick an apple off your head with it, like whatsisname.'

'Tell.'

'I just told.'

Gleeson walked him round the shed, pointing out various areas: Perishables, Dries, Refrigerated, and so on. Occasionally he'd introduce him: there was someone called Tan who appeared to be Chinese; someone called Casey, tall, long-haired and even surlier than Gleeson; a couple of drivers, and someone who's name Duffy forgot. Then Gleeson told him to wait around in a corner of the shed until someone asked him to do something. Like being stood in the dunce's corner, Duffy thought. Occasionally throughout the morning Gleeson gave him orders: he had to load and unload things; a couple of times he was asked to move a large packing case just a few yards, to a point which seemed no more sensible or useful than where it had started from. Duffy didn't ask; he just did it. Maybe it was some sort of initiation; maybe they were just buggering him about.

When the dinner whistle went he had just finished loading up a Transit van with Casey, who muttered what sounded like 'Canteen', and sloped off. Duffy followed and soon found himself hunched over pie and beans. Casey was eating double pie and double beans. Duffy stared at Casey's hands. The first joint of each finger of his right hand had a letter tattooed on it: H A T E was what they spelt. Always on the right hand, of course, on the fist used for persuading people. Duffy knew what he'd see on the other hand – L O V E it read – but this time there was a slight variation. The 'O' on the second finger of the hand had a sophisticated addition, a cross on the top of it: Ö. Pretty high-class tattooist, thought Duffy; wonder if he knows what it means. Casey did. As he tumbled his knife and fork on to his plate at the end of the pie and beans, he leaned across to Duffy and wiggled his second finger up and down in front of Duffy's nose.

'Courting finger,' he said, laughed, and squeaked back his chair. Two minutes later he was back, with a double sago pudding and custard. Duffy watched in silence (he felt it tactful not to be too gabby with this one) as Casey slurped it down. When he had finished putting it away he exhaled loudly.

'You courting?' he said.

'Yes,' replied Duffy straight away.

'My mistake.' But Casey's tone was still closer to belligerence than apology. 'Picked you for a wrong 'un.'

'Sorry, can't help you there,' said Duffy. He sensed that it wouldn't help him to wear a big pink star on his back around this place.

It was comforting to see Carol. For one thing, she was always so keen that it was now. She insisted by her natural mood that it wasn't the past any more, and that it wouldn't be the future until at least tomorrow. And that you didn't deserve the future until you'd made a reasonable job of the present. It was odd that she had this effect so forcefully on Duffy, because in many ways she did represent the past – the time when they were colleagues in the force, when they were going around to-gether, when they were sleeping together successfully, before Duffy was framed out of his job and his girl friend one nasty evening that he mostly tried to forget. And Carol helped him with this, refused to let him brood, insisted that he think about today, worried with him about his work. Sometimes she stayed the night, sometimes she didn't; though since he'd moved further west, out to Acton, she stayed a bit more often than when he'd been in Paddington.

They were sitting in his kitchen eating cheese on toast, and Carol was trying to stop Duffy leaping up every minute to tidy things away. Duffy was anal: there was no doubt at all about that. If he could, he'd do the washing up before the meal; Carol knew he'd secretly prefer her to hold the cheese on toast in her fingers so that he could wash up the plate. And then, when he'd done that, he'd probably hover near her with a damp J-cloth in his hand to catch any crumbs she might drop. And as for the refrigerator – it was just as bad as the last one, the one in which all the food was double-wrapped as if it were trying to escape and had to be straightjacketed; the fridge she'd called Colditz. This one, in his new flat, was no better: you opened it and saw nothing but plastic everywhere. No food, just plastic: Tup-perware boxes, plastic bags, sometimes Tupperware boxes inside plastic bags, sometimes plastic bags inside Tupperware boxes.

'What's the distinction, Duffy,' she'd once asked, 'between the things that go in polythene bags and then into Tupperware boxes, and the things that go into Tupperware boxes and then into polythene bags?'

'Ah,' he'd said. 'Ah. Now, I'm sure there's a reason. I'm positive there's a reason.' He gazed at the ceiling, trying to remember.

'Duffy,' she bellowed at him after three seconds of his reverie, 'you really think I want to know, don't you? You really think I want to know.'

'But you asked,' he replied, puzzled and mildly offended.

'Forget it. For-get. For-get. O.K.?'

'O.K.' He still couldn't work it out.

That evening he told her about Hendrick (though he didn't mention how he'd been put on to him), and about his first two days at the shed.

'Sounds like it could be a long job.'

He grunted. She felt apprehensive when he grunted. It usually meant he was about to say something she might not like.

'Can you do a couple of things?'

'I might.'

'Lend me your car in the evenings. I might need to follow someone and they'd know my van from work.'

'Maybe.'

'I mean, swop. You can have mine.'

There was a bit of a silence. Duffy had vaguely broken the rules. How would he know how to give it back at the end of the evening? Or where to give it back?

'Maybe, Duffy. But it'd have to be day-to-day. You'd have to ask each time.'

'O.K. And can you get me the traffic report on the accident this McKay had?'

'I shouldn't think so.'

'You could, though, couldn't you?'

'I might be able to get someone to read it to me. But it's not in our rules.'

'I just thought,' said Duffy quietly, 'that someone might want to do the same to me.' God he was unfair. She went and fetched her overnight bag. He knew what he'd done and felt shitty. Not about using her to get information, but about frightening her.

'Please stay.'

'No, sorry. Busy day tomorrow, beauty sleep and all that.' She ruffled his hair as if to say, It's all right really, it's just that it's not all right enough now. 'And I hope they're nicer to you at work tomorrow.'

'Oh, yes, I forgot to say – they were quite nice to me today. I mean, they weren't, as I told you, for almost all the day, and then they were.'

'Explain.'

'Well, I had to do most of the work, like yesterday, and nobody spoke to me much, and they made me do things I knew weren't necessary, and they knew I knew weren't necessary. And then at the end of the day, guess what? I looked in my locker and what did I find? Fifty quid. In very used notes.'

3

The next morning, the jumbos weren't using the M4. The whisper had got around and they were all following the North Circular. People said it was just the wind that made them land from a different direction, but Duffy knew better. Yesterday they'd obviously dug up so many divots in the runway that they were being forced to land on another one. And they wouldn't tell the passengers. That was another reason why Duffy would never fly: you never got told the truth. He'd heard enough stories from his mates to know that the first rule of any airline was, Don't scare the customers, they might yet live to come back and use us another time. So it was 'Just a little turbulence' when half the passengers could see that one of the engines was on fire; and it was 'Sorry, the captain's forgotten his Kleenex' when the hydraulics collapsed and the plane panicked back to base, jettisoning all its fuel over the Thames Estuary as it did so.

While he drove, he wondered idly about the Hendrick job. It looked like a money-earner, that was all it looked like: one of those jobs where you do your best until the client decides he's poured enough money down your drain and he'll try something else, or something better, or go to the police, or learn to live with his losses. He'd had this sort of job before. It would obviously take him some days more to work out exactly how the freight firm operated, how the terminal's security worked and how it could be bypassed; and that was just basics. He didn't know what was likely to be stolen (since in Hendrick's description it changed every time), and he didn't know who was best placed to rip it off.

So what did you do in the slow cases, the nit-picking cases, the sit-on-your-bum-and-keep-your-eyes-open cases? Well, you went back to basics, and you got the little legs working. What did he have? He had a car crash. He had a – from what he heard – badly smashed-up freight worker, whom he couldn't very well go and talk to in case he was a villain. He had a series of thefts at about monthly intervals. He had a shedful of people who weren't particularly charmed by his company – though there was no reason why they should be, if he believed Mrs Boseley, and he had no reason (apart from not liking her) not to believe her. And he had fifty quid. That was what he had most.

Cash in the locker was an old trick, of course. Everywhere in the world that there was a fiddle going – even in the place with the nice, comforting blue light outside – there was cash in the locker. For a very good reason: it sorted you out. It gave you an instant choice, and it instantly compromised you. If you handed it in, there were two problems: you might hand it in to the wrong person, someone who didn't know what was going on, someone who'd create a great stink as a consequence, and as a further consequence you might get your head rubbed up against the brickwork in some alley after work. Or you handed it in to the right person, the person who'd more or less given it to you, and then you were saying to him, 'Nice to know you're a villain; I'm not as it happens, but I do so hope we'll still get on', and then even if you were a bit bent, but just didn't want to join in this particular package scheme, this Butlins of fraud, it made you look as if you were super-clean, nothing less than old Mister White the vicar's son. And the consequence of *that* was that all the dirty jobs going somehow seemed to keep coming your way, and the sump oil just happened to get tipped down the trousers of your best suit, and the night shift fell into your lap just a bit more often than it did anyone else's, and sometimes in the canteen your arm got just a little jog as it was ladling some beans into your mouth, until finally you thought, stuff it, and you couldn't complain because you'd sound like a schoolgirl, and what had they really done to you anyway?

So, often, simply because it was easier – or because the wife wanted some new curtains, or so that you could afford a double for a change while you watched the darts match – you took it. Duffy quite understood. He didn't approve, but he didn't have any difficulty in understanding.

In the present case, he hadn't wavered for a moment. As soon as he'd seen the green bundle with the rubber band round it, he'd tucked it into the top pocket of his denim jacket. There could be someone watching, you never knew. And if there was, it was a good idea to show them a picture of instant and willing corruption.

Just to be on the safe side – there might, for all Duffy knew, have been something tiny but incriminating attached to one of the notes – he stuffed them into a brown envelope, put the date and place of finding on the outside, and gave it to Carol for safe-keeping. Now, as far as that side of things went, you just had to wait. You didn't go poling up to Gleeson, or the China-man, or whoever you guessed it to be, and say, 'Thanks very much for the money; what do I do now?' Or you didn't unless you were very stupid. You just hung around, and then after a bit, who knew how long, you'd be standing in the sun minding your own, when a voice behind you would say, 'Nice to have you with us,' and you'd turn and nod and keep your own counsel and think, so it *was* him.

But that was obviously not going to happen today, thought Duffy. Just get on with your job and keep looking around, those were the rules. He had been allotted his dunce's corner, and he was expected to sit there until they wanted him. There wasn't anything special about the corner, he realised, except that he could be watched easily, especially by Mrs Boseley in her little glass hut. Duffy trundled his trolley when asked, and found that his day consisted of the usual mix of short, back-breaking bursts of work interspersed with tedious periods of inactivity. Except that there was always something else to do. With a casual eye and a little bit of bored wandering about, he managed to work out the security system of the place. The alarm, and then on top of it the hidden trigger alarm which goes off if anyone tries to tamper with the main one: not bad, a middle-price item from about five years ago. And somewhere there'd probably be a buzzer to alert the terminal people.

At one point he wandered over to Mrs Boseley's eyrie when he noticed she wasn't there. He half-opened the door, and pretended to look inside; well, she might be under the desk or something. Then he stood politely outside the door, though the glass meant that he could see most of what he wanted to.

'Yes, what are you doing up here?' Mrs Boseley had suddenly reappeared.

'Oh, Miss, er, Mrs, I wondered if there was any work. I haven't had anything to do for a bit.'

'*I* don't give you work. Mr Gleeson gives you work.' You needed gloves to talk to her.

'Sorry, sorry. Only trying to be helpful.' And he walked cravenly back to his corner. But he'd checked the door lock, and worked out where he thought the alarm buzzer would probably be.

When the dinner whistle went, he tagged along with Casey to the canteen. It was a bit early to call it a friendship: it was more that Casey didn't actually punch Duffy's head in for following him about. They sat opposite one another while Casey consumed twice as much food as Duffy. Why didn't he get fat? Maybe he took a lot of exercise; maybe it was nothing to do with how much you ate, anyway. Duffy feared getting fat, so he didn't eat much and he took as much exercise as he could handle; he even ran up stairs sometimes – well, if he was in a hurry. Mostly, though, he just worried, and worrying about getting fat seemed to keep him thin. For the time being, anyway.

Duffy stared at Casey's long, sallow face, the thin moustache inspired by some old Charles Bronson film, the rocker-revival hairdo. Was anything going on under that hairdo, he wondered. Casey never addressed him – not that Duffy minded – but as a token of incipient toleration he deigned to answer questions, as long as they weren't asked while he was eating. As he laid down his knife and fork, swabbed at the baked-bean juice on his moustache and exhaled loudly, Duffy asked him,

'You hit many people?' He indicated Casey's right hand with a deferential gesture, to fill out the inadequacy of his words. Casey looked at his hand, and as he looked it formed itself into a fist, seemingly without the authority of its owner.

'Only when I 'ave to,' he replied.

'You got any more tattoos?' Duffy asked this quickly, sensing Casey's impatience at the protractedness of their conversation.

This was one Casey could answer without words. He reached to the neck of his shirt, and pulled open the top two jeans poppers. A line of dashes ran round his throat, interspersed with letters. Duffy read:

- - - - C - U - T - - - - - H - E - R - E - - - - -

Casey's Adam's apple formed a chunky punctuation mark in this complex instruction, whose implications he allowed Duffy to take on board while he went off and fetched himself two sweets. Duffy watched him demolish them and tried to keep his mind off the idea of getting fat. He imagined a balding, middle-aged version of himself turning up to offer security assistance and being laughed away. 'We don't want a *fat* security man,' they shouted at him; 'whoever heard of a *fat* security man?'

At the end of the sweets Duffy knew he was allowed to speak again. He adopted a tone of one decidedly less brave than Casey but trying hard to put on a stiff upper lip.

'Is there – is there much violence around here?'

Casey almost smiled; that's to say, he seemed to strain a

smile through his face, and the sieved remnants of it came out the other side.

' 'ad a mate,' Casey replied, 'Big nose. Big nose.' Casey tapped the side of his own conk to help Duffy out. 'Fahnd 'im in one of them big fridges. In wif the toolips.'

Casey fell silent, looked almost reflective; then just when Duffy was about to offer his condolences, he went on loudly, with a rolling laugh:

'Didn't need to send that sod no flahs.' And he kicked Duffy hard under the table by way of emphasis.

On his way back to the shed Duffy stopped off at the telephone box and made three calls to breakers' yards in the area. Two didn't answer; they must have been out to dinner. To the third Duffy described McKay's car, and explained that his hospitalised friend had left something in it.

'Nothing like that here, mate.'

'You sure?'

'Sure I'm sure. Look, I might not be able to recognise a tiger in yer tank, but I can tell one when it's all over the cowing car, can't I?'

'Sure. Sorry, mate.'

'Any time.'

He'd have to come back to that later. Another afternoon, and then it would be Friday. Maybe he should do it this weekend – break in. He could be here for days before he picked up how the shed operated; or before he even knew the full range of stuff they transported. All he'd need was a couple of quiet hours; it wasn't as if he was going to smash anything.

But of course, he didn't need to break in. He could get Hendrick to give him the key. Assuming that Hendrick himself was on the level. Duffy never forgot about the client's angle. But if Hendrick was on the fiddle, why call in Duffy at all? Maybe there were two fiddles, one Hendrick's and one somebody else's? *It's Fiddle City, Duffy*, Willett's voice repeated in his head. Yes, but even so, Hendrick wouldn't call him in if he were on the fiddle himself, would he? Would he?

Anyway, what did it matter – if he asked Hendrick for the key, and Hendrick refused, then he threw in the job; if he asked, got it, and then something happened which made Duffy think there was more to Hendrick than he'd been told, he'd throw in the job even quicker. And then he'd take Carol out on the fifty used oncers.

Friday's work was like Thursday's, and Wednesday's and Tuesday's. When the dinner whistle blew he hopped it to the telephone box. He told Hendrick's secretary that he was still worried about the papaws. He hoped the job didn't last beyond the end of the papaw season, otherwise he'd be in trouble. She put him through.

'Mr Hendrick, it's about those papaws.' (It was always useful to remind the clients of their own pathetic security ploys; they liked that.) 'I think I might need the key.'

'The key to the papaws? Oh, you just cut them open with a knife.'

'Very amusing, Mr Hendrick.' (Very wasteful on my 10p, Mr Hendrick.) 'I'm not finding things out quick enough. I think I'd better take a look round this weekend. Can you let me have the key?'

'Er, yes, I don't see why not. But you'll have to come and collect it from my home.'

'No trouble, Mr Hendrick, it all goes on the account.' (It was also useful to remind the client of your expenses.)

Hendrick gave him an address in Fulham and asked him to call on the Saturday morning. Duffy then rang the other two breakers' yards; one of them was still out to lunch from the day before, the other, at Yiewsley, thought it might have seen the car, but couldn't remember where it was. Maybe Duffy would like to call round sometime? Yes, they were open Saturdays: until four.

So far, so good. Duffy walked quickly to the canteen where he found, to his surprise, that Casey had kept him a chair. Not that the gesture appeared to mean he was going to unbend in any other way. The same silence continued while the serious business of eating was undertaken. Except that when Casey finally thundered his sweet spoon back into his bowl, he actually addressed Duffy, for only the second time in their now burgeoning relationship.

'Where j' get the ring, then?'

'What?'

'Where j' get the ring, then, if yer not a wrong 'un?'

Ah, that; so that was what had been preying on Casey's mind all this time: the stud.

'Girl I'm courting gave it me.'

Casey in reply gave his delayed exhalation.

'Only I fort you was a wrong 'un.'

Perhaps I've made a friend, Duffy thought.

Friday afternoon was pay-day. They lined up, all six of them, at four o'clock precisely, outside Mrs Boseley's office, and went in one by one. Duffy, as the most recent recruit, was last in the queue.

'I hope my work has been satisfactory, Mrs Boseley,' he said, in a manner which he hoped might seem not too openly ingratiating. Mrs Boseley gave him one of her specially refrigerated glances, and went back to counting his wages. As she handed them over, she said,

'I wouldn't know, I haven't been watching.'

Which was only partly true, because occasionally in the last four days Duffy had looked up from his dunce's corner of the shed and noticed her blonde semi-beehive pointed in his direction. She certainly made Duffy feel watched, whether he was or not.

He went and sat on a packing case in his corner. He gazed back at the glass cubicle. Where did a woman like Mrs Boseley come from? Did she have a Christian name, for instance? Did she have a past? Did she have parents, or did she simply drop in through the roof of Hendrick's shed one day, trim and fortyish and avid to run things? She can't always have been an office manager; and she clearly didn't work her way up in Hendrick's. What could she have done before? Duffy thought of her scraped-back hair, her neat but to him unappealing figure, her bland, well-boned good looks; then he took ten, fifteen years off it, put her into a uniform (without watching while she undressed), and there she was: a stewardess. Or, as they called them then, an air hostess. That was it, that made sense. She was an ex-stewardess; they always retired them at – what was the age, he didn't know; but it was like Playboy bunnies. Rather unfair, Duffy thought; one day you're worth the free trips and the businessmen's glances, and the next it's sorry, no one wants to look at *you* any more, no there's nothing wrong, but isn't the skin round your jaw a little looser than it used to be, perhaps, and, anyway here's a nice little ground job which doesn't involve any travelling except to the loo and the canteen.

What did old stewardesses do? What did old anything do? Old golfers never die, they only lose their balls. Where had he read that? And what about old security men? What about Duffy when he got fat and old and stopped being smart any more? Would he become a nightwatchman and sit in a hut roasting chestnuts over his fire, waiting to be peed on by punks who called him Grandad? And would he perhaps be shuffling one midnight along the corridor of some factory, not because he was suspicious or anything but because he was bored and his legs needed the exercise, when some over-enthusiastic cowboy decided to take him out with the wooden end of a shotgun? It was always happening.

'Car keys.'

Duffy gave a start. Gleeson was standing next to him, chewing slightly, and making his mutton-chops shift softly up and down. Gleeson was one of those chubby people who look as if they are naturally friendly; in his case looks were deceptive.

'Your car's parked in the wrong place, can I have the keys?'

'Sorry, I'll move it.'

Duffy had his hand in his pocket and was making off when Gleeson intercepted his arm.

'Your car's parked in the wrong place.'

'Yuh, I heard.'

They stared at each other for a few seconds. Duffy found himself wondering why they'd taken all day to ask him to move it; and surely it couldn't be . . .

'Your car's parked in the wrong place.'

God he was stupid. Christ he was stupid. He wordlessly dug out his keys and handed them over. He might have hoisted it in more quickly if he hadn't been mooning over his old age, but even so . . . He felt almost ashamed of himself. You take the fifty, you wait for the connection, and then when it comes, you don't recognise it. Maybe you are getting fat, Duffy.

In a couple of minutes Gleeson returned. Duffy half expected him to say something, though he didn't quite know what; something, perhaps, like, 'Meet you behind the third frigo-container on the right.' But instead, Gleeson merely tossed the keys to Duffy from a distance of four yards and turned his back. As he caught them, Duffy looked down the shed towards Mrs Boseley's office. Did he catch a flash of blonde as a head looked away?

Well, at least something was happening. Better something than nothing, even if you don't understand it. Duffy couldn't wait for 5.30, to see why they'd wanted to move his car.

However, when the whistle blew, he loitered a bit. He changed slowly, and didn't hurry on his way to the shed door. Anyone who wanted to fall in casually beside him was more than welcome as far as Duffy was concerned. But no one did. Outside, in the small forecourt, his van was in exactly the same position as he had left it in the morning. This didn't surprise him in the least. He walked slowly across to it, waiting perhaps to be hailed by Casey, who was climbing into his Capri. But nothing happened. So Duffy eased himself into the van. Nothing on the seat. He flicked open the glove compartment: nothing there either. Nothing on the windscreen shelf. He looked over his shoulder into the back, but that all looked the same as ever. Maybe they've sawn through something in the engine, thought Duffy; but dismissed the idea as paranoid.

228

Then, as he was backing out of his parking space, he slipped his hand into the driver's door pocket. Polythene. Ah-hah. He lifted a package on to his crotch and didn't look at it until he was in second gear. Then he shifted his glance downwards. Calculators. Six pocket calculators; still in their boxes; still in their polythene bag.

How very kind, Duffy thought. Fifty oncers on the Wednesday, six pocket calculators on the Friday. That thought contented him for not more than half a second, then he changed up a gear into third and slowed the van until it deliberately stalled. He pulled into the side of the road, quarter of a mile from Hendrick's and half-way to the gate. Then, just in case anyone was watching, he put the van in first and turned the ignition. It fired, the van heaved forwards, and stalled again. He repeated this twice, then climbed out with a not-this-again expression, and threw up the bonnet.

He fiddled a bit with the plugs as he worked out quite why he felt unconvinced. He didn't know how these things were done, but he felt sure that they weren't done like this. You got the fifty quid, and then you got the connection; or you got the calculators and then the connection; you didn't get both and then nothing. It couldn't work like that; you had to do something to earn something. What's more, the calculators were still in their original packaging; the polythene had a couple of stickers on; even a police cadet would be able to work out where they came from.

Duffy slammed down the bonnet and climbed back into the driving seat. He took a duster and a pair of driving gloves out of the glove compartment. He pulled on the gloves, and with the duster rubbed very hard all over the polythene packing; it would be nice to leave Gleeson's dabs on it, but there was no way. Then he wrapped the package in the duster, took off the gloves, started the car, looked lengthily in the rear-view mirror, then drove off quickly. He turned sharp left, left again, right, and braked sharply in front of the Gents as if he didn't know whether or not he could hold it any longer. He ran up the path to the Gents, dived into a crapper, climbed on to the seat and tucked the calculators behind the cistern. One of these days, he thought, public crappers will go over to low cisterns like we have at home, and then where will we all be?

He smiled to himself as he drove slowly back towards the gate. He didn't mind at all being picked out at random by a security man and flagged into a special lane where a policeman was waiting. Of course he understood it was all routine. Sure, there's a lot of it about. Search away. Glove compartment, under the seats, don't miss the driver's door pocket. Brief body search, this way please, no problem, might even enjoy it he said to himself. The policeman patted him all over, and as he worked his way up the insides of his legs Duffy said to himself, Don't get too cocky. The policeman was very friendly as they went back outside to the van, where the security guard had just finished his work; he was also nice to Duffy. Duffy was nice back. He quite understood, didn't mind at all, any time, feel free, see you again soon.

As he drove off, Duffy remembered Willett and said to himself: random nose, or scientific nose? Or a bit of help?

Hendrick opened the door to Duffy with a preoccupied expression. He walked him silently down the hall and into the kitchen, scattering before him a pair of small daughters whom he instructed to go and play outside. As the back door banged, Hendrick fretted over whether he ought after all to let Duffy have the key to the freight shed. Duffy knew the situation well: first you employ someone to help you on the security side, and you tell him all your troubles, and then you start wishing you hadn't. It was a familiar psychological pattern. And there was an equally familiar way round it. You didn't stand on your dignity and get petulant and thrust your credentials down the client's throat; you just went quiet for a moment to show him you weren't as put out as he expected you to be, and then you tickled the businessman in him.

'Just as you wish, Mr Hendrick, I mean, it's really up to you.

I can't swear to you I'll find anything of use if you lend me the key. It's just that, given the sort of job this is, it'll definitely cut down the bill if I can get round the shed when there's no one there. But it's entirely up to you, of course.'

It was almost criminal the way this always worked, Duffy thought. Hendrick crumbled, apologised, agreed, dug out the key and handed it over.

'Two things, though, Mr Duffy.' This bit was familiar as well; it sprang from the need to reassert oneself as the employer, as the layer-down of conditions, the paymaster. 'First, I want to know precisely when you're going over there, and how long you'll be. And second, I want the key back as soon as you've finished with it.'

'No problem.' Duffy was deferential, as the pattern called for. 'I'm a bit tied up today, so I reckon I'll go round Sunday afternoon – middle of the afternoon; three o'clock, shall we say? I'll only be an hour or two. Can't be more exact, I'm sure you understand why' (appeal to ally, to fellow-conspirator; Hendrick duly nodded) 'and then I'll be able to give you the key back by about six, I should say. I'll stick it through your door if you're not in.'

Hendrick began to explain in unnecessary detail how to stop the alarm system being triggered when you opened the side door. Duffy half listened to this, just in case it contained anything new, and pretended to concentrate by gazing out of the kitchen window into the back garden. There was a nice crazy-paving patio outside the back door, then a bed of geraniums, then a kids' play area. There was a sandpit and a paddling pool and a slide. The two girls, who seemed about seven or eight to Duffy, were noisily playing on the slide. One of them was standing up on the top of it now. Duffy winced: it wasn't far to fall for an adult, but for a child? On to the concrete? It worried Duffy. He shifted his gaze to the brick wall at the end of the garden, which was only about a dozen yards from where he was standing, and found that there was another worry in his head, one he couldn't identify, one which had something to do

231

with the last few days but which he couldn't pin down. Meanwhile, Hendrick came to the end of his instructions about the alarm system, and Duffy nodded as if, with some difficulty, he'd just about managed to understand. Clients liked that. It made them think they had a secure system.

The first thing Duffy did as he drove west was to call at a locksmith's and get a duplicate key made. He didn't want to rely on Hendrick's vacillating assessment of his reliability if he wanted to make another visit; and besides, it was a bit of a traipse over to Fulham.

He'd lied to Hendrick about the timing of his visit to the shed. Just in case Hendrick wasn't entirely level with him, he'd decided to go at once. He reached the shed at 11.30 and opened the side door with the key he had just had made (best to check it, in case he had to take it back for refiling). The alarm worked on a trigger-delay of twenty seconds: enough time for Hendrick to toddle up a half flight of stairs and flick the cancel lever.

Duffy began by the big double doors at the southern edge of the shed. The floor was marked out with coloured lines like an indoor sports arena, and the goods were stacked on their rust-painted racks within differently sized squares and rectangles. Some areas were set aside for regular customers, and had their names on placards hanging above them: Fraser Matthews, Bamco, Holdsworth & French, and so on. Regular shipments thus went to exactly the same place in the shed week after week, month after month, making things easier for Hendrick's men – or the customers themselves, if they were collecting.

Duffy examined the freight more carefully than he was able to in the daytime, but didn't learn much. The documentation tags on the goods were informative to the person with the right to know, and deliberately uninformative to anyone else – like himself. Carrier, weight, number of packages, airway bill number, destination (which meant airport, rather than importer or recipient). Well, that was fair, if unhelpful, enough. Name, rank and number: especially number. Some of the cases announced what was inside them. Calculators here (that was a mistake – Duffy could see signs of interference with one of the cartons), American weekly journals there, refrigerated fish down the far end. Packing-cases, tea-chests, compressed-cardboard boxes, hessian-wrapped bundles. Hendrick was right – what the hell did Duffy think he was going to find just by wandering around? Did he think he was like Alice in Wonderland with her Eat-Me cakes and Drink-Me drinks: that he'd find a big packing case marked Steal Me, and all he'd have to do would be to climb into it, wait for someone to pick it up, then leap out with a pair of handcuffs dangling from his belt and shout 'Freeze'. Is that what he thought it would be like?

Still, if this bit was disappointing, he could move on to the next bit. He passed his dunce's corner and strolled over to the lockers. There were six people working there and a bank of ten lockers. With a small knife he opened the ones he'd seen his fellow employees going to: each contained a set of overalls, plus extra male appurtenances which were either useful at work or couldn't be taken home: fags, chewing gum, booze, the occasional dirty mag, greasy sweaters. Casey's locker contained a bottle of Listerine mouthwash, which took Duffy aback; perhaps there was a secret Casey he didn't know about, one who combed cologne into his hair and shaved his armpits?

Duffy then opened the four lockers which he'd never seen anyone use. Two were empty; one contained a copy of the *Sun* from two years ago, the other an unopened tin of dog food. Duffy closed them all carefully, and moved off. Then he had a hunch. He walked back and opened his own locker and looked inside. Hmmm. He nodded to himself. Exactly as he had left it yesterday. So much for hunches.

The lock on Mrs Boseley's door detained him for about a minute and a half. Again, he had to move quickly to the cancel lever on the alarm. Then, having checked the precise location of the alarm buzzer under the desk, he sat down in her chair and surveyed the shed from Mrs Boseley's angle. Yes, there was no doubt you could see a lot better from up here, even if it was only about four feet above the level of the rest of the shed. Over there was that turd Duffy's corner; that was where we made the little bugger stand; that was where we made him push his trolley and eat shit. Have some calculators, Mr Duffy. Don't forget to declare them at the gate, Mr Duffy. Few weeks in prison do you, Mr Duffy?

He stopped himself. He didn't like Mrs Boseley, but he had no reason to believe that she had anything to do with the calculators. The fact that he wanted her to meant that he ought to be doubly careful before concluding that she did. Stop hating her, Duffy. Go through her desk instead.

He took out a notebook and started slowly working his way through the desk. He went through box-files full of invoices and copied down the names and telephone numbers of what seemed to be the regular clients. Business looked pretty healthy, as far as Duffy could judge, though he had to admit he wouldn't recognise a book-keeping fiddle if it stood up and played a tune for him.

Then he went through the recent correspondence and saw why Hendrick had decided to employ him. One wholesaler of furs had decided to take his business elsewhere – it wasn't that he wasn't insured, it was just that if it happened once, it might happen twice, Mr Hendrick, mightn't it, and it's so inconvenient (nothing personal, of course) – and a general dealer had said how seriously unhappy he was about the loss of a case of Italian sunglasses.

In the top left-hand drawer he found Mrs Boseley's dressing-table: powders, lotions, creams, lipsticks, combs, mirrors; if he looked hard enough, he'd probably find the collar-stiffeners she put inside her cheeks before talking to him. Instead, he went on to the next drawer, where he found her address book. This detained him for some time, though with little profit: no names which made him jump out of her chair; many of the regular clients' numbers, which was hardly surprising. He looked up the addresses and phone numbers of all Hendrick Freight's employees, and copied them down. He rechecked B for Boseley, but she appeared to know no one else of her own name. He flipped to the fly-leaf and copied down the home address and telephone number of Mrs E. Boseley. That 'E' was the only thing about her he'd found out so far. E for Eskimo.

He carried on through the drawers and encountered only the normal paraphernalia of office life – a stapler that had conked out, some perished rubber bands, the unused packet of Pritt Buddies. In the third drawer down on the right-hand side, however, he found something which was clearly peculiar to this office: a photograph in a frame, placed face-down in the drawer. Duffy very slowly turned it over, as a magician turns over his predictably surprising card. As he did so, he vibrated his tongue against his palate to make a quiet drum-roll noise, then went 'Ta-taaaaaa TUM' as the face turned the right way up.

It was no one he knew. The photo showed a round-faced man in his forties; balding, with little round gold-rimmed glasses, and an indulgent smile on his lips; he was wearing a chalk-striped suit with a rather elaborate buttonhole. A wedding photograph, perhaps? Mr Boseley? Was there a Mr Boseley? It was a recent photo; had the office manager got married in the last five years? He didn't know. The most probable solution was, of course, the simplest: that it *was* Mr Boseley, and the fact that Duffy wanted it not to be – wanted, indeed, for it to be some brutish lover with a fully equipped torture dungeon – made him wary of going along with this fancy. One slight question lingered in his mind. It was understandable that you didn't want to put such a photo on your desktop – people would only smirk at it and Mrs Boseley didn't look the sort who cared for smirks, but if you put it in a drawer, so that you could reach down and take a look whenever you felt glum, or beset, or sexy, or curse-ridden, wouldn't you put it in face upwards?

Duffy reset the alarms as he left and drove to the breakers' yard. He'd rung them about this mate's car, the customised Cortina. Not me you talked to, squire. Cortina, eh? Painted to look like a tiger? Well, I'd remember *that*, wouldn't I? Think you're out of luck, squire. Well, all right, if you insist. Into the hut, check the books. Yes, we had *a* Cortina, but it's about this size now (gesture like a fantasising fisherman). Amazing how small these crushers can get things, isn't it? You sure it was sent on here?

Still, it was a bit of a long shot anyway. And by seven o'clock it didn't matter. Carol rang.

'Sorry, I tried to get you yesterday, but you seemed to be out.'

'. . .'

'It's about that car.'

'Good.'

'I had the report read to me. As far as they could work out there must have been some sort of collision before it went over the barrier. There was paint on the offside rear wing from another vehicle, and quite a severe dent in the side where the point of impact was.'

'Puncture?'

'They said the tyres were fine.'

'Steering?'

'They said the car was in good nick. Apart from being crashed, of course.'

'And nothing on the other vehicle.'

'Not a thing. No one stopped. No one saw anything.'

'That's a great help, love. Thank you.' Carol smiled at the telephone. You didn't get those two words out of Duffy very often. She mused fondly on him.

But Duffy was musing elsewhere. He was thinking: what do you kill for – as near as makes no difference? Do you kill for a case of Italian sunglasses? Do you kill for a couple of boxes of smoked salmon?

4

'Right on time, Mr Hendrick.' It was always a good idea to point out your own virtue to clients.

'Ah, yes, thank you, Duffy.' Hendrick stood on his front door step and held his hand out for the key. He didn't look particularly pleased to see Duffy.

'Wondered if I could have a quick word, actually.'

'Hmm? Oh, very well.' He led Duffy down the hall and into the kitchen, gloomily shooing the children into the garden yet again. This time they seemed more reluctant than last time. Maybe they got shooed into the garden too much for their own liking. And was there a Mrs Hendrick around?

'Suppose I should have asked you before, Mr Hendrick, but do you mind if we run through your employees? Fill me in on them?'

'Fine, go ahead.'

'Mr Gleeson.'

'You don't suspect Mr Gleeson?' Hendrick looked across at Duffy as if he'd got Gleeson handcuffed to him already, gold bars pulling his pockets out of shape and diamonds dripping out of his turn-ups.

'I don't suspect anyone, Mr Hendrick, anyone in particular yet. But if you don't start by suspecting everyone then you start suspecting no one, and then you don't see anything.' It wasn't really true, any of this, but it was the formula the clients seemed to like; it made them feel all right about telling dirt on their favourite employees. And Duffy had deliberately started with someone whom Hendrick probably trusted, so that they wouldn't have to go through the argument again when it came to Mrs Boseley. 'There are certain routines of investigation which may strike you as irritating, but I'm afraid if you want a professional job done they have to be gone through.' They liked that line too: it appealed to a shared professionalism, as well as to the small boy in them.

'Of course, of course. Well, Gleeson's a splendid chap. Been with me four years. Hard-working, never missed a day, gets on with the others.'

'Tan – Chinese, is he?'

'No, Malaysian, I think. Well, he's very oriental, isn't he? Yellow and doesn't say much.'

'Maybe that's because he doesn't speak the language too well.'

'Oh, he does, born and brought up here. Nice chap, works hard. Very strong. Does that thing with his hands they all do out there . . . '

'Origami?' (Careful, Duffy, he thought to himself, don't get too smartass; but Hendrick didn't blink.)

'No, that smashing bricks and things with the side of your hand.'

'Oh yes, I know what you mean.' Well, thanks for the warning.

'Casey?'

'Nice chap,' (oh, *come on*, Mr Hendrick) 'works hard. Bit slow on the uptake sometimes. Good driver.'

Duffy asked about the other two – Botsford and McAndrew – then, slightly apprehensively,

'And, you know, just as a matter of pure routine – Mrs Boseley?'

Hendrick looked at him sharply, and Duffy gave him the we've-talked-about-it gesture.

'Oh yes, very well. Splendid lady, very efficient, completely trustworthy, never misses a day, gets on with the employees very well.'

And runs a wolf-cub pack in the evening, no doubt, under the name of Akela or something. Hendrick was useless. He obviously had a group of model employees – clean, hard-working, honest, healthy, and so on. It was just that one of them was nicking his stuff, that was all. Duffy switched his tone, as if the professional side of the talk were over, and they were now man-to-man over a couple of beers.

'I'm bound to agree with you, Mr Hendrick, she's a terrific lady. I certainly knew where I was right from the beginning. She been with you since you started up?'

'Oh yes, five years Mrs Boseley's been with us.'

'What did she do before? Just out of interest. I was wondering what that sort of lady would have done before.'

'I think she was a senior stewardess on one of the big airlines.' Hendrick spoke with the tone of one saying less than he knew.

'Why didn't she stay on? She could be running B.A. by now, couldn't she?'

'Well *I* think she could, naturally, but I suppose she thought that if she couldn't do what she wanted to do, it was best to get out. They don't let them go on being hostesses after a certain time, you know. Silly rule.'

'I agree. I suppose . . . ' Duffy's tone became even more bottom-of-the-glass, 'I suppose there's a Mr Boseley?'

Hendrick laughed, which was a rare occurrence, and his corpse's suit juddered about at the unexpected upheaval within it. A dirty lock of blond hair fell across his face.

'Now I see where you're leading, Mr Duffy. I'm afraid the answer is, I don't fancy your chances.'

Duffy persuaded his voice to join in the laugh. 'Oh, it wasn't for myself I was asking. I just thought, you know, pity such a splendid lady has to earn her own living.'

Hendrick still looked roguish, still clearly disbelieved him. 'Well I gather there is one, but I think he's an invalid. One doesn't like to pry, but they do say he's in an iron lung. Poor Mrs Boseley.'

Poor *Mr* Boseley, thought Duffy; not only in an iron lung, but having Mrs B. as your ray of sunshine. He shifted his tone back to the professional one.

'What about McKay? What was he like?'

'Oh, very hard worker, good driver, been with us some years.' Helped run Mrs Boseley's wolf-cub pack, no doubt. Very handy with a tent-peg. Drove old ladies across the street in his tiger car. Did a lot of work for charity.

'So what we have, Mr Hendrick, is that all your employees have been with you for some time – at least a couple of years?'

'Yes.'

'And thefts only started about six months ago.'

'Yes.'

'Hmm. And one other thing. I suppose none of your employees have criminal records?'

Hendrick pushed the dirty blond lock back where it belonged.

'Oh, but I'm sure they're perfectly rehabilitated.' Uh-huh.

'Tell me, Mr Hendrick.' Duffy was getting extremely pissed off, but tried to sound merely reproachful.

'Well, Tan did knife someone once; but he was very young, he didn't know what he was doing. I'm sure it was under extreme provocation. That's why he's taught himself to do that thing with his hands.' (So that he breaks their bones instead of having to knife them.) 'And Casey has hit a few people in his time.'

'How many convictions?'

'Four, actually. But it was always a six-and-two-threes situation, from what he tells me. I mean, I don't think he'd hit anyone just for the pleasure of hitting them.'

'Don't you think I ought to have known this before?' Bloody clients.

'Oh, well, I didn't think it was relevant. I mean, none of my employees have any convictions for stealing. And none of them have got into fights – not on my premises anyway. I'm afraid I thought it might only prejudice you if I told you earlier.'

'All I can say is, Mr Hendrick, you're a very fair-minded man.' And a fucking fool.

He supposed he believed Hendrick. He thought he was pretty wet and pretty naïve; but he supposed he believed him. In a funny way, too, Duffy almost agreed with him. The public always thought, once a criminal, always a criminal; they also thought that once you've committed one crime, then it's as if you're in a great supermarket – you just pick any crime you fancy off the shelf. Duffy knew it didn't work like that. Some crimes go with other crimes, some don't. White-collar criminals, for instance: they usually stuck with white-collar crime (who wouldn't, it was so lucrative). And arsonists, they were really odd buggers. Just liked committing arson, all the time; nothing but arson. Have a house burnt out and it's no good rounding up the cosh men and the bank robbers; you have to find a nut with a box of matches, someone who used to like watching the fire engines go by as a kid, someone who's probably quite timid and entirely law-abiding – except that he likes burning people to death.

So, theft and assault? Well, there was a much closer connection there. But not a necessary connection. Sometimes you hit people to steal from them; sometimes you stole and then had to hit people to get away. But an awful lot of people liked hitting other people just for itself. They liked it. It made them feel good. And it stopped the person they hit from carrying on irritating them. Duffy understood that. If you were a Malaysian brought up over here, didn't feel particularly Malaysian, just bloody looked it all the time, you'd get fed up after a few years of school with all the kids pulling slit eyes at you and talking in sing-song voices and aiming kung-fu kicks at you which might just occasionally land, and most of all pointing out all the time that there were more of them than there were of you, and that's how it was always going to be, and that's a nice biro, Chinky-

Winky, I fink I'll have that. Wouldn't you fancy carving a few stitches into someone after a bit of that? And if you did, and had, it wouldn't necessarily make you want to start nicking Italian sunglasses ten years later, would it?

Hmmm. Duffy could see the Hendrick view, but at the same time it was a bit wet-panted, a bit sentimental. You could just as well argue the line that, if Tan knifed someone at school, then afterwards the kids would probably have treated him differently. Don't tangle with the crazy Chink killer: the eye-pulling and the kung-fu kicks would have fallen off. Kids respect violence and madness – not wet, introverted madness, of course, but crazy, outgoing, killer-madness. No doubt Tan got an easier ride at school after the knife episode. And no doubt he could have concluded that crime, in its funny way, does pay. That would be just as logical, wouldn't it? And the logic would continue with the idea: it pays even more if you don't get caught. Duffy knew from experience how to read a criminal record. He did it as policemen always do: reading any acquittals as convictions, doubling up the number of convictions, seeing the guilty pleas for what they probably were – a way of getting off a heavier charge – and filling in between the recorded convictions all manner of other, undetected crimes.

Duffy was letting his mind freewheel because of an acute shortage of facts. All he could do was play about with the few he had. He wouldn't have minded a bedside chat to McKay, but that was far too risky; too many possible connections. Instead, he rang Carol and asked her to run half a dozen names through the computer. He wanted to check the record against what Hendrick had given him. As an afterthought he added another name – Hendrick's. You never can tell.

Carol didn't want to do it. She didn't like the way Duffy just used her as part of the service he offered clients. It was also strictly against police regulations. She could be fired on the spot. Duffy exaggerated the importance of the check, and she finally agreed. It wouldn't, after all, be that risky; and he did need it for his work; and he was, really, in the same line of business as her.

He also asked if she would lend him her car that evening; but she refused. He could have it the following evening, but not tonight. Duffy agreed, rang off, and imagined her down at the roller-disco with John Travolta, who was excuse-me'd in mid-shuffle by Robert Redford, who squired her off to an operatically candlelit dinner (why was she still wearing her uniform in his fantasy?) and then, later, back at his place, made her weep and croon with joy and delight. Meanwhile, Carol was thinking: well, I *could* have put off Auntie this one time, but you've got to have some principles with men; especially with Duffy.

At work, on the Monday, there was a tricky thing to be done. Gleeson. Duffy hoped he wouldn't balls it up. It was a question of getting the right manner as much as anything. It was also a question of not bringing it up too soon, so that they had a little sweat about what might have happened; but also not leaving it too long, so that they thought nothing at all had happened. Duffy spent some of the day wondering whether Malaysians needed sunglasses in the English climate; and then, about mid-afternoon, he thought he'd better do it now before he'd thought about it too many times. He spotted Gleeson, clipboard in hand, checking some cases and wandered casually over to him.

'Can you give me a hand with my car?'

Gleeson didn't look up, and went on checking his list.

'It's parked in the wrong place.'

Gleeson ignored him.

'It's parked in the wrong place.'

Still Gleeson ignored him. He pursed his lips over the clipboard and the mutton-chops shifted forwards.

'It's parked in the wrong place.'

'Fuck off, Duffy,' said Gleeson in a quiet, seemingly friendly tone.

If you couldn't get him to come outside, you'd have to say it here. Or you could try something different, to stop him telling you to fuck off. In almost an undertone Duffy said,

'I take it you were wearing gloves, Gleeson, because I certainly was.'

Then he wandered slowly away, out through the double doors and round to the car park. A minute later they were standing side by side peering into the engine of Duffy's van. Gleeson's mere presence told Duffy something extra: that he hadn't been wearing gloves.

'Now, what about Friday?'

'What about Friday?'

'The stuff in my car.'

'What stuff?'

'The calculators.'

'What calculators?' Christ, it was like an English lesson for foreign students; repeat everything I say but turn it into a question.

'There were calculators in my car on Friday.'

'You been nicking calculators, mate? Better watch I don't report you.'

'You put six calculators in my car on Friday.'

'Now why would I do a thing like that? 'Snot your cowing birthday or anything is it?'

'And quite by chance I was stopped by a random check at the gate.'

'Very good, the security round here. Tight as oats.'

'You borrowed my car keys on Friday.'

'Did I, mate? Expect I wanted to move your car or something.'

'You didn't move my car.'

'Then why would I want to borrow your keys? Be logical, mate.'

Duffy felt he wasn't quite on top of the argument. 'Why did you come out here as soon as I mentioned wearing gloves?'

'Is that what you were saying? I could hear you muttering something. I thought you wanted a hand with your car. That's why I came out. Now you start telling me you've been nicking calculators. I think maybe this job's getting too much for you, Duffy.' Gleeson smiled in a friendly way; he knew how to look friendly as long as he didn't mean it. The only thing to do was to change course.

'O.K., let's start the conversation again. Let's pretend the car's fixed. Let's pretend you moved it on Friday. Let's pretend I don't somewhere have a package which might or might not have someone's fingerprints on it.' (Not that that would prove anything, Duffy realised.) 'Let's pretend I wasn't given a shakedown at the gate on Friday, and that in any case if I was, it was completely random. O.K.?'

'I think this job's getting too much for you.' Duffy kept doggedly on.

'So we're starting now instead. I need this job, Gleeson. I don't like it any more than any other job, but I need it. It's not a good time not to have a job. Now, I don't mind the fact that you give me shitty things to do, and make me move packing cases which you and I know fucking well don't have to be moved. I don't mind the fact that you give me a shitty corner of the shed to stand around in. I don't want to join in your card games because I don't play cards. I don't even care why you don't want me to work here; that's your business. All I'm telling you is I'm working here, and I'm fucking going on working here, and you can bleeding well get used to it. And if you try and fuck me around, then I'll fucking fuck you around, I can promise you that.'

Duffy hoped the way he veered from pathos to aggression, and then to manic insistence, would have some effect. The trouble was, he didn't really have any threats in his locker. 'Or I'll let your tyres down . . . ' 'Or I'll stamp on your shoe-laces . . . ' – that was what it sounded like to him. He just hoped it sounded more convincing to Gleeson; he hoped the existence and current location of the calculators might give him just a little leverage. All he could do would be to hang on, keep his head down and watch out for people trying to fuck him up.

At least Gleeson was looking serious as they walked back to the shed. His bushy eyebrows were pushing together in thought. As they came through the double doors he turned confidentially to Duffy.

'By the way, I shouldn't nick any more of them calculators, Duffy. I mean, you can't work more than one at a time, can you?'

As Duffy got on with his work he reflected that this conversation, necessary as it had been, would also have the unwanted effect of freezing things. Gleeson (assuming that it was just Gleeson, or 'they' if there were a 'they') would know that Duffy would be on the lookout for being fucked up, for having a dead cat stuffed up his exhaust pipe, or whatever. He'd be watching them (assuming 'them'), and they'd be watching him. They might try and fuck him up; they'd most probably just leave him alone in his dunce's corner; what they certainly wouldn't do would be to follow up the fifty quid in the locker (assuming, of course, that this is what the money was about in the first place; on the other hand, maybe it was just a bit of preliminary bait so that he'd accept the calculators). Whichever way, Duffy realised that he was going to be hard pushed to get a break from this end of things. He'd just have to see if his out-of-hours legwork turned up anything.

So began an extremely boring fortnight for Duffy. Every other day he phoned the third breakers' yard, but they never replied. He borrowed Carol's rusting Mini on the nights it was available, and each evening tailed one of four people; Gleeson, Tan, Casey and Mrs Boseley. That's to say, he drove his van round to Carol's, picked up the Mini, drove to one of the addresses he'd listed in his notebook, and sat around waiting for something to happen. It wasn't much good as a technique for getting to know their routines; it was, in fact, only just marginally more useful than staying at home and pulling his wire; but at least he felt, as his bum grew more numb by the hour, as if he was more or less earning his money.

The flaw in the schedule, of course, was that by the time he got into position outside where they lived, they'd often gone out for the evening already. Casey, for instance, seemed to turn round after work in just a few minutes – a quick rinse with Listerine was probably his idea of slipping into something loose. Two evenings were spent fruitlessly outside Casey's squat in Heston before Duffy realised that he had already gone out and was probably exercising his specially tattooed courting finger in some cinema car park. The third evening Duffy took a risk and followed him straight from work in his van. That evening, of course, Casey decided to stay in. The next day he asked Duffy over double pie and beans,

'Seeya figh' last nigh'?'

Duffy regretted that he hadn't; Casey assured him it had been a figh' inna million.

With Gleeson he had to sit outside a large semi in Uxbridge; there was a Mrs Gleeson and, by the sound of it, a baby Gleeson. Maybe this explained why they didn't go out much. At least, they didn't go out on the nights Duffy chose. The only thing that slightly surprised him was the two cars shunted up against each other on the small concrete parking space: the Viva which Gleeson came to work in, and a big Granada, V-registration. Maybe Mrs Gleeson had private means.

Tan was a bit more interesting. He lived with his family on the edge of Southall. He went out most evenings with his girl-friend – though, fortunately for Duffy, not before he'd had a good Malaysian meal with his parents first. Duffy imagined this meal while munching a pork pie and driving as fast as he could from Carol's flat back to Southall. If he hurried he'd get there in time to follow Tan taking his girl friend to a cinema, or to the pub, or once, for a walk in the park.

Mrs Boseley lived in Rayners Lane, which was marginally more convenient for Duffy – out along the Western Avenue and then cut through. She seemed to like watering her front garden in the evenings, which meant that Duffy had to park some way off. The other thing she seemed to enjoy was having friendly chats with her neighbours. It didn't seem very much to report back to Hendrick about.

This routine was heavy on petrol. It was also heavy on Duffy's patience. Nine nights of it on the trot and he couldn't stand any more. He gave himself the evening off and went down the Gemini Club. This was where he trawled when the Alligator was feeling a bit stale, when he was tired of the same old faces sipping vermouth, when he wanted a bit more of the unexpected, a bit more of the chase. It wasn't rough at the Gemini, but it was a bit more competitive. You had to work for your trade down there, spend a bit more; but the merchandise was a lot more varied. Duffy had a very nice Swede snaffled from under his nose (it was a members' club, but foreigners were allowed in on presentation of their passports); he got home eventually with a shy publishing trainee who flirted quite hard, got Duffy to buy him too many drinks, told him in the van that he'd never done anything like this before (Duffy didn't believe him, but assured him it wouldn't hurt), and then got scratchy about leaving his watch in the Tupperware box. He walked around the flat, naked and drunk, with his watch still on, exclaiming, 'But I want to time us, I want to time us.' Eventually, when Duffy expressed impatience, the guy pulled a long face, trudged obediently to the bathroom, dropped his watch in the box and was promptly sick into it as well. As Duffy was rinsing the sick off the watch and listening to the snores from the settee, he vowed his loyalty to the Alligator once more.

The next night but one something happened. Mrs Boseley went to town. At 8.30 she came out of her front door and gave Duffy a shock. She didn't have a watering can in her hand; she didn't look around for a neighbour to chat to; she walked straight to her car and drove off. What's more, she had put her hair down.

She was a confident driver, but he followed her without much difficulty into the West End. She clearly knew her way around; Duffy knew his even better. Three years as a detective-sergeant in Soho and he still remembered every alleyway, every one-way street, and most of the possible crimes. Mrs Boseley parked in Great Marlborough Street; he drove past her, stopped thirty yards on, and watched in his wing mirror as she got out and locked the car. He tailed her down Poland Street, along Broadwick Street, a left and a right, and then she suddenly disappeared into a club. He stood around some twenty yards short of the entrance for a few minutes, then crossed the street and strolled slowly along the pavement on the other side.

Dude's, it was called, and even from across the street it didn't look the sort of place which Mrs Boseley would know about – not the Mrs Boseley he'd met anyway. There was a maroon awning over the entrance with 'Dude's' written on it in three-foot-high copper-plate handwriting. There were velvet curtains in the windows, held back with lace ties; but though the curtains were drawn back, you couldn't see through the window because there were shutters as well on the inside, and these were closed. To work out what it might be like you had to consult the large display cases on either side of the entrance, which contained big colour transparencies lit from behind.

Duffy crossed the road and quickly took them in. There was a picture of a curving bar with lots of stools, none of them occupied; there was a picture of what might have been a dining area, showing various booths with waist-high slatted swing doors. There were also two pictures of very pretty girls, one dark and one blonde, each with bare shoulders. At the top of the display box on the left Duffy read: 'DUDE'S – WHERE GENTLEMEN RELAX'; at the top of the right-hand box he read: 'DUDE'S – FOR THE BEST IN COMPANY'.

He walked on, and took up a station some thirty yards beyond the club entrance. After about an hour Mrs Boseley emerged, and without a glance began to walk swiftly back towards her car. Duffy tailed her for long enough to guess with safety that she was going home; then he turned off, drove the Mini back to Carol's place and swapped cars. He pushed the keys through the door; Carol had insisted on that. As he drove off, Duffy stared balefully at the cars parked near by. Wasn't that one Paul Newman's?

At work the next day he found himself occasionally looking down the shed to Mrs Boseley's glass eyrie. Well, well, well, he thought. The regular, reliable job, the little house in Rayners Lane, the watering can, the husband in the iron lung – and suddenly, hair down and off to the tacky club. What did it mean; what *did* it mean? Was she turning the odd trick on the side to help with her husband's medical expenses? If so, would it be worth it, driving all the way into town for just an hour? You'd have to do something incredibly filthy to make it worth your while, Duffy thought. And when she came out, she didn't look as if she'd just done something incredibly filthy.

Maybe there was an entirely innocent explanation. There never was, in Duffy's experience; but try. Maybe her brother worked there; or something like an illegitimate daughter. Did you visit your illegitimate daughter at work? And why did she put her hair down? She looked, Duffy had to admit it, better with her hair down, less frosty. Almost like someone who wasn't nasty.

The enigma kept Duffy happy all day. What's more, he knew that tonight it wasn't going to be following Tan to the Malaysian disco in Hayes, thank you very much. After work he rang Carol to check if he could call by; no, he didn't need her car. What he did need was the brown envelope he'd left with her. He didn't reckon that Gentlemen Relaxed for peanuts. He also reckoned that they didn't relax in green suede blousons with big plastic zips up the front and polo-neck sweaters and jeans. Part of Duffy thought, Stuff it, I'm paying, why shouldn't I dress as I please? The more sensible part thought, don't stand out any more than you have to. He dug into the very back of his wardrobe and came up with a real copper's suit, a delicate mud colour with tight trouser-bottoms and lapels as narrow as the triangles on a backgammon board. He pulled it on and didn't like the feeling around his waist; he undid the two elasticated button-fastenings at the sides, but that didn't seem to make any difference. Just filling out with maturity, he said to himself; but the other voice whispered, Getting fat, Duffy, getting *fat*.

He found a tie as thin as a runner bean and pulled it round his neck. As he was doing it up he felt like a suicide; Christ, fat *neck* too. Then he examined himself in the mirror. He looked ridiculous. He looked like a member of a 1960s band which had modelled itself on Gerry and the Pacemakers and got nowhere; he twiddled some drumsticks to himself. The last thing he looked like was a Gentleman about to Relax. Should he take the stud out of his ear? Should he change his desert boots? Hell, no – he'd compromised enough already. Wait till they saw the colour of his extremely used one-pound notes: then they'd know who they were dealing with.

When Carol saw him she burst out laughing.

'Where you going, Duffy? Revival disco?'

'That bad, is it? I thought I looked quite smart.'

'Duffy, you look chronic.' And she kissed him on the lips in sheer delight at how awful he looked. His waistband was cutting into him and made him want to pee. When he returned, Carol said,

'Oh, I checked out those names for you. Sorry it took so long, but I didn't want to take any risks.'

'Sure. Thanks, love. What did you find?'

She handed him a piece of paper. He read it quickly. Exactly as Hendrick had said. And Hendrick himself was clean. Still, he'd better be grateful.

'That's very useful, love. That's just what I needed.'

'How's it going?' She hadn't asked any more what 'it' was, because she didn't really want to know. But she worried about Duffy's career in a general way.

'Not very well. Slow job. Still, it's paying.'

'That's the main thing.' She went and fetched his brown envelope. He took out the money and stuffed it in his pocket. As he left the flat – Carol was suppressing a giggle at the sight

251

of his flat-cut jacket bottom, like something out of an old gangster film – he began to feel like a man of means. He could very well pass for a Gentleman, in the dark with the light behind him.

He parked in Great Marlborough Street and walked away from the car with a pair of flapping hands inside his stomach. He made his way down to Dude's, which was new since he had left the patch. What would it be like? Would it be posh? Would it be dirty? Whatever it was, it would beat sitting in a rusty Mini at Rayners Lane.

The double glass doors said Dude's on them. The custom-built doormat said Dude's on it. The inner double glass doors said Dude's on them. They were certainly good at letting you know where you were. Inside, it seemed very dark to Duffy at first. On his left was a cloakroom opening with a girl standing in it. He might have stopped anyway, but he definitely stopped now. Her breasts were completely bare, and very nice too, he thought.

'Your hat, sir,' she said.

'I don't have a hat.'

'No; your hat, sir.'

He moved closer towards her. Was he being very stupid? Was it O.K. to look at her breasts?

'I'm sorry,' he said, 'this is my first time here.'

'That's quite all right, sir,' she replied with a toothpaste smile. 'You will be taking one of the girls downstairs, of course.'

'Oh, of course.'

'Twenty pounds, please, sir.'

'Oh, of course.'

He slowly counted out two-fifths of his bundle and wondered what he was paying for. Wondered who he was paying for as much as anything. Where was downstairs? And where were the girls?

He needn't have worried. As he turned away from the hat-check girl he saw them. To his right was the long curved bar

252

pictured outside, though it seemed smaller and less luxuri-
ously appointed than in its photograph. There were about
fifteen girls variously clustered round the bar, five or so of
them attending to a fat man at the far end. There were, he
noticed, many different types of girl here, including a token
black girl and a token Chinese (or perhaps a token Malaysian),
but they all had one thing in common: their breasts were bare.
Except for one, that is, who wore a leotard. As Duffy walked
across towards the bar this girl mechanically lowered the top of
her leotard so that he could see her breasts; they swung slightly
from the movement of the undressing.

The eight or ten girls at his end of the bar made way for him,
guiding him to a barstool merely by breaking ranks. The extremely large barman instructed him to have a drink, and he
couldn't have agreed more. He ordered a whisky.

'Four pounds, sir.' You didn't argue with that voice; if
anything you felt like saying, Is that all, can't you make it a bit
more, here, have seven pounds. It was an extremely small
whisky. He was now almost half-way through his roll.

'I'm sorry, I don't think I can afford to stand you all a round,'
he said apologetically to the girls around him. He had never
seen so many different-sized and different-breasted girls at the
same time in his life. It made him feel funny. It didn't make
him feel particularly dirty; it made him feel a bit as if he were in
a zoo.

'That's all right,' said the girl on his right. 'Ours are on the
house.' They were mostly drinking orange juice. He took a sip
of his whisky. He felt the conversation was beginning to die.

'So, what do you all do?' he said nervously, as if he were at a
party. It was probably the least necessary question he asked in
his whole life. The girls giggled.

'And what do you do?' countered the one on his left, a dark
girl with a northern accent and breasts which seemed about
half-way between the two extremes on offer.

'I'm a . . . I'm a . . . ' One or two of them began to giggle
already. Presumably the men always lied, that was one of the

253

rules, and the girls always knew it. Finally he said, 'I'm a . . . couturier.'

They howled at that one, and a girl on the fringes of the fat man detached herself and moved across to Duffy's group. Conversation languished again. He was nearly at the end of the whisky.

'Right,' said the girl on his left. 'That's enough browsing. Which of us are you taking downstairs? The suspense is killing.'

'Oh.' Duffy reached for his whisky and gulped the final teaspoonful down. He felt shy about examining them all in front of one another, even if he had paid his twenty pounds. He ducked his head and said, 'Oh, well, you I suppose,' to the girl on his left.

They stood up, and as they did so the girl in the leotard pulled up her shoulder-straps and tucked her tits back into place. They'd stay there till the next customer. He followed the girl he'd chosen across the room towards the stairs. She was, he noted, wearing black velvet pants which finished at mid-calf level, so that he seemed to be following the legs of a gondolier; and below them, gold-strapped sandals with high heels.

As they walked downstairs, it seemed to get even darker. There was a strong smell of incense. They reached the other room pictured outside, the one with the separate booths and the slatted swing doors. After a little peering around, the girl found an empty booth and they settled in. She pressed a bell and said,

'What's your name, love?'

'Nick. What's yours?'

'Delia. Terrible name, innit? Call me something else if you want to. Most people do.'

'No, that's fine, it's . . . perfectly all right.' He didn't reckon he'd have much cause to use her name; there wouldn't be much shouting across crowded rooms during this encounter. A waiter appeared with two glasses and a quarter-bottle of champagne; it wasn't so much on ice as on melted water.

'Ten,' the girl whispered to him, and he counted out some more of Gleeson's money.

The girl poured two glasses and clinked with him. He drank from his; she put hers down on the table.

'Where j' get the clothes then?'

'D'you like them?'

'Yeah, I think they're really nice. They're really Fifties, aren't they?'

'Uh-huh.'

'Where j' get them?'

'Oh, this little shop I know. Does Fifties revival clothing.'

The girl smiled at him, almost a normal smile, he thought.

'Why the smell of mothballs, then?'

'That's just my cologne. That's coming back too. Haven't you heard of it – mothball cologne?'

'Yer kidding.'

'No. I'm not.'

'Yer funny.'

'Uh-huh.'

'You can hold me tits if you like.'

'Oh.'

'You paid for them, after all. That's why they're out. They're not for looking at.'

'Of course not.' It was, he supposed, marginally more exciting than being asked to hold a bag of caster sugar; she certainly knew how to drain the invitation of eroticism. He stretched out his hand and curled it round her right breast. She seemed almost relieved, as if the proprieties of the occasion were at last being observed.

He looked at the table. Apart from the champagne there were three things on it: a lighted candle; a bunch of exotic-looking flowers which he guessed were plastic; and a puffing joss-stick.

'They're real,' she said. She probably wasn't still talking about her tits.

'Are they?'

'Yeah – have a sniff.'

255

He would. He considered the logistics of it and realised he couldn't lean as far as the flowers without first removing his hand from Delia's breast; as it was he'd been sipping his champagne left-handed and getting in a tangle of arms every time. He released his grasp on her breast and bent his head towards the flowers. As he did so he caught a quick movement out of the corner of his left eye. He sniffed them; they smelled vaguely lush, though with the overlay of joss-stick it was hard to be precise.

He straightened up and returned his hand to her breast: again the right one, which was nearer; it seemed over-familiar, or complaining, to reach across for the far one.

'What sort are they?'

'Dunno. They're fresh. Fresh every day. Mr Dalby has them flown in every day. Flown in from abroad. Fresh flowers for my little flowers, he says.'

'Why did you throw your champagne away when I was smelling them?'

'Oh, to get rid of it and order another bottle. Actually, I don't really like the taste any more. I've gone right off it since I started working here. Would you like me to toss you off?'

'Er, not just now, I think.'

'It's ten if you're worried about the price. Look, quick, better order another bottle, here comes Mr Dalby.' She pressed the bell in the wall and Duffy took his hand off her breast to reach for his money. A man had come out of an office up a few stairs at the far end of the room, and was slowly walking along between the booths. He was being discreet, looking out of the corner of his eye, but his soft-footed presence made the girls leap to their bells and order more champagne.

'I'll drink yours as well this time, if you don't mind.'

'All right, but don't dawdle over it, you'll have to drink it as quick as if we was both drinking it.'

'All right.'

Mr Dalby was almost level with their booth. He walked a bit like an old man, but maybe that was because he was trying not

256

to scare the customers. In fact he was about forty, with a round face and little round glasses and a pink complexion and a chalk-striped suit. Duffy looked away, and it wasn't punter's guilt that made him do so. Mr Dalby was the man in the drawer.

5

'Is that the boss?'

'Yeah, that's Mr Dalby.'

The second quarter-bottle of champagne arrived, leaving Duffy with six of Gleeson's pounds left.

'You been dahn the dogs?'

'What?'

'The dogs – that where you got all them pound notes?'

'No,' he said, 'Hardy Amies always pays me like this.' She giggled. He quite liked her. No, that was an exaggeration. He didn't mind her. He placed his hand, damp from the champagne bottle, back on her right breast. Were you allowed to rub, he suddenly thought, or was that extra? Not that he particularly wanted to.

'What's he like, Mr Dalby?'

'He's all right. He sticks by the rules. If you don't like the rules you don't have to work here, so that's fair enough.'

'Do you have to go to bed with him?'

'Yeah, course. Not very often. And he always pays you. You can say No if you like as well, that's one of the rules. Not that anyone would, of course.'

'Uh-huh.'

'And anyway he doesn't really like it much, so that makes it better for you.'

'He doesn't like it?'

'No, not really. He does it a lot, but he doesn't seem to like it.

258

He's the sort of fellow always puts two tonkies on first cause he's scared of catching something, know what I mean?'

'Mmm.'

'And then it's stick it in, pull it out, wipe it off and straight into a bath.'

'You're joking?'

'No. Straight up. He's got a little flat up there – office, bedroom, bathroom. He always runs the bath first, it's all part of his routine, so he can jump straight in afterwards.'

'What else does he do?' Did Mrs Boseley know all this, he wondered.

'Well, sometimes he sniffs some stuff before doing it.'

'What sort of stuff?'

'Well, there's two sorts. There's some stuff in a little capsule which he keeps by the bedside, and then just after he takes his socks off he sort of breaks it under his nose and sniffs it. And sometimes he gets some powder and sniffs that instead. But it doesn't seem to make him enjoy it any more.'

'And what do you do?'

'I just lie there waiting for him to get on with it. I mean, it's all preparations and then washing as far as he's concerned. Not that *I'm* complaining – I wouldn't mind if all my gentlemen were like that.'

Duffy was feeling very pleased with himself. He was beginning to feel glimmerings of understanding. After nights in Carol's cramped Mini, this was his reward. He felt good. Now, if he put some of his own money with the rest of Gleeson's . . .

'How much did you say you charged?'

Delia smiled at him in a puzzled way.

'Ten, love,' and her hand landed on his thigh in a commercial caress. Six of Gleeson's oncers, a fiver of his own, take back one of Gleeson's . . . he put it on the table. When she saw the blue five pound note she chuckled.

'Hey, Mister Big Spender.' Weren't men odd? You never could tell what they'd get off on. Here he was, all friendly enough to talk to but not exactly the grope of the month, and then tell him about fucking Mr Dalby and all of a sudden he's finding he's got deeper pockets than he knew.

Apart from anything else, Duffy was glad to get the waistband of his trousers undone; it had been killing him. He unzipped his fly and let her dig out his cock for him. Quickly and diligently, she milked him out on to the carpet.

Duffy thought, no wonder they need so many joss-sticks, what with the stuff that gets dumped on this carpet; first the champagne, then the spunk. Maybe they have carpet tiles down there, where it was too dark to see, and change them once a week. The candle was burning down. The unnamable flowers looked just as fresh, though he still couldn't smell them. Duffy wondered, just wondered, who freighted the joss-sticks.

The exhilaration of the previous evening had already ebbed away by the time Duffy got Hendrick's call.

'Been wondering how you've been getting along.'

'Oh, fine, Mr Hendrick, fine. Bit of this and that, lots of surveillance.' (They liked that word, even if most of them couldn't pronounce it.) 'Lots of sitting around in cars, you know what the job's like.'

'Yes. But have you been getting anywhere?'

'Well, I'm a lot more clued up than when I started.'

'It's quite expensive, hiring you, Mr Duffy.'

'Uh-huh.'

'And you haven't caught my thief.'

'No.'

'And there haven't been any more thefts since you arrived.'

'Now, Mr Hendrick, you wouldn't want there to be, would you?'

'No, of course not.'

'So maybe my presence there is putting them off.' Duffy felt this was a wonky line as he produced it.

'Yes, but if you're putting them off, then they aren't stealing anything and you aren't catching them, are you?'

'No.' Hendrick was clearly all logicked up at this time of the morning. It wasn't fair. Duffy was still on his first cup of coffee.

'You see, I can't afford to pay you just to be there to see that they *don't* steal things.'

'Of course not.'

'I mean, that would be even more expensive than just letting them help themselves once a month to whatever they fancied.'

Duffy grunted.

'And you have been there almost a month, haven't you?'

'Well, it must be coming up for their time again, then.'

'I don't know whether to hope it does or hope it doesn't.' Ah, Hendrick's logic was beginning to tire at last.

'Put it this way, Mr Hendrick, it is entirely your decision, and naturally I respect whatever you think it's best to do. I would just ask for a little more time, though. I can see your point of view – you haven't had anything for your money yet. On the other hand, you haven't lost anything for your money yet. And I take it my work in the shed is satisfactory.'

'Oh yes, quite satisfactory. In fact, Mr Duffy, if you were thinking of giving up your present employment . . . '

'That's very kind of you. So' (you always had to get the next line in before the client did) 'we'll leave it as it is for a bit, shall we?'

'I suppose we'd better.'

As he rang off, Duffy thought, well, that's a bit more time; but not much. And if the worst comes to the worst I could always tell him I've got a criminal record; that way he'd probably promote me straight over Mrs Boseley's head.

It was funny, he reflected, as he drove to work. Some bits of it always were funny, that was what kept you going. The eager guy from the Gemini had ended up painting his insides into the Watches box; and the girl in Dude's had been the one who'd drawn the double cream. You'd never have guessed *that*, said Duffy firmly to himself; you'd never have guessed *that* if I'd given you the options beforehand.

But in other ways, it wasn't particularly funny, or neat, or comprehensible. As he drove to work, the jumbos were following him again. Duffy read the news to himself. 'All 352 people . . . ' 'All 113 people . . . ' 'All 2,345,918 people . . . ' That was always how they began the news of aircrashes. Never just '254 people . . . ' And as soon as Duffy heard that first *All* on the radio, he knew how the sentence was going to continue: ' . . . were killed when a DC-10 of Cockroach Airways flew straight into the side of a mountain near Lake Honky Tonky. Wreckage was strewn over a wide area. As far as is known the plane was on course and experienced no mechanical trouble . . . ' Presumably they just had a tape ready and fed in the minor details that made this crash different from any other. And always they began with that *All*.

As the Cockroach Airways jumbos queued up for their go at crashing, Duffy thought about yesterday's exhilaration and today's disappointment. The exhilaration came from being carried away by a hypothesis; the disappointment from examining the facts as he knew them to be. And they were still uselessly thin.

Start at the beginning. Hendrick had some goods stolen; that we believe, don't we? Yes, for want of any contrary evidence. McKay was crashed. *No* – McKay crashed, that's all you know: he sideswiped something, or something sideswiped him, and he ran off the road and is all fucked up in hospital. Could have been accidental, could have been deliberate; just because the other vehicle didn't stop doesn't make it a contract job; people often don't stop if they think they can get away with it.

Next, he got fifty quid in his locker and six calculators. To bribe him into something, to pay him off for something, to set him up for something? He couldn't tell, and his exchange with Gleeson under the bonnet of the van had probably closed off finding out any more about that.

Next, there were two people working for Hendrick with criminal records. So – the sun still rises in the east.

Next, nothing more had been stolen since he got there. That

could mean that he'd been fingered; or that McKay had been the thief; or that there hadn't been anything particularly tempting since he'd arrived.

Next, he'd had a good look round the shed on his own, had gone through the accounts, kicked a few packing cases, snuffled about, and come up with nothing. He'd also sat outside a few houses and come up with nothing there too. Except . . .

Except that beyond this point it was all hypothesis, probably based on the fact that he disliked Mrs Boseley as unreservedly as she did him. And some prejudice like that always got the old hypotheses scurrying off in all directions.

Mrs Boseley kept a photograph of Mr Dalby in her office drawer; face down. Mrs Boseley went up to Dude's with her hair loose, and stayed there an hour. Mr Dalby – he'd checked in his notebook – was one of Hendrick Freight's regular customers. Mr Dalby popped the odd capsule of amyl nitrate before getting on the job; perhaps he had ignition trouble. So what else was new? And what did a really smart fellow conclude from this set of facts? That Mrs Boseley was having an affair with Mr Dalby, which was quite understandable: if you lived in Rayners Lane with an invalid husband and had once had a fruity career as a stewardess, wouldn't you occasionally fancy putting your hair down and taking a trip into town? It would be worth driving all that way for *that*, wouldn't it? It always seemed to be. Duffy had driven further himself. And this would explain why the photo was face down – the touch of shame, the decorum of adultery. And as for only staying an hour, well, the girl had given Duffy the lowdown on Mr Dalby's brevity of indulgence. Besides, he had a business to run, especially at the time Mrs Boseley had called: must get out there and keep the girls hitting those bells. Duffy felt almost sorry for Mrs Boseley.

Argued this way, the hypothesis – and Duffy's assumption that there were two strands of action at Hendrick Freight, not one – fell apart. The only thing that made him want to keep on nagging at it was his dislike for Mrs Boseley's character and Mr Dalby's prices. Fifty quid – no, fifty-four quid – for a hand-job, a small amount of champagne and a whisky which you could only see was there because it was coloured brown; ask for a vodka at the bar and they could give you an empty glass and you wouldn't be able to tell the difference.

So, what had seemed, in the exhilaration of drink and spending someone else's money and not having his clothes laughed at and feeling like getting lucky, to be some sort of a break, now struck Duffy as little more than an extra insight into the way shits lived. Nothing more than that. If he wanted to hold on to the job – and it did keep him off the streets – he would either have to find out more, or make something happen.

Or both, perhaps. At lunchtime he rang Willett and invited himself over after work for a question-and-answer session; still just background work, but maybe with a more precise focus than before. And in the afternoon he got down to some thinking about the morning's telephone conversation with his irritatingly logical employer. Hendrick said there hadn't been a theft since Duffy was hired, and his tone seemed almost complaining. Well, if a client wanted a theft, who was Duffy to stand in his way?

'Catch any stuffers this week?' asked Duffy as they sipped coffee in the bazaar of the imperial city. Willett gave a creased smile.

'No – couple I wouldn't have minded having a good rummage in, though.' He gave his old Waterguard's grin. 'Best thing that happened was to a mate of mine down at Gatwick. Bit of old Pakki-smuggling.'

'That still going on?'

'Sure – God knows why, but they still want to come. Costs them about five thousand each, too, that's the going rate. Some of them do it on H.P. – you know, something down at the start, and then a few quid a week over twenty years or so. Twenty years when the guy they're paying can decide to up his rate, or just turn them in if he gets bored. They must really want to come.'

'Well, it's a Tory paradise here, isn't it?'

'I'll ignore that one, Duffy. Some of them, of course, never get here. They get as far as Rotterdam, hand over all their money, and then the little boat in the night never turns up; the decent chap who promised to help them and told them how scandalous the immigration laws were has just buggered off. There's a lot of penniless Pakkis in Rotterdam.' He nodded sagely, as if advising Duffy not to go off and join them.

'Anyway, this mate of mine down in Gatwick. He has this great container of stuff to search. All jumbled up. You know, you can hire part of a container, you don't have to have the lot, and this one had been split up among lots of firms, and there were all sorts of cases and packages and whatnot in it, and it was pissing down with rain, and he really thought, you know, you get those nights sometimes – he thought What *am* I doing here? So he just bashes on this big cabinet and says, "You all right in there?" and a Pakki voice comes back, "Yes, fine, thank you very much".'

Duffy burst out laughing, then guiltily tried to calm down as a tiny Asian cleaning-woman floated past. It was pathetic, of course, and all that; but it was fucking funny as well.

'That's the way it is, you see,' went on Willett. 'The blokes we're dealing with are either too clever by half, or they're so thick you feel sorry for them. And even the ones who are normally clever often turn thick when they decide to smuggle something; they're just not up to it. Take all the Iranians we were picking up last year. Bloody smart back in their own country, doing well, nice pot of money, then along comes the old Ayatollah Whatsit. Bad news, time to leave. Only trouble is, currency restrictions: you can leave, the old man says, but two Crunchy bars each, that's the limit. So they think, aha, well, we won't take it out in money, let's take it out in heroin, after all the Ayatollah doesn't think much to that anyway, so he isn't going to mind us taking some with us.

'They fill up a suitcase, bung in the heroin, jump on a plane, and turn up here. And what do we see? One wealthy Iranian businessman in a lightweight suit, straight off a flight from Teheran, just a small case and sweating like a pig. He's only just realised that if we catch him and pop him back on the next plane, it's not going to be Oh, you are a naughty boy, it's going to be a couple of quick paragraphs from the Koran, and then Bang bang. So the fellows with gold rings round their sleeves take a quick dekko at him, then look at each other and say, "After you, Claud; no, after you, Cecil".'

Duffy nodded, and got down to business.

'If I was you . . . No, if I was *me* and looking for something, where would I look?'

'That's a bit vague.'

'If I thought something was coming in, but didn't know what it was.'

'That's still too vague, Duffy. I mean, you'd have to use your nose, wouldn't you? And you can only learn nose, so that wouldn't be much good. Still, if you want to know, you start by standing there and seeing how people react to you as they go past.'

'It's hard to do that with freight.'

'Ah, now he mentions it. Well, freight's always a bugger. There's the very occasional tip-off, and the usual amount of luck, which means not very much. And grey matter still works. Sometimes you spot something suspicious when you go round a shed.'

'For instance?'

'Well, say there's something wrapped up in hessian, you might give it a gentle kick, put the toe-cap in, and see how it feels underneath. Normally you'd expect cardboard. So if you feel metal underneath, you start wondering: why wrap something in hessian when it's already in a tin box? So you might very well want to take a gander.

'Or you might get a line on things from the documentation. Why is someone importing four thousand cuddly toys from

Ghana when you happen to know there isn't a cuddly-toy industry in Ghana? You're looking for things that don't feel right. Why is someone bothering to import something when the shipping costs exceed the declared value of the goods? That sort of thing.'

'Lots of paperwork.'

'Well, we do have LACES. The computer.'

'But a computer can't tell you what to search.'

'You'd be surprised. I mean, often that's exactly what it does do. It sorts the stuff into channels for us – like the green and red channels for passengers. With freight it's Channel One, scrutiny of documents; Channel Two, scrutiny of documents and examination of cargo; Channel Three, clearance within one hour.'

'How does it decide?'

'Well, every airline gives us a cargo manifest for every flight, saying what they're carrying, and we feed it into LACES. We have a read-through of it at the same time – the cargo's usually still in the air at the time, sometimes it hasn't even left – and if we spot something we think we ought to take a look at, we key in a 97. That's an inhibitor: tells the computer to route the cargo to Channel Two, which is then done automatically.

'But it does a lot by itself as well. There's a whole lot of things keyed in all the time: suspect importers, for instance, or cargo from what we call the Badlands. All new importers are picked out automatically the first couple of times, and so are any one-offs that come through. Plus what I just told you about: if the declared value of the goods being shipped is less than the shipping costs, the computer turns that up for us, and we take a look. Often that means quite innocuous things get examined, like samples of booze being sent from a factory abroad back to the home country for analysis. Still, it's a useful check.'

'What about random sampling?'

'Oh, the computer does that for us too. It diverts something like one per cent through Channel Two on a purely random basis. We get a printout, an E1, telling us the reason the stuff's been picked out. Then we take a look.'

'Hm.' This might have made things easier for the likes of Willett, but it didn't seem to help Duffy much. 'So nobody smart would use a one-off shipment for smuggling? They'd know you'd look more closely at it.'

'They might, yes, if they knew how we worked. But then . . .'

' . . . ?'

'Well, it's all bluff and double-bluff, isn't it? I mean, sure we look at the one-offs as a matter of routine. But we also have to look at the regular stuff just because it's regular. You have to be always on the hop. It's like them being either very clever or very thick. Or like the way they hide stuff. To start with, they put things in the least obvious place, then for a bit in the most obvious place, then back in the least obvious place.'

'What would you look for if you were me?'

'Well, I don't know. You're still vague as vague. But if you know what you're looking for, then you can work a bit from the origin of the goods and their destination. And it's always a good idea to look out for something that's being freighted unnecessarily. I mean, it's expensive, air freight: so you should think, Why are they importing this fruit from Ghana when they can get it more cheaply from Italy, or wherever, so you have a bit of a rummage and maybe you find something. It's like that big drugs haul they had down at London docks. There were a couple of Volkswagens coming in on a boat from Malaysia; perfectly normal, all the papers were O.K., no problems. Except one of the officers thought: Why are they importing these two rather old Beetles when the shipping costs are greater than the cost of buying similar cars over here? So they stripped them down and found them full of Chinese Number Three.'

Duffy felt the conversation was drifting in one particular direction; that was the one he'd intended, but he thought he'd better clear some ground first. He went and got them a couple more coffees.

'Let me start at another angle. What do they kill for? What do they think about killing for?'

'Oh – varies. Depends how nasty they are. Depends what you've done to them. Depends how easy it is to do it. I don't come across it myself, but then I wouldn't.'

'Gold?'

'Nnnn. Not much of that about nowadays. Most of the money stuff is all paperwork. You know, altering documents so that the goods appear to have come from one place instead of another; then you pay less import duty or whatever. That sort of thing. Gold's really tight nowadays. Not like the Fifties – that was the Gold Rush. You'd have pilots and stewardesses with special shirts, everyone was mad and greedy; just one run, they'd say, and I can retire. Just one run. And sometimes they'd try and take a double load, and just keel over with nerves. Or heat. One chap I remember, keeled over on the tarmac at Calcutta Airport. Shirt pockets full of gold. Got seven years in Calcutta jail. Lasted a couple, then just died. Poor bugger.'

'Porn?'

'No. It's not that nasty a business, from what I hear. Not that I see too much – the big shipments come in by road. It's so heavy. We don't get much here except private consumption stuff: half a dozen fladge mags down the Y-fronts, that sort of thing.'

'So, if – and it's only if as far as I know – someone, say, arranged an accident for someone, then, unless it was personal, it might be what . . . drugs?' After the meandering of the sentence Duffy pronounced the last word sharply.

'There's more *ifs* in that sentence than when I'm trying to get the wife into bed, Duffy.'

'Well, let's assume some ifs.'

'O.K., what do you want to know?'

'Where would I look?'

269

'Turn it round. You're not you, you're them. Where would *you* put it?'

'Dunno, that's why I asked you.'

'Well, think about it.' Willett suddenly seemed severe, as if Duffy were one of his stumbling assistant officers who'd just let the French Connection through. 'You tell me how you'd bring it through, and I'll tell you an improvement on what you suggest.' He was proposing a game, Duffy realised. He sipped his coffee and imagined himself – with extreme difficulty – on a plane descending to Heathrow. *All* 256 passengers . . . was what came into his head.

'I'd . . . I'd have a special pocket sewn in my clothes.'

'Go to Pakistan,' said Willett dismissively. 'They'll sell you ready-made shoes, all built up with special compartments in the heels and soles. Buy them with or without the dope inside. Of course, we'd pick you up straight away. Had one only the other day: Pakki and his small son, teetering along, both wearing them. Walking awkwardly, but never looking at their feet. No problem.'

'I'd dress smart and walk through the customs next to a hippie.'

'Not bad – if you can find one on your flight. They're not as common as they used to be. I'll tell you a better one. You hire a couple of couriers, one smart, one a bit scruffy; actually, it doesn't matter what they look like, but you need two. You give a small amount of stuff to one, and all the rest to the other. Then you tip off the customs about the first guy. They wouldn't think there'd be *two* couriers on the same flight.'

Duffy was impressed. Willett meant him to be.

'I'd bring it in by car.'

'What, in the boot? Don't make me laugh. Not when compressed cannabis resin can be shaped like fibreglass. You can get yourself a whole new car wing. Like in *Goldfinger* – only much more plausible.'

'I'd . . . fly in from some unsuspicious airport.'

'There aren't any. All airports are suspicious. You might

have two passports, though – one to get you to Paris and back like a weekender and one to fly you on from there to pick up the stuff. That's quite clever.'

'I'd check in two suitcases with identical sets of clothes, one with the stuff in. Then if I were stopped, I could go back to the carousel and pick up the other suitcase.' Duffy was quite pleased with this, but Willett only chuckled.

'Moses was busting them with that trick crossing the Red Sea. What about the baggage tickets? Anyway, you're only allowed one bag each on a lot of flights nowadays. What's more, if you did, you wouldn't put the same clothes in each case. The case you left on the carousel would have *your* clothes in; the one you took through should be full of dirty knickers and Tampax spilling out when we opened it, so that it *obviously* wasn't yours. How about that?'

There was a competitive light in Willett's eye. Duffy felt the rules of the game were a bit unfair. After all, he'd never even been in a plane, and wasn't going to start now. He said rather grumpily,

'I give up.'

'They don't.'

No doubt Willett was trying to teach him something. No doubt he was right to try to do so. Duffy gave his friend the benefit.

'So where do I look?'

'I wish there was an easy answer. You look everywhere. There's nowhere it can't be – within reason. If it's cannabis, then it's bulky, you've got that on your side. But if it's hard stuff . . . You can get half a million quid's worth of heroin between the back light of a car and the boot. That's where you'd have to be looking, and that's what it's worth to them to hide it.'

'The hardest places.'

'And the easiest places. And the hard–easy places. What do opium sticks make you think of? Cigarettes, right. So you wouldn't look for them there. We had opium sticks the other month hidden inside the cigarettes in a sealed carton of duty-free Marlboro, which as far as anybody could see had been bought in transit at Frankfurt.'

'Has anything changed much since I was last chasing the stuff? Like where it comes from. Is the Golden Triangle still producing as hard as ever?'

'It's a quadrangle, Duffy. Bits of Red China as well. No, the stuff's just the same – only there's more of it. Iran's pretty well closed down – I suppose you have to hand that to the old Ayawhatsit. But as against that, the Pakkis have just cracked how to refine theirs much better. Their stuff used to be crummy, I expect you remember; the best was only about thirty per cent. Now they've made the breakthrough: it's up to ninety, all of a sudden. Swings and roundabouts, isn't it – except that they're making the roundabouts go faster.'

Duffy felt glum. Five, six, seven years ago he'd pounded up and down Gerrard Street, in and out through the Chinese area of Soho like one keen young copper. He used to imagine wizened old Chinamen in back rooms puffing dreamily away at opium pipes, only disturbed by the zealous young Duffy bursting through the door, truncheon in hand, quipping, 'Not Rothman's Number Two again, sir?' It had all seemed picturesque; at first, anyway. He used to stroll along Gerrard thinking: Down these chow mein streets a man must go. None of it had hit home until a couple of years later.

'Dead babies,' said Willett sharply. Duffy looked up, and saw no longer the familiar garrulous old joker, but a serious customs officer.

'Dead babies,' he repeated. 'I can imagine what you're thinking, Duffy, and I've had it a lot of times myself. I'll never find it, you think. What's the point – if they want it that badly, let them have it. I catch myself going down that track sometimes, and I always stop myself before I get too far by thinking about dead babies.' He took a swig of coffee. 'You'll remember there's quite a lot of heroin goes across the border between Thailand and Malaysia? Well, couple of years ago the smugglers came up with a new system. They buy babies. Sometimes they kidnap them, but often they just buy them: they say there's some rich, childless woman in Singapore wants to adopt a kid. Why shouldn't a poor peasant sell one of hers; she's got enough and some over. So the peasant sells one: seems a good opportunity, like sending the kids to college. But of course they don't ever get to this imaginary rich childless woman in Bangkok. The smugglers kill them, take out their internal organs, and stuff them with bags of heroin. Then they give them to a "mother" who cradles them in their sleep and carries them over the border. Simple as that.'

Duffy felt sick, but Willett hadn't finished. 'Of course, it's got to look as natural as possible. So they only use babies which are under two years old – otherwise their sleeping pattern might seem unusual. And the other thing is – don't forget this, I don't – they always have to be got across the border within twelve hours of being killed. Otherwise the colour will have drained out of their faces and they won't be any use.'

Duffy didn't need the details – he didn't need them at all; but he knew it was good for him to have them, however sick they made him feel. Willett certainly knew how to get to him. So all he said was,

'Thanks.'

The only thing that stopped Duffy brooding at work the next day was planning his switch. From among the clients who regularly came to collect their own goods he picked out his target: a couple of pile-it-high, sell-it-cheap hifi villains. They were full of shoulder-slapping, bracelet-chinking, fell-off-the-back-of-a-lorry bonhomie, and wouldn't think twice about anything that came their way by mistake; in Duffy's opinion, they thought honesty was just a plant that grew in the garden.

Their pile of hifi equipment came in to a regular bay in the shed, quite near Duffy's corner; so far he'd always been the one instructed to load their van. In the course of the day, while seemingly doing no more than he was told to, Duffy managed to shift a small case of Japanese cigarette lighters across the shed until it was in the bay next to the hifi equipment.

The whole of Hendrick Freight always heard them coming: they drove with the side doors of their transit van hooked back, and Capital Radio at full blast. Their arrival was the nearest thing to an event in the week of loading and unloading. If the flashier of the two was driving, he'd always look for little patches of oil on the floor of the shed, and try to put the van into a skid by stamping on the brakes.

Towards the end of the afternoon they arrived with a roar and a squeal, backed the van up to their bay, turned the engine off but left the radio on. With a 'Hiya, wack' at Duffy they clattered off to flirt as successfully as anyone could with Mrs Boseley, and in the process exchange receipts with her. Duffy loaded up six boxes of tape-decks, six boxes of turntables, six boxes of tuners, six boxes of amplifiers, and one smaller case of Japanese cigarette lighters, from which he quickly ripped off the documentation: didn't want to give them an attack of conscience, however unlikely. He stuck the lighters between the turntables and the side of the van, so that they would be invisible when Gleeson checked off his list.

The hifi villains clattered out of Mrs Boseley's office, Gleeson wandered over with a clipboard and checked the van, the driver shouted, 'Didn't forget the smoked salmon, did you, wack?' at Duffy, who bellowed, 'It's under the seat', in reply, and they roared off. What they would make of the place where the lighters were stuffed Duffy didn't know; in all likelihood they didn't unload themselves; there was probably an old man with two withered arms employed to do that for them.

The lighters were due to be picked up the next day, and they were in Casey's area of the shed; so Duffy didn't need to worry about that. It could take care of itself.

With the switch safely concluded, and not much work for the rest of the day, Duffy started brooding again. He found himself gazing across at Mrs Boseley's blonde hair in the glass office and thinking violent, unprofessional thoughts for which there was at present no possible justification. All because Mr Dalby occasionally snorted a little coke before screwing his hostesses, and because Willett had told him various unpleasant truths.

Duffy's moral outlook had always been pragmatic. Three years in the force had made it more so, and it wasn't going to change now. He wasn't idealistic about the law, or about how it was implemented. He didn't mind a bit of give-and-take, a bit of blind-eye, a bit of you-naughty-boy-on-yer-bike and forget it. He didn't think the ends justified the means – except that sometimes, just occasionally, they did. He didn't believe all crimes were equal; some he couldn't get worked up about. But always, at the back, there were absolutes. Murder was one, of course, everyone agreed on that. Bent coppers was one; but then, Duffy had a little private experience of that, and could be expected to feel strongly. Rape was one; Duffy was disgusted how some coppers thought it was little more than a mild duffing up with a bit of pleasure thrown in. And heroin was one as well.

Seven years ago, Duffy had thought about sweet old Chinamen puffing away in poppy dreams; but he didn't think of that now. And Willett hadn't needed to push him with the dead babies, because Duffy was more or less there already, ever since Lesley. He'd laughed at the idea of Pakkis tripping over their built-up shoes, but it didn't mean he wouldn't cut their legs off at the ankles given half the chance. He knew all those colourful Chinese phrases they used about smoking heroin – chasing the dragon, playing the mouth organ, shooting the anti-aircraft gun – but they didn't charm Duffy; not since Lesley.

She had been a pretty, long-faced, serious-looking girl with dark hair and large eyes who had lived in the same block of flats as he had shortly after he'd been kicked out of the force. He vaguely fancied her but didn't do anything about it because he was all crazy from the shock of breaking up with Carol and the best he could do at the time was trail madly back to the Caramel

Club and drink too much and pick up any old rubbish and do whatever they wanted. She vaguely fancied him but didn't do anything about it because she was a junkie.

He remembered how avuncular, how responsible it had made him feel when she told him. He had a romantic picture of the two of them, bruised by the world, mending each other's hurts. Then she stole his camera. She came back and told him how sorry she was, it was just a question of priorities, and weighing her need against his camera there was really no argument. He accepted it immediately, it wasn't even a matter where he had to 'forgive' her or anything; he simply hadn't realised that junkies had weak characters. Now he knew; now he'd be prepared.

For an addict she was comparatively in control of her life. That's to say, she started thinking about what she needed to do to support her habit at least a day before her supplies ran out. Sometimes she stole; sometimes she worked in a massage parlour; sometimes she managed to get modelling jobs. Duffy continued to like her just as much as when they'd first met. Then she stole his tape recorder; and this time she was quite a bit less sorry. Why had he left it lying around his flat like that? He knew she only had to nick his duplicate key to get at it.

Sometimes she went off for cures which her family arranged, but always she came back. Her legs got thinner and her eyes got bigger; even the freckles on her face seemed to get bigger, stretching themselves into blotches. Her flat got filthier and her carpet began to stink. The carpet stank because when she pulled the syringe out of her arm with its residue of blood, she'd clean it by filling it up with water and then squirting it with a giggle at the patterns in the weave.

Duffy moved away because he knew that the cure rate for heroin addicts was one in ten, and that Lesley was going to be one of the nine. He moved away because he feared doing everything he could to help and still failing. It wasn't a decision he was proud of, but the self-obsession and weakness of addicts is catching: how can I defend *my*self, you begin to think after a while. He moved away because he was fond of her and didn't ever want to hear that she had died. She was twenty-two.

At one end of the chain there were dead babies in Thailand; at the other end there were Lesleys fixing themselves to death. She'd told him once that her one great fear wasn't dying, but that soon she'd have nowhere left to fix. The veins in her arms had gone; the veins in her legs had gone; she was fixing in her wrists and hands at the moment, which was more painful than she'd imagined possible. Soon, she said, she'd be fixing in her groin.

Duffy thought he'd hang around Hendrick Freight for a bit longer; just in case.

6

The next afternoon there was a sudden bustle at work. Duffy was looking down the shed from his dunce's corner when Mrs Boseley came skidaddling out of her office, pushing the door open with her right hand and still clutching the telephone in her left.

'Gleeson,' she yelled, 'GLEESON.'

She went back into her office and shut the door. Duffy could see her phone conversation taking a rather animated course for the next couple of minutes. Then she put the phone down, Gleeson arrived, and they closeted themselves together for a good ten minutes. After that Mrs Boseley picked up the phone again and made a call. Gleeson came out of the office and strode over to Casey's area of the shed. Duffy concluded that things were looking up. He ambled over himself. As he arrived, Casey was ripping open the top two press-buttons of his shirt. He pointed to the CUT HERE and made a slicing motion with the edge of his hand.

'Guides' honour,' he said, and did a wolf-cub salute to Gleeson.

'Fucking look some more,' said Gleeson.

Duffy coughed.

'Excuse me, Mr Gleeson. Anything the matter?'

'Fuck off, Duffy.'

'Anything I can do to help?'

'Fuck off, Duffy.'

He turned and began to wander off.

'No, just a minute. Help Casey search. Two half-brains are better than one, I suppose.'

'Charming,' muttered Duffy as Gleeson marched off to consult Mrs Boseley again.

'What are we looking for?'

'Case of sparks.'

'Ah. Get lost, did it?'

Casey didn't answer except by kicking a tea chest. Duffy assumed that meant Yes. Kick the tea chest for Yes; punch the packing-case for No; butt your head against the refrigerated container for Don't Know. That was probably the local vocabulary.

'Who were they for?'

'Mucks.' This was presumably Casey's abbreviation for Muxton and Walker.

'Who loaded them?'

Casey grunted indeterminately, but Duffy already knew the answer.

'Who signed them out?'

'Gleeson.'

'Who drove them?'

'Gleeson.'

Better and better, Duffy thought. He hadn't counted on that bonus. Normally, if the customer didn't collect, one of Hendrick's two drivers delivered the goods. That day, one of them had been off sick, the other had a heavier schedule as a result, and that morning Gleeson had obviously decided to do the delivery to Muxton's himself.

Duffy was still pretending to help Casey look for the missing case of sparks when a bottle-green XJ6 drove into the shed and parked in the most inconvenient place. Hendrick got out, looking extremely pissed off. After ten minutes in the eyrie, he, Mrs Boseley and Gleeson all came over to the area where Duffy, Casey, and now Tan as well were pretending to search. They were only pretending now, because they'd combed the

279

whole of Casey's area twice and it was perfectly obvious that the sparks had flown – upwards or wherever.

'Afternoon, Mr Hendrick,' said Duffy as the three of them arrived. He was, after all, meant to be his ex-odd-job-man. 'Sorry to hear about this spot of bother.'

'Fuck off, Duffy,' said Gleeson before his boss could open his mouth, 'just fuck off back to your corner.'

Duffy tried looking phlegmatic, as if this was the sort of way Gleeson always treated him (not that it wasn't), in the hope that Hendrick might give his shed foreman a little talking-to about industrial relations. It was a distant hope; but Duffy's line in such circumstances was, Anything to stir it a bit.

As he stood in his corner he thought what he'd give for a duplicate set of invoices for the goods freighted to Dude's. He'd taken a good scout round in the course of the day, and read lots of bits of documentation stuck to cases, and loitered for a while in the refrigerated section in case he could make out the flowers whose scent was destined to be drowned by joss-sticks; but all to no avail.

At 5.30 he was changing by his locker when Tan came up to him.

'Mrs Boseley want see you before you go,' he said.

Aha. A regal audience. He finished changing, and bounded up the steps to her office.

'Oh, take a seat, please, Duffy. I won't be a minute.'

She bent over some paperwork and appeared to be adding up a line of figures. She did it once; she did it twice; then she sighed, and fished out a calculator from her top drawer. Duffy noticed that it was the same brand as the six he had left behind the cistern in the Gents, but he didn't jump to any conclusions. Or rather, he jumped to them straight away, and then rejected them. Whatever Mrs Boseley was messing with, he guessed, it wouldn't be just a little something to help her do her sums.

He glanced round her office. It looked much like any man's office, except that there wasn't a girlie calendar. Why didn't they make dirty calendars with men on them? All they seemed to make, if Mrs Boseley was anything to go by, was National Trust calendars.

Hey, come on, I've been here ten minutes, I could be dodging the jumbos on the M4 by now. He looked out into the shed. The double doors were closed for the night. Everyone seemed to have gone home. Except for him and Mrs Boseley. What *did* the E stand for? Elizabeth? Elspeth? Eva? Yes, probably Eva – changed her name to that of her great heroine, Eva Braun. Dyed her hair to look as Aryan as possible. What did she want to see him for? he wondered. She couldn't . . . oh no, that would be silly, wouldn't it? That would be just too corny. Handsome lady office manager falls for muscular young manual worker. Her initial air of frostiness only a poor, sad mask to hide the feelings which lurked within her . . . Secretly, she longed to . . .

Come on, Duffy, that's enough of that. And if she did, you know what you'd be? Sodding embarrassed for a start. You wouldn't know where to put yourself. You've never exactly appealed to that type of lady, have you? Not exactly a regular feature of your track record, are they?

So it was a surprise when Mrs Boseley finally laid down her calculator, looked up, and smiled. She did look better when she smiled, there was no denying that. The only fly in the ointment was that she wasn't smiling at Duffy; she was smiling past his shoulder.

'All locked up,' said Gleeson. The phrase gave Duffy a jolt: it took him straight back to his early days in the force, when he found such lines gave him an extra bit of swagger. 'On yer bike,' he'd gruff at a clearly bikeless hobo curled round the remnants of a bottle of sweet sherry; 'Yer locked up,' he'd shout at some particularly nasty bit of fighting rough, and just pray he didn't get the reply, 'You and who else?'

Duffy hoped he didn't show any reaction to Gleeson; hoped he just carried on staring with dulcet expectation at Mrs Boseley, as if she were about to award him a wage rise. When he heard Gleeson turning the key, however, he thought he had the right of any other normal citizen to swivel in his chair and issue a long, puzzled glance. Gleeson pocketed the key and came and stood behind Duffy's chair. Duffy didn't like that. It reminded him of the sort of coppers who enjoyed doing that to people they were questioning; and it reminded him of what occasionally happened when they did.

'Any complaints, Mrs Boseley?' he enquired, like any other normal employee who's been kept late, locked in, and has a big man with mutton-chops standing right behind his chair. She didn't deign to reply. Don't give up, he said to himself, keep the dialogue going – that's what they said whenever there were those street sieges, wasn't it? 'We are keeping the dialogue going with the gunmen.' Duffy decided to keep the dialogue going. It didn't strike him who was taking which role.

'I hope there haven't been, Mrs Boseley. Any complaints, I mean. I'm really enjoying my work here, you know. I meant to pop by and say so only the other day, but I looked in your office, and you were . . . you were on the phone.'

Mrs Boseley finally seemed to be giving attention to his presence, though not, as far as he could tell, to his words. She looked as if she were going to speak. He waited dutifully. She couldn't be going to sack him, could she?

'You're a man of many talents, Mr Duffy.'

Oh, well he didn't expect her to say *that*. If only Gleeson weren't there he might think she *was* about to make a pass at him.

'Yes, M'm?' Why did he never know what to call her?

'Principal among which, in my view, is the ability to mow concrete.'

'. . .?'

'You mow concrete, Mr Duffy.' It was spoken in the tone of one reminding a recalcitrant child about a multiplication table. Nine sixes, you know you know nine sixes, Mr Duffy.

'Beg yours?'

'You mow concrete. Up and down. And all the concrete

clippings go into the concrete box on the front of the mower. Wuuuuaaah, Wuuuuuaaah,' went Mrs Boseley all of a sudden, imitating the noise of a lawn mower. 'Or maybe – maybe you use an electric: then of course you don't have a concrete box on the front do you? You just have a rotary thing, don't you, and all the little bits of concrete go flying out of the side, and you leave them lying on the top and that acts as a fertiliser. Is that what you use?'

Duffy was bewildered. She was cracking up. All that wielding of a watering can in Rayner's Lane had finally cracked her. He squirmed round in his seat and looked at Gleeson by way of enquiry, but he only seemed to be staring back at Mrs Boseley in a headily admiring fashion, as at some prophet who promised to teach him how *he* could part the waters, too, and no sweat. When Gleeson became aware of Duffy's movement he reached down a fat palm and twisted Duffy's head back to face Mrs Boseley.

'I think we're on different wavelengths, Mrs Boseley,' he stammered.

'No, I don't think so, Duffy. You mow concrete. At least I think you do. Let me put it to you directly: do you mow concrete, Mr Duffy?'

'NO,' he replied loudly. He'd had enough of this. She looked disappointed. At least, she acted looking disappointed, which wasn't at all the same thing.

'Oh dear, I'd quite counted on you mowing concrete. You see, you said you did at your interview.'

Duffy looked blank.

'I asked you what your qualifications were and you said you did odd jobs for Mr Hendrick. I asked you what. You said you . . . lifted things. I remember letting that pass, though I did want to ask whether your expertise extended to putting things down again as well, or whether we were being asked to hire someone who went around all the time with stuff stuck in his hands because he hadn't yet learnt about putting down. And then I asked you if you mowed Mr Hendrick's lawn.' Uh-huh,

283

thought Duffy, or rather he thought UH-FUCK-A-DUCK-HUH loud inside his head. 'And you said you did.' Duffy remembered the inexplicable sense of unease that he'd had when he'd visited Hendrick and looked out through his kitchen window at the children playing on the slide. Standing up on the top of it. Maybe he'd thought he was feeling uneasy about the kids falling off, but he wasn't; he must have been feeling uneasy about the future of Duffy.

'Now Mr Hendrick's lawn, as you would know if you had ever been anywhere near Mr Hendrick's house, is not made of the usual grass. Part of it is made of crazy paving and part is made of concrete. I engaged you, Mr Duffy, on the firm understanding that you could mow concrete. I'm very disappointed in you.'

'I'll learn,' Duffy found himself saying, 'I'm sure I can learn.' There was a faint, nasal snigger from behind him, a stern glance from Mrs Boseley which went over his shoulder, and then a hard, flat-handed clout across the top of his head from Gleeson. It hurt. It wouldn't have hurt at all if he'd known it was coming. That, doubtless, was the point.

'I don't think you'll learn quickly enough for me; it's a very difficult trade to learn. I don't think you'll master it quickly enough. If I hire a concrete-mower, Mr Duffy, I expect to get a concrete-mower. I'm afraid I'm going to have to dispense with your services.'

'Oh dear,' said Duffy. Oh dear not about being sacked – was he being, anyway? – but about the rest of it.

'But before you go, just tell us all about yourself.' Mrs Boseley put on what was quite clearly meant to be a violently insincere smile. She was quite an actress, Duffy had to hand it to her. Maybe it came from years of traipsing up and down the aisle with a 'Would you like tea or coffee, sir?' always on your lips, and getting pissed off with the fat men in bursting jackets with snowdrifts of dandruff on their shoulders quipping, 'I'd rather have you, darling' as if they were the first man ever to say it; and if at first you gave a polite half-amused smile, you would, after a few years of it and its equivalents, learn a real putdown of a smile, wouldn't you, a horrible parody of a smile, a fuck-you-Jack smile? Mrs Boseley had learnt one, anyway.

Gleeson hit him across the back of the head again. It hurt just as much as the first time.

'I'm just an ordinary fella,' he said.

'Who are you, Duffy?'

'I'm me.' It sounded weedy, lost.

'What are you, what do you do?'

'I'm me, I work, I work for you.' He put more pathos into it this time; it seemed to come quite naturally.

'You've never been to Mr Hendrick's house, have you?'

'Yes.'

Gleeson flat-slapped him again.

'You do something else, don't you?'

'No.'

'How did you meet Hendrick?' The 'Mr' had gone.

'I worked for him. Odd jobs.'

'Why were you loitering near the flowers today?'

'What?'

'Why were you loitering near the flowers today?'

'I don't know what you're talking about.'

'Why didn't you take the calculators?'

'I beg your pardon?'

'WHY DIDN'T YOU TAKE THE FUCKING CALCULATORS?' Mrs Boseley screamed at him. 'WHY DIDN'T YOU TAKE THE FUCKING CALCULATORS?' He hated that; he hated women screaming at him. He thought, That'll make Gleeson hit me again. But it didn't. It made Gleeson do something else instead. Something that made Duffy wish he'd been cuffed around the head after all. Something that made him feel altogether more uneasy.

It was a little click in his left ear, accompanied by a little pull on the lobe. He turned his head very slightly, and felt something cold against his flesh there. Out of the corner of his eye he saw Gleeson, who had moved round slightly to the side of him. When the second cold touch came, he worked out with no difficulty that Gleeson was gripping the gold stud in his left ear with a pair of pliers.

'Up,' said Gleeson, tugging gently with the pliers. Duffy didn't dispute the instruction. When he was standing, he was moved back a pace or two and his chair kicked away from behind him. Mrs Boseley came round from behind her desk and began to go through his pockets. He thought, briefly, of making a sudden dramatic leap at the woman, but he didn't fancy the consequences. And in any case, she was welcome to his pockets. Duffy wasn't smart for nothing. The notebook with the names of regular customers was at home; so was the spare key to the shed. She was welcome to a dirty handkerchief, some change, a small comb, a wallet which contained an out-of-date credit card and which was singularly lacking in little bits of white pasteboard announcing 'DUFFY SECURITY', a biro and half a packet of Opal Fruits. She piled all these between them on the desk.

'Down,' said Gleeson, kicking the chair back into Duffy's knees. He sat, a position which even without the local difficulty around his left ear gave Gleeson a considerable advantage. 'I might have to change hands now and then,' Gleeson informed him, 'But we won't try anything silly, will we?'

'I won't if you won't,' said Duffy.

'Right,' said Mrs Boseley, surveying the pile of Duffy's possessions as if she'd just tipped out half a dozen used contraceptives and a dead vole. 'Now let's start again.' Duffy looked at her with genuine apprehension. Part of this sprang from not knowing how to play it. He couldn't give them nothing. He couldn't give them everything up to his hypothesis. He'd better give them a bit, but not too much. And of course, how much he gave them depended a bit on Gleeson's activities round his left ear. Duffy was smart, but he was no braver than anyone else.

What he decided was, play it along for a bit, then as soon as Gleeson does anything that hurts, babble out all you're going to give them and then stick by it. Sticking by it was obviously going to be the tricky thing. What the pain, if it came, would be like, Duffy had no way of estimating. In fact, as he knew, you could pinch someone's earlobe quite hard and it didn't hurt; it was one of those semi-dead areas of the human body. So having his stud gripped by Gleeson's pliers didn't actually hurt – indeed, even the cold metal had now warmed up against his skin.

Or rather, it didn't hurt in his body. It hurt a lot in his mind. So it was better than it could have been and a lot worse, both at the same time. If Gleeson had been hurting him in a normal way – punching him in the face, say – and promising that it would get gradually worse until Duffy did or said something, then he'd know where he was, would be able to guess what he could endure. This way, it was the anticipation of pain, not present pain, that made him fearful; and that was a lot worse.

'Name?'

'Duffy.'

'What are you?'

'I work for you.'

'Where'd you meet Hendrick?'

'At his house.'

'Why were you loitering by the flowers?'

'I wasn'toooooooOOOOOOOWWWWWWWWWWWW.'

And that was just a little twist, a sudden half-turn on the pliers by Gleeson. It didn't feel very life-enhancing to Duffy.

'I never liked this fancy-boy's ear-ring of yours,' said Gleeson. 'But I never thought it would come in handy. That was just a little twist, just a little wiggle really. I wonder what would happen if I pulled a bit.'

Duffy thought, Shit, I hadn't known it was going to be like that. And knowing isn't going to make the next round any easier. I think it may be time to crack. He could feel Gleeson taking a fresh grip on the pliers. Yes, it's probably time to do the decent and crack.

'Name?'

'Duffy.'

He felt a little pull on his ear. Just a little pull hurt a great deal now. He closed his eyes as if he were making a last effort to hold himself together.

'What are you?'

He didn't answer, inviting another pull on the pliers, but not the sort of vicious, mind-blanking tug he'd get for an obvious lie, or for cheek. He wanted no more than a sort of this-is-a-reminder tug, the sort that would give him a justification for cracking. He got precisely that. He decided to crack.

'I run a security firm. Well, there's only me,' he babbled on. 'I'm a one-man band, I'm the firm, there's just me.' For that he got a sharp twist on the pliers, not quite a you-sodding-copper twist, but almost.

'Where'd you meet Hendrick?'

'In a club.'

'Why were you loitering by the flowers?'

'I was looking at the air waybills.'

He was pointing down at the desk, avoiding Mrs Boseley's eye in the way that villains who cracked avoided the copper's eyes: they told their shame to themselves, that was the theory, and the copper was just overhearing it. That way they still retained a scintilla of self-respect. Duffy's theory was slightly different: he could lie better with his head down.

'Right, now let's amplify things. Where was this club?'

'It's called the Alligator. It's in Fulham. It's a gay club. I met him there.'

Time for some broken-man-spills-all details. 'It's a nice place, very quiet, I was having a drink, he came in, we had a chat, he told me he was having thefts at work, I offered to help, he gave me the job. Then we decided to say I was his odd-job man, but I guess we didn't prepare our story well enough. I didn't think you'd interview me properly.'

'Odd-job man,' said Gleeson. 'I bet you were his odd-job man. Poof.' He switched the pliers to his left hand and belted Duffy again with his right. The blow jarred Duffy's head against the pliers; he thought he felt a trickle of blood easing its way down the side of his neck.

'Hey, lay off, will you. I'm answering. Lay off.' It was an appeal to Mrs Boseley, and it seemed to work.

'Yes, don't do that, Gleeson. There wasn't really any call for that.' She turned back to Duffy. 'And what did Hendrick say?'

'He said he'd been getting thefts. Fairly regular. About once a month. Said he didn't want to go to the police because they'd upset the shed.' A sudden thought came to Duffy: maybe Mrs Boseley had persuaded him not to go to the police? At first, anyway. And then maybe, after a while, he decided he'd go half-way.

'And what have you found out?'

'Well, it's got me rather baffled.' He didn't want them to think he was a particularly smart security man; and they were into a tricky area. 'I mean, I looked around a bit, and it seems to be a very efficiently run firm.'

'Spare us that,' said Mrs Boseley. Shit, overdoing the praise.

'Well, I mean *I* couldn't see how anyone could fiddle the system.' That put the blame back on his own slowness of mind, which was probably better by them. 'So I reckoned it was McKay. I reckoned he'd been using some system I couldn't work out because I wasn't around then. And that's as far as I'd got, except that now I suppose it must be Casey after all.' Though his head was still pointing at the little pile of his possessions on Mrs Boseley's blotter, he caught a glance on its way to Gleeson. *They'd* obviously thought it had been McKay as well; his switch yesterday had clearly thrown them.

'I don't think Casey's as thick as he looks. Did you know he'd got two O-levels? He told me over dinner. And the lighters went from his part of the shed. I don't know where the earlier stuff went from. But I reckon it's Casey. I was going to follow him home from work tonight, only I seem to have got held up.'

'Why were you loitering by the flowers?'

'I didn't know I was. I mean, no more than loitering by anywhere else. I was mooching around, working out the system, you know.' He very much didn't like the idea of telling them he thought there might be two fiddles, not one. But he had hopes. He had hopes he'd just about covered the exits. They were definitely worried by the latest theft, he could tell that. It had made them jumpy. He just had to keep them quiet, play them along a bit, and maybe he'd get out of the wood. That's what he thought.

'You're sacked, by the way.'

'What?'

'You're sacked. As of now.'

Duffy, rather to his surprise, said, 'Employment Protection Act.' He heard Gleeson give a nasal snigger of disbelief. 'Week's notice, I get a week's notice, I've got the right.'

'I don't think you've got any rights,' said Mrs Boseley. 'False pretences,' she added, as if quoting a subsection of the act.

'Week's notice,' repeated Duffy, as if quoting a different subsection. He didn't have the slightest idea what was in the act; and he guessed she didn't either. 'It's only fair. Week's notice. Then I might be able to stick it on Casey. And it wouldn't surprise the others so much. I think another week here and I could really stick it on Casey.' This was his best line. Presumably they knew, or at least thought, that McKay had been the thief; they'd had him crashed to stop him drawing attention to Hendrick Freight; and now they were jumpy that it might not have been McKay after all. Crashing two out of a firm of eight would be a bit much, even by their standards. But letting Duffy land Casey might appeal to them. 'You can sack me first thing tomorrow,' he said. 'I'll be late. Give me a week's notice in front of everyone.'

Mrs Boseley was thinking it over. Duffy thought he was almost home and dry.

'And you met Hendrick in a gay club?'

'Yes.'

'Are you . . . gay, as you call it?'

'Yes . . . sometimes.'

'And is Hendrick gay, as you put it?'

'Yes . . . sometimes.'

'Whatjer mean, *sometimes*?' said Gleeson ferociously from

behind him. 'You're a fucking poof or you aren't a fucking poof. You can't be both.'

Duffy should have said, Yes, sorry, Gleeson, you know about these things much better than me, I made a mistake, I am a fucking poof, that's the long and the short of it, I've always been a fucking poof, I am a fucking poof, a whole poof, and nothing but a poof. Instead, thinking he was home and dry, and so not thinking, he said,

'It's been scientifically proved that all men are to some degree bisexual.'

Half his head came off. First his ear came away completely, then half his jawbone, and a litter of teeth, and one eye and most of his nose and a good part of his brain. That was what it felt like. In fact, Gleeson had merely tugged on the pliers with the long clean pull of a gardener starting a motor mower. Duffy put his left hand up to his ear, beyond screaming, and felt the blood drip into his palm. And while his head was very slowly shuffling back into position, he felt the pliers clamp on his right earlobe, the naked one, the only one he had left. Oh my Christ, he thought. Gleeson bent to that ear and whispered,

'Not me, poof. Not fucking me.'

Duffy slowly looked up at Mrs Boseley. She didn't look in the least surprised. She didn't look pleased or displeased. She stared at him as if he were a newscaster on the television. He reached out his left hand, palm upwards, showing the blood; but all she did was pick his handkerchief off the blotter and hand it over to him. He swaddled it over his left ear and feared for his other one. Gleeson was holding it in a firmer grip than was absolutely necessary; but then he would, wouldn't he?

Fortunately, Mrs Boseley had made up her mind.

'You'll be late for work tomorrow, you'll be given a week's notice, you'll clear up Casey within that week, and you'll stay out of our way. That's enough, Gleeson, really; I wish you didn't enjoy it so much.'

The grip on his ear relaxed, then disappeared. Duffy wanted to say either, Thank you very much indeed, or, I'll fucking fix you, but wisely stuck to a middle course and stayed silent. He stood up, gathered his things from the blotter and stuffed them into his blouson. He heard the office door being unlocked behind him, but he didn't look at it, or at either of them. He clasped his handkerchief to his ear, ducked through the door, crossed the shed, pulled open the side door and went out into the evening. He thought that it would be night, that this was the only thing it would decently know how to be, after what he had been through. But it wasn't. It was still, cheekily, a bright, clear evening, and another fucking jumbo was coming in to land.

The houseman who stitched his ear at Uxbridge Hospital smelled faintly of lavender water.

'Well, it's not the best place to stitch, but then again it's not the worst. I don't need to tell you what the worst is.'

Duffy just wanted him to get on with it. He'd waited an hour and a half in casualty already, piqued that his injury was judged so unimportant, and that any old housewife who rolled up with half a television set embedded in her stomach could immediately jump the queue.

'ow,' he said, loudly. He'd run out of the day's stock of courage and didn't care any more.

'Yes, well it would,' said the houseman. 'You know, it's odd you coming in with this. I don't think I've ever done an ear before.' Thanks a lot, just fucking shut up and get on with it. 'And I did my first nose only a few weeks ago.'

I don't want to hear about it, Duffy thought; just tell me about a nice clean aircrash instead, to keep my mind off things. '*All* 246,000 passengers aboard a pedal cycle of Cockroach Airways were killed this afternoon when . . . '

'I'd never done a nose before. Very nasty; all sort of sliced through as if someone had cut it with a penknife. Mind you, that was the least of his troubles. He'd been in a terrible car smash, and he was, ooh, in a shocking state, but they patched him up, all except for his nose. I suppose it must have been hidden under the oxygen mask or something. Anyway, I got the hang of it eventually. I dare say I will with this. How did you get it?'

'I got it.' Duffy had already told the casualty registrar various lies, so that he wouldn't think it was a criminal injury and feel obliged to ring the police. Something about an ear-ring catching in a fence as he was running along. No, he didn't have the ring for the registrar to examine. He didn't have his stud either, for that matter.

'You don't have to tell me if you don't want to.' No, of course I don't. Duffy felt tired. Still, who gives a stuff one way or the other.

'I wear a stud in it. Some people who don't like me pulled it out,' he said.

'Oh God,' said the houseman, and carried on poking with a needle that felt the size of an oar. 'Well, I think we should all stick together,' he added, leaning a bit more heavily on Duffy's shoulder. The smell of lavender water recurred. Duffy smiled very faintly to himself.

'I think I'm feeling just a bit tired tonight,' he said.

'Did they do something to the other as well?' asked the houseman. 'There's a bruise coming up.'

Duffy felt tired, but it wasn't depressed-tired, so he didn't let it count. His ear throbbed. The houseman had wrapped the bottom half of it tenderly in cotton wool and gauze and plastered it down. Duffy glanced in the mirror and thought he looked like Van Gogh.

He drove back to his flat in Acton and turned round in two minutes. All he needed was his key and his notebook. Then he started back towards Heathrow. He normally made a bit on petrol, but he doubted he would on this job: too much town driving, too much stop-and-start, and then full pelt down the motorway. He was usually late getting up in the mornings, and a steady, petrol-hoarding forty-five became out of the question. Tomorrow he could dawdle, though. Tomorrow he could be as late as he fancied. He could cheek Mrs Boseley as well if he wanted. Might as well be sacked for a wolf . . .

He reached the shed and let himself in with the key as softly as possible, just in case Gleeson was Black-and-Deckering his way through a few more recalcitrant employees. It was all quiet. He neutered the alarm system and padded across to Mrs Boseley's eyrie. Inside, he looked for traces of what had happened only hours before. Was that a drop of blood on the carpet, or just an oil stain? It didn't make any difference. 'Mrs Boseley, we have reason to believe that there is a spot of blood on your carpet.' 'Yes, several of the men keeping coming to me with nose bleeds.' Or whatever. The Highland stag gazed benignly down from the National Trust calendar. Duffy flicked it a V-sign.

He found the invoice file where it had been last time he looked. He found the file of forthcoming shipments underneath it. He spent some time copying into his notebook. Then he wandered round the shed, occasionally kicking at hessian-wrapped cases, on the principle expounded by Willett. But only cardboard answered him, never metal. He searched out various shipments and peered at the documentation tags on them. Then he went home, and straight to bed. Fuck it, he thought, I don't like sleeping on my right side.

7

Duffy slept late and got up slowly. His ear didn't feel too good. He rescued some muesli that had been trying to escape from its triple straightjacket of polythene bags, and chewed his way through it without real enthusiasm. He never trusted muesli to be what it said it was. He couldn't believe there weren't jokers in the muesli factories who occasionally slung in a box of sawdust, or a bagful of wood-shavings, or a sack of hedge-clippings, just to see if anyone noticed the difference. They wouldn't, of course. The worse it tasted, the better it was for you: that's what everyone believed.

At ten o'clock he went to the telephone and dialled Carol. She came sleepily to answer it: she'd been on the old shit shift again, six till two in the morning. Yes, she'd love to come round that evening. Anything special? Were they going out? That was a joke, even though she never said it as one. They never went out. Or rather, to be more precise, he never took her out. What did you do last night, Carol? Oh, Duffy didn't take me out again, that's what we did. Her girl friends smiled, because she looked a bit embarrassed. That Duffy, they thought, a real terror in the sack, *we* can tell. We know what *she* means by staying in.

But of course, it wasn't like that. They stayed in, and Duffy cooked her dinner while she teased him about how he always scrubbed the vegetables clean enough for a moon shot; about how the food was trying to escape, and how the knife gave a better reflection than her make-up mirror. They pottered around each other like an old couple. And, contrary to what her girl friends thought, they didn't go to bed together – also like an old couple. They watched television, and chatted, and sometimes, but not necessarily, Carol would drop her watch in the Tupperware box and cuddle up to him for the night. She'd stopped expecting anything to happen. Well, it happened elsewhere; and it was surprising how, after a while of not expecting it, you really didn't mind. You even gave up quietly trying to rub yourself against him. You suspected he didn't like it anyway – brought back too many memories.

Next, Duffy called Willett and asked if he could drop by after work. He had a questionnaire in response to the one old Willett had given him the other day. There was a chuckle of assent. Then he rang a new number, one from his notebook.

'Could I speak to Mr Dalby?'

'I'm afraid Mr Dalby's not available at the moment, sir.' No: probably a bit early. All that late-night pounding up and down Dude's, making sure the corks and the cocks are popping off regularly: it must take it out of a fellow.

'When would be a good time to ring?'

'Well, you could try about eleven.'

'Fine.' That would also make him nice and late for Mrs Boseley; help her pretend to work up a fine head of steam. At eleven o'clock he rang again.

'Mr Dalby in?'

'I'll just see. Who's calling?'

'Oh, just say it's Lord Brown's assistant.'

'Just a moment, sir . . . Putting you through.' They always did, Duffy reflected.

'Hallo, Dalby here.' A precise voice, with neutral intonation, ready to switch to bossy or deferential as the occasion demanded.

'Good morning, Mr Dalby, it's Jeffrey Marcus here, Lord Brown's assistant.' Duffy could do a perfectly unstreet voice if he wanted to. 'It's a private matter, actually, not to do with Lord Brown.'

'Yes.'

'I've been talking to Christopher, and he tells me you're doing business again.'

'Christopher . . . ?' Dalby sounded puzzled, as well he might.

'I know him as Christopher, he's used that to me for a couple of years, but I daresay he uses another one for you. No flies on Christopher.'

'If you say not . . . '

'So if you're doing business again, I'd like to come and see you this evening.'

'Can you be more specific?'

'I don't think that would be wise, do you? Not on this line . . . '

'Oh, I suppose not . . . '

'Shall we say nine o'clock, Mr Dalby? And I'll come to the front door, shall I?' Duffy hoped he'd say, No, not the front door, and give him an alternative, but his confident, almost hectoring tone with Dalby had clearly worked too well.

'Yes, nine o'clock, yes, all right, Mr Marcus, well I'll expect you then.'

At least that had gone smoothly. Duffy regarded the success of the call as moral payment for the damage to his ear; that's to say, the first, extremely small down-payment. As long as the rest of it went as smoothly. As long as he could continue to sweet-talk Dalby in person; as long as Willett came up with the right answers; as long as Mrs Boseley stuck to her agreement and didn't have a frame-up and a copper waiting at the door for him when he turned up to work; as long as plan A – which involved tidiness, intelligence, acuteness and an enormous amount of luck – worked. And if it didn't, he'd have to fall back on plan B, which involved being really rather nasty, cutting a few legal corners, and relying on only a fairly enormous amount of luck.

Duffy ticked off his rosary to himself as he drove slowly to work in the late morning; he felt it wouldn't be good for the van today to exceed forty-five, and dawdled along the M4, tugged at occasionally by the slipstream of airport buses as they swooshed past. The rosary went: fresh flowers, joss-sticks, tinned lychees, pistachio nuts, fresh clams, miscellaneous. Dalby must own a restaurant somewhere as well. He ticked them off, turned them over in his mind, went through them again, forwards, then backwards. It would have to be 'miscellaneous'. His morale sank a bit at the thought. But maybe Willett would tell him differently.

Looking back on the previous evening, Duffy shook his head at himself for the remark about all men having a slice of gay in them. Especially to someone like Gleeson, the inside of whose locker door was a papier mâché of Page Three girls several centimetres thick. And he'd kept his tongue under such good control up till then. It was the sort of remark you might toss at someone offensive you met at a party who was already quite sozzled and had a caliper on his leg, but not at a muscular page-fucker who had your pecker in his pocket, or at least your ear in his pincers. Dumb, Duffy, dumb.

But at the same time, behind the sensation of having half his head torn away there had been a thought struggling out, and the thought was quite simple. It went: Gotcha. Gotcha. That final impulse of Gleeson's to pull Duffy's head off may have been simple queer-bashing; but everything before and after was about something else. The fact that Duffy's ear was at risk in the first place told him that it wasn't just about who he was and where he had met Mr Hendrick. The violence came from nerves, from jumpiness, from a willingness if necessary to wipe out the whole freight shed if that's what it took to get what they wanted; a willingness haunted by a fear that if they did, this might blow it all. Which was why – though Duffy's tail was in any case fairly well covered – they wanted to believe him. They desperately wanted him to be no more than what he had confessed to being when he cracked.

And this jumpiness, coupled with their keenness to sack him on the spot, made Duffy convinced something was going to happen pretty soon; that some shipment or other was on its way. That's why they had been so thrown when the new theft occurred and that's why they wanted to believe Duffy's rather thin, hopeful assurance that he'd fix Casey for them before the end of the week. *They* had no evidence on Casey, or even any knowledge of Duffy's competence; but their worry made them believe they had both.

So Duffy wasn't surprised when Mrs Boseley played her part as arranged. As he was stripping off his jeans top at his locker, Tan was suddenly beside him.

'Missus Bosey see you now soon.'

'Thanks, Tan, I'll think it over.'

'No, now, soon soon, she say.'

'O.K. Tan, O.K.' He stretched self-indulgently, putting on an act for Tan. 'That woman gives me a real pain in the melon, I don't mind telling you.'

'. . . ? You cut yourself?'

'Yeah, I cut myself. Ear today, gone tomorrow. Oh, forget it.'

Tan looked mystified, as well he might, by the different Duffy that had turned up today. This new man slouched across from the lockers to the raised office, pushed open the door and stood just inside it. Both he and Mrs Boseley kept their voices raised so that anyone hanging around could hear.

'You wanted to see me?'

'Yes. Sit down, Duffy.'

'I'm happy here.'

'You're late.'

'So?'

'Don't you *so* me, Duffy, I demand an explanation. Other men have had to do your work until you decided to show up.'

'Well, that makes a change. Normally I get their shitty jobs to do all day. Now they're doing their own for a change.'

'If you're not happy in your work you'd better find another

job. I can't say you'll be missed here.' They were shouting at each other quite loudly by now; out of the corner of his eye Duffy could see a baffled Casey, plus one of the drivers, looking up at them.

'I wouldn't mind it if there weren't so many *cunts* around this place.' That should be enough, he thought; however much they dislike Mrs Boseley, they'll see that as a sackable offence.

'You're fired.'

'It can't be soon enough as far as I'm concerned.'

'I want you out in a week. Now get back to your work.'

Duffy kicked at the glass door but found that it was wisely reinforced. As he clattered down the steps he shouted over his shoulder, 'Needs a cowing union, this place.'

Though the bravado was fake, it still somehow infected Duffy. He was playing a game with Mrs Boseley, but he still enjoyed bawling her out in front of the shed. He sat in his dunce's corner feeling quite chipper for most of the morning. And when the dinner whistle went a surprising thing happened. Casey lolloped across to him and punched him on the bicep.

'Canteen,' he said, clearly and loudly. Duffy felt like an animal experimenter who had finally taught one of his charges to imitate the sound of the human voice. The effort, however, took a lot out of Casey, and over his double spaghetti hoops and chips he slumped back into his normal taciturnity. When he threw his spoon down after his double plum duff and exhaled loudly, Duffy thought he might pick the conversation up.

'What a day,' he said. 'Nearly slice me ear off shaving, and then get the boot.'

Casey frowned. He appeared to be thinking for a very long time. Then he said, in a tone of extreme confidentiality, 'Like the way you call 'er cun'. Herher.'

Duffy felt almost moved. Casey was, he guessed, expressing a sort of affection for him. What a pity it had taken so long. What a pity they would only be lunching together for another week or so. What a pity Duffy might have to dump Casey in the shit.

After work he rolled along to Terminal One again, to the Apple Tree Buffet. The same air of mass panic reigned, as ever, only transferred to a new set of damp-palmed passengers.

'A couple of factual points,' he said to Willett, 'and a quiz.'

'Fire away.'

'Factual point one. You find a bag of heroin. Doesn't matter where, Chinaman's bum or wherever. What happens?'

'Well I guess we'd pull it out first.'

'And then?'

'We do a field test on it. We've got a little kit. Just to make sure it isn't contraband salt or something they're trying to smuggle in.'

'And that tells you what it is.'

'More or less, yes. Then we send it to the Government Chemist. Under seal, of course, so that the courier doesn't get too merry. They analyse it for us and report back.'

'And what can they tell?'

'Well, they tell you what it is. They tell you how old it is. They tell you where it comes from. That's one of the more satisfactory sides of it all: the analysis is incredibly precise. It's helped, of course, by the fact that no two batches will ever be the same – unless they're made at the same time in the same factory, of course. And as so much of it is cottage-industry work, well, that's a help. I mean, you wouldn't get two batches of heroin the same any more than you'd get a pair of salt-glaze plates coming out the same.'

Duffy didn't need the comparison. For a start, he didn't understand it.

'And if . . . supposing, say, the courier had a bag – say there were two bags, and they got split up, on the plane or wherever, and they were found some distance apart: would the Chemist be able to prove that they were part of the same batch?'

'Oh yes. No problem. It's often the only evidence we've got

that, say, a couple of dealers are connected. But it's very strong evidence.'

'Hmmm. Good. End of part one. Ready for the quiz?'

'Yes.'

'You are a smuggler.' It seemed only tit for tat: Willett had made *him* play a customs officer. 'You have a certain amount of heroin.'

'What form?'

'What do you mean, what form?'

'Well, it's not just powder necessarily. It can be dissolved into a solution, made into paste. Can I do what I like with it?'

'You can do what you like with it. All you have to do is get it through customs – through me. I'm a keen but relatively new assistant officer.'

'No problem.'

'No, you have to do it in one of six ways. You're freighting in six sorts of cargo, and it has to go in one – or perhaps more than one – of them. Ready?'

'Ready.'

'O.K., here's your starter for ten. Pistachio nuts.'

'Are those those little green buggers?'

'Yuh.'

'Sort of half-open but you still break your fingernails on them? Some of them are open and you break your fingernails; some of them are closed and you break your teeth?'

'Yuh.'

'Shouldn't be too difficult.' Willett thought for a minute or so. 'Powder form. Break out some of the half-open ones, fill the shell with stuff, glue the two halves shut.'

'What, individually?'

'Sure. You get enough in each to buy a car with. Once it's cut for street selling. And they're sort of dusted over with salt or something, aren't they?'

'Yes.'

'That'll help. No trouble. We've got them through. Next?'

'Joss-sticks.'

302

'Hmmm. How do they come?'

'Oh, not sure. Let's say, packets of, what, twenty, thirty? Few dozen packets to the case.'

'What sort of packet? Paper?'

'Yeah, O.K. Well, cardboard box, say, and a paper label.'

'That's trickier. Couldn't exactly drill the sticks. Making it into sticks and painting it? No. No – it'll have to be the packaging. Not too difficult, but long and messy as the boxes aren't that big, but O.K. Soak the labels off, make the heroin up into paste, and paste them back on. That should get through you.'

'Tinned lychees.'

'Tins. Can be good, can be bad. Depends entirely on the state of your ancillary technology. If you have a little canning factory on the side, of course, no problem. Three ways, I suppose. You could use the paste method on the label. Or you could use a draining method: that's to say, you take off the label, bore a tiny hole in the can – no, I suppose you'd need two, wouldn't you, one for the air – and pour off the liquid. Then you refill with dissolved heroin – just bung it in with a syringe. Stick the label back on and Bob's your uncle.'

'What about the lychees?'

'Oh, you just leave them in. Unless, of course, heroin and lychees set up some sort of chemical reaction I don't know about. But dissolved heroin's very popular. You've no idea how many bottles of soya sauce and Chinese wine we've opened to no very good effect.'

'And the third way?'

'Well, what's easiest for the man at the other end is if you can interfere at the canning stage – either that or have the technology to take out the can lid and then reweld it. Then you just dump the bag of heroin inside, fill up with a few lychees until you get exactly the same weight as all the other cans, and reseal it.'

'How does the person at the other end recognise the can?'

'No trouble. Simple code – say, a couple of tiny pinpricks in the label, in prearranged places. Unless we get tipped off – or unless we open every single can that comes through – there's no possibility of our spotting it. And if we tried opening every can that came through whose label wasn't in absolutely perfect nick – well, we'd have to have a whole separate department, wouldn't we?'

'Fresh flowers.'

'What sort?'

'Er – various.'

'In that case – various possibilities. If they're exotic, you know, big fleshy stems, you could work a thin plastic straw of stuff up the inside of the stalks. You could use the packaging in the same way as with the joss-sticks – paste form. You could – though this would depend on where they were coming from and how long they were taking – use cloth or maybe cotton wool soaked in heroin solution, to look as if they were keeping the flowers damp. It's a bit of a long shot, but that sort of thing has been done. Oh, and there's another clever thing with flowers I heard once. Not in this country, though. They got a local artist – must have been a very skilled fellow – to paint on to bits of paper what looked like the bottoms of the inside of flowers: you know, the sort with big bells to them. Then they stuck these inside and had what was in effect a false-bottomed flower; room for a fair amount of stuff between the two bottoms.'

'Like a suitcase.'

'Exactly. Bloody clever. You wouldn't look there, would you?'

'No. Fresh clams.'

'I don't really know what they look like; I'd have to have a gander at them first. If they're closed up – or if some of them are – you can just use the pistachio nut principle. If they're open: bit trickier, might have to use the shells in some way. Well, if that's too hard I'd just go for the packaging.'

'Uh-huh. And last of the six: Miscellaneous.'

'What do you mean?'

'Well, that's what it says on the documentation.'

'Bits of everything?'

'I suppose so.'

'Well, then it's my birthday, isn't it – looking at it one way. I mean, if you've got a case with a dozen different things in, I'll find you a dozen different methods, and then I'll pick the best, and you'd never find it, except of course that you might.'

'Why might I?'

'Because you'd look quite closely at something coming through called Miscellaneous. It seems a bit too likely, given that you've got any suspicions at all. It's just the method some not-too-professional guy might use for a big one-off shipment.'

'Uh-huh. So which of the six would you use?'

'Well, don't forget I might well come up with better methods for each of them, given a bit of time. I mean, that's what it's all about. Those guys out there spend months, sometimes years, thinking up something which we either spot or don't spot in seconds or minutes. It's not very good odds. And they're always changing. As soon as any method is busted – and often, if they're smart, before – they move on; the clever guys never use the same system once it's been blown, wherever in the world.'

'So which would you use?'

'I don't like the clams, though I'd have to have another think about them. I don't like the joss-sticks because that might make some keen young assistant officer start thinking of opium dens or whatever. As I said, I don't like Miscellaneous. I'd go for the nuts, the tins, or the flowers. At that stage it depends on your personality as much as anything. Flowers if I were a bit more fanciful than I am; tins if I had the technology; nuts if I had the patience. But don't misunderstand me – I'd get past you. I'd get past *you*, anyway.'

Duffy pondered. Was that a quiet appeal? A don't-do-anything-on-your-own-lad bit of advice? Possibly. If you were Willett, you wouldn't enjoy the thought of amateurs trying to play customs men; you'd expect a tip-off, an appeal to the professionals. Fair enough – except that Duffy had no details: no shipment time, no specific goods to watch, just a hypothesis. Officer, open that hypothesis at once. Just as I thought: a false bottom.

He decided to half-respond to Willett's appeal.

'If I got on to anything . . . '

'Yes?'

'How far does your authority run?'

'Everywhere.'

'You mean, outside the bonded area? As far as Hendrick Freight?'

'No, I mean everywhere. You don't get an amnesty just because you've got something through the customs. If goods are prohibited or dutiable they stay that way. We'll come looking you up wherever you are.'

'Ah. Well, in that case I don't think I'll try. I'll dump my stuff overboard from the cross-Channel ferry.'

Willett's creased face crinkled up a little more.

'Well, watch the currents is my advice.'

' . . . ?'

'Case a few years ago. Some fellow in a private aircraft got cold feet. Flying in with a nice bale of stuff that wasn't exactly feed for his cattle. Hay content pretty low, as you might say. Anyway, got cold feet, dumped all the stuff in the Channel. Landed, went home, felt a lot poorer but a lot more relieved. Few days went by, and the tide washes up this great bundle of dope on the Dorset coast. Somebody's birthday, the old farmer thinks, and smokes a fair bit of it before he realises it's that funny stuff they're always going on about in the papers. Calls us in, we trace it, and do the pilot for illegally importing it.'

That seemed a bit thick to Duffy. He grunted, and went on.

'This is factual point number two, by the way. If I got on to anything, I could give you a call?'

'You'd be mad not to.' Willett was proud of his profession, proud of the way Heathrow had moved in recent years. It had got a lot tighter. Of course, this meant that the clever guys were trying elsewhere – Luton, for instance, and soft, package-tour airports where bandits swirl through the green channel in a bustle of tired perms and duty-free Tia Maria. But even so, that was grounds for local pride.

'I could be . . . quite general, could I?'

'Oh yes – often we just get tips along the lines of: Jamaica, some time this month. But it gives us more of a chance.'

'Or if . . . I was very specific?' Duffy, as always, was keen to cover his tail.

'Second locker along, top shelf. We wouldn't object to that, mate.'

'And what about my position if I rang you – or someone else if you're not on duty?'

'Well, if I'm not around, ask for Dickie Mallett: first-rate chap. As for you: I couldn't be absolutely positive, I'm not a lawyer. But I'd say that you'd have at least as much immunity as was necessary for us to make sure we'd get the information.'

That sounded nice and legal: in other words, muddled and incomprehensible. Duffy tried again.

'If I rang you up, and didn't say who I was, just said, "I'm an interested member of the public" – say I said exactly that, but you knew I was me, and then I tipped you off. Would you have to pass on that you knew it was me?'

Willett realised that this wasn't part of the quiz (not that the quiz hadn't been for real, he reflected); he was being tested. He gave it a few moments' thought.

'I think I'd think,' he replied eventually, 'that if you used that formula, you'd be stating your terms, and I'd have to accept them. I'd also argue, for form's sake, that if I didn't guard your identity the first time round, then there wouldn't be any hope of there being a second time round.'

Duffy smiled. He didn't think there was much chance of a second time – he didn't much want to work around airports again. But he'd got his deal.

He'd got his deal, but Willett had also blown Plan A for him.

Well, it had been naïve of him in the first place to expect that his friend would just reply, No, No, No, No, No and then Yes, it'll be in the third clam on the right in the next delivery but one. That was stupid; but he'd gone along with half-believing it because he wasn't too keen on Plan B. Then he touched the bit of his left ear that was allowed to protrude from the house-man's tender swaddling, and he got a bit less unkeen on Plan B.

Christ, he'd double-booked Carol. Should he call her, or pretend that the Dalby business had cropped up subsequently? Well, in a way it had, he supposed. Think about it later, he said to himself. There are a couple of calls to be made first, and a couple of connections. One of which meant very bad news for somebody.

As he dialled Geoff Bell's number, he worked at his opening gag. Bell was a friend whom Duffy used occasionally for help on the technical side of things. He could bug a phone merely by scowling at it; he could photograph through brick walls. Duffy had once foolishly bet him a fiver that he couldn't get a photo of him, Duffy, in his underpants, within a week. Duffy went around for two days being extremely careful where he dropped his trousers. He needn't have bothered. On the third day in the post he got a blurred, grainy but unambiguous snap of himself and a friend from the Alligator. In a very post-underpants condition. Bell's covering note read: 'I'll keep trying for one with the underpants if you like.' As there were four days to go on the bet, Duffy didn't rate his chances and paid up.

Bell recorded every incoming telephone call, so Duffy always began his in satirical vein:

'Ah, Geoff,' he said when he got through, 'this is AQ35B about the Tripoli connection. If we put the plastic under the second oil-well rather than the third, then we could use the lighter detonators and run the fuse straight across the Med to Malta.'

'Duffy, how are you? Haven't heard from you for ages. Not

since that wipe-job you gave me.' Sometimes Duffy despaired of Bell. What was an introductory game to Duffy was an entirely serious test to Bell.

'Got something rather tricky coming up, Geoff, wondered if you could help.'

Duffy had something rather simple coming up, as a matter of fact; it was just that Bell didn't get excited by simple jobs.

'Are you free tomorrow night?'

'Yes.'

'I'm going to need a body-recorder some time around six, and then a bit later, not sure when, I'm going to need three copies done and taken to three different addresses as quickly as possible. I'll probably be dodging bullets at the time,' he added melodramatically.

'Well don't use a police vest, you can shoot Rice Krispies through them. If you've got the right weapon, of course. Like a pea-shooter.'

'What about the taping?' Trust Geoff to seize the inessential first.

'Well, we'll do it in series, so that you get the same quality on each instead of a slightly deteriorating one, and . . . ' Geoff went on for some time, but Duffy didn't listen: Bell was talking to himself really.

The second call he made was to Christine, a nurse he'd met a few months ago. Physically, she overlapped with Carol a bit too much for Duffy to feel it was O.K. to fancy her; so he just took her out a few times, now and then, feeling a bit bad towards Carol when he did so. She, in turn, was quite pleased that Duffy wasn't a doctor, and that gynaeological examination wasn't going to be called for before the first half can of beer had been downed, the first packet of crisps finished. Duffy never asked for that. Indeed, this time, on the phone, it was the first time he'd asked for anything. He said he needed what he needed for some amateur dramatics; well, actually, for a comic sketch he was doing with some friends at a pub. Could she come? No, he'd be embarrassed in front of her, he'd freeze; but if he did it again, sure she could come. Could she borrow one for him? Christine said it was strictly against hospital regulations; but they were always throwing them away, and if it wasn't for use . . . No, said Duffy, but it must look as if it could be used – there might be some doctors in the audience who'd complain if it didn't have the right end on it. And he could pick it up tomorrow? Lovely.

At 7.30 Carol arrived in her Mini.

'What's it to be tonight, Duffy? Cheese on toast, or grilled bread with a cheese topping? Christ, what have you done to your ear?'

'Shaving. It's all right, doesn't hurt. I'm having moussaka and chips, and you can have whatever's on the menu under four quid.'

'Duffy . . . ' and there was a curve of surprise and delight in her tone as she drew out the name, 'we're not going out, are we?'

'All right.'

'You should have told me, I'd have changed.'

Duffy looked embarrassed. Carol thought this was because he felt guilty about how long it had been since he'd last taken her out. But he went on looking embarrassed.

'Duffy,' she said sternly, 'what's the catch?'

'Nnn?'

'What's the catch, Duffy?'

'Eh? No catch.' But she could tell there was. 'I've got to see a man on the way, that's all.'

'Duffy, you are a bugger.' He gave her a wary grin.

'I know.'

At 8.30 they left and drove slowly into town. When Carol saw the direction in which they were going, she turned to him and said, 'You're not taking me to work, are you, Duffy? I mean, I don't need to clock in till tomorrow morning.' That made him look even more embarrassed.

They drove much closer to Dude's this time, and parked about thirty yards short of it.

'That's where I'm going,' he said, pointing down the street. 'Shan't be long.'

'You *are* a dirty bugger, Duffy. If I see one of my mates tootling past, I'll send them in just to see you aren't up to any monkey business.' But she didn't really mean it. If Duffy wanted to spend his money in posh massage parlours, then that was up to him. She couldn't disapprove. And at least it was with women.

There was a different hat-check girl tonight. Blonde, and with breasts . . . no, Duffy didn't really want to look at them. There was something about this place that made you feel a lot dirtier, and at the same time a lot less interested. Fifteen pairs of breasts ought to be fifteen times more exciting than one pair; but it didn't work like that. Even in the booth with the girl he hadn't really felt much interest in her breasts, because they didn't seem to be hers: they seemed to be part of the club's fixtures and fittings. Clipped on, and then put back on the shelf at two in the morning when the last puffing punter was given his hat and eased out into the street.

'Do you charge?' he said to the girl, suddenly curious.

'Twenty pounds, sir . . . '

'No – no, I mean for leaving your hat.'

'Your hat? Not many gentlemen have them nowadays,' she said.

'Or your coat. Does the cloakroom charge, is all I'm saying.'

'Oh *no* sir, certainly not.' She seemed quite offended. 'Though of course, you can always tip us,' she added. Of course. Always. The pound change from the price of a single whisky – that would be about right. He felt irritated.

'Appointment with Mr Dalby,' he said, rather curtly.

'Oh, well, sir, I'll have to see if he's free.'

'The name's Marcus.'

'Marcus what?'

'*Mister* Marcus.' Duffy realised he had picked himself a pseudonym made out of two Christian names. Like Eric Leonard. A name that wasn't serious.

'Oh, of course.' The girl seemed abashed. Duffy felt like a bully. That was probably just as well; he had to get into the right mood for bluffing Dalby.

He rather hoped he wouldn't be recognised by the girl with the northern accent and the breasts which were located in the middle of the graph. Still, how long did a punter stay in their minds – ten minutes? And besides, he looked different now; instead of Fifties revival and tincture of mothballs, he was all velved up. Blue jacket, blue trousers – a close enough match in this light to pass for a suit – boots, and a mauve shirt open at the neck. Did he look like Lord Brown's assistant? Did he look like a dealer? Well, it was up to him to turn those equations round: he didn't have to look like either of them if he made both of *them* look like *him*.

He gave a hooded glance at the girl-strewn bar as he was led towards the stairs. The same smell of joss-sticks. Just as dark downstairs. The booths with their slatted half-doors; the hands clamped to the breasts as if with superglue; the wet bottles; the fresh flowers; the artificial tones of hostess conversation; the balding husbands with good suits and bad consciences.

'Mr Marcus, a pleasure.' Dalby had come out of his office to greet him, and paused briefly to inspect the scene below. You couldn't actually hear the peeling-off of ten pound notes; but you could imagine it well enough from here, Duffy thought.

At first Dalby's office seemed floodlit, but it was only the contrast. Duffy sat in a high-backed tapestry-work chair across the desk from the club owner. He took his time, and looked around the office for a few seconds as if he were thinking of buying it. He took in the standard lamp, the sofa, the small bookcase, the series of large prints round the walls. They looked like early woodcuts which, for modern reproduction, had been enlarged about twenty times; they showed pastoral scenes. The one behind Dalby's head depicted a large tethered horse, a cow, a sheep, and a couple of thatched cottages. Centuries, and worlds away from Dude's. Unless, of course, the tethered horse belonged to Ye Olde Opium Dealer who had called in at one of the cottages to make a connection.

Dalby coughed, and Duffy permitted his eye to return slowly to the cougher. Dalby was watching him rather damply from behind his little round gold spectacles. Duffy decided that he momentarily had the initiative; and this was the way it was going to stay. If you bluff, bluff big, he thought, and bluff aggressive. Also, as a sign of confidence, leave out the shifty, ambiguous half-language of the trade. Dalby looked the sort of dealer who lived by circumlocution and might fret at straight talk.

'The room's clean,' said Duffy sharply, in his unstreet voice. It was an affirmation rather than a question.

'Oh yes.'

Duffy looked across at the open door past Dalby's left shoulder, which led, presumably, to his bedroom, and the bathroom with the post-coital tub. He let his held glance act as his second question.

'We're quite alone,' Dalby assured him.

Duffy then talked quickly and confidently, as befitted Lord Brown's assistant.

'I've got two hundredweight of grass coming in fairly soon, though from what I hear of you you won't be very interested in that. Can't say I blame you, it's such a long-winded drug, isn't it; and personally I find cigarettes a disgusting habit, though I cast no aspersions. I've got a moderate amount of coke coming in next week or so. And I've just had some excellent Chinese Number Three which is being cut at the moment. That's my shopping list. Why you? Because I need money now for my next import, which is quite substantial. I wouldn't go outside otherwise. I hear you're reliable and honest – that's what I hear, anyway – and if you don't mind my saying so, you're British, which makes a nice change. Of course, if you aren't – I don't mean British, I mean the other things – I don't advise you to deal with me.'

Duffy gazed at Dalby impassively while awaiting his reply.

'Er . . . um . . . um . . . ' He seemed thrown by such direct-ness. Thrown enough, Duffy hoped, not to go into the ques-tion of who the invented 'Christopher' might be.

' . . . er . . . price?' he said eventually, as if forcing himself to use a dirty word.

'The coke or the smack?'

'The er . . . former.' (Which meant that he was interested only in the former; or that he had his own supplies of the latter on the way?)

'Sliding scale, depends on purity. I'll have to wait and see when it arrives. My rates are middle-of-the-market. Twenty to thirty a gram. You want some?'

'Er . . . yeees.'

'Good, fine,' said Duffy, as if he had another few calls to make that evening. He got up and extended his palm.

'It's all on the handshake,' he said. Dalby took it as if it were an honour. 'Oh, by the way, I seemed to disturb some of your customers on the way in. Is there another way out?'

'Oh yes, this way.' He took Duffy out of the office, along a corridor away from the booths, down a passage and out through a back door. No alarm system, simple door: Duffy was laugh-ing. Dalby held the door open; Duffy nodded, but without looking at him, and strode out into the dark. That had been a strain.

'Did they do wonderful things to you?' Carol asked as he slid into the van. It was a half-serious tease. It was also near a dangerous subject.

'Wonderful,' replied Duffy in a dreamy voice. 'Only costs fifty-four pounds.'

'Will you take me some time?' she asked. But Duffy only chuckled to himself.

Later, as they sat over kebabs and tried to make themselves heard above the Zorba music, he said, 'I might let you go on your own.'

'Where?'

'That place – Dude's.'

'What do you mean?'

'Well, I was just wondering who you might be having dinner with tonight.' Carol looked puzzled. Duffy winked.

'I'll pay, of course, but if you take the bill, then you can charge it, can't you, if it works out?'

She leaned over and tapped her knuckles on the top of his head, as if to restore order in there.

'I mean, it's a way of repaying you really, isn't it?'

Sometimes, she didn't understand him at all, even when she looked back on it later.

'Your kebab's getting cold.' Why was he smiling at her like that?

He drove her back to Acton, since her car was there already, and as it was late she decided to stay the night. They went into the flat and Duffy turned all the lights on, even though they were going straight to bed. He always liked to have a last look round. It made him feel more secure about going to sleep.

'Duffy,' she said to him as she cuddled into his back.

'Mnnn.' He was almost asleep.

'I like that velvet suit.'

'Mnnn.'

'Pity it doesn't match.'

8

The next day, when he arrived for work, Duffy was again greeted by a punch on the bicep from Casey, and a chortle of 'Cun''. This flutter of affection from the Tattooed Man touched Duffy, and he began to wonder if he could unfix Casey. If he didn't have to fix him, if he could leave all the thieving with McKay where it truly belonged, then that would square him with Hendrick. And if he unfixed Casey, then that would also be another promise broken towards Mrs Boseley, and that couldn't be bad. It might be just worth a try, as long as it didn't put him out too much.

At lunchtime he telephoned the hifi villains. If they had any sense, they wouldn't have rushed straight round to their nearest middleman with the stuff; they'd wait a few days just to see if there wasn't going to be any follow-up. He got the driver who liked the oil patches. Duffy's voice was tuned to its streetiest.

'It's Duffy 'ere, from 'endrick, 'eafrow. 'Bout that case of sparks I frew in by mistake the uvver day. O.K. if I come rahnd this evening?'

'What, mate?'

'Case of sparks you got wiv yer hifi. I loaded for yer. Frew 'em in by mistake.'

'Sparks?'

'Ligh'ers, you know, snout ligh'ers. Frew in a case. Gotta ge'hem back or get the cowing sack.'

'Can't say I remember any, mate.'

'Awri', well, you prob'ly didn' unload them. Prob'ly still sittin' wivver hifi. But we go'hem booked aht t'ya, see?'

'I'll just go and check, old cock.'

'Awri'.'

He was away several minutes, and Duffy was afraid of running out of 10p pieces before he returned. He sounded displeased.

'We found them, mate, they were in with some tape-decks.'

'Fanks, oh fanks a lot, you saved my skin.'

'Well, I'm afraid one or two of them are missing. Someone seems to have been helping himself round here.' The hifi villain's pound of flesh, Duffy thought.

'Lock 'em up till I get rahnd, willya? And fanks. You saved my skin.'

'Any time.'

He didn't sound as if he meant it.

It was going to be a busy evening, he could see that, so he decided to start early. Skipping off work at half four would irritate Mrs Boseley a great deal, which was of course an end in itself, but it would also enable him to get to the hifi villains in Ealing before they closed.

He picked up 140 of the original gross of lighters which he had switched, and drove home. Then he went to the nurses' hostel and collected a small item from Christine. Home again, he packed a holdall with everything he thought he'd need and set off for Geoff's flat. As he rang the bell, he pulled down his zip, and let his trousers gape. He did this every time he called on Bell.

'Do your flies up, Duffy,' said the entryphone. Duffy smiled. He'd never been able to spot the camera. Most people liked to let you know you were being spied on, through the fish-eye lens in the door, or the not-so-hidden camera; it gave them a sense of power as well as of security. Bell got his pleasure from knowing that you didn't know you were being examined.

'Armpit, groin or back?' was his greeting. Duffy groaned to

himself. It was always like this. He tried to show as much interest as possible in Bell's techniques, but the fellow did exaggerate. There were fifteen miniature tape recorders laid out for inspection on the work bench. Duffy imagined the arguments about their respective merits that would doubtless ensue: arguments not between Duffy and Bell, but between Bell and Bell.

'Does it matter?'

'Of course it matters. It's the first question. Where do you want the mike, where do you want the recorder?'

'I don't know. Are there any factors that make any difference?'

'Course there are, Duffy. Who are you taping? And where? I don't want to be told, of course, I just want to be told enough. How long do you want to record for? How far away will your friend be? Will you both be stationary? Is there going to be any background noise? Will you be able to slip away and change the tape?'

'I see,' said Duffy, but Bell had only paused for breath.

'Will you want to change your clothes? Is it as important to record you as it is your friend? Will there be any third parties? And then, of course, there are the physical matters.'

'What do you mean?'

'Is anyone likely to try and kick you in the balls? Or punch you in the back? Will you want to hit anyone while you're recording? Or before you're recording? Will you want a stop on the recorder so that you can pause the tape, hit someone, and then go back to recording?'

'You don't think I'm very nice, do you, Geoff?'

'What? What do you mean?' Bell, Duffy realised from his surprised expression, had been talking from a purely technical angle. Hitting someone, as far as he was concerned, was merely a factor which might interfere with sound quality.

Duffy began to outline what he needed. He'd estimated that the visit might take forty minutes; in the event it took two hours. He emerged feeling as if he'd just had all his ribs bandaged at Uxbridge Hospital. A recorder the size of a crispbread was plastered into the small of his back; wires ran into each of the pockets of his blouson: switch in the right pocket to start, switch in the left pocket to pause. He'd better remember *that*.

It was dark now as he drove along the M4. All that survived of the mad, self-destructive jumbos were a few twitching lights in the sky; red, green, white. It was their fault if they crashed now, Duffy reflected: going out in the dark like that. It shouldn't be allowed.

At the shed he unloaded the cigarette lighters and dumped them close to his dunce's corner. He'd think up a story for Hendrick later. First, though, he had to get through Plan B. He flicked the top of his left ear and made it throb. That made him feel better about Plan B. He picked his way across to Mrs Boseley's glass office, dumped his holdall beside the desk, sat in her chair, steered his foot well away from the security buzzer, took a deep breath and picked up the phone.

Come on, come on, answer it, you've been in every time I've watched you, don't go out tonight, maybe you're polishing that big Granada of yours in the drive, come on, ah –

'Gleeson, it's Duffy. Yes, Duffy from work, that's right.'

'What the fuck do you want?'

The main thing was, to get it in the right order, not give him anything which would make him ring off before he saw he had no choice but to pick the course of action Duffy was leading him towards.

'I called Mrs Boseley, but her husband said she'd gone to stay with a friend for the night.' Get *that* into his skull for a start.

'Where did you get my number from? Why are you calling?'

'I got your number from a big book which is sitting in front of me called E–K. All right?'

'Why are you calling me?'

'I found some heroin today at the shed.'

'You *what*? Duffy, where are you?'

319

Duffy let that pass. He paused. He rather felt he had Gleeson's attention for a while.

'At least I thought it might be. So I took a bit of it – you may have noticed I left early – and I showed it to a friend, who said he thought it probably was, and we'd better hand it in or something. I said I'd better ring the people at Hendrick Freight, so I got out the phone book . . . ' He enjoyed spinning it out.

'Where on earth did you find it?'

' . . . and I rang Mr Hendrick.' Pause at that.

'What did he say?' Gleeson didn't sound too secure.

'Oh, he wasn't there, he's out for the evening. Then I rang Mrs Boseley as I said, and she's out for the night, so I thought maybe you'd know what to do.'

'Quite right, Duffy. Let me think.'

Duffy gave him about four seconds' space and then said, 'Shall I call the police?'

'Let's not rush anything, Duffy. Let me think. I mean, we don't want it to look bad for Hendrick Freight.' That set it up nicely.

'I don't care the fuck how bad it looks for Hendrick Freight. What do I owe Hendrick Freight? How much is Hendrick Freight giving me for my fucking ear? I'm going to ring the fucking police.' He let his voice climb towards the hysterical.

'Don't, Duffy,' said Gleeson. 'Stop, let's think it out. No, of course you don't care about the company, why should you? But I don't want to be hasty.'

Duffy reckoned he had him now. He put on a calmer tone.

'Well, *if* you want to think it over, I suppose I could show you where it is. I mean, I've got a key to the shed.' The hook was going into the roof of the mouth: would he notice?

'You what? How?'

'Yeah. Didn't ever use it, but Mr Hendrick gave me one when he hired me.'

'O.K., that's a good idea. It'd be awkward tomorrow with all the other people around. Where are you now?'

'I'm at home, but I can get out there in about half an hour. If I get there before you I'll let myself in and turn on one of the small lights. I shouldn't think it's a good idea to turn them all on.'

'No, quite right. I'll set off straight away now. Oh, and, maybe you could bring that bit of the stuff you took this afternoon. Then we can put it all back together.'

'Of course.'

Duffy put down the phone. Then he took a chair from Mrs Boseley's office and placed it beneath the one light he had turned on, about a third of the way down the shed. Next to the chair he put his holdall, having first extracted a couple of items which he stuffed down the front of his blouson. Then he went over and waited near the side door for Gleeson to arrive. He'd have two advantages: Gleeson wouldn't know quite where he was, and it was very dark in the shed. It was even darker than in Dalby's wankpit. Twenty minutes went by.

'Duffy.' The side door clicked shut and Gleeson stood there blinking into the murk.

'Over here,' said Duffy from about ten yards away. Gleeson walked towards him, and Duffy immediately said, in as peremptory way as possible, 'This way.'

He turned away from Gleeson and set off fast across the shed. That's what it looked like to Gleeson, anyway, who trotted in pursuit. Except that after taking four paces Duffy wheeled round, and, as Gleeson came up to him, punched him extremely hard at the top of the stomach. Gleeson's momentum increased the effect of the punch: he bent half-forward, gasping for breath. Duffy wasn't much of a believer in the left-uppercut, right-cross-to-the-point-of-the-chin school of fighting. If you had hurt someone in a particular place, it always seemed logical to Duffy to hurt them some more in the same place. This time he used his knee. Then he used his fist again.

Gleeson didn't fall over. He just stood there, all gorilla-armed, eyes popping, as if he was in the middle of a heart attack. He barely noticed as Duffy dug into his blouson and handcuffed his wrists. He racked them up tight, the way he used to do with villains he really disapproved of. Then he dug out a length of rope and sat on the floor by Gleeson's feet. He looped the rope round the far foot and pulled it until it was next to its partner, almost toppling Gleeson in the process. Then he tied the ankles together.

Duffy took a while to get his breath back. Gleeson took longer. Duffy gave him time for the heart attack to subside. He wasn't a sadist. Not yet. Then he said,

'Hop.'

Gleeson stared at him, half-scared, half-puzzled. Duffy pointed across the shed at the chair set up under the light.

'Hop. Oh, and by the way, if you feel like shouting, I'll put a gag in your mouth and pour half a pint of Castrol down your nose. All right?'

Gleeson hopped, like a child in a school race. He looked pathetic. He looked as if he'd gone in for the sack race and someone had stolen his sack. Duffy didn't feel sorry for him. He thought he could hold that sentiment at bay for as long as it took. For ever, come to think of it.

Gleeson hopped as far as the chair, looked at Duffy, and sat himself down in it. Duffy got out some more rope and tied him to the chair.

'Right,' he said, 'here are the rules. If I tip you over from this side, you smash the back of your head in. If I push you over from behind, you smash your face in. If you start screaming, I pour Castrol down your nose, O.K.?'

Gleeson could have worked most of that out for himself. But Duffy wanted him to know that their minds were as one. Gleeson nodded. He looked scared. He was right to be.

Duffy pulled over two empty packing-cases and placed them just outside Gleeson's kicking range. He sat down on one, and unpacked his holdall on the other. He did it in an order which, he hoped, would keep Gleeson guessing for as long as possible. First a box of matches. Then a lemon. Then a candle. Then a knife. Then two saucers. Then a small tin of Marvel milk.

Then a plastic bottle. Then a spoon. Then a small polythene bag of white powder. Then an oblong cardboard box. He opened the box and took out a hypodermic. Then he lit the candle. Then he looked at Gleeson. Then he said,

'Right.' And flicked out the match.

'I don't know anything about this,' said Gleeson.

Duffy barely paid attention to him. That's what they all said. Some of them used to say it whimperingly, pathetically, when they'd been caught with their pants messed and the half-dressed child on their knee; some of them said it confidently, aggressively, when they'd been picked off the street outside Fine Fare and thought they'd just cleared the goods through the fence in time, and they knew their fucking rights and Bendy Benson, lawyer to crooks for twenty years, would be round to fix them bail pretty soon.

Gleeson said it midway between these two points. But even if he'd said it at the top end of the scale of confidence, Duffy wouldn't have been perturbed. No Bendy Benson would be popping into Hendrick Freight tonight, with his soiled brief-case and paralysing attacks of fairmindedness. And Duffy wouldn't exactly be fretting about the Judges' Rules. He might even have to trot round the back of Gleeson from time to time and see how he liked *that*.

'I don't know anything about this,' repeated Gleeson, in the sad mumble of a drinker into his beer.

'Gleeson, this isn't going to be complicated,' said Duffy, still not bothering to look at him. 'It may be painful, but it isn't going to be complicated. Oh, one thing first, though.'

He dug into Gleeson's inside jacket pocket, leaning close to his face as he did so but again pretending he wasn't there, and pulled out Gleeson's wallet.

'Fair amount of folding in here. I should be careful where you go, carrying this lot around.' He reached in and took out twenty pounds. 'That's for the stud, Gleeson. I reckon that's what it'll cost. And you're lucky I'm National Health, otherwise it would have burned you a sight more.'

Gleeson falsely discerned a lightening in Duffy's tone.

'I didn't really mean to do it,' he said.

'That makes it worse, not better,' replied Duffy coldly. He walked round the back of the chair, noted where the useful parts of Gleeson's back were, and readjusted him so that the crossbar didn't protect his kidneys too much. While he stood there he flicked the Start switch in the right-hand pocket of his blouson.

'Right. Now you're going to tell me everything you know, from the beginning.' A stab on the Pause button in the left-hand pocket. 'And if you stop, or hesitate, or lie, I'm going to hurt you. And if you scream or shout, you'll get Castrol down your nose.' To indicate that this wasn't a figure of speech, Duffy dug into his holdall and placed a round, one-pint tin of the oil on the packing-case.

'I don't know what you're talking about.'

'You're going to tell me all about the heroin, and Mrs Boseley, and Dalby, and how it comes in, and where it comes from, and who it goes to, and when the next shipment's coming through.' Always ask them more than they're likely to know, that was one of the rules.

'I just work here.'

Duffy walked round the back, flipped the Pause button, punched Gleeson hard in the kidneys, waited, punched him once more, and started recording again.

'It's a nice big Granada you've got in your drive. Wife has private money, does she?'

'Pools,' he grunted. Why didn't they ever think up anything better than that?

'How often do the pools come through?'

'Don't know what you're talking about.' This was getting tedious. Duffy flipped the Pause control and punched Gleeson again. Then he changed tack. Escalate quickly, that was one of his rules.

He sighed, strictly for Gleeson's benefit, picked up the hypodermic and held the point of the needle briefly in the candle flame. Then he made as if he was having second thoughts, turned towards the Castrol tin, and carefully rubbed the needle in the accumulated dirt round the pourer.

'You need it explaining? I'll explain it. When we've finished, I'm going to use this spike to inject you. Now, as far as you've got a choice, here it is. This little bag,' he pointed at the polythene with the white powder, 'is, they assure me, ninety per cent pure. No, of course I didn't find it in the shed,' he replied to Gleeson's questioning glance, 'I went out and bought it. Now, I've only got their word for it, but as far as there are straight dealers, they've always proved straight. You might like to take a risk on how pure it is, but then again you might not.'

He let Gleeson puzzle at that for a while, then continued.

'If you feel you're unable to co-operate, or if you lie to me, or if you hold back, I'm going to inject this ninety per cent pure straight into your arm.' Which would kill you; he didn't need to tell him that. 'If you feel you can co-operate, then, when we've finished, I'm going to cut the smack with Marvel.' Which would make you feel you'd been hit with a sledgehammer, but wouldn't actually kill you. 'Whether or not I drop the needle in the dirt a few times before I inject you depends very much on how I feel the evening's going.'

'You wouldn't kill me, Duffy.' There wasn't much bravado in the voice.

'I would kill you with no second thoughts.' What did another death on the route matter, especially that of someone who shifted the stuff? He said again, in a perfectly level voice, 'I would kill you with no second thoughts.' He left Gleeson to work out the angles, to imagine himself sitting roped to the chair, with a smear of blood on the inside of his forearm where the spike had come out, pop-eyed with fear, even after death. And the police would come, and they'd put it down as another small score being settled by someone on the heroin trail; and then they'd go into Gleeson's bank account, and then they'd watch Hendrick's shed for a while, but of course they wouldn't catch anything, and after a while they'd decide to keep it on file, which is another way of saying they'd wash their hands of it, and what did it matter anyway, just a fat pusher with mutton-chops roped to a chair, waiting for the dawn. It wasn't a nice death, either; you shitted yourself, you got a comic erection, you drowned in sweat. There was nothing to be said for it at all. Duffy's thumb flicked in his right-hand pocket.

'I didn't know what it was at first. I didn't, I swear I didn't.'

'How long ago was this?'

'About two years – two and a half years. One day Mrs Boseley comes up to me and says, "Would you mind delivering this case personally? I wouldn't want it to get lost on the way." It was something to go to Dude's. So I said fine – I like the driving, anyway. So I took it – I don't even remember what it was now – and I drove it to Dude's and forgot about it. And the next day Mrs Boseley gives me forty quid. Forty quid! "Just a little cash bonus, Gleeson, for delivering that case so well." Well, first of all I think, Christmas is early this year, then I think, Does she fancy me or something, then I sort of forget about it. Then it happens again, only this time it's fifty quid I get, and Mrs Boseley thanks me very nicely, and I think, Well if she does fancy me she's going a very funny way about it.

'The third time it happens I decide to ask. So after I've made the delivery I go to her office and say, "It's all right, what I'm doing, is it, Mrs Boseley?" and she says, "I'm very satisfied." And I say, "But, I mean, what is it I'm delivering?" and she says, "Are you sure you want to know?" and I think it over and I say, "No, I don't think so." And I say to myself, that's the last time you do this, Gleeson.

'And then a few months later Mrs Boseley tips me the wink again, and I say, "I think you'd better find yourself another driver," and she gets up and closes the door of her office. I remember her doing that. Then she sits down and says, "No, you're my driver, Gleeson." And I say, "I just resigned." And she says, "I'm afraid you can't." I say, "Why?" and she says, "Because I'd never find another driver as reliable as you," and I say, "Bullsh", or words to that effect, and she just says, "And in any case I can't let you." And it makes me feel there's something up. So I say, "Why not?" And she says, "Because you're in it now, like it or not. Stand or fall together," she says. I say, "What have I been taking to Dude's, then?" And she says, "Small amounts of heroin for medical purposes. Just small amounts; just for someone's old grandfather who became a heroin addict in China and has to get some stuff regularly, and the import regulations are so silly about it." And then she gives me a hundred pounds. In advance.'

Duffy hadn't heard the story before, but he'd heard the pattern of confession a million times – across an interrogation table, from the witness box, in a police cell. First it was I'm Just Mister Nice Guy; then it was Look What They Made Me Do. You wanted to say, if you *were* Mister Nice Guy you wouldn't have let Them Make You Do it. But that would be wasted breath. Duffy more or less believed Gleeson's story; at least, he didn't disbelieve him enough to hit him.

'Go on.'

'Well, it's sort of carried on from there. I just deliver. I just get paid for each run.'

It could be right, but Duffy didn't think so. There was always a first point at which a villain decides to halt his story. He thinks, they can't prove any more than that, so I'll stop there. That was what Gleeson was doing. Except that the circumstances were different. Duffy didn't have to prove anything. The burden of proof had shifted. Gleeson had to prove to Duffy that he'd told him everything he knew.

'And why was McKay crashed?'

'He was nicking things. He very nearly nicked the last shipment. By chance. We couldn't take the risk.'

Duffy picked up the knife and cut the lemon in half. He felt like a genteel tea-lady as he squeezed a little juice into the tablespoon. He looked across from the spoon to Gleeson. His guest didn't look at all happy.

'Go on.'

327

'Go on what?'

In response, Duffy tipped out the small amount of white powder from the polythene bag on to the saucer. Then he picked up the tin of Marvel, began to lever off the lid with the handle of the knife, seemed to have second thoughts, and banged the lid back down. Then, in case Gleeson got any ideas about sneezing or suddenly blowing hard, he put the spare saucer upside down over the one with the powder in it.

'Who, how, where, when?'

'There's only Mrs Boseley and Dalby, I don't know anyone else, Mrs Boseley doesn't tell me.' That was probably correct: heroin trails were normally run as tightly as possible. So Duffy merely said, for the tape's benefit as much as for the state of Gleeson's soul,

'And you.'

'And me. The stuff comes in about every three months or so. I take it to Mr Dalby.'

'Always?'

'Always. No one else.'

'And you deliver personally to him?'

'Yes. Mrs Boseley makes a call before I leave and he's always at the door when I get there.'

'Which door?'

'What do you mean, which door?'

'What does it look like, this door?'

'It's just a door, wooden door, says 61 on it.' Uh-huh; the back way, of course.

'And he pays you?'

'No, he just says, "Thank you, my fine fellow", or something snotty like that, and then shuts the door.' That was three of the four questions. Now the vital one.

'How?'

'How what?'

'How does it come through?'

Gleeson paused. Duffy unscrewed the plastic bottle and poured a small amount of water on top of the lemon juice. He could sense Gleeson's popping eyes following the operation.

'It varies. Sometimes it's in one thing, sometimes another. They never use the same system.'

'What is it next?'

'I don't know. Mrs Boseley knows.'

'How does Mrs Boseley know?'

'I don't know.' But he didn't sound confident about not knowing. Duffy picked up the tin of Marvel and put it down on the floor. On the other side of the packing-case. Where he might easily forget about it.

'It's marked on the air waybill number. There's always a double-four in them.'

Duffy got up and headed off towards Mrs Boseley's office. After a couple of steps he stopped, turned round, came back, lifted up the Castrol tin, waved it under Gleeson's nose, set it down again, and went off, all without a word. He returned with the file of invoices referring to Dalby's business, and with the file of forthcoming shipments.

'Show me.' He ran his finger down the first page until Gleeson nodded; then they went down every page in turn. All the shipments, as Gleeson had said, had a double-four in their air waybill number. Duffy opened the Forthcoming file. Again, he let Gleeson do the work, merely running his finger down until the nod came. It came very soon. 783/5236/144. One case tinned lychees. Port of origin: Hong Kong. Arrival date: Thursday. The day after tomorrow. No wonder they had been getting jumpy.

'That's the one?' said Duffy, and read the file number into the record.

'Yes.'

'And where's the heroin in them?'

'I don't know. They wouldn't tell me something like that. I wouldn't want to know anyway. It'll be somewhere in one of the tins, I suppose.'

'How many tins?'

'It's on the invoice.' Duffy showed him the file again and let

329

him do the reading. 'One gross eight-ounce tins of Chung Mon lychees.' Thanks very much. Duffy reached inside his right-hand pocket, switched the tape off, and began to get excited. Quite visibly so.

'Go on,' he said.

'Go on what?' The pitch of Gleeson's voice was rising with his panic.

Duffy began to warm the spoon over the candle.

'The rest, tell me the fucking rest, you scumbag.' His tone was getting a bit hysterical, though his hand wasn't shaking. It wasn't shaking either as he uncapped the saucer and carefully tipped half the white crystals into the spoon. Then he carried on warming it.

'There isn't any rest.'

But Duffy was scarcely listening to Gleeson any more. He was thinking about dead babies cut open and stuffed with bags of heroin and hurried over the border before they lost their natural colour. Dead babies who had to be under two years of age to be any use. Get past two and you're safe: you can grow up like any other kid. Grow up to be an addict if you feel like it, or a pusher; it's a free country.

And he was thinking about a serious-looking girl with dark hair and eyes which grew larger as her body wasted away. A girl intelligent enough to recognise that her own weakness of character was killing her. A girl with a carpet that smelt from her washed-out syringes. A girl he had run away from in case he found out what happened to her.

These two thoughts concentrated Duffy's mind wonderfully.

'There isn't any rest,' Gleeson whimpered. 'Mrs Boseley wouldn't tell me any more. I don't know where it comes from.'

Duffy stared at the dissolved liquid in the spoon. He didn't give a fuck about Gleeson, any more than Gleeson would have given a fuck about Lesley. Or any of them. He put down the spoon, and roughly wiped the dirt off the end of the hypodermic. He moved the tip towards the spoon.

330

'Marvel,' was all Gleeson said. Then again, softly, 'Marvel.'

Duffy put down the syringe, walked round the packing-case to where the powdered milk was, and kicked the tin very hard. Gleeson heard the tin land fifteen yards away, behind his back; then heard it roll for a while, hit something, and stop. That was the last he heard of the tin. His throat produced an involuntary squeak.

'There isn't any rest,' he repeated. He was speaking very softly, as if he feared the Castrol just as much as the hypodermic. Duffy dipped the end of the syringe in the solution and pulled back the plunger. The liquid was sucked smoothly up into the transparent plastic barrel of the hypodermic.

Briefly, Duffy laid the syringe down. He reached into his holdall and took out a pair of dressmaker's scissors and a piece of string. He sheared straight up Gleeson's right forearm, cutting through the jacket and the shirt at the same time. He pulled the flapping bits roughly back, and tied the string round his arm just above the elbow. He watched for a moment and saw the veins come up on the forearm. Gleeson still had good veins in his forearm, healthy, plump, fixable veins. Maybe he should fix Gleeson in the wrist, just below the handcuff. Or in the groin.

Duffy felt he was bursting. His ear throbbed. He picked up the hypodermic, held it at an upward angle, and pressed lightly on the plunger. The solution sprayed out in a fine curve, spotting the packing-case on which he had been sitting. He imagined the spray from Lesley's spike as she cleaned it out crazily on to her carpet. Then, with a sudden mental jump, he found himself remembering the spray from his cock as he sat downstairs in Dalby's crepuscular wankpit. Spraying up, out and over the carpet; just the same. Duffy felt excited; he felt a bit crazy.

The veins on Gleeson's wrist offered a wide choice. Duffy approached them. He held the arm down firmly with his left hand, and moved towards a broad, meandering vein with the tip of the needle. Gleeson passed out; his shifting weight nearly toppled the chair over sideways.

Duffy's ear hurt. His back hurt too. So did his hand; he was quite out of practice at punching people. He replaced the hypodermic and walked down the shed to where the tin of Marvel had landed. He picked it up, walked back and tucked it into his holdall. Then he put the other things back – the lemon, the bottle, the saucers, the full hypodermic. He unlocked the handcuffs and put them away. Then he untied Gleeson's feet. Now he was only loosely roped to the chair. Duffy waited for him to come round. It took about five minutes, but that didn't matter; Duffy needed time to recover as well.

Gleeson opened his eyes, and made his mutton-chops waggle as he shook himself back to consciousness. The first thing Duffy did was to turn round in front of him, haul up the back of his blouson, pull his shirt out of his jeans, and show him the tape recorder. Gleeson clearly couldn't work out why he wasn't dead; but Duffy didn't feel like giving him a hand with that one.

'Right,' he said. 'I've got all that, and I'd say, given the current attitudes of the judges, you'll get at least ten years. Unless you land a softy who might give you eight. Now, you've got two choices, the clever choice and the stupid choice. The stupid choice means that you don't do as I say, and as a result you get ten years, and Boseley and Dalby might just bugger off scot-free. The clever choice means that we get Boseley and Dalby and if we can wangle it that way, you get off; if they shop you, then you'll have to go down, but I'll speak up for you about how you came forward and volunteered information. You might get four or five.'

Duffy assumed that Gleeson would pick the clever way, and told him precisely what he expected of him. As he finished, he added,

'And by the way, just in case you're not happy with being clever, but want to get clever-clever, I'll have three copies of this tape made within an hour, and they'll all be on their way to different addresses.'

Gleeson nodded. He hadn't said anything at all since he saw the needle coming towards him. Duffy hoped he hadn't been struck dumb by the shock; he might be needed in the witness box, after all.

'The ropes are pretty loose,' he said as he walked off. 'Put the chair back where I found it, will you? Oh, and turn out the light on your way.'

Duffy drove fast to Bell's flat – not out of need, but out of exhilaration. He dumped the tape and left Geoff to get on with the copying and the distribution. Then he went back to his flat and unpacked his holdall. He squirted the contents of the hypodermic down the sink. Then he took out the polythene bag with the unused half of the crystals, and carefully, delicately poured them back into the salt cellar, where they belonged.

9

The first thing he did next morning was to ring Hendrick.

'Oh, it's Duffy, Mr Hendrick. Good news. I found the lighters.'

'You *what?*'

'I found the lighters. I was checking out the shed yesterday and I found them in the toilets. I reckon kids must have got in one dinnertime. They nicked a few, I'm afraid, but they're almost all there.'

'Good, Duffy, well *done.*'

'So I think we can say it was probably McKay.'

'I suppose we must conclude so. Poor fellow. He seemed so trustworthy too.'

'Yes, well, you never can tell, can you?' If McKay had had eight convictions for burglary and ten for handling, that would probably have made Hendrick trust him even more.

'No, you certainly can't.'

'So I'll get the lighters sent on, shall I, and we can call it a day. As a matter of fact I've managed to get myself the sack from Mrs Boseley, so it seems to be quite convenient all round.'

'Oh dear, I'm sorry to hear that, Mr Duffy, how did it come about?'

'Well, I think she probably did the right thing, to be honest. I wasn't really happy in my work.'

'Oh. Some of the chaps adore it, you know.'

'Yes, they've told me so.' He thought of Casey punching

him on the bicep with a 'Cun', herher'. 'So you'll get my bill in the morning, Mr Hendrick, and I hope you won't mind my mentioning that prompt settlement would be appreciated. These aren't easy days, as you doubtless know only too well yourself.'

'No, indeed. Well, thank you. Goodbye.'

Duffy dug out his Yellow Pages and looked up Food Importers. Three calls produced a near miss, a bugger off and a wrong number. He ploughed on. Eventually he got a yes: or rather, the three yesses he needed. Size, brand, and availability. Then followed two yesses of his own. Yes, a gross. Yes, he did have a lot of Chinese friends. And one no. No, he didn't need anything for the first course.

He collected them on his way to work. Sixty-five quid's worth of lychees rattling around in the back of the van. That put him in debt for the job, and he'd already spent – thoroughly spent – Gleeson's well-worn oncers. He supposed he could always eat some of them.

The man on the Cargo Terminal gate waved him through. Funny, there hadn't been any of those spot checks recently. He wondered why. A case of lychees wouldn't look all that probable, so he'd better take good care of the receipt from the Sino-Pak Food Company.

Dalby's shipment wasn't due until the next day, Thursday, but Duffy wasn't taking any chances. Freight had been known to arrive early, so he was covering that possibility.

But it didn't. Cockroach Airways were keeping to their schedule. 'All 144 tins of lychees were killed,' Duffy began to himself, 'as a DC-10 . . . ' That would be ironic. He'd worried about friends going on planes before now – Carol going off for ten days in Sicily with Somebody – but never before about freight. Don't take off in the dark, he found himself whispering in the direction of Hong Kong.

The Wednesday was quiet. Duffy stayed out of Gleeson's way, stayed out of Mrs Boseley's way, even stayed out of Tan's way for no particular reason. He had his normally convivial lunch with Casey, and afterwards found himself nervously checking the back doors of his van. Yes, they were locked.

On the Thursday he rang Willett and Carol and asked them what their work schedules were over the next couple of days. Willett answered in a tone Duffy recognised: the tone that said, I'm not asking and You're not telling and You haven't made this call. Carol answered with a tone equally familiar to Duffy: the tone that said, Are you asking me round, Are you asking me out, and which sounded disappointed at the end when he rang off without being specific.

When he got to work he felt nervous. He parked his van half-way between the Terminal entrance and Hendrick Freight, down a little cul-de-sac leading to the shed of a now bankrupt forwarding agent. He walked to work and was overtaken on his way by Casey, who greeted him by hooting, accelerating savagely, mounting the pavement and swerving away at the last minute as Duffy thought he might have to jump on the bonnet or climb a twelve-foot wall.

'Gotcha,' said Casey as Duffy arrived in a state of irritated shock.

'Cun',' grumbled Duffy.

'Herher.'

The trouble was, for the next few hours it was up to Gleeson. They hadn't spoken since their evening in the shed; they'd barely looked at one another. The only outward sign that anything had happened was that Gleeson was wearing a different jacket from the one he normally came to work in. Duffy wondered how he'd explained that to his wife: the neatness of the cut, the slashing of the shirt as well. Still, that was the least of Duffy's problems. And certainly the least of Gleeson's.

At eleven Duffy found Gleeson tucked away behind a pile of cases, ticking off a list on his clipboard. Nobody else was in sight. Duffy passed the van keys over to him. A nasty thought crossed his mind, so he just said, quietly,

'The tapes came out really well.'

He left it at that and wandered back to his dunce's corner. For

336

the rest of the day he paid no obvious attention to the running of the shed. He trundled his trolley, loaded and unloaded at command, made what was to be a farewell visit to the canteen with Casey, and kept his head down. The last thing he wanted to do was make Mrs Boseley suspect that he was in the slightest degree interested in a certain shipment from a certain part of the shed. Nor did he fancy getting ankle-tapped by a forkie at this stage. At two o'clock he tried very hard not to watch as Mrs Boseley bustled out of her glass hutch and spoke to Gleeson. Indeed, he deliberately went and fiddled in his locker so that he wouldn't see Gleeson fetch one of the company vans and back it up against a certain heap of newly arrived freight.

But after that, he couldn't keep his mind off what was meant to be happening. Gleeson would be backing up the cul-de-sac about now. He'd be opening the van doors. He'd have to make his decision *now*. The one decision Duffy had to leave to Gleeson, as he couldn't foresee how Dalby's lychees would be packaged. Gleeson either had to switch the documentation on to the case that Duffy had bought, or he had to open both cases laboriously, and transfer one gross of tinned lychees in each direction. And not drop one particular tin (which in the circumstances he wouldn't recognise, or get careless halfway through.

Now he was driving down the M4. Mind that lorry. Mind that bridge where McKay got crashed. Mind that bus. Mind that tricycle. Mind that cockroach. Careful that pigeon doesn't shit on the windscreen. Looks like rain – put your wipers on, Gleeson, *wipers*. Don't jump those lights. Smoothly. Mind that policeman. Well done, here we are, Number 61. Ring the bell, grovel as usual, hand it over, tug the mutton-chop deferentially to Mr Dalby, that's right, back in the transit. Careful on the way back – you've still got my van keys on you. Nothing fancy. Change down into third. Yes, doing well. Through the gate. Into the shed. Disengage gear; handbrake; ignition. Brill.

Gleeson walked over to Duffy and from a distance of a foot or so flung the van keys at him quite hard. Perhaps on the way back he'd been thinking of an angle Duffy hadn't mentioned to him: what if Dalby discovers straight away that he hasn't got what he thought he'd got? Duffy had his answer ready, just in case. It would obviously take Dalby a while, going through all those tins; and he might not do it till he got home, in any case. And then what would he find? The right tins, the right documentation, but no smack. He'd hardly pin that on the Heathrow courier; at least, not that quickly. He'd probably assume something had happened at the Hong Kong end.

But Dalby might be on the phone to Mrs Boseley sooner than anticipated. So Duffy decided it was time to sever his connection with Hendrick Freight. He sauntered up to the glass office and sat down opposite Mrs Boseley without being invited. She looked up: the high bones, the scraped-back hair, the cold, dead eyes. He found himself thinking, I hope you come out *grey*; I hope you come out fucked up; I hope you come out with nightmares which make you have to take little coloured pills and I hope you get hooked on them and eat more and more and lose weight until your polar eyes pop out of your face. Duffy didn't have a forgiving nature. But all he said was,

'Well, I'll be off now.'

'What?'

'I thought I'd be off now. Get out of your hair. Collect me cards. You can pay me off. I don't fancy coming back here tomorrow.'

'Nothing would give me greater pleasure.' She paid him, and gave him his cards. She seemed more relaxed now than at any time since he'd been in the shed. Yesterday she'd been jumpy – as well as very puzzled at the way he'd 'found' the cigarette lighters. Now she seemed, not exactly serene, but her normal self – dauntingly in control. He couldn't help taking a little stab at her as he left.

'By the way, Mrs Boseley, what's the E for?'

'I beg your pardon?'

'Is it Eva?'

She stared at him in an icily unamused manner.

'Elizabeth? Egbert? Ethelred? Eskimo?'

'It stands for Eff off, Duffy.'

He grinned at her as irritatingly as he could, and clattered down the stairs. When he got to the van he had an unpleasant thought. What if Gleeson had driven straight there? What if he had slipped away and was even now on his way out of the country or something? I mean, it wasn't exactly far to the airport, was it?

But the tins had been changed, and Duffy reflected how fanciful his anxiety had been: men like Gleeson didn't run. They didn't like abroad for a start. They'd rather sit in an English prison for a few years and read the morning paper and eat the local food than skip to some hot country where the grub was spiced and the natives unfriendly. Not that Duffy felt superior on this count: he'd rather take a long lease on an English cell than paddle in the wildest foreign luxury.

He drove home with care, absurdly solicitous about the welfare of the tins. He lugged them into the kitchen and put them on the drainer. He dug out his tin-opener and excitedly opened the first tin. Two lychees bobbed on the surface. He plunged in a forefinger and twirled it around. The fruit had an eerily smooth feel to them: it was like plunging your finger into a tin of eyeballs. He picked one of them up and bit into it. It had a fragrance as much as a taste: it was like eating the smell of roses. Duffy didn't much care for eating the smell of roses. He thought he was going to have a lot of tins left over at the end.

He was about to throw the first tin away when he had an unsettling thought. What if the heroin *had* been dissolved, as Willett suggested. What if it were swilling round in one of the tins, or several of the tins? That would screw things up. Depressed suddenly, he went on to the second tin. Then the third. On the fourth his fingers, sticky from probing the cans, slipped and the tin-opener skidaddled across the floor. Shit. This wasn't going to be an exercise which would leave him in a good mood.

He lined up the opened tins on the kitchen table in rows of ten. Ten, twenty, thirty. Duffy had seen enough lychees to last him a lifetime. Forty, fifty. Yet another good reason for not going abroad – cut down the chances of getting given lychees. Sixty, seventy. Duffy discovered his definition of hell: flying on a jumbo of Cockroach Airways and being fed meals of lychees. Eighty, eighty-six, eighty-seven. Uh-huh. Uh-HUH.

Beneath the three lychees bobbing on the surface of the syrup there was a package. Carefully, Duffy lifted out the three fruit and piled them on top of tin number eighty-six. Then he washed his hands. Then he laid out a double thickness of kitchen towel on the table next to tin number eighty-seven. He'd have put down a strip of red carpet if he'd had it handy.

He put in three fingers and lifted out a squat plastic bag. He laid it on the kitchen towel and held the tin up for inspection. There was a small tear at one point in the wrapper, and what seemed to be a pinprick in the curve of the 'g' of Chung Mon. No more than that, unless Duffy was missing something. From this direction, a pinprick in the lettering looked, well, almost obvious; but from the other angle, from the customs end? Duffy tried to imagine that as being their only clue in shipment after shipment of tinned goods. They'd be coming through regularly, month after month, and then suddenly there'd be a tin with a pinprick. What chance did Willett and his colleagues have?

Duffy swabbed the plastic package dry. It was fastened tightly at the top with thin wire. He removed the wire, and opened the top of the package. Another one was inside, upside down. He pulled it out; tied as tightly as the other, this time with string. Inside it, yet another bag, this time with a wire tie. Duffy imagined Carol's voice: Hey, Duffy, is that smack trying to escape? He smiled to himself. He looked inside the third bag, and there it was: lying contentedly, feeling safe. He licked a finger and tasted the fine white powder; it was bitter and salty. He closed the top. He weighed it in his hand; allowing for the three lychees put in as padding, and the juice, there were maybe six ounces here.

Then he went back to the cans. It was hard on the fingers. Maybe he should buy himself an electric can opener. No, maybe not: there can't be too many jobs like this. In can 117 he found another bag. He dug it out and put it on the kitchen roll beside the first one. Then he ploughed on. The rest of the cans proved, if only in one sense, fruitless. Finally, he stared at his kitchen table. One hundred and forty-four opened, dripping cans of lychees yawned back at him. It looked like one of those fairground games where you have to throw a ping-pong ball at a cluster of goldfish bowls: the ball bounces around the rims for a while, and if it falls into a bowl you win a prize. Duffy had won two.

He fetched two big black plastic refuse bags and poured all the lychees into one of them; then he threw all the tins (after carefully closing the lids) into the other. Then he mopped up the kitchen table, and changed the kitchen towel under the bags of heroin, as if it were a nappy. Then he sat down and stared at them for a while.

He was going to leave each portion in its own bag, until he remembered what Willett had told him. If by any chance the two bags had come from different factories, then that would screw things. Carefully, Duffy emptied their contents into a jam-jar. He shook it vigorously for a couple of minutes. Then he redistributed the heroin: he had six little plastic bags to share it among. Half he put back into one bag, which he tied with wire. The other half he distributed between the other five bags, and tied their tops. Shared out that way, they were only about half a centimetre deep when pressed down. That should do it.

He thoroughly washed the jam-jar and scrubbed the kitchen table. Then he had a thought. He reopened the black refuse bag which had the tins in it and took out a couple. He untied the wire from the top of Dalby's little package and dripped some of the lychee syrup into the heroin. That would ease things along

341

a bit. Short of typing out arrest warrants, this was as helpful as Duffy thought he could be. If the Government Chemist was as shit-hot as Willett had said, he'd soon identify the liquid that had leaked into Dalby's smack. Oh yes, Mr Dalby, and did you on such-and-such a date take delivery of one gross of lychees? Duffy imagined Dalby's reply: Yes I did, and I opened every single one of them myself and *none* of them had my heroin in it. Thank you, Mr Dalby. The Crown rests its case.

Duffy put down his black bags on the way out to the van. He hoped the one with the fruit in didn't burst. Seventy-odd pounds of sweet eyeballs rolling down the street, tasting of the smell of roses: that was all he needed. With relief he humped them into the back of his van. Then the tins. Then he pulled on his driving gloves and went back into the flat. He wiped the plastic packages very carefully and slipped the five slim packets into his right-hand blouson pocket. He could take Dalby's with him as well; but decided against it and put it in the fridge instead.

Last van to Fiddle City, he thought, as he idled along the M4. It was 9.30. The jumbos were back to being just coloured lights in the sky; as they hung there, scarcely moving, Duffy kept expecting them suddenly to go out, like the last trailing sparkles of a rocket. But they didn't. No, they wouldn't, would they, not as long as they had Duffy to annoy: that gave them a reason for living. And of course, all the pilots had decided to use the M4 route tonight. 'Well, I had thought about the North Circ, but I decided to waggle my wings at Duffy one last time – you know, suddenly lose a few hundred feet, cut the jets, and steer in his direction. He didn't like it much, you know. Swerved straight on to the hard shoulder and dived in a ditch. Funny fellow.'

At the shed it was quickly done. Third drawer down on the right, that was all he was interested in this visit. He unclipped the photo frame, and tucked the five thin bags in between the backboard and the photo of Dalby; then he did it up again. It was a bit tighter than before, but he doubted Mrs Boseley would notice. She would have eyes only for that plump English face, that sweet bald head, those cute little round gold glasses. When did she look at it, Duffy wondered: when the day was going well, or when the day was going badly? Why *did* people have photos on their desks? Duffy didn't know. Duffy didn't even have a desk.

Back at the flat he had a few more hours to kill. He rescrubbed the kitchen table, rewashed the jam-jar, ate a pork pie and sat watching television. The trouble was, he had to keep switching channels. He was enjoying a rerun of *North By Northwest* until it struck him that Eva Marie Saint was perfect for the part of Mrs Boseley. He button-punched away from a comedy duo because the fat one kept waggling his face around and Duffy only had to paint on a pair of mutton-chops to be with Gleeson. And then a forty-five minute BBC-2 film about a social worker, which Duffy was intensely bored by, but thought was entirely safe, suddenly blew up in his face during a case conference; one of the other social workers looked just like Lesley. He stopped watching television, rechecked Willett's and Carol's schedules, and tuned in to a late-night radio phone-in. It was all about the distribution of Britain's North Sea oil revenue, and proved harmless.

At one in the morning he stuffed the single bag of heroin into his blouson and set off. He'd had a long stare at the lock on the door of Number 61 and had marked off half a dozen keys to try first. He was fairly confident one of them would do the trick. He didn't fancy standing on the doorstep too long and hearing the distant tread of some keen young copper: some updated version of the younger Duffy. Attempted burglary while in possession of heroin didn't sound the sort of offence for which he'd get an unconditional discharge.

But the door yielded at the third key. Now all he had to hope was that Dalby wasn't romancing one of his employees, wasn't taking a post-coital header into the tub at this very moment. The office was empty; the bedroom behind was empty; out of curiosity Duffy looked at the bath. Hmm, looked just like a normal bath; disappointing. He took the bag of heroin out of his blouson pocket and had a think. Then it came to him. Where might plump little Englishmen put their treasures? Where childhood's magic used to unfold. Duffy tucked the bag of heroin underneath Dalby's pillow. The tooth that once fell out could turn into a sixpence. The heroin could turn into thousands of dreams, thousands of sensations, millions of sixpences. It could also turn into some dead people. Or, in this case, it could turn into a long prison sentence.

He left Dalby's office and looked down the few steps at the wankpit. The candles and the joss-sticks were dead, the champagne and the spunk in the carpet were slowly drying out. The smell of it was pretty bad, even from here. You probably would want to take a lot of baths if you ran a place like this. He thought of his hand, wet from the champagne bottle, being politely reapplied to the girl's nearer breast. 'You can hold them,' she'd said. 'You've paid for them. They're not for looking at.' Duffy turned and left.

At eight o'clock the next morning he made the first of two phone calls.

'W.P.C. Lucas, please,' he said in a strong Welsh accent.

'Carol, some Taff for you,' he heard a voice shout, while a hand was inefficiently cupped over the mouthpiece.

'Hallo?'

'*Don't* say my name, it's Duffy. Or rather, it's your anonymous Welsh informer. That place I made you sit outside the other night – Dude's. I'd say there might be some heroin in there somewhere. The fellow probably uses it just before he goes to bed, or maybe when he's in bed.' He told her where Dalby's private door was, so that the ferrets could start at both ends. 'Oh, and your anonymous Welsh informer will be ringing you next week about a celebratory meal.'

'Oh, D . . . '

'*Don't* say my name.' Christ, she'd nearly blown it then. 'I mean, we're not necessarily going out' (after all, he'd taken her out only recently) 'but we could stay home. I could cook you something. I'll learn a new takeaway.'

'Thank you for your information,' replied Carol correctly.

Then he rang Willett and directed him, without being too specific, towards the task of ripping Mrs Boseley's desk apart, and preferably her with it. After he'd rung off, he regretted he hadn't just said, 'There's half of it in the photograph frame, and half of it up Mrs Boseley's bum.' That would have made her eyes swivel.

He hung around the flat for a bit, not knowing what to do. He didn't want to be around when the raids took place. Certainly not there, and not even here, at the end of a telephone. One of the troubles was, he could never leave a ringing telephone unanswered. If only he could train himself to do that, he could sit around the flat all the time.

What did other people do when they had nothing to do, Duffy wondered. Visited their old mums or something, he supposed. Duffy didn't have an old mum. But he had one small thing to do, at least. He drove round the North Circular for a few miles, turned off into a stretch of London which was being slowly gentrified, and found himself a skip. He dumped the lychees and the tins. Then he bought himself a pub lunch.

He drove slowly home and called at a couple of kitchen shops on the way. He bought some plastic bags in the one size he was getting a bit low on. There didn't seem to be anything else he wanted to buy. Carol had this picture of him as someone who kept squirrelling away kitchen equipment. Duffy thought this was unfair; he just wanted to have enough of everything. He hated the idea of running out.

Why didn't he feel excited, he wondered, at the end of this job? It *was* the end, after all: Carol and Willett would struggle briefly with their consciences, would worry a bit over whether Duffy had just been very smart or whether he'd been fiddling things, but would accept what they'd been given; hell, they might even get commended for their smart cultivation of con-

345

tacts – so why should he worry? And as for his methods: well, Duffy thought, when in Fiddle City . . .

Even so, the job did leave him feeling depressed. Depressed at the thought of a world which had dead babies at one end of it, dead girl fixers at the other, and in the middle a swarm of tireless operators who just sat around for a few months, and then, with a pinprick in a tin label, did what they wanted to and got away with it. He was depressed, too, at parts of his own reaction to it all: for instance, at the way he'd wanted to kill Gleeson. He realised soberly that he might very well have done so if he'd had the real thing in his syringe.

Well, there weren't any new methods of stopping feeling depressed; there were only the old methods. He spruced himself up and headed off to the Alligator. He got there right on opening time, six o'clock. He drank double whiskys, not very fast, but fast enough. It wasn't so much that after a while he began to stop feeling depressed; it was more that he started to feel very drunk. At nine o'clock there was a shuffle at the next barstool and a cough.

'My dear Sir Duffy.'

He turned. Slowly, don't overshoot the stool. Uh-HUH:

'Eric.' It was that Eric fellow. Why had Duffy thought of him as unhealthy-looking? He'd never seen a fitter man in his life. He looked very healthy. He looked very neat. He looked very nice too.

'Drink for my friend,' Duffy shouted in what he judged to be more or less the direction of the barman.

'I knew I'd win one day,' said Eric, and ordered a triple vodka and tonic. 'These bar measures,' he said to Duffy by way of explanation. Christ, Duffy did look drunk. He should have ordered a quadruple.

'Well, Sir Duffy, what have you been up to today?'

'Ah,' replied Duffy, and turned back towards the bar, partly out of modesty at his exploit and partly so as to hold on better. 'I caught Lord Lucan today.'

Eric winked at the barman as his drink arrived.

346

'Another triumph for Duffy Security. How did you manage that?'

'Well, you see . . . ' (Christ he really *was* pissed) 'he was flying this jumbo b'longing to Crock . . . to Cook . . . to Cruc . . . to Cockr . . . '

'To *who*?'

But Eric never found out. Duffy suddenly keeled over into his arms, knocking Eric's triple vodka to the floor as he did so. With the help of the barman, Eric hauled him back on to his stool. Duffy was very heavy, pulling his full drunk's weight. Briefly, he opened an eye, and smiled seraphically across at Eric. His lips fumbled their way into action.

'Your round, I think.'

PUTTING THE BOOT IN

To Antonia and Martin

If I had the wings of a sparrow,
    If I had the arse of a crow,
I'd fly over Tottenham tomorrow,
And shit on the bastards below.
                                    Old Song

Warm-up

There are too many ways of breaking a footballer's leg. Too many, that is, from the footballer's point of view. Others may find the freedom of choice encouraging.

Duffy patrolled the edge of his penalty area and wondered what had happened to Danny Matson. That was where it had started. Danny Matson in the underground car-park. The first sign of the whole business going public. And after it had gone public, and really threatened to become a bit serious, there had been more things to worry about than poor little washed-up Third Division Danny. Who remembers yesterday's footballers? Who remembers even the famous ones – the ones with the hacienda-style house, the Merc and the wife that's a genuine blonde, the ones who get to partner fat comedians on the TV golf? They slip the mind as soon as they stop playing. Pampered swaggerers, they strut the floodlit pitch for the last time, salute the fans, and disappear down the tunnel. Suddenly, they find it's colder there, and they don't feel so tall, and no one applauds; there's a faint smell of piss and Ajax, a 40 watt bulb overhead, and a concrete floor underneath. No grass any more: if you fall, this time it will really hurt. And that tunnel is the rest of your life. So if it feels like this to the players at the top, what chance was there for the Danny Matsons?

Time to stop worrying; or to start worrying about something different. That speedy little ginge had got the ball again. Duffy retreated towards his goal. Close him down, for Christ's sake close him down. Bell was too slow, as usual, but Maggot got near enough to threaten a little GBH, so the ginge whipped the ball out to the left instead. Duffy checked his angles, got up on his toes, banged his gloves together and

355

started inching out for when the winger beat the right back. He would beat the back, of course: he'd done him three times already, no trouble. Once going inside, once outside, once nutmegging him in a show of public contempt. Which would he go for this time?

He went for simple pace – the cruellest method there is. Show the full back every inch of the ball, give him a couple of yards, then just hare past him as if to say, Give it up, this game, don't bother, you're too fat, you're too slow, you're not smart enough. And that left it up to Duffy. Come out fast, narrow the angle, cut down the winger's options, make him pick one way or the other, don't go down too soon, but when you do go down, really spread yourself. Duffy was muttering the coaching manual to himself for company; there wasn't much other help around. The winger was closing fast. *Now*, thought Duffy, and started to spread himself. Just as he did so, the winger gave a little jink to the right, and took off at speed to the left. He beat Duffy, who couldn't lay a finger on him, legal or illegal; but in doing so ran himself out of space. Too close to the line, and with a red-faced defender thundering back, the winger tried a finely-angled cross-shot which missed even the side-netting. He spat angrily and interrogated the turf, as if the ball had bobbled unexpectedly at the last minute. Duffy got up calmly, trying to look as if he had masterminded the whole thing. Honour seemed even, except that Duffy knew there would be a next time, quite soon, and that this fellow had more tricks than the Magic Circle.

Duffy was a worrier. They say goalkeepers tend to be worriers. Some start off like that, and choose to play in goal because it fits their temperament. Others start off calm, capable fellows and then get frazzled up by their own leaky back four, or by a sudden loss of form when their handling goes and they sweat at the thought of a high cross, or by some psychotic striker with Aberdeen Angus thighs who doesn't seem to know whether it's the keeper or the ball that he's meant to be putting into the net. Further up the park and you can hide; you can even blame others. But a goalkeeper is exposed. Everything he does wrong is vital. Ten men can win you the game and one berk can lose you it; that's what they say. You can get your own back a bit by shouting at the other ten: keepers are allowed to shout, and can sometimes shift the blame after a goal by picking out the least forceful member of the defence and giving him a rollocking. But mostly you're on your own, shuttling between boredom and fear.

Duffy had been a worrier long before he started playing for the Western Sunday Reliables. He'd been a worrier since – oh, he couldn't remember. He worried about that too: was his memory going? When other keepers went about their business, they worried about playing badly, and losing, and letting the side down, and getting kicked, and facing penalties, and getting called a wally. Duffy worried about all this too, and then some; he even worried about why he'd become a goalkeeper in the first place. Perhaps he wasn't really a worrier; perhaps he was a fully-fledged neurotic.

One of the reasons he liked goalkeeping – and one of the reasons he worried – was that he liked things neat. He liked the neat box of the penalty area; he liked the way it marked out his territory, his manor. Everything that happens inside this box is *your* responsibility, Duffy; he felt like some young copper being given his first beat. He also liked the way everything in his manor had corners: the penalty area, the goal area, the woodwork; even the netting was made in squares. He liked these right-angles: they reassured him. The only thing on his patch that didn't have corners was the penalty spot. A great big round chalky mess, as if some bloody enormous pigeon up above had decided to unload right into the middle of Duffy's manor: *splat*. Somebody ought to clear that mess up, Duffy thought. It bothers me. He didn't like the penalty spot. For a start, it was much too near the goal.

He found himself looking down at his legs, at the white bits, the bits that were getting cold. A late March wind was blowing across the recreation ground. He wasn't looking for goose-pimples, though; he was looking for little brown blotches. Still doing so, after all these months. He was probably safe now; probably. But at the time, when that whole business was going on, it had been just another thing to worry about. Actually, to get shit-scared about. There were a lot of very frightened people down at the bars and clubs then, and Duffy had been no exception. There were days when someone had only to put a hand on his arm for Duffy to send his jacket to the cleaners. And the funny part of it – yes, it was funny, he decided, looking back – was the thing about Carol. The thing with Carol. Very odd. Duffy smiled.

Christ, that ginge again. Anyone would have thought the chief scouts of Juventus, Benfica and Manchester United lay concealed among the mute crowd of eight spectators that the game had attracted. Close him down, close him down, Duffy found himself yelling, even though the ginge was still in his own half. Bell had a go, with the usual lack of success, Maggot was caught too wide, everyone else backed off or stuck tight to the man they were meant to be marking, and suddenly the ginge was free and heading straight towards Duffy's manor. He came out fast. Where was his defence? Where was his fucking defence? Duffy had only one idea – get out there, outside the area, and bring the ginge down.

Perhaps the Benfica scout really was present. Duffy came roaring out, and had almost reached the edge of his box when he noticed something odd. The ginge had stopped running towards him. In fact he'd stopped running altogether. He'd put his foot on the ball. Before Duffy could cover another yard the freckly little fellow had flipped the ball up a couple of feet and volleyed it dippingly over the oncoming keeper; he was already turning away, index finger raised in modest triumph, by the time the ball hit the back of the net. One–nil.

Christ, thought Duffy. And they're only meant to be a pub team. Where had *he* sprung from? Had they brought in some cowboy specially? That didn't seem likely: everyone knew you didn't need cowboys against the Western Sunday Reliables. Perhaps he was some minor-leaguer coming back after injury and getting in a bit of extra match practice. Or perhaps he was just a chap who drank at the pub and happened to be a class above everyone else on the pitch. Somebody would certainly have to give *him* a whack pretty soon, or he'd be getting above himself.

The Reliables didn't even go through the motions of blaming one another. One or two nodded at the ginge as if to say 'Good goal'. Duffy wondered if he would have had any chance of touching the shot if he'd been taller; or if he'd jumped. The only trouble was, it wasn't so simple to jump when running full tilt; and if you did so, you'd probably signal it so obviously that the bastard would just toe-poke the ball along the ground underneath you instead, and then you'd really look a wally. This was one of the problems with goalkeeping. You needed to be several different sizes all at the same time. If you were tall, you could pick out high crosses all afternoon but got beaten by low volleys. If you were small, your ground work might be terrific but you often made the net seem invitingly large to opposing forwards. If you were chunky, there was a lot of you to spread in front of someone with the ball, but you might not be so nimble about the box. And if you were slim, you might move fast, but you might also find yourself on the end of a lot of agg when they brought up the big men for the corners. Duffy was medium-sized – just tall enough for the copper he'd once been years ago – and stocky. This seemed to him to be the worst of all worlds. It worried him.

One–nil. There goes my clean sheet, thought Duffy. He liked that phrase: 'keeping a clean sheet'. It made you understand the way goalkeeping was all about neatness, tidiness. He sometimes imagined conversations which went like this:

'How did you get on yesterday, Duffy?' 'Oh, clean sheet again.' He had to imagine these conversations because they very rarely took place. Not many people asked him about his football; and when they did he wasn't very often in a position to give the response he dreamed of. Clean sheet. It was a funny expression. He gave a small smile. The only time he'd kept a succession of clean sheets had been when he was searching his legs for brown blotches and taking his temperature every other day; the time when the Alligator and all the other clubs were running scared.

The Reliables weren't the greatest outfit Duffy had ever played for. Some of them were a bit fat, a bit bald, a bit heavy in the leg; one or two of them were distinctly old. But they were keen; they turned up. It's all very well having a teamful of ball-playing wizards, but if only nine of them show up, and one of those nine happens to run into a skilfully-placed elbow early on, then you're in trouble. Duffy had kept goal for a few Sunday teams like this. The trouble with Sunday is that it follows Saturday, and as likely as not the creative midfield dynamo has been creatively on the piss until all hours the previous night, while the hunky ballwinner is gazing round some strange bedroom for the first time and realizing that he has six and a half minutes to get across London *and* he hasn't got his kit with him. Duffy had had enough of such teams; for a start, they tended to leave their keeper a little short of protection. Whereas with the Reliables, you could always count on there being four players in the back four. When the team had been founded, all of three years ago, they'd called themselves the Western Sunday Casuals. It sounded pretty smart, and even hinted that they were some rather posh outfit who'd been going since the days when everyone wore pyjama tops and shorts down to their calves; but it didn't really suit, and after a few months the Casuals had quietly become the Reliables.

One–nil with ten minutes to half-time. A couple more scares for Duffy, but otherwise not too bad. They'd really have to sit on the ginge, though; maybe kick that winger about a bit too. And perhaps last night's beer might catch up on the pub side in the second half. Just keep the concentration going and don't try anything clever in the last couple of minutes. Go two down and they'd be sunk. Lost. Lost without trace. Like ... like Danny Matson. Where was Danny Matson now?

First Half

There are too many ways of breaking a footballer's leg. If you want to make quite sure, of course, you can simply drop a few hundred in the right direction and the delivery man will come round with a junior sledgehammer in his pocket. That's a bit noisy, of course, but then it's surprising how many people don't mind being a bit noisy. If you want to be quieter, you might look up the right fixture, look up the right player on the other side – someone with good strong legs himself, for a start – and send a runner round to suggest a way of earning a little nest-egg. All for one awkward, mistimed tackle, a bit of over-the-top for a fifty-fifty ball, probably wouldn't even get a yellow card. However, there are even quieter ways.

Danny Matson was a bit pissed; even he would have admitted that. But the men who stopped him from taking his car out of the underground park that night weren't primarily concerned with cutting down the number of drunken drivers on the roads. Later, Danny couldn't even be sure how many of them there had been. 'How many would you estimate?' the detective-sergeant had asked him. 'Too bloody many,' was all Danny could reply. It had puzzled the detective-sergeant. Danny had only been carrying about thirty quid: hardly enough for a couple of lagers each nowadays.

Danny had been feeling pretty good that Saturday. His twelfth first-team game on the trot. He'd fitted in; he'd done the business; and he'd laid on the pass for big Brendan to knock in the equalizer. He'd done some fancier things in the other games – five goals in eleven matches can't be bad for a midfielder, and especially when the team's struggling – but this time he'd been pleased with his all-round game. The lads had been pleased. The Boss had been pleased. They'd got a result. One–one against Barnsley wasn't rubbish in anyone's language. 'I see light at the end of the tunnel, lads,' the Boss said afterwards. The Boss always had this posh way of talking.

And the nice thing about getting a resu.t, for a change, was that it made the rest of Saturday more lively. Sure, they'd get drunk regardless; but getting drunk to celebrate one–one against Barnsley was so much better than getting drunk to forget about getting thrashed. It also meant that you could look the bouncer in the eye when you turned up at The Knight Spot.

That was another nice thing about making the first team: they gave you free entry at The Knight Spot. Free entry; the first drink on the house; and at some point Vince would wander over and have a chat about the game. The time Danny had tucked away that header at the far post and given Athletic their first win in eight outings, Vince had come along with the ice-bucket and the champagne. Personally. That was one reason people liked The Knight Spot: Vince wasn't above doing things himself.

So they'd had a bit of a knees-up that Saturday. A few of the lads were there and more than the odd Bacardi got drunk. Danny was even asked to dance by a girl called Denise, a bouncy, dark girl with more than a fair handout of flesh: most of it showing, and some of it pressed against Danny. Tasty. I wonder what two–one against Barnsley would have earned me, Danny reflected. He thought Denise looked more than all right under the strobe lights.

When Monica turned up – Monica that he'd dated a couple of times recently – Denise chased her off. Not pushy; just firm. A few more Bacardis got themselves drunk, and when it was time to go Denise seemed to be with him. As far as the door, anyway.

'You fetch the car round, love, there's an angel,' she whispered, shivering a little and parting from his arm, it seemed, with the greatest reluctance.

Whoops, he thought, steady now, as he had a little trouble with his feet. They were getting uppity; didn't seem at all keen on walking him to the car-park. Perhaps they knew something he didn't.

He got to the first basement level and set off in an approximately straight line towards his old Cortina. He hoped Denise wouldn't be too disappointed. Just waiting delivery on the new Capri, he thought he might mention. There were lots of things wrong with the Cortina. Like the way its keys kept playing hide-and-seek in your pockets. Ah, there they were. Now, mind that puddle. Funny how they never worked out the drainage in these car-parks. There were always great lakes of oily water around even when it hadn't been raining for days. Now, which way up did the key go?

He thought they hit him on the head first, but later he couldn't be sure. They certainly knocked him down and gave him a bit of a kicking and rolled him in the water and messed his suit and nicked his wallet and tore off his watch. He was drunk enough to find it a matter of curiosity why they were doing all this to him, and why they were being so rough when they already had his wallet. Why were they still holding him down, one of them sort of pushing his face into the oily water, and another one holding him by the leg. Perhaps he was trying to kick them; he wasn't sure. There was no noise except for some scuffling and panting, and by the time Danny thought to let out a bit of a shout they had given him good reason to do so. Maybe he had been kicking or something, because all of a sudden he felt this tremendous thump on the back of his ankle, just down near the heel. Then another, sharper this time, and another, and another, and suddenly more pain than he'd had from any injury in his career so far, even that shoulder he'd once put out at Scunthorpe. He screamed, and when he stopped screaming the men had gone, and his suit was messed, and his Rolex was

367

stolen, and Denise had given up and gone home, and his career was wrecked.

Jimmy Lister was in his first season as manager of Athletic, and quite possibly his last as well. Fourth from bottom of the Third Division with ten matches to go. Every manager in the land knew what that meant. They wouldn't sack you before the end of the season because anything, they reckoned, was better than nothing as a manager; and no new fellow would take on the job at that stage. So you had the next ten games. If the team was relegated, you were slung out – no question. On the other hand, if you saved the team from relegation, that didn't make you a hero. Thanks but no thanks. Well done, Jim lad, good effort over the last six weeks, but I think we'll be making other arrangements at the start of next season. No hard feelings?

There were a lot of jokes about Jimmy having no hair left after a year in charge of Athletic; but the fact was, he didn't have much when he joined. He'd lost most of it by the time he'd finished as a player, so the stress that was getting to him now was probably going somewhere else. Ulcers, he expected.

He'd had a good run, on the whole, had Jimmy Lister. Started off as a wing-half in the days when such things still existed. Not quite the best, but pretty classy all the same. Three England B caps; a dozen years in the First Division, then three in the Second; and he'd come out of it all with a good reputation. Bit of a thinker, they said of Jimmy; bit of a card, too. He curled a nice cross-ball into the box, did Jimmy. A good reader of the game, they said; never played the obvious ball; always ghosting in from deep positions without being picked up. They said a lot of other junk about Jimmy Lister's game, and he was crafty enough never to deny it. Go bald and they immediately think you must be brainy; well, if that's what they wanted.

He made the jump into management early, and avoided

that depressing slide through the divisions towards some Mickey Mouse team in the Toytown League. Two years as assistant, then three in charge of a Second Division club in the West Midlands. Sixth in the table when he took over; nineteenth when he left. Not brilliant. Not disastrous, either; not really. And there'd been the usual frustrations: not enough money to buy new players, because not enough people through the turnstiles; not enough people through the turnstiles because no exciting new players for them to come and see. Too many sag-bellied senior citizens nearing the end of their careers; a number of new lads coming along, but not coming along all that quickly. One really good find, quick lad, clever as a monkey, and the Board sells him to pay off the overdraft. One reason we've got an overdraft, he told the Board, is that we're selling lads like this one before they've had a chance to pull in the crowds. We admire your loyalty to your players, Jimmy, they told him; but we've got a loyalty to someone with a big stick called the bank. You'd rather have a bank manager than a football manager, he'd said. Don't get cheeky with us, Jim lad, or we'll have to let you go.

Just before the end of his third season somebody had tipped off the local paper about him and the physio's wife. All that free booze poured down the sports page and look what they do to you when you're on the ropes. The job went; Mrs Lister thought she'd call it a day too; it was a bad time. He had a year away from the game: did a little schools' coaching, just to keep his eye in; wondered about going overseas; and for a year he didn't buy himself a new shirt. When the call came from Melvyn Prosser he was finding it easy to get depressed. He didn't know who to thank, so he thanked Melvyn Prosser. Whoever he might be.

Athletic's trouble had always been that they were one of the least glamorous teams in London. Cup semi-finalists in the middle Thirties, decent run one year in the League Cup, a few bits of yellowing silverware in the boardroom; but year in, year out, a team of huffers and puffers who never looked like blowing anyone's house down. The Board's answer had been Melvyn Prosser (or at least Melvyn Prosser's chequebook); and the new chairman's answer had been Jimmy Lister.

Jimmy had decided to play this one a bit more high profile. Image isn't everything, but it's not nothing. You buy a foreign player, for instance: he isn't necessarily better than someone you could have picked up for less money in Scotland, but a Dashing Dane or a Swanky Slav makes good copy in the local paper, and brings a few more in through the turnstiles, if only out of curiosity. It was the same with a manager. It couldn't do any harm to let them know there was a bit of a character loose among them, could it? And this time, he promised himself he'd keep his hands off the physio's wife, however tasty she might turn out to be.

He dressed himself carefully: the blue double-breasted blazer, striped shirt, scarlet tie, grey slacks, white shoes. A sort of bald Robert Redford, he thought. And always the white shoes, even in the rain. He'd thought of a fedora, but that had been done before; besides, the bald head was an item in itself. And the white shoes were a good touch. He did well by the press; he was always available; he opened a couple of shops in the first week after taking over; and he was pictured in the local paper with Miss West London sitting on his lap. He rang up the Playboy Club and asked for the loan of eleven Bunnies to do a photocall with the first team. He was given to understand that Athletic were not considered glamorous enough to merit the loan of Bunnies. But that's why I want them, he answered, to make us glamorous.

When he told Melvyn Prosser of this snub, the chairman said, 'I expect we could get the Dagenham Girl Pipers.'

Melvyn and Jimmy understood one another. Instead of the Bunnies, they hired a biplane to fly over the ground at half-time with a big banner attached to its tail reading COME ON YOU BLUES. The Blues were two–nil down at the time, and

370

some of the crowd suggested that the plane's petrol money should have been kept in the piggy bank and put towards a new player. So the next week six girls dressed in Athletic strip came out before the game and each kicked a free football into the crowd 'with thanks from Melvyn Prosser', as the public address announced. Two of them were thrown back.

Athletic started the season well, with three home wins on the trot; they got through the first two rounds of the Cup without any trouble, but had the misfortune to land a tough set of Second Division cloggers in the next round. Away from home; robbed in the last minute by an offside goal.

'Pity about that, Jimmy,' said Melvyn. 'Nice little cup run would have done us a world of good.'

'Still, it leaves us free to concentrate on promotion,' said Jimmy. The remark was a little speculative, given that Athletic were then fourteenth in the table.

'You didn't say relegation, did you, James?' Melvyn inquired.

'No, no.'

'I'm glad to hear it. For your sake as well.'

The only trouble with concentrating on promotion was that there were many other sides in the Division with better powers of concentration. The bad weather came; they redesigned the players' strip, and got a decent news story out of it; they tried bingo in the official programme; but the team continued to slide. In early February Melvyn called Jimmy into his office. He had a way of standing, did Melvyn; sort of not quite looking at you, as if you weren't really central to his scheme of things, as if he was really addressing some misty figure a few yards behind you who might well turn out to be your successor. It unnerved Jimmy a bit.

'Jimmy, you know the trouble with this team I've bought?'

'I'm always listening.'

'It's a dog. That's what's wrong with it. A bow-wow.'

371

'So what do we do about it?'

'What *we* do about it, James, is that *I* tell *you* what to do about it. If it's a dog, then there's only one thing to be done.'

'Chief?'

'You must teach it new tricks.'

'Yes, chief.'

It was time to take risks. He pensioned off a couple of senior citizens whose legs were falling behind their brains, introduced Danny Matson and another scrapping youngster, pushed big Brendan Domingo further forward, demanded more fight, sympathized with players shown the yellow card, and indicated more openly than before which of the opposing players he expected to be shut down at all costs. His job was on the line, and this was the bottom of the Third Division. Keep it tight, take no prisoners, and push the big men forward whenever you get a corner. Back to basics.

None of this gave much pleasure to the former England B wing-half, who could still curl a ball in more accurately than those he managed; and it gave him mixed feelings when the change of tactics worked. They picked up a few points, climbed a couple of places, but still weren't out of the wood. Little Danny Matson had worked, though: come on fast, seemed to have struck up a real understanding with big Brendan. The coloured fellow was gaining a lot of confidence from having Danny always prompting him; he'd pointed this out to Melvyn, and Melvyn had agreed. He'd pointed it out because even Melvyn could see most of the other changes Jimmy had made – like the fact that his team were fouling a lot more vigorously than they used to – but you had to have a bit of a smell for the game to see how Danny and Brendan were knitting together.

What an idiot the boy had been. Jimmy had seen it before with lively little players like him. Full of fire on the pitch, can't believe it isn't the same off it. Put a win bonus under their belts and a few Bacardis in their bellies – or even the thrill of a draw plus a half of lager – and they start picking fights. The worst ruptured Achilles tendon he'd seen in twenty years of professional football. At least six months out of the game; possibly more. What they said about the Achilles tendon was always true in Jimmy's experience: however well it mends, you always lose a yard or two of pace afterwards. And Jimmy had seen enough football to know that Danny's game was all about pace.

Jimmy knew something else as well: that when the day came for him to be sacked, Melvyn would be very nice to him, and would call him James.

Duffy had had the flat in Goldsmith Avenue, Acton, for three years now. It looked as if he had moved in two days ago and the rest of his stuff hadn't arrived yet. But there wasn't any 'rest of his stuff', this was it: bed, table, kitchen, telephone. These, along with the rusting F-reg van outside, were the entire visible assets of Duffy Security after its initial operating period of six years. It didn't bother Duffy: the less you had, the easier it was to keep tidy. It might have bothered a few clients, but they never actually got to visit the 'offices' of Duffy Security. Duffy explained the condition of his van – if he caught one of those looks which said, 'Why did I pick *you* out of the Yellow Pages?' – by saying that it made surveillance work easier. Any wally can buy himself a new motor and put it against tax, Duffy would add confidently. In his early days he would sometimes joke, when the clients seemed unimpressed by his van, that he was still saving up for the dog. He soon found out that clients didn't like jokes. They also, in a funny sort of way, wanted dogs. Duffy didn't want a dog. Dogs bit. Dogs worried Duffy.

Other things worried him more.

'Can you look at me back?'

'Nnn?' Carol was only half-awake. It was eight o'clock on a Sunday morning and she'd come off duty at two.

'I've looked at me legs, can you look at me back?'

Carol slowly opened her eyes and looked him up and down from shoulders to bum.

'It's all still there, Duffy, it hasn't run away.'

'Does it look the same?'

Carol squinted again, as carefully as the time of day allowed.

'You've got hair on your shoulderblades, Duffy, did you know that?'

'All the same otherwise?'

'It's disgusting, you know, Duffy.'

'What is?' Christ, had she spotted something?

'I should shave it off if I were you. It isn't a bit sexy.' Oh, that. 'I wouldn't mind doing it for you, Duffy. I mean, it's never going to be a feature.'

Duffy had gone back to sleep; Carol too, but less easily.

Over breakfast that morning he suddenly said to her, 'Do you know where to look for lymph nodes?'

'Some sort of cereal, are they, Duffy?'

He'd scowled a bit, and got on with his muesli. Carol knew it never did any good asking. Either he'd tell you, or he wouldn't tell you. Perhaps it was something to do with his football. He liked to start fretting quite early before a match.

'You be here when I get back?'

'Don't think so, Duffy. Stuff to do.'

'I see.' He knew not to ask things as well. Sometimes, they seemed to spend their time not asking. He looked across at the pretty, dark, Irish morning face of WPC Carol Lucas, and thought how even after all these years it was something nice to see in the mornings. He didn't tell her that, either. 'Only, you see, I thought we might ... do something.'

Do something? What did he mean? They never did anything. When had they last done anything? That Greek meal the previous summer? Or had he taken her for a drive in the van since – yes, that time when he had something worth nicking in the back, and one of the door locks didn't work, and he'd had to see a client on the way to somewhere else. Carol had sat in the van guarding a cardboard box containing she didn't know what for half an hour. That was the last time they'd 'done something'.

Her friends assumed they didn't go out much because they were always in bed. She'd told them Duffy did a bit of weight-training (well, he had a couple of dumb-bell things too heavy for her to lift which he kept in the fitted cupboard in the bedroom) and they'd jumped to the obvious conclusions. 'Pumping iron again, last night, was it?' they'd sometimes ask. That was very far from being it, but Carol always smiled. She and Duffy had held the world chastity record for – what? five years? It didn't bear thinking about. Odd that she could still go for him, she thought. Odd that he still wanted her around. When that terrible thing had got him thrown out of the Force, when they'd framed him with that black kid who claimed to be under-age, he'd stopped being able to get it together with her. Tried everything for a bit, but no good. That would have been it for most people; but in a funny way they'd stuck together. Only by not asking a lot of questions, though.

'I could come back tomorrow if you like,' she offered.

'I've got a new dish I heat up in the oven.'

'That sounds smashing, Duffy. I'll put on my best dress.'

As he drove to the game, though, he started worrying if Carol had looked properly. Little brown irregular blotches, that was what he had read. Duffy shuddered. It had a nasty name, too. Kaposi's sarcoma. That didn't sound like something you got better from. Who the hell was this Kaposi guy? He had a name like one of those old Hollywood movie stars. Bela Kaposi.

Of course, there was nothing to show that he'd got it. But on the other hand there was nothing to show that he hadn't got it. This didn't strike Duffy as a very good deal.

At first, it had just been a scare story in the papers. KILLER PLAGUE HITS U.S. GAYS. One of those things they have over there, he thought, like Legionnaire's Disease. WHAT KILLED GAY PLAGUE MAN? Over-indulgence, Duffy thought, as he read the headline and passed on. U.S. CHRISTIANS SAY GOD IS PUNISHING GAYS. And so it continued. NO HELP YET FOR AIDS VICTIMS. Then: SHOULD GAYS CHANGE THEIR LIFESTYLE? And finally, dreadfully, one morning: KILLER GAY PLAGUE AIDS IS HERE.

Duffy soon learnt what the initials stood for. Acquired Immune Deficiency Syndrome. Attacks Homosexuals, Heroin Addicts, Haitians and Haemophiliacs. Everyone with an H in their name: like only eating shellfish when there's an R in the month, or something. Homosexual includes Bisexual, Duffy read. Duffy had been pretty bisexual in his time. Well, all that would have to stop. If he'd picked it up, though, everything would stop. Everything. One hundred per cent death-rate after three years or so for all diagnosed cases. No way of knowing whether you were going to get it, no way of knowing whether you'd already got it, and no cure.

Promiscuous homosexuals especially at risk. Passive homosexuals especially at risk. Well, of course he'd been promiscuous. He'd also been promiscuous with women – did that help in any way? He'd been very promiscuous after things had all gone wrong with Carol; in fact he'd made a rule only to have one-night stands, because he didn't want to get involved. He also wanted to hang on to Carol, and having nothing but one-night stands, however many of them, was in a funny way being loyal to Carol. Not many other people would probably see it that way, but Duffy did. He'd had a year or two of being, yes, well, up for anything that moved, really. Then it sort of settled down, and he was just averagely promiscuous now. He didn't necessarily keep to his one-night-only rule, because he didn't feel his relationship with Carol was under threat any more. At least not from his side. Her side was another matter. He didn't like to think about that.

Passive homosexuals especially at risk. No comment, Duffy muttered to himself.

First you get infected, they said. Someone who's been on a package tour to San Francisco; a tasty American who's found the Alligator Club in his *Spartacus Gay Guide to the World* and dropped in for a trawl. Then nothing happens. That was the scary bit. Nothing happens for six months or so. Then you feel a bit unwell, you get night sweats, lose a little weight, get the runs, have a high temperature; and these lymph node things swell up. That'll go on for a bit – perhaps as much as a year – and suddenly it goes away. Completely. You feel fine. Never better. Back down the Alligator and no problem. The only problem is, your entire immunity system has been wiped out. No resistance left: a common cold blows you away, or some odd form of pneumonia. Or, most likely of all, this Bela Kaposi comes along with the old sarcoma, and the brown blotches start, and that's it. You might as well put your head in a polythene bag and save the National Health Service some money.

Had he felt unwell in the last year or so? Of course he had. Of course he sometimes woke up sweating in the night; who didn't? Temperature? Occasionally. Weight-loss? Yes, but he thought that was a good thing at the time; he didn't want to get fat, so he'd started pumping iron and watching his diet. Bit of a health-food kick, almost. Diarrhoea? Who doesn't find himself doubling back to the toilet once in a while? You don't keep a record, though, do you?

Or on the other hand he could still be in the six-month incubation period. The first cases in Britain were only just being officially confirmed. But by 'cases' they meant deaths. And these 'cases' wouldn't have lived their last couple of years any differently from how they'd lived the earlier ones. So think of all those six-month incubation periods stacked up one behind the other, waiting to burst out. No wonder people were getting so jumpy down at the clubs. No wonder anyone with an American accent couldn't even get a drink.

Duffy still called in at the Alligator; there wasn't any reason to boycott the place – it wasn't as if they put AIDS in the beer there, though some people behaved as if they did. But he always went home alone, nowadays.

No more men. Not for a bit. Watch out for night sweats. Try and find out where your lymph nodes are.

It wasn't Duffy's brightest game for the Reliables that Sunday. He missed a punch on a corner: one–nil. He came out far too late when the back four was caught square: two–nil. He got an elbow in the side at a free-kick and was too winded to see who'd done it. And he ended up being scooted round by a fat midfielder who picked the ball out of the net for him, and proudly announced that it was his first goal in eighteen months: three–nil.

He didn't feel too bright in the shower afterwards, either. There had been times when he would glance around the flesh on display and have a quiet smile to himself. Pity they're all *straight*, he'd think. Now he half-closed his eyes as the shorts were dropped, and winced as all these pink, healthy, heterosexual bums came waltzing confidently out of the shower. Herpes was the most they'd be worrying about.

One of the bums belonged to Ken Marriott – Maggot, as he was affectionately known to the team, because of the way he kept getting under opponents' skins. There was something about Maggot that really riled other outfits. Probably the way he kicked them; they never did seem to get used to that. Maggot was tall and thin and bad-tempered-looking, and didn't have much hair left: most of it had been worn off on all those strikers he'd butted. But then, if he hadn't been a touch on the physical side, he probably wouldn't have kept his place with the Reliables. For Ken suffered from a terrible affliction: he was a thinker. He worked on the sports desk of the *West London Chronicle*; perhaps that was where he got his ideas. He talked a lot about 'vision', and 'changing the point of attack', and 'spreading the ball wide'.

'He's got great vision, our Maggot,' said Karl French after one match. Karl French was the fittest, youngest and smartest member of the Reliables, and they were lucky to get him. 'Great vision. Only trouble is, the ball doesn't go *anywhere fucking near* where he wants it to.'

Maggot was always trying to play subtle chips round the edge of the box, or back-heel the ball at speed, or lay it off one-touch with a caress of the boot. The Reliables forgave him these delusions of grandeur because of his defensive qualities. He could mistime a tackle like no one else in the team; and since he was tall and thin and looked a bit unco-ordinated, the ref often let him get away with it.

'I know I'm a bit rugged,' Marriott had once explained, almost apologetically, after an especially vicious game, 'but I've got this vision as well, you see.'

'Course you've got vision, Maggot,' said French consolingly. 'Anyone can see that. Great vision. It's just a question of whether the rest of us can adapt our game to fit in with you.'

Maggot thought he had made a friend for life.

As they were leaving the ground, Marriott asked Duffy for a lift back. Despite his vision, he'd so far been unable to persuade any driving-test examiner to allow him on the road unaccompanied.

'Been seeing a bit of Jimmy Lister lately,' he began, as he untangled his seat belt.

'Uh-huh.'

'Now there's a man with problems.'

'Uh-huh.' Not like mine, thought Duffy. Bet Jimmy Lister doesn't get night sweats. Or if he does, they're only about something short-term, like losing his job.

'Ever met him?'

'No. Liked him as a player. Bit of a berk as a manager, isn't he?'

'You try managing Athletic with Melvyn Prosser breathing down your neck.'

379

'What's he earn? Fifteen thou? Twenty?'

'Something like, I should think.'

'Well, I'd let Melvyn Prosser breathe down my neck for that money.'

'Pressure, Duffy. That job's all about pressure.'

'Why does he wear white shoes if he isn't a berk?' said Duffy aggressively. He had more things to worry about than Jimmy Lister's employment prospects. They drove on in silence for a bit.

'How's business, Duffy?'

'All right.'

'Good.'

'It's all right.'

'Turning down work?'

'Not exactly.'

'Want a job?'

'Thought you'd never ask.'

'Ah.'

'What is it? Nannying the rest of Lister's mob so they don't all go on the piss and get themselves into fights?'

'Anyone would think you didn't want work, from the fuss you make.'

Duffy grunted. Maybe he should pack it in and take it easy for the last couple of years or so of his life. Perhaps he'd marry Carol on his deathbed at the hospital. Except that he might not even get admitted to the hospital. He'd read about some doctors and nurses refusing to treat AIDS victims. Too dangerous. Not enough known about the way the disease spreads. Filthy queers, anyway. Duffy wouldn't be surprised if, by the time he got his Kaposi thing, all the guys with AIDS were being packed off to some leper colony in the Welsh mountains. Made to wear little bells round their necks so people could hear them coming. Ding-dong, ding-dong. No, dear, that's not the ice-cream van, it's the man with AIDS come to dig in our dustbins. *Do* go and turn the hose on him again, will you? Or why not just shoot him this time, darling?

Jimmy Lister was wearing black shoes. He was also wearing a polo-neck sweater and an old pair of jeans. Obviously Miss West London wasn't going to come and sit on his knee for the benefit of the press this morning. He'd filled out a bit since Duffy had last watched him from the terraces; but you could see the remains of a lean, elegant player of the sort that Maggot deludedly supposed himself to be. Above his ears a few bits of sandy hair were still left. He got up, smiled and shook hands with Duffy, who found himself thinking, Maybe you aren't a berk after all.

'Ken Marriott told me you ... looked after things.'

'I'm not a minder.'

'No. I mean, you looked *into* things.'

'That's more like it.'

'Call me Jimmy.'

'All right.'

'What shall I call you?'

'What do you want me to look into?'

Lister glanced across at Duffy. I'm not surprised you don't get too much work, my lad, if this is how you go about it. Where are the customer relations? What about a little smile? Fat chance of that, he could see. Duffy had a small, tight mouth set in a broad face, and it moved only to speak. His hair looked as if it had once been in a brush-cut, and then had been allowed to fend for itself.

'You follow Athletic much?'

'No.'

'Any particular reason?' Jimmy didn't mind going in for a bit of customer relations, even if this strange chum of Marriott's didn't.

Duffy thought about this one for a moment; Lister was almost on tenterhooks.

'I don't think they're much good, that's why.'

'Charming.'

'Anyway, QPR's my team.'

381

'QPR? With that nancy-boy pitch of theirs?'

'Fifty quid a day, plus exes,' was all Duffy said to this. He put his thumb to his left earlobe, felt the ridged scar and rubbed it. He had worn a gold stud in that ear until one day someone had done something nasty to it. He was still debating whether or not to have his right ear pierced and start again. The chances of the same thing happening twice were pretty thin; but then the chances of having your earlobe being nearly torn off in the first place by a maniac with a pair of pliers aren't exactly high, are they?

'You read about Danny – '

'Fifty a day, plus exes.'

'Sure, sure. I'll have to clear it with the chairman, but I reckon it'll be OK. You read about Danny Matson?'

'Uh-huh.'

'What did you think?'

'I didn't think. I wasn't being paid to.'

'Look, er, Mr Duffy ... '

'Duffy.'

'Duffy, thank you.' So he did answer questions eventually. 'What I thought at first was, he got himself into a fight. Maximum he got mugged. Extreme maximum some of those Barnsley fans were still hanging around for some reason and decided to work him over. I mean, they need the points as badly as us.'

'Is he out of the game for long?'

'For good, I'd say. At this level. Bit of Southern League stuff left in him if he's lucky. He's only twenty.'

'Poor sod.' Even so, that still left him with an average life expectancy of another fifty years; he had that to look forward to. 'But now you don't think he got mugged?'

'Well, this isn't the smartest end of town, I know. But if it was a fight, if he was trying to kick out, he wouldn't kick out backwards, would he?'

'Not unless he was a horse.'

'Quite. I think someone did Danny.'

'What changed your mind?'

'Several things. Partly this.' Lister reached into his desk and fetched out some long papers, folded in half vertically. 'It's a writ. Or rather, it's three writs.'

'You need a lawyer.'

'Thanks. I'd never have guessed. It's three writs. All from people living in Layton Road. Sueing the club for persistent trespass by our loyal fans, various amounts of damage by the same loyal fans stretching back over a period of years, and applying to the court to get the Layton Road entrance closed on match days.'

'Is that bad?'

'The first two bits aren't so bad. We don't mind paying out a bit to keep the locals sweet. Customer relations, it's called, Duffy.'

'Never heard of it.'

'The Layton Road entrance, as you might not know, being a supporter of the wrong team, is where all our bad boys go in. So that they can shout rude things from the Piggeries end.'

'How bad are your bad boys?'

'About as bad as you can get.'

'It's not like that at QPR.'

'Really? I suppose all your bad boys just sing nursery rhymes, applaud the referee, and line up for fingernail inspection afterwards?'

Duffy grinned. 'That's about it. Nice family club, QPR. So anyway?'

'So if home and away fans have to go in at the same entrance, there's bound to be a bit more aggravation, isn't there?'

'Still, if I lived in Layton Road and had to put up with all your bad boys, I'd have done the same myself before now.'

'Point taken. But why now? It's not as if it's the start of the season. There's only half a dozen home matches left.'

'Hmm. Anything else?'

'You seen one of these before?'

Lister passed him a crudely printed handbill. It read:

WANTED!

ARE YOU YOUNG? ARE YOU STRONG?
ARE YOU BRITISH?
ARE YOU FED UP WITH THE WAY
THIS COUNTRY HAS GONE SOFT?
ARE YOU FED UP WITH THE WAY
THIS COUNTRY IS PUSHED AROUND?
DO YOU THINK THE RACES CAN
LIVE SIDE BY SIDE?
DO YOU BELIEVE IN REPATRIATION?
ORGANIZE!
STRENGTH WILL WIN!
JOIN THE RED WHITE AND BLUE
MOVEMENT!

'Never had any of this stuff down here before,' said Lister. 'At least, that's what the physio says, and he's been here for years. Never anything like that.'

'Not very nice,' said Duffy, after reading it and looking in vain for a printer's name at the bottom. 'How long have they been dishing these out?'

'No idea,' said Lister. 'Weeks, months? They made the mistake of giving one to some student the other Saturday; he sent it in to us. Said he felt a bit relieved he'd left off his Anti-Nazi League badge for the afternoon.'

'What's it got to do with football?'

'In theory, nothing. We don't mind how many whackos we let in through the turnstiles as long as they pay their money. And as long as they behave themselves.'

'These don't?'

'Not sure. Don't know how long they've been handing these things out.'

'What's the Red White and Blue Movement?'

'Never heard of it. But I remember something similar down at Millwall a year or two ago. What happens is that

384

these, what do you call them, neo-Nazis or whatever, start using the grounds as recruiting centres. Wanted – Big strong white men to beat up small brown men: that's about what this says, isn't it?'

'More or less.'

'So the Nazis recruit the thugs, and the thugs all watch the football together, and the thugs go to the Nazi rallies, and bring more thugs along to watch the football. And the thugs drive away the fans. Why should anyone come along here and pay a couple of quid to stand in the rain and see his side lose and then get spat at by some fourteen-year-old skinhead as he's leaving the ground?'

'It doesn't happen at QPR,' said Duffy.

'Well it's not going to bloody happen here. I don't train a team to play in front of a crowd of yobboes who might or might not give us a passing glance when they take a breather from stabbing one another and ripping the safety barriers apart.'

'I see the point, er, Jimmy. But it's a little long-term, isn't it?' Lister, he thought, was clearly a worrier.

'I'll give you the short-term, then. The news hasn't exactly crept into the papers yet, and it's your friend and mine Ken Marriott who's helping keep it out at the moment. But there've been quite a lot more fights at the last few home matches. Quite a bit more boot than usual. Now what this means is, more policemen. I don't know if you know much about how the police work – '

'Not much.'

' – but they don't just turn up to our matches out of the kindness of their hearts and because they want to see a good game of football. For a start, this is private property, and we have to invite them in to get them. Second, we have to have a weekly conference about how much work we think we're going to give them. And third, we have to pay them. Saturday afternoon is overtime rates, as well.'

Duffy remembered all too well. Pulled out of his Saturday

rest day and bussed up to North London. However much you frisked the thugs, they still managed to find things to throw at you. Once, he was in a line of eight coppers – eight neat helmets standing in a row – when someone on the terraces had heaved half a brick at them. As it whizzed through the air, about a hundred friendly supporters started chanting, 'Coconut! Coconut!' He hadn't thought much to those Saturday afternoons.

'So more thugs means more fights means more police means more money. Closing Layton Road means more fights means more police means more money. And there's another thing. They've started booing big Brendan.'

'Brendan Domingo?'

'Yup. Never happened before. He's used to being booed at away games, that's normal. But he's been in the team for nearly two seasons now, and always been popular at home. Now the Layton Road end has started booing him.'

'Is he out of form?'

'Brendan? He's playing like a dream. Never better. That spell of a dozen games with Danny really sparked him. Lovely control. Silky skills. He's our best player now. Whether he'll stay like that if the Layton Road end keeps it up ... It's very demoralizing, Duffy, being booed by your own supporters. Makes you wonder why you should give a monkey's.'

'I know.' Duffy had been booed one Sunday by the entire Reliables supporters' club; both of them.

'I mean, if *I* were him, I wouldn't give a monkey's.' Lister sighed. He was looking worried again. Duffy decided to sum up.

'You think someone's out to get you, don't you? The club, that is.'

'I think I do.'

'So what you want me to do is find out who clobbered Danny Matson, find out why the Layton Road residents are suddenly cutting up rough, stop the neo-Nazis gathering at home matches, stop the thugs booing Brendan Domingo, stop Brendan Domingo losing his form, save you from relegation – and help you keep your job.'

'Sounds as if you've got your hands full.'

'I'm saving up for a dog,' Duffy threw in light-heartedly, and immediately regretted it. Shit, why did he say that? Why had it slipped out again? He thought Jimmy Lister had a sense of humour. Listen, Duffy, *no* client has a sense of humour, remember? Even if he laughs a lot.

'Any questions?'

'Well, I'd like to meet the chairman.'

'He's not in till the day after tomorrow. I suppose he might see you at his headquarters if you asked nicely, though.'

'Thanks. No, that'll do for the moment.'

They got up, and Lister showed him towards the door. Duffy noticed that there weren't any cups or trophies in the office. Nothing silver at all. Perhaps all that stuff was kept in the boardroom. Or perhaps Athletic had never won anything.

'You play in goal, I hear?'

'Uh-huh. You don't happen to know where your lymph nodes are, do you?'

'No idea. Ask the physio.'

'Right.'

They shook hands.

'Oh, er, Jimmy?'

'Yes?'

'Why aren't you wearing the white shoes?'

'I'm not a berk, Duffy.'

'Right.'

Danny Matson was sitting in a purple armchair with his leg up on a footstool. A copy of the *Sun* had been placed on the stool so that his plaster cast wouldn't mess it up. Mrs Ferris kept a clean set of digs; always had, since she'd started taking in boys for Athletic a dozen years ago. The club liked to look after its players. The best way of looking after them, of course, was to see that they got married. A player needed stability, the club always said: all that rushing around and adulation, best thing for him is a nice wife at home, a couple of toddlers, a car to take down the car-wash and a garage to paint in the winter. Stops them losing their heads, stops them taking to the booze and the birds too much (mind you, even the married ones got a bit naughty sometimes: take them off on a pre-season friendly tour to some hot country and you wouldn't believe the high jinks). But you couldn't force them to get married; so until that time the club liked to put them in reliable digs with careful, motherly ladies who were always given a pair of free tickets to the home games. They weren't there to spy on the lads; they were there to look after them; though, of course, if one of the boys was having a bit of trouble that the landlady thought the club ought to know about, then they'd be more than grateful for a quiet hint on the side. Who wouldn't be?

The club liked to lodge the lads in pairs. 'The animals came in two by two,' as Mrs Ferris would tend to shout out from her kitchen when her couple of boys had some trouble with the front door after a hard Saturday night on the Bacardi. The boys were company for one another; they talked about the game a bit, and it was surprising how often their understanding on the park improved if they roomed together. Danny Matson roomed with Brendan Domingo. When Duffy called, Brendan was out: down at the ground doing his sprints, lifting his weights, trying one-touch stuff with the player they'd brought in to replace Danny, practising corners and free-kicks, or simply off at one end of the pitch by himself improving his silky skills. Danny sat with his big white foot up on a copy of the *Sun* and waited for Brendan to come home. The whole business really rather pissed him off.

He looked a slight lad to Duffy: pale, long face, with black hair in a curly perm that was just beginning to grow out.

Footballers always looked a little smaller off the pitch; this one was no exception. He waited for Duffy's questions with politeness – the Boss had phoned ahead and asked him to co-operate in any way he could – but a sort of cheerful boredom. He didn't care any more who had done his leg. It was done, wasn't it? Snapped. Danny thought of all the players who'd had Achilles trouble. They were never quite the same again, even if they were still good. Look at Trevor Francis. Blistering speed he used to have; blistering. Then the trouble, and the lay-off, and at least a yard of pace had gone by the time he came back. Still a fine player, in Danny's view – don't get me wrong, still a fine player – but not world class any more. Not world class.

They went through the incident in the car-park; the police had already done that with him a few times. Duffy asked if there was any detail he might have forgotten; then asked him a lot about the girl who'd picked him up, or who he'd picked up (the precise order of things was still a bit blurry). Did the men say anything? How long did it take to walk from The Knight Spot to the car-park? Who was on duty at the pay-out? And so on.

'If you don't mind my saying, mister, I've been asked these questions before.'

'Well, there might be something you've forgotten. Some little detail. That's why I'm asking them again.'

'But the coppers have already done that. Asked it once, then sent someone else back a bit later in case there was anything I'd forgotten.'

'Well, third time lucky, perhaps.'

But it wasn't third time lucky. The men hadn't said anything; he hadn't seen their faces; they hadn't taken anything more than his wallet and his watch; no, he couldn't remember anything more about this Denise girl. Black hair, he'd said, black dress and showing quite a lot. Sure he'd liked her; but that didn't mean he could re-member much about her. Sure he'd recognize her if he saw her again, he wasn't thick.

'Danny, I wonder if you'd do something for me. I wonder if you'd go down The Knight Spot with me one evening and have a look for her.'

'Well, that's very smart thinking, if I may say so, Mr Duffy, but you see I've already done that with the coppers. Twice. And she wasn't there.'

This didn't surprise Duffy too much. He was only an ex-copper himself: he was bound to do some things the same way as the coppers. Neither did the girl's disappearance surprise him: if she'd been genuine, and really was a nice ordinary girl, she'd probably have got in touch with Danny. The attack had been in all the papers. Why hadn't she dropped him a line saying she was sorry she hadn't waited but it had been perishing cold, and she was sorry about his accident, and maybe she could pop round in her nurse's outfit and ruffle his hair? But on the other hand, the fact that she hadn't written didn't necessarily make her a phoney. Perhaps she just liked her footballers all in one piece.

'I expect you'll be going to see Vince,' said Danny.

'Who's Vince?'

'Vince runs The Knight Spot.'

'Right.'

'And Fat Frankie?'

'Who's Fat Frankie?'

'Fat Frankie's the bouncer.'

'Expect so.'

'Well, Fat Frankie can't remember one person going out of the club from the next. Not unless they make trouble. Plus which, he's got a bit of a lager problem. Vince didn't even see me with a girl all evening.'

'How do you know?'

'The coppers checked it all out. How else?'

'Danny, will you come down The Knight Spot with me once more?'

'No. No. Look, I'd like to help, obviously. But ... the

390

plain fact is I promised myself I wouldn't go back, not till I was in the first team again. It made me feel bloody awful going down there with the coppers, I don't mind telling you. Going in on bloody crutches, seeing all those people dancing. I even ran into one of the lads.'

'Yeah, I see.'

'I mean, it's not like I got this going for a fifty-fifty ball or something. I'd just be sitting there in plaster and they wouldn't be thinking, "Oh look, isn't that Danny Matson up there, pity about the injury, brave lad isn't he, wonder how long he'll be out, why don't we buy him a drink and cheer him up?" No, it wouldn't be that, it'd be, "Look at that Matson kid over there, what a wally, gets himself pissed and beaten up just when the team needed him most, makes you sick, doesn't it?" '

That's probably what they would be thinking, Duffy silently agreed. But Danny was a willing lad – apart from anything else he seemed glad of company – and eventually they struck a compromise. Duffy would pick him up one evening; they'd park outside The Knight Spot and just watch the customers going in. Danny thought he could handle that; and the Boss had asked him to co-operate as best he could.

'You follow the game much, Mr Duffy?'

'A bit. QPR's my team, though.'

'Ah well, now, QPR. Don't let the Boss catch me saying it, but QPR's a classy outfit. Classy.'

Duffy nodded. They lapsed into silence.

'It's a funny old game, Mr Duffy, isn't it?' Duffy agreed. 'I mean, I haven't been in it long, not really in it, not at first-team level, but already it's taught me a thing or two.' Duffy nodded. 'It can be a very kind game, Mr Duffy, it can give you lots of things.' Duffy nodded again. 'And it can be a very cruel game. It can build you up; and then it can knock you down. It's a bit like life, really, isn't it?'

Duffy concurred.

'Have a feel in that pocket over there.' Danny was pointing to his blazer, which hung on the back of the door. Duffy reached in and pulled out a square of slightly shiny paper. On a nod from Danny he unfolded it and laid the two pages side by side. Spread across most of them was a large photograph of a sitting room. Crouched in the middle of a huge area of brightly patterned carpet was a smiling, dark-haired man holding a small child. The child was half-balanced, rather precariously, on a football.

'That's Trevor Brooking's room,' said Danny. 'I got it out of one of the posh Sundays.'

Duffy examined the photograph. He saw a couple of large wooden cabinets, mostly full of silverware; a large yellow leather armchair, matching a large yellow leather sofa; a carved fireplace; a low glass-topped coffee-table.

'Very nice,' he said.

'That's Warren. With Trevor. He's nearly four. Well, he was nearly four when the photo was taken. I suppose he's a bit bigger now. And there's Colette, she was seven. And there's Hilke, she's Finnish. That's Trevor's wife. Hilke keeps the place really tidy, it says.'

'Very nice.' Duffy liked the sound of Hilke.

'Look at the picture Trevor's got over the fireplace.' Duffy could just make out a gold frame; inside it, a family, standing somewhere.

'That's Trevor getting his MBE at Buckingham Palace. With Hilke, and Warren, and Colette. They have this photographer standing outside, and he takes the picture, and then you have it framed.'

'Nice.'

'Do you see the decanters? And look at that fireplace. It's not a real fireplace, actually, there isn't a chimney, but Trevor likes fireplaces so he had it put in. It's electric.'

'Nnn.'

'And look at the way the stereo's built in. That must have cost a bomb. And the chess set. And the candlesticks on the coffee-table. I bet they're real silver.'

'It's a very nice room, Danny.'

'His wife's Finnish. She's called Hilke.'

'Very nice.'

'He's one of the all-time greats, Trevor Brooking, don't you think?'

'No question.' Duffy refolded the pages carefully. 'Better be on my rounds, Danny. Might call back some time if that's all right?'

'Sure. Any time. One thing I can't work out – do you think the room's really as big as that, or do you think they took the photo with one of those wide-angle lenses?'

Duffy unfolded the pages again.

'It's hard to tell.'

He turned to go. It was only about four feet from the middle of the room to the door. If ever they came to do Danny Matson's room, they'd certainly need a wide-angle lens.

Three phone calls. The first to Jimmy Lister, asking what the club's policy was on the Layton Road residents.

'Delay, Duffy. Delay the case as long as possible. I mean, it's coming up in court this Friday, so they can try and close the gates for Saturday. But even if it goes against us, we can try appealing, or whatever.'

'Has anyone been down to talk to the residents?'

'No. We thought about it. But we decided the best way of making sure everything happens as slowly as possible was to do it through solicitors. Then if it all works out in the end we'll bung them a few free tickets, something like that.'

'What about the press?'

'Complete news blackout, that's our policy on the press, Duffy.'

'No one been sniffing around?'

'No one.'

The second call. To Ken Marriott at the *Chronicle*.

'Ken, if I asked you whether or not you'd heard a particular story and you hadn't, that wouldn't necessarily be the same as me telling you the story, would it?'

'How do you mean?'

'I mean, you could hold off for a day or two, and pretend I'd told you later, couldn't you?'

'I suppose so. It'd depend a bit on copy day, and what the story was. This week – this week I could give you forty-eight hours easily. Unless there's a lot of work to do on the story.'

'Did you know about Athletic being sued by local residents?'

'No. Interesting. Which residents? Where? What for?'

'Forty-eight hours?'

'As long as you come back to me and no one else.'

'Right.'

Third call. To the Anti-Nazi League.

'Oh, it's Ken Marriott of the *West London Chronicle*. *West London Chronicle*. Wondered if you can help us. We're doing a story about neo-Nazis recruiting at football matches. We think it might be starting up at the Athletic ground – some outfit called the Red White and Blue Movement. Just wondered if you had any information on them?'

They had, it seemed, more than enough information on the Red White and Blue Movement. Especially about its affiliation to other, similar groups, most of whom Duffy had never heard of, and about its exact political position, which sounded pretty nasty, and about its organizing members, their backgrounds and criminal records. It was an impressive dossier, and Duffy pretended to be taking it all down. What he mainly wanted to ask, though, was how long the Movement had been in existence, and where it operated from. Six months, and an address in Ealing were the answers. Duffy offered fraternal thanks, and rang off.

Layton Road consisted of two low terraces of red-brick Victorian villas. They were neatly kept; some of them had been freshly painted. It looked a houseproud little street.

394

Duffy approved. He took out a notebook and started at number 37.

'Oh, good morning, sir – '

'No.'

'But I'm – '

'No samples, no religions,' the man said. He was small and fierce, with crinkly grey hair and a jutting chin; he looked like a retired PT instructor.

'I'm from the *Chronicle*. The *West London Chronicle*.' At least that stopped the door being shut in his face; just.

'Oh yes.'

'Yes, Mr – Mr – ' Duffy pretended to search his notebook for the name.

'What do you want?'

'Sorry to hear about the trouble you've been having.'

'How did you hear about it?'

'That's what we're paid to do.'

'Snoopers,' said the man. Duffy didn't feel he was getting anywhere. Suddenly the door was opened wide, the PT instructor came out, took him by the arm and marched him the four yards to the gate. Oh well, all in a reporter's day, he reflected. When they got there, however, the fellow kept hold of Duffy's arm and pushed him gently against the gate.

'Bullivant,' he said, answering a much earlier question. 'Look at it,' he went on, pointing at the street. 'Nice, isn't it? Nice little houses. Very clean, very quiet. See all these cars? Nice cars. Every home game we have to move them quarter of a mile away. Freer access for the crowds, that's what the police say. Stop them getting vandalized by the yobboes, that's the truth of it. Look at these front gardens. Notice anything odd about them? Nothing in them. Just hedges, nothing else. No flowers, no plants. No point having flowers, the yobboes just pull them up. No point having window boxes, the yobboes knock them off. No point *chaining* your window-boxes to your window sills, that just excites them some more. Animals.'

'Can you tell me why you haven't complained before?'

'Have complained before. Makes no bloody difference. All they do is send you a couple of free tickets for the next match. Who wants free tickets to watch a bloody awful side like Athletic? Send me free tickets to go and watch Tottenham and you're talking. Anyway, the only time I feel happy about those yobboes is when they're all locked up inside the ground making their animal noises. What on earth makes the club think I want to go inside as well and listen to their obscene chantings from a bit nearer?'

'Ever had a chicken take-away through your door? Course you haven't. Disgusting food. Even the dog wouldn't eat it. Ever had a yobbo doing his ablutions through your letter-box? Course you haven't. Ever had a yobbo doing his business in your front garden? Course you haven't. You don't know what's going on, my lad, you with your sharp pencil and big fat notebook and not writing anything down in it I see. You just don't know what's going on. You know another thing they like doing. They like ringing on the door and asking if they can use the toilet. Course you can't, you say, use the one at the ground, and you close the door on them and there's a bloody great explosion. Know what they've done? They've stuck a lightbulb in the door just as you're closing it. Done that twice to me. Great sense of fun, the yobboes. Then they do their ablutions in your front garden because you wouldn't let them use the toilet. Haven't got any free tickets for Tottenham on you by any chance, have you, my lad? No, I thought not. Good morning to you.'

And Mr Bullivant marched back up his path and slammed the door.

Duffy crossed the road to number 48. The door was opened a couple of inches, as far as the chain would permit.

'Arthur's not in.'

'Good morning, madam, I'm from the *Chronicle*. I was talking to Mr Bullivant – '

'Arthur's not in.'

396

'Could I talk to you instead?'

'He'll be back later.'

'When would be a good time to call?'

'Not now.'

'Thank you for your help.'

At number 57 a red-faced lady in a tight perm and a pinafore answered the door.

'Oh, the *Chronicle*. Very nice. Always read it. If I'd known you was coming I'd have taken off me pinny. Will you be wanting a photograph?'

'Er, not today perhaps.'

'Oh, be sending him round later, will you? That'll give me time to get tidied up. But you'll be the one with the cheque?'

'I'm sorry?'

'You mean I haven't won the Lucky Numbers? No, I can see I haven't. Oh well, another fortune slips through my fingers.' She looked quite cheerful about it.

'No, it's about the trouble with the fans, Mrs – '

'Davis. That's D-A-V-I-S. Right.' She leaned over Duffy's arm while he recorded the first piece of information to enter his notebook. 'Yes, that's right, without an E. No, I don't really mind them myself. They're not bad lads. Not really wicked, just a bit high-spirited. I mean, we were all young once, weren't we?'

Duffy thought he still was young. But perhaps it was a sign of middle age that you felt no inclination to stuff half-eaten take-aways through people's letter-boxes. Yes, that must be it.

'I was just wondering why you all decided to go to law, especially as there are only a few home matches left in the season.'

Mrs Davis looked momentarily flustered, then gathered herself.

'I'm afraid my husband deals with all the bills. He earns the money, he gives me the housekeeping I need – he's a very fair man, my husband, don't you go thinking the contrary – and when the bills come in, he deals with them. Always keep a bit back for a rainy day, that's what he says, and he's quite right too.' Politely, she closed the door.

Duffy was puzzled. In one way, of course, it was all quite straightforward and understandable. The yobboes were getting worse and worse – Jimmy Lister had said they were fighting more on the terraces as well – and the residents had decided enough was enough. But *these* residents? If the yobboes were getting out of hand, they might go to the police. They might complain to the local paper. They might write to their local councillor, if they could remember who that was, or even to their MP. But going to a solicitor and having a writ served? They might go to a solicitor to get divorced, or to make a will. But if someone like Mr Bullivant wanted to stop the yobboes doing their ablutions through his letter-box, then he wouldn't go running to a solicitor. Someone like Mr Bullivant would be far more likely to get out his toolkit, file down the metal edge of his letter-flap until it was really sharp, wait by his door until some heavily-lagered boot-boy stuck his whatsit through the flap, and then *smack*. Very nasty too. Much nastier, and much more satisfying, than running to a pinstripe.

'I'm afraid Mr Prosser isn't too pleased,' said Jimmy Lister. Duffy had called in on his way to see the chairman. 'Not pleased at all. Thinks I'm way out of order hiring you, Duffy. Says he won't be putting this through the firm's books.'

'What does that mean?'

'It means that if I want you, I pay for you, Duffy.'

'So am I still in work?'

'Just. But I've done the calculations, and what I'd be paying you, Duffy, would be pretty much my entire salary; once the Taxman's been to call, that is. On top of which I'm currently into an alimony situation. Would you take thirty-five?'

'Oh all right.' Duffy thought he really must master this haggling business, one day.

'And you'll keep the expenses down?'

'No Concorde trips, I promise.'

'Just so we understand each other. Now I'll take you to meet Melvyn.'

Melvyn Prosser's boardroom was where they kept the club's silverware. One yellowing double-handled pot and a couple of shields. The pine-panelled walls of the large oblong room were covered with photographs: of the various Athletic teams down the years, and of the various Athletic Boards of Directors. The directors seemed to change as often as the teams and, in terms of wallspace, to be equally important.

Melvyn Prosser was standing by his desk in his camel-coloured overcoat giving a very decent impression of a busy man. Either he'd just arrived from somewhere, or he was just going somewhere; or perhaps he'd slipped on his overcoat especially for them, so that they'd realize how precious his time was. Having established the heavy suggestion of other priorities, Melvyn Prosser was prepared to be affable. He had a broad, fleshy face, with a vertical crease in the middle of his forehead which might possibly have been old scar tissue. It had been a quick climb, from blue collar to white collar to boardroom, and it couldn't have been achieved if Melvyn hadn't known how to smile while stamping on your fingers.

'James, welcome back. And Mr Duffy. Welcome. Sherry, beer? A pint of hooch, Mr Duffy, perhaps?' Duffy shook his head. It was quarter to eleven in the morning. 'Quite right. I'll abstain as well. Now James has told me about his curious decision to hire you, and as I expect you've heard, I very nearly said you may do the hiring, Jimmy, but I do the firing. Still, as the financial aspects have been sorted out I don't see any objection to you hanging around if you want to.'

'Thanks very – '

'Though I wouldn't mind being allowed to give you my

view of the matters which Jimmy has doubtless already laid before you with a different emphasis.' Prosser gave a chairman's pause, the sort of pause which expects some sycophant to mumble, 'Go ahead, please, Mr Chairman.' When none of this was instantly forthcoming, Prosser continued. 'I've heard what Jimmy's had to say and I'll tell you what I told him. I don't go in for conspiracy theories. I think we're chasing our own tails. I think *we* – that's a polite way of referring to my manager – are looking for excuses. I think *we* are in danger of losing our concentration on the matters in hand.'

'You don't think – '

'I would be as reluctant to criticize James as the next man, but I'm bound to say that he is in danger of looking for excuses. The club is not in the happiest of positions currently in the matter of League table position – in fact, if you'll pardon the phrase, it's all a bit dicky. But the way out of the maze is not to be found among the boot-boys on the terraces or among the residents of Layton Road. At least, that's my own ill-informed opinion. The way out of the maze is to be found on the park. Nowhere else. What I worry about is that our friend James's concentration on the matters in hand is in danger of going down the karzy, if you see what I mean.'

'You don't think anyone's trying to ... ' Duffy wasn't quite sure how to put it.

'Trying to waggle the digit in the wrong orifice? Tell me who. Tell me why. Who cares if the club gets relegated? I do, Jimmy does, the Board does, the players and their wives do, and a few hundred of the older-style fans do. But why should anyone else care one way or another? I think we're in danger of looking for excuses, as I say. We're taking our minds off what really matters: how the players are playing. Jimmy's job, as I see it, is and always will be to do Jimmy's job.'

'Can I ask if you have any particular enemies, Mr Prosser?'

Prosser laughed, and then smiled a little patronizingly at Duffy.

'Did you see the car on the way in? Corniche, right? Gold Rolls-Royce Corniche, right? Now you don't get one of those in this society of ours without treading on a few toes, I'll give you that for nothing.'

'Anyone in particular?'

Prosser laughed again.

'Listen, if anyone was out to get *me*, they wouldn't do it through the club. It's nice having a club and all that, and believe me I'm committed to its future, but if I was the Big Bad Wolf out in the bushes looking to make it hot for Mel Prosser, I'd be going after some of his other business interests. Much easier. I wouldn't be bothered to start by duffing up his Davey Matsons.'

'Danny, chief.'

'Danny Matsons. How is the lad, Jimmy?'

'Bit down in the mouth, chief.'

'He's a good lad. Must be a bit of a blow, losing his first-team bonus.'

'But if,' Duffy persisted, 'there was someone ... some enemy – who would he be?'

'Vic Rivers, Solly Benson, Wally Mountjoy, Fiddler Mick, Steve Wilson, Charlie Magrudo, *Mrs* Charlie Magrudo, Dicky Jacks, Michael O'Brien, Tom Clancy, Stacky Stevenson, Reg Dyson ... ' Prosser spread his hands. 'How many more do you want? My friends are my enemies. I like them, but I'd do them; same goes for them the other way round. I'm a businessman, do I make myself clear?'

'Anyone in particular?'

Prosser looked irritated. He looked as if he was being asked to squeal on a friend. He was, in a way.

'*Maybe* Charlie Magrudo. Maybe. I did him a bit of naughty a year or two ago.'

'What sort of naughty?'

'Not very naughty. Heard he was trying to line a few council pockets and fix himself up with a contract or two.' Melvyn smiled at the memory. 'So I dropped him in it and walked off with them myself. He didn't like it much. But I'm sure he's forgiven me by now.'

'Did he go down for it?'

'Go down? Good God no. I wouldn't do *that* to him. No, it was all kept within the old cream paint of the Town Hall. And then I got the contracts by laying out just half what Charlie had laid out. I liked that.'

Prosser turned his mind back to Duffy.

'And what have we found out so far that our friends in blue have missed? Any little leads? Giving young James his money's worth, I hope.'

'Not really. I'm trying to jog Danny Matson's memory. And I've been down Layton Road.'

'You've been down Layton Road? Harassing our residents and loyal supporters? That's a bit out of line, I'd say.'

'I wasn't harassing them. They were very co-operative.'

'Oh yes?'

'Yes, they wanted to tell me all about what the yobboes did through their letter-boxes.'

'It's a terrible area, this,' said Prosser, hunching his shoulders in melodramatic resignation. 'Born and brought up within the sound of Sainsbury's supermarket, but it's sometimes hard to be loyal to it.'

'Mr Prosser, can I try out something else?'

Prosser checked his watch.

'You have three minutes and forty-five seconds.'

'Is the club making a profit?'

'You need to ask? No, the club is not making a profit, the club is making a healthy loss. It's the thing this club does most efficiently. James and I had various schemes at the beginning of the season with which we hoped to allure the paying customers, but I fear it was all pissing in the wind. We're lucky to get three thousand for a home game, and I'm afraid we're not one of the League's top attractions when we travel. What did we get at Rotherham? Under fifteen hundred, as I recall. No Cup run worth speaking of ... '

'Putting it bluntly, Mr Prosser, are you paying most of the bills out of your own pocket?'

'Answering it bluntly, Mr Duffy, yes I am.'

'Would the club be a viable proposition in the Fourth Division?'

'Duffy, those are words we do not utter anywhere on these premises, do you understand? No one, but no one, mentions those words.'

'Sorry. Sorry. But I was just ... Look, in the extremely unlikely event of ... of the worst coming to the worst, what would happen? I mean, what would actually happen?'

'Well, if a certain sad day in the history of this distinguished club were to come to pass, the first thing to happen is that Jim-boy here would be on his bike and looking into his career prospects. Sorry, Jimmy.'

'You've always been level with me, chief. I wouldn't expect anything else.'

'And then?' said Duffy.

'Then it would be a matter for the Board.'

'Or at least for its major shareholder.'

'Yes I am as a matter of fact. Clever of you to guess. Well, yes, there would be various options to consider.'

'Any you'd care to share with us? Purely in the unlikely event of, naturally.'

'Naturally. Well, the chairman would have to resign.'

'Melvyn,' said Jimmy with genuine surprise. 'You couldn't ... Not after all you've done for the club.'

'James, let's not get sentimental. All I've done for the club in my two years as chairman is foot a not inconsiderable wages bill, redesign the players' strip, appoint you, preside over a four-figure decline in attendance, and watch us go down the table from tenth to twenty-second.'

'And what else?' asked Duffy.

'Are you always so persistently gloomy, Mr Duffy? What else? Well, I imagine the Board would go through the usual motions, there would be much wailing and gnashing of teeth, the playing staff would be reduced, the best players would be sold off, we might start looking for a cheap manager. Or we could just wind the whole thing up.'

'If the chief shareholder said so.'

'The chief shareholder would obviously have an influential say in the matter.'

'You couldn't do that, Melvyn,' said Jimmy protestingly. 'It's not as if we were bottom of the unmentionable and applying for re-election.'

'Times have changed, James. Times are hard. Every division has half a dozen clubs scraping along on the breadline, with some indulgent chairman holding them up by the bootstraps. Just because you aren't bottom of that division which we agree not to mention by name doesn't mean you're safe. Who's going to pay the wages? Where are they going to find another Melvyn Prosser from? I don't mind telling you I've tried looking around a bit in the last few months, and I reckon I've got about as much chance of unloading this club as I have of selling choc-ices to the Eskimos.' There was a silence. 'But I'd better be on my way, before I cheer you up some more. Still, what I've just said ought to persuade you of one thing, Mr Duffy.'

'You tell me.'

'That if there is a Big Bad Wolf out to get me, his best tactics are to make sure we avoid relegation so that I carry on being bled dry paying the bills for another year.'

'Point taken,' said Duffy, as Melvyn Prosser swept off for an appointment with his gold Rolls-Royce Corniche. Jimmy Lister was head down, and flattening his remnants of sandy hair with his fists. Duffy felt sorry for him. Eventually Jimmy stopped rubbing his head and spoke.

'Bit of a choker, that.'

'Sorry if I led him on a bit.'

'No, no, it's best to have the cards on the table. Just to check that you don't have any trumps. It's all going wrong, isn't it? All going wrong for me, all going wrong for Melvyn.

It must be costing him a packet.'

'Hmm.' Duffy wouldn't commit himself this early. 'Just out of interest, how did he get involved in the club?'

'I don't know, why does anyone want to do anything as daft as own a football team?'

'Try telling me,' said Duffy.

'Well, sometimes it's in the family. There are a few clubs that are almost like family businesses. Father to son, old aunt Mabel with the casting vote on the Board and so on. Can be very friendly places to work for, big happy family and all that; or they can be bloody awful, with the chairman picking the team. Then there are the people who want to own a club simply because they're football nuts. Love the game, watched it from the terraces, made a pile, and can't wait to have a set of toy footballers to play with, like the toy soldiers they used to have as a kid. They're really keen on the game, come to all the matches, don't bother too much about the bottom line. If things go well, they're probably the best sort to work for.'

'Judging from the way Mr Prosser can't even get the names of his players right, I gather we wouldn't classify him as a football nut?'

Jimmy laughed.

'Well, he does his best, old Melvyn. No, he really tries. He likes saying things like "Class ball" and "Super skills" and "Screamer" – though truth to tell this old team doesn't give him much opportunity to use his vocabulary. No, I think even Melvyn would admit that he's the third sort of owner. Local boy made good, done well for himself, got all he wants, got the big house, the business, the money, and doesn't know what to do with it all of a sudden. Buying the nearest team seems the answer. Nice bit of fame, picture in the paper almost whenever you want it. Local hero and all that. Takes you out of yourself as well – it's a different world, seems glamorous at first, even if it seems a lot less glamorous after a couple of years. And everyone dreams of the Cup run –

Wembley, the twin towers, sitting in the Royal Box, all the stuff that never comes.'

'So what does the club need now, if Melvyn Prosser's thinking of pulling out?'

'It needs another nice sucker like Melvyn Prosser,' said Jimmy ruefully.

On the drive to Ealing Duffy suddenly remembered Don Binyon. Stocky, balding, and with an unkind sense of humour, Binyon had been an occasional drinking companion down at the Alligator. Duffy hadn't fucked Binyon – didn't really fancy him – but he'd enjoyed his company. Nice sense of humour, if a bit cutting. Liked to tell people the truth about themselves; very keen on doing that. One evening Duffy, who had been feeling a bit sorry for himself and was punishing the shorts more than he should have done, got a bit talkative. Even tried to explain himself in some funny sort of way. Went on about Carol, and the frame-up, and who he went to bed with. It was a mistake trying to explain himself; not just a mistake, but cheeky as well. Binyon was the guy who explained people. Binyon knew Duffy better than Duffy did.

'Thing about you, Duffy,' said Binyon rather impatiently after his companion had begun to ramble a bit and repeat himself. 'Thing about you, Duffy, is: you're queer. Don't give me any of this bisexual shit. I've heard it all before. It's just a way of saying, Oh no, I'm not really – I'm not really *that*. It's a way of trying to pull back when you're already in it up to your whatsit. You're queer, Duffy. I've seen you operating here often enough to know what you are. You're queer, Duffy. *I'm* queer, *you're* queer, let's have another drink.'

They had another drink.

'But if I'm queer,' said Duffy, who was beginning to feel the strain of the conversation, what with all these shorts, 'if I'm queer, why do I like Carol more than anyone else?'

406

'Nothing odd about that. Most queers like women. Most women like queers. I'm sure she's a very nice girl, heats a tin of soup up something wonderful. That's got nothing to do with it. And the proof of the pudding, if I may briefly allude to the matter, is the fact that you have a winkle problem with her.'

'But that's because – *that*'s because of that thing that happened ... '

'No, Duffy, the thing that happened just brought it all out into the open. Your winkle problem is your body's way of saying you're queer.'

'But I've been – I've been with girls since,' said Duffy, feeling unaccountably shy all of a sudden.

'How many, eh? How many?' Binyon was almost jeering. Well, not as many as ... but the reason was obvious ... I mean, given that ... Duffy's brain was running out of petrol. Binyon patted him gently on the shoulder. 'Don't fret yourself, Duffy. And I'm not even trying to get off with you. But you don't fool me, and I don't see why you should fool yourself. If you're not queer, then I'm Selfridges.'

That conversation had worried him. In fact, the next person he'd been to bed with after it had been a girl; but no doubt Binyon would have had an answer for that too. Was he simply gay (Binyon, though gay himself, always preferred the word 'queer', as if he were telling some brutal truth)? In a way, Duffy didn't mind if Binyon was right. He just disliked being regimented like this. You lot stay on this side of the street, and you lot over there keep to that side of the street. No jay-walking; use of the zebra crossing forbidden; and if you try leaping over the pedestrian barrier you'll get run down by a balding man with an unkind sense of humour.

Duffy had remembered this conversation from a couple of years back because of his current preoccupation. Bela Kaposi and his travelling sarcoma. Certificate X. They said you could get AIDS if you were either homosexual or bisexual. Presumably if you were bisexual there was a smaller chance, in basic statistical terms: every girl you'd been to bed with meant one percentage point, or tenth of a percentage point, less chance of night sweats and swollen lymph nodes. On the other hand, there were probably some bisexuals who ended up going to bed with more guys than some homosexuals did. Like himself, for instance. He'd always said that for him the difference between having a girl or a guy was the difference between bacon and egg and bacon and tomato. He still thought that was true. He also had to admit that he'd eaten a lot of breakfast in his time. He looked at the backs of his hands on the driving wheel. Still all clear there, at least. If only he'd known at the time, he could have asked Binyon where your lymph nodes are. It was the sort of thing Binyon would have been sure to know.

Staverton Road, Ealing was a short cul-de-sac of inter-war mock-Tudor semis. Each stretch of pavement supported a pair of lime trees, freshly pollarded. At the end of the street, in front of a decaying brick wall that sealed it off from the railway line, was a car up on blocks; it was shrouded in grey plastic sheeting and its wheels had been removed.

It wasn't hard to spot the headquarters of the Red White and Blue Movement. One of the semis had a flagpole in its small front garden and was flying the Union Jack. Duffy didn't even bother to check the number he'd been given by the Anti-Nazi League.

The door was answered by a middle-aged man with a red face and small piggy eyes. For someone answering his own front door at eleven o'clock on a Wednesday morning, he was very smartly dressed. He wore the waistcoat and trousers of a dark three-piece suit, a white shirt caught above the elbows by a pair of elasticated metal armlets, a regimental tie, and well-polished black shoes. He also, for some reason, was wearing a bowler hat. Was this Mr Joyce, the organizing secretary, answering his front door; or was it perhaps some bailiff on the way out?

'Mr Joyce?'

'Yes.'

'I wanted to ask about the Movement.'

'You press?'

'No.'

'You from the Communists?'

'No.'

'Come in.'

Mr Joyce turned away, hung his bowler on the hat-rack by the front door, and led Duffy into a sunlit kitchen. Duffy had deliberately not overdone the sartorial elegance this morning: denim jacket, denim trousers, lumberjack shirt, heavy boots. He didn't look exactly like one of the Layton Road gang; but he looked fairly tough. He also tuned his voice to a plausible frequency.

Joyce sat him down at the small kitchen table and went off into another room. He returned with a fountain pen and what looked like an application form of some sort. As he took a chair opposite Duffy and gave a perfectly normal smile, he suddenly looked less like a bailiff. More like a doctor about to ask your details. How long have you been homosexual, Mr Duffy? How long have you been bisexual? Would you prefer to be homosexual or bisexual? How long have you had this winkle problem? Maybe I'd better have a look at this winkle for you. No, I think I'd better have a look at this skin discoloration first. Yes, rather as I thought. No point worrying about the winkle problem now. Nurse, fetch me a large bowl of Dettol and the humane killer, would you? Aaaargh.

'And what do you want to ask about the Movement, Mr – er – ?'

'Binyon.'

'Mr Binyon.'

'Well, I suppose I want to ask if I can join.' Duffy had decided that he would play things a bit tough, but indicate that he could be respectful if need be to the proper authorities. Like Mr Joyce.

'How did you hear about us?'

'Well, some of the lads on the terraces were talking a bit at half-time. Down at the Athletic on Saturday, down the Layton Road end where I always go; these lads were talking about it at half-time, and I thought, that's the sort of thing for me.'

'May I ask what your politics are, Mr Binyon? First name?'

'Terry. I'm British and proud of it, that's my politics.'

'Yes, well that's a beginning.' Mr Joyce was looking fairly benign, but Duffy couldn't glance up without feeling that the little piggy eyes were examining him very carefully. 'And tell me, what do you think the aims of our Movement are?'

'Beating up the niggers and the Pakkis,' said Duffy with a wolfish snigger.

'Oh dear,' said Mr Joyce, laying down his fountain pen, 'we don't seem to have a case of advanced political development here.'

'Nah, it's all right, Mr Joyce, sir, I was just having you on a bit. From what I could gather from the lads and the way they were talking, it's about being a patriot, isn't it?'

'Yes, you could start like that.'

'I mean, I may be out of order here, Mr Joyce, but as far as I understand it, one of the problems with this country is all the politicians are corrupt. Lining their own pockets, going around in big cars, never listening to the people. I mean, if the people want something, then it's their job to give it us, isn't it? I mean, that's what they're there for. Like hanging. Everyone wants hanging, but they won't give it us.'

'I'm with you on that,' said Mr Joyce.

'Or repatriation. Everyone wants that, but they won't give it us.' Duffy tried to remember the handbill he'd been shown by Jimmy Lister. 'I mean, my generation' – Duffy lopped ten to fifteen years off his age, and hoped he could get away with it – 'My generation, it's all, you know, apaffy, that's what it's like. Apaffy. What's the difference between one set of liars and another set of liars? What we need is where the politicians listen to the people and do what they tell them, that's what we need. I mean I want to be proud of being British. I *am* proud of being British,' he added hastily, 'but I'm pissed off with the way this country's been dragged through the mud lately. It is *Great* Britain, isn't it?'

'It is indeed, Mr Binyon. And how are we going to put that Great back into the name of our country?'

Duffy appeared to give the matter some thought.

'Well, I'm only guessing, here. I mean, you must know a lot more about all this than me. But it looks to me that you've got to kick out all the politicians and get in a new set. And it's gotta be Britain for the British. And repatriation. And putting the Great back into Great Britain. And also if they give you too much agg, then it's beating up the niggers and the Pakkis.'

This time Mr Joyce allowed himself a conspiratorial chuckle. Duffy felt he wanted a wash.

'But only if they give us, as you put it, too much agg, Mr Binyon.'

'Oh yeah. I mean, fair's fair, isn't it?'

'Fair's fair indeed.'

Mr Joyce unscrewed his fountain pen and began to take Duffy's details. To Binyon's name he added a false address in Paddington and a false age. He confessed to being unemployed. He denied, truthfully, any earlier political affiliation to any other movement. He promised to pay ten pounds annually, or five pounds half-yearly, or three pounds quarterly, and handed over three pounds. He signed where indicated. Then Mr Joyce went away again and returned with two books, one held in each hand: the Bible and Shakespeare. Duffy was asked to stand, and to lay one hand on each book.

'I solemnly swear ... '

'I solemnly swear ... '

'That I shall be loyal to Her Majesty the Queen ... '

'That I shall be loyal to Her Majesty the Queen ... '

'And follow the aims and principles of the Red White and Blue Movement ... '

'And follow the aims and – what?'

'Principles.'

'Principles. Aims and principles of the Red White and Blue Movement ... '

'And obey its officers.'

'And obey its officers.'

'Very good. Now we have the medical. Take off your shirt.'

'What?'

'Come on, come on, take off your shirt, just a quick once-over. I am a qualified doctor.'

Duffy reluctantly stripped to the waist.

'Yes, very nice, won't take a minute. No sickle cell anaemia, I hope? Ha ha.'

'Eh?'

'Don't worry, don't worry, no chance of that with *you*.'

Joyce produced an aged stethoscope and applied his attention to Duffy's pectorals. He laid cold fingers on his shoulderblades and tapped. He made Duffy extend his arms full out and checked his fingertips for tremble. Maybe the bloke was a doctor. As well as being a whacko, of course.

'Fine, fine. Don't bother to get dressed again for the moment.'

As Duffy was wondering what came next, Joyce opened his fridge and took out a loaf of sliced white bread. He extracted two pieces and slipped them into the toaster.

'I've had breakfast, Mr Joyce, sir.'

'This isn't breakfast.'

'I think I'd better be off.'

'You've just sworn to obey the officers of the Red White and Blue Movement. Sit down again, Binyon. This won't take long. We've had the medical. Now we're going to have the physical.' Duffy looked at him. Mr Joyce looked at the toaster. '*This*,' he announced, 'is the amusing bit.'

He cleared the few remaining things off the kitchen table and wiped it down with a J cloth. When the toast was done, he lifted the slices out, buttered them thickly, and spread a lot of marmalade on top. He carried them to the table and placed them in the middle, about two feet apart. Then he wiped his hands on the J cloth.

'Arm-wrestling,' he announced. 'Just a little fad of my own. You could call it an initiation ceremony, if you like.'

'Can I put my shirt on?'

'Let's stay as we are, shall we?'

Mr Joyce, one steel armlet glinting in the sun, extended his elbow to the middle of the table, white-shirted forearm rising vertically. Duffy, naked to the waist, put forward his own arm.

'Just a moment,' said Mr Joyce, and carefully adjusted the two pieces of toast. Then he repositioned his elbow next to Duffy's; they locked palms and thumbs.

'On a count of three, shall we say? I leave you the count, Mr Binyon.'

Right, you fucking whacko, thought Duffy, and said very quickly, 'One two three.'

Duffy was fit, extremely fit; and the weight training had no doubt strengthened his forearms. But his initial surge made no impact on Mr Joyce, who held the vertical without trouble. Mr Joyce had clearly done this before. So had Duffy, though probably not as often. After the opening surge that failed, Duffy applied steady pressure, but the opposing arm remained immovably vertical. A minute or so of this, and Duffy changed his tactics. He released his pressure, let his arm fall back from midday to one o'clock, and then sharply reapplied the kick. The first two times he did this he got back to the vertical position with no difficulty, but couldn't make any further progress. The third time he tried it, his arm remained stuck at one o'clock. The next time, it was pressed smartly down to two o'clock. The marmalade was only a couple of inches away. Duffy didn't look at Mr Joyce. It was

413

clearly the time for heroics, he decided, for the killer punch. He gathered his strength and surged. Half a second later his forearm was being mashed into the marmalade.

Joyce got up, wiped the palm of his hand on the J cloth, and tossed it to Duffy.

'I didn't want to mess up that nice shirt of yours,' he said.

On their way to the door Joyce explained about the monthly newsletter and about next week's march from Tower Hill. Duffy couldn't get out of the house quickly enough, and gained a yard or so on Mr Joyce in the short corridor leading from the kitchen. He opened the door and turned to say goodbye – or if not goodbye, at least Fuck off. When he turned, he noticed that Mr Joyce was wearing his bowler hat again.

'You know, there are some days when I feel quite normal,' said Duffy.

'Don't let it worry you, love,' replied Carol.

While they were waiting for Duffy's latest culinary creation – frozen pizza from Marks & Spencer – to cook, he told her about his visit to Ealing.

'Lucky he didn't keep his hat on while you were wrestling, Duffy,' she said. 'I don't think you'd have been able to handle it.'

'Do you think I *am* normal?'

'What's normal? There isn't any normal, is there? And if there was, no you wouldn't be normal, course you wouldn't.'

'Oh.' Suddenly, Duffy wanted very much to be normal, even if normal didn't exist.

'But you're not crackers, if that's what you're asking. You're not even odd. Not to me any more. I mean, you probably *are* odd, but I suppose I've got used to it.'

Duffy took the pizzas out of the oven, and put the baking tray to soak before he sat down to eat.

'Very good, Duffy. Delicious. I like the way you've arranged the bits of green pepper.'

Duffy smiled, and accepted the compliment. They often played this game. He liked playing it. For himself, he thought he'd overdone the pizzas. The base was all crispy. Sure, it was *meant* to be crispy, and he'd cooked it for precisely the length of time it said on the box; but it was so crispy that when you cut into it with your knife bits of it went in all directions. Bits of it even went on the floor; and if there was one thing Duffy hated, it was food trodden into the floor. Not that you could exactly tread things *into* a tile floor, but you could certainly squash them on to it, which Duffy didn't like, and you could also pick them up on your shoes and walk them into other rooms, which Duffy liked even less.

'Ever heard of Charlie Magrudo?'

'No. Should I have?'

'No reason. He's apparently some sort of legit villain around here.'

'No. Too far out for West Central to know about him. Unless he was really big.'

'Sure.'

Carol didn't really like hearing about Duffy's jobs. He talked so little about them that when he did she felt she ought to listen, because there was probably something worrying him; but she didn't really like it. It stirred memories. Old memories of when they'd been colleagues at West Central; courting colleagues. And every so often, Duffy would ask her for a bit of help. Help which meant her breaking police regulations. She didn't like that either. She didn't like divided loyalties. She wished he'd got a job which was quite different, which had nothing to do with the Force. She wished he kept a pub – that was what some ex-coppers did. Except that the brewing companies probably weren't looking for publicans whose careers in the Force had ended the way Duffy's had. She hoped he wouldn't ask her for help; if only because she knew she'd probably give in.

'Oh, Duffy, by the way, I found out about lymph nodes.'

'Uh-huh.' Did he really want to know now? Put to the test, he wasn't sure.

'Yes, I asked someone at the station and they said to ask Dr Hawkins.'

'Uh-huh.'

'They're sort of clumps of things. Under your arms and in your neck and in your groin. That's where they are.'

'What are they for?'

'I couldn't really follow it, but they sounded sort of ... useful, from what Dr Hawkins said.'

'Did he say how big they're meant to be?'

'How big? No, I don't think he did. I mean, I think they're pretty small from what he was saying. Do you think you ought to see the doctor?' Carol didn't mention the word cancer, which had come into Dr Hawkins' explanations.

'No.'

'I mean, if you're worrying, I think you ought to see the doctor.' By 'worrying', Carol meant 'worrying more than usual'. If Duffy went to the doctor every time he worried, he might as well rent space in the surgery for a camp bed.

Duffy knew he shouldn't have asked about lymph nodes in the first place. That was always the trouble: you always found out just enough to make things worse, never enough to make things better. Still, at least he knew where these node things were now; that was one step forward. On the other hand, he didn't know how big they were meant to be, so how could he tell if they were swollen? That was one step back. If you could actually feel them, did that mean they were swollen? Or did that mean they were normal, and that if they got any bigger, then they were swollen?

Still, he wasn't going to any doctor, thank you very much. He didn't want them getting out the leper's bell and packing him off to the Welsh mountains.

'No, I'm not worrying, love, I'm fine. Really, I feel fine.'

She looked as if she didn't believe him, so he came round and bent over her and put his arm round her shoulders. He looked at her and smiled, and in a funny sort of way almost felt like kissing her; but they washed up instead. She washed, and he wiped; her wiping was still a bit hit-or-miss, in Duffy's judgment, though her washing was fine. Very thorough.

Carol had an early start the next morning, and by the time Duffy came to bed she was almost asleep. As he climbed in and settled down, he felt something sharp against his leg. He turned on the bedside light again and felt round the sheet a bit. He might have known. He might have known. A small piece of pizza crust. That's *exactly* what he meant. He really would have to give the pizzas five minutes less the next time. There's nothing wrong with soggy crust. People with false teeth must always cook it like that. Unless ... unless you didn't kill the bacteria properly if you didn't cook it for the length of time they said on the box. Perhaps Dr Hawkins would know about that. He'd get Carol to ask him. He snuggled up to her back and half-curled round her.

Duffy fell asleep quickly, and the dreams came quickly too. He saw Binyon standing on the bar at the Alligator wearing a black bra and knickers, suspender belt and black stockings. He saw yobboes marching down Layton Road carrying Union Jacks. He saw Binyon and Mr Joyce arm-wrestling. He saw himself keeping goal for the Reliables and every time he went to pick the ball out of the net it had turned into a soggy pizza. He saw Binyon again on the next barstool at the Alligator turning to him and saying, 'The thing about you, Duffy, is that you're a lymph node. You may pretend not to be, but that's what you are.' He saw Melvyn Prosser in his gold Rolls-Royce Corniche reversing over Danny Matson's leg. He saw ...

He woke up suddenly. He was still curled close to Carol, but two things were different from when he'd gone to sleep. Two things had happened. He was sweating, that was the first thing. He touched his forehead with his fingers and thought, *That*, Duffy, is sweat. *That* is a night sweat.

The second thing which had happened was that he had an erection. He didn't believe this either, but a check with the same fingertips confirmed the fact. *That*, Duffy, he said to himself, is a hard cock. Remember? The first one to come out of hiding for years. With Carol, that is.

There must be some explanation. Perhaps the two surprises were connected. Perhaps his cock was just a lymph node, and it was swollen now because he was going to die in a year or two of this terrible disease. But even so, that was definitely a hard cock.

Thank Christ Carol was asleep.

The next day was one of legwork and small chores. Bits and pieces stuff. He began by dropping round at Danny Matson's digs to invite him down to The Knight Spot that evening. Danny Matson didn't get many invitations, and even a few hours sitting in an old van was better than nothing.

'They found my wallet, by the way. The coppers did.'

'Oh yes? What did they take?'

'Money. Credit card. There wasn't much else. Lucky I didn't have my Trevor Brooking photo in it. They might have taken that.'

'Mmm, they might.' Especially if they'd been Barnsley fans. 'How's the leg?'

'Still there.'

'Keep laughing.'

Then it was back to Layton Road, doing the houses in the opposite order.

At number 57 Mrs Davis answered the door again in her pinafore.

'Oh Wayne,' she called out on seeing Duffy, 'it's that fellow from the *Chronicle* again.' Suddenly she had disappeared and a skinhead in braces took her place. He pushed his face close to Duffy's: either he had bad eyes, or he liked to greet visitors with a head-butt.

'Bugger off, you. You right upset me mam with all that talk of winning the Lucky Numbers.'

'Is your dad in? No, all right, forget it,' Duffy added hurriedly, as the skinhead visibly pondered the need for hostile action.

At number 48 Arthur still wasn't in, and the voice behind the chain gave him even less time than before.

At number 37 Mr Bullivant bounced to the door.

'Yes?'

'Mr Bullivant, it's me again.'

'I can see that, laddie.'

'It's just a couple more questions the office wanted me to check out with you.'

'Well, *check them out* then,' said Mr Bullivant, sneering at the phrase.

'Er, how long would you say this trouble's been going on?'

'Since the day they built the ground.'

'But it's got worse in the last – what? three years? one year? three months?'

'Yes.'

'Yes, which, Mr Bullivant?'

'Yes all three.'

'I see. Now, Mr Bullivant, assuming you win your injunction, that might not necessarily be the end of the matter. The club could appeal. How far are you prepared to go with this action?'

'As far as we have to.'

'All the way, you mean.'

'As I said.'

'Mr Bullivant, is the street behind you on this one?'

'No it's right in front of me, silly bugger. Yes of course it is.'

'Have they – had a whip-round for you?'

'Why do you ask?'

'Well, it could cost you a lot of money. If the club fought it all the way.'

'That's our business. Whose side are you on?'

'I'm just trying to find out what's happening. Mr Bullivant, I wondered if perhaps you had a sponsor.'

'How do you mean?'

'Well, is there someone who's sympathetic to what you're doing and who's said he'll cover any expenses you may incur by bringing this action?'

'I wouldn't tell you if there was.'

'Why not?'

'Why should I?'

'Why shouldn't you?'

'Are you what they call a cub reporter?'

'Well, yes, I suppose I am.'

'Thought so. Still haven't written a word in your notebook in two visits. No wonder there's so many lies in the bloody papers. Good day to you.'

Home; and then a call to Ken Marriott. Could Duffy drop by the *Chronicle* to give him the story? Sure. And in exchange, could Ken wangle him into the newspaper's library for ten minutes or so? No problem.

At the *Chronicle* the 'library' turned out to be a false room built into the open-plan office by setting up four walls of filing cabinets from floor to ceiling. Ken found him the file on Charlie Magrudo and left him alone with it.

There were about a dozen items altogether, covering fifteen years. Each had been cut out and glued to a sheet of foolscap paper. Apart from one substantial profile, most of the items were small. LOCAL BUSINESSMAN DONATES SUNSHINE COACH TO VARIETY CLUB and NEW SUPERMARKET TO BE BUILT ON SCHEDULE, PROMISES CONTRACTOR: that sort of thing. From the clippings, Duffy assembled a picture of a hard-working, home-loving, socially aware, charitable, generous and concerned local businessman who was equally loyal to his employees, his family, the Church and the Rotary Club. From time to time other journalists wandered in to use the library. One looked over Duffy's shoulder.

'Charlie Magrudo, eh?'

'Yes.'

'Why are you interested in him?'

'Oh, he's trying to get a contract up in Islington, and we'd heard he wasn't the cleanest thing that ever drew breath.'

'Charlie Magrudo? Charlie Magrudo's as clean as a whistle. Someone must have been having you on. Pillar of the Rotary Club, and all that.'

'So I'm discovering,' said Duffy. 'Who are you?'

'I'm the chief crime reporter.'

Ken Marriott was quite keen on Duffy's tip-off about the Layton Road residents, and promised he wouldn't let on where the story had come from. Duffy suggested that Ken try to find out if anyone was bankrolling the residents, and added that he had been down there already to ask a few questions; he hoped this didn't affect Ken's chance of getting a good story.

'Don't you worry, old son. I'll get them eating out of my hand. It's surprising how people open up when you tell them you're a journalist.'

'I didn't find that,' said Duffy.

'But you aren't a journalist,' Ken pointed out.

'That's true enough. But you see, I thought the residents mightn't want to talk to me ... '

'Yes?'

'So I said I was you.'

When Duffy got back to his flat there was a message on his answering machine to ring Jimmy Lister. The manager suggested that if Duffy was free he might like to come over to the ground in the next ninety seconds or so.

'Duffy,' said Jimmy as he showed him into his office, 'meet Brendan Domingo.'

'Hi. I hear you're the rising star.'

'Pleased to meet you. Nah, it's all about teamwork really. Get the right set of lads around you and that's what counts.' Brendan looked at the floor. He was large and heavily

421

muscled; though born in Britain, he had very little chance of joining the Red White and Blue Movement. Duffy thought his loyalty to the other players in the Athletic team rather touching. Jimmy Lister had already passed on to Duffy Melvyn Prosser's supportive opinion about his eleven players: this team's a dog, the chairman had said.

'No, if anyone's going to save our necks, it'll be Brendan,' said Jimmy Lister.

'Thanks, Boss,' said Brendan Domingo, still looking at the carpet.

'I gather some of the yobboes are booing you,' said Duffy.

'Yeah. Not very bright of them, is it?' replied Brendan, looking up at Duffy for the first time. Looking up, and then looking down: there was a good seven inches between their heights.

'Does it bother you?'

'Nah,' said Brendan. 'The first time it happened, the very first time, I thought, why don't I just pick up the ball and walk off the pitch? Then I thought, why give them the satisfaction? Second time, I thought, here we go again, and I got rid of the ball a bit quickish. Third time I thought, no that's what they wanted me to do last time, so I showed them a couple of tricks and hit the post from about twenty-five yards.' Brendan was smiling now, and at ease.

'Tell Duffy what you told me.'

'Well, there's not much to tell really. I was in this pub and there was a geezer there and I think he was trying to fix me.'

'Fix you?'

'Yeah, you know, give me a few hundred quid or something. Not that we got around to money after I showed him I wasn't interested.'

'Tell me from the beginning. All the details you can remember.'

'Well, like I said, I was in this pub – '

'The Albion,' put in Jimmy Lister.

' – the Albion, right, having a beer and a couple of pies

after training, and this fellow comes up. Watched me from the terraces, he says, could he buy me the other half, he says. As I was drinking pints – sorry about that, Boss – I said don't mind if you do. So we started talking about the team, and the results, and this and that, and he finally got around to saying that he had a proposition to put to me. If he hadn't said it was a proposition I probably wouldn't have noticed, he did it really clever.'

'What did he say?'

'Well, he said I was the star of the team, blush, blush, and how what would happen if Athletic got relegated, and I said we weren't going to get relegated, we're going to stay up. So he said he liked my attitude, and he said he expected other people would like it too. I ask him what he means, and he says, well look, son, you're under contract, aren't you, two years, three years, five? I tell him three more to go. Well, he says, look at it this way, if Athletic save themselves from relegation, then obviously you're going to carry on in the team, aren't you? Course I am, I say. *But*, he says, suppose some terrible tragedy occurs and you do all go down the toilet, then what's going to happen? The club needs some cash, and the obvious thing to do is to sell their gifted striker. Meaning me. Well, apparently, the word's out on me, he says, people are interested. Nice little Second Division outfit up North, he says. Mid-table, very safe. Couple of years there and I'd be ready for the move into the First Division. So that, he says, is how he sees my career. Choice between another three years slogging along in the basement of the Third Division, or a quick bye-bye and off like a rocket for Brendan. I said I still wasn't getting him, and that's when he said it.'

'What, exactly.' Duffy leaned forward.

'He said that the gentlemen he represented would be more than a bit willing to give a little up front on their investment. On their gifted striker. Meaning me.'

'Very nice,' said Duffy.

'Not very nice is what I thought,' said Brendan.

'No, I meant clever.'

'Yeah, well it wasn't that clever, was it, cause I told him to hop off.'

'Now, Brendan, tell me exactly what this fellow looked like.'

'Oh man, I can't do that. You know, he was sort of average.'

'Old young, big little, well-dressed scruffy?'

'Sort of pretty small; sorry, I mean about your height; oldish – fifty I suppose; thinnish, quite neat, had a mackintosh. But I told him to hop off so he did.'

'How did he talk?'

'Normal. I mean he didn't have a stammer or anything.'

'Colour of his eyes?'

'Man, I don't look at things like that.'

'Hair?'

'Yeah.'

'What do you mean?'

'I mean, like, he had some. He wasn't bald. Look, I'm sorry I don't remember him better. I was eating my pies. And anyway, you know what they say.' He looked up a little mischievously, as if not sure whether to voice his thought. 'All you white folks look the same.'

That evening, Duffy sat in the van with Danny Matson outside The Knight Spot gazing at another collection of white folks who all looked the same. They all looked the same because they all weren't the one person Duffy and Danny were looking for. There were short girls, tall girls, old girls, young girls, girls with cleavage down to their waists and girls as mysteriously shrouded as the car that stood in Mr Joyce's cul-de-sac; but there was no Denise amongst them.

After a couple of hours' waiting, Duffy decided that she might possibly have gone in before they'd arrived. He set off for the entrance to The Knight Spot bearing in his head Danny's less than full description: Denise, dark hair, black dress, showing quite a bit of flesh, dances close to you, hangs around, chases off the other girls, leaves with you, waits while you get the motor, then scarpers. Well, someone was bound to recognize who he was talking about from that, weren't they?

But there was a problem getting into The Knight Spot that evening. The problem was Fat Frankie. Fat Frankie pointed out to Duffy that he wasn't properly dressed for West London's premier club. Fat Frankie pointed out that he wasn't wearing a tie. Fat Frankie said he was the scruffiest bugger who'd tried to get in all evening. When Duffy wanted to remonstrate, Fat Frankie took a lager can and scrunched it up in his great big fist. This impressed Duffy because the lager can was full at the time. What's more, the pressure of Fat Frankie's attentions made the ring-pull burst, and a certain amount of Carling Black Label landed on Duffy's denim jacket. Fat Frankie pointed out that Duffy looked even scruffier now. Duffy wanted to point out to Fat Frankie that he looked like a council rubbish dump; but he took the wiser course of silence.

When he got back to the van, Danny said, 'My leg hurts.'

'Sure,' said Duffy. 'The day's been a dog, anyway. I'll run you home.'

Saturday was match day. Bradford City at home. Duffy rang Jimmy Lister, and apologized for bothering him, but had he had any more thoughts on who might be trying to poach Brendan Domingo, assuming that the attempted bribery had something behind it? Jimmy said he had a short list of three nice little mid-table Second Division outfits up North, and that he'd get on to them first thing on Monday. He knew one of the managers involved, and thought he might get a straight answer.

'But the trouble is, Duffy, when it comes to poaching players, no one obeys the rules. I mean there are decent clubs with decent managers who are still prepared to give a third party a pretty loose budget and turn a blind eye as long as he delivers the goods. We're not talking First Division and six-figure transfers here. We're talking little deals between clubs who are feeling the pinch and can't pay top wages; if some third party persuades a certain player that he'd be happier off with you than where he is, then you wouldn't be human if you didn't thank the party concerned.'

'Yeah, I see that.'

'Coming to the match?'

'Wouldn't miss it.' The first match Athletic had played since Duffy started sharing Jimmy Lister's pay-cheque.

'Do you want to see it from the directors' box?' The directors' box was a rectangle of faintly padded seats in the main stand. 'I'll be a bit busy myself. Or I could bung you a ticket at one of the turnstiles.'

'Thanks. No, I'll go down the Layton Road end. I'll give you a wave. No I won't, you'll be able to pick me out easy. I'll be the one cheering Brendan Domingo.'

'Right.'

Duffy made himself a cup of strong coffee before phoning Ken Marriott.

'Maggot, it's Duffy.'

'Duffy? Pull the other one. I'd know that voice anywhere. Isn't it that cub reporter on the *Chronicle*? What's his name, Marriott?'

'Sorry about that. Hope I didn't drop you in it.'

'Nothing I couldn't handle.' Maggot was sounding pleased with himself. 'No, I just went along the street apologizing for the extreme ineptitude of the cub we'd foolishly sent along to talk to them. Mr Bullivant was less than impressed by your journalistic skills, I'm afraid, Duffy.'

'Uh-huh.' He'd better let Maggot say his say on this one. It was only fair.

'Said you didn't take a single note. Big fat pad, nice new biro, didn't take a single bloody note.'

426

'I thought that's the way journalists normally behaved, Maggot.'

'Cheeky. No, Mr Bullivant was very unimpressed. But fortunately I was able to reassure him that your working days at the *Chronicle* were definitely numbered. He said you looked as if you needed a sharp dose of unemployment.'

'Was Mr Bullivant a PT instructor by any chance?'

'Why do you ask?'

'I just thought he looked like one.'

'Duffy, *just thinking* isn't good enough if you're to continue your brilliant career all the way to the pinnacles of Fleet Street. No, Mr Bullivant is not a PT instructor. He's a retired plasterer who does faith healing and osteopathy in his spare time.'

'How'd you find that out?'

'I asked him, Duffy, I chatted him up and asked him.'

But if Maggot had found out about Mr Bullivant's employment record and skill with stiff joints, he hadn't been able to add much to the small pile of Duffy's knowledge. Number 48 still wouldn't unchain the door; number 57 revealed a rather unforthcoming husband of the pinafored Lucky Numbers player; while Mr Bullivant disclosed no less, and no more, than he'd disclosed to Duffy.

'They could be genuine, you know, Duffy. I mean, I thought they were genuine. Those yobboes can be pretty unsavoury when the fancy takes them.'

'I'm not denying *that*, Maggot, I'm just thinking perhaps there's a Santa Claus somewhere slipping them some advice, and most of all some cash.'

'There's a lot of money in home osteopathy and faith healing. Especially if you don't declare it.'

Perhaps. Duffy didn't think that was the answer. And besides, would number 57 think of sueing the club over the yobboes when the son of the house turned out to be a prize yobbo himself?

At opening time Duffy went to the Albion and bought the

barman a drink. Sure, he worked here every lunchtime. Yes, and yesterday lunchtime. Littlish fellow, fiftyish, neat, mackintosh? No, don't remember him. He wouldn't have been a regular. How do you know? Well, the regulars are the ones I remember, and the ones I don't remember aren't regular. Simple. Anyway, Duffy went on, this bloke in the mac was with Brendan Domingo. Who? Brendan Domingo, big fellow, very muscular, dark skin. Oh, you mean, coloured fellow? Yes, that's Brendan Domingo. Oh that's *Brendan Domingo*, is it? No, don't remember him, he can't be a regular. Who *is* Brendan Domingo anyway? Tell you this for nothing, all these coloured chaps look alike to me. Cheers!

Rather than face the Albion's lukewarm meat pies, Duffy went home for a slimmer's lunch. There'd been a lot more brown bread and yoghurt around Duffy's kitchen lately. Duffy was worried about getting fat. Duffy was also worried about not having enough to eat and losing his strength. So he had the brown bread and the yoghurt for stopping getting fat; and he had some streaky bacon, cheese and a bottle of Guinness for making him not lose his strength. That was about the right balance. After lunch he felt his neck and his armpits; then undid his trousers and dabbled in his groin. The trouble was, there seemed to be little lumps everywhere. Maybe his lymph nodes were really getting out of hand. Maybe he only had a couple of hours to live. That night sweat he'd had felt a real killer. It had even, as he recalled, given him hallucinations about other parts of his body.

By a bit of lawyer's know-how, the club had managed to delay its courtroom confrontation with the Layton Road residents for a few days. Even so, this might be the last time the yobboes would stomp down the street, Duffy thought, as he joined the crowd. There seemed to be quite a few policemen around; a couple even standing right outside Mr Bullivant's house. Perhaps the club had made a few suggestions to the coppers, and a special ablutions watch was being kept on number 37.

Just inside the ground the coppers were searching everyone who was young, male and not obviously in a wheelchair. Anyone wearing big boots was taken aside and had his toes introduced to a constable's heel. Just checking for steel toecaps, Sir. The police took away everything that could be thrown, everything that could be drunk, and everything that could be used for sticking into someone else. No metal combs, no beer cans, full or empty; no, you won't be needing that set of darts this afternoon, lad, come and collect it afterwards. A mound of potentially lethal junk was piled behind the police lines. Lots of stuff got smuggled in all the same – that was why they had a WPC searching the occasional tough girl who dared to stand at the Layton Road end – but at least this caught some of the heavier ammunition. If the coppers didn't search every single yobbo every single time, they'd be bringing in Armalites and assembling do-it-yourself bazooka kits on the terraces before you knew where you were.

Past the police lines and the ground began to display its smells and sounds and sights. A hamburger stall stood near the entrance to the toilets: the two smells not cancelling one another but mixing together into a richer, denser brew. The screechy public address system churned out pop records which the club secretary – who preferred Herb Alpert and the Tijuana Brass himself – imagined that the better class of customer wished to hear. Programme sellers in booths labelled PROGRAMMES bellowed 'PROGRAMMES!', to help anyone partially sighted who might be in the vicinity. Fans rushed past as if their favourite place on the terracing was about to be stolen, even though the ground held fifteen thousand and the expected attendance was two and a half. A man dressed in the club's blue-and-white waved a board of rosettes and badges, but was meeting some dogged consumer resistance.

A light drizzle was beginning to fall as Duffy made his way up the couple of dozen concrete steps leading to the terraces. The Layton Road end was also known as the Piggeries end, for some forgotten historical reason; though in recent years the nickname had become appropriate again with the arrival of the yobboes. From time to time they would acknowledge the fact with a jolly chant of 'ATH-LE-TIC-OINK-OINK-OINK.'

Up on the terraces, away from the smells and the programme sellers, even a run-down little ground like this had its charm. There it was, all laid out: the bright pitch, the fresh markings, the nice rectangular goals. Apart from a few advertisement hoardings, you couldn't see anything that wasn't to do with the game. Just the pitch, the terraces, the fans; beyond, only the sky and the floodlights rearing up at the four corners of the ground. Duffy felt excited.

He took a position half-way up the Piggeries terrace and a bit to the left, where he could watch both the game and the yobboes without too much trouble. The exchange of pleasantries between the Athletic fans at this end and the Bradford fans at the other had already begun. 'ATH-LE-TIC' – 'SHIT' – 'ATH-LE-TIC' – 'SHIT' – 'ATH-LE-TIC' – 'SHIT'. And then, a bit later, the welcoming reply: 'CIIIII-TY' – 'SHIT' – 'CIIIII-TY' – 'SHIT' – 'CIIIII-TY' – 'SHIT.'

After a while, both sets of fans began to tire of this. The City supporters, whose club occupied a safe position in the top ten of the Division, decided to predict Athletic's fate come the end of the season. 'GOING DOWN GOING DOWN GOING DOWN,' they chanted, 'GOING DOWN GOING DOWN GOING DOW-OW-N.' The Layton Roaders couldn't think up any immediate riposte, but after a while they sketched a lively self-portrait for the City fans. 'WE ARE THE ANIMALS – OINK OINK OINK. WE ARE THE ANIMALS – OINK OINK OINK. WE ARE ... ' and so on until the two sides trotted out. The public address cheerfully cut off Cilla Black in mid-phrase and began running through the teams. Each Athletic name was dutifully cheered by the home fans and booed by the away fans; all except that of Brendan Domingo, which was booed by both sets of fans. Duffy noticed that Brendan didn't even pause in his warm-up. He carried on nonchalantly laying the

430

ball off to a chunky midfielder, sprinting a few yards and taking a return pass. I'd move on, mate, if I were you, thought Duffy. Nice little Second Division outfit somewhere. They might even have another black player in the side. Not that you probably need the company; it just makes it harder for the animals when they find they're booing almost one-fifth of their own side. Duffy had two solutions for Brendan and Jimmy Lister and Melvyn Prosser. One: sell Brendan, make the club a few bob, advance the player's career and get him into a less unsavoury outfit (though this, he recalled, was exactly what someone seemed to be trying to do already). Two: keep Brendan, sell the other ten players, and buy ten new black players. That would sort the Piggeries end out; it might be just a bit too much for their poor brains to handle.

The match was one of those uneven, end-of-season bouts between differently-motivated sides. Athletic needed to win if they were to have any chance of lifting themselves out of the bottom three in the table; City didn't need the points, and were already turning their thoughts to next season. This ought to have given the advantage to Athletic, but it didn't: they were fretful, wound-up, over-eager; they pressed too hard and left themselves open at the back; two players would often go for the same ball in their keenness to do something, anything. City, on the other hand, with only their win bonus to worry about, were more relaxed; they tried a few little tricks, but didn't worry if they failed to come off. One side was jumpy and frantic; the other ambitious but lethargic. The midfield became clogged, and for all Athletic's anxious bustle they never troubled the City goalkeeper. The most effective piece of action in the first half came from the coppers: perhaps they were as bored as most of the spectators. On a given signal, twenty of them suddenly sprinted up the Layton Road terrace, burst their way into the phalanx of yobboes, made a path to its centre and stood there, four deep and five across, watching the game and chatting up the yobboes. Duffy laughed a bit at this. It was obviously a new tactic since his days in the Force. Just standing there, in the middle of the boot-boys, watching the game and gassing away. Not trying to be nice to the yobboes – that wasn't the point; just embarrassing the hell out of them for ten minutes or so. Then the coppers eased themselves away and went to look elsewhere.

The first half was what Melvyn Prosser would have called a bow-wow. City were clearly the more skilful side, but weren't too bothered either way; Athletic didn't seem to have any ideas about attacking except to win throw-ins and occasional corners, tactics which City had clearly seen before. At half-time, as Cilla Black took up her song from the beginning again, Duffy moved across to the fringe of the yobboes. They looked young to Duffy: very young, very unhealthy, and very tough. He saw lots of grey skins and pimples and unformed faces; yet he bet most of them would run Mr Joyce closer at arm-wrestling than he had done. None of them wore a rosette, or a badge, or anything indicating support for Athletic. Hair: short. Height: normal. Special characteristics: zero consumption of yoghurt and health foods.

Duffy picked out a largish youth wearing a Union Jack T-shirt and sidled up to him. He decided not to start by praising the skills of Brendan Domingo.

'Playing rubbish, aren't they?' he said casually.

Union Jack didn't reply.

'You wiv ... the Movement?' he tried next. This got a reply.

'You what?'

'You wiv the Red White and Blue? You going down Tower Hill next week?' A couple of those nearby were now listening to the exchange.

'Haven't seen you down this end before.'

'Name's Des.' He was getting through a lot of names this week, he thought.

Union Jack, Duffy noticed, had a gold stud in his left ear.

But there seemed little chance that he was a regular at the Alligator.

'Haven't seen you down this end before.'

'You going down Tower Hill next week?'

There was a long pause. Three of the yobboes on the step below had turned round and were staring at Duffy. Union Jack was ignoring him, and gazing down at the pitch. Finally he found something to say.

'I don't fink it's good for your elf, standing ere.'

Duffy retreated.

The Layton Roaders seemed to enjoy the second half more. Waddington, City's tubby left-back, tried a long-range shot and nearly hit the corner-flag. 'OOOOOOH, WANKY-WANKY, WANKY-WANKY-WANKY-WANKY WA-DDING-TON; OOH, WANKY-WANKY, WANKY-WANKY-WANKY-WANKY WA-DDING-TON.' The referee failed to give a penalty when an Athletic midfielder tripped over his own feet in sheer excitement at getting in the opposing area. 'KILL THE REFEREE, KILL THE REFEREE, EE-AI-ADDIO, KILL THE REFEREE.' Brendan Domingo took a lofted ball from the wing, killed it on the inside of his knee, let it roll down his calf, and laid it off swiftly to give Danny Matson's replacement a scoring chance. 'BRENDAN IS A FAIRY, BRENDAN IS A FAIRY, BRENDAN IS A FAIRY.'

With ten minutes to go, and the City fans setting up another chant of 'GOING DOWN GOING DOWN GOING DOWN', Athletic fiddled a corner. Short to the near post, headed on, headed out, turned back, miskicked, headed back in, not cleared, twenty-one different players to choose from, and Brendan, off-balance, toe-poked it home from about five yards out. The City fans were silent; the Layton Roaders were silent; Duffy, despite his promise to Jimmy Lister, decided not to draw attention to himself; there were a few claps and squeaks from the main stand, repeated at about the same volume when the public address announced the scorer's name. Move on, Duffy whispered to Domingo, move on; this lot don't deserve you.

Ten minutes later, Athletic had gained victory and three points; when news of the other matches came through, it was confirmed that they were out of the bottom three. They were still in the bottom four, but looking at the points won and the games to play, it meant that at least the future was in the side's own hands. If they got the results, they'd stay up, no matter what the other teams did.

Jimmy Lister was still smiling when Duffy wandered into his office.

'Good result,' said Duffy.

'The lads did the business. They did the business. What more can you ask?'

Danny Matson, who could handle coming to the games if not going to The Knight Spot, was sitting in a chair by the Boss's desk and smiling too.

'Big Bren came good just when we needed him.'

Big Bren and ten other damp-haired players had the biggest smiles of all.

'Hey, Boss,' Brendan shouted across the room, 'I hope you saw how I planned the whole movement.' Everyone laughed.

'I'm proud of you, lads,' said Jimmy Lister. 'Never stopped battling. Full ninety minutes. Real team effort. Proud of every one of you.' And he went round the room slapping the players and punching them playfully.

'Hey, Boss, OK if I have a few beers tonight?' shouted Brendan.

'You can have as many halves as you like,' said the Boss.

Brendan had quite a lot of halves that evening. Duffy had a tomato juice followed by a low-alcohol lager. Well, he'd never been a Saturday-night raver; or at least, not Saturday night rather than any other night. What about Carol, though, he wondered, as he divided their boil-in-a-bag cod dinner into two portions. Maybe she wanted to be taken out on a Saturday night?

Later, as Carol was falling asleep and Duffy lay tucked up with her, he got another erection. He held his breath. She stirred slightly, and moved her bottom a little.

'Duffy,' she murmured, 'is there anyone else in this bed apart from the two of us?'

'Not that I know of,' he answered. He was feeling – almost hearing – a slow, fat, deadly drop of sweat begin to trickle down his temple.

'Then I must be dreaming,' she said, and slipped off into sleep.

Brendan Domingo, despite the opinion of the Layton Road yobboes, was not a fairy. Brendan Domingo, like Duffy, had an erection. Whether this was a good idea or not, he wasn't to know at the time.

Half-time

'Shhh,' went Geoff Bell; and the whole team obeyed.

Bell was not one of the Reliables' star players. He was heavy in the leg, didn't train enough, and secretly preferred rugby. He also wore glasses, but left them in the dressing-room, which was a handicap; he'd tried contact lenses, but they irritated his eyes a lot, and he was afraid of losing one on the pitch. They used to tell him that if he could get used to lenses he might develop into a player with vision, like Maggot; but they didn't really mean it.

Geoff Bell usually occupied a loose, freeish position in midfield. It was free because however many instructions you gave him, he never managed to follow them. It was a mystery why he ever wanted to play the game. It was a mystery to opponents why the Reliables ever bothered to pick him; but then opponents never saw the Reliables more than once a season, and they normally assumed Bell was a last-minute substitute. Bell was never a last-minute substitute. If it was a home game, his was the first name to be pencilled in; if it was an away game, his was the first to be left out.

Home matches were always played at the recreation ground, and the Reliables, partly by being so reliable, were routinely allotted pitch A, alongside their own small changing-hut. There were two tiny rooms, three showers and a toilet. According to a long-established and friendly ritual, the two sides would retire to the hut at half-time, where the away side would find in its room a small tray bearing six halved oranges, a packet of chocolate wholemeal, four pints of milk and half a bottle of whisky. At first some of the teams were suspicious about the whisky, but most of them worked out that a half bottle between eleven wasn't going to make anybody's game woozy; it was simply a nice gesture, and it made teams look forward to playing the Reliables at the recreation ground.

Partly it was a nice gesture; but it also ensured that opponents didn't decide that the macho thing to do at half-time was stay out on the pitch and get in some shooting practice.

Geoff Bell was crouched on a bench with his hands pressed tight to his ears. Anyone would have thought he was sunk in gloom at the memory of his first-half performance. Anyone who thought that would have been wrong. For seven of the fifteen minutes that half-time occupied, the home dressing-room was entirely silent. Then Geoff Bell sat up, took out an earphone and said, 'Right. Got it.'

The other ten waited attentively. This was Bell's moment of importance, and he played it for all it was worth; he was dry, authoritative and irrebuttable.

'Right. For a start they know they've got the skinning of our right-back. Sorry about that, Tommo; the winger says he's got you on toast. Second, they think that someone called Phil, who I think must be that ginge, has got the complete run of the midfield, but they want him to push a lot further forward in the second half. They say it's all very well walking over the midfield but it's no good unless it puts you in business on the edge of the penalty area. They're not very impressed by my play; in fact I think I caught the phrase "complete wanker" at one point.'

The other ten laughed. This was just like Geoff. He could easily have edited that bit out, but he seemed to have some curious determination to tell everything that went on. This made them not mind so much when he didn't tone down some of the comments about the rest of them.

'Maggot, there was also a bit about you.'

'Oh yes?' said Ken Marriott hopefully.

'Yes, they say they think you're a psycho.'

'Oh. Didn't they say anything about my vision?'

440

'Just that you're a psycho and that the first three times you get the ball in the second half they're going to give you a whacking.'

'Oh dear.'

'They think that only Barney – at least, I think that's who they must mean by the bald smarmy one – sorry about that, Barney – is any threat to the defence. They say he's a bit slow but turns nicely for a fat man, and might have pinched one right on the whistle if they hadn't closed him down in time.'

Barney smiled. He didn't mind being called fat and smarmy in the least as long as they had picked him out as the most subtle and venomous operator amongst the Reliables.

'Anything about me?' said Duffy.

'They said they think you're a terrific keeper, very fast, very brave, reflexes like a cat and a lovely pair of hands. The only thing stopping them give us a real hiding.'

Duffy grinned to himself with quiet pleasure; until he noticed that all the others were grinning with very noisy pleasure.

'Sorry, Duffy, nothing at all.'

'Oh, well.'

'They're pretty confident they've got the beating of us, but they're going to play it fairly quiet for the first ten minutes or so, apart from stomping on our psycho, that is, and then push a couple more men forward for quarter of an hour to see if they can nick another goal, and then whatever happens they'll pull them both back again. One will be wide on the right, the other one I think is the big centre-back who's going to be allowed to come forward whenever he feels like it. That's about all. Oh, and they said that someone they call the young lad – I guess that must be you, Karl – looks quite sharp, but they think he's a bit out of his depth at this level of the game.'

'Fucking hell,' said Karl French. 'They're only a pubload of wankers.'

'Just passing on what the man said.'

'Which one said that,' asked Karl, 'which one? I'll bloody do him, second half.'

'Just voices, voices,' said Bell.

'Quite,' said Micky Baker, captain and left-back of the Reliables. 'For a start, you won't do anyone, Karl. That's not the point of the whole thing. That just undoes everything. Now, quickly, lads, we've only got a couple of minutes, so concentrate.'

Barney checked that the door was quite shut, and Micky gave his instructions.

'First, we'll swap our full-backs over. I was thinking I'd have to take that winger of theirs anyway. OK Tommo? I'll follow him, and if he switches wings, we switch. You take my chap, he's a bit less tricky. Always tries to go on the outside, too; I think he's only got one foot. Next, we don't give Karl the ball for ten minutes.'

'Come off it,' said Karl.

'No, I'm serious. You didn't get much of a sniff in the first half, so they don't know what you can do. We know what you can do. So for the first ten minutes while they're keeping it tight, we keep it tight, and any ball that comes to you, you get rid of fairly quickly. Then, when they push the extra men forward and are only watching out for Barney, who they think is a bit slow anyway, we try to get the two of you forward quickly on the break. Anyone gets the ball midfield, look up and try and spot Karl, whip it up to him quickly and let him run at them. Give them the shock of their lives if he does the business on them.'

Karl grinned. 'I like it.'

'Now, what else?'

'What else?' said Maggot. 'What else? They're going to beat me up, that's what else.'

'No they're not,' said Micky soothingly. 'We can't stop them trying – I mean, not without letting on that we've been eavesdropping – but we can give them a bit of their own back. Every time they have a dig at you, we clobber the ginge.'

'That won't make *me* feel better,' complained Maggot.

'No, but it'll stop the ginge, which has to be priority number one.'

'You're a hard man, skipper.'

'Come off it, Maggot, we won't let them do anything too bad to you.'

'They want to destroy my vision,' said Maggot mournfully.

'Shut up, Maggot,' most of the team counselled. Micky Baker unscrewed the cap of the home team's half-bottle of whisky and, as was the custom, offered the first gulp to Bell. 'Nice work, Geoff.'

Duffy grinned across at Bell. It had been Duffy who'd first suggested him for a place in the Reliables. Geoff was a sort of friend, though more of a business associate – someone to run to for advice on the technical side of things. Geoff Bell was good with machines, and cameras, and recorders, and electricity, and all the things that Duffy was bad with. His expertise, however, wasn't quite so great when it came to estimating the distance that a spheroid object of known weight would travel when struck by his own boot; and for the first couple of games Duffy had watched with some embarrassment as terrible things kept happening in the vicinity of Geoff Bell.

'Still struggling with his form, is he?' asked Micky Baker after Bell's fourth game.

'Well, you know how hard it is coming into a strange team playing a different system,' Duffy replied defensively.

'Yeah, I suppose it must seem like a strange system to him – kicking the ball along the ground to someone on your own side and then trying to get it into the opposite net.'

Even Duffy had thought Bell lucky to get a fifth outing with the Reliables. On that occasion they were four–nil down at half-time and Bell sat with his head in his hands, apparently absorbing the various reproaches that were flying around. In fact, he was listening on an earphone to the small bug he'd placed in the visiting team's dressing-room. Suddenly he upped and told them the whole of the opposition's plans – and their predicted result of eight–nil.

At first the Reliables hadn't known how to react; but given that they were four–nil down and carrying this joker in midfield, they decided that the only thing they could do was treat it all as a giggle. So they had a good laugh, and then they thought, Well, if this mad passenger of ours really has found out this stuff for us we may as well try using it. They went out for the second half in rather a humorous frame of mind, and they came back in rather a serious frame of mind, having reduced the deficit to four–two and come very close to squeezing a third goal. Then they sat down and had a think, and decided that since other sides were always doing things which weren't quite in the spirit of the game – like including the odd cowboy to inject a bit of class – why shouldn't the Reliables have their own little way of doing things? It wasn't as if they were breaking rules on the pitch, or bribing the ref. A few of them felt uneasy about it at first, but they soon got used to it; and the fact that they didn't play Bell away from home (where you normally just stood shivering on the pitch at half-time) made it all seem more acceptable. It became a jolly part of the home-game ritual, along with the oranges, the milk and the whisky.

As they walked out again, one–nil down against the pub side and expecting a certain amount of agg, Geoff Bell caught up with Duffy.

'I'm afraid they did say something about you.'

'Oh yeah?'

'Only as it wasn't of direct tactical relevance I didn't pass it on in front of the others.'

'Oh yeah?'

'They said you were rather small for a goalkeeper.'

'Thanks, Geoff. Thanks a mil.'

444

Second Half

'Good three points.'

Brendan looked up.

'Oh. Yeah. Thanks.'

Brendan was sitting by himself in a corner seat of the Albion saloon bar. It was a Saturday night, and the pub was at its fullest; a noisy game of darts was whooping away in one corner, and the evening's serious drunks were beginning to feel a bit combative. The more the noise rose, the more people had to shout, and the more the noise rose. Saturday night's husbands were squeezing another pint into their elasticated stomachs before toddling home for the weekly legover. Saturday night's smokers had bought themselves a cigar for a change, just to make the air thicker. Saturday night's solitary drinkers felt the more solitary as those around them rowdily demonstrated that, whatever else they might lack in their lives, they certainly didn't lack friends.

All except Brendan. To Brendan the Albion seemed almost quiet, and he didn't mind in the least being alone. Perhaps this was because he'd come on from Benny's after leaving the other lads to it. Benny's was where some of the team went when The Knight Spot began to feel a bit of a chore, a bit like another public appearance. Benny's was small, deafening and cheap; while the girls, as Athletic's keeper had once enthusiastically explained to Brendan, were very, very slaggy. Brendan used to go along, simply because being with the lads helped him come down after a match; and then, an hour or two later, he'd plead early bedtime, and the lads would say, Hey, we know you Brendan, you just don't like our girls, you're popping down The Palm Tree for a bit of your own, aren't you, let's all go down there, lads, big

Bren'll get us in; and he'd smile and say, No, really, it's early bedtime, and then paying them back a bit he'd say, Anyway I wouldn't take you down The Palm Tree, you guys ain't *classy* enough to mix with the chicks down there, and they'd all roar and slap him about a bit and shout Good old Bren, and then he'd slip away for a couple of quiet halves down at the Albion.

'Mind you, it wasn't exactly a great spectacle, if you don't mind my saying so.'

Brendan laughed.

'And I wouldn't mind betting you didn't know where you were putting it when you scored.'

Brendan laughed again.

'Well, I knew it wasn't going to be an own goal.'

'Can I buy the conquering hero a drink?'

'Pleasure.'

'Bacardi and coke?' she suggested. Was she teasing?

'Half of best, thanks.'

'Half of best it is.'

She was called Maggie, she said, and she dressed in black. Shoes, tights, shortish skirt that was almost a ra-ra but not quite, turtleneck sweater. Probably she did it because she had lots of blonde hair; Brendan had to admit that the contrast was striking. Footballers are meant to prefer blondes, he knew that. It wasn't so much true nowadays, but there was a time in the Sixties and early Seventies when every footballer wanted a blonde wife to go with the Jag and the ranch-style house out Chingford way. They used to say that you could tell if a footballer was First Division or not by looking at the roots of his wife's hair. If you saw little black quarters of an inch you knew the fellow was Second Division. If you could see from across the room that the wife had been doing it herself with peroxide, then he was probably Third or Fourth. There was an awful lot of dyeing in those days: some of the supporters' clubs could have opened a ladies' hairdressing business on the side.

Maggie knew a bit about football. Not a lot, she admitted; she'd only really got keen on the game this season, but she came to all the home matches. She was a good listener, and she didn't ask stupid questions. That was the trouble with fans, Brendan had to admit to himself. At first he'd thought all fans were a good thing – anyone who liked the game was a good thing, and anyone who thought Brendan was a great player was an even better thing; but after a while you could get enough of the fans. Or at least, you could get enough of two kinds of fans. The first lot were the know-nothings, who giggled and nudged one another and wondered if that wasn't big Brendan Domingo over there and mustn't it be smashing to be a professional footballer and wasn't that a screamer of a goal you scored against Port Vale, when it had only gone in because it had bounced off your knee and the keeper had been out of position and fretting about his mortgage repayments. The second lot were the know-alls, who'd seen Stanley Matthews years before you were born, lad, who could tell you exactly what was wrong with the club, the management, and most of all with you and your play – too deep or too far forward, too wide or too central, holding the ball too long or getting rid of it too quickly. Sometimes Brendan thought that these two kinds of fans were the only ones who ever came to the matches. Football was, in a way, simpler than either of them imagined. You practised a lot, and you went out there and did your best, your very best, every week; it was a job, but a job that you liked; and though you were pretty good at it, there were lots of other people who were better. That was how Brendan saw the game.

'Does it get to you when they boo you?'

'No. Yes. Well, not at the time, because you're concentrating, and you don't want to give them any satisfaction. But afterwards, I suppose, yeah, it does get you down a bit.'

'Why do they do it?'

'I think they don't like my blond hair and big blue eyes,' said Brendan.

That seemed to relax them a bit. It was as if he'd said, You see, one of the things about me is, I'm black; you may not have noticed, but I thought I ought to point it out to you. And when she'd joined in his laugh, it had meant, Funny you should say that thing about being black; I thought there was something about you, but I just couldn't put my finger on it.

Brendan stood up.

'Can I get you a small gin with a half-bottle of tonic, twist of lemon and plenty of ice?' It was his tease back.

'Drambuie and lemonade,' she said, and they both laughed. He much preferred the Albion to Benny's. And truth to tell, he wasn't all that keen on The Palm Tree.

They stayed until nearly closing time, and Brendan thought, I could go for you. Problems, of course; but I could go for you.

'Do you feel·all drained after a match?'

'Depends. If you lose, you do. Just want to put your head in a bucket. Wish you didn't have to get through Sunday before you can go back to the ground and start working on things. If you win you just feel, give me half an hour, and I'll go out and play another game. You feel kind of set up. I dunno.'

'Well, I'm glad you won today.'

'So am I. Those three points are gold-dust.'

She lived just off Twyford Avenue; would he drop her? Sure, of course, he said, noting that she said drop rather than run home or see home, or any of those other phrases that you listen out for very carefully. But as he put the handbrake on and left the engine running, she said, 'I haven't any coffee, but I've got some Drambuie and lemonade in the fridge.'

'When in Rome,' said Brendan with a laugh.

They sat in the kitchen and had a few more drinks than they ought to have done; there wasn't any doubt about that. Maggie was mixing them, and it seemed to Brendan that each one was a little stronger than the last. When on about the fourth, he said, 'Hey, is there any lemonade in this one?'

She came over to his chair, sat herself down on his knee, stroked her hand against his cheek and said, 'Is this the big centre-forward calling for more lemonade?'

Brendan thought, I'm not exactly a *centre-forward*, you don't use words like that. He felt it highly important to pass on this piece of information.

'I'm not exactly a centre-forward,' he said very seriously, 'It's more that I play up front. I'm a target man.'

'Oh, you're a target man, are you? Well, all I can say is, Bull's-eye!'

Brendan laughed, and felt uneasy at the same time. This was the awkward bit; this was the bit he'd have to leave up to her. True, she was sitting on his lap, but something always held him back a bit with white girls. Sure, he was meant to be all relaxed and sexy and macho, and limbo-dance under her bed or whatever; but it wasn't like that when it came down to it. He hadn't even put his hand on her leg yet, even though her leg was very close to his hand, and her skirt was almost a ra-ra. That Drambuie definitely did need some more lemonade in it. The thing was, of course, he really did rather like her.

'It's all right,' she said, leaning into him until her head was on his shoulder and her mouth not far from his ear. 'It's all right. It's only called going to bed.'

He chuckled.

'Oh, is that what it's called? I thought only the grown-ups did that.'

She got off his lap, pulled him out of the kitchen, pushed him into the bedroom and disappeared, shutting the door behind her. For a moment he wasn't entirely sure what was happening – perhaps she'd gone off to sleep on the couch? – but at any rate, here was a bedroom, here was a bed, and here he was expected to sleep. So he undressed, climbed into bed, smelt the sheets, and thought, It's been a good day, Brendan, say what you will, three points plus a nice girl has got to be better than relegation and a wank, hasn't it? He wasn't quite sure what to do about the overhead light. He'd left it on when he got into bed. Should he get out, turn it off and put the bedside lamp on instead? He didn't yet know whether or not he was going to get company. He supposed the lads were still boozing down at Benny's. He hoped Danny Matson wasn't waiting up for him at their digs. He liked Danny, but they'd somehow seen less of one another since Danny's leg went. He'd better make more of an effort for Danny. Must be awful. Maybe Maggie's got a friend who likes footballers with their legs in plaster?

There was a distant noise of water running through pipes, then a door was shut, then another door was opened. This door, thought Brendan, who had an arm across his eyes to shield them from the overhead light. Then the light went off and the door was closed. He felt a pull on the sheets and a press of flesh and a knee hit him in the thigh and he apologized, even though it wasn't his fault.

'Do you remember, in the pub,' she said.

'What's that?'

'We were talking about the match and I said I thought you didn't know where you were putting it when you scored.'

'Yeah.'

'Well, I hope you do now,' she said, and pressed even closer.

'You dirty girl,' he said, pushing her on to her back and kissing her for the first time, and not very accurately, given that the light was off. 'You dirty girl. Have to wash your mouth out with soap.'

'Or something,' she said. As she reached down and grabbed his cock, he heard a faint chant in the back of his head. 'Brendan is a fairy, Brendan is a fairy.' If the Layton Road enders were interested, then Maggie was holding Exhibit A.

Yes, that was a good feeling, Brendan thought, as she eased him inside her. That was a good feeling. The good feelings went on, for a bit, at least. Then Brendan thought Ow. The good feelings returned, until Brendan thought Ow

452

again but laughed a bit, because it was only her nails in his ribs, and that was all part of the game. The next time it happened it was much harder, and he said, 'Ow, that hurts, you know.'

She didn't reply. It was dark; the curtains were thick; she had given up saying things to him that were a bit dirty; they were just there, in the dark, silent, fucking. Lots closer, and yet a bit more distant, Brendan thought; but he didn't think much, and they carried on fucking.

They started getting a bit noisier. She scratched at his ribs a bit more and he whispered, 'Maggie,' but she didn't seem to be hearing him. She reached up and got hold of his ears and seemed to be telling him what to do by pulling on them; and that seemed to be nice too, until suddenly she reached round the back of his neck and pulled his head down very hard and there was a cracking sound as his forehead hit her nose and he felt as if he'd gone for a fifty-fifty ball and a defender had booted him in the face, but still she didn't say anything or make a sound. Brendan felt uneasy, but there didn't seem to be any point in not carrying on. Christ his head hurt. Why ever had she done that? He wouldn't let her get hold of his ears again.

She didn't get hold of his ears again. She reached up and dug both her hands into his cheeks and dragged both sets of nails across his face and howled while she did this. She was attacking him and howling, and Brendan found it definitely a bit scary but also, somewhere, he had to admit, a bit exciting. She reached for his face with her nails again and he pushed her hands away and said 'No,' and she reached again and he stopped her and she suddenly got noisier and reached again and howled and he thought Christ she's hysterical and the next time she reached he hit her across the face, and she said, 'Fuck me, hit me,' and after she went for him again it didn't seem such a bad idea, and especially when he felt blood on his face and she was really going at him with her nails and he hit her again and she shouted, 'Fuck me, hit me, fuck me, hit me,' and everything seemed to get noisier and more painful and more exciting because that was what she was telling him to do, and with a lot of bellowing he came inside her and then she suddenly stopped. Just stopped everything. She lay completely still and said nothing, and it was utterly dark and he wondered if she was having a fit or had passed out or needed a glass of water or something, and he rolled off her and whispered, 'Maggie?'

She reached across with an arm and patted him on the nearest bit she could find, as if to say, 'It's all right, I'm all right,' and after a while he felt the bed shift and heard the door open and close. A minute or two passed, and he waited for the sound of water running through pipes, but it didn't come. What he heard instead was the slam of a door, so loud that it shook the walls of the flat, and then, close at hand, too close, much too close, the sound of someone screaming. Brendan thought that maybe things weren't all right after all. When he switched on the bedside light and saw the blood on the pillow, and the blood on his hand, and looked in the mirror and saw the blood on his face, he knew that things weren't all right in any way. He ran for his clothes, and started putting them on in a panic, and they were all in the wrong order, and none of them seemed to fit – Hey, why am I getting into someone else's clothes? – but he struggled and tugged and finally made it, and ran for the front door and slammed it, not caring, and got to his car. As he turned the ignition key he knew, without the least doubt, that things weren't ever, ever going to be all right again.

The detective-sergeant thought it strange that he was calling at the same set of digs for the second time this month. Bloody footballers. Bloody football. Horrible game, played by thugs, watched by yobs. Cricket was the detective-sergeant's game. When was the last time you heard of a cricketer getting into trouble? Whereas football . . . maybe it was all the adulation they got; made them think they could get away with anything. Half the footballers in London probably had a criminal record, if you looked closely enough; had, or at least jolly well ought to have. And here were another lovely couple. Sharing digs, choice pair of rotten apples. The Irish boy who likes to pick fights and the coloured boy who couldn't get it into his head that No meant No. That girl had been in an awful state. Three to five years, thought the detective-sergeant, given the current climate of sentencing.

The police were very correct with Brendan Domingo. Even if the barman at the Albion didn't know who he was, they did. Don't lay a finger on him, whatever you feel like. This case is going to get publicity enough by itself. We'll even call him sir for a bit; until we've charged him, that is. We'd like you to come with us and make a statement sir. Brendan was very polite back. He thought he ought to ask for a solicitor, but he didn't know any solicitors, so he asked if he could telephone the Boss. Later, son, no problem, you can do it from the station; let's just get the statement over with first, then you can call whoever you like. Brendan said OK, and went with them, wondering how long it would be before Danny and Mrs Ferris realized that when he'd said he'd had a bit of a fight, it was only in a manner of speaking.

Yes he knew someone called Maggie. No he didn't know her surname. No he hadn't known her long. Yes, that was correct, they had met last night in the Albion for the first time. Yes, he had been to her flat. Yes, he had had sexual intercourse with her. Yes, it had been with her consent.

'How did you get those marks on your face?'

'She scratched me.'

'Scratched you quite a lot from the look of it.'

'Yes.'

'I see. And did you at any time while you were in her flat assault her?'

'Assault her? No.'

'Did you hit her at any point?'

'Yes, I hit her a few times,' said Brendan quietly.

'Why did you hit her?'

'Because she asked me to.'

'Because she asked you to?' The detective-sergeant looked across at the officer who was making notes of the interview. We've got a cheeky one here, he thought. Bold as brass.

'Yes.'

'And why ever should she ask you to do a thing like that?'

'I don't know. It seemed to be ... her thing.'

'Her ... thing?'

'Yes, well we were in bed you see, and she asked me to ...'

'You were in bed with her at the time?'

'Yes.'

'You didn't hit her before you raped her? You just hit her while you were raping her?'

'I didn't rape her. I didn't rape her. I only hit her because she asked me to. It seemed to be ... her thing.'

'You hit her when she refused to have sex with you, that's what you're saying, is it?'

'No, that's not what I'm saying at all. I ... I liked her.' It sounded pathetic, but Brendan felt he had to say it. It was part of the truth, and if he told them the truth they'd be bound to understand sooner or later.

'You liked her?'

'Yes. Course I did.'

'She's got a broken nose, severe bruising to the left side of the face, and one of her molars is loose. If that's what you do when you like people, sunshine, I wonder what you'd do if you fell in love with them.'

A broken nose? Christ.

'I only slapped her a few times. Because she asked me to,' he repeated.

'Apart from the head-butt.'

'The what?'

'The head-butt. Come off it, Brendan, that's what you footballers are good at, isn't it – the head-butt? Wait till the ref's looking the other way and then in with the nut. It may

456

not be a criminal offence when you're playing for Athletic, but I can assure you it's against the law anywhere else.'

'I didn't butt her. She got hold of my ears and pulled my head into her face.'

'And the sun shines out of my arse.'

'It's true, she got hold of my ears and pulled my head on to her face.'

'Hard enough to break her nose?'

'I suppose so. If that's what happened.'

'That's what happened. Now you tell me, Brendan: why ever would she want to do a thing like that?'

'I don't know. She just ... did it. I don't know.'

'You see, son, we can help you a bit. Not much, but a bit. I mean rape's a very serious charge, especially nowadays, what with all the hoo-ha about it. A few years ago you might just have been able to get away with something like this, assuming you hadn't knocked her around so much, and assuming you'd thought up a better story. But as it stands, we're looking at five years, old son. Five to seven, I'd say. And that's not going to be too good for the old career, is it?'

Brendan looked down at the table. He somehow hadn't thought about not playing again. He'd thought about everything else, but he somehow hadn't thought about not being allowed to play football again. He didn't think he could stand it.

'So if I may offer a word, Brendan, I think we'd better go for the truth in the present instance. You just tell us what happened, and we'll do the best we can for you.'

Brendan didn't say anything.

'I suppose she was a bit of a tease,' said the detective-sergeant. 'Led you on a bit?'

'No,' said Brendan, 'she didn't.'

'This is hopeless.'

'Can I ring the Boss?'

'Later, Brendan.'

'Isn't it my rights to ring the Boss?'

'I don't think so, Brendan. I don't know where it's written down if it is. Do you know where it's written down if it is?'

Brendan shook his head.

'Perhaps we should ask the other officer?'

Brendan and the detective-sergeant looked across at the other officer, who had remained silent throughout the interrogation. He didn't speak this time, either, but merely shook his head slowly from side to side.

'No, he doesn't think it's written down either.'

Brendan was confused. The police didn't believe him, that was obvious; but they were being almost nice to him. Well, fair, anyway. They hadn't hit him, or called him a black bastard, or told him to go back to the trees. He remembered an incident from last season, only his second game for Athletic, playing away up North, and someone had thrown a banana on to the pitch right near him. If he could have found that fan, he might have head-butted him. But apart from the odd yellow card, he'd always stayed out of trouble on the pitch; took a bit of stick, dished some out, but never tried to do anyone deliberately. Stayed out of trouble off the pitch, as well. Until this. Just when everything seemed to be going a bit right.

They took him into a small room, told him to strip and left him. He sat around in his underpants for half an hour until the police doctor arrived. The doctor told him to remove his underpants, then had a good look at him. All over. Neither of them said a word as the doctor went about his business, occasionally stopping to make a note. He was particularly interested in Brendan's face, his ribs, and his cock. Why is he looking at my whatsit like that, thought Brendan. I haven't denied what we did. Perhaps the doctor was queer or something. Brendan felt weary, and also felt that nothing would surprise him any more.

Eventually, the doctor spoke.

'You can get dressed again now.'

After an hour or so, he was taken back to the two detec-

tives. Again, the same one spoke. The other one was for
beating you up, Brendan supposed.

'Well, this is a sorry mess.'

'Yes.'

'I bet you're wondering how you got yourself into it.'

Brendan didn't think that was a question, so didn't reply.

'I said I'm sure you're wondering how you got yourself
into this?'

'Yes.'

'Well, let me give it a guess for you, Brendan. You picked
up this girl in the pub, you thought that was a good start; she
invited you in for coffee, you thought that was the green
light; you had a bit of a kiss and a cuddle, she said it was a bit
late, you said never too late for this, darling; she said No, you
thought she meant Yes; she said No again, you hit her a bit
and she hit you back, then you head-butted her and she went
quiet, and because she didn't say anything you thought, Well
if she isn't saying No she must mean Yes, and then you had
your way with her. Give or take a few details which you'll
now correct me on. Am I right or am I right?'

'I didn't pick her up; we just got talking. She didn't invite
me in for coffee; she didn't even have any. She didn't say No
or Yes or anything; it wasn't like that. I never hit her at all
except when she . . . she told me to.'

'Well, Brendan, I can't say you're being exactly co-
operative. At the moment we've got rape and grievous bodily
harm, and when we've looked over the girl's flat we may find
we've got burglary as well, and if we can't have that we might
settle for attempted burglary just to make up the three. I
always like to charge in threes, you know; it's sort of neater,
somehow. So you go away, my son, and you sit in a nice room
for a few hours with a constable to keep you company, and
you give your big woolly head a shake, and then you can
come back and see me and I'll charge you.'

Brendan had wondered when they would get around to the
fact that he wasn't the same colour as his interviewers.

'And then can I phone the Boss?'

'Then you can phone the Boss. If you think the Boss wants to hear from you after what you've been up to.'

In the end Brendan didn't phone the Boss. By the middle of Sunday afternoon, when Mrs Ferris had called the station for the third time and been told that Mr Domingo was still helping them with their inquiries, Danny Matson rang the Boss. Jimmy Lister got round to the station at six o'clock but was not allowed to see his player. No, he's still helping us with our inquiries, though all Brendan had done for the last three hours was stare at a radiator and wonder why Maggie had behaved the way she had. When Jimmy Lister mentioned that he'd be back in half an hour with a solicitor, the police said that was absolutely fine with them, but wasn't it a bit much getting a solicitor out on a Sunday night when nothing more was going to happen until the morning? If Mr Lister brought a solicitor along at ten, they could both be present when Mr Domingo was charged. How do you know he's going to be charged? He'll be charged all right, said the desk sergeant. You should have seen the state of that girl. He'll be charged even if he can prove he was in Alaska last night.

By the time Jimmy Lister returned with his solicitor, Duffy was off following a small idea. It was one of several small ideas he'd had, all of them so far useless; the trouble was, there weren't any big ideas around at the moment. All the questions that were there when he started sharing Jimmy Lister's salary were still no nearer solution. Why should anyone want to put Danny Matson out of the game? Why should anyone want to do down Melvyn Prosser? Why should anyone want to see the club relegated? And those three Whys were accompanied, naturally, by three Whos. Six questions, no answers. It was like arm-wrestling with Mr Joyce: you couldn't get past twelve o'clock, and the marmalade sandwich seemed inevitable.

Had Mr Joyce something to do with it? Was the Red White and Blue Movement backing Mr Bullivant and his Layton Road residents in some way? Was some other club trying to strong-arm its way out of the relegation zone by putting the heat on Athletic? That seemed a bit far-fetched. It couldn't just be that someone wanted to buy Brendan Domingo and was hoping to pick up a bargain at the end of the season when Athletic would be desperate for cash? Brendan was a good player, very honest, Duffy thought, and skilful for a big man; but he wasn't an undiscovered genius. Duffy doubted if he was even First Division material. What else? Perhaps he needed to ask Melvyn Prosser a few questions about the club's finances or something – assuming Melvyn Prosser was still giving him the time of day. That was the trouble. Football clubs were very public in some ways, but very private about backstage matters; they didn't need to tell anyone anything, and they usually chose not to as a matter of principle. BOARDROOM RESHUFFLE AT CITY you would read; but unless someone had been garrotted in the directors' box before several witnesses nothing ever came out. People retired 'for reasons of health'; new positions were created 'to give the Board a more effective cutting edge'; the chairman was changed 'to bring in some fresh blood'; and after six months or so everyone had forgotten, and there were a few embittered men in cashmere coats scattered around the district who could tell you a story if you had the time. But most people didn't have the time.

At the town hall they told him to follow the signs. Through the gloomy bits of Victorian Gothic, out into a courtyard, across some asphalt to a purpose-built Sixties block: the planning department. The members of the public who got this far tended to be nuisances: that's to say, they actually wanted to check up on things that the planning department was doing, or was about to do, or had done. The planning department couldn't send them away – it had its statutory obligations; but there were times when public consultation and democratic access to files were simply other ways of saying the word time-wasting. Still, at least this character in the green suede blouson seemed to know what he wanted.

The assistant planning officer brought him the file. And there it was: an application for outline planning permission for an area covering the whole of the Athletic ground and two adjoining sites. The drawings which Duffy slowly unfolded showed a clean and stylish future for the place where the Layton Road enders currently stomped: a shopping mall, a leisure centre, an eight-storey block of flats with offices underneath; fully-grown trees, fountains, zig-zag black-and-white pavements. Even some swanky, architect-designed pigeons taking off into the sky.

'Christ,' said Duffy.

'That *is* what you're looking for?' confirmed the assistant planning officer. She was amused, even gratified, by Duffy's reaction. Normally people just held the drawings upside down and grunted.

'Can you tell me what this means?'

'Well, it means that outline planning permission has been applied for.'

'How soon could they build this?'

'That's a long question. This is just a first step. It's an essential step, but it's only a first one. This is just for outline. That has to be granted, then there's full planning permission, and that has to be granted.'

'But basically, the club just gets one of these, then one of the next ones, and then goes ahead and knocks itself down and builds this instead?'

'Sort of. I mean, there might have to be a public inquiry; it depends on the project and whether there are any objections. But in any case I don't think this has anything to do with the club.'

'Eh?'

'Well, the application's in the name of Hess House Holdings. Unless that's the company name of the football club, which I shouldn't think it is.'

'Tell me if I'm following you. Someone can apply for planning permission to develop land which they don't in fact own?'

'Oh, yes.'

'So I could put in an application to turn Buckingham Palace into a gay club and the application would be duly received and considered?'

'You might have a problem with Crown Lands, but in principle the answer is Yes.'

'Why would I want to do such a thing?'

'I don't know. I'd have thought there were enough gay clubs anyway.' She smiled rather unenthusiastically at Duffy. Even some of the sensible ones were nutters.

'No, I mean, what are the advantages in terms of planning?'

'Well, it would speed things up. That's why most people apply for planning permission on land they haven't yet bought. It sort of primes the pump. Means you can start work as soon as the change of ownership comes through.'

'What else would they have to do at this stage?'

'Well, this is a big scheme. There'd obviously have to have been some consultations with council officers first. You know, fire, access, drainage. They'd have to have some idea of what might be allowable.'

'Private consultations?' Duffy heard the rustle of fat bribes.

'Private? Of course. There's nothing sinister about that. It's quite normal.'

'Sorry, I wasn't suggesting any irregularity.' Duffy was trying to work out how far some operator could get without anyone sniffing what he was up to. 'And how long would it be before any of this would be bound to become public knowledge?'

'Hard to tell. It depends a bit on the planning department's schedule of meetings. Things are always a bit slow in the summer. I'm only guessing, but I'd say we'd have to publish this scheme in, what, three or four weeks' time.'

Just after the end of the season. Neat.

'And how long would it take from the present stage to laying the first brick?'

'Couldn't tell you. Depends on too many things.'

'But if, say, things went really smoothly. Say there weren't any objections. Could they get a lot done in ... three months?' June to September, the summer lay-off. Even the yobboes were away, kicking heads in Ibiza. Cor, look, Wayne, someone's nicked the Athletic ground while we've been away. So they cowing have.

'You could probably get through a lot of the paperwork, yes.'

The next stop was Companies House, City Road, where they assumed Duffy was an investigative journalist from a radical underground paper. Up to a few years ago you always used to get respectably dressed people who knew what they wanted. Nowadays you got any old – or, worse, young – crackpot walking in, wanting this, wanting that. 'Hello, I'm from the *Monthly Paranoid*, we're a bit short on city scandal this issue, can you dig me out a nice conflict of interests, please?' – it was almost as bad as that.

Duffy flipped through the microfilm catalogue, paid his pound, and waited half an hour in the search room until his microfiche came through. Hess House Holdings. Registered 1974. Registered Office, Hess House W3. List of Directors. Dee-dum, dee-dum, Duffy read. Dee-dum dee-dum, dee-dum dee-dum. And then, well, well, well, Mrs C. R. Magrudo. He checked the profits as an afterthought. No profits declared for the last two years.

When he phoned Jimmy Lister that afternoon the Boss sounded rather far away.

'I think I've got something, I definitely think I might have got something,' said Duffy.

'Oh, yes. Crown Jewels turn up?'

'I won't tell you what it is now. I'd rather come round and see you.'

'Oh yes.'

'Is that all right?'

'Sure it's all right. But whatever you've got, Duffy, it won't make any difference. They just charged big Brendan with rape.'

Jimmy Lister ought to have been out on the pitch with the lads planning free-kicks or something at the time Duffy arrived; but he was still sitting at his desk, mournfully waiting for the next bad thing to happen.

'It's all over,' he said, as Duffy sat down opposite him, 'it's just all fallen apart. First Danny, then Brendan, now the residents have got their injunction ... '

'When did they get that?'

'First thing this morning. Layton Road entrance closed till the end of the season. Leave to appeal granted, but not until it's too late. It's all over, Duffy. The club's going down the U-bend. You should have seen the lads this morning when I told them about Bren. End of the world, they knew it. And I don't think my glorious reign of management here is exactly going to bring the offers flooding in from Abu Dhabi.'

'How's he taking it?'

'Bren? Not too badly in a funny sort of way. I mean he says he didn't do it. *Course* he didn't do it – I know Bren like I know my own boy. He just seems to think that if he goes on saying he didn't do it, they're bound to believe him in the end. What he doesn't realize is that if he carries on saying he didn't do it they'll end up thinking he's being cheeky.'

'When does he come up?'

'Well, tomorrow, first time. Then there'll be a remand, then another remand, and so on.'

'Any chance of bail?'

'Not much, the solicitor said. Not nowadays. You know what the headlines are like – ACCUSED RAPIST FREE TO STALK

THE STREETS, and all that. Even with Brendan always being a good boy, I don't think they'd do it.'

'If we got him bail, would you play him?'

'Come off it, Duffy. No way. No way. It wouldn't be fair on the lad. It just wouldn't be fair. Can you imagine what they'd do to him from the terraces? They'd roast the boy. I mean, remember Bobby Moore.'

Duffy remembered. The 1970 World Cup, the England captain, an incident in a jeweller's on another continent, and all the next season when he walked out on to the pitch he heard the tune of 'Clementine', and the fans singing, 'Where's the bracelet, where's the bracelet, where's the bracelet, Bobby Moore?' And he was as innocent as the breeze.

'I couldn't play the lad, Duffy. I don't know what I'd be more scared of, the fans away from home or the loyal supporters at the Layton Road end. He'd get crucified.'

'When do you see him next?'

'Tomorrow, next day. I'm not sure. I mean, it's obviously not just a club matter, it's a family matter as well. I can't go stomping in saying Please can I have my Bren back when there's his old mum sobbing her eyes out and seeing her boy getting set for five or six years behind bars.'

'When you see him, find out the name of the girl and where she lives.'

'What for?'

'Just find it out, Jimmy.' Lister was surprised by Duffy's attitude; it had suddenly become very businesslike. This wasn't altogether surprising. The more things that went wrong for Jimmy, the more things there were for Duffy to work on.

'Isn't that breaking the law or something? I mean, isn't there a big thing about protecting the anonymity of rape victims?'

'That's only about publishing her name in the papers. Look, you don't think Bren did it, do you?'

466

'No,' said Jimmy Lister, though in truth he thought Bren might have done it.

'Nor do I,' said Duffy, though as a matter of professional principle he never put anything past anybody. 'So if we know he's innocent, we've got to find why he's being fitted up, haven't we?'

'If you say so.'

'Get me her name, get me where she lives. Either from Brendan, or from the solicitor. They'd probably have to tell him if he asked.'

'All right, Duffy. I was going to say, please can I have my salary back; but I reckon I'm not earning it, so you may as well.'

'Ta. Now, is the chairman about?'

Melvyn Prosser was standing by his desk in his overcoat, just as before. This time, however, he didn't look like a businessman in a hurry; he looked like a sea-captain whose ship is going down, and who thinks the best way of handling it is to put on his pea-jacket.

'Still with us, Mr Duffy? Isn't it all a bit out of your hands now?'

'Parts of it, I expect. But I think I might be on to something.'

'Some magic way of getting us three points from each of our last six games?'

'Wish I could, Mr Prosser, wish I could. No, I don't know what made me think of it ... ' He looked at Melvyn Prosser carefully as he said the next words. 'But I found out about the planning permission.'

Melvyn Prosser's broad, fleshy face with the vertical scar on the forehead disclosed to the keen observer only that Melvyn Prosser was still worried stiff about Brendan Domingo.

'What planning permission?'

'Did you know about the application for outline planning permission for the whole of the Athletic ground and two adjoining sites in Meadow Lane?'

'No, I didn't, Duffy. What sort of thing are we talking about?'

'Big development. Shopping centre. Offices, flats. Leisure centre.'

'Sounds like a good idea,' said Melvyn Prosser evenly. 'Sooner they wipe this shambles off the map the better.'

'Hey, *chief*,' Jimmy Lister protested.

'Sorry, Jim boy, you know how much I love this club. I love the game, I love the club. I'd do anything for this club, but you can't help getting a bit discouraged, sometimes.'

'Sure, chief.'

'I mean, don't think I overvalue my contribution. Any club – it's the players, it's the team, isn't it? The players, the fans, that's what counts. And the results. You can't have a happy club if you aren't getting the results. But I've always been right behind this club, and any little something I've been able to do, I've done.'

'Course, you have, chief, course you have. Pulled the club up by its bootstraps.'

'No, no, I've just done what any other chairman would have done in my place.'

Like pay all the bills, Duffy thought. Like pay Jimmy Lister's wages, and thus, indirectly, mine. Duffy noticed that in Melvyn Prosser's basic outline of a football club no mention was made of the manager's role. He wondered if Jimmy Lister had noticed this.

'Anyway, Mr Prosser, shall I go on?' Duffy felt that the excitement of his discovery was being rather deflated by Melvyn Prosser's philosophizing.

'Oh, go on, yes, sure.'

'Outline planning permission for the entire Athletic ground and two adjoining sites has been applied for by a company known as Hess House Holdings.'

'Never heard of them,' said Prosser.

'Hess House Holdings have an interesting Board of

Directors,' said Duffy. 'One of them is listed as Mrs C. R. Magrudo.'

'Charlie's wife?' Melvyn seemed delighted. 'Charlie's wife?' Then he burst out laughing. 'The cheeky bugger. Cheeky Charlie Magrudo. You've got to laugh, haven't you?'

'Why?'

'Why? Because it's one of Charlie's jokes. You sure there wasn't something else on the plan? Like a lighthouse or a pier or an airport or something?'

Duffy was a bit pissed off with Melvyn Prosser.

'Look, Mr Prosser, correct me if I'm wrong. Someone's trying to fuck up this club. I asked you if you had any enemies. You mentioned Charlie Magrudo. I find out that Charlie Magrudo, through his wife, has applied for outline planning permission on this site.'

'Yes I'm sorry to laugh, Mr Duffy,' said Prosser, and carried on laughing none the less. 'But what do you deduce from this?'

'That Charlie Magrudo is trying to fuck up this club to buy it cheap and develop it like he's asked for.'

'Hmm. Yes, I'm sorry not to take your theory with the seriousness it warrants, and do please watch your language by the way, we're not in the team bath now. The point is, Charlie Magrudo hasn't got two beans to rub together.'

'What do you mean?'

'If he wanted to rub beans together, he'd have to take out his sole surviving bean and cut it in half first. He's a bankrupt. Not officially, of course, but as close as you can get without the men coming round for your three-piece suite at eight o'clock in the morning. That's why Mrs Charlie's name's on everything. She holds the surviving bean in her little bean-bag, and takes it out occasionally and lets poor old Charlie count it.' Melvyn was off into chuckling again.

'You did him some naughty, you said, over some contract.'

'Oh, that. No, that wasn't much; just normal business

469

procedure. The real naughty I did Charlie was with Mrs Charlie, and that was years ago. It's all blood under the bridge and I'm sure we've forgiven one another.'

'What was that bit of naughty?'

'Oh, you don't have to ask, do you? What do you do with your middle stump?'

'Sorry.'

'Not very bright today, are we? Look, the point about Charlie Magrudo is that if this whole club came up for sale he might, if the bank gave him a loan – which is less than likely – be able to bid for a half-share in the toilets. Maximum.'

'Couldn't he . . . I don't know, get backing or something?'

'Not with Charlie's business record.'

'But . . . but I read his file down at the *Chronicle*. They said he was a thriving local businessman.'

'I'll tell you how he does that. It's called buying the reporter a drink. It's called not turning up with dandruff on your collar. It may, or it may not, be called passing the wine list across to the reporter with twenty-five quid inside it – I wouldn't want to cast any aspersions on the lawfully wedded husband of Mrs Charlie or on the integrity of the gentlemen of the press.'

'Oh dear.'

'It's also called not believing what you read in the papers.'

'Oh dear. But why would he do it?'

'As I say, it's a typical Charlie joke. Well, it's typical of what he used to do, anyway. I haven't seen him for years, to tell you the truth. But it sounds like he's getting his own back for that little bit of council business I dropped him in. He puts in this plan, and then waits a bit, and then one day when he's a bit low or something, he gets someone to ring up the *Chronicle* and say, Did you know they were going to knock down the Athletic ground and build a racecourse? And they're bound to do a big story, whatever, aren't they? Front-page splash, if it's a boring week. And then Charlie gets to think about what my face will look like when I pick up the paper. Typical Charlie.'

'Oh dear.'

'Well, nice try, anyway,' commented Prosser benevolently.

'Uh-huh.'

As Duffy drove home, he thought, Typical. Bloody typical. Spend all morning chasing a really bright idea, find exactly what you're looking for, get back and what happens: something much more important has turned up, and your own bright idea is transformed into a real poodle.

Carol seemed to be coming round more often lately. Duffy couldn't work out whether this was because of him or her. Had he been asking her more, or had she been just turning up more? Perhaps those parts of her life he didn't like to ask about weren't so busy at the moment; perhaps Robert Redford was away on location and not able to ask her out so much. On the other hand, it might be that since his activities down at the Alligator were a bit curtailed at the moment, he'd been inviting her round more without noticing. Or it might be a mixture of the two.

'What're the chances of getting bail for rape nowadays?' he asked over dinner.

'Rape? Pretty thin. I mean, there's always a chance, because of the overcrowding in the cells. But it's not the sort of thing that happens very often. The bench doesn't like to get egg on its face, especially not with rape nowadays.'

'What if the accused has got a nice smile?'

'No previous?'

'None of any kind. Clean as a whistle. Simple conflict of evidence.'

'Well, it's possible. It's always possible. A smart lawyer might swing it. I mean, he might be able to suggest bail conditions that would satisfy the court.'

'Like having his cock chopped off?'

Carol grinned.

'I think they'd accept that.'

Duffy didn't think Brendan would, though. Then he noticed that Carol was looking at him and smiling. Oh dear, he thought: were things going to stop being neat again?

'You wash, I'll wipe.'

Carol sighed.

'You don't have to say it, Duffy. That's what we always do.'

Later, in bed, he realized that he hadn't worried about his lymph nodes all day. Well, that was something. Carol seemed wide awake, but Duffy had had enough. Another dog of a day. Another real bow-wow. As he lapsed into sleep, he remembered the last time Carol had stayed, and how he'd won himself a night sweat and an erection. The second of each. He could hear that man reading the sports results on the telly. Erections 2, Night Sweats 2. Replay on Monday.

When he woke up he realized that he'd got through the eight hours without a night sweat. He'd also got through the eight hours without an erection. Perhaps the two *were* connected in some way. Perhaps you couldn't have one without the other. That worried him.

There were four weeks of the season to go, and six games left for Athletic. Fourth from bottom of the table, and with everyone in the relegation zone having played the same number of games, their future was, as the lads kept telling one another and the manager kept telling the lads, in their own hands. If they won every single remaining match, they wouldn't be relegated. Of course; but you might as well say that if they'd won every single previous game in the season, they'd be in the Second Division by now. Who, for instance, fancied Athletic's chances away from home to top-of-the-table Oxford? That was the trouble at the end of a season. The clubs at the top were still chasing promotion, and you didn't expect any favours from them; while the clubs at the bottom were trying to escape the drop as much as you were.

This left the clubs in the middle, the clubs who'd had an average season but were safe for another year. In theory this made them easy pickings: kick them about a bit in the first twenty minutes, and they lost interest and started to think about their summer holidays. But it didn't work out like that: just because they were safe for another year, they were more relaxed, more ready to try things, less depressed if they went a goal down. All footballers like to play a bit of fancy stuff if they can; they like to score goals; and they like to win matches. Middle-of-the-table clubs at the rear end of the season aren't any different in these basics. And if you tried kicking them, well, who likes being kicked, especially by some no-hoper with his luggage packed for the Fourth Division? Middle-of-the-tablers can kick back just as well; they might even mind a little less than you do about being sent off.

'Mr Bullivant, good morning.'

'You again, laddie, I thought they'd fired you.'

'Yes, well, you see, I'm still learning.' Duffy took out his notebook, uncapped his biro, and tried to look as if he were about to take down the Sermon on the Mount.

'Well, you can't come and practise on me every day.'

'How's the osteopathy going?' Duffy thought it a good idea to establish some rapport before asking his real questions.

'Very well, thank you.'

'How do you feel about getting the injunction?'

Bullivant didn't answer. Instead, he continued to stare at Duffy's notepad.

'You haven't written anything down yet, smiler. Aren't you going to write down that the osteopathy is going very well?'

'Oh, yes, sorry.' Duffy started writing, then looked up. Mr Bullivant was grinning at him.

'You're a real berk, aren't you?'

'Mr Bullivant, how do you feel about getting the injunction.'

473

'I would just like to say on this one, that British justice is the finest in the world, and you can quote me.'

'You think this will be the end of the trouble?'

'The British police are the finest in the world and I have every confidence that they will carry out the duties entrusted to them to the best of their ability. Write it down.'

Duffy wrote it down.

'Do you think you are in any way damaging the prospects of the club at this vital stage of the season by your actions?'

'Soccer hooliganism is a reflection of a wider violence which affects all parts of our society. You cannot merely consider soccer hooliganism by itself. You must look at the breakdown of respect for law and order generally, and the lack of self-discipline in a society that has gone soft. Going too fast for you?'

Duffy dutifully copied all this down, then read it through.

'What's that got to do with my question?'

'Just checking to see if you'd write down any old rubbish.'

'Mr Bullivant, will Mr Magrudo continue to support your action even if the club appeals and goes to a higher court?'

'How's that again?'

'Will Mr Magrudo continue to foot the bills if the club appeals?'

'Who's that?'

'Mr Magrudo.'

'Who does he play for? Italian World Cup squad?'

'Mr Bullivant, I happen to know that Mr Magrudo is paying your solicitor's bills.'

'Why would some Italian footballer pay my bills? Athletic aren't in the European Cup are they, or haven't I been reading my papers lately?'

'Mr Bullivant ... '

'You're a real berk, you know that? A real berk. Write it down. B.E.R.K., that's right. I think I like the yobboes more than I do you.'

'Well, at least you'll be able to plant flowers in your front garden, Mr Bullivant, now that the yobboes have gone.'

'Bye-bye, tulip,' said Mr Bullivant unexpectedly.

Well, that was another idea gone. Perhaps he should go over to Ealing to the house with the flagpole and ask Mr Joyce if he was being paid by Mr Magrudo. He'd be sure to tell him, too. Yes, Mr Magrudo the well-known near-bankrupt who just has enough money to buy himself flattering mentions in the local paper, yes as a matter of fact he is supporting the Red White and Blue Movement, and when he's built his nice new leisure centre with all the money he hasn't got he's going to let us have a recruiting booth outside and also a reviewing stand so that we can have march-pasts and he'll be giving us a lifetime's supply of toast and marmalade, you really are a berk, Mr – what was it you said your name was this time?

At least with Danny Matson he could be himself. Danny still had his foot up on the stool. Terrible about big Bren, wasn't it? Terrible. No, he hadn't seen or heard him come in. Must have been real quiet; unless it was late, of course. In the morning they – Danny and Mrs Ferris – had found him sitting downstairs at the breakfast table in his club blazer, club tie and best trousers. Just staring ahead of himself, frowning a bit, with these big scratches on his face. Said he'd been in a fight. Wouldn't say any more. Just sitting there, waiting. Ate his breakfast like normal; didn't want to talk about the game at all; just waiting. And then the coppers came. Yes, sure, he said. Will I need any clothes or anything, he said as they took him off. Poor Bren. Anything else? No, nothing else. Just wouldn't talk about it. He's a class player, you know that? Class. Very nimble for a big fellow. Got it up here, too. Danny tapped the side of his head, indicating brains.

The Magrudo Construction Company turned out not to be quite as grand as its name. It was a small builder's yard off Copton Avenue, and yes, the receptionist was sure Mr Magrudo would be free some time before lunch if he didn't mind waiting. Mr Magrudo was always happy to see people from the *Chronicle*. Take a seat.

Charlie Magrudo arrived at about twelve in a four-year-old Granada which looked as if it stalled if it heard the word car-wash. Ten minutes, quarter of an hour, sure, no problem. He was a round, friendly man, dark hair, and rather tight in his suit; comfortable-looking, like some middle-rank snooker player who'd never quite made the top fifty, but was more than happy doing the rounds of the little clubs.

'We haven't met before, Mr Marriott?'

'No.'

'No. I've seen quite a bit of Ron down the years, Ron Grayson. And Gerry Douglas, of course. Old friends.' Old recipients of small bribes, thought Duffy. 'You new?'

'Newish. I'm sort of doing a bit of everything. Sports pages mainly, but they've also given me a few stories to do about planning, roadworks, things like that.'

Duffy tried to make it sound low-key. He also hoped that Charlie Magrudo wasn't a keen reader of bylines, in which case he might have known that Ken Marriott had been on the sports desk for four years, and never once gone near the other pages.

'So how can I be of assistance? Always ready to help the gentlemen of the press.'

'It's about this application for a development on the site of the Athletic ground.'

'Yes, sure. What do you want to know?'

'How realistic would you say it was?'

Mr Magrudo thought it was very realistic. He gave Duffy a run-down on the plans as if he'd been going through them only that morning with the architect, and was shortly off for a working lunch with an American bank to clean up the last details of the financing. He gestured a lot, and as he talked his hands seemed to create the shopping centre, the eight-storey block of flats, the piazza, the fountains, the trees in tubs, the lively bustle of a successful commercial project.

Duffy thought it all sounded wonderful; but he also thought it time he added to Ken Marriott's academic qualifications.

'Mr Magrudo, I hope you don't think this impertinent of me ... '

'Fire away. Ask me the hard questions. Be my guest.'

'Well, before I did my three-year planning course, I read economics at university. Now I expect I'm a bit rusty, but I'd say we're looking at a project high in seven figures, maybe even eight. It sounds a splendid idea, even if it does mean Athletic losing their ground and having to look for a new one. But the hard question I have to ask is this. You don't even own the site yet, and I simply don't see how you can raise the money.'

Charlie Magrudo was about to answer, but Duffy went swiftly on. He didn't want to get Charlie blustering and then forced to defend an indefensible position. There would be more chance of the truth if Duffy played it a bit tough. In the nicest possible way, of course.

'You see I've had a little look at Magrudo Construction and its associates. It's a very solid little family firm, if you don't mind my saying so. You'll be able to change that Granada for a new model this year or next, I should say. But we're talking seven figures just for the site, Mr Magrudo, and I couldn't help noticing at City Road that you haven't declared for the last couple of years. Now that's not on. In fact it's so much not on that, if you don't mind my saying so, I think it must all be about something else.'

Charlie Magrudo spread his hands and smiled.

'They would send you, wouldn't they? I mean, just my luck to get the brainiest fellow on the *Chronicle*. If they'd sent Ron or Gerry, I reckon I could have done enough pulling of the wool. Look if I don't say another word, have you got a story?'

'Sorry, no.'

'Not even a paragraph? A paragraph? We could have lunch about it?'

477

'Sorry. I'm afraid it's either a big story or it's nothing. It seems to me it isn't a big story any more; it's just a question of whether you want to tell me what it's all about, though there's absolutely no reason at all why you should.'

'Fair cop,' said Charlie, 'fair cop. I just hoped it might work. It's a joke, actually.'

'A *joke*?' Duffy really put on the amazement. Anything to let Magrudo know that his plan was at least causing some reaction.

Then Charlie told him about Melvyn Prosser, and old rivalries of a kind which were sometimes friendly and sometimes a little less friendly. The name of Mrs Magrudo, Duffy noticed, did not come up. The version of events concerning the council contract was also a little different from Melvyn Prosser's. But the story was essentially the same.

'How did you think Mr Prosser would react?'

'Well, I hoped that for one minute, just for one minute or even less, he'd be scared shitless,' said Charlie Magrudo. 'I just had this picture of him opening his paper and thinking his lovely new football club which he was so proud of was going to be bulldozed down and concreted over. I just wanted him to be scared shitless. Perhaps even for longer than a minute.'

'Do you think he would have believed it?'

'He might have. He might have. I mean, we haven't seen each other for quite a few years now. He might have thought I'd done some good business, made a little pile, and was just about to come bursting in all over him.'

'Well, I'm sorry to have spoiled your joke, Mr Magrudo.'

'Oh, don't worry. It was a bit of a long-shot. What did you say your name was?'

'Marriott. Ken Marriott.'

'Nice meeting you, Ken. We must have that lunch some time.'

'I'd like that, Mr Magrudo.'

'Charlie from now on, son. Tell you what, I think you'll go

far in your chosen profession.' And Mr Magrudo gave him a big wink.

Well, that was another door closed in Duffy's face. Sometimes it seemed to him that there were more doors closing than had ever been open in the first place. Still, at least Mr Magrudo thought he was a good journalist. Duffy quite wanted to get Charlie Magrudo and Mr Bullivant together and listen to the pair of them discussing the merits of Ken Marriott, *Chronicle* journalist. He'd like to have Maggot listening in on the conversation as well.

All he could do now was push on the only door left that was slightly ajar. The next day Jimmy Lister, with some reluctance, released to Duffy the name of Maggie Coleman, and the address off Twyford Avenue. Duffy realized he had to play this one very carefully indeed. If there was one thing the coppers didn't like it was outsiders coming in and hassling rape victims. They got very cross about that sort of thing. There were a few sections of the criminal law especially designed to deter people from leaning on prosecution witnesses; and the coppers certainly wouldn't mind using them. Much as he liked Brendan, Duffy wasn't ready to join him in the next cell just yet. So he started low-key. He started by ringing Geoff Bell.

'Atom sub 24 degrees South 22 degrees East request permission instant destroy query PM waiting urgentest.'

'Hallo, Duffy,' said Geoff. 'That was a bit over the top even for you. Is it about the match on Sunday?'

'Wondered if you'd be interested in a little photographic assignment?'

'Very nice.'

'It's pretty difficult, actually, Geoff. I mean, there are certain aspects to it which could turn tricky.' You always had to do this with Bell. He couldn't get interested in easy assignments, somehow; you always had to dress them up. Duffy found it a bit tiresome.

'Try me.'

Duffy tried him, emphasizing the possibility that there might be an incredible number of plain-clothes men around, that Maggie Coleman might be living locked in her flat with the curtains drawn, and so on.

'Leave it with me,' said Geoff. 'Oh, and Duffy?'

'Yes?'

'Those co-ordinates are all to cock. Who'd put an atomic sub in the middle of the Kalahari Desert?'

'I'll do better next time, Geoff.'

There was another thing he could do when the doors were closing in his face. He didn't like doing it, but he somehow always fell back on it. He asked Carol to check out three names for him on the police computer: Maggie Coleman, Charlie Magrudo and Melvyn Prosser. Carol always said No, and Duffy bullied her a bit, and then she finally said Yes, and they both got a bit silent. Duffy always felt bad, but there it was. He tried being as nice as he could to Carol afterwards, but she remained silent and a bit distant; she stayed the night, but there weren't any cuddles. No cuddles, no swollen cocks, and no night sweats.

On the Saturday Athletic were away to Oxford, and Duffy turned on the radio to catch the result. Oxford 2 Athletic 1. Oxford now assured of promotion, Athletic drop back into the bottom three. Pitch invasion by Oxford fans, some scuffles when travelling Athletic fans come on to the pitch as well. Eighteen arrests, one policeman slightly injured.

'It was a sickener,' said Jimmy Lister at the ground next morning. 'The lads really did their stuff. I mean there we were, biggest crowd of the season, ten thousand or so I'd say, a real promotion–relegation number, and this Brendan business hanging over their heads. They really battled, those lads. Came in one–nil down at half-time, none of them needed lifting, we had a little talk and thought if we could match them a bit more in midfield and then get just a good bounce of the ball, there wasn't any reason why we shouldn't share the points. I was really impressed by the lads' attitude.

It was as if they were doing it for Bren. It was funny, no one mentioned his name, not once, but I'd lay money that every one of us on the coach had been thinking about big Bren all locked up in his little cell. In a funny sort of a way, it seemed to bring out the best in the lads.

'Second half, they really did the club proud. Got hold of the midfield, lots of pressure, and we nicked one back after twenty minutes. Not the cleverest goal we've ever scored, but a goal we deserved all the way. I really did think the lads would do it then. I really thought if they got one, there's no reason why they can't get another. Or at least come away with a result. What happens? Ten minutes to go, the lads pushing up in search of a winner, breakaway goal. Not even trying to play the offside trap, just caught a tiny bit square and their number eight was straight through. Speedy little bastard. What a sickener.'

'Still, it sounds as if they've got the right attitude, at least.'

'Bags of character, Duffy. Maybe I've been wrong all season. You know how I like to get teams to play. Maybe that was wrong. They'll never be very fancy on the ball, this lot, but they've got guts hanging out of their ears. I just should have recognized it earlier.'

'Don't blame yourself, Jimmy. What do you think the chances of staying up now are?'

'Worse than they were before. I mean, it's not just up to us any more, is it? We've got to rely on one or two of the others slipping up as well. Just got to keep battling, haven't we? Just got to keep battling.' Jimmy Lister wondered gloomily what they did to you in Abu Dhabi if they caught you with the physio's wife. Chopped if off, most likely.

On Sunday the players who had been hurt the previous afternoon came in to see the physio for treatment. Duffy wandered down to the physio's room to the echo of Jimmy's words. Keep battling. Good attitude. Guts hanging out of their ears. It was odd to hear the elegant England B international of ten years ago coming out with all the old football manager's clichés. But there was truth in them, even so. They expressed what Athletic had to do for the next five games. No point doing anything else. It was also what Duffy would have to do, because Duffy's position was no more promising than Athletic's. He just had to keep on battling and hope for a bloody great brainwave. Or a bloody great stroke of luck. Or both at the same time, thank you very much.

Throughout this business Duffy had felt a bit like the goalkeeper he was. He felt useful, but only in a defensive way. All goalkeepers have spells of envying the outfield players – they want to rush out of the area, surge upfield and have a kick at the opposing net. But they're stuck, penned into their neat little box, their square-cornered territory: you're doing a nice job, let's leave it that way, don't get ideas above your station. Keepers only get a crack at the other side's net when they're allowed to take penalties: Duffy, for all his occasional hints, had yet to be entrusted with a spot-kick by the Reliables.

There was, however, a freak way in which a goalkeeper could score: Duffy had seen it happen once on television. The keeper advances to the edge of his box and gives the ball a bloody great hoof; a following wind catches it and whisks it further than anyone had anticipated; it fools the defenders, bounces, catches the opposing keeper too far off his line, and lobs over his head into the net. Incredibly lucky, of course: it depended on a strong boot, a helpful breeze, a lethargic defence and a rash goal-minder. But it could happen. It was the sort of break Duffy needed in the present business; very much indeed.

Saturday's injuries had been light: one aggravated groin strain plus one slightly ricked knee.

'Not bad for this stage of the season,' commented Reg Palmer the physio. 'Normally you get a lot of extra little tears and niggles, especially with the older players.' He strapped a tension bandage on a midfielder's knee. 'All the injuries seem to be happening off the park for some reason.'

Duffy hung around, waited until the two players had been patched up, and chatted away to Reg Palmer. He was a thin, wiry man of uncertain years and terrifying fitness. He had been at the club for thirty years. Seen it all. Managers come and go. Promotion, relegation, good players, bad players, pitches all over the country and injuries all over the body. Boardrooms come and go, yes, that too.

'What was it like before Mr Prosser arrived?'

'Oh, it was all right. Bit of a shambles; no one quite knew who was giving the orders. It's a bit clearer under Mr Prosser.'

'Has he made changes?'

'Well, he brought Jimmy in, didn't he? And it's always nice having someone new, isn't it? Full of enthusiasm, especially at first. Offered me all sorts of machines – you know, sonic whatsits, infra-red and all that. Happy to spend quite a bit on the physio room, if I wanted it. But I said No, I'll stay with God's two hands and my bag of tricks. Still, it was a nice offer.'

'Does he – I don't know – does he interfere much?'

'Interfere? Not that I've noticed. One thing he does do is ring me every Sunday afternoon, four o'clock, without fail, and ask me exactly what lads I've got under treatment and how they're getting on. Most chairmen would think they were a bit too grand for that, but not Mr Prosser. He may not get their names right, but he does ask after them.'

'Is he popular?'

'Yes, he's popular. I mean, every club's got to have a chairman, haven't they? I've known quite a few, and I've known far worse. No, Mr Whatever-your-name-is,' and Reg Palmer looked sternly at Duffy, 'you won't hear anything against Mr Prosser from me.'

'I wasn't asking, Mr Palmer. I just wondered. I was also wondering, if he's an improvement on what went before, then why is the club doing worse?'

483

'Well, he's not picking the team, is he? He's not picking and training the team.'

Or maybe Duffy wasn't looking to boot the ball hopefully upfield, see it catch a following wind and bounce over the opposing keeper's head. Maybe he wasn't looking to lean against a half-open door just in time to stop it shutting in his face. Maybe it wasn't a matter of battling away, showing bags of character, and having guts hanging out of your ears. Maybe it was more like seeing a little chink in a wall, and inserting a chisel or a screwdriver or something, and giving it a little twist, and watching the whole wall tumble down. The whole front wall of a shopping centre, leisure complex and block of offices-cum-flats, with or without the addition of piazza, fountains, tubbed trees, lighthouse, pier, airport, racecourse or whatever.

On the Monday morning he telephoned Hess House Holdings. This called for the posh voice.

'Jeremy Silverlight here. Is Mr Magrudo going to be in today? It's a touch urgent.'

'Hold the line, sir, please.'

Pause.

'He should be here about two-thirty. Can I take any message?'

'No, I'll call again. Two-thirty, you said?'

'Yes, sir.'

At ten minutes past two he rang Hess House Holdings again and asked to be put through to Charlie Magrudo's secretary. He didn't know if Charlie had a secretary at Hess House, but that didn't matter. The way these places operated, they usually made up a 'secretary' on the spot, especially if you sounded like money down the other end of the phone. They wouldn't say, 'Oh, Mr Magrudo hasn't got a secretary, actually the firm's not doing well enough for that, there is a girl somewhere who we think slept with Mr Magrudo – well, Charlie to all of us girls – but she's down the corridor putting nail varnish on a run in her tights at the moment so I'll get her to call you back when she's finished.' No, they wouldn't say that. What they would say is this:

'Trying to connect you.'

And after a minute or so (perhaps the girl was putting nail varnish on a run in her tights):

'Mr Magrudo's office.'

'Jeremy Silverlight. I gather Mr Magrudo's going to be with you shortly.'

'Yes, he's expected.'

'It isn't actually Charlie I want to get hold of. Well, I wouldn't mind a word, but that can wait. It's Mel Prosser. He's a devil to track down. His office thought he might be on his way to Hess House with Charlie. Do you know about that?'

'I'm afraid I don't.'

'Hmm. Look, sorry to be a pest, but perhaps you could check Charlie's book and see if he's expecting Mel this afternoon?'

Pause.

'There's nothing in the book, sir. Though of course that doesn't necessarily mean that ... ' She sounded helpful as well as helpless.

'No, of course. Actually, I wouldn't put it past Mel to tell his office he was going to see Charlie when he was actually going somewhere else. He's more than a touch crafty, our Mel. Still, I don't want to bore you with the ins and outs of how old Mel Prosser carries on business. We could be here all night.' The rambling was deliberate, and the question it provoked was more or less forced.

'How can I help you, sir?'

'Look, I'm not going out of my tiny, I hope. I mean, correct me if I'm wrong, but Charlie does see quite a lot of Mel, doesn't he?'

'Oh, yes, sir. He's always round. Well, not always, but

485

he's been round a lot lately. He just sort of drops in. That's why we don't really put him in the book.'

If there is a book, thought Duffy.

'Well if he does turn up, could you ask him to give me a bell on 205 3637. You've got the name?'

'Silverlight, yes sir.'

'I mean, don't bother if he doesn't turn up this afternoon. I can catch him at home in the evening.'

Phew. Being a bit posh down the phone always took it out of Duffy. And at the same time he felt a little surge of satisfaction. Is that the chink in the wall? And if so, which way do I turn the chisel?

Ten minutes later, the phone went. Duffy jumped, almost expecting it to be Melvyn Prosser. In a way, he wished he'd left his real number, just for a laugh.

'Watch the birdie.'

'Sorry?'

'Click, click, watch the birdie.'

'Oh, hello Geoff. Sorry, wasn't concentrating.'

'You should have warned me about the lenses.'

'Geoff, I thought you were best left to work that out for yourself.'

'Well, you could have given me some idea. I mean, I needed at least the 200 and probably the 400, and there I was stuck with a piddly little 35 to 80 zoom on and I just had to decide, well do I shoot or do I change and I thought anything was better than nothing so I shot.'

'I think that was the right decision.'

'So I've got you some earlies, anyway, and I know the answer is not to have just the one camera body but three. I suppose in a way I'm as much to blame as you.'

'I'll be right round, Geoff.'

'Well, I warn you, I had some trouble blowing them up. And if you'd told me the flats faced west ... '

'I'm truly sorry.' Sometimes Duffy thought that Geoff was even more of a worrier than he was.

486

The photos, of course, were almost perfect, just what Duffy had asked for. They showed a girl with blonde hair emerging from a block of flats, looking around her, and setting off down the street. Pity about the dark glasses. He didn't know what sort of shape Maggie Coleman was in, but he always thought wearing dark glasses was the stupidest way of trying to go unnoticed. It just made you look like some Cabinet Minister's moll, or a star witness in a divorce case. 'And here, leaving her block of flats near Twyford Avenue, Acton, we see Maggie Coleman, the doctor's wife accused of administering a lethal dose of weedkiller to her husband, who has just been flown back to England by the Spanish authorities after vacationing in Marbella with Pedro the handyman.'

As against that, the glasses did make it harder to see what her face was like. Duffy spread out the photos and stared at them.

'Oh, and I did get this one, but I didn't really have time to focus, and with all that business of the lenses ... '

It was a sharp, well-focused picture of Maggie Coleman raising her glasses. You still couldn't see her eyes, because they were cast down, looking at something out of shot; but it was exactly the sort of photo Duffy wanted.

'I just got it in time. Lucky I changed the lens first, before I followed her. And then, even so, it was pure chance that I parked where I could see between a couple of vans. She took off the glasses to see if some fruit was ripe in the greengrocer's.'

'Does it look like her?' Duffy asked.

'What do you mean?'

'Well, would you say it was a good likeness?'

'Look, I'm sorry, if I'd known you wanted Lord Snowdon ... '

'Sorry, Geoff. Sorry. They're terrific, they're just what I wanted.'

'They may be just what you wanted, but they're not

terrific. Technically, they're pretty much in the Third Division.'

It was always a bit like this with Geoff. He didn't care whether he was photographing a politician's moll, or a child murderer, or even some girl in the street that you fancied. He was only interested in whether he should have stopped down a bit more, or whether there was enough density in the negative. Look, Geoff, here's a picture of the entire Royal Family with no clothes on. I think they should have lit it more from the side, Duffy, and that crop is terrible.

'Thanks, Geoff. See you Sunday?'

'We're playing away.'

'So we are. Sorry.'

Duffy went first to the Albion, since that was where Brendan had picked Maggie up, or vice versa, depending on whether you were a policeman or one of the rare Athletic fans on his side. The barman who couldn't remember Brendan Domingo couldn't remember Maggie Coleman either. No; well, anyway, she can't be a regular, because I remember the regulars. But she was with a regular: she was with Brendan Domingo. Who's he? Brendan Domingo, he's the footballer I was in here asking about a couple of weeks ago, asking about the fellow in a mackintosh he'd been drinking with. Oh, the coloured fellow? That's right. No, he hasn't been back here since. What, the man in the mackintosh? No, the coloured fellow, the Brendan fellow, he hasn't been back since you first came and asked me about him. Why, he done something or something?

Hopeless. Duffy drove to the Athletic ground, waited until training was over, asked Jimmy Lister's permission, which he granted reluctantly, and showed the photos to the lads.

'That's her? The one who did Bren?'

'The one Bren did, you mean.'

'Tasty.'

'Wouldn't mind a bit.'

'Worth a year or two behind bars.'

'Always knew Brendan could pull them.'

'Where's she live, Duffy? You got her address?'

In a way, Duffy wasn't surprised. Footballers were very sentimental, but they were also pretty tough. They had to be to get through. Footballers in the first team couldn't afford to think about footballers who weren't in the first team. Healthy footballers couldn't afford to think about footballers whose legs had been broken, whose backs had given way, whose tendons had snapped. Footballers in form couldn't afford to think about footballers who had lost their form. Being a first-team player meant not being a lot of other things – like someone sitting in a purple chair with his leg up, or someone sitting in a cell with a bucket in the corner – and you couldn't let those other things get on top of you.

Kennie Hunt was the only one who thought there was something vaguely familiar about Maggie Coleman.

'Can't remember her, eh, Kennie? You can't have forgotten all the lucky ones.'

'I think I've seen someone like her.'

'Kennie just wants to keep the picture. Fancy her a bit, do you Kennie?'

'Any idea where you might have seen her?' asked Duffy.

'All the same in the dark to you, aren't they, Kennie?'

'Not sure. Maybe down at The Knight Spot.'

'Give him the picture, Mr Duffy, that's what he's after.'

'Hang on to one of these. See if it helps you remember.'

'That's what he wanted. Here, give us another look, Kennie.'

Duffy drove to The Knight Spot and rang the bell. Fat Frankie was no doubt still sleeping off his lagers, but Vince was there, in early, doing the books. Yes? Oh, any friend of Jimmy's, any friend of the Athletic. Vince was as worried as anyone about the chances of Athletic going down to the Fourth at the end of the season. Third Division footballers were OK, I mean close your eyes and they were almost in the Second Division, and that's class. But Fourth Division? Come to my wonderful fashionable West London club and gaze upon a special table of wallies who manged to get themselves relegated at the end of last season? Girls, get yourself picked up by the cream of the Fourth Division! It didn't sound much of a selling point to Vince.

The pictures? Well, we get a lot of girls in here. The thing about girls is, I don't really notice them unless they don't fit in somehow. You know, if they're too classy or too trampy. Otherwise, they all look the same. It must be the hair or something – you know, if they all dress the same and have the same hair, you can't tell them apart. Unless it's just that I'm getting old. It could be that. This one, for instance, this one you're showing me, she's very familiar. She is? Yes, she's very familiar because she looks like a thousand other girls. Not too trampy, not too classy. I wouldn't know her even if I'd passed the time of day with her a dozen times. I simply wouldn't know. Do you think Athletic have got any chance of staying up?

The trouble was, Duffy hadn't any idea where the best places to ask were. He didn't want to get too close to Twyford Avenue in case it got back to the coppers that someone whose credentials weren't exactly kosher was asking about Maggie Coleman. But if he stayed away from Twyford Avenue, where did he look? She'd met Brendan in the Albion, but that didn't necessarily mean she liked pubs. Even so, he tried the Bell and Clapper, the Rising Sun and the Duke of Cambridge. No go. Then he tried Benny's, where for a change they remembered Brendan, but where they had never seen the girl before. Then, as a long shot, he tried The Palm Tree, where a couple of sleepy West Indians shook their heads, and at the name of Brendan Domingo said, Brendan Domingo? Haven't seen him for a year or so, used to be a bit of a regular, gone to stay with the white folks since he's got so famous. Even if he does live just round the corner, he still prefers the company of the white folks.

So Duffy went just round the corner to see the white folks; or at least to see one of them – Danny Matson. As he walked into the tiny room with the purple chair, Duffy felt a bit depressed. Danny was still there, foot up, as cheerful as he could be, and pleased to see Duffy; but it was still depressing somehow. Depressing because here was a footballer who wasn't playing football. Duffy recalled the feelings of the Athletic players when shown Maggie Coleman's photo. Make a joke of it, lads, something like this could happen to you. Anything could go wrong at any time, remember that. Stay fit, play well, don't get into any trouble, and with a bit of luck you might stay off the scrap-heap until you are thirty-five. But there are a whole lot of junior scrap-heaps all the way along the line to thirty-five. Duffy couldn't understand why footballers didn't worry a lot more than they did. Or perhaps worrying was another thing that was bad for you: if you worried, you ended up on the worriers' scrap-heap, the scrap-heap kept specially for the indecisive footballer who dishes himself by thinking too much. Maybe you could only get to the top and stay at the top by having certain strong traits – single-mindedness, tenacity, cruelty – and cutting everything else out.

'This is a joke, Duffy?' said Danny Matson, looking serious.

'Eh?'

'This is a joke? You are pulling the one with bells on?'

'Come again?'

'This is the girl big Bren is supposed to have raped?'

'Yup. Maggie Coleman.'

'Oh. Maggie Coleman, eh? She told me she was called Denise.'

The trouble with putting a chisel into a wall and twisting is, of course, that the whole blade might break off. And that could be a great waste of time.

491

'Mr Prosser?'

'Oh. Still with us Mr Duffy?'

'Wondered if I could have a word.'

'That usually means more than one. How long do you want.'

'Ten minutes?' Duffy really wanted twenty or thirty.

'That usually means twenty or thirty.' Prosser smiled. 'If you can find your own way back from North London you'd better come in the car with me.'

'Thanks.'

'Turn round.'

Duffy turned round.

'Lift your feet.'

Duffy raised first one foot, then the other, displaying the soles of his shoes to Mr Prosser.

'Right. Fine. Hop in. Only you can't be too careful, what with all the dogshit around nowadays.' Duffy rather liked Melvyn Prosser. Well, approved of, perhaps he meant. Well, sympathized with, perhaps. Well, recognized another neurotic when he saw one, that was nearest the truth.

'Drink?' Melvyn said, while Duffy was still awed by the amount of room in the back of the Corniche. As big as a hotel suite. Certainly as big as Danny Matson's room. Lovely carpet – I'd make them wipe their feet too. Gold upholstery. Telephone. Little control panel with buttons at Mr Prosser's elbow. Lovely. 'You don't get one of these in our society without treading on a few toes' – that's what Prosser had said. Whose toes?

'Tonic water, please. Lovely motor.'

'Thank you. Let's see, one tonic water.'

'Have you got Slimline?'

As Melvyn Prosser poured the tonic into a nice bit of cut glass, Duffy gazed at the carpet. Beige, with flecks of brown in it. Little flecks of brown. Was that what Kaposi's sarcoma looked like?

'Well you've had two minutes already.'

492

'What do you think of the lads' chances tonight?' At home to mid-table Wigan. Could be a difficult match. Thrashed four–nil up there in the early part of the season. Bound to remember that, some of the lads, that's what Jimmy Lister had said.

'You didn't ask for a lift all the way to Muzzie Hill where you aren't going in order to ask me that.'

'How much are you worth, Mr Prosser?'

'Ha ha. Yes. Well, I wish I knew. But it's the old saying, I'm afraid. I make the money, and I pay others to count it.'

'But we're talking well into six figures, aren't we, Mr Prosser? I mean, I'd say well into seven figures.'

'That's very generous of you.'

'You must be quite used to things being a success?'

Melvyn Prosser chuckled.

'I'm very glad I'm not footing your bill, Mr Duffy. I think it's very funny, the idea of Jimmy Lister paying you, what is it, fifty quid a day plus expenses to ride in the chairman's Corniche and ask him tricky questions. This is the bit, I suppose, where I say, Yes I am used to success and look all smug and pleased with myself and then you say something I wasn't expecting and I break down and admit I'm the Boston Strangler and Jack the Ripper and Colonel Gaddafi.'

'I'm not trying to ask you tricky questions. I'm just trying to get some background. For instance, there you are, rich man, used to success, and you find yourself with a real loser on your hands like the Athletic. Isn't that a bit aggravating?'

'Nice of you to care. Obviously, I'd prefer it if the club were making a profit. But there are two answers to your question. First, I suspect that you have a rather crude picture of the way businessmen like myself operate. We look successful, because looking successful is all part of being successful. But we don't have any magic formula. We don't always back winners. We throw a lot of bread upon the waters which simply goes soggy and gets eaten by seagulls. It's partly a question of knowing what to get into, partly a question of knowing when to get out, and partly a question of just pretending to know what you're doing.

'And the second thing is, I didn't buy this club because I wanted to make money. Of course, I'd prefer it if we roared up the table and were entertaining Juventus or Borussia Münchengladbach every other week, and building new stands et cetera. But if I'd been thinking return on capital, I wouldn't have sunk whatever it was into Athletic. I'm just nuts about the game, that's the fact of the matter. Ever meet a kid who didn't want to own a football club? Wildest dream.'

'Used to play the game, did you, Mr Prosser?'

'Wanted to. Wanted to. You may not believe this, but as a kid I was too fat. Too fat and too brainy.'

'I'm a goalkeeper,' said Duffy. Sometimes he thought he was prouder of being goalkeeper for the Reliables than of any other thing in his life. Well, perhaps that wasn't surprising: what would be number two source of pride?

'You look a little short for a goalkeeper,' said Mr Prosser. 'Also a bit – how shall I put it? – a bit stocky for a goalkeeper. Is that why you're on the Slimline?'

'So you're seven-figure rich and you're pouring money into Athletic ... '

'Not pouring, Mr Duffy. A little dribble. And you've no idea how useful a loss can be here and there in the books.'

'And you've absolutely no enemies.'

'What a silly word that is.'

'Can we start at the beginning again, Mr Prosser?'

'Wherever you like. As long as you don't charge poor James for the petrol. The Corniche can be a little heavy on fuel, especially in London traffic.'

Duffy took a swig at his tonic water. Nasty crack, that, about the Slimline. He was just in training, that's all. In training twelve months of the year. In training for not getting fat.

'OK. So we have a football club. Third Division, slipping

a bit. Slipping quite a bit. Deep down in the relegation zone. Scrambling for points. Gates dropping, not enough money coming through the turnstiles. New manager unable to stop the rot. Some hopeful signs, though, especially the way young Danny Matson is playing, and the understanding he's striking up with Brendan Domingo. Not out of the wood yet, not by a long way, but there's a little bit of light at the end of the tunnel, as the manager keeps saying.

'Then, what happens? The clever little midfielder who happens to be prompting the revival walks into a good kicking in an underground car-park. Rather a lot of them doing the kicking if they were only after thirty quid and a Barclaycard. They didn't even borrow his motor, either. They just made sure he wasn't going to be out playing one-twos for quite some time.

'Very unfortunate for the club, just when they were beginning to pull round a bit. Still, they say crisis brings out the best in everybody, so what happens next? Young Brendan Domingo starts taking more responsibility, the other lads chip in, and Danny Matson isn't missed that much. Is this a bit more light at the end of the tunnel? It might be, but someone comes up to Brendan in the Albion and suggests an early wage packet for seeing to it that Athletic gets relegated. In the nicest possible way, of course. Big Bren tells him where to shove it, and what happens? A few days later Bren gets fixed on a rather clever rape charge. It may not work out in the end, but it'll be enough to keep him out of the game until the end of the season, and perhaps for several seasons to come. No Danny, no Brendan, no Athletic.

'And just in case this isn't enough to do for the club, there's bits of agg off the pitch as well. Like a very nasty bunch of yobboes up one end, who all of a sudden start turning against one of their own team's star players. A very nasty bunch of yobboes organized by some neo-Nazi nutter funded by we know not who. Could be anyone. Plus which there's another bit of agg from a normally very quiet set of residents, who for some reason take it into their heads to sue the club and close the Layton Road end. Thereby ensuring that the yobboes get more chance of mixing with the away fans, and that the club has to pay out more money for more coppers, and that the average home fan thinks twice before taking his wife and kids down to the ground. How does it sound so far?'

'It's like listening to Jimmy Lister. Another Slimline?'

'No thanks.'

'Probably the wise decision. Well, it doesn't sound anything to me, Mr Duffy. It sounds less than anything. Are you suggesting that I ought to be more concerned than I am?'

'I don't know how concerned you are, Mr Prosser.'

'I'm very concerned about this club being relegated. But what are you telling me? That there've been two criminal acts relating to members of the playing staff over the last few weeks. Quite right there have, and they're both being looked into by the police with what is I am sure a proper diligence. Whether the criminal acts are as you described them, though, seems dubious to me. Matson was always a bit of a hothead, and he admitted he was drunk at the time; what more natural than for him to get into a fight? And how do we know there were these dozens of unidentifiable men descending on him? Perhaps there was only one. With Matson in the condition even he admits he was in, one would have been enough. It might have been a schoolgirl. Some schoolgirl in need of thirty quid for the hairdresser or something.

'As for Domingo, I'm sure he'd be touched by your loyalty, and I'm sure there are two sides to the story, but until it comes up in court it seems to me that we have to accept the police's view. I've always liked Domingo myself, both as a player and as a person. I don't know him that well, of course; though I know him a lot better than you do. And since we're hazarding reckless guesses, I'll give you my guess. Brendan had been booed rotten by the Layton Road end all Saturday afternoon. Then he'd got us the winning goal, and only the directors' box applauded. He's had this treatment for weeks – you may even have seen my note in the programme a couple of weeks ago deploring the loutish behaviour of certain untypical groups of so-called fans. He's always pretended it didn't affect him, but how much self-control can you have? So he's been made to feel unwelcome, to put it mildly, all afternoon, and then after the match which he's won for us he goes down the boozer, meets a girl who invites him back to her place, and just when he thinks the whole white world isn't against him after all, she suddenly turns unwelcoming as well; starts going on about a woman's right to choose, or whatever. He isn't the conquering hero after all, he's just a big black fellow who scores goals and then gets kicked around and jeered and turned down. So for once in a while he kicks back, his self-control snaps – and very unfortunate it is for all concerned.

'So what does that leave us with? The yobboes. Well, I'm sure you wouldn't say that yobboes are unique to this club. Or even the Red White and Blue Movement. I gather something similar happened down at Millwall, and I expect it happens elsewhere as well. We club chairmen are always trying to think up new strategies to combat hooliganism, I can give you my assurance on that one.

'The Layton Road residents? Well, I can't say I blame them, given the way some of our so-called fans behave. I'm surprised they've been so long-suffering. The other thing, the bribery? Deplorable, of course, but not unusual. There's always a shortage of class players, and now there's a shortage of money as well. No club chairman is going to turn up his nose if some third party wants to earn himself a little drink.'

'So you're saying it's all coincidence?'

'I'm saying that when a club, or a business, or a marriage, or anything is in trouble, then you'll always find that it never rains but it pours.'

Duffy grunted, and reached into his pocket.

'But what if there's someone up there making the clouds?'

'I wish I knew who it was who invented the phrase "conspiracy theory". It's been responsible for so much sloppy thinking.'

'Did you know her?'

'No. Should I? They're very good pictures. I didn't know you were a photographer Duffy.'

'She's called Maggie Coleman. Or at least, she sometimes is. She's the girl Brendan is supposed to have raped. But she's not always that. Sometimes she's called Denise. When she was called Denise she picked up Danny Matson at The Knight Spot, fought off the other girls through the evening, made sure he left with her, sent him off to the car-park alone while she waited at the club, and got him beaten up.'

'Is it really the same girl?'

'It's the same girl.'

'Well, she must like footballers.'

'Bit of a coincidence, isn't it?'

'Is it? There *are* girls who like footballers, you know, Duffy. I mean, I don't know if the outfit you play for is famous enough and, if I may say so, sexy enough to attract groupies, but it's no rare phenomenon in the Football League. Both Matson and Domingo are attractive to women, I should imagine. I don't think we should disapprove of her morals just because she allowed herself to be taken home by both of them. Indeed, perhaps she should have our sympathy, given that neither of her romantic evenings with the stars of the local team went according to plan.'

'They didn't go to plan for Danny and Brendan either.'

'Then we must sympathize all round.'

'Don't you think it's a bit iffy that she had dark hair and was called Denise when she met Danny, and had blonde hair and was called Maggie when she met Brendan?'

'Duffy, I'm not responsible for this young woman's behaviour. Ask her hairdresser, ask her mother, ask her psychiatrist, ask ... '

'Whoever's paying her?'

498

'No. Ask the girl herself.'

'I'd love to. Except that I'd get locked up for doing so.' Duffy put his glass down and started on the harder bit. 'And then we have the question of the planning permission.'

'The planning permission? Oh, Magrudo's joke. What's that got to do with anything?'

'Can I spin you a line, Mr Prosser?'

'Go ahead.'

'I mean, you won't take offence, or anything?'

'I can't promise not to.'

'Fair enough. Well, let's try this line. You bought the club, what, two years ago? It was pretty run down, losing money, falling gates, hadn't won anything for years. Everyone thinks, Ah, here comes the saviour. Local hero. Pump money into the club. New blood. All that sort of stuff – I remember reading it at the time myself. What they got wrong was, you never intended to save the club. In fact, you intended the opposite. You aren't interested in football, though you're very good at going through the motions. You've got away with looking like a chairman trying to pull the club up by its bootstraps, but all the time you've been letting the plug out on it.'

'Really? And how've I been doing that?' The tone was mild, polite, interested. Melvyn Prosser didn't look at all ready to admit being the Boston Strangler.

'Well, you appointed Jimmy Lister for a start. Very good player, nice man, rotten manager. Had a good little Second Division outfit and what did he do with it: in a couple of years he nearly got it relegated. Then out of the game for a year. That's not called bad luck, that's called the whisper going round about Jimmy Lister. And it wasn't a comment on his morals – they weren't worrying about their physios' wives. I bet he wasn't even offered a non-League team in all that year. You picked him up because you thought he was good at getting clubs relegated. And you gave him his head with all that silly stuff about kicking balls into the crowd and

Bunnies sitting on his knee or whatever it was, which is all very well if you're riding high and pretty pathetic if you aren't. But that sort of thing makes people expect more from a club, so if you let him get on with it and then the club doesn't do the business on the pitch, then the manager looks more of a berk and the club looks even sillier.'

'I didn't know I was such a deep thinker,' said Melvyn Prosser. He was smiling at Duffy and following attentively, just as if he was being told a wonderful story he'd never heard before.

'I'm not sure I'd put it that high,' said Duffy. 'But you do look ahead. I think when you first got into all this you had some idea of how it might turn out. How you might make it turn out. Most people who look at a football ground see just that. A bloody great place where they play football. Something that's always been there, and always will be, even if it's looking a bit tatty at the time. You don't knock down a football stadium any more than you knock down a church.'

'They're knocking down churches nowadays.'

'Well there you are. That's what you saw. It looked tatty, and you thought, if I bought that, I could make it into a wonderful bit of development. So you started running the club down. And the worse it got, the more dependent on you it became. You didn't mind paying the bills because if any-one came along and was at all interested in buying it they'd take one look at the books and see how much it was costing you and they'd run away. You bought this club and instead of giving it a blood transfusion you cut its throat.'

'James will be saddened to hear that the fellow whose wages he is paying has such a low opinion of his professional capacities.'

'I think we have about the same opinion of Jimmy Lister, you and I, Mr Prosser.'

'So what do I do next?'

'Well, next you get Magrudo to apply for outline planning permission for the site.'

'Even though I haven't seen him for years.'

'Even though you haven't seen him for years except that you forget to tell various people like the staff at Hess House Holdings that you haven't seen him for years.'

Melvyn Prosser chuckled. He actually chuckled.

'I'm sorry. I didn't realize I was on oath when I spoke to you.'

'Then you get the permission and are all set on that side of things. Except that Jimmy Lister isn't quite running down the club quickly enough. He's done his best, but you can't actually be sure of relegation. So you decide to hurry things along. With Danny, and Brendan, and the residents. I don't know about the Red White and Blue – that might even be a coincidence.'

'Suddenly you're admitting there is such a thing as coincidence?'

'Yes.'

'Well, all right.' Melvyn handed him back the photographs. 'And that's my wife, by the way,' he added sarcastically.

'Then I suppose – not knowing as much about the business as you do – but I suppose you then have some system worked out with Charlie Magrudo. He's the front man, you're the money man; you sell him the ground for peanuts, then buy it back from him. I don't know how these things work – '

'Evidently.'

'But perhaps you bung him some work for his construction company as a thank-you present. Give him the contract for the leisure centre or something. Nice little leg-up for a business which hasn't always enjoyed the best of fortune.'

'I see. Is that it?'

'Yes. More or less.'

'And how do you rate my chances of getting detailed planning permission?'

'I don't know.'

'And what sort of profit am I looking to make?'

'I don't know.'

'Oh dear, how disappointing. And what would you say if I told you that you're living in cloud-cuckoo-land?'

'I wouldn't believe you.'

There was a pause. They were somewhere north of Camden Town; Duffy wasn't exactly sure where. He couldn't understand Melvyn Prosser at all.

'Can I have another Slimline?'

'Of course. Would you help yourself? I always try and do the first drink and then let guests help themselves.'

Duffy poured out his tonic water.

'Yes. Definitely too small for a goalkeeper, I'd say. Even though I know less about the game than you, as you've so carefully pointed out.'

'I'm quite a good goalkeeper, actually,' said Duffy. 'Why aren't you angry?'

'Angry? I don't get angry. Not in business. Not even outside business. It doesn't ... work, I find.'

'But I've just accused you of committing grievous bodily harm and conspiring to pervert the course of justice.'

'Yes, I was thinking about that. If only I'd had the partition down and Hobbs had been listening, I could have sued you for slander.'

'I've put everything in my wife's name,' said Duffy. 'Like Charlie Magrudo.'

'Really? How interesting. For some reason I'd always thought you were queer. I do apologize.' Melvyn Prosser touched a button on his armrest console and the glass partition descended.

'Hobbs, will you stop in about two hundred and fifty yards' time.'

'Yessir.'

The partition slid up again, and the Corniche came smoothly to a halt.

'If I let you out here, Mr Duffy, I think you'll find you're exactly half-way between two tube stations. I'm afraid I can't take you any further.'

'Thanks for the lift. See you at the game.'

Duffy got out on to a damp pavement somewhere between Tufnell Park and Archway. Why did he almost like Melvyn Prosser? He should try and stop almost liking Melvyn Prosser. It was a funny feeling: you put the chisel into the wall and twist, and nothing happens. The chisel's intact; the wall hasn't shifted an inch; everything's the same.

'Cheers, mate,' said a passing figure.

Duffy realized that he was still holding a cut-glass tumbler containing half a Slimline tonic.

Duffy woke up, and went through his ritual lymph-node check. Groin, armpits, neck. All the usual little bumps and knobs, as far as he could see, but nothing actually in raging motion. Night sweats? Erections? No, the score was still the same. Erections 2, Night Sweats 2, after extra time and several replays. No doubt Binyon could have explained it all to Duffy. 'You get the night sweats, Duffy, because you've got AIDS, and you've got AIDS because you're queer. The erections are merely a hysterical reaction designed to convince yourself that you might after all be straight, or at least – what's that quaint expression of yours? – bisexual; that's it. Your sweats are telling you the truth, your dick is lying.' Something like that.

The trouble was, if Binyon were sitting on the next barstool at the Alligator, Duffy would have been inclined to believe him. But at the moment he only had himself to do the explaining. So, with the full bravery acquired by one who has successfully got through a whole night on his tod, Duffy decided that he had got the night sweats – only two, after all – because he was really worried about something. What he was really worried about was getting night sweats. Nothing unusual in this; it was rather like having a hysterical pregnancy. Not that Duffy had had one of those ... And as for the erections, well, he thought, let's take the simplest course. You had an erection in bed with Carol because you fancied her: there's nothing complicated about that, is there? So why hadn't he had one the last two nights she'd stayed? Well, the second night we were a bit distant with one another because I'd bullied her into looking those names up on the computer for me; and the first night ... The first night? I don't know, maybe I had a headache or something. Oh yes? Go tell that one to Binyon.

The evening before, Athletic had lost two–nil to Wigan. Duffy had watched the game from the Layton Road end, where the yobboes still congregated after kicking their way through all the other fans, and there was little to take heart from. It wasn't a case of the mid-table club being more relaxed because they didn't have any promotion or relegation worries, and fretful Athletic being over-anxious. It was just a case of one team being better than the other: quicker, cleverer, more willing to contest the ball in midfield, and sharper in finishing. 'No excuses,' Jimmy Lister told the *Chronicle*, 'they were the better side on the night.'

'Is it back to the drawing-board, Jimmy?' asked Ken Marriott (the real Ken Marriott).

'No, it's not back to the drawing-board. No one's going to give us a new set of pencils at this stage of the season. We're not going to panic. It's just a question of battling away. The lads know what they have to do, and they know that the chairman and the management are right behind them.'

The lads knew what they had to do: they had to win every game. They also had to hope that the other teams immediately above them would continue to drop points. And short of sending hit squads round the country to maim half a dozen fiery little midfield schemers and frame half a dozen skilful black strikers, there was no certain method of making that happen.

Ken Marriott had also had a brief interview with the chairman of Athletic. Yes, he was right behind the lads who were battling away but just not getting the breaks. No, he hadn't given up hope of Third Division football at the Athletic ground next season. Well, he didn't want to talk about the other possibility because he didn't want to put the lads under any more pressure than they were; but everyone knew that the club was making a considerable loss, and that while the chairman was happy to sustain that loss until the end of the season, he'd obviously have to reconsider his own position, and indeed the club's whole future, if Athletic were relegated.

Well, that was clear enough, thought Duffy. It was also a bit clever: while claiming he didn't want to put the lads under any more pressure, Prosser was doing just that: saying that he'd pull the plug on them if they went down. And he would, too: this was the first time he'd gone into print on the subject, and Duffy was sure he meant more than every word. Melvyn Prosser would slit the club's throat.

And what could Duffy do about it? Nothing, unless he could get the team playing again. After all, if Athletic somehow managed to stay in the Third Division, that would be a considerable embarrassment to Prosser. He might sack Jimmy Lister – though that probably wouldn't get him anywhere if he'd chosen Jimmy in the first place because he thought he wasn't any good; replace Lister and the club might find itself with a real manager who'd push them to a safe place in mid-table. But how could Duffy get the team playing? He couldn't exactly mend Danny Matson's leg with superglue, or dynamite Brendan Domingo out of his cell.

He could try and stir things up a little, though.

'Maggot?'

'Yeah.'

'Ready for the game on Sunday? Honing the vision?'

'Sometimes I think you're taking the piss, Duffy. Actually, I'm more worried about Saturday's fixture. If they lose again, anything could happen.'

'Yeah. Tell me, Maggot, me being only a cub reporter and all that, tell me, would it be a story,' Duffy tried to sound as if he really wasn't sure, 'if there were plans to knock down the Athletic ground and build a shopping centre all over the top of it?'

'I think it'd be a sensation. Are you taking the piss again?'

'Promise not. I've done a little work on it myself' – he heard Maggot groan – 'No, not like last time. I mean, I was me, and I wasn't from the *Chronicle*.'

Duffy explained about the outline planning permission. Well, if Prosser and Magrudo had both been assuring him it was just a little joke so that Charlie could think about Mel's face when he opened the papers, why not give them both the thrill? Duffy acted the cub reporter a bit with Ken Marriott, but wasn't short of advice. He mustn't fail to point out that Prosser and Magrudo were old friends and business associates, and that staff at Hess House Holdings had confirmed to a reporter that the two men had been having a lot of meetings lately. Duffy wondered if Maggot would hint that Melvyn Prosser had been an old friend of Mrs Charlie Magrudo. He didn't think the *Chronicle* would stretch that far, but he threw it in anyway. He warned Marriott that both the chairman of Athletic and the managing director of Magrudo Construction would claim that it was all a joke. Duffy even had the temerity to suggest that Maggot could take some line about whether the Athletic players and the Athletic fans would see the humour of the situation, given the club's current plight.

The story appeared on the Friday. ATHLETIC GROUND FOR REDEVELOPMENT? ran the headline on the inside-page splash. ITALIAN STYLE PIAZZA LOOK it said underneath, which Duffy liked, as it would bring out the patriotism of the fans; and underneath that, in smaller capitals but still prominent: CHAIRMAN DENIES CLUB TO FOLD. Ken Marriott had done the job well: Prosser and Magrudo's suggestion that the whole thing was 'a joke' was slipped in just at the right moment, making them seem to be either outright liars or at best people with a very sinister sense of humour.

On the Saturday, Athletic were at home to Bristol Rovers, and as Melvyn Prosser took his seat the main stand booed him. Duffy, from the Piggeries terrace, had a quiet smile. On the other hand, it wasn't that funny: it meant that the only well-behaved part of the home crowd was now joining in the fun of turning on the club in some way. The yobs would have booed Brendan if he'd been there; but he wasn't, so instead the season-ticket holders booed the chairman. To any outsider it would seem that the whole place was falling apart, and it didn't seem to do the home team's confidence much good. Bristol Rovers unstitched them comprehensively in midfield, fooled them with a free-kick ploy just before half-time, and never looked like losing. One–nil, Athletic second from bottom, and though he'd been booed, Melvyn Prosser might well have found it a rewarding day in the stands. Duffy didn't know whether he'd come out ahead on his ploy with the *Chronicle*, or further behind.

On Sunday morning there was a ring at his door. Duffy felt nervous. No one had tried to beat him up yet. No one had tried to frame him for rape. Prosser would have known that Duffy had been behind the *Chronicle* story. Perhaps he'd sent round some heavies. The doorbell rang again.

'Who is it?'

There was a loud bellow from outside in an American accent.

'Open the door, schmuck, or I'll break it down with this pick-axe.'

Phew. That was a relief, thought Duffy, and opened the door immediately.

'You had me worried, just ringing the bell like that. Come in.'

Geoff Bell wandered in and started looking around Duffy's flat as if he expected it to be bugged.

'Like the way you keep this place, Duffy. Not too much

stuff around. Bit of a challenge to plant something on you.'

'Well, you know, Geoff, I like to think of all eventualities.'

'Mind you, that door of yours is chronic. No one in his right mind has a door like that. I mean, you might as well just leave it wide open when you go out.'

'I'll look into it. I promise. Social call?'

Geoff Bell never made social calls, as Duffy well knew. Quite what Geoff Bell did for a social life – apart, that is, from turn out in home matches for the Reliables every other Sunday – was a mystery to Duffy. One day he'd ask Geoff, though Geoff might well not understand the question.

'Thought you might like to see these.'

There were about two dozen large black-and-white photographs, and Duffy almost didn't glance at them, since he knew he'd have to sit through a lengthy explanation of lighting conditions, lenses, depth of field and film-speed first. But the top picture immediately caught his attention. It showed Maggie Coleman, or was it Denise given that she had dark hair again, leaning back against a wall with her shoulders and pushing her hips out towards a man in a mackintosh whose cheek she was stroking. It appeared to be raining, but Maggie's own raincoat was unbuttoned at the front, and her skirt was very short.

While Geoff droned on about the difficulties of choosing film-speed when using a 200mm lens in poor light, Duffy shuffled slowly through the photographs. You didn't need to be a copper who'd once done three years in Soho to know that Maggie Coleman was more than just an average friendly girl with a striking sense of fashion. There were photos of Maggie getting in and out of cars (Geoff had usefully included the number-plates in one or two of the shots), Maggie accosting, Maggie raising the middle finger and shouting at some punter who'd probably said she wasn't worth *that* much. Back at work so soon after a broken nose? Maggie Coleman must have a lot of grey-haired old mothers to support, or a very grabby pimp. On the other hand, it wasn't so surprising. Maggie wouldn't need her nose to ply her trade. Whores don't kiss.

'Where were these taken, Geoff?'

'On the back.'

Times, dates, places, all written neatly.

'You see I wasn't really happy with that first set I did for you. I could tell you weren't happy either, Duffy. Wanted to know whether they were good likenesses or something, I seem to remember you saying. Well, these are good likenesses.'

Duffy wasn't sure whether Bell was teasing or not. Knowing him, quite possibly not.

'Would it be possible to run me off another set, Geoff? I know we're playing at twelve.'

'*You're* playing at twelve.'

'Sorry.' Duffy should have remembered that Geoff still believed he ought to be included for away matches as well. Not for his skill in surveillance, but for his skill on the pitch.

'Well, I thought you might ask,' said Geoff, producing another large brown envelope.

'You're brilliant, Geoff, do you know that? You could probably tell me what I'm thinking.'

'You're thinking, I wonder if he really does care about being left out of away games. And the answer is yes I bloody do. I'm just as good defensively as Maggot, and I don't have half so many potty ideas as he does.'

'Quite wrong, Geoff. I was wondering how much Maggie Coleman charged.'

'Liar.'

'You're brilliant, Geoff.'

'Yeah.'

As Duffy drove to the game, he thought about the photographs. Of course they weren't conclusive. Nothing in this whole business had ever been conclusive. But they were something extra. They certainly threw a little doubt on Melvyn Prosser's theory that Maggie Coleman was just a nice girl who liked footballers – unless, that is, all the gentlemen in Geoff Bell's photos were footballers. Sure, thought Duffy, the whole of the First Division out on a coach trip.

Of course, just because Maggie and Denise Coleman were two girls of distinctly flexible morals didn't mean that the coppers would throw out the charges against Brendan. Judges and coppers no longer assumed that all women secretly wanted to be raped, that girl hitchhikers deserved everything they got, and that whores were outside the protection of the law. Whores got raped, just as housewives got raped: even the coppers were beginning to acknowledge that. On the other hand, this didn't make the coppers feel that whores were deeply misunderstood girls with nice honest natures; it didn't make the coppers step in when a girl was arguing prices with a punter and say, 'No, she's worth more than that – more than she's asking, in fact. Go on, Maggie, put your prices up, you're something special.' No, the coppers wouldn't be doing that for a while yet.

What they might do, if they saw these photographs, was have a much closer look at Maggie Coleman's evidence. And what they might do, if they also were in possession of a statement from Danny Matson that Maggie was also Denise, was have a much closer look at her motives, her background, and her business associates. They might put the Matson case and the Domingo case together and start digging – and do it with a few more resources than Duffy had at his disposal. And if Jimmy Lister's solicitor was smart, and if he made the right noises about possible conspiracy but didn't make them too loudly, and if they weighed in with Brendan's blameless past, and if the police solicitors could be persuaded to drop their objection to bail, then the magistrates might just be persuaded to open the slammer next Wednesday and let Brendan out into the sunlight. Bail for rape was a tricky decision, but if the magistrates could shift their responsibility on to the police solicitors, it could just be swung. Whether that would make any difference, Duffy didn't know. Would

Jimmy Lister dare play the lad? And in any case, what would Brendan's fitness be like after ten days walking up and down a little cell?

The Reliables played well that Sunday, and were unlucky to lose by the only goal of the game: Maggot's vision induced him to square-pass across his own penalty area, and then, when the pass was intercepted, to bring down the opponent with a rugby tackle. The penalty was whacked past Duffy, who didn't feel too bad about it: keepers are never blamed for penalties. They may be made to look silly, but they aren't blamed.

On Sunday evening Carol came round and they had pizzas again.

'I like the way you've done the peppers,' she said. 'You've arranged them just exactly the way you did last time. Did you realize that, Duffy?'

Duffy grunted.

'Only if I could make a very tiny criticism this time, they're not as crisp as they ought to be. They're a bit soggy.'

Duffy grunted again. It was just that he didn't like sleeping with half a pizza in his bed. Couldn't anyone understand that? For Christ sake, what did other people do? Move the fridge into the bedroom and throw a few packets of frozen peas in between the sheets, just for company?

'Mine's all right,' said Duffy.

'Delicious,' muttered Carol. Why had he done the crust like that? Another thing added to the list of what she couldn't ask him about.

She'd had a quiet Sunday at West Central; quiet enough to check out the names Duffy had asked her about. Not much help, she was afraid. Melvyn Prosser and Charlie Magrudo were clean. Maggie Coleman had one charge of soliciting, about a year ago, in Shepherd's Market. Come down in the world since, thought Duffy. Oh well, every little helps; the coppers wouldn't object to being reminded of that.

On the Monday Duffy went down to the Athletic ground,

keeping a sharp eye out for gold Corniches which looked as if they might want to run over his foot, and showed Jimmy Lister the dossier on Maggie Coleman. Then he bullied him. He had to bully him quite a lot. Jimmy Lister was wary of the coppers, and wary of solicitors, and Duffy had to remind him quite hard that as the club was paying the solicitor's bill, the club had a say in what the solicitor did.

'OK, OK, I'll do it,' said Jimmy eventually. 'But playing the lad is another matter.'

'You don't think he'll be fit?'

'No, I shouldn't think he'll have lost much being locked up. Sometimes a lay-off at this stage of the season actually sharpens them up.'

'Well, there you are.'

'But would it be fair on the lad? I mean, would it be fair? Just think what a roasting they'd give the lad from the terraces.'

'They give him a roasting anyway. He gets booed every time he touches the ball here. He gets booed away from home. What's the difference?'

'They can be very nasty, you know, the fans.'

'What do you think Brendan will want to do?'

'He'll want to play, of course he will.'

'Then let him. It's his career.'

'Yes, but as manager I've got to look after the boy. I've got to think about his long-term interests.'

'What about everyone's long-term interests?' asked Duffy.

'How do you mean?'

'I don't think you've got a choice. You're getting relegated at the moment, no doubt about it. You need all the points you can get. Nine from the last three matches and you could well be safe. Six and there's an outside chance. Three or less and you're sunk. Fourth Division and a salary drop for all the lads; that is, if the whole place doesn't get concreted over first. Slow plane to Abu Dhabi for Jimmy Lister, except that the Abu Dhabi offer somehow doesn't seem to be coming through. And if you do drop, not that it will then be a matter of concern to you, the club loses Brendan. Some Second Division outfit is sure to snap him up. Play him and you might just have a chance of staying up – and keeping Brendan. Don't play him and you lose him, and maybe everything else as well: the team, the job, the ground.'

'Put like that, Duffy ... '

'Yes?'

'But I'm still worried about the fans. They can say the cruellest things, you know, Duffy. Things you wouldn't imagine they could think up.'

'Earplugs,' said Duffy sharply. 'Earplugs.'

While Jimmy Lister went off to see the coppers, Duffy drove off to the group of five streets whose names were on the back of Geoff Bell's photographs. The lunchtime trade on a Monday was always a bit slack – punters were slow recuperating from the weekend – so there was a fair chance he might find her. As he slowed the car and started a bit of furtive eyes-left, he wondered what the going rate was nowadays for impersonating a police officer. Or for blackmail.

He lowered the passenger window in preparation. Then up and down, round the square, eyes half on the road, half squirting off in search of those gaudy, lounging figures who pecked at the pavement with their high heels. Up and down again, round the square: no wonder the residents objected. It wasn't just that respectable women got propositioned by thick punters; it was having to bring up your children in an atmosphere of pure exhaust fumes. Now, once more, and, and, what about ... *There* she is.

'You doing business?' It was probably the least necessary question Duffy had ever asked; but he said it routinely, as if establishing his credentials. Maggie – or perhaps Denise as she still had dark hair – was already checking the car: inspecting the back to see that there wasn't a second punter lurking on the floor, checking the driver to see that he wasn't an obvious psycho.

'Twenty-five,' she said. This wasn't the smartest end of town. What would she have been pulling down in Shepherd's Market? Four times that? Six times? Ten times, perhaps; especially if she landed an Arab. Maggie Coleman had come down in the world.

'Hop in, darling.'

She got in quickly, filling the car with a scent like air-freshener. Perhaps it was air-freshener, given some of the punters she'd have to consort with at her current going rate. She put her hand on Duffy's thigh and said, 'Twyford Avenue, you know it? Money first.'

'Course, darling,' said Duffy. 'What's yer name?'

'Sharron.'

Duffy waited until he had got up enough speed for it to be inadvisable to jump out, then murmured, 'Well, Sharron, I shall call you Denise if that's all right.'

'Whatever you like.'

'Or maybe I shall call you Maggie.'

'Call me the Queen of Sheba if that's your thing.'

'And you can call me Detective-Sergeant Hawkins, C Division.'

She reacted to that, at least.

'You shit, you fucker, you pulling me in for that? Copper. Fucking *copper*. You'd think I could smell fucking copper by now, wouldn't you?' Duffy gave a little smile. 'You pulling me in for that? You fucking came up and *asked*, copper. It's not soliciting if a copper comes past with his truncheon hanging out of the window.'

'Well, maybe I'm not pulling you in, Maggie.'

'I see. You want a bit of free, too? Listen, I give out so much free to you coppers I might as well come down the station one day and do it there. Save breaking up my working day, wouldn't it?'

'That's not a bad plan.'

'Listen, I've got this baby girl ... '

'Shove it.' Duffy stopped the car. 'Do you know who lives over there?'

'Course I don't, copper.'

'Danny Matson.'

'Who?'

'He sits in his chair all day with his foot up on a stool.'

'What, does he need a girl or something? You treating him?'

'He'd be very pleased to see you.'

'It's thirty for, you know, cripples and so on.'

Duffy usually quite liked whores. This one he found less appealing.

'You set up Danny Matson, you framed Brendan Domingo. Who paid?'

'Friends of yours, are they? Never heard of them meself.'

'Who paid?'

'What do you mean? Punters pay. Only coppers get it for free, copper.'

'Danny's out of the game for life, Brendan's facing five years, now who paid?' Duffy was squeezing the driving wheel hard; afraid that otherwise he might be squeezing something else instead. Somebody's windpipe, for instance.

Silence.

'Was it Prosser? Was it? Was it Magrudo?'

Silence.

'OK, I'll just have to throw the book at you, Maggie.'

'There's not much in your book, copper.'

'Soliciting, GBH, attempting to pervert the course of justice.'

'Don't make me laugh.'

'Well, we'll see who the jury believes – you or Brendan. It's five years for one or the other of you.'

'You're just a dry wank, copper. You can't scare me. Who would a jury believe, a tart or a nignog? They'd just tell us to

515

bugger off and not make so much noise next time we're screwing.'

She wasn't stupid; that was a pity. She wasn't stupid, and she didn't scare. Duffy tried to think of another line of attack. He failed. She didn't.

'But I'd plead guilty to the soliciting. I'd do that. And I'd throw myself on the court's mercy and say I was terribly, terribly sorry and that it would never happen again and was there anything they could do to stop the boys in blue asking for so much free?'

'Get out, Maggie.'

'You're a dry wank, copper, you know that? A dry wank.'

'Cheers,' said Brendan Domingo when the police released him and explained the terms of his bail. 'Cheers,' said Brendan Domingo when Jimmy Lister said he'd risk him in the first game, see how it went, and then make a decision about the last two. 'Cheers,' said Brendan Domingo when Duffy explained his idea about the earplugs.

At home to Newport, away to Hull, at home to Preston. Win all three and they'd have a real chance of escaping relegation. Lose more than one and they were for the drop. Something in between and it all depended on how their fellow-strugglers got on.

Duffy stood on the Layton Road terrace for the Newport game, and the yobboes were not well behaved. They may not have had the full powers of concentration when it came to spelling, but they could all certainly read. Read the headlines in the local paper, at least. 'OH, NAUGHTY-NAUGHTY, NAUGHTY-NAUGHTY-NAUGHTY-NAUGHTY BRE-HEN-DAN' was one of their politer chants. Others were more specific; they turned on Brendan's colour, and the African jungle, and the function of his middle leg. Every time Brendan touched the ball, several hundred yobboes booed, and several hundred yobboes' fists went up in the air and made wanking gestures.

Brendan, his ears blocked, didn't notice. Duffy was more

worried about the effect the noises might have on the rest of the Athletic side; but they appeared not to notice either. Having Brendan back seemed to relax them; and for a change, the opposition clearly had their minds on their summer holidays. After forty minutes Athletic won a free-kick on the edge of the Newport area. Brendan took a long run and smashed it straight at the wall. It took a deflection off a defender's shoulder, lobbed into the air, spun across the goal area with a deceiving bounce, and was sliced off a Newport defender's boot into an Athletic chest, from where it cannoned unstoppably past the keeper. A real end-of-season goal; one–nil; three points.

'I think we can do it, Duffy,' said Jimmy Lister after the match. 'I really think we can do it.'

'How's Brendan taking things?'

'Oh, a bit subdued, you know. Just thinking about his game, I suppose.'

'What did the police say?'

'They said, Score a hat-trick and we'll drop the charges. Funny sense of humour, I thought.'

'Yes, well, they're like that.' They were; Duffy remembered some of the things that seemed funny to coppers. 'Two more wins, then, Jimmy?'

'On my granny's life, I promise you.'

However, both of Jimmy Lister's grandmothers had been dead some time, and the midweek away game at Hull confirmed it. Two–nil down at half-time, three–nil down after fifty minutes. Jimmy pulled off a midfielder and put on a wide man; Brendan took out his earplugs and threw them at the bench; but neither move made any difference. The Athletic midfield was underpopulated; the wide man didn't get a kick; and Hull walked in another goal. 'We were beaten by the better side on the day,' Jimmy told the *Chronicle*. 'But the season's never over until the final whistle's been blown.'

Events the next day in the North of England unexpectedly made things easier for Athletic; or if not easier, at least clearer. Port Vale finished their season with a handy defeat leaving them still only two points above Athletic. So if Athletic lost or drew their final match, they'd be relegated; if they won, by however fine a margin, they stayed up. 'The lads know exactly what they have to do,' said Jimmy Lister. 'It's all down to us now.'

On the morning of the Preston match, Duffy got Carol to have another look at his back.

'It's still there, Duffy, like it was last time I looked.'

'Thanks.'

In the bathroom, before he shaved, he did his lymph-node check. No movement on that front. No blotches on his legs either. No more night sweats. How long before he could count on being safe? Six months? A year?

When he came back from the bathroom he was whistling. Carol smiled at him. She wondered why he kept wanting her to check his back. She wondered why the pizza he'd cooked her the night before had been even soggier than the previous one. Were the two eccentricities connected? Did he think crisp pizzas brought you out in a rash? He was an odd one and no mistake. Always worrying about something. Always on the move. Why couldn't they sometimes have a nice lie-in, like other people?

'Duffy, one of these days, will you bring me breakfast in bed?'

A puzzled look came over Duffy's face, followed by one of horror as he thought of toast-crumbs in the sheets.

'Of course not,' he said. 'Never.'

'Oh well. I suppose not. What about in a hotel?'

'What d'you mean?'

'Have you ever had room service in a hotel, Duffy?'

'Of course not.' What a ridiculous idea.

'Neither have I.'

Duffy was puzzled. He didn't know what Carol was going on about. Perhaps she wanted something.

'Do you want to come down the match with me?'

'What, the Reliables?' Carol was usually forbidden from watching Duffy play; it made him nervous, he claimed.

'No, the Athletic. Against Preston.'

'The Athletic? Against Preston? Of course not. I've got some standards, Duffy.'

'Uh-huh.' That can't have been what she wanted, then.

On his way to the ground, Duffy took a short diversion and knocked at number 37 Layton Road.

'Mr Bullivant.'

'Ah, it's the laddy with the big pencil and the small brain.'

'Mr Bullivant, I wonder if I could have a quote from you about the proposed redevelopment of the Athletic ground?'

'Now why ever should you want a thing like that? Can't you use one of those other remarks of mine I remember you copying down into your book?'

'But are the residents happy about the proposed scheme?'

'This particular resident doesn't give a tinker's, sonny.'

'Why's that?'

'Because by next season I shall be able to go for a short walk from my home and watch a class outfit by the name of Tottenham Hotspur.'

'You're moving? You're selling your house?'

Mr Bullivant winked. 'Sold it two months ago, laddy.' And then he shut the door.

The Preston match was never going to be easy. Duffy knew what he wanted – a three–nil win with Brendan scoring a hat-trick – and he knew what little chance there was of getting it. Besides, the Preston management had just announced that its first-team squad would have to be reduced next year. Every place was up for grabs; it was going to be musical chairs with five seats short instead of just the one.

The crowd was bigger than it had been for the last ten home games. The twin possibilities of relegation and redevelopment had brought an extra two hundred through the turnstiles. Two hundred ghouls, keen to witness a death.

The Piggeries end were in good voice, but the rest of the crowd was subdued. A hot spring sun made the football seem unreal, and time went quickly. Two corners, a free-kick and a couple of throw-ins, it seemed, and the referee was already blowing his whistle for half-time. Nil–nil. No good at all to Athletic. No sign, either, of what they could do about it. Brendan had been a bit subdued; neat, but subdued. Duffy wondered what Melvyn Prosser was thinking. Forty-five minutes from ... from what? From the sound of Charlie Magrudo's bulldozers?

Athletic were playing towards the Layton Road end in the second half; though most of the action was taking place in the clogged midfield. Slowly, it seemed, Preston were beginning to batten Athletic down. They won a couple of free-kicks in dangerous positions, and then a corner. Everyone went deep into the Athletic half except for Brendan, the big Preston centre-back, and the Preston keeper. The corner was an outswinger, the Athletic keeper committed himself too early, and was dragged further and further out of his goal in pursuit of the ball. To everyone's relief he caught it, somewhere near the penalty spot. Three strides and he was at the edge of his area and giving the ball a hoofing drop-kick. Chase that one, you buggers, he seemed to say, and eighteen players did. Two, however, had a good thirty yards start on them. Or rather, suddenly, just one: Brendan. The big Preston defender had tripped, somehow – did anyone see what happened? – and was lying on his back near the centre-circle. Brendan was sprinting alone towards the Preston goal, his head cocked as he watched the ball descend towards him. The keeper, seeing his centre-back on the ground, came out fast. Bring him down, Duffy found himself whispering; and he was talking to the keeper, not Brendan. Both players went up in a flail of arms; both players came down in a flail of legs; the ball, quietly, bounced over their falling bodies and continued its unimpeded progress until it settled in the back of the Preston net. One–nil.

No one knew where to run. Half the Athletic team ran to their keeper; half to Brendan. Most of the Preston team besieged the referee, claiming offside, a foul on the centre-back or a foul on the goalkeeper, according to their temperament. A few went over to the linesman and expressed doubts about his eyesight, parentage and sexual habits when alone. A couple bent over the prostrate keeper, who was feigning injury quite well and worrying about next season's first-team squad. One–nil.

Preston, not surprisingly, seemed to resent the goal, and attacked with an additional muscularity. Brendan, for his part, found himself on the end of some close attention from the big centre-back who had earlier mysteriously lost his footing. There would be bruises to count on the Sunday morning. But Athletic weren't eager to throw away their sudden gift. They scrambled, they hoofed, they scrapped, they battled; they were not above getting a touch physical themselves; and their keeper, spurred on by his first goal ever in League football, saved them twice with full-length sprawls. Suddenly, it was all over. One–nil. Athletic were safe.

Ten members of the Athletic team ran towards Jimmy Lister's dug-out. There was hugging and shouting, and a few tears were shed, before they all turned to the main stand for acclaim. But the attention of the main stand was temporarily elsewhere. They were watching Brendan Domingo. So was Duffy, and he was a lot closer.

When the final whistle blew, Brendan had stopped where he was. He offered his hand to the Preston centre-back, who refused it, and carefully took out his earplugs. Then he began trotting very deliberately towards the Layton Road end. On his way he passed the Preston keeper and offered his hand, and was refused again. Slowly, he walked round behind the net until he faced the phalanx of yobboes. Duffy wondered what Brendan was going to do next, but he clearly had it all planned out. He began clapping the yobboes, as if thanking them for their kind advice in telling him to go back to the jungle. The yobboes were puzzled by this; but they were less puzzled by Brendan's next gesture. He turned his back to the Layton Road end, bent and lowered his shorts. The two white straps of his jock seemed to emphasize the blackness of his bum. He stayed like this for some five seconds, then pulled up his shorts, turned round, and started clapping the Layton Road enders again. Slowly, tauntingly. Duffy thought Brendan was extremely brave, even if there were a few coppers around.

Then, suddenly, Brendan was felled. He clutched the top of his head and keeled over heavily. The coppers, who had been looking on almost as puzzled as the yobboes, took this as their cue and waded into the terracing. The rest of the Athletic team, who had only caught the end of Brendan's performance, were already rushing over. The fans in the main stand started booing the yobboes at the Layton Road end. Must have been a coin, or a brick or something. The physio came running across and bent over Brendan. The police were vigorously bidding an end-of-season farewell to the yobboes. The main stand carried on booing, until, after a couple of minutes, Brendan got slowly to his feet; then they started cheering. While Jimmy Lister and the ten other players began a lap of honour, Brendan, his arm round the physio's shoulder, made his way groggily to the tunnel. Everyone knew exactly what had happened. Everyone except Duffy, that is.

An hour or so later he stood in the Athletic boardroom clutching a Slimline tonic and wondering whether he ought to be there. But Jimmy Lister had insisted. 'Might be the last time I can invite you up. Next year, who knows? Abu Dhabi?' It was clear to both of them that Abu Dhabi was a euphemism for the scrap-heap. Jimmy Lister hadn't yet established whether the Board was going to treat him as a hero for saving the club from relegation, or as a villain for having got them into trouble. Duffy didn't think this was the moment to float his private theory about why Melvyn Prosser had hired Jimmy Lister in the first place.

He had three conversations as he sipped his Slimline. Two of them were of professional interest, and related closely to the events of the last few weeks; and yet it was the third which intrigued him the most, and which he later wanted to tell Carol about.

The first conversation was with Ken Marriott, who was as surprised to see Duffy there as Duffy was to see him. Maggot told him, in an undertone, that soon after his article about the possible redevelopment of the ground had appeared, a number of long-time club supporters had founded a Reform Group.

'Not much chance of reforming things around here, is there?' said Duffy.

'Well, you can't be sure. The embarrassment factor is always worth something. And I'll be giving them quite a few inches on the sports pages. Better than nothing.'

'Sure.'

Duffy wasn't quite so sure after his second conversation. A hand took him suddenly by the elbow and turned him through 180 degrees. Melvyn Prosser. What's more, Melvyn Prosser smiling.

'Good to see you, Duffy. Make free with the Slimline. Didn't the lads do well?'

'Very well, Mr Prosser.'

'Can't thank you enough for getting Brendan out when you did. Without him I do declare we'd be in that place which we aren't allowed to mention inside this club.' Meaning the Fourth Division.

'I expect so.'

'You saved us, Duffy. I have to give you that. Maybe we should keep you on the payroll.'

'I'm not on it.'

'No, so you aren't. Well, come over here anyway, there's someone I'd like you to meet.' Prosser led Duffy across the boardroom towards a chunky, dark-suited man who had his back to them. Prosser elbowed him in the side to attract his attention.

'Duffy, I'd like you to meet my business partner, Charlie Magrudo. Charlie, this is Duffy, I was telling you about. We're thinking of putting Charlie on the Board.'

'Oh, yes,' said Duffy. 'Congratulations.'

'Haven't we met before?' asked Charlie, shaking him by the hand.

'I've got a brother,' said Duffy, 'I've got to go.'

What was all that about, he wondered. Was it a sneer? Was it a show of strength? Was it saying, You don't understand me, Duffy, and you never will? Was it saying, Fuck you, Duffy? He really didn't know. He wished Melvyn Prosser weren't almost likeable. For a villain, he nearly had a sense of fun.

'Hey, Duffy.'

'Brendan. How you doing?'

'Fine, terrific, never better. Thanks for the earplugs tip.'

'Thanks for the floor-show.'

'Yeah, well, I kind of lost me rag.'

'That's probably what most people would have thought.'

Brendan looked at him carefully.

'Meaning?'

Duffy smiled. 'Nice party, isn't it?'

'No, meaning? *Meaning?*' Brendan put a big, friendly arm round Duffy's shoulder and squeezed. Brendan was a lot bigger than Duffy.

'Meaning, well, I was standing pretty close to the yobboes, and I was watching you, and I didn't see anyone throw anything.'

'Duffy, didn't you see the way I went down? I was pole-axed.'

'Yes, I saw you go down, Brendan. I saw you go down like a striker in the box. The other thing I saw was that a club can hardly expect a player to abide by the terms of his contract

524

with however many years left to run if he's just been felled by his own fans.'

Brendan's arm tightened round Duffy's shoulder.

'You know, man, you're a pretty clever fellow.'

'So are you.'

Brendan gave a deep chuckle.

'One of these days I might take you down The Palm Tree. Only trouble is, you're a bit scruffy.'

'One of these days I might come with you. Only trouble is, I'd steal all your girls.'

Duffy wondered why that made Brendan laugh so much.

'I expect because he thought you were one of the other sort,' said Carol when he related the conversation to her.

'The what? Oh. Uh.' Everyone seemed to think he was the other sort. Brendan thought so. Melvyn Prosser thought so. Binyon thought so. 'Do you think I am?'

'I don't know, Duffy. I don't really think about it much,' she said, lying.

'No, I don't think about it much either,' he said, telling the truth.

'Well in that case ... '

'Yes ... '

'We'd better do the washing up, hadn't we, Duffy?'

'Of course.'

'I thought you might say that.'

So they washed up, and then they put the things away, and then they wiped the draining-board and the kitchen table, and then Duffy put the catch down on the front door, and then they went to the bathroom one after the other, and then they got into bed and turned out the light, and then Carol felt Duffy probing surreptitiously in his armpits for his lymph nodes, and then they both tried to go to sleep. This is what being married for a very long time must feel like, thought Carol.

And then Duffy got an erection. At first Carol thought it might be his hand that was moving, looking for another lymph node somewhere. But they were lying like spoons so closely that there wasn't room for a hand. She tried to breathe very gently, and listen to see if he was awake. Did she want him to be awake or not? She didn't really know. That other time, she couldn't be sure she hadn't imagined it. But this time, this time ... She tried not to breathe at all, so that she could listen to Duffy's breathing. It wasn't giving anything away. Oh, this was just silly.

'Duffy,' she said quietly, 'Duffy, am I awake?'

He stirred slightly.

'You're awake,' he said finally, 'I'm dreaming.'

Extra Time

Extra Time

The first ten minutes of the second half were a bit lively. Both sides were deliberately playing it tight, and both had a victim marked for special attention. After two minutes Maggot, who had been looking a little jumpy since the whistle went, surrendered to his wilder instincts and tried to sandbag one of the pub team's midfield. Oooff, went Duffy, as the midfielder seemed to forget about the ball and just drove through Maggot, one knee right on line for the wedding tackle. Oooff. Then, a minute or so later, in clear retribution, the speedy little ginge was slowed down by a well-contrived sandwich between Barney – bit of elbow there, too, Barney? – and Micky Baker. It almost made you glad to be a keeper, seeing bits of agg like that. But the funny thing was, by the end of the match everyone would be shaking hands and looking forward to next year's game; being generous in defeat and modest in victory.

Was that what Melvyn Prosser had been doing, a year or so ago in the Athletic boardroom, when he had smiled, and checked that Duffy had enough Slimline, and introduced him to his 'business partner' Charlie Magrudo? And if so, which was Prosser being – generous or modest? Was he admitting Duffy had outsmarted him over the Brendan business, or was he, by introducing Magrudo like that, saying, Nice try, you little short fat goalie, but I laid out this game so that whatever happened, I won. Was that it? He tried to remember what Prosser had said to him in the Corniche. Something about throwing a lot of bread on the water and most of it getting soggy and being eaten by seagulls. And then something else, about the important thing in business being to look as if you knew what you were doing, even if you didn't. Was that how Melvyn was deliberately behaving for Duffy's benefit?

He must have been right, mustn't he? It must have been Prosser trying to fuck up the club? Nothing else made sense. The planning permission, the connection between Prosser and Magrudo which they'd both tried to deny, the appointment of Jimmy Lister (that *had* been a clever move, he had to hand it to Melvyn), the use of Maggie Coleman to fix both Danny and Brendan, the Layton Road lawsuit. Yes, this had been the final bit of confirmation, when Mr Bullivant had winked and told him he'd sold his house a couple of months before. Sold it before the case came to court, in fact. Well, he wouldn't have bothered, would he?

Proof? That's what they always said, wasn't it – where's your proof? Well, there was proving and knowing, which were two different things in the eyes of the law, but the same thing in the eyes of people who weren't in the courtroom. For instance, take the spectators at this Reliables game: that middle-aged man and his wife, both swaddled in toning sheepskin jackets of a mid-brown colour. If they had watched the first half attentively, and then the first ten minutes of the second half, they would know, wouldn't they, that the pub team had decided at half-time to sit on Ken Marriott, and that the Reliables had decided to sit on the speedy little ginge? They wouldn't be able to *prove* it, and they wouldn't understand about Geoff Bell's technology, but they would see it and know it. And they'd be right, too, wouldn't they?

Uh-huh. The first ten minutes were over, with both the ginge and Maggot slightly the worse for wear. Now came the tricky bit. Two extra men pushing forward, looking for the killer goal. No time for mistakes, no time for Maggot's vision. Still, the Reliables had swapped their full-backs over, and that seemed to be making a difference: not too much coming down the flanks at the moment. They seemed to be shooting from a bit further out, too. Like that – whoops, thought Duffy, as the big pub centre-back who'd been pushing up tanked the ball from thirty yards out. He started moving right and down, but suddenly the ball wasn't coming. It had struck Geoff Bell on the hip and squirted sideways to Maggot. Duffy, from where he lay on the ground, watched Maggot look up, pick out Karl French up front, measure his pass, and hit it quickly.

What had young French said? 'Great vision. Great vision. Only trouble is, the ball doesn't go *anywhere fucking near* where he wants it to.' Maggot's pass went quickly off course, but as Duffy got to his feet again, he saw that the ball had unerringly picked out Barney, the Reliables' other front man – the one characterized as fat and smarmy, according to Geoff's earpiece. Barney gave a fat sideways glance and smarmily transferred the ball to French. Christ, he *was* fast, thought Duffy, as young Karl set off. Took three yards out of his marker in the first ten. Thirty yards out, only the full-back and the keeper ahead of him. Getting pushed too wide by the full-back – no, that was just a bluff, and suddenly French had cut back into the middle and skinned the back in the process. Closing on the keeper – Duffy didn't know who to root for. On this occasion professional solidarity lost out. Do it, Karl, Duffy found himself urging. Do the biz. He almost couldn't look. Karl did the biz – drew the keeper, waited for him to go down, slid the ball under his diving body. One–one. 'GOAL,' roared Duffy from his unpopulated end of the pitch, 'GOOOAAAL.' Karl French had turned away from the prostrate pub keeper, and stood with both forearms raised in triumph. His team-mates descended and embraced him. I suppose that's what they call French kissing, thought Duffy. Perhaps one or two of the team ought to take French lessons.

Ha. Maggie Coleman. That was where he'd blown it. Of course, she was one tough tart, but he should have known that, shouldn't he? You can't put the arm on tarts that easily. Still eager to play the copper after all these years, Duffy.

Sure, he'd had excuses – the real coppers would have closed down Maggie once Jimmy Lister had given them Geoff Bell's photos – and he'd wanted to clear up his bit of bother before they did theirs. What he'd done, he now saw, was to screw both sides. She wouldn't tell him who was paying her; and then, before the real coppers could get to her, she'd disappeared. Done a runner; packed up a few things from her flat off Twyford Avenue and scarpered. Never seen again. Moved up East, perhaps, changed her name – who knows? It meant, of course, that the charges against Brendan were officially dropped, but there would have been more satisfactory ways of doing that in the first place. Like by getting Maggie sent down for conspiring to pervert the course of justice and seeing Melvyn Prosser go down with her.

The breeze was freshening behind Duffy. The corner-flags to left and right of him were pointing straight up the touchline. Well, that should wear down the pub side a bit. No one likes facing a stiff wind in the second half if they haven't had the benefit of it in the first: some elementary sense of justice makes you feel affronted. Still, that didn't seem too ... oh shit, the ginge, oh, ooooh, aah, *now* ... a thump on his wrist as Duffy dived to his left and the ball pinged away for a corner.

'Save, keeper.'

'Great stuff, Duff.'

Duffy bounced about on his goal-line while the tallest pub defender stood directly in front of him and tried to block his view of the corner. It was an outswinger – he could tell that from the start. He came for it, the wind got hold of the ball, and Duffy was being dragged far out of goal. The all-or-nothing ball the keeper hates: the point at which you're either a hero or a wally. There's nothing in between. Not a wally, Duffy thought, *not a wally*, as he snatched the ball from the path of an approaching pubman. Four steps and he was at the edge of his area. A memory of Athletic's last game of the previous season flashed at him. With the breeze behind, he hoofed a drop-kick at the ball. Oh shit. Well, sometimes a wally, he reflected: the ball skidded slightly as he struck it, and flew directly into touch on the half-way line. Sometimes a wally, Duffy, sometimes. But I do have this vision, you see.

Mel Prosser had vision – vision of a fortune. Charlie Magrudo had vision of a parkful of bulldozers and changing his filthy Granada more often. Jimmy Lister had vision of Athletic playing cultured one-touch stuff in the lower reaches of the Third Division. Brendan Domingo had vision of not being booed every time he touched the ball. Mr Joyce had vision of a country where Brendan Domingo had no place at all.

What about Mr Joyce and the Red White and Blue? That was the one bit Duffy was prepared to put down to coincidence. An awkward coincidence, but it might well have been one: on the whole, he thought Prosser a bit too clever, and a bit too careful, to get tangled up with psychos like Mr Joyce. Unless – was he that clever? Duffy had once been picked up by a chubby journalist at the Alligator who had told him, 'Never over-estimate your opponent.' He'd thought it just a smart line at the time, but it had some truth. Prosser, after all, had said that the thing about business was looking as if you knew what you were doing. And Prosser, when it came down to it, hadn't succeeded in his main ambition: fucking up the club he owned. You'd think, wouldn't you, that anyone would be able to do that? Maybe he wasn't so clever?

At the start of the present season Melvyn Prosser had made a great noise about having every confidence in Jimmy Lister. Perhaps he meant that he had every confidence in Jimmy Lister's ability to get Athletic relegated second time round. So Jimmy started the season as boss, and a slightly different boss from the previous year. He was even quoted in the *Chronicle* as saying, 'I don't want any fanny merchants in my squad. Hard work is what wins matches.' No cultured England B wing-halves for Jimmy Lister.

Half-way through the season hard work had helped Athletic into a decent mid-table position, Jimmy had bought himself six new pairs of white shoes, and Melvyn Prosser had sold out. Just as there are always new players coming through, there are always new businessmen coming through, and Melvyn Prosser found Ricky De Souza, a bright lad with a chain of grocer's shops and a sense that owning a football club was about the most English thing you could do. Ricky De Souza reached an understanding with the Reform Group, which quite frankly had been pissing Melvyn off with all the agg they'd been giving him, and the deal was struck.

The sick joke of it all was that as soon as Melvyn handed the club over to Ricky, Athletic began to slide. One or two injuries, a run of tough away games to top clubs, two–one defeats that could as well have been two–one victories, and suddenly the club was in the bottom six. And this time round, Jimmy Lister didn't have Brendan Domingo to pull the side together. Brendan's little floorshow had won him what he'd hoped: release from the terms of his contract. Brendan was now snuggling down with a nice mid-table Second Division outfit up North, where they had two other black players in the first-team squad, and where the local yobboes appreciated his silky skills. 'Silky Domingo' they'd taken to calling him, with something close to affection.

So this time round, it might be serious for Athletic and Ricky De Souza. Duffy would watch the results of their last ten games this season with more than a little interest. But if they carried on at their present rate, by this time next year Athletic would be in the Fourth Division, Jimmy Lister would be on a slow camel to Abu Dhabi, Ricky De Souza would be thinking he'd bought a real dog of a club, and Melvyn Prosser would be kicking himself very hard indeed.

Odd how there was always some consolation. Most of the time you didn't win five–nil, and you didn't lose five–nil. Often things ended in a sort of draw. Duffy's match with Melvyn Prosser had ended in a sort of draw. One–one, you could say. You could say it with even more certainty about the present game: Reliables versus Pubmen. Technically, there were still a few minutes to go, but the ref was running short of wind and wouldn't mind at all getting home early for his dinner, so he blew and waved his arm in a big circle over his head like the refs did on TV, and the players trooped off, and Ken Marriott shook hands with the speedy little ginge, and the pubmen thought, well it's not a bad fixture, this, what with the half-bottle of whisky, and they don't push us *that* hard do they, still, pity about that soft goal we gave away, real sucker punch. Duffy thought, if it hadn't been for that ginge I'd have kept a clean sheet.

'Nice work, Geoff,' he said as he walked off with Bell.

'Yeah, thanks, I really upped my workrate in the second half.' Duffy had actually been referring to the nice work Geoff had done at half-time, but didn't like to withdraw the compliment now.

'Did they really say that thing about me being a bit small for a keeper?'

Bell nodded.

'Afraid so, Duffy. Sorry about that. The only thing I made up was the bit about Karl French.'

'What, about him being out of his depth in this class of game?'

'Yeah, that bit. Well, I thought it might gee him up. He hadn't done much, first half, had he?'

'You clever old thing.' Duffy was genuinely admiring.

'Well, I'm not just a pretty face.'

They clattered up the two stone steps to the changing hut, into an atmosphere of steam, and shouting, and snapping wet towels, and fake screeches, and first cigarettes, and the odd hip-flask, and bare, scrubbed bums which didn't give Duffy a momentary twitch. Odd that, he thought, because I must be in the clear now: I won't end up tinkling my leper's bell on some Welsh mountainside. He checked his armpits, looked down at his legs in a ritual way, but he felt, after all this time, that he was almost certainly in the clear. Maybe it took some time before you got your confidence back, he thought. It can't be that I don't fancy guys any more. Things don't change that quickly. I hope they don't, anyway.

Things did change that quickly for some. As he sat on the hard, slatted bench waiting his turn in the shower, Duffy remembered a long, pale face and a curly black perm that was beginning to grow out. Danny Matson. A dozen first-team games, a sniff of the big time, free entry to The Knight Spot, striking up an understanding with big Brendan, photo in the papers, popular with the girls, waiting delivery on the new Capri, and then ... *phut*. You're a small feature in somebody else's plans and your career goes down the toilet. Never knowing why, never knowing who. Left with a few thoughts about football being a cruel game and a folded picture of Trevor Brooking's room. Where was Danny Matson now?

GOING TO THE DOGS

To Ruth and Don

BUCKINGHAMSHIRE/BEDFORD-SHIRE BORDERS. Classic rural neighbourhood with easy access M1. Outstanding detached period residence standing in 40 acres of its own land. Substantially modified in mid-1960s but many original features remain. Three reception rooms, 8 bedrooms (2 with en suite bathrooms), study, family room, kitchen/dining-room, billiard room. Gardens comprise own wood and lake. Outbuildings include stable block and former squash court (currently recording studio for well-known pop star who must sell) with opportunities for reconversion.

Freehold. Sole Joint Agents: Madley and Burton Wood. Viewing and offers by arrangement.

1 • LIBRARY

There was a body in the video library. It was hard to miss, as these things are, and Mrs Colin spotted it the moment she pushed open the panelled light-oak door on which someone had humorously painted a large pink *trompe-l'oeil* keyhole. Mrs Colin recognized Ricky at once, recognized equally that he was dead, and put her hand to her throat. Beneath the white poplin blouse she had ironed that morning at 6.30, she felt the bump of her crucifix. She always wore Our Saviour inside her clothes, next to the skin, and the few people who knew wondered if it was because she was ashamed of her religion. Mrs Colin was not ashamed of her religion, but she was often more than embarrassed by some of the things she found herself looking at in the course of her daily duties at Braunscombe Hall. If you had been born in Davao thirty-five years ago and were sending money home every month, you did not question the way people chose to behave on the Buckinghamshire/Bedfordshire borders. But this did not mean you should allow such behaviour to be inflicted upon Our Saviour, even upon an image of Our Saviour. There were times, as Mrs Colin set the breakfast tray down in certain bedrooms, when the gold figure at her throat seemed to burn in anger, and with the pressure of her hand she would try to reassure it that such things had nothing to do with her, and that she would in due course pray for the slumbering sinners. Part of the money she sent back to Davao always went to the Church of Our Lady of Penitence, where the holy sisters regularly chivvied the Lord about the moral safety of those in service overseas.

This time, however, as Mrs Colin gazed into Ricky's cold, dead eyes, the crucifix did not burn, and after the first shock she began to look calmly round the room. The several thousand videotapes – a collection of which Vic Crowther was exuberantly proud – lay undisturbed. They were enclosed in special boxes with tooled plastic spines, and had their titles printed in gold leaf. This made them look, Vic would explain, as if they were real books. Some of the tapes were pretty rare, and some of the fruitier items in Vic's collection masqueraded under such titles as *Chess for Beginners: The Middle Game*, or *Cooking with Spices, Part 2*. But whoever it was that had killed Ricky hadn't been interested in old films, or the middle game

543

in chess, or cooking with spices, or even in what really lay behind such innocent titles.

The curtains over the french windows were drawn back, which was not unusual in Mrs Colin's experience: nobody in this household seemed to bother much about keeping out the dark, or the light, or the draughts. But the fact that the curtains were open meant that when the man, or men, had thrown Ricky's body through the window, it, or he, had travelled further into the room than if the curtains had been there to slow his, or its, progress. This elaborate thought took some pedantic time to travel through Mrs Colin's brain, and it was swiftly followed by the awareness that standing there trying to work things out was not at all her job. She shook her head at herself, released her grasp of Our Saviour, quietly closed the door of the video library and went in search of Mr Crowther.

Belinda Blessing was also Mrs Vic Crowther, but she preferred to keep her professional name. It always seemed a bit silly when some sly gawper still at work on his first moustache turned shyly to her in the pub and asked, 'Excuse me, you *are* Belinda Blessing?' for her to slap his face with a 'No, I'm Mrs Crowther.' Belinda stopped on her way to the video library and checked her side view in a long mirror. She'd always known she'd look good in riding clothes, but they also did something to her bum that she wasn't entirely happy with. Jolly girlfriends used to say that you couldn't have too much money or too much bum, but she wasn't sure, and stared quizzically into the mirror, shifting from one leg to the other, studying the effect on what Vic would jokingly refer to as her other pair. Belinda smiled, as if to camera, tapped her riding crop against her thigh (naughty, naughty), and walked quickly to the library, where she found those members of the household who believed in rising by 8.30 on a Sunday morning. She cast a quick look at the body, coughed sharply and observed, 'Looks like he was thrown through the window.' Then she turned away and went off to ride. A good gallop, with some of your long black hair escaping from underneath your hat and flowing out behind so that you might be recognized from a distance, made you forget all the nasty, sick things in life, she found.

Jimmy thought this was rather hard on Belinda's part, but then no one had ever compared Belinda to a duvet, except in respect of where she frequently used to find herself; at least in the old days. Now . . . well, Jimmy wondered a bit about all that, how Vic and Belinda were managing in the bedroom department after what was it, seven, eight years? Had there been a bit of extra-curricular activity? I mean, given their pasts, and given the fact that Vic's rev-counter probably didn't climb into the red zone all that often these days, what would you expect? It was a subject to which Jimmy occasionally turned his mind. He was not bright, Jimmy, and with a head that sloped away at top and bottom he didn't look bright either; but he was a tenacious thinker. For instance, he some-times reflected on the fact that he came from a good family but seemed, as far as he could work out, not to have a bean to his name, whereas old Vic Crowther, his host, who was as common as muck (well, that was Jimmy's phrase – Vic would have preferred something like salt of the earth), had large amounts of the folding stuff which bought you a jolly good time. In short, he was stinking rich. Harry stinkers, in fact, as Jimmy would have put it. He dragged his brain back to the matter in hand, a process which made his right arm naturally extend and firmly enclose the shoulders of Angela. This was a harder business than it sounded, since Angela was crying a lot and shaking up and down. The grieving widow, thought Jimmy, and watched his arm being propelled up and down by Angela's back, as if he were operating a pump on the village green.

It was rather like that: Jimmy's arm pumping up and down, and water sluicing out of Angela's eyes. The bastards, the bastards. She'd loved Ricky. The tears were now interfering with her proper view of Ricky's body, but she didn't have to see him to feel the presence of those gentle eyes, that sweet expression, that lovely curly hair. The bloody bastards. She'd paid, and they hadn't ever mentioned Ricky, so why had they done it? The bloody bastards. What had Ricky ever done to anyone? Her sobs became fiercer, and Jimmy felt her pulling at his arm, as if she wanted to throw herself on the body. We can't have this, Jimmy thought, and held on more tightly, at the same time catching Mrs Colin's eye and making a drinking gesture with his free hand. Mrs Colin quietly disappeared.

Nikki, who was six, and who had been rather surprised when her mother had simply walked off, held her father's hand and wondered if Ricky was in Heaven. Mrs Colin had said she wasn't to go into the video library but everyone seemed a bit distracted so she had just slipped in and put her hand into her father's. What a mess the window was in, all broken like that. She wondered if this meant she wouldn't be able to come in and watch videos for a few days. She usually said she wanted to see *Bambi* or *Supergran* or *The Hundred and One Dalmatians*, but recently she'd found that if she climbed on a chair, some of the other films could be a lot more interesting. She didn't tell anyone about her discovery, though that Mrs Colin had caught her the other day and threatened to tell Mummy. Nikki had had to cry a lot and pretend a video had got in the wrong box by mistake. Nosey Mrs Colin. Actually, she thought she'd recognized Mummy in one of those films, but she didn't have the right colour hair, and Nikki couldn't be sure. She held her father's hand, looked at Ricky's stiffened limbs, and wondered if he was in Heaven.

Vic Crowther, a stocky man in his mid-fifties, had a ruddy complexion, chain-store clothes, and a cheerful expression which the coppers always used to take for cheeky. On this occasion he wasn't looking so cheerful. 'I'm going to have to bollock Duffy about this,' he said to Jimmy. 'Christ, try to give a mate a leg-up and look what happens.'

'Who's Duffy?'

'Fellow who put in the alarm system. This was his big break. Never exactly been the John Paul Getty of the security business. But there it was, nice job, big country house, don't count the pennies. Told him he'd be doing tripwires at Buckingham Palace next. And what happens? He screws up. Someone throws poor old Ricky through the french windows and the bell doesn't even go off. I'm going to give that Duffy a right bollocking.'

'Maybe it's out of guarantee.' Jimmy's suggestion was made in a worried voice.

'Guarantee? Guarantees are a guardsman's tit where I come

from.' Vic was sounding really angry. 'Guarantees are for stockbrokers and schoolmasters. I don't count the pennies and I don't keep files, but if someone does me a job of work, then someone does me a job of work.'

'Check,' said Jimmy.

Vic grunted. He didn't count the pennies, and he didn't keep files, and he did despise stockbrokers and schoolmasters – indeed, sometimes he'd have a chuckle about how he'd started lower than the lot of them yet ended up in the big house with a girl they'd give their right sperm-bank for. But he wasn't really thinking about this, and he wasn't even thinking about Duffy. What he mainly felt, as his daughter's hand squirmed like a mouse in his palm, was relief that no one had gone messing with the films in his video library. What if someone had come through that bloody great hole in the window and nicked his tape of *Naked as Nature Intended*? That was a real collector's item, that was. One of these days those old naturist movies were really going to come back into fashion.

Mrs Colin was not a drinker. She was a good Catholic who had come all the way from the Philippines to the Buckinghamshire/Bedfordshire borders and who regularly sent half her wages back to her mother, some of which was forwarded to the holy sisters at the Church of Our Lady of Penitence. You didn't come all this way to waste money on yourself, least of all by pouring it down your throat. Even after five years with the Crowthers, two in London before Miss Blessing retired and three in the country, she was still amazed at how much people drank in this cold, damp, grey-green land where the money was good. Perhaps they did so precisely because it was cold and damp and the leaves seemed to be falling off the trees all year round. In her country, among her people, they drank San Miguel beer, and that was enough. Here they drank everything, and more kinds of different everything than Mrs Colin had ever imagined. She stood behind the sitting-room bar – all deep-buttoned leather with brass accessories – and wondered what to get for Miss Angela. The array of bottles and tins and mixers and squirters, the prodders and crushers and pokers and pounders, plus the cheery colours of all the different drinks, made her feel like a pharmacist in a dispensary. Maybe that's why the English said things like, 'What's your medicine?' or, for a change, 'What's your poison?' Perhaps Miss Angela needed a little of each of her favourites. Mrs Colin poured an inch of crème de menthe into a large tumbler, added an inch of white wine, and topped it up with an inch of gin. She paused, thought of Miss Angela's tear-lined face, and added another inch of gin. She picked up one of Mr Crowther's novelty cocktail stirrers – a policeman's helmet at one end to hold it by, and a big pair of policeman's boots at the other with which to do the agitating – and mixed Miss Angela's medicine. Then she hurried back to the video library. Jimmy took the glass from her, raised an eyebrow at the colour, and wordlessly held it in front of the now quieter Angela, who drained half its contents without comment. It seemed to Mrs Colin that she had chosen wisely.

Almost in an undertone, but with a firmness of enunciation which made all those who heard it realize that it was an instruction, Vic Crowther said, 'I don't think we'll inform the gentlemen of the law just yet.' Then, one by one, those who had risen at Braunscombe Hall by 8.30 on a Sunday morning filed out of the video library with the cautious step of penitents leaving church. Mrs Colin closed the door and was alone with Ricky.

The fact of the matter was, Mrs Colin had always disliked him. He had frightened her. She hadn't ever told anyone, and it was probably more to do with something that happened once in a backstreet in Davao after dark than with Ricky himself; but there it was. Now, looking at him stretched out in death, she felt a little guilty about having disliked him. His eyes were empty of life, and his limbs were stiff, all four of them, and his tail would never wag again.

2. DRIVEWAY

It was 8.45 on a Sunday morning on the Buckinghamshire/ Bedfordshire borders when Mrs Colin from Davao slipped Ricky into a large blue plastic laundry-bag, stood for a minute or two pondering the etiquette of putting him in the freezer, decided against it, and went instead to the back cloakroom. Nobody much visited the back cloaks. The room contained a large number of wellington boots, none of which appeared to fit members of the household, a fairly new croquet set which Belinda had ordered and quickly become bored with, a wash-basin with a dripping tap, and a Victorian lavatory whose porcelain interior was decorated with a dark-blue flower pattern. A botanist, even an amateur one, would probably have been able to identify the flowers etched into the porcelain, but Mrs Colin had never tried: there were certain things, she thought, which ought to be decorated, and certain things which oughtn't to be, and lavatories fell into the second category. She had never heard of decorated lavatories in Davao. Ignoring the decadent bowl, Mrs Colin looked instead at the row of hat-pegs on the right of the cloakroom. On one of them hung a mud-splashed trench coat which some weekend guest had never bothered to claim. Occasionally, a shooting friend of Vic Crowther's would give him a brace of pheasant, and it was here – two pegs along from the discarded trench coat – that they always hung for a few days. Mrs Colin lifted the plastic laundry-bag and was about to slip its handle over the pheasant peg when she wondered if in some way this might be wrong; she hesitated, and chose the next peg along instead. Ricky's tail, or at least six inches of it, protruded from the bag. Mrs Colin tried pushing it down, but without any success.

Duffy's laundry-bag was made of bright yellow plastic, and at 8.45 on a Sunday morning he was carrying it down Goldsmith Avenue, Acton W3. A stray policeman on the lookout for murdered dogs would have found the contents of his bag innocuous. In legal terms, that is, though some of the contents were far from innocuous where the sense of smell was concerned; some of them might have constituted a minor health hazard; some of them – had the right public official been handy – might even have been taken away from Duffy and buried in a lime pit. Duffy was aware of this problem. It wasn't that he didn't change his clothes often enough; it was simply that he didn't get down to the launderette often enough. He carefully stacked his dirty clothes away in plastic bags at the bottom of his fitted cupboard; after a few weeks, when he thought the bags must be so familiar with one another that they might start breeding, he would empty their contents into his yellow laundry-bag and set off down Goldsmith Avenue.

Duffy quite liked this Sunday chore. Partly it was the release from guilt; partly it was the quiet of the streets. Saturday night had gone home. Saturday night was still snoring away in bed waiting for Sunday morning's hangover to come and wake it up. There was nobody about as Duffy turned in to the huddle of shops which contained the launderette. Lightheartedly he kicked at a few discarded styrofoam burger boxes. Some careful drunk had stacked up a pile of eight empty lager cans on the pavement outside the bookie's. Some less careful drunk had decided that the recessed entrance to the bookie's was well-suited for use as a urinal because, if it wasn't to be the bookie's it would have to be the next shop along anyway, and hadn't he lost a tenner on some three-legged nag here only last week? Duffy wrinkled his nose, aware that the reek from his laundry-bag came in a close second to the pong from the doorway, losing only by a short head.

Duffy consigned his clothes to the tender chomping of the wash, crossed the empty street and pushed open the door of Sam Widges. Sam was a middle-aged Chinese, who had always been called Sam and who had spent thirty years in the British catering business. After ten years in its lower echelons, he had acquired his own establishment, whereupon he changed his surname by deed poll to Widges. At the time Sam Widges had, not surprisingly, sold nothing but sandwiches. In the last ten years he had extended his cuisine, and was now proud of his skills with the microwave; but he remained stuck with the name.

'The usual, please, Sam.'

'Righty-ho-coming-up.'

The usual was a British breakfast cooked in the British way.

It had taken Sam some years to master – visits to rival eateries had even been necessary – but now he was able to handle the separate skills of undercooking the bacon while overcooking the egg, allowing the tomatoes to collapse while the sausages stayed *al dente*, and making sure that the baked beans, when they hit the plate in a sticky mass, retained the original shape of the serving spoon. As Duffy was a favoured customer – indeed, at that time of the morning he was the only customer – Sam threw in a slice of British fried bread: thick-cut, sopping in grease, not too crisp, not too brown.

'Delicious,' said Duffy, thinking a little about his pre-season training. Duffy played in goal for the Western Sunday Reliables and the first match was only five weeks away.

'Thank-you-coming-up.'

The fried bread slipped around the plate as he pursued it with his fork and left a broad snail-trail of grease. Duffy thought of young Karl French, lean as a whippet, who would be out pounding the road even now. Still, you didn't need so much speed to be a goalkeeper, Duffy consoled himself. You needed . . . solidity. He trapped the delinquent sausage against the curve of his plate; with a mixture of cunning and brutal strength he succeeded in piercing its skin.

On his way back up Goldsmith Avenue, with the yellow laundry-bag held rather more proudly beside him, Duffy pondered the eternal question posed to those who frequent launderettes: what happened to the other sock? You put twenty-four in, you got twenty-three back. You put thirty-six in, you got thirty-five back. You put two in, you got one back. At least the machines were fair: they stole equally from those rich in socks and those poor in socks. At first you merely assumed that you had left one stuck to the washer or the drier like a piece of chewing-gum, but this obviously wasn't what happened. However scrupulous you were – you counted them all out and you counted them all in – you always lost one sock. Perhaps there was a little trap-door at the back of each machine, which opened for just long enough to snaffle it. Perhaps this was the owner's way of increasing the profit-margin on these establishments. Duffy had long since given up trying to fight the extra tariff. Instead, he played along with it. He owned only two kinds of sock: the black cotton/ nylon mix from Marks & Spencer, and the red cotton/nylon mix from Marks & Spencer. That way, if you lost one, you didn't worry too much, and when you lost another you were laughing.

'Telephone,' said Carol sleepily as he shut the door of the flat.

'Breakfast,' Duffy replied to the mound of curly black hair on the pillow. He got the yoghurt, the muesli and the skimmed milk out of the fridge, fetched the granary bread, the brown sugar and the honey from the cupboard. You needed your health and strength, that's what everyone said. The breakfast at Sam Widges' was for his strength; this one was for his health. Besides, you should always give yourself a reward for going to the launderette.

As water began to gurgle in the bathroom, Duffy switched on his answering-machine. The message was brief, and easily understood. 'Duffy, this is Vic Crowther. If I pay four figures for a fucking alarm system I expect it to work. Now get your fat bottom down here.'

Fat? What was Vic going on about? Vic Crowther hadn't seen his bottom for three years, so how could he tell? Duffy thought of himself as short, admittedly, but muscular; his face was broad, sure, but jowl-free. He examined his hands: square-ended, a little stubby, but no sign of podge. Nervously, he took an extra spoonful of yoghurt, as if that would help the problem. Well, at least it might help the anxiety about the problem, which was a beginning.

'I'm off to see Vic Crowther,' he said as Carol poured her second cup.

'So you're not taking me out to Sunday lunch?'

Duffy grunted. Of course he wasn't. When had he ever taken her out to Sunday lunch? How long had they been together, or half-together? Seven years, something like that? Ten years? Eighty-four years? He'd *never* taken her out to Sunday lunch. Why was she suddenly expecting it? He looked across at her; she was grinning.

'Well, at least you've got some clean shirts,' she said. 'Or is it black-tie country down there now? Iron your cummerbund, sir?'

'It's work,' said Duffy. 'The alarm's buggered.'

'Probably Vic trying to break into his own house for the insurance.'

'Now, now,' said Duffy, suddenly protective about his former client. 'Vic's never been sent down for anything.'

'Nor was Pontius Pilate,' said WPC Carol Lucas.

'Really? You know, I never knew that. How did you know that?'

'It's on the police computer, Duffy, what do you think? Pilate, P., age, very old, distinguishing features, Roman nose, suspected attempting to pervert the course of justice, manslaughter and going equipped for crucifixion.'

'No, how do you know that?'

'I don't know, Duffy. Telly, I expect. They said he killed himself in the end, but no one's ever proved it.'

'I don't see Vic taking a handful of pills.'

'Or falling on his sword.'

'I didn't know he had a sword.'

'Duffy.' Carol leaned across the table and rapped gently on the side of Duffy's head, 'Is there anyone in today?'

'Oh, I get it.' All that laundry had clearly taken it out of him.

'By the way, how's Miss Tits?'

Duffy wondered briefly if he ought to feel guilty. He didn't think he knew anyone who particularly answered to this description at the moment. 'Eh?'

'Little Miss Tits. Belinda Whatsit.'

'Ah. Blessing.'

'Blessing. What a terrible name. Belinda Blessing. You'd have to take your clothes off if you were called that, wouldn't you?'

'It's not her original name. She had it altered.'

'So that she could take her clothes off.'

'Suppose so.'

'I wonder what else she had altered at the same time.'

'*Carol*. What's got into you?' He looked across at her pretty, morning Irish face with its frame of dark curls.

'You?' She grinned again.

'Ca-*rol*.' He got up. 'There's stuff in the freezer. Pizzas. And some fish bits with a low-calorie sauce.'

'Terrific. Drive carefully. Kiss.'

Duffy would have driven carefully even without Carol's advice. For one thing, he wasn't crazy about the M1: biggest unofficial race-track in the country, if you asked him, full of mad lorries and flashing headlights; even your family saloons thought it the right place to have a crack at the world land-speed record. For another thing, he was driving his new Sherpa van, sitting high in the seat and worrying about getting sideswiped. It had been a relief to junk that rusting F-reg number and get something new. Well, 'new' in the sense of new to him, not absolutely new: he wasn't doing as well as that. So, if it hadn't been for the other traffic, he'd have enjoyed sitting up proud in his white Sherpa with DUFFY SECURITY painted on each side, heading up the middle lane at a steady fifty-five.

There'd been that good scam up the M1 not long ago. Duffy, as an ex-copper, didn't really approve of coppers being villains; but he couldn't find it in him to do anything but laugh at this one. Some petrol company, instead of giving away wine-glasses or little koala bears to hang in your rear window, had come up with a different scheme for attracting customers. Every month they circulated their garages with a list of car numberplates, fifty or so. If you owned a car whose plate number was on the list, you could win anything from a hundred quid to a thousand. Of course, you had to buy some petrol at the garage first; the cashier wouldn't let any old Tom, Dick or Jimmy Fiddler run his finger down the numbers.

The scheme certainly brought in the customers, but it also set a few philosophers thinking. In particular, a group of coppers based near the M1 who liked a little challenge. All done in plain clothes, of course, and mostly out of hours. Two of them would drive to a garage, buy some petrol, all above board, and ask for the list of numbers. They might not find their own, but would come away having memorized a couple of others. Of course, if they'd only bought a gallon or two of petrol, they soon might need another garage, and be forced to squint at the numbers again. The next day, back in uniform, they might find themselves – in the course of duty, what else? – obliged to check the odd numberplate with the police computer. Owner's name and address, please. And then, if it was in the area, they might drive over and ask the fellow if he knew how he could pick up a couple of hundred quid, quite legit, all for a short drive? Of course, there'd have to be a drink in it for them, let's go halves, shall we, after all without us you wouldn't be picking up a penny, would you? They didn't even need to say they were policemen.

Duffy supposed it was dishonest, but found it hard to get indignant. Who was losing? Not the petrol companies, who were risking that amount of money anyway. Not the motorist who couldn't be bothered to check the numbers every month and was now getting a bonus: half of something was always more than nothing. Nor were the boys in blue exactly losing. They were merely showing the spirit of commercial enterprise which was supposed to be the making of the nation. Who was losing, who was actually losing? That was what crime was – one person gaining wrongfully from another. Here there were only winners. Until the day it had all come out, and a few bottoms had been smacked. Then the petrol company closed down the scheme for a bit, and everyone went back to collecting wine-glasses and miniature toy koala bears instead, which was a lot less fun to Duffy's mind.

Cruising the middle lane at fifty-five, he turned his mind to Belinda Blessing and Vic Crowther. Little Miss Tits, Carol had called her. Duffy smiled. The Little applied only to the Miss, not to the Tits. Very much not to the Tits. Belinda Blessing had been one of the earliest Page Three girls unleashed on the nation. At several million breakfast tables men would have a quick glance at the headlines, then turn the page to be coshed with delight and awe by Belinda's . . . by Belinda's . . . well, tits, you couldn't call them anything else: Tits, in fact, with a capital letter. There would be throat-clearing at a million breakfast tables across the country, and sometimes there would be crossing of legs. Belinda had done her morning's work again.

She had long black hair, a neighbourly face, eyes of an

indeterminate colour, which didn't matter as Page Three was in black-and-white, plus what the caption-writer ingeniously referred to on her first appearance in the paper as BELINDA'S BLESSINGS. Not surprisingly, the invented surname allowed the roster of caption-writers full scope to demonstrate their inventiveness. BELINDA COUNTS HER BLESSINGS, followed – just in case the reader didn't get it – by ONE! TWO! Then there was BLESS ME - IT'S BELINDA and a dozen others. Readers became fond of her and wrote in to complain if they hadn't seen her Tits for a month or so. Cynical detractors, loosened by a couple of jars, maintained that Belinda without her Blessings would be just an ordinary-looking girl. But that, her passionate defenders across the beer-mat replied, was exactly what was special about her. She looked really friendly, you know, sort of girl who might have poured that pint for you, who you might have grown up with, who you could show off to your mum without worrying – that sort of girl. Except, except that she had these . . . Blessings.

After six months or so of newspaper fame, Belinda's Tits sacked their agent. They acquired instead a career promoter and personal publicist, who was only one person and still took the same twenty per cent. But he got her a celebrity spot at the Motor Show (she wouldn't lounge about on any old car), he had her opening a few supermarkets, he stage-managed her front end for photographers outside night-clubs, he was thought to have been behind that incident when she threw champagne at a well-known actor who had tried to go snorkelling in her cleavage, and he got her on to a number of TV chat-shows. Here her effervescent homeliness and prepared jokes endeared her even to those who had expected to disapprove. She acquired a boyfriend, and soon after disacquired him. The boyfriend sold his memoirs the following month to a rival paper: 'Why did I buy an MG? Well, I thought I needed a topless car to go with my topless bird.' Readers of Belinda's paper were loyally shocked at this vile piece of opportunism and applauded her magnanimity in not immediately taking revenge by telling the world what a tiny cock the fellow had.

Belinda, flattered by crimpers and lensmen, enjoyed every minute of it. But she also remembered her mum and two sisters that she'd only just managed to move out of the council house, and she knew the time would come when fellers would no longer be quite so interested in seeing her without her bikini top. What would happen then? Would she be able to make the jump to being a proper celebrity? From somewhere inside her came a mutter of fear and doubt. She looked around the men she knew and saw only two kinds: the ones who were scared of her fame, and the ones who were turned on by it. The first type you had to lasso even if you only wanted to have tea with them; the second type were merely booking you for another notch on their bedstead.

And then she met Vic. Oh, of course people said the obvious things; that Belinda had lost her dad when she was a teenager and was still looking for a father figure; they said she broke up Vic's marriage; they said she deliberately got pregnant. But it wasn't really like that. She and Vic just got on from the start; he made her laugh – that's always important, isn't it? He wasn't scared of her because she was famous; he was a success in his own field, so he didn't feel threatened; and when she said to him, 'You know, Vic, sometimes I just want to throw it all up and live in the country and have a horse,' he didn't say, 'Silly cow,' but just nodded and patted what he called her other pair and answered, 'That'd be nice.'

Of course Vic's marriage had been on the rocks for years, and she didn't deliberately get pregnant: it was just one of those things that happens when people fall in love, wasn't it? It had given her publicist a bit of a headache, too, but what in other circles might easily have been HUSBAND ABANDONS WIFE FOR PREGNANT GIRLFRIEND was transformed into BELINDA'S LOVE-CHILD, and that made it all more acceptable. Of course, the modelling dropped off a bit, though there was a patch of leotard work, showing young mums-to-be how to keep fit; but Belinda's heart wasn't really in it, and as she grew fatter with little Nikki she sometimes looked forward with dismay to getting the weight off and seeing if they still wanted to look at her without her top now she was a mum. She carried on doggedly for a year or two after Nikki's birth, until one day, as she was uncapping the piña colada mix, she said, without really meaning it any more than usual,

'You know, Vic, sometimes I just want to throw it all up and live in the country and have a horse.' To which Vic gave a grin and said, 'Well, I have seen this little place, you know.'

Exit 13, that's the one, Duffy thought, and cautiously edged his white Sherpa van into the slow lane. He hadn't ever really gone for Belinda – not even when she'd come out at him from the newspaper like a police snatch-squad. And when he'd turned up to install the alarm system three years ago, she'd been a bit too Lady Muck about the place for his taste. I mean, Braunscombe Hall may not have been one of your top-drawer, ermine-and-pearls country houses, but it was still Braunscombe Hall. And Belinda Blessing and Vic Crowther were still very much Belinda Blessing and Vic Crowther, weren't they? You had to laugh really, and in his quiet way Vic did have a chuckle about it; but it seemed to Duffy from his first visit that Belinda Blessing had solemn ambitions to become Belinda Braunscombe, Dowager Lady Muck.

Vic wasn't likely to change. For as long as Duffy had known him (and that was going back a dozen years), Vic had been the same. He'd played at being over fifty – one who'd examined a lot of life and wasn't going to be impressed any more – when his birth certificate still insisted he was under forty. He coupled this with a cheery public manner of the kind that union negotiators affect when chummying up to the T V camera. Such stolid affability made those with ungenerous minds suspicious. Duffy had once tried to run Vic Crowther in, years ago. Vic, apparently uninsulted, had just laughed, then called in Laski & Lejeune, his favourite firm of bent solicitors, to explain how the watches in their client's warehouse may very well have been quite by coincidence a perfect match to the ones in Duffy's report, but they still weren't stolen, oh dear me no, fat chance.

This had been in the old days, when Duffy was a junior South London copper and Vic Crowther was . . . what, exactly? On his occasional appearances in the paper, he was always referred to as 'local businessman Vic Crowther'; but when asked to specify what sort of business he would give his candid smile and answer, 'Oh, a little bit of this and a little bit of that.' He'd started in the building trade, and switched to installing fitted kitchens when he spotted that construction work was nicer if someone else did the hard part for you first. Then he began to reckon that it was always nicer if someone else did the hard part for you first Franchises, sub-leases – this seemed to be Vic's favourite area: get the other fellow to put up his life savings, take ten per cent and, if the operation folds, well mugs will be mugs, won't they? At one stage Vic had owned a string of launderettes: hey, thought Duffy, I bet it was Vic who dreamed up the idea of the washing-machine that nicks one of your socks every time. There had also been a couple of Crowther-operated funeral parlours; he'd had a bite of the local fast-food business; and stepped into video-hire pretty early on. Quite how legit he was had often been a matter of debate among the local CID, but no firm conclusion had been reached except the obvious one: that if Vic Crowther was clean, then the Queen of England peed standing up. A few coppers had tried to pin things on him, and Vic had always been friendly, then a bit less friendly, then called Laski & Lejeune, who were downright off-putting. If Vic did walk both sides of the street, it was probable he'd be just as canny when being wicked. And no doubt the principle remained the same: franchises, sub-leases and, if the operation folds, well mugs will be mugs, but I was down at the Duke of Clarence at the time, Officer, as most of the Rotary Club will confirm.

Duffy stopped his van at the turn-off to Braunscombe Hall. Those entrance pillars are new, he thought. Two square red-brick jobs, each topped off by a flaking stone globe; the right-hand one had a stone animal, also flaking, clamped to its curving side. A weathered ferret, as far as Duffy could see. There was something odd about the mixture of bright, new brick and old, pitted stone. Duffy stared at the fat orbs until they brought back the days when he used to open his paper and get a double-barrelled blast of Belinda between the eyes. Hey, perhaps that was it. The family arms of Belinda Blessing and Vic Crowther. Two Tits Rampant with an old ferret crawling over them.

Duffy was still grinning at this as he stomped on the brake and scattered the gravel in front of Braunscombe Hall. Vic Crowther came out to greet him.

'Do you want me to go round the back, boss?' asked Duffy cheerfully.

'This isn't the bloody British Grand Prix,' said Vic. 'Look what you've done to my gravel. I'll have to get that raked.'

At this moment a small woman in glasses, who Duffy thought must be Japanese, came round the side of the house in a half-run. 'Mr Crowther,' she said as she got up to them, then stopped and assessed Duffy before continuing. 'Mr Crowther, sir. Someone just stole Ricky.'

3• KITCHEN/DINING-ROOM

The eye-level cupboards in the kitchen were much posher than any Vic Crowther had ever fitted in the old days. They were made of polished German oak, and their price implied that the polishing had been done by little men in lederhosen rubbing their bottoms around on them for thirty days or so. Beneath the cupboards lay a smart bank of domestic machinery which might have been nicked from Mission Control at Houston. What could they all be for, wondered Duffy, whose own kitchen leaned towards the spartan. A plump middle-aged woman, evidently not from the East, whom Vic identified as Mrs Hardcastle, pirouetted from one machine to another, occasionally springing open some hatch and plucking from it another glistening pie, another bubbling quiche. With a kitchen like this, you could start a hotel.

'Planning a big family?' asked Duffy.

'There's only Nikki,' said Vic. He was a bit heavier and a bit ruddier than Duffy remembered; perhaps he was getting to like his booze. 'I think Nikki's the lot. I think any more might interfere with the riding.' He sighed, and looked as if he were going to say more, but the various permanent and temporary inhabitants of the house began drifting into the dining area. If the kitchen was Mission Control, the dining-room was tourist/rustic. There was a long refectory table, oak beams which Duffy reckoned must have been at least two years old, an open fireplace whose surroundings were emblazoned with horse brasses, a cast-iron chandelier which had either been converted to electricity or most likely had started off like that anyway, a set of wheelback chairs and a pair of petit-point footstools. In the corner stood an oak spinning-wheel, just in case Vic and Belinda wanted to start making their own clothes or something.

The ex-Page-Three girl shook Duffy's hand and gave him a distant, chatelaine's smile, as if completely puzzled why Vic had asked him to eat with them: surely he had a pickled onion and a slice of cheese wrapped up in a red spotted handkerchief which he could take out and eat on the back steps while the farm dogs chewed his boots? My my, thought Duffy, she has come up in the world; mind you, those jodhpurs didn't exactly do wonders for her bum.

'This is Duffy,' said Vic to those already seated round the table. 'Old mate. Come to fix the alarm system.' The five guests all seemed to be in their thirties, and you could be sure they hadn't yet in their lives touched kitchen installation or the franchising of launderettes. Duffy was presented to Angela, who seemed rather puffy about the eyes and whose red hair had a strange gild to it that might have come from a large bottle; Jimmy, balding and slightly short of chin, who stood up and shouted, 'How d'ye do, officer'; Damian, in a velvet suit, who didn't rise, but turned instead to the blonde Lucretia, who nodded briefly at this tradesman who'd come to share their lunch; plus Sally, a cascade of giggles and black curls, who said, 'Is that your van?' As Duffy was about to sit down, Nikki skipped in, came across to him and looked up at his face. 'Shall I do my dance for you?'

'Later, sweetheart,' said Vic quietly.

'But I want to do my dance. He hasn't seen my dance.'

'Lunch,' Belinda insisted. Nikki sat down grumpily, and when Mrs Colin tried to adjust the napkin round her neck, stabbed the Filipino woman in the arm with a fork. Mrs Colin didn't complain; nobody rebuked the girl, or seemed to notice. Duffy noticed.

'Where's Taff?' Vic asked. 'Where's Henry?'

'Taffy took a sandwich to the woods,' said Damian, as if it were the quaintest piece of behaviour he'd ever heard, 'where he is attempting to slaughter the local wildlife with the help of a carbine. Though why he doesn't simply pick up the poor little furry things and bite their heads off with his metal teeth, I'm sure I don't know.'

'And bloody Henry's bloody not here,' added Angela.

Every so often through lunch Duffy had to stop himself from nearly choking – a reaction which would not have been caused by Mrs Hardcastle's pies. Damian did most of the talking. He had long lashes and wavy brown hair, and the tip of his nose waggled very slightly from side to side as he spoke. His chubby face seemed to shine with the simple pleasure of being Damian. He held forth about topics and people unfamiliar to Duffy, occasionally breaking off to wave aloft an empty bottle of wine as if he were in a restaurant; whereupon

566

Mrs Hardcastle would come and replace it. Jimmy listened to him with his mouth hanging agape, and laughing just a little after the others. Vic didn't speak; Belinda spoke, but not to Duffy. Well, if they wanted him to play the tradesman, that was fine by him. Fix the alarm after lunch and join the mad-men back on the race-track. He wondered if Carol was having the pizza or the fish in low-calorie sauce for her lunch.

'Is that your van?' It was Sally, from across the table. She had lots of black curls down to her neck and large black eyes which didn't seem to be focusing exactly on Duffy. Maybe she needed glasses; or maybe it wasn't that at all. In either case, it was the second time she asked him that question.

'Mmm,' he replied.

'Duffy Security,' she continued, drawing out the syllables and giggling when she reached the end of the phrase. 'Are you secure? I like a man that's secure.' She giggled again. 'Are you secure?'

Duffy didn't know what to answer. What did she mean? Did he have any break-ins at his place? Did he have a mort-gage? Did he have a steady girlfriend? Cautiously, he answered, 'Sometimes.'

'I always assume,' said Damian in a voice that addressed the whole table while somehow ignoring Duffy, 'that policemen and all those people who deliver one's money to the bank in crash helmets, all that Wells Fargo crew, must have very peculiar sex lives. I mean, *truncheons* for a start.' Sally giggled. 'And *handcuffs*. What one could do with handcuffs . . . And those lovely big *dogs* . . .'

Angela, who had been silent for most of the meal, stood up suddenly and ran to the door. There was a silence.

'Berk,' said Lucretia.

'Oh, *whoopsie*,' said Damian. 'A bit tactless. But it just slipped out, as the actress said to the bishop. Oh God, I'll have to eat humble pie now. By the way, Mrs Hardcastle,' he raised his voice towards the kitchen area, 'the pies are magnificent.' Mrs Hardcastle smiled. 'My felicitations to the chefette.' She smiled once more; she looked quite fond of Damian.

'Have you got a dog?' It was Sally again.

'No.'

'I mean, for the business. You must have a dog for the business.'

'No.'

Sally took a while to assimilate this response. She was seen thinking it over carefully. 'I suppose the fact of the matter is that your dogs have been taken over by technology. Technological advances have eliminated . . .' She paused; these long words were taking it out of her. '. . . your use . . . for . . . the dog.'

'No, I just don't like dogs.'

Sally thought this the funniest thing she'd heard in ages; she yelped, she whinnied, she yodelled with laughter. 'He doesn't like dogs,' she repeated, and her eyes seemed to diverge even more from the parallel. Duffy squinted down the table. Lucretia was watching him impassively; she didn't blink when he caught her eye, merely continued to examine him. With her flowing blonde hair and firm, neatly cut features, she looked the sort of girl you only came across half-way through a fashion spread in one of the posh magazines. The models there had spent months being coached in the art of the frank, disdainful, fuck-you glance; this girl had it in real life. She looked way out of his league.

'Given that you don't like dogs . . .' It was Damian, addressing Duffy for the first time. '. . . then perhaps you're the fellow we're looking for. Can you explain your whereabouts on the night of . . .'

'Knock it off,' said Vic rather sharply. 'Ricky's gone. I mean, Ricky's body's gone. Mrs Colin put it in a laundry-bag and hung it in the back cloaks and someone nicked it.'

'Well, you do make a lot of meat pies around here,' said Damian brightly. 'Perhaps the moving finger of suspicion points at Mrs Hardcastle.' He pretended to examine a large home-made chicken-and-ham pie, then acted a bout of nausea.

'Leave it, Damian, old son,' said Vic. 'I suppose someone had better go and fetch Angela.'

Belinda went to look for her, and after a few minutes they returned together. There was trifle, plus fried-up Christmas pudding which must have been in the deep freeze for eight months or so. As coffee was being served, the door opened and a large, red-faced, square-headed man of about forty came in. He was wearing a bright hound's-tooth check suit, a mole-skin waistcoat of ancient cut, a check Viyella shirt and a red spotted bow-tie. He looked enthusiastically across the table at his fiancée.

'Henry darling, where have you been?' said Angela, with a sweetness Duffy hadn't thought anyone at the table capable of. 'I've been trying to get hold of you for hours.'

'Sorry, old girl,' Henry replied. 'You know how it is. Had to see a man about a dog.'

Angela screamed. The room fell silent. Henry shifted awk-wardly from one fat brown brogue to the other. 'What have I said?'

●

After lunch, Vic took Duffy along to the video library. A large sheet of brown paper had been taped over the hole in the french windows.

'That's where they threw Ricky through,' Vic explained.

'Cor.' In a curious, distant way, Duffy was rather impressed. Coppers, and ex-coppers, get so familiar with crime that any minor innovations are almost to be welcomed. Duffy had certainly never seen this before. 'Big dog, was he?'

'Mmm, well,' said Vic. He looked a bit vague and helpless. 'He was, sort of, you know, dog-sized.'

'Gotcha,' said Duffy. 'Was he any particular make?'

'They're not called makes, Duffy, they're called breeds. Even I know that. No, well I expect he was, he was just a sort of standard . . . dog. Curly hair, tail.'

'Four legs?' asked Duffy.

'Yeah. One of those ones with four legs. I can't say I'm a great student of dogs.' This was one of Vic's less necessary remarks.

'Was he dead when he came through the window?'

'Well, he was certainly dead by the time Mrs Colin found him.' He paused a moment. 'I suppose you don't get finger-prints on a dog?'

Duffy considered the question briefly. 'Not if it's disappeared.'

'Right.'

'So, when do the coppers arrive?'

'Coppers? I'm none too keen on coppers.'

'So I remember.' Duffy smiled. He wondered how much of a villain Vic had been in the old days, how much of a villain he still might be. Did the launderettes and the funeral parlours and the video-hire shops pay for a place as big as this? Or had there been the odd source of income on the side?

'And in any case, now that Ricky's disappeared, it'd just be a waste of their time coming, especially at the weekend. I thought, I just thought I'd . . .'

'. . . let sleeping dogs lie?'

'That sort of thing,' said Vic, and chuckled. 'You know, it's always nice to talk to someone who speaks the same language.'

'Not many of *them* were born in Catford,' said Duffy, nodding back in the direction of the dining-room.

'Yeah, well, they're mainly Belinda's friends. Anyway, you have a big house, you meet the other people from big houses. They're not as bad as you think,' said Vic. 'They're a bit loud sometimes, but they're young.'

'Well, I guess I just don't like posh people.'

'They're not all that posh.'

'They're all posher than me,' Duffy insisted rather grimly.

'That's usually a fair enough starting-point with everybody, I'd say.' It was Duffy's turn to chuckle. 'I mean, that Damian, for instance. He's just a vicar's son, clever boy, went to college somewhere, got in with a smarter crowd. *Damian*'s not a posh name.'

'It's posher than Vic.'

'Right, but that's your England nowadays, isn't it, Duffy? Your Vics can mix with your Damians, and your Damians can get to know your Hugos. All this class stuff, it's out the window now. It's what you are, not who you are. I mean, Belinda and me, look at us. When I grew up – you remember, no, you'd be too young to remember, but when I grew up there used to be silver threepenny pieces.'

'Heard of them,' said Duffy.

'People used to put them in the Christmas pudding. You know, hide them and make a little mark on the side of the pudding so they knew where they were and the kids got them. Well, we didn't have threepenny bits like that in our house. My Dad used to wrap farthings in silver paper. That's what we got. Probably got a dose of metal poisoning as well. And now here I am in a big house. That's England,' said Vic, coming out of what was clearly a set speech with a slurp of grateful patriotism. 'That's England. And look at Belinda. It wouldn't have happened in the old days. You know I dote on her, but she couldn't have done it in the old days. People would have looked down their noses because she took her clothes off for the papers. Now people don't mind that. She goes hunting with people who fifty, no, twenty years ago wouldn't have let her hold their horse. That's England, and bloody good too, I say.'

'Well, maybe I'd like posh people more if I had a big house like this,' said Duffy.

'No need to be chippy, old son. I mean, the house is a good example. Know who I bought it off? Do you remember The Filth?' Duffy nodded. The Filth had been briefly famous in the early sixties: three or four top-ten hits, never quite made Number One, but picked up a good following, who stayed with them for some years. Not as good as the Hollies or The Tremoloes in Duffy's book, but still . . . 'Remember the one who played keyboard?' Duffy vaguely recalled a velveteen elf with a doggy grin, who always performed with a large feather protruding from the back of his trousers. 'Izzy Dunn? Remember? That's who I bought it off. Point is, houses like this are being owned by people like us' – Vic paused, and slightly adjusted his phrase – 'by people like me, anyway, into your second generation. I mean, the house got a bit knocked around when Izzy was here, he was paranoid about people watching him eat, so he boarded up the minstrels' gallery, and he turned the squash court into a recording studio and he put in quite a few picture windows and he even tried out piranha fish in the lake, but it's still a nice piece of house. I get tourists coming past looking at me like I'm the lord of the manor.

Have the Crowthers been in this part of the world for many centuries? I can hear them asking it.' Vic chuckled.

'By the way,' said Duffy. 'Those stone balls you've got on your entrance. What's that ferret doing climbing over one of them?'

'Duffy, you don't deserve to live in a big house like this. It's not a ferret, you wally, it's a salamander.'

'Is that a sort of ferret? Anyway, it's got bits missing.'

'It's a fully weathered salamander, Duffy. Looks like it's been there for ages, doesn't it? I'll let you into a little secret. There's a place you can go where you get them pre-weathered. Like pre-shrunk jeans, you know. Well, saves you the bother, doesn't it? They've got all sorts, bears, pelicans, you can take your pick.'

'Why did you choose a salamander?'

Vic looked a bit sly. 'Well, to be honest, I didn't know it was a salamander either when I first saw it. I mean, I could see it was a lizard or something, and I said to the fellow, "What's with the lizard?" He said it was a salamander, and that in the old days people thought it was special; they believed it could walk through fire without getting burnt. And you know, I said to myself, that's a bit like old Vic Crowther, is that salamander. He can walk through fire without getting burnt, touch wood, so far anyway. So we got it.'

'Why isn't there one on the other ball? Did it fall off?'

'No, it didn't. You only have one. It's heraldry, or something,' said Vic vaguely.

While they were talking, Duffy had been looking round the room and remembering the system he had installed three years previously. He excused himself briefly and went to examine the control box fitted behind a piece of fake panelling in the master bedroom. On his way he passed Mrs Colin, who was trying to take Nikki out for a walk, and getting kicked quite a bit. When he came back he was feeling irritated. He shut the door of the video library. Sunday afternoon, too; bloody hell.

'We talked it all through at the time, Vic. Doors, windows, pressure plates. We decided not to alarm the windows because all you need is a strong wind and the whole system keeps going off. We agreed on alarming the doors and having pressure plates underneath the ground-floor windows. Only you decided not to have a pressure plate in the video library because it was a small room and someone might want to stay up pretty late there and you didn't want them setting everything off when you'd all gone to bed. Obviously the glass isn't alarmed. But if they'd tried to force the window, all hell would have broken loose.'

'So the flaw in this pricey number you fixed me up with is that if people throw dogs through this window I won't know until Mrs Colin does her rounds in the morning?' Vic was smiling at him as he said this.

'Not if you don't hear the crash. I could install a pressure plate if you liked.'

'No, I shouldn't bother.'

Duffy was feeling pissed off. 'While I'm here I'll check the system anyway.'

'Yes, that's a good idea,' said Vic. 'It might take you some time. And on second thoughts maybe you could install a pressure plate. And I expect you haven't brought all the bits and pieces of equipment you need in your van. And, of course, it's a Bank Holiday tomorrow.'

'I don't understand,' said Duffy.

'Even if they'd forced the french windows last night nothing would have happened,' said Vic. 'I didn't turn the alarm on.'

'I don't understand,' Duffy repeated.

'I hope you will, son. I hope you will.'

At that moment the door of the video library opened and a flirtatious Nikki appeared. She looked up at Duffy and said, 'Can I do my dance for you now?'

'Later, sweetheart, later,' said Vic.

'Can I do my dance for Taff when he comes back from the woods?'

'That's a nice idea, sweetheart. Off you go now.'

Vic unlocked the french window with the brown-paper patch in it and stepped out rather heavily on to a flagged terrace. Duffy followed him. Growing between the square stones were little plants – probably herbs or something – which Duffy didn't recognize. A couple of large urns, which may have been pre-weathered or may have been the genuine pound note, contained a bright array of geraniums. A bumble-bee droned slowly past, flying awkwardly as if weighed down by shopping. Hesitantly, Duffy sniffed the air. He felt like someone asked to taste the wine in an expensive restaurant who doesn't reckon his chances on knowing whether the stuff is meant to taste like that or not.

'Smells different,' he announced cautiously.

'Funny, that, isn't it?' said Vic. 'I notice it, too. It's all these years of being in London. Doesn't smell real, does it, the country? Smells like it comes out of a can. Old God up there with his aerosol thinking, "What shall we give them this morning: puff of Spring Flowers, squirt of Autumn Fragrance?" You know, I often come out here and feel like having a smoke, just to put some real smell in the air. And I don't even smoke any more.'

By this time they were leaning over the stone balustrade at the back of the terrace. Duffy's eye was caught by a movement away to his right. A figure had turned the right-hand corner of the terrace and was coming towards them. He was crawling, quite fast, with his elbows stuck out and his toes kicking at the ground. Head down, he passed five feet below them without taking any notice, scuttled towards the far end of the terrace and disappeared from view.

'Looked a bit like a salamander,' said Duffy knowledgeably.

'Jimmy was in the Army,' Vic explained. 'Loved it, always loved it. They said he wasn't bright enough. He's always going on at me to let him build an assault course in the grounds here. He thinks guests might like to try it – you know, squeeze through those big sewer pipes and swing across the lake on ropes – before they earn their gin and tonic.'

'What's he do now?'

'I think it's called being an estate agent,' said Vic sceptically. 'But I don't think I've ever heard him talk about it.'

He led Duffy to a rustic seat which confirmed Duffy's suspicions about the discomforts of the country.

'Spit it out, Vic,' said Duffy.

'It's Angela. We're a bit worried about Angela. Belinda and me.'

'Is she the one with the red hair?' Out of a bottle, Duffy silently added.

'Right. We've known her ever since we moved down here – longer than any of the others. She's best mates with Belinda, and I'm very . . . fond of her.'

'Does that mean what I think it means?'

Vic ignored him. 'I don't know how to put this, but Angela's always been a bit . . . rackety. She's been around a bit, as they say, by anyone's standards. I mean, that sort of thing's more noticeable in the country. No one cares where anyone sticks their chewing-gum in London, but you have to be slightly more careful out here. And she's never been a careful girl. Do anything, try anything, that's always been her motto.'

'So she screws around a lot and takes drugs,' said Duffy, keeping a professional voice on. 'What else?'

Vic shrugged. 'She might look a tough cookie to you at first glance, but she isn't. That's one of the reasons she gets on with Belinda. You know, they both look like they know the way everything runs, but deep down,' Vic's voice shifted register slightly, 'they're just girls at heart. Little girls lost in the wood.' He paused. Duffy didn't exactly feel a torment of sympathy for the two maidens adrift in the bracken.

'Take a squint at her wrists if you get the chance. Looks like Clapham junction with all those lines. That was the second time, about a couple of years ago. The time before that, it was the pills. They pumped her out, tried to cheer her up, told her not to do it again, and she went on exactly as before. Two years ago, as I said, shaving her legs in the bath, takes the blade out of the razor and . . . Someone found her an hour or so later. It was a miracle she wasn't dead.'

No, it wasn't a miracle, thought Duffy; or not exactly a miracle. It sounded more like incompetence. Duffy had come across quite a few attempted suicides in his days as a copper. People always said that if you failed it proved you didn't really want to die. Duffy disagreed. What it usually proved was that you weren't very good at doing it. People thought cutting your wrists was easy, so they just slashed across at right angles, but often the weight of your hands just closed up the cuts again. The people who were really serious cut their wrists diagonally.

'Poor kid. Why did she do it?'

Vic shrugged. 'Said she wanted to be dead. Said no one loved her. You know, the usual stuff. The parents split up when she was a kid, that may have something to do with it. They're dead now.'

'How old is she?'

'Thirty-seven, thirty-eight. Looks younger, doesn't she? They do nowadays. She's a sweet kid underneath it all.'

Duffy grunted. People were always saying things like that. *She's a sweet kid underneath it all.* So why does there have to be all that stuff on top, Duffy always wanted to ask.

'So, you get the picture. Things definitely a bit dodgy.'

'She got money?'

'She got money. Anyway, a bit dodgy, and all the usual things had been tried, doctors and clinics and you know what, and lots of promises, followed by lots of promises being broken. Even if you're fond of them you can get a bit fed up with people like that. So, about a year ago, she meets Henry.'

'Was that the one who said he'd been to see a man about a dog?'

'Check. Henry's been around for a long time. Comes from one of these country families that goes way back.'

'Vic,' said Duffy. '*All* families go way back. I've got just as many ancestors as the next man. So've you. So's a ferret.'

'Don't start getting chippy again. You know what I mean. Henry's about forty-five, and everyone had pretty much given up on him. In the marriage stakes, I mean. He's a bit funny, you know, you don't quite suss what makes him tick. Anyway, contrary to all expectations, he went for her. Perhaps because she was different. I mean with Henry, it'd always been girls with headscarves and green wellies whose idea of fun was to pull the shooting-stick out from under him at the point-to-point.'

'So it's wedding bells, is it?'

'Three weeks' time. The church is booked.'

'Well, that's all right, then,' said Duffy, prodding.

'She lives in this cottage, just outside the village. About two months ago things started happening. Just little things. Noises in the garden and you can't tell if it's a dog or something else. One day she finds a dead bird on the step – well, it could have been a cat leaving it there. Knockings in the night. Then one morning a stone comes through the window. That did it. She took a handful of pills to calm herself down and passed out. That's when we told her to move in here.'

'Where does she get all the pills? And the other stuff for that matter.'

'Rich people can always get pills, Duffy. Anyway, the point is, she's really on the edge now. She quietened down a bit when she got here, then she got worried about the cottage and went back, and do you know what she said? She said she thought the whole woodpile had moved about two yards. The whole pile. Just got up and walked. That set her off, and not knowing whether she was imagining it didn't help.'

'What does Henry think about all her . . . activities?'

'We think he's had the cleaned-up version. I mean, I don't think he gets off on that side of her. He probably just thinks girls are like that, one day they're a bit excited and one day they're a bit quiet.'

'So she's on the edge.'

'She's really on the edge. I mean, I don't know what it's about, and I don't know how much she's imagining, but I do know we've got to keep her in one piece for the next three weeks. This is her last chance, Bel and me both think so. Henry's her last chance. Getting her up that altar is her last chance. We just think she'd fall apart if she doesn't make it.'

'So the dog didn't help.'

'The dog did not help. Who'd do a thing like that, Duffy. Poor innocent creature . . .'

'I thought you didn't like dogs.'

'I didn't say I did. I just said they were poor innocent creatures.'

'Right. What else?'

'She says she's being blackmailed.'

'Now he tells me. Who, why, how much?'

'Wouldn't say. Just clammed up. You don't like to push her in case . . .'

'Sure,' said Duffy. 'Call the coppers.'

'She wouldn't talk to the coppers. And I'm not having coppers around if I can help it. Old habits die hard.' Yes, and coppers with sharp noses might arrive bringing big dogs with sharp noses. They stood up. 'So you'll stick around for a few days?'

Duffy nodded. 'I charge higher rates for posh people.'

Vic shook his head sadly. 'You're such a bad businessman, Duffy. I'll pay you your normal rates.'

'All right.'

They walked slowly round the outside of the house, as if inspecting it for possible ways to break in. When they reached the drive Duffy swore. Bloody hell, someone had been fiddling with his van. It was all at a funny angle. He walked across the gravel, half looking across to the house as he did so. His two offside tyres were flat.

●

Minder to a slice of posh, Duffy thought. Well, if that's what they wanted to pay him for . . . In Duffy's view, Braunscombe Hall didn't need Duffy. It needed the coppers, and it needed a psychiatric nurse, and it needed a good spring-clean, one long squirt with some giant aerosol which made selected humans go around for a couple of minutes buzzing like a dentist's drill before falling down with their legs in the air; but it didn't need Duffy. On the other hand, who did you hire if you wanted to make sure someone got married? Were there wedding enforcers in the Yellow Pages? Perhaps they'd ask him to give Angela away, just to make sure he could accompany her all the way to the altar. Would he have to manacle her for the trip? Yes, sir, and with the grey morning suit and the gloves and the topper, we recommend this nice pair of silver-gilt handcuffs. Very discreet, as you can see, sir. No, everyone's getting married in them nowadays. As the bridegroom slips the ring on the bride's finger, the security adviser unlocks the manacles and throws the key to the posse of waiting girls. First one to catch it is next up the aisle.

Still, it was the client who was paying, and forty a day plus expenses (no, he shouldn't have used that line about charging more for posh people – he should just have upped his rate) also bought, for a brief initial period, the benefit of the doubt. And he hadn't really examined this Angela, just seen her bolt from the room at the mention of a dog. He'd obviously have to watch his tongue about the place. Not say 'Woof Woof' at the wrong moment. Customer relations, Duffy, he thought, customer relations. It wasn't his strong point and he knew it.

'Duffy's staying on for a couple of days,' Vic announced casually as dinner began. 'The alarm system's all cocked to hell.'

'Maybe it was a bad installation,' said Belinda sarcastically. Thanks a bunch, Bel, thought Duffy. He tried to imagine the conversation between Bel and Vic when the latter had informed her that Duffy was going to hang around for a bit. He wondered where he'd be sleeping. Probably in some attic with newspaper on the floor and a broken window, if Bel had her way.

'Well, that's very jolly,' said Damian, looking evenly at Duffy. 'You can make up a four at bridge.' He batted his long lashes and gave the tip of his nose what seemed like an intentional waggle.

'I don't play,' said Duffy.

'Then we'll have to make you dummy, won't we?' Damian smirked and Sally, the one with big squiffy eyes who always giggled, giggled. You watch it, my son, Duffy wanted to say, or you'll get your nice velvet suit all muddy. Instead, he looked around the table and said, 'Who's been mucking with my van?'

'Mucking?' replied Damian. 'With your van? I wouldn't muck with somebody else's.'

'Two of my tyres got let down. That's dangerous. And if the rim's gone through the tyre that's criminal damage as well,' he said, trying to sound a bit more authoritative.

'Round up all the usual suspects,' bellowed Jimmy, as if he had just thought of the line. Bald twerp, thought Duffy, and remembered Jimmy scuttling along below the terrace like a salamander. No, like a ferret.

'I thought you were meant to be secure,' said Sally. 'Duffy Security,' she repeated, and grinned at him.

'I'll pump up your poor little tyres if you'll play bridge with us,' said Damian in a tone of mock weariness, as if this really was his last offer and nothing Duffy did would make him improve it.

'Round up all the usual suspects,' repeated Jimmy. Lucretia was silent.

'Put it on the bill if there's any damage,' said Vic, 'and stop messing about if it was any of you kids.' He treated them like an uncle who had too much patience, Duffy thought; as if smacked bottoms and tears before bedtime were bad ideas.

Turning slightly as he ate, Duffy tried to get a squint at Angela's forearms. Wrists like Clapham Junction, Vic had said. Well, Clapham Junction was wrapped in tarpaulin: a beige rollneck sweater also rolled its way all down her arms and covered the first inch or two of her hands. She didn't talk much, this woman he was meant to be minding.

At that moment, the door opened and a short man in a black turtleneck number entered. His neatly cut black beard made him look a bit like a member of a weekend jazz band who played trad at minor festivals; but the shape of his body made this unlikely. His top half was almost triangular: his swelling shoulders embarrassed his head with their size. His upper arms were powerfully developed, but his hands were quite small. His waist was narrow, and he moved delicately.

'Taffy,' said Vic. 'We wondered where you'd got to.' The black-haired man silently raised one of his hands and showed the table three pigeons, their necks tied together with string.

'Pigeon pie,' he said, in a very quiet voice.

Duffy expected some elaborate sally to come from Damian's curvy lips; but all he said was, 'I like pigeon pie.'

It was only when the pigeons had been handed over to Mrs Hardcastle that Duffy remembered. Christ, you're getting slow, he thought; you'd never have been that slow when you were on the beat. But, then, you'd hardly have expected to run into this particular pigeon-slaughterer on the Buckinghamshire/Bedfordshire borders. Taffy was a Welshman, Taffy was a thief, Taffy came to my place and stole a side of beef. Except that, in this case, Taffy was an Englishman, and his name was a shortening of Tafford. Taffy was an Englishman, and a bit more than a thief.

There must have been a time when Taffy was appearing on the front page of the same tabloid in which you could find Belinda aiming her upper storey at you from Page Three. Neither of them much resembled their photographic images. Belinda didn't look at all like the sort of girl who would romp across the room, plant herself wigglingly on your knee and teasingly undo your top button; while Taffy, seated across from her and neatly slicing his roast veal, didn't look at all like what certain headline-writers enthusiastically referred to as Public Enemy Number One. Where was the glazed hunter-killer look which had helped sell so many newspapers?

Taffy's career went way back and began, like most criminal careers, in mediocrity: a little pilfering, a little taking and driving away, a little gentle robbery. He didn't steal much, he wasn't particularly violent, and he got caught quite often. What with the constant interruptions to Taffy's schooling, there was little chance of him getting into university. He was in his middle twenties before he finally broke out of the self-defeating cycle of small theft, small violence and small spells in prison. He worked out that the amount you could steal was often directly related to the amount of violence you were prepared to use. This key discovery led to his career breakthrough: the very nasty roughing-up of a husband-and-wife in Sussex, in return for which he obtained a large quantity of Georgian silver, not all of it on obvious display. Taffy also worked out that if you stole more at one time, then you didn't have to steal so often, and the fewer times you went to work, the less often the lads in blue uniforms had a chance to nab you. As a result, Taffy was for some time able to live a normal social life; though he never did get into university.

What put him on the front page helping Belinda sell copies for the same press proprietor was a touch of over-enthusiasm with an iron bar during a slack period for news. He'd been serving two years in Maidstone for being over-fond of what didn't belong to him when he suddenly went stir-crazy, brained a prison officer with a piece of railing and did a runner. Where he'd got the weapon from nobody found out. The photo of the officer with blood all over his face looked rather fetching to the professional eye of front-page layout men; and it was swiftly followed by a picture of Taffy himself, definitely not looking his best. For a few summer weeks he became a brief celebrity. One newspaper offered a reward for his recapture; another speculated that he had escaped with the intention of making some public protest – perhaps he planned to interfere with the minor royal wedding two weeks hence. The public quickly deduced that Taffy was on the run, eager to inflict maximum violence on anyone who stood in his way, and plotting to blow up the entire royal family. A Welsh reader wrote to *The Times* pointing out that Taffy was not one of his fellow-countrymen.

In fact, Taffy was the opposite of on the run: he was holed up with a bit of female company and a crate of his favourite beer, both of which he'd been badly missing in prison, and like any other loyal citizen he watched the royal wedding on the telly and reckoned we did these things better than anyone else. He guessed he'd get another five for braining the warder, and get beaten up a bit by the other screws, which was fair enough; but, when he turned himself in, he did it cleverly, by claiming the newspaper's reward for his own recapture, and arranging for what the newspaper imagined was a secret rendezvous in a public place to be covered by several other papers, and even by television. He didn't get the reward, of course; but he copped a lot of publicity, some of which hinted that here was a human being who, though evil, might be reclaimable for society. So he went back to prison, and he got beaten up a bit when nobody was looking, and he got the five he'd anticipated; whereupon he began attending chapel regularly, and started taking an Open University course in sociology, both of which activities eventually impressed the parole board. He was released quietly, at dawn, with a damp mist in the air, and he never went to church again.

Taffy was very quiet over dinner, not saying much and laughing at other people's remarks. His neck and shoulders were enormous. Duffy had seen that sort of muscular development before in ex-cons. The ones who didn't go all apathetic in prison often took to furious keep-fit activity; but

since the opportunities for this were usually a bit limited –
especially if you were doing a spell in solitary – it often ended
up with you doing pull-ups and push-ups in your cell. You
could easily get a bit obsessive about this, and the obsession
eventually showed itself in the shape of your body.

'You're a bit of a chancer,' said Duffy when he got Vic on
one side after dinner.

'How do you mean?'

'Taffy.'

'Taffy? Don't you like him?'

'You know who he *is*, Vic?'

'You mean, do I know who he *was*? Of course I know who
he was.' Vic shook his head a little sorrowfully. 'Don't you
believe in rehabilitation, Duffy? Society offering a helping
hand to the offender? "Come unto me, all ye who have done
more than five years inside." Don't you believe in any of that?'

Duffy couldn't tell how far Vic was taking the piss, so he
ducked the question. 'I notice he kills wild animals,' he said
neutrally.

'A pigeon is not an animal, Duffy. It's a bird. You're in the
country now. And if you want to lock up fellows who kill
birds you may as well begin with all the dukes and marquises
and whatsit.'

'That'd make a good start.'

At this moment Mrs Hardcastle came up to them. 'I know
this sounds silly, Mr Crowther, but I thought I should mention it. Some of the cutlery has gone missing.'

4. BILLIARD ROOM

Duffy pushed open the kitchen door and edged cautiously out on to the terrace. He sniffed the air apprehensively. He knew what Vic meant about wanting to light a cigarette to make the place smell proper. Country smells were all a mixture of you didn't know what: flowers and trees and grass and stuff. People in the country put their heads back and gargled with their noses; they stopped beneath trees for a snort of pong; they held blind tastings of roses. Flowers were all right to look at in Duffy's book, but he thought it a bit degenerate to go sniffing them. Already he felt nostalgic for the smells of the city: the dieselly reek of a hot bus engine; a dense noseful of fried onions escaping from a burger bar; the monoxide of stalled traffic.

Vic had told Duffy to give him ten minutes or so and then to join him in the billiard room for a chat with Angela. Duffy wrinkled his nose. That was another thing about the country he didn't like: it was full of dead animals. Someone had put a dead bird on Angela's doorstep; someone had tossed her pet dog through the french windows; a well-known ex-con walks in with three dead pigeons. In Duffy's experience, all work involving dead animals was likely to be messy. There'd been that case of his in Soho some years back, which had started with something very nasty being done to a cat down in Surrey. Something to do with the spit-roast attachment on the cooker. Duffy didn't like to think about it even now.

Braunscombe Hall looked to the distant or ignorant observer as if it might be an Elizabethan manor, but in fact it was built in the 1880s for a banker who didn't quite make it to Lord Mayor of London. In the normal way, one section of the ground floor had been tacitly reserved for men: smoking-room, gun room, billiard room; and beneath all three lay a large vault where the not-quite Lord Mayor cellared vintages which he did not live to enjoy. There was no longer a gun room, only a gun cupboard, to which Vic kept the key; the smoking-room had long since fallen victim to female emancipation; while Vic's idea of cellaring a vintage was to get enough Vinho Verde from the supermarket to see them through the weekend. Only the billiard room retained its original function, and even that had seen some renovation when

Izzy Dunn, who played keyboard in The Filth with a feather sticking out of his bottom, had owned the house. Izzy had got a bit paranoid about a stretch of green baize, twelve feet by six, and he'd got even more paranoid about his inability to get the fucking balls in the fucking holes, man, so he'd swapped it for a pool table; while into the square divisions of the barrel-vaulted white plaster ceiling he'd stuck twelve by eights of his favourite brothers-in-arms of the music business, and that made it all a lot jollier, didn't it? Vic, who had known a time when the temperance billiard hall above Burton the Tailor's was the best place to spend a wet afternoon, had reverted to tradition and got a mate to knock him out a reconditioned table for not much more than four figures, with a set of super-crystallate balls and half a dozen cues thrown in. Belinda had insisted on smartening the room up a bit, so instead of that awful heavy shade coming right down over the table there was a set of spotlights recessed in the ceiling; she put a pink chintzy sofa at one end in case anyone wanted to watch, and she took down Izzy's photos of rock stars and picked out the cross-bars of the barrel-vaulting in a matching pink. But, all in all, and even though they tended to call it the snooker room rather than the billiard room, it was pretty much like old times in there.

Vic yielded his place on the chintzy sofa to Duffy. Angela didn't seem to register the substitution. As Vic headed for the door, casually rolling a ball up the snooker table as he went past, Duffy examined her profile. Squarish jaw, fullish around the cheeks, a little pouchy under the eyes, brown eyes, pale cheeks which emphasized the glow of hennaed hair and made it seem more artificial. She was a good-looking woman in need of a ten-thousand-mile service.

'Vic tells me you've a spot of bother.'

She looked up brightly. In full face her jaw became less square, her nose slimmer, her large brown eyes even larger. A brief crackle of current buzzed through them, and she seemed animated, laughing, sexy; definitely not one of your green-wellies brigade. Then she clouded over again as the question seemed to get through to her. 'Everything's absolutely fine,' she replied in a monotone.

'Sorry about the dog. Who could have done such a thing?'

'There are a lot of perverts around nowadays,' she said vaguely.

'But don't you want to find out who did it?'

Angela shrugged. 'What's the point in finding some pervert who likes to kill dogs?'

'So that he won't do it again. So that he'll be punished.'

'We all punish ourselves, don't we?' said Angela, giving him a lethargic half-smile which may or may not have been intended to appear mysterious.

'Do we? Look, I know it's none of my business . . .'

'No, it isn't any of your business. Everything's fine, I've told you.'

'Someone's blackmailing you.'

'No they're not. Everything's fine. I'm getting married soon. Do you smoke?'

'No. Yes, I heard. Congratulations. Vic told me you were getting blackmailed.'

'Wherever did he get that idea? He is sweet, old Vic. Must have misunderstood something I said.'

'He's not stupid, old Vic.'

'No, he's not stupid, he's sweet. But he doesn't always understand things.'

'But he did understand that you needed looking after? That's why you moved in here, after all.'

Angela continued looking away from him, her hair shimmering a little in the spotlights. 'Well, we all get nerves before the Big Event, don't we? Nerves, that's what I had.'

This isn't getting us anywhere, Duffy thought. At the same time he didn't know how hard he could push her. Going on this way was exhausting; it was like bump-starting a hearse. That first sparkle of animation seemed gone for ever.

'About your dog. It was you that stole him, wasn't it?'

'What do you mean?'

'You stole him out of the cloakroom so that you could take him off and bury him. Properly, you know.'

'That's a very stupid suggestion.'

'Is it?'

'Yes it's very stupid.' If it was very stupid Duffy would

have expected her to be cross with him. But she didn't seem to be. She was just reacting as if his interest in her life was completely irrelevant, which from her point of view maybe it was. There was a click as the door opened.

'So *there* you are. Little tête-à-tête? *Do* let me play gooseberry.'

'We've finished, Damian,' said Angela, getting up and slowly leaving the room.

'Chatting up brides-to-be,' said Damian. 'Naughty. I'll have to report you to big Henry.'

'Is she all right?'

'Angela? In the pink, don't you find?'

'I don't know her. Where's Henry?'

'At home, I should think. In his *house*,' Damian added, as if Duffy were too dense to understand the term 'home'.

'Where's that?'

'About three miles away.'

'What's he doing?'

'What do you mean, what's he doing? Rogering livestock for all I know. Actually, he's probably playing Scrabble with his mum.'

'No, I mean, why isn't he here with Angela?'

'Old English tradition. Probably doesn't apply where you come from. Husband and wife in the weeks before marriage see less of one another so that their transports of delight may be the fiercer after the nuptials. Fancy a quick frame?'

'I think I see,' said Duffy. Damian was rattling the reds into the triangle; he closed one eye to line them up, then topped off the pyramid with the pink. 'No, I'm a bit tired.'

'Oh well, poor little Damian will have to play with himself. Story of my life,' he added mournfully. If Sally had been there, she would have probably found this the funniest thing she'd heard since the last funniest thing she'd heard. Duffy disappointed Damian by not responding. 'Go on, you break off for me at least.' Duffy placed the white ball in the D and decided to show him some fancy stuff. Off two cushions, miss the black, and roll gently into the back wall of reds. That was the plan, anyway, but something about the cue, or the lighting, or the cloth, or most probably Duffy's state of mind, sent the cue ball scuttling sweetly into the black.

'Seven away,' cried Damian mockingly.

'I think I'm a bit tired,' said Duffy. 'Perhaps tomorrow.'

'Promises, promises,' murmured Damian, pinging the cue ball off the corner of the pack and taking it safely back into baulk.

As Duffy closed the billiard-room door he thought, 'You're the sort who gives my sort a bad name.' Quite what Damian's sexual orientation might be wasn't clear, and there were frequent occasions when Duffy wasn't sure about his own; but he'd seen enough of Damian to know that if he, Duffy, had been just a regular up-and-down bloke he'd have put this velvety fellow with the wiggly nose down for a screaming faggot. Duffy, of course, was far from being a straight up-and-down bloke; indeed, he had enjoyed what Damian archly termed transports of delight on both sides of the street. Still, this very tendency to cover the waterfront meant that he was impatient with coyness, with not saying what you are; and if he'd run into Damian down at the Alligator or even the Caramel Club, and found him sitting on a bar-stool with a laundry-bag of handkerchieves in his back pocket and a car-thief's clump of keys dangling to his groin, he'd still have had the same reaction. Duffy wasn't keen on camp, and when clever fellows who'd been to university were camp, he was even less keen. People who know long words had a duty to be straightforward, that's what Duffy thought.

He strolled along a dark corridor past what had once been the butler's pantry but which was now a garage for various types of Hoover, and felt a bit lost. He'd never been in a house this big, and one of the disorienting things about it was that you never knew where anyone was. Where was Angela? (Gulping down something that was bad for her?) Where was Taffy? (Stripping the lead off the roof?) Where was Belinda? (Practising her accent with a Sony Walkman and a set of Teach Yourself Posh tapes?) You couldn't keep track of them all, and it bothered Duffy. Where he came from, if anyone left the room and they weren't in the kitchen then they must be in the toilet, so there was no problem. Braunscombe Hall had more lavatories, as he'd heard even Vic calling them, than there were rooms in where Duffy came from.

In what the estate agents had designated as the family room, but which Vic tended to call the lounge, Duffy found Lucretia. She was leaning half-sideways on a sofa, smoking and reading a copy of the *Tatler*. A tumbler of watered whisky stood on a small brass table which Belinda might have picked up in Burma but more probably in Marbella.

'Where are the others?'

Lucretia waved a hand in the air, presumably signifying that they were looking after themselves quite happily just as she was.

'What are you doing?'

Lucretia glanced up and gazed at him levelly. She seemed very smart to him, as if a coachload of tailors and crimpers and grooms had left only a moment ago. He still didn't know what she looked like when she smiled. 'I'm reading a fairly good restaurant critic called Basil Seal in a magazine called the *Tatler*. I don't suppose that's part of your regular culture.'

'No.'

'He's writing about a restaurant called L'Escargot. What do you think of the food at L'Escargot?'

Duffy paused. He wondered if it was a catch question. Finally, he said, as casually as he could manage, 'Very nice last time I was there.' Lucretia smiled, just a little. He wondered what she was like when she smiled a lot more.

'Only you see, if in your feeble way you are attempting to chat me up, you ought to be vaguely aware of what field you're operating in.'

'Check. Actually, I think I'll turn in.'

Lucretia returned to Basil Berk writing about the Golden Sausage in the *Wankers' Monthly*. Oh well, thought Duffy. The funny thing was, she was being pretty frosty with him and he didn't mind. At least it was a change after Damian. And if she liked restaurants, why didn't he take her down Sam Widges while they waited for his laundry to get stolen over the road? Double fried bread, Sam. Righty-ho-coming-up.

Duffy retreated to his bedroom. Despite his fears of what Belinda might inflict upon him, it was quite a nice room:

carpet, comfortable bed, curtains, pile of magazines, only about a quarter of a mile to the nearest bathroom. But perhaps this was Belinda's point: she gave him the worst room, and he still thought it was very nice – which confirmed what she thought about him. Oh well, Belinda was probably the least of his worries. He went to the window, which didn't have any broken panes, opened it a few inches and sniffed. No, he'd had enough of that stuff already, he thought, and closed the leaded casement firmly.

He lay down on his bed in the cast-off shortie dressing-gown that Vic had loaned him and read a copy of *Country Life* in about forty-five seconds. He didn't like the smell of that either: a photo of a posh girl in pearls about to undergo Damian's transports of nuptial delight, lots of pictures of posh furniture, then a letters page with people writing in to ask how they could stop their hedgehog running away. The magazine might as well have been written in a foreign language for all that Duffy could understand it.

He lay on his back and tried to work out what he thought of Angela. Apart from the fact that she obviously wasn't tell-ing the truth, he didn't work out much. Why would anyone want to kill her dog? Was it connected with the blackmail she wasn't admitting? But why should the corpse go missing? Was the dog-killer the same person as the body-snatcher? Was it something to do with the illegal substances that were pre-sumably being consumed on the premises, though he hadn't actually seen any direct evidence of this, your Honour, it was only hearsay so far. Why had someone let his tyres down? That was pretty needless, wasn't it; it might even be construed as provocative, as if someone was saying, 'Fuck you, Duffy, with your silly white van and your alarm system that doesn't work.' And now the cutlery was going for a stroll as well.

It was one o'clock on Duffy's digital by the time he decided to call it a day. He'd better hitchhike down to the nearest toilet first. He'd told Vic to isolate the pressure plates and only alarm the external doors so that he could, if he wanted, creep around the house and spy on people; but even so, he walked along the corridor's paisley-patterned carpet as if there were pressure plates every yard. He felt a bit of a wally in his shortie dressing-gown; it was royal-blue silk and flapping its wings on the back was some big gold bird which looked like an eagle, only fancier. He'd have to ask Vic what it was. The dressing-gown was also more obviously short than he'd initially reckoned: if this was where it came down to on him, then where the hell did it come down to on Vic, who was three or four inches taller than Duffy? Perhaps there were some trousers to go with it that he hadn't been loaned.

When he came out of what was obviously a lavatory as it was a lot posher than any of the toilets he'd ever used, he felt wide awake. The house appeared silent, though an occasional light placed here and there meant that you could see your way round if you wanted to. Perhaps they left the lamps on all night as a sign that they were rich. You woke up in the middle of the night, saw a strip of yellow shining underneath your door, thought, well that's a relief we've still got money to burn, and went happily back to sleep. Or perhaps they left the lights on for the convenience of bed-hoppers.

Duffy decided to slip down to the family room and borrow that glossy mag Lucretia had been reading. He obviously needed to put in some homework on restaurants. He crept gently down the stairs. Carpet all the way: no wonder Vic told him he wouldn't need to borrow slippers. Moving quietly, for no particular reason except that it seemed polite, he made his way to the family room or lounge. He picked up the *Tatler* from a low glass-topped coffee table, then paused. You can be a bit smarter than that, he thought, put the magazine down again, looked around for the newspaper trough and went through it until he found an earlier month's issue. Yes, that's a lot less obvious.

He was about to put his foot on the stair when he thought he heard a noise. Yes, muffled, but a noise. He walked along the corridor and past the former butler's pantry where the Hoovers slumbered and entered what had once been the gen-tlemen's part of the house. As if nodding to this dead tradition, the carpet gave out at this point and was replaced by hessian matting which wasn't so kind to Duffy's bare feet. Ouch! He stood on one foot and rubbed the sole of his left foot against the swell of his right calf. As he did so, the lower halves of his dressing-gown pulled apart and he stood there exposed, like a flashing stork. Should have kept your pants on, Duffy. Yes, the noise was coming from the billiard room, definitely. Gently, he pushed open the heavy door and walked in.

There are many variations to the game of snooker, and Duffy knew a few of them. There were obscurer ones only played in London clubs by men with braying voices, and with these Duffy would have been understandably unfamiliar. But the game being played on the Braunscombe Hall table would not have been found in any snooker manual, however obscure. Immediately in front of Duffy a velvet-trousered figure was bent over the baulk end of the table, lining up on the blue. In the far corner away from him, and from Duffy, Sally was sitting on the table, her coccyx thrust into one of the bottom pockets. Her skirt was a mere frill around her waist; one leg was pressed against the side cushion, another against the end cushion, forming an angle of ninety degrees. This made it apparent, even from Duffy's distance, that she wasn't wearing any knickers. It also made it quite clear where Damian was trying to put the ball. Various previous attempts lay marooned against her thighs. Sally was on a roller-coaster of giggles. She also, Duffy couldn't help noticing, had kept her shoes on, which were digging into the cloth.

Damian played the blue and made it cannon off a red that was close to Sally's thigh. This deflection took it straight to its target. 'In-off,' he shouted.

'Ooh, I wish you'd warmed the balls,' she said.

'Filthy girl,' he said, fetching the white ball back and lining up another shot. '*Filthy* girl.'

It was clear to Duffy that both of them were aware of his presence, and both of them were determinedly ignoring it. He turned to go. Just as he was about to close the door, Duffy heard Damian murmur, '*Hate* the dressing-gown.'

●

Vic's idea had been that Duffy should spend a few days at Braunscombe Hall pretending to repair the alarm system, while all the time keeping an eye and an ear open. The trouble was, if Duffy kept diligently taking up the floorboards to check the wiring and the pressure plates, it made it hard for him to pad round after Angela and see that nobody sand-bagged her. On the other hand, if he nosed around too much, it wouldn't look good professionally, and it would make old Vic look a bit of a wally: first he hires this old chum who installs a faulty system, then when it breaks down he hires him again to mend it, and what does he do? Start wandering round the house like a tourist; starts enjoying the free break-fasts. Do you know, I caught that maintenance man nicking a copy of the *Tatler* from the family room at one in the morning? What is England coming to?

Duffy reckoned he'd have to spin out the repair dodge for as long as he could get away with it, and then they'd either have to think up another excuse or level with people. Still, it was Bank Holiday Monday, and perhaps the sight of anyone even vaguely working would impress some of those around. When he'd been at school it had always been said that you could stroll through any part of the buildings at any time of the day as long as you were carrying a note in your hand: all the teachers assumed that some other teacher had sent you on an errand, and you never had to explain yourself. Duffy hadn't tried this line before; now he found, rather to his surprise, that if you wandered around looking thoughtful, with a piece of wire in one hand and a pair of pliers in the other, stopping occasionally to examine a wall or a window, people assumed that you were in some unfathomable way hard at work, and tried not to disturb you in case they broke your concentration. Perhaps that's what professional electricians did all the time.

In the billiard room he found Mrs Colin pulling a fat indus-trial Hoover round after her. He looked at the table, wonder-ing if what he'd seen last night had been some sick, chippy dream. '*Hate* the dressing-gown' – the words came back to him. He looked at the small figure of Mrs Colin tugging at the large steel vacuum cleaner, and wondered why they didn't make special ones for houses this size. When he'd been a kid and gone down the recreation ground he'd always been impressed by those motor-mowers which the parkies used to just sit on and drive; none of that sweaty pushing. They ought to make Hoovers like that. He imagined Mrs Colin driving across the rugs and parquet of Braunscombe Hall, occasionally hooting at you to get out of the way.

'Mrs Colin. Do you mind if I ask you a question?' Mrs Colin switched off the Hoover and waited. 'Why are you called Mrs Colin?' She smiled at him, looked away, switched the Hoover on again and went back to work. Perhaps that was a hint. Duffy continued his exploration of the house. He pushed open the cellar door and went down some concrete steps. He expected it to be damp down here, but it wasn't; instead, there was a dry, musty smell. Rows of wine-bins, in which the not-quite Lord Mayor had cellared the vintages he had not lived to drink, stretched away underneath the house. Vic had made an unconfident attempt at emulation: in the two nearest bins there was a case of Vinho Verde and one of pink champagne. Duffy took out a bottle of the latter and examined the label. On the wall nearby hung a very old thermometer, presumably placed there by the not-quite Lord Mayor so that potentially harmful fluctuations of temperature could be monitored. Duffy reckoned that Vic's wines wouldn't be in the cellar long enough for potentially harmful fluctuations of temperature to get at them.

In the kitchen he found Belinda in her well-stocked jodhpurs, and Vic, to whom he suggested a potential modification of the alarm system which could best be discussed if they went out on to the terrace, down across the lawn, well away from the house and out of earshot of everybody else. Before they left, Duffy asked Belinda if she could spare him a word or two later in the day perhaps.

'I'm afraid I leave the wiring to others,' she replied. He looked at her as if to say, come on darling, you know what we're talking about. She looked back at him as if to say, course I know what you're talking about, but I couldn't resist it, could I?

Down on the lawn with Vic, where no one could hear them unless Jimmy had already dug a series of tunnels as part of his assault course and installed listening devices (which was always a possibility), Duffy said, 'You'll have to give me more background.'

'Be my guest.'

'Why do you let all those people sponge off you?'

'Duffy, you watch your tongue, lad, or someone will cut it off and put it in a pie. Those are my friends, my guests.'

'Belinda's friends, your guests.'

'Maybe. So what? I like people round the house. I'm not short of the odd penny. Anyway, we've got Angela to think about.'

'Is that what they're for?'

'Well, no, not all. I mean, that's Damian and Sally, really, they're the ones I got to take her mind off it all.' Duffy wondered where Angela was when Damian and Sally were taking their own minds off things on the snooker table.

'What about Lucretia?'

'She's a friend of Angela's. She's been down quite a lot. I suppose she's helping with the wedding dress . . . or whatever they do.' Vic sounded vague.

'Jimmy?'

'Oh, Jimmy's sort of . . . around. He doesn't always stay here. He's got a camp in the woods.'

'Are you serious?'

'Sure. I mean, he's got a house a couple of villages away, and he stays here a bit, but he's got this sort of camp, you know, hide, up in the woods. He likes it there. Must remind him of the Army or something.'

'Is that where he runs being an estate agent from?'

'I don't think Jimmy sells that many houses, to be perfectly level with you,' said Vic.

'And Taffy?'

'Oh, Taffy's a . . . house guest.' Vic didn't sound as if he was completely accustomed to using the phrase yet.

'Well, it must make a nice change from being a house guest in Maidstone or the Scrubs.'

'You're so unforgiving, Duffy.'

'No, I just think that if you're harbouring a known criminal and the spoons go missing, then you ought to put two and two together.'

'You know, that's a very posh word for you, Duffy, *harbouring*. I've never much liked it myself. And I don't think

Taffy's much interested in nicking my cutlery. Never steal from your own, that's what they say, isn't it?'

'So Taffy's your own, is he?'

'Duffy, I'll be straight with you. I've known Taffy some time. I knew him before he made the front page. And I'll tell you, he's changed. He's a reformed character.'

'Oh yes?'

'Sure. And I'll give you the proof of it. He's got boring.'

'What do you mean?'

'It's that sociology course he did when he was inside. He's always trying to explain things nowadays. He used to just nick things because someone else had them and he wanted them. Now if you showed him a bank with an open vault he'd want to read a history of Wall Street before he made up his mind whether it was OK for him to help himself.'

'It's a good front, anyway.'

'You're too cynical, Duffy, that's your trouble. I always knew coppers were more cynical than villains. I tell you something, I bet villains give a lot more to charity than coppers ever do.'

'That's because villains earn more.'

Vic laughed. 'You see, I couldn't have a chuckle with Taffy about this sort of stuff. He'd always be wanting to prove something or other.'

'How long's he been here?'

'A month or two, I suppose.' Duffy raised an eyebrow. 'It's hard for him to get a job at the moment. You'd be surprised how prejudiced some people get.'

'Well, make sure he doesn't get institutionalized. You know, can't live anywhere except in country houses.'

'That's my problem.'

'And your bank manager's.'

'I'm all right, Duffy. Don't start worrying about me.'

'OK. So tell me what drugs people are on.'

'Nicotine, I'd say. Bit of alcohol, maybe.' Duffy waited. 'I don't know, and I don't ask. I don't ask who's sleeping in whose bed, and I don't ask if they're using funny tobacco.'

'Permitting your premises . . .' Duffy began, as if reciting a charge sheet.

'Oh, fuck off, Duffy. I'm paying you, you're not turning me over, right?'

'Right. Then who's had it off with Angela?'

'Well, Henry I hope. But as I said . . .'

'Come off it, Vic, saying you don't ask doesn't mean you don't end up knowing.'

'Right.'

'So?'

'Well, Jimmy had been very keen on Angela for years.'

'Was he cut up when she got engaged to Henry?'

'Hard to tell.' Duffy snorted in irritation. 'No, it *is* hard to tell with Jimmy. He did spend quite a bit of time in his camp in the woods afterwards, I remember. But . . . you know, it was a nice summer, and perhaps there were a lot of rabbits around.'

'You've really convinced me. Anyone else?'

'She's been around, like I told you.'

'Damian, Taffy?'

'Do you think Damian's that way inclined? Taffy? Not since she got engaged to Henry, I mean, she wouldn't risk it, would she?'

'You?'

'Duffy, what's this, flattery?' Duffy waited. 'Don't you remember the old seaside postcard? When you're twenty to thirty, tri-weekly. Thirty to forty, try weekly. Forty to fifty, try weakly. No? No, you'd have to see the card, I suppose.' Duffy still waited. 'You *are* serious, aren't you? Listen, if you had Belinda, you wouldn't need Angela, I can promise you that.'

'Right,' said Duffy. 'That'll be all for now, sir,' he added, coming over all copper, 'but don't leave the area without informing us, will you? And we'd like you to surrender your passport.'

'Cheers,' said Vic.

'Oh, and just a couple more questions while we're about it. Why is Mrs Colin called Mrs Colin?'

Vic grinned. 'When she was first with us there was a fellow she was keen on, well he was keen on her anyway, and we kept saying to her "When are we going to be calling you Mrs

Colin?" and it sort of stuck. She broke up with him — we never knew the details — and we sort of thought we ought to stop calling her that, but when we tried she got cross. Funny, that. She's been Mrs Colin ever since.'

'I see. And the other thing. That dressing-gown you lent me. What's with the eagle on the back?'

'It's not an eagle, it's a phoenix.'

'Is that heraldry again?'

'Yeah.'

'I don't think I'll ever crack heraldry.'

'Well, the phoenix . . .'

'Don't tell me, Vic. I don't want to know.'

Duffy walked back up the lawn, round the side of the house, and crunched across the gravel towards the stable block. The Elizabethan-style half-timbering was a bit skimpier here, but the block still seemed to Duffy about the size of a very large detached house in the London suburbs which was being lived in by posh people. The stables at Braunscombe Hall were occupied by two horses, three cars plus Mr and Mrs Hardcastle. The horses had the best of the accommodation, and no doubt saw the gentler side of Belinda, such as it was; but the Hardcastles still had two up, two down and as much parking space as they liked. Duffy hadn't yet set eyes on Ron Hardcastle who apparently functioned as gardener, handyman and stable lad; and he didn't set eyes on him now, either. Mrs Hardcastle answered his knock.

'Oh, I'm going over the alarm system, and Mr Crowther was wondering whether it ought to be extended to the stable block. Do you mind if . . .'

'Poke around,' said Mrs Hardcastle. 'I'm just off over to the house to do the lunch. Ron's off somewhere. I don't think we've got anything worth stealing.'

'Yeah, I don't know, maybe it's the horses . . .' Duffy realized this sounded a bit feeble. Or maybe it didn't: protect the horses against thieves, but not Mr and Mrs Hardcastle. Yes, that would probably be Belinda's line.

He walked round the stable block, steering well clear of the part where the horses were. Horses bit. They had these sort of half-doors on where they lived, and they lurked among their straw until you put your nose in and looked for them, and then Snap! they had your nose off and probably half your face with it. Instead, Duffy looked into the garage, where he saw a cream Range Rover, a red MG and a Datsun Cherry of some purply colour he couldn't put a name to. He continued until he came to the Hardcastles' end of the building. They also had one of those two-part front doors like the horses had. He reached inside and unbolted the bottom half.

It was a neat little house: kitchen and telly room downstairs, bathroom and two small bedrooms upstairs. Duffy poked around in a professional way; that's to say, he didn't enjoy it much. There were some people's places you enjoyed poking round in: these were usually people who were richer than you, or nastier. Oh, so *that*'s what you do with all the money you made by fiddling the books, is it? And you'd pick up some horrible tapestry cushion as if with tongs. But with ordinary people, or poor people, or nice people, you didn't get that sort of pleasure. You felt what it would be like if someone was rifling through your own stuff. Duffy looked briefly into the two bedrooms, then went downstairs and out of the front door. Just in case anyone was watching him from the house, he stepped back a few paces, scanned the upper windows and the roof, then nodded his head. He walked round to the back, past a neat little kitchen garden. Behind the house was a coal bunker, a wood store and a small lean-to shed. Automatically, Duffy put his hand to the door; it was locked. Just as automatically, Duffy looked around for the key. There was always a rule about keys: if they weren't in the obvious place, they were in the second most obvious place. Not under the big stone? Try under the little stone. Or, in the present case, not under the big flowerpot? Try the small flowerpot. Duffy picked up the rusting key and pulled open the shed door. Various forks and spades and diggers and whatsits that people who had gardens needed were arrayed in front of him, but Duffy didn't really look at them. He reached in to the back of the shed and pulled a large piece of sacking off a square mound. Well, well. He hadn't met Ron Hardcastle, yet, of course, and he might indeed turn out to be a man who knew his Asti from his Spumante; but just for the moment Duffy registered the fact that Ron's wine-cellar was twice as big as Vic's. Two cases of Vinho Verde, to be precise, and two cases of the same pink champagne that Vic had a fancy for.

He locked up, and as he did so thought he registered a slight movement at the periphery of his vision. Nonchalantly, he put the key back underneath the small flowerpot, turned and began to saunter towards the end of the Hardcastles' garden. A small path led across a corner of the wood and back towards the lawn. He followed the path, treading as lightly as he could, listening out and wishing he'd been in the Boy Scouts. When he reached the edge of the lawn, he sat on a bench and continued listening. Just at the appropriate moment, he said,

'Jimmy?'

'Damn. Damn, damn, damn.'

Duffy turned, and saw Jimmy flat on his stomach about three yards away. He was wearing a camouflage jacket and a small home-made hat plaited together from ferns. 'Damn. When did you spot me?'

'Oh, only right at the end. I think you must have, er, disturbed a twig or something.'

'Ah. But how did you know it was me?'

'Well, it was either you or the Boston Strangler.'

Jimmy, lying in the bracken at the edge of the wood, appeared to give the alternative possibility some serious thought. 'Well, it couldn't have been *him*,' he said finally and came to sit beside Duffy on the bench. 'Damn,' he repeated.

'Sorry if I spoiled it.'

'No, you were quite right. Tell you what, why don't you try following me now?'

'Maybe not today, Jimmy. I've got to mend the alarm.'

'Oh, right. Did you find what you wanted?'

'What I wanted?'

'Yes.' At the top of his head Jimmy's bald pate fell away, and at the bottom his chin fell away, but in between his slightly popping eyes were fixed firmly on Duffy. Don't assume he's as thick as he's painted, Duffy thought. 'What you wanted. In the shed.'

'Not unless there was a dead dog in there I missed.'

'Oh. Right.'

'Have you been looking for him?'

'Who?'

'Ricky.'

'No. Why?'

'Oh,' said Duffy, 'I just thought that if we could find him, between the two of us, say, we could give him a proper burial. Seems a bit unfair that first he gets killed and then he disappears. I'm sure Angela would appreciate it.'

'See what you mean,' said Jimmy. 'That's something I could get on to. Not much happens in these woods that gets past old Jimmy.'

Duffy nodded conspiratorially, happy that Jimmy had bought the feed so quickly. There was no point Duffy tramping through the woods and looking for freshly moved mounds of earth and getting nettled and bitten and stung when old Jimmy could do it for him. Perhaps being in Vic's house infected you with Vic's philosophy: sub-contract, never do the work if some prat will do it for you, and if it all comes to nothing, well, mugs will be mugs, won't they?

'I suppose Angela's pretty cut up about this business,' said Duffy after a pause.

'She's a grand girl,' Jimmy replied, 'she's a grand girl.' Whether or not this was intended as an answer to the question, Duffy could only guess.

'You've, um, you're obviously, um, fond of her.'

'Loved her for years,' said Jimmy, 'loved her for years. Poor old Jimmy. Nothing doing there. Washing her car, that's all I'm good for. Not bright enough. Not that women mind that,' he commented ruminatively. 'No oil painting, either. Not that women mind that. No money. Not that women mind that. No prospects. Not that women mind that. I suppose what women mind is the combination of all four. Poor old Jimmy.'

'That's tough,' said Duffy. He wondered if washing her car also included other duties. Running up to London for things to keep her merry, for instance.

'Will she be happy with Henry?'

'Got money – doesn't need prospects,' said Jimmy rather bitterly.

'What's Henry like?'

Jimmy considered the question at some length, gazing across the lawn to the distant glint of the lake. 'He's all right if you like people like him,' he said finally.

'Check.'

They sat on the bench for a while longer. Then Duffy had another thought.

'I suppose you can probably swim.'

'Rather.'

'Probably got a snorkel and some flippers.'

'Rather.' Jimmy looked across at Duffy, then followed his gaze towards the lake. 'Right. Yes. Good thinking.' He stood up. 'Enjoyed the chinwag.'

'Oh, and Jimmy?'

'Yes?'

'Mum's the word.'

Jimmy paused in his departure and half-wheeled back towards Duffy. 'You know I often wonder why people say that. My mum talked *all the bloody time*.'

At that moment a gong summoned them in to lunch. Duffy felt uneasy throughout the meal. When he looked at Jimmy, he half-expected him to blurt out their plan of combing the woods and the waters for Ricky's corpse. When he looked at Lucretia, he wondered if last night's plan of reading posh magazines to impress her could possibly have been serious. When he saw Mrs Hardcastle passing another bottle of Vinho Verde to Damian, he wondered if what he'd seen meant what he thought it meant. And when he looked at Damian receiving the bottle, he wasn't sure what he felt. Embarrassment? Disapproval? Nausea? And what, for that matter, did last night's little incident suggest about Damian's sexual preference? Was his little game hetero or homosexual, randy or contemptuous? Perhaps neither; perhaps it was just a moment's sport which laughed at sex, which said it was about as serious as snooker. He could try asking Sally, except she was probably too smashed at the time to notice.

Whatever Damian felt about it all, embarrassment wasn't at the top of the list. When he caught Duffy's eye on him, he

605

looked straight back and said, 'By the way, you won't forget our little game tonight?'

'Game?'

'You promised me a couple of frames.'

'I did?'

'I assumed that was why you were creeping around the house late last night in your frightful dressing-gown. Wanting to get in some practice before the big match.'

'That's my dressing-gown, actually,' said Vic.

'Oh dear,' said Damian brightly. 'Foot in mouth time again for Damian. All I can say is, I bet it looks *much* more fetching on you, my dear Vic.'

'You could talk your way out of a roped sack,' said Vic.

'I'd just *thcream*,' said Damian. 'Thcream and thcream.'

After lunch Duffy was working in the video library fixing the new pressure plate – well, at least some part of the overhaul could be authentic – when he heard the door open. He looked up and saw Sally. She was either still pissed from lunch or starting her aperitifs early for dinner; or perhaps she'd mixed some private cocktail of her own.

'Thought I'd find you in here,' she said, half falling on to the sofa. 'Got an apology, you know.' She giggled as if apologies were almost as funny as jokes. 'Let down your tyres.'

'You?'

'Yeah. Sorry, right? Well, it wasn't my idea. Damian said why don't we let down his tyres, you do the ones on that side I'll do the ones on this side, but by the time I'd done mine he'd buggered back into the house. Said he thought he heard someone coming.'

'Why did you do it?'

'Seemed like a good idea. Fun. Sorry, right?' She turned her head to one side and her heavy black curls flopped round the side of her face. Clearly, she was bored with apology now.

'By the way,' said Duffy, trying to keep his voice in neutral, 'I should take your shoes off next time.'

'Next time? I wouldn't do it again. It wouldn't be worth it. Anyway, you'd guess it was us.'

'Not the van. The snooker table. Heels are bad for the cloth.'

She paused, thought, and remembered the previous night as if it had been a month ago. 'Oh, right.' Now that she was clear what they were talking about, she began to laugh again. 'I'll take them off next time. Ooh, those balls were cold.'

'You shouldn't do things like that,' said Duffy. He hadn't meant to say it, he'd wanted to stay cool. It had just slipped out. Anyway, he meant it.

'Do what I like,' she replied sulkily.

'You shouldn't let . . . *him* do things like that to you.'

'Oh, you mean, like he won't respect me?' Duffy grunted. 'You're neolithic, you know that, neolithic. Anyway, what makes you think I want to be respected?' Duffy hadn't quite meant that, but he couldn't find the words for exactly what he did mean. 'It's fun,' she added listlessly.

Duffy thought it didn't matter too much what he said to this girl; she probably wouldn't remember anyway. 'You shouldn't drink so much.'

'It's fun,' she replied.

'It's not fun for others.'

'You're the first to complain, Mr Neolithic.'

'And you shouldn't take whatever it is you're taking.'

'It's fun,' Sally said, 'it's fun, it's fun, it's *fun*. It's not fun here any more. No fun with you. How old are you anyway?'

'Old enough to be your brother.'

'Then don't come on like my fucking father, right?' She screamed this last part.

'Right.'

Sally stomped off, and Duffy carried on wiring up the pressure plate. He felt depressed. It was always the same problem. The same problem whether you were at Braunscombe Hall or in the back alleys behind some South London comprehensive where the crime figures were higher than the national average. Duffy had still been a copper when the first scares about glue-sniffing had started up. Kids putting their heads in plastic bags and sniffing away at solvents. It sounded like a really dumb thing to do. Duffy had read all the reports in the papers. Glue-sniffing gave you headaches, it gave you sores round your nose, it made you apathetic. It made you do badly at school and it screwed up your home life because all you were thinking about was getting outside with the plastic bag and the aerosol. And that was just the start. The end was that you OD'd on solvent. You died. Kids of ten, twelve, thirteen dead on the streets, and all their own work. Duffy couldn't fathom it. You blame the parents, you blame the teachers, you blame the shopkeepers who ought to know better than to sell the stuff to users, and you blame the kids themselves. But after all this blaming, you still don't understand.

Duffy had wanted to understand, and one day he'd found a couple of kids in an alley who hadn't run away from him. He wasn't a teacher, he wasn't a social worker, and they weren't old enough or canny enough yet to smell a copper. He got round to asking them why they did it. Fun, they said. What sort of fun? Different sorts of fun, they said. Fun looking forward to it, for a start: you never knew what was going to come out of that bag when you sniffed. And what did? All sorts of things, they said. Sometimes you saw things, like giant frogs jumping over the houses, that was magic. And you hear great winds rushing around you but you're not cold, and you see colours, fantastic colours, and you feel good, you feel good. It's fun. What's it like after? It's not so good after. You come down, and it's not so good. But there's always the next time. It's fun.

That's what you don't want to accept, thought Duffy, but that's what you've got to. They do it because it's fun, whether it's behind some railings with a plastic bag in the rain or whether it's in a comfortable toilet, sorry lavatory, on the Buckinghamshire/Bedfordshire borders. It seems to you that the fun they get can't be worth it, you can see that it can't be worth it. To them it is worth it. You can call it addiction if you like, but you mustn't duck the other truth: they do it because it's fun.

⬤

'Belinda.'
    'Just hold her a minute.'
    '*Hold* her? Where?'

'Not by the tail, you berk. *There.*'

Duffy got hold of one of the metal bits with leather attached which in his view were altogether too close to the horse's mouth and held on. Christ, they were big, horses. Much bigger than on the telly. A huge eye bulged at him; a colossal vein ran down the snout; lips like sofa cushions pulled back to reveal vast yellow teeth. Why did they need such big teeth if all they ate was grass?

'Thanks,' said Belinda. Duffy nearly shook his head to clear his ears. Had she said thanks? Had he done something right at last?

She had slipped to the ground while he held the horse – or rather, while he stood there and the horse very decently decided not to run away – then took charge of it. She led the way into a stable and indicated that they could talk while she gave the horse a rub-down, or a shampoo, or whatever people did after riding. Duffy stood apprehensively just inside the horse's two-part front door. That was the other thing about stables: they reeked of horse-shit.

'How's Angela?'

'Fine.'

'How's Angela?'

'She's taking rather too many anti-depressants. She's up and down all the time. Most nights she comes in and sleeps with us. She's very apathetic. And she doesn't take any bloody exercise at all.'

'She sleeps with you?'

'Not the way your perverted mind assumes. There's a bed – well, it's a sort of large cot, really, in our room, and when she's feeling bad she just comes in, doesn't even wake us usually, and climbs into it. Find her in the morning sleeping like a child.'

'Do you think she's . . .'

'. . . a danger to herself, as the doctors put it? I can't say. Got it wrong twice before, didn't we? She's my oldest mate – well, my oldest mate down here – but I don't know what's going on inside her.'

'Who do you think's trying to tip her over?'

'No idea.'

'But you think someone is?'

'Could be.'

'Does she have anyone – I dunno, anyone who's mad at her?'

'Not that I've heard.'

'Old boyfriends? Someone she's jilted?'

Belinda stopped rubbing down the horse and laughed. '*Jilt*? I haven't heard that word in years. You mean, someone she's stopped screwing?'

'Well, it's a bit more than that, I suppose.'

'What, gave him back his engagement ring, that stuff?' She laughed again. 'No, Angela hasn't *jilted* anyone.'

'Is she OK for money?'

'As far as I know she's still comfortable.'

'And what about Henry?' Duffy had only glimpsed him briefly so far, a large, square-faced county fellow with clothes Duffy wouldn't have been seen dead in.

'What about him?'

'Well, for instance, is she in love with him?'

'I hope you're better at fixing alarm systems than you are at asking questions. Jilted? In love? Look, Duffy, if you're a girl, and you're thirty . . . thirty something, shall we say, and you're falling apart at the seams, and you've never even had an engagement ring on your finger before, and the chap is presentable and he's got a farm and he comes from an old family, then you're in love.'

'Is that what it is? And what's it like for the chap?'

'See what you mean. Crafty little girl and all that. Well, what it's like for the chap is this. If you're a chap, and you're forty-three, and you're still living at home with your mum who isn't very keen on being left alone, and you don't have the greatest track record with the girls in green wellies and headscarves, and you don't really have any friends that anyone knows about, and all of a sudden you meet this sexy girl who isn't married to someone else, who's got a bit of money and actually doesn't mind moving in and living with your old mum after you're married, and she knows how to drive a car, then you're in love.'

'I think I get it,' said Duffy. 'And then they'll have babies and live happily ever after?'

'I don't know if they'll have babies,' said Belinda. 'They'll have to get a move on if they're going to. And they'll live as happily ever after as anyone else.'

'Meaning?'

'Meaning you can't tell beforehand. After a while it's not a question of love, as you like to put it, but stamina.'

'Like the three-day event?'

Belinda looked up across the horse's back in surprise. 'Very good, Duffy. Where did you get to hear about three-day eventing?'

'I must have seen it on the telly.' He remembered a big country house somewhere and lots of men with flat caps and shooting-sticks. There'd been Land Rovers everywhere, riders falling off at the water-jump, and a commentator whose tongue sounded as if it was wearing a flat cap and was supported in his mouth by a shooting-stick.

'There's nothing wrong with my alarm system, anyway,' he said suddenly. He didn't want people passing the news on.

'No. Right. Vic told me.'

'So don't go around saying so.'

'I thought that's what we had to pretend?'

'Well, don't say it like it wasn't a big surprise to you when it went wrong.'

'OK.'

At that moment they heard a loud and regular noise on the gravel, a sort of thumping, not like the sound of someone walking. Belinda came across the stable and stood at the half-door with Duffy. Someone was marching across the drive-way. Someone, what's more, in a wet suit, with flippers on his feet and a mask on his face. Someone carrying a snorkel under his left arm like a swagger stick. Jimmy. He noticed Duffy and Belinda standing at the stable door but didn't break step. Instead he yelled, 'Special Boat Squadron . . . Eyes . . . *right*' and snapped his head across on his neck. When he had passed them he eyes-fronted again and disappeared on to the quiet grass in the direction of the lake. Duffy wanted to laugh but Belinda looked serious. No, perhaps it wasn't funny. And perhaps poor old Jimmy had really thought about it. If you want to dive in the lake secretly, how do you do it? By diving in the lake obviously. Maybe he's been reading Sherlock Holmes.

'And Taffy?'

'What about Taffy? He's a house guest.' She said it with considerably more ease than Vic did.

'Mrs Hardcastle says the cutlery's going missing.'

'Duffy, number one, Taffy is our friend, number two, Taffy is a reformed character, number three, if Taffy was still into nicking, he'd go for the Range Rover or the house or something, not the spoons.'

'Right.' Unless he couldn't get it out of his system. Unless he was just keeping his hand in. No, that wasn't very likely.

Duffy left Belinda, thinking she wasn't necessarily as bad as he'd imagined, in fact quite a bit less bad, and went in search of Vic. When he'd been given the directions he needed, he set off round the back of the house, dodged behind a hedge, and slowly worked his way towards the wood. As he tiptoed cautiously up the path, expecting everything that wasn't obviously a nettle to be a camouflaged nettle, he wondered about Taffy. Just a house guest. Quiet, polite, a bit boring, liked to talk about the individual's relationship to society, looked like a weekend jazz-player. Fine, except that he had a habit of beating people up and braining screws with iron bars. This, of course, was precisely what gave him his social pull. It was well known that London café society welcomed major criminals, so why shouldn't country society welcome minor villains who'd once made the front page for a couple of weeks? In the words of his host, England had become a place where your Vics could mix with your Damians, and your Damians could hob-nob with your Hugos. Why shouldn't your Taffys rub shoulders with your Vics, your Damians and your Hugos? Besides, it wasn't just about social mobility. Crime was sexy. This was another truth that Duffy, as an ex-copper, found it difficult but necessary to accept. Drugs were fun and crime was sexy; not always, but often enough. You read about East End villains splashing around in pink champagne at those restaurants written up by Basil Berk in the *Tatler*. You read about

– you'd even seen – ex-cons (as long as they were really violent ex-cons who'd really scared people) pulling girls as easy as shelling peas. It wasn't fair, Duffy thought. Why weren't coppers sexy?

What a way to spend a Bank Holiday Monday afternoon. The path had got steeper suddenly, and the bracken thicker. Vic had said there was a bit where the path seemed to go straight on but there was a little nick in a beech tree and a track you normally wouldn't notice off to the left. Was that a beech tree? Was that a nick? Was that a track? If only he'd been in the Boy Scouts. He'd probably need to know a few posh knots before the week was out, and how to light a fire by rubbing two Girl Guides together.

This seemed to be the place. Vic had said you had to go past and then look back, otherwise you'd never notice it. Yes, there it was. Even Duffy could appreciate that Jimmy's camp, though only ten minutes from the house, was well hidden. The leaves on the ground gave way beneath him like posh carpet, and he approached the hide with caution. He had a sudden memory from a kids' book, or maybe the cinema, of the sort of traps Red Indians or Africans or whoever used: all of a sudden the ground gave way, you fell ten feet and got a sharpened stake up the bum. You lay there like a piece of meat on a kebab stick until the locals turned up, piled lots of wood around you, and had you for dinner. Duffy! Duffy! That's enough. Even so, he half-wondered, as he approached Jimmy's camp, whether he shouldn't have a long stick with him, and be poking at the leaves as he walked.

It wasn't exactly a camp, more a sort of hide from which you watched birds, or a place thrown up for the night by a particularly tidy soldier in a war film. A large piece of tarpaulin had been stretched over stakes at a point where the ground shelved away; bracken and stuff had been piled on the roof. It didn't at the moment look particularly concealed – there was even a patch of burnt earth by the front door where a fire had presumably been – but it looked as if it could be very concealed if necessary. Duffy dodged sideways down the slope for a closer examination.

The hide was about eight feet long and consisted of two

rooms. Not that there was a division between them; it was just that six feet of the space was clearly the bedroom, and the other two the kitchen and bathroom. At one end was a bedroll wrapped in a sheet of polythene and staked to the ground. At the other Duffy found a small primus stove, various square green tins and a mirror. He opened the tins: shaving equipment, canned food, a few bits of biltong wrapped in foil, and some cutlery. Not, however, the cutlery that had taken a walk from Braunscombe Hall; only one of those knife-fork-and-spoon sets with a screw through the middle to hold it all together.

In a corner of the sleeping section, by the bedroll, was another row of green tins. Bedside reading, thought Duffy facetiously. In the first tin he found a small paraffin lamp; in the second a large jar of presumably paraffin plus a small jar of what smelt like methylated spirits; in the next three copies of *Playboy* wrapped in a polythene bag. He looked at the date: they were several years old. The fourth tin he nearly put the lid back on as soon as he'd flipped it open: what business was it of his? Well, you could never tell what might turn out to be business. On top lay a photograph of a small boy with a receding chin; he was dressed in some uniform, maybe Boys' Brigade. Next came proof that the child hadn't changed much fifteen or twenty years later, by which time he was in a grown-up uniform, that of the Army. Then a much older photo of someone's wedding: a smiling bride, a severe groom, looking from their lapels and hairstyles as if it were just after the war. Jimmy's parents, presumably. Underneath was a picture which Duffy had no trouble in identifying: Angela, with large eyes looking away from the camera, and what smelt like a bit of touching-up around the jaw. Clearly a studio job; Duffy flipped it over, but the photographer hadn't bothered to stamp the print. Finally, a clipping from a newspaper which puzzled Duffy until he read the caption: only then did he realize that it was a story from the local *Mail & Advertiser* about Henry and Angela's engagement. He hadn't been able to grasp this at first because the clipping was punctured by several dozen circular burns. The sort of burns you make with a cigarette at the end of an evening when you've only a four-year-old copy of *Playboy* to tuck up with. Duffy stared at the tortured photo and found an extra reason why it worried him: the burns obliterated not only Henry's face, but also Angela's.

When he emerged from the wood, having miraculously managed to avoid the bear-traps, the killer spiders and the Iroquois, he wandered to the lake's edge. A gesture brought Jimmy swimming over to the bank. He stood up, water streaming from his wetsuit, and raised his mask. He was better-looking with his head all swathed in rubber.

'Any sign of Ricky?'

Jimmy shook his head. 'Nothing.'

'Must be lying doggo,' said Duffy.

'I don't think that's funny.' Jimmy pulled down his mask, adjusted his snorkel, turned and trudged back into the lake.

'No, maybe it isn't,' Duffy muttered to himself.

He lay on his bed waiting for the dinner gong with a copy of the *Tatler* open at the society pages. Miss Olivia Fartface marrying the Hon. Peregrine Pokerupthebum, the couple to take over the ancestral home at Much Gelding where he will live off inherited wealth and she will bear a royal flush of laughing children fit only for the finest schools. Duffy wondered idly about the joke he'd made to Belinda: marriage as a three-day event. Maybe it wasn't a bad comparison. It started with that section where the horses were all got up to look their best. What was it? Dressage, that's right. They skittered around on tiptoe, all primped and shiny, doing very formal manoeuvres ever so tidily. That was like the courtship part. Then there was the main bit, the cross-country. None of that pointing the toe and looking good, you just ran, or cantered if that's what they called it, out across the open country, and that was fun and a release, except that every so often there'd be these hurdles you had to get over, some of which were pretty steep, and there were great muddy banks with water at the bottom of them, and you might be inclined, if you'd had enough, to throw your rider. What's more, it went on and on, this cross-country bit, miles and miles of it. Finally, it was over, and they took you back to your stable and you had your dinner, and thought you'd done pretty well – or if not well, at least you'd done your duty. Then the next day, just when you were thinking about putting your four legs up, they took you out again and made you jump all these obstacles, even though you were really knackered. And all you did in the show-jumping was lose points. You never gained points at this stage, you only lost them.

Was it like that? It looked a bit like it from the outside. Duffy had never tried marriage, never been tempted by the three-day event. Of course, having quite a spell of being queer hadn't improved his chances. Or, if not being entirely queer, at least walking both sides of the street. Had he ever been in love? He wasn't sure. Well, if he wasn't sure, he couldn't have been, could he? He remembered how he'd felt about Carol when they'd first started going around together; he'd felt as if he was beginning to understand things, and as if there'd always be something for dinner. Was that love? Maybe you called it this because you reckoned it was the best you were going to get. Maybe Belinda had been right to laugh at him. In the real world you married not for love but because some-one else would have you, because there was someone out there who could bear to be with you, and because if you didn't you were lost. Perhaps he ought to phone Carol.

Instead of phoning Carol, he flipped back a few pages in the *Tatler* until he got to the restaurant column. What was Basil Berk writing about this month? Duffy read the page with rising incredulity. Call this a job? You went along to some wallies' rendezvous – in the present case one of three fish restaurants in Chelsea – had a jolly good nosh-up, took Lady Berk along with you, copied down the menu, made up some joke or other and pretended Lady Berk had said it to you across the fish-knives and went on to the next restaurant. And the prices . . . You could get seven good dinners at Sam Widges for the price of a single fish snack in Chelsea.

He threw down the magazine and yomped to the nearest lavatory. Then he went downstairs and into the family room. Lucretia was in her accustomed position on the sofa, blonde hair cascading down the back of it, cigarette and watered whisky on the go. She nodded expressionlessly at Duffy. He sat in a chair opposite her and found himself, rather to his surprise, clearing his throat. He was almost as surprised by what he said next.

'I find the sauce is very good at the Poison d'Or.'

'What?'

'I find the sauce is very good at the Poison d'Or.'

'The what?'

'The sauce. The way they put saffron in it.' (Had he got that right?) 'It's very nice.'

'Where's this?'

'The Poison d'Or.'

'Now,' said Lucretia briskly, 'after me. *Poisson. Poisson.*' As she said the words her lips parted and then came together in a way that was really very, well, nice, Duffy thought.

'Poisson.'

'*Poisson. Poisson.*'

'Poisson.'

Lucretia gave him that half-smile which made him wish he could somehow get her to give him the full version. 'Promise me one thing. Don't ever go into a French restaurant and ask for the fish, all right?'

'Promise.' He looked at her. 'How did I do?'

'You're funny, you know that? You are funny.'

Was that good in her book? Either way, Duffy felt a little less out of his league with this girl. He was about to turn the conversation suavely on to topics of wider interest – like whether she enjoyed horses and had she ever been for a ride in a Sherpa van – when there was a commotion at the door. Jimmy ran into the room, with dripping hair, though fortunately no longer in his wet suit, and stood between the two of them, his back to Lucretia, and winking furiously at Duffy.

After about a dozen of these facial contortions Duffy finally got the message.

'Oh, er, excuse me, Lucretia.' Silent, she waved a hand at him in dismissal.

Excitedly, Jimmy led him round the house to a bit of undergrowth by the lake. There, by a discarded wet suit and a pair of flippers, lay a blue plastic laundry-bag with a tail sticking out of it. The handles were tied together.

'Had to cut the string,' said Jimmy. 'Probably tied round a stone or something. Couldn't bring that up as well, though.'

'Great stuff,' said Duffy, and clapped Jimmy firmly on the shoulder. It wasn't at all the sort of phrase or gesture that came naturally to Duffy, but he supposed he ought to speak Jimmy's language. The snorkeller beamed, and began to explain in more detail than was necessary how he'd divided the lake up into sections with markers on the bank and removed each marker as he cleared each section. Duffy heard him out and at the end repeated, 'Great stuff.'

'Ange will be pleased, won't she?'

'I'm sure she will, Jimmy. But perhaps we won't tell her immediately.'

'Oh.' His face fell, which was easy given its shape.

'You see, I've been thinking.'

'Right.' Jimmy seemed to fall in with Duffy's idea even before it was explained to him, as if anyone who had been thinking automatically deserved respect and obedience.

'The point is, someone threw Ricky into the lake because they didn't want Angela to bury him. Maybe they didn't want us to have a good look at him. And whoever did it can't be that far away. So, if we just tell everyone about it, the same thing could happen all over again. Ricky would go for walkies. Permanently, this time.'

Jimmy was nodding slowly. 'So?'

'Well, I suggest we put him in a safe place for a bit. Until we can think about what to do.' Duffy had already thought about what to do.

'Where's a safe place?'

'Well, my van, for instance.'

'Is that safe?'

'Well, it says DUFFY SECURITY on the side, it ought to be.'

'Is it alarmed?'

'No, it isn't as a matter of fact.'

'Righty-ho, well I'll leave it in your capables.'

Jimmy picked up the wet suit and flippers. Duffy belted him on the shoulder in congratulation once again, and he headed off towards the house. Duffy, the laundry-bag in one hand, worked his way stealthily round Braunscombe Hall until he crossed the driveway at a point two-thirds of the way to the stone balls with the salamander on top. There he left Ricky in a ditch. He jogged back to the house, climbed into his van, and set off down the drive. He returned after ten minutes, which was longer than necessary. Ricky was safe; but Ricky was not in the back of his van.

The gong had gone by the time he returned, and everyone was seated round the refectory table.

'Been putting in some practice?' asked Damian.

'Eh?'

'Been making pretty patterns on the green baize in antici-pation of our nocturnal showdown?'

'No. I've been checking the van.'

'You know,' said Damian, again managing his trick of addressing the whole table while excluding Duffy, 'it always amazes me that the lower classes have taken to snooker with such ferocity.'

'Why's that?' asked Vic. He could tell when Damian needed to be stoked up with the obvious question.

'Glad you asked. Because it's so élitist. I mean, can you imagine, some of the balls are actually more valuable than others. The black's always worth seven, the pink's always worth six, and the poor little reds are only worth one point each. It's like people having more money than one another, not just for a bit but for always. I bet if this was *Russia*,' he said emphatically, '*all* the balls would be red, and *all* of them would be worth one point each. You'd probably prefer that, wouldn't you, Duffy?'

'It wouldn't be such a good game,' he replied. Don't let him rile you, he thought; don't let him rile you now, and don't let him do it on the table either.

'But it would be more democratic, wouldn't it?'

'I don't think that's relevant,' said Duffy.

'He isn't going to rise,' put in Lucretia.

'That's your problem, sweetie, not mine,' said Damian. Sally giggled violently at this, and Jimmy looked blank.

Henry was at dinner that night, and Duffy was able to get his first good look at him. He was large, square-headed and fleshy, with big red hands and a mouth that turned down at the corners; he looked straight at you when you addressed him, but still seemed to keep something in reserve. He wore a farmer's jacket with a check big enough for even a myopic noughts-and-crosses player to be able to manage, and a yellow silk handkerchief cascaded out of his top pocket; the same spotted bow-tie continued to clash with the same Viyella shirt. He didn't say much, not even to Angela, though when she addressed him he would turn slowly towards her and beam in a benign sort of way. Duffy thought he looked just right for the green-wellies brigade; which was perhaps why Angela had come as such a bright surprise to him. Angela, for her part, seemed calmer in his presence; neither hyped-up nor apathetic, but more or less normal, which was probably as normal as she got.

Occasionally, Damian would address the odd remark to Henry, as if trying to bring him into the conversation. 'Dipped many sheep today, Henry?' he would ask brightly, whereupon Henry would reply, 'It's not the time of year for that. You dip sheep . . .' but before he could tell Damian when you dipped sheep, his interlocutor had gone on with, 'Well, you must have shot some pheasant then?' And as Henry started up again explaining that no, he hadn't done that either, Damian danced off to another topic.

Duffy thought this a bit unfair, and at one point turned to Henry and did his best with, 'Have you got a large farm, Henry?' but Henry wasn't allowed to answer. ' "How many acres have you got?" is the better way to phrase it, Duffy,' cut in Damian, 'but that's a boring question anyway, because everyone but you knows the answer to it already, so why don't you stick it down your jumper until you're alone with Henry and ask him then. I do think conversation over dinner ought to involve as many people as possible.'

'Are you always like this?' asked Duffy.

'Like what, like what?' Damian was expectant.

'Do you always go on like a prat?'

'Ah, aaah,' Damian moaned. 'Stabbed. A poniard in the vitals. Such a turn of phrase, such a pretty turn of phrase.'

'Knock it off, kids,' said Vic.

After dinner Damian tried to get everyone to watch the

Braunscombe Hall snooker final, but something about his jocular over-enthusiasm – 'Roll up, girls, and listen to the clic..ing of balls' – seemed to put people off. Vic and Belinda went to bed; so did Angela; Taffy went off to watch a television programme hosted by a female rabbi about whether or not we choose to do evil; and Lucretia disappeared without explanation. Duffy was a bit disappointed by this. Still, maybe when she was next in town she'd like to watch him play in goal for the Western Sunday Reliables; she probably enjoyed football.

So it was only Henry and Sally, sitting at opposite ends of the pink chintz sofa, who watched Duffy break off – none of this fancy stuff, just a normal prod with a touch of right-hand side – in the best-of-five Braunscombe Hall snooker final. When Damian offered a little bet, Duffy replied, 'I should have thought the satisfaction of winning was enough.' When Damian started chatting to Sally, Duffy suggested that such conversation as there might be should only be about the frame in progress and not about whether Petronella Pipedream's Pimms Party was on Tuesday or Wednesday. When Damian left his cube of blue cue chalk on the rail, Duffy pointed this out as a breach of etiquette and asked him to remove it before his next shot. Duffy played it very cool, and he also played it carefully, suspecting that Damian was one of these players who might auto-destruct when under the cosh.

Sally retired to bed, or so she said, but maybe it was just for more supplies, when Damian was leading two frames to one. Despite the fact that Angela must now have been alone between the sheets for almost an hour and a half, Henry stuck solidly on the pink chintz. Duffy pulled back the fourth frame with the help of a canny bout of snookering, but was always behind in the fifth. By the end, he needed blue, pink and black to win, and his attempted safety shot on the blue sent the white rolling gently into the middle pocket. 'In–off,' cried Damian for the second successive evening in Duffy's hearing. Duffy racked his cue as an admission of defeat. '*Must* tell Sally,' said Damian. 'Excuse me for a little gloat.'

All through the match Henry had sat silently. You couldn't tell from his expression whether he could follow what was going on in front of him or not. Now he rose, picked the longest cue from the rack, put the white back on the table, and said, 'I think you're not staying down on the shot long enough.' He mimed the little head-jerk which Duffy knew was an all-too-frequent feature of his cue action; indeed, he played the same shot twice for Duffy's benefit, missing the pot on the blue by a couple of inches when using the special Duffy head-twitch, and rolling it home without touching the sides of the pocket while using his own personal set-in-concrete head-positioning. Then he potted a long and difficult pink, and followed it by doubling the black the length of the table into the top pocket.

'You're very good,' said Duffy. 'You must play a lot.'

'Billiards. Billiards with Daddy from an early age. Never really played snooker. Daddy thought snooker was a degenerate game.'

'Played by yobs,' suggested Duffy.

'No, not that. It was more that the game itself decided how long it went on. Daddy thought billiards was a gentleman's game because the players decided how long it lasted. More subtle, too, of course.'

'Anything else apart from the head?' asked Duffy.

'I think you're holding the cue too far back. Small chaps often do. The forearm isn't hanging vertically enough.'

'Anything else?'

'I think you should have gone for the first frame more. The first frame's vital.'

'I know. I was going for it.'

'Oh well.'

They sat on the sofa, Duffy still wondering what Henry was doing downstairs. It must be nearly half-past eleven.

'How's Angela?'

'She's fine.'

Why did everyone keep saying that to him. 'She's fine.' Did they think he was an idiot? Or were they just telling him to mind his own business?

'The Ricky thing must have upset her.'

'Ricky was a lovely dog,' said Henry, not quite answering the question.

'Was he Angela's or yours, or both of yours?'

'No, he was hers. Mind you, he was everybody's around here. They all loved him. Sally loved him, too.'

'Sally?'

'Yes, I should think she took him for walks as often as Ange did. Probably more often.'

'Damian?'

'I don't see Damian as a dog-walker.'

'Check.' There was a pause. The evening was coming to its end. 'Well,' said Duffy, turning to Henry in what he hoped would sound like a jolly male stag-night tone, 'Only a couple more weeks before you tie the old knot. Can't be too soon, I shouldn't think.' Duffy wondered if he should elaborate his new theory of marriage as three-day eventing, but thought it might not be appropriate, or at any rate might take too long.

Henry didn't react for a while, then smiled distantly and got up. 'Oh well, Mother calls.' He clapped Duffy on the shoulder for no obvious reason, then shook his hand, grinning all the while. Duffy was left alone in the snooker room, practising a few shots and supposing it was normal that Henry went home to his mother instead of staying with his girlfriend.

The next morning, over breakfast, Duffy made the noises he and Vic had planned about how he had to go down to London to get some pieces of equipment for the alarm system which were obviously unobtainable on the Buckinghamshire/ Bedfordshire borders. He might be back that night or he might not. One thing he'd make sure to bring with him, he thought as he crossed the gravel, was his own dressing-gown. Not that he worried about Damian. In fact, if he had any sense he'd forget about Damian altogether. Three–two. Damn. If only he hadn't been over-ambitious on that long red in the final frame and let old Waggly-Nose in for a break of twenty-two. Perhaps he should get some practice. That was a thought. Maybe when he got back to London he'd call the local hustler and get himself seriously beaten.

He walked casually round his white Sherpa van, inspecting it with care. At least Sally hadn't retired early last night in order to let down his other two tyres. He examined the locks and the join of the rear doors to see if anyone had tried

623

inserting a metal instrument and wrenching. No sign of anything. Well, this proved one negative at least: that Jimmy had kept quiet about finding Ricky. The Sherpa started at the second touch, and Duffy drove off taking a deep breath. Perhaps he'd wind the window down, swear a lot, play some junky music on the radio, and stop off at a motorway caff for some real food of the sort that would make Basil Berk throw up all over Lady Berk.

First, though, he had to retrieve Ricky. Duffy turned off the road a couple of minutes east of Braunscombe Hall, and went up a quiet track still marked by his tyres from last night. Blue plastic was quite a vivid colour, so he'd carefully piled a few branches and lots of bracken on top. Such a brilliant piece of camouflage he almost missed it. Go on like this, Duffy, and you'll get your woodcraft badge. He picked up the laundry-bag and put it in the back of his van. Ricky was already beginning to pong a bit and some of the hair had fallen out of his tail. Duffy wondered if he'd better stop and grab himself a hamburger with lots of extra onions just to make the van smell nice.

When he got back to the flat he made a few telephone calls. There wasn't anywhere obvious you could go – Yellow Pages weren't any help – but eventually he tracked down someone from his past, someone from forensics who'd always done a bit of freelancing. Then he drove to an address in Kensington near the Natural History Museum and handed over the laundry-bag. He recognized Jim Pringle at once, while noting that he was losing his hair almost as fast as Ricky.

'Sorry about the smell,' said Duffy.

'You should take something for that, you know. Might start interfering with your social life otherwise.'

'Check.' Jim was always like that. Didn't mind who he said what to, either. Perhaps that was why he hadn't had the promotion he deserved. Still taking in laundry after all these years.

Duffy explained what he wanted, asked Jim not to make too much of a mess, in case Ricky had to be returned to the grieving widow, and left a couple of telephone numbers. As he turned to go, Jim said, 'Do you want him stuffed as well?'

'Eh?'

'Stuffed. Stuffed and mounted. I could do you an all-in price. The thing is, if you've got to cut him open anyway . . .'

'Jim, I'll get back to you.'

'It'd be cheaper if I knew now.'

Back at the flat, he opened the freezer to see if Carol had eaten the fish with the low-calorie sauce. No. She must have eaten the pizzas, then. No. What had she been eating? Where? Who with? She'd been seeing that Robert Redford again and that Paul Newman and that Steve McQueen . . . No, he was dead, she wouldn't have been eating at the Poison d'Or with Steve McQueen. Duffy's brain skedaddled off on its usual track of mild paranoia. Look, if he had rights, she had rights . . . Sure, sure. And if you don't have to tell, she doesn't have to tell . . . Sure, sure. And if it doesn't mean anything serious for you and doesn't affect the relationship, it's the same for her, too . . . Sure, sure. I just want to know why she didn't eat the fish in the low-calorie sauce.

'You didn't eat the fish,' he said rather sharply when Carol walked in.

'Been having an affair with Paul Newman, haven't I?'

'Why didn't you eat the fish?'

Carol was tired. It had been a long shift, and there'd been that midday alkie. You'd have thought daytime drunks would have had less of a skinful than evening drunks; that they'd be less belligerent. But they weren't, and she'd had to radio for assistance. She didn't like having to do that, not in a crowded street, anyway. She kicked off her shoes and fell on to the sofa. 'They're your rules, Duffy,' was all she said. 'Kiss?'

Sure, kiss. And they were his rules after all. Perhaps they ought to discuss things again. They hadn't done so for years, it seemed to him. But that's what they'd agreed. In the old days there'd been explanations and openness and No-you-just-go-ahead, but that hadn't worked. Then there'd been discussions and rules – the main rule being No Discussions. Had that worked better? Duffy kissed Carol again and she yawned, but politely, and he went to transfer some chicken Kiev from the freezer to the microwave.

'So how's old Vic doing?'

'Vic's doing all right for himself. Bum in the butter. Don't know where he gets the money from.'

'No one ever did. And how's Little Miss Tits?'

'Belinda. Very horsey. She'd be all hoity-toity if you called her that. You could say she's putting her front behind her.'

Carol laughed. 'Bet you thought that one up in the van on the way down.'

He had, too. 'You know me too well,' he said.

'It's not bad, knowing you too well, Duffy.'

He kept his head down and picked at his dinner. It tasted a bit funny to him. 'Do you think the sauce needs a touch more seasoning?'

'You what?'

'Do you think the sauce needs a touch more seasoning?'

This time Carol really laughed. Much louder than at his joke. She got up, went to the fridge and came back with a bottle of Heinz. 'Here, have some red stuff in it. That'll make it taste different.'

'Do you ever want to go to a really pricey restaurant?'

'If you'll take me, I'll go.'

'There are some nice fish restaurants in Chelsea.'

'Duffy, I think you've been mixing with too many Hooray Henries.'

He grunted. 'More like Hooray Nigels. Bit of a mixed bunch, really. Mind you, what's going on is a bit of a mixed bunch. We've got dead dogs, stolen spoons, blackmail except everyone's denying it, a bit of drugging except everyone's denying it. My main job is to see that someone gets married.'

'Don't they want to get married?'

'Sure.'

'Then what's the problem? Can't afford the ring?'

'No. Well . . . no.' That was another rule. Not to bring too much work home with you. Carol always obeyed that particular rule. Duffy was less good at it. 'Got beaten at snooker last night. Three–two. On the blue. I had this problem with my head . . .' Carol smiled, but Duffy didn't notice. Without specifically – or even generally – being asked, he talked her through each frame, describing the key shots, characterizing his opponent's style of game, discussing aloud

where he might have gone wrong. At one point she murmured, 'Sounds as if you deserved to win,' but the irony was
lost on him, and he explained, again with vivid detail, how
that was indeed more or less the case.

He packed a holdall, twice checking that he'd included his
towelling gown that came down to well below the knee, and
put it by the front door for the morning. As things turned
out, this was a sensible move. They went to bed early, but
Carol's encounter with the drunk had taken it out of her, as
perhaps too had Duffy's extended account of his snooker
match with Damian. She lay turned away from him, a heap
of dark curls on a pillow, all just visible in the orange burn of
a street light filtered through a curtain. Duffy was propped
on one elbow, smiling at her in the dark, when the telephone
rang.

'Get your arse up here, Duffy, and pronto.' It was Vic.

'What's happened?'

'Angela's disappeared.'

5. GROUNDS

Which did he prefer, the daytime drivers on the M1 or the night-time ones? It was like asking Carol whether she preferred tangling with an aggressive drunk in a crowded shopping street or in a deserted alley lit only by a smudge of sodium. There wasn't really much in it. Duffy joined the other half of the Le Mans 24-hour Race, with the maniacs driving just as fast and just as close, yawning away as the radio disgorged some disc jockey with a voice as smooth as yoghurt, and only shaking themselves awake again when their heads hit the steering wheel. He kept to a steady fifty-five, the same as in the daytime, but now found himself being shunted across into the slow lane. That told you something.

Vic was standing in the porch when Duffy arrived. 'Where've you been?' he grunted, adding wearily, 'Look what you've done to my gravel.'

'Have you found her?'

'No.'

'When did she go missing?'

'Don't know.'

'What do you mean you don't know?'

'We don't know when she went missing. No one *saw* her go missing.'

'When did you last see her?'

'Lunch.'

'When didn't she turn up?'

'Dinner.'

'Have you called anyone?'

'Only Henry. To see if she was there. She wasn't. He's here.'

'Who saw her last?'

'Everyone. At lunch.'

'Called the coppers?'

'You know me.'

'Right, we'll search the house.'

'We've searched it.'

'We'll search it again.'

They left Sally, Damian and Belinda having stiff drinks together in the kitchen. Vic, Henry, Jimmy, Taffy and Lucretia started in the not-quite Lord Mayor's wine-cellar. They looked in all the spaces large enough to contain Angela, then in all the spaces large enough to contain half of her. Duffy directed the other five and together they lifted sofas, turned over beds, climbed up to look on top of wardrobes, moved large industrial Hoovers, even – you had to be logical, however silly – opened the doors of grandfather clocks. By four o'clock they had established that Angela was not in the house – not unless she'd been dodging round them all the time. The others wanted to call it a day, but Duffy insisted that they carry on and clear the outbuildings. Partly they had to do it, and the sooner the better; partly, this was something he knew about, and doing it with Lucretia's eye on him wasn't entirely displeasing.

They shifted the horses to one side and poked around among their bedding. They looked through the garage and opened the boot of each car. They knocked up Mr and Mrs Hardcastle, who were awake anyhow, and apologetically rummaged through their cottage. In a criss-cross of flashlights they examined the coal bunker and the wood store. They got to the garden shed.

'This open?' asked Duffy rather gruffly. He hadn't told Vic about Ron Hardcastle having exactly the same taste in wine as his employer, and he wasn't sure that now was the time, but there was no avoiding it.

'The key's under that flowerpot there,' said Ron. 'No, the little one.'

Duffy opened the shed and pointed his flashlight round it. Spades and forks as usual, and a square mound covered by some sacking. Vic was beside him as he pulled the sacking away. Piled neatly underneath were six slatted boxes of freshly picked apples.

By a quarter to five the sky was getting light and they had found no sign of Angela. As they walked across the gravel Duffy said to Vic, 'Call the coppers.'

'Suppose there's no other way,' Vic replied.

Everyone assembled in the kitchen, where Sally and Belinda were still patronizing the whisky bottle. Vic's speech was short and to the point. 'We haven't found her. I'm going to call the coppers. The coppers will have to search the house again. If any of you have got anything you think it might be a bad idea for the coppers to see, I suggest you get rid of it no w. I also suggest that if we all leave the room at the same time, then none of us will start thinking naughty things about the others.'

There was a shuffle of chairs. Belinda asked, 'You didn't find anything?'

'Not really,' said Vic. 'Oh, we found the cutlery.'

'The cutlery?'

'Yeah. It was under Mrs Colin's bed.'

Duffy caught Vic by the elbow as the others were leaving. 'When you call the coppers, better tell them they might need a diver.'

●

Detective-Sergeant Vine had not had a good Bank Holiday weekend. The roses had needed pruning, the grass seemed to have grown a foot, the kids wanted to be taken to the public baths, and the one-day cricket final, which was about the only thing he'd actually been looking forward to, was rained off. He was glad to get back to work, and there were worse ways of doing so than dealing with a disappearing female. They said they'd searched the house, in fact they said they'd searched it twice, but they were only amateurs, so he got Constable Willey to do it in a professional manner.

Whether or not they yet had a missing female on their hands was a matter on which D/S Vine was currently suspending judgement. People went off on long walks sometimes, and just forgot what time it was. People had rows. People played hard to get. People played that old game of Miss Me, Miss Me. This particular female didn't even live at this particular address, and the inhabitants of this particular address – who looked a pretty strange crew, not just because they'd been up all night – hadn't even checked Miss Angela Bruton's home address. Well, they said they'd telephoned, but there was no reply, and since her car was still at the Hall and she wasn't known as a walker, they'd assumed . . . That was the trouble with the public, they always did assume. So Detective-Sergeant Vine and Constable Willey and the lady in question's fiancé drove round to the cottage. They knocked a bit, then quizzed the neighbours and finally pushed in a back window. No, after you, Constable. Constables and children first, I always say.

But she wasn't there and by late morning it had been established securely enough in D/S Vine's mind that the woman in question was, as they said, of a nervous disposition, which translated into normal language meant that she was barking mad and liable to top herself at any minute. So at about half-past eleven on an otherwise very pleasant morning the police frogman lowered himself into the lake and D/S Vine began the boring task of taking statements from the household; statements which, he knew from experience, would either express complete surprise at the fact that Miss Angela Bruton had gone missing, or else complete surprise that she hadn't gone missing a lot earlier.

It was while he was interviewing the Filipino woman, who kept clutching at her throat and going on about some spoons or other which the Detective-Sergeant wasn't the slightest bit interested in, that a short fellow with a broad face and a grown-out brush-cut came into the room.

'Later, sir, if you don't mind.'

'Duffy, West End Central. Used to be, anyway. Freelance.'

'Put in your six-penn'orth.'

The intruder nodded at the Filipino woman, who was dismissed. Duffy was cross with himself for not having thought of it earlier. He hadn't because it was a possibility which implied a gloomy view of human nature. But that was exactly the view he had been trained to take – which was why he was now cross with himself.

D/S Vine put his head round the door and told Constable Willey, who was standing outside, to make sure everyone waited their turn in the family room, and not to let anyone into the video library where he was conducting his interviews. Then he and Duffy slipped out through the french windows, one of which was still to be mended, and crossed the terrace.

Vine, a plumpish young man with sandy hair and a dark moustache, was obviously much more at home in the woods than Duffy was ever likely to be. Silently, they followed the path as it rose through the thickening bracken. This time, Duffy knew where the nick in the beech would be and instantly turned left. He didn't need to walk past the hide before turning back to spot it. This time he simply cut his way firmly down a nettled slope until he and D/S Vine came out opposite the low entrance to the camp. What they saw made them break into a run.

She was lying on her front on a piece of tarpaulin with a brown-paper bag over her head. Her wrists were tied together behind her back and her ankles were roped as well. To ensure that she couldn't turn over, each elbow was lashed to a short stake like a tent peg which had been hammered into the ground. She made a noise in her throat as they approached, which at least allayed their most obvious fear. Their next most obvious fear was not allayed: her skirt had been pulled up over her back, and her tights pulled down to her knees, leaving her naked from waist to lower thigh.

'It's all right. You're all right, we've found you. It's OK. It's Duffy. We've found you.' It didn't matter much what you said, you just have to say it in the right tone. Duffy babbled, and alongside him D/S Vine also babbled, two streams of meaningless comfort as they undid the loose piece of string holding the brown-paper bag in place, then unfastened the gag and the blindfold and cut away the ropes. She sat blinking for some time, and the two men rubbed at her wrists, then she sat up, which made her skirt fall back into place, and when Duffy whispered, 'Pull your tights up, love,' she did as she was told. But she didn't look at either of them, and she didn't reply when D/S Vine asked her gently if she knew who'd done this to her.

They helped her to her feet and she stood there wobbling like some new-born animal. Then after the detective-sergeant had taken a good first look round Jimmy's camp the three of them set off down the path. At first Duffy tried holding Angela round the waist, but she didn't want that; then he tried taking her arm, but even this amount of physical contact seemed unacceptable; so they came through the wood in single file, with Angela silent between the two men. At one point

635

she began shivering, but as soon as D/S Vine touched her shoulder from behind, she stopped.

They came out of the light bracken and made their way across the lawn towards the house. There was at first only one face at the large picture window in the family room, then there were several. One of these suddenly broke away, and a few seconds later the kitchen door was thrown open. Duffy and D/S Vine, more baffled than curious, watched as Jimmy ran across the terrace, down the steps, across the lawn and hurled himself straight into the lake. As there was a police frogman on duty there at the time, it proved easy enough to arrest him.

Duffy joined the others in the family room. They would all now have to wait longer to be interviewed. Priorities had changed. D/S Vine would be back probably the following day, but in the meantime no one was to leave, right? 'What about calls of nature, Sergeant,' asked Damian. 'I don't think this is a time for levity, sir,' replied Vine.

They let Jimmy change into some dry clothes, but he still looked damp and wretched as they took him away. Angela followed in Mrs Vic Crowther's red MG, driven by Belinda. Going off to be interviewed about kidnapping and rape in a red MG with the hood down, driven by former model Belinda Blessing, didn't look or sound quite right to Duffy. He knew who it would sound pretty good to: the tabloids.

'We're going to have a problem with the papers,' said Duffy. 'They're going to love this one.' Big house in the country, missing girl, posh people, ex-Page-Three girl, rape, the old villain – sorry, local businessman – Vic, the young villain Taffy; all they needed was sex and drugs, which they could probably find without even needing to use a telephoto lens, and they were well away. Every neighbour interviewed, every speculation indulged. It would keep all those what-is-the-country-coming-to? columnists happy for weeks.

'Yeah, well, I might be able to hold it off for a day or two,' said Vic, and left the room.

There was a silence. Somehow, Duffy expected the first direct question to come from Lucretia. He was right. 'How did you know where to go?'

'What, the camp?' It was easier to lie with Vic out of the room. 'Oh, Jimmy told me about it. Roughly. It wasn't too hard to find.'

'No, I don't mean that. Why did you think it was Jimmy?'

'I wasn't particularly thinking it was Jimmy. I was just thinking of places she might be. I suppose you could call it a hunch,' he added, using the professional term.

'Do you think Jimmy did it?'

'Well,' said Duffy. He wasn't sure whether it was tactically better to be fair or unfair to Jimmy. 'We don't know what anyone "did" yet. Angela didn't say anything on the way down, so we're just assuming. I mean, it looked like something had happened, I have to admit that.' It could only have looked more like something had happened, Duffy admitted to himself, if they'd actually caught the fellow still zipping up his fly. 'And Vine did have a poke around when we were up there. Jimmy had these tins. With things in.' He looked at Henry as he said the next bit. 'There was an engagement photo of you and Angela, from the paper. It had burns all over it. Like it had been done with a cigarette.'

Henry didn't reply. Duffy went on. 'The funny thing was, he hadn't just put burns all over your face, he'd done it to Angela's as well.'

Henry wafted his hand from side to side in disbelief. 'I don't understand any of it.'

'Come on, Henry,' said Lucretia. 'It's called jealousy.'

'He never told me he was jealous of me.' Henry made this sound like a full answer to the problem. He took his floppy handkerchief out of his breast pocket and blew his nose loudly.

'They don't,' Lucretia explained. 'They don't. That's the point about it.'

'But I didn't steal her from him. He's a . . . he's a . . . friend.' There obviously wasn't a nearer word Henry could lay his hands on.

'Henry, *everyone* stole her from him.' Lucretia's emphasis made Damian chuckle; a response which irritated her. 'No, I don't mean *that*. I mean everyone had more chance with her than Jimmy. The milkman had more chance with her.'

'The milkman has more chance with everybody, I'd say,' smirked Damian.

'So I just happened to be the one at the time? But why didn't he do something to *me* if he was soft on Ange?'

'Maybe that's the point,' said Lucretia. 'It could have been you, it could have been anyone, if not quite the milkman. But it was always going to be her. There was always going to be Ange around. I suppose poor old Jimmy couldn't take it any more.'

'Poor old Jimmy,' Sally mimicked crossly. 'What about poor old bloody Ange?'

'He had been behaving a bit oddly lately, I suppose,' said Henry.

Lucretia demurred. 'No odder than usual I'd have thought.'

'What was he doing in that frogman's suit yesterday? Everyone saw him, but from what you say he was going on as if he was the Invisible Man.'

'He was looking for Ricky,' said Duffy.

'Looking for Ricky? That was a bit potty, wasn't it?'

Duffy shrugged. He didn't feel he'd confess who'd put Jimmy up to it. 'Well, it doesn't seem so strange to me. If you're soft on someone, you probably think their dog needs a decent burial.'

'Yes, old Jimmy would be just like that,' Damian spotted a chance to annoy. 'I can just see him saluting on some rain-swept hillside with the Last Post on a bugle and a damp little headstone. Ricky: He Barked His Last.'

Henry cleared his throat. 'One of these days, Damian, someone's going to thump you.'

'If only they would,' sighed Damian, 'if only they would.' Henry moved approximately a foot closer to Damian, where-upon the latter yelped and jumped over the back of the sofa. 'I didn't mean it. Nice dog. Nice doggie. Woof, woof.' Sally giggled, and Vic's return to the room was fortunately timed.

'They'll do what they can,' he said, making Duffy wonder if the local papers up here also described Vic as a 'local busi-nessman', and if so what they thought his business was. 'At the moment the coppers can say there's no story because they don't know that any offence has been committed.' Sure, thought Duffy, long-term open-air bondage is all the rage among posh people nowadays.

'What about a couple of frames before lunch?' Damian suggested.

'I think I've been up all night,' said Duffy.

'About those cigarette burns on the photo,' said Lucretia. 'Jimmy doesn't smoke. And another thing I don't understand.' Duffy rather wished Lucretia would shut up. No one else seemed to be thinking at the moment, which suited him fine. 'If Jimmy killed Ricky, why was he looking for the body?'

'Because he's potty.' This was Henry's suggestion.

'No, no, my dear Watson,' said Damian. 'Don't you see, he did it to throw suspicion off himself. Who would ever suspect he was the murderer if he was the one that found the body?'

'Brill,' sighed Sally in genuine admiration.

'Only one thing wrong.' It was Lucretia with another correction. 'He didn't find it. The body. If he'd hidden it, you'd think even Jimmy would know where to look.'

'Maybe it's not helping anyone, going over things like this,' Vic suggested. 'Why don't we break it up and have a spot of lunch?'

The women and Damian led the way. Duffy turned to Henry. 'Have you still got your Dad's billiard table?'

'Of course.'

'Look, say if you think this is a bit silly, but if I'm stuck down here for a couple of days, what about you giving me a couple of lessons, secret, you know. Then I could really take that Damian apart.'

Henry grinned, looked serious for a bit, then grinned again. 'Well, I suppose it depends on Mother a bit. And Ange. But I'd like to.'

'Then you wouldn't have to thump him.'

'But I quite want to thump him.'

'So do I. But I wouldn't mind thumping him with a side-bet.'

Despite Vic's suggestion that going over it all wouldn't help things, there seemed nothing else to talk about. Henry's presence inhibited some of the preciser speculations on what might have been done to his fiancée, but the character and career of her assailant were thoroughly examined. Jimmy's professional reputation as an estate agent was confirmed as not being of the highest; in fact, no one had ever known him sell a house. His less than moderate success with women was apparently known through two counties. His mother had died young, and his father had pushed him hard. He'd really enjoyed the Army, but the Army hadn't enjoyed him. He was a loser, a wimp-out, and at thirty-five it had all just got too much for him.

'There's something else I don't understand,' said Lucretia. Shut up, shut up. 'If Jimmy was clever enough to start fishing for Ricky's body to put us all off the scent, why was he so stupid as to run away when the police brought Ange down from his camp?'

'Because he's potty,' said Henry.

'Ah.' Lucretia had aimed the question at Damian, who briefly got going. 'The psyche of the criminal is indeed a Hampton Court maze. But perhaps . . . My dear Taffy?' Damian lobbed the question on to the man in black with the triangular torso.

'Well,' Taffy began. 'He looked as if he was running away, didn't he?'

'Yes,' various people replied with various emphases.

'I've been reading up on this, you see. Sometimes, the psychologists say, running away isn't what it looks like. Running away isn't running away, you see. Running away is really wanting to be caught.'

'Isn't it easier to stay where you are if you want to be caught?' Lucretia swept her blonde hair off the side of her face in a manner which implied polite scepticism, if not that Taffy was the biggest fucking fool she'd listened to for quite some time.

'No, not necessarily. There has to be a moment of symbolic fugue followed by symbolic reintegration into society.'

'You mean running away and getting arrested?'

'If you want to use the layman's terms. You see, the offender isn't any different from most of us round this table.'

Well, he isn't any different from *you*, thought Duffy. 'The offender is always seeking his place in society. It's just that he sometimes uses unusual methods.' Like hitting people with iron bars. 'But what he's seeking is reintegration, or rather the integration he never had in the first place.' Duffy looked across at Vic; he wondered if Vic's move to the Buckinghamshire/Bedfordshire borders had been a symbolic fugue in quest of a symbolic or actual reintegration.

'So Jimmy ran into the lake,' Lucretia said slowly, as if only just following Taffy, 'because it was a sort of public gesture which would provoke a forceful reaction which he might not knowingly want but which would bring him what all his life – since his rejection as a child – he'd secretly been looking for.'

'More or less,' nodded Taffy.

'I think he did it because he's potty,' Henry repeated stolidly.

After lunch Duffy and Vic were on the terrace, sniffing the dangerous air.

'I like those red flowers,' said Duffy politely.

'Yes, they're nice those red flowers,' replied Vic, 'but I don't know what they're called either. They're full of those great hornet things, though.'

'Bumblebees,' stated Duffy authoritatively.

'Bees.'

'Wasps?'

'Bluebottles?'

'You have to have the odd chuckle, don't you, with all this going on?'

'What are you going to do about Mrs Colin?'

'Mrs Colin? Hadn't thought. It's up to Belinda, I expect. I should think she'll have to go. I mean, that's the first rule of employing people, isn't it?'

'I wouldn't know.' And if it were, Vic might have to let the Hardcastles go as well. Duffy wondered when to mention the matter of Ron's taste for pink champagne; he also wondered where Ron had shifted the stuff. He couldn't have drunk it all in the time. 'Maybe you could give me a day or two on that one?'

Vic grinned. 'Are you sure you're up to it? The case of the

missing spoons which have turned up anyway in the possession of the culprit who has given a fortnight's notice. I mean, I'm not sure this isn't out of your league.'

'I thought I might be able to pin it on Jimmy.'

'Yeah. Get him a parking ticket at the same time. Actually, I'm not sure why you're still here, Duffy.'

'Detective-Sergeant Vine told us all to stay, didn't he? And you're paying me daily rates.'

'Am I?'

'A gentleman's word is his bond.'

'Do you think those red things are called salvias?'

'Bound to be. Unless they're not, of course.'

'Yeah.'

Mrs Colin's attic room looked very bare; though whether it was always like this, or whether Mrs Colin had already started putting things away in her case, Duffy couldn't tell. There was a small crucifix above the bed, a mirror on one wall, a pile of magazines which Mrs Colin had saved from the waste-paper baskets downstairs, and a framed colour print of people in Davao drinking San Miguel beer on somebody's birthday.

'Is it . . .?' Duffy hovered by the door. Mrs Colin had been crying, but she waved him in and pointed at a small Lloyd Loom chair. Duffy didn't know whether or not she would think it proper for him to shut the door; he hesitated, then firmly did so. Yes, that was probably the right approach. 'Mrs Colin,' he began, and it was a statement not a question, 'you didn't steal those spoons.' She didn't reply. 'I don't think you stole those spoons.' Not unless it was a symbolic gesture aimed at achieving social reintegration, in which case Duffy would just climb into his van and drive away. 'I'll tell you why you didn't do it,' said Duffy. 'Because you wouldn't do so. Because you don't do things like that. And because anyone who did anything like that would be daft to leave them under their bed.'

'They found them,' said Mrs Colin. 'You found them. I have to go.'

'Are you happy here?'

'Yes. Happy here.'

642

'How do you get on with Mr and Mrs Hardcastle?'

'Oh, very nice.'

'They aren't . . . I don't know, jealous of you?'

'Jealous?'

'Jealous, sure.' Well, why not, it seemed to be the flavour of the day. 'They don't think you work too hard? They don't think you're too popular with Mrs Crowther?'

'No. They are normal. Mrs Crowther, she is nice.'

'What was that run-in you were having with Nikki? What was she shouting at you about ?'

'Oh, she's a bit spoiled, Miss Nikki. No, that's normal. I just caught her in the video room watching something she shouldn't be watching, so I send her off. That was a few days ago, but she's still cross with me.

'What about Jimmy?' Well, he'd promised Vic he'd try and pin it on Jimmy.

'Mr Jimmy, what's he done?'

'We don't know yet.'

'Mr Jimmy, he's a *gentleman*,' she said forcefully. 'He helps with things.' Maybe Jimmy could go into business designing Hoovers you drove around on, Duffy thought, and Mrs Colin could do the advertisements. Maybe he could; when he gets out in six or seven years.

'Mrs Colin, if I did something for you, would you do something for me?'

'I do something for you anyway. What you want done? These shoes don't look too clean.'

'No, well, that's how I like them. Look, don't just go off or anything. I mean, the police will want to talk to us all, I expect.'

At the mention of the police Mrs Colin reached for her handkerchief. 'No, no, Mrs Colin. About Jimmy. They'll want to talk to you about Mr Jimmy.'

'Mr Jimmy, he's a gentleman,' said Mrs Colin.

'Sure.'

Whether or not Mr Jimmy was a gentleman was a matter much discussed over dinner, and speculation became the freer because Henry, after telephoning Detective-Sergeant Vine, had obtained permission to go home and look after his aged mother. Angela and Belinda had returned at about six o'clock; Angela had been put to bed with a large drink, a meal on a tray, a portable television and a bell to ring if she wanted company; now Belinda's report of what had emerged at the station gave things a new impetus.

The first point was that Angela hadn't seen who had attacked her. She'd been walking at the edge of the woods, sometime in the middle of the afternoon, she couldn't say when, and had been attacked from behind. A hand was over her mouth, a knife which she didn't see and couldn't describe was at her throat. She didn't resist as she was dragged, blind-folded, and gagged. Strong, that was all she could say about the man, he was strong. She didn't see his hands, might have glimpsed some bit of greeny-buff sleeve but she couldn't swear to it. No, she absolutely didn't recognize the man who'd made her walk to Jimmy's camp. That's what she said. How did she know it was a man, then? Well, it would have had to have been an incredibly strong woman. And a woman couldn't have done what happened at the camp.

That was the second point, the one that led to the main part of the discussion. Angela hadn't been raped. There was a genuine exhalation of relief when Belinda revealed this piece of information; and Duffy heard Mrs Colin's voice in his head – 'Mr Jimmy, he's a gentleman.' Angela had been dragged the last few yards, then thrown down on to what didn't feel like the ground and turned out to have been a tarpaulin. She heard a hammering noise quite close. She didn't try and kick, or stand up, or do anything, because she realized how hopeless things were; and she also thought that this was perhaps what the fellow wanted her to do. After a minute or two she found her elbows being roped tightly to whatever had been banged into the ground. Something extra was put over her head. Her ankles were tied together – she did try to kick out against that – and her tights pulled down. When her skirt was hauled up round her waist she lay there and expected the worst. She expected worse than the worst. Then nothing happened for a while, though she thought she heard some distant noises, some scrabbling, perhaps. After a few minutes she felt some-thing, perhaps a knee, against the outside of her right thigh, and shortly afterwards something wet began to fall across her buttocks. It wasn't rain. After that, there had been waiting, and feeling cold, and thinking about suffocation, and wondering if anyone would find her, and wondering what would happen if someone else, someone who didn't want to rescue her, found her instead.

There was a silence around the table. 'The thing I couldn't get over,' said Belinda, 'was that this fucking policeman kept asking her about her knickers.'

'I thought they got policewomen to do the questioning.' Another nasty job for WPC Carol Lucas, thought Duffy.

'Yeah, well, we're a bit backward in the provinces.' Belinda didn't hold back on the sarcasm. 'They got in some trainee girl, I don't know, she had the uniform but I shouldn't think she was more than seventeen, and obviously Ange didn't want to talk to her, cause she knew she'd have to go through it again with the detective fellow, so she just asked for him.'

'Bloody plucky.' Damian for once was looking subdued.

'But what he seemed to be most interested in was where her knickers were. "He pulled down your tights. Can you tell me what happened about your knickers?" She said she didn't wear knickers, just tights. He was incredible, I thought he was getting off on it. "What happened about your knickers?" – he came back to it later. Like either Jimmy had stolen her knickers and if they went through his pockets and found them they'd have him all locked up, or else she was a tart because she went around only wearing tights, and so she got everything she deserved.'

No, it wasn't like that, Duffy thought; but he didn't say anything. You had to ask, and you had to repeat the question. Stealing knickers was a completely normal thing to do – given that you were the completely abnormal person who'd already done everything else to Angela.

'They're all perves, coppers,' observed Sally.

'Now, now,' said Damian, 'I bet there are some really sweet ones somewhere.'

'Why did he do that?' Lucretia asked suddenly. 'Why did he just wank off on her? Why didn't he rape her?'

No one answered for a bit. Duffy remembered the

four-year-old copies of *Playboy* in the green tin. Maybe that was what he liked doing best, and doing it with a real person was even better than doing it with magazines. Maybe, for all the brutality leading up to it, he just didn't have the guts to go ahead and rape her. Maybe, in a funny sort of way, he thought it showed he loved her. A very funny sort of way, admittedly.

'Perhaps Taffy can give us a line on this one,' said Damian mischievously.

'Never did understand sex offenders,' Taffy shook his head gravely. 'They're not like your ordinary offender. They always keep themselves to themselves when they're inside.' Duffy thought this the understatement of the decade. If sex offenders didn't keep to themselves in prison, they lived a very short life. They got it from the screws, and they got it from the other inmates. Everyone thinking, that could have been my girlfriend, my daughter, my little boy. It wasn't, but it might have been. Thump. Filthy pervert.

'Perhaps it's all about humiliation,' Lucretia tried answering her own question. 'That's what they say, isn't it? Maybe he reckoned it was more humiliating this way. Sort of, I could have raped you but you aren't even worth doing that to. Does that sound likely?'

'Sounds likely,' said Belinda. 'The only thing is, can you see old Jimmy thinking like that?'

'Who knows what went on in old Jimmy's head.' Vic was rueful. 'I was wondering. Maybe I should have let him build his assault course. Work it all off, sort of.'

'Did she actually ever, you know, go out with him?' Duffy asked.

Damian chuckled, and his face shone. 'Isn't it funny how people say "go out with" when what they really mean is "stay in with".'

'No,' said Belinda. 'She never teased him or anything. He was always around, sort of useful, could you shift that, Jimmy, please, and so on, but she never showed him any leg or anything.' Not like an experienced Page-Three girl might have done.

'So he knew it was hopeless all along?' This was what Duffy

had been told by Jimmy, but you never took people's word on things like love and sex.

'Suppose so. No one ever thought, "If Ange breaks up with So-and-so, there's always Jimmy." No one got anywhere near thinking that.'

'Perhaps that was the trouble,' said Vic.

'Hey, look, what about Ange, all right?' It was Sally, almost violent. 'I mean, fuck Jimmy, that's what I say. What about Ange?'

Ange, it seemed, had made her statement to Detective-Sergeant Vine in the presence of Belinda and the woman police constable who wasn't meant to be old enough, then said they could talk to her again tomorrow if they wanted to, and asked Belinda to take her home. By home she presumably meant Braunscombe Hall. She didn't speak on the journey there, nor did she weep.

'Christ.' Belinda suddenly got up from the table and ran upstairs. Everyone else must have been thinking roughly the same; they didn't look at one another, and just waited. A door banged, and they heard Belinda swear. Then there was silence, and no one knew quite what to do. After a minute or so, Belinda could be heard coming slowly downstairs again. The silence continued; people began wondering whose fault it might be.

'Christ,' she said. 'It's all right. Christ, I got a shock, though. She wasn't in her room. She's in the cot. Fast asleep.' She turned to her husband. 'Early night, Vic? She might need us.'

'Sure, Bel.' Vic threw his napkin down on the table in a lordly way, a mannerism recently learnt.

Duffy caught Lucretia's eye as the others politely rose and followed the example of their hosts. When they were alone, she said, 'I hope you don't want to discuss restaurants.'

He grinned briefly. 'Where's Henry?'

'At home. With Mum.'

'I don't get it. Your girlfriend's been missing and nearly raped and he's at home with Mum. Does it make sense to you?'

'Oh yes,' said Lucretia. 'You haven't met Mum.'

'Bad as that?'

'And you don't know Angela.'

'What is there that I don't know about Angela?'

'Well, that Ange's USP is understanding about Mum.'

'What's a USP?'

'Sorry. Unique Selling Point. Worked in advertising once,' she explained.

'So it's apron strings all round?'

'Tied in a double bow.'

'And Angela will put up with that after they get married? No, don't tell me, I've already had the lecture about love from Belinda.'

'Which one's that?'

'About how love means just about being able to put up with the other person.'

'Do I detect a Romantic?' She was teasing him now; he could guess that.

'Dunno. I'm no good with flowers and things.'

'That's not what it's about,' said Lucretia firmly.

'Oh, well maybe I am, then. I'm not good at candlelit dinners, though.'

'Is that a back-handed way of asking me out?' This time she sounded less teasing. Was she serious, or was she just trying to draw him out so she could have a good laugh at him?

'Dunno.' He couldn't really ask her out to dinner, not when he almost never took Carol out for a meal, could he? Or could he? Why hadn't Carol eaten that fish with the low-calorie sauce? This running joke they had about her going out with Paul Newman and Robert Redford: you didn't have running jokes that meant nothing, did you? And she hadn't explained about the fish. Maybe . . . maybe . . . Then he realized that Lucretia's eyes were on him. He wondered how much of all that she could read.

She didn't let on. Instead, she lit a cigarette and said, 'But anyway, the matter in hand.'

'They aren't seeing so much of one another before they're married because it's an old posh custom.'

'Who told you that?'

'Damian.'

Lucretia laughed. 'Well, for once, Damian's giving you the censored version. Which is probably only because he doesn't know the uncensored one.'

'Which is?'

'You know that thing that people do?'

'Sorry?'

'That thing that people do. When they're alone. People of opposite sexes. Two of them. The thing they do.'

Did he blush? He cleared his throat and said, 'Gotcha.'

'They haven't done it.'

'*What*?'

'That's right. They haven't done it. Angela told Belinda and Belinda told me. Girls' talk. You know, it goes on, while we're waiting for you and Taffy to finish your port and tell the one about the nun with big tits.'

'But . . . but . . .' But Angela's meant to be a right little goer is what he wanted to say; in the circumstances it didn't seem the proper phrase.

'Yup. Henry,' she said, with a lecturer's emphasis, 'is saving himself for marriage.' Something about the way she pronounced the phrase suggested that it had been used originally by Henry and dutifully transmitted down the female line.

'Christ.'

'Yup. You're a pretty weird bunch, you men, I'll tell you that for nothing.'

'How long have they been going out together?'

'Which in this case does not mean staying in together. About a year.'

'Hmm. Still, if it takes two to tango, it takes two not to tango as well.'

'That's a funny way of putting things but I suppose I see what you mean.'

There was a pause. Duffy wasn't sure if he was on dangerous ground or not. 'Do you know,' said Lucretia, 'with horses, really top horses, the ones that race, they don't get any sex. They aren't allowed it. Then if they turn out to be good at racing and they're worth breeding from, they're sold to stud. By that time they've usually forgotten what they never learnt. Have to be helped to do it.'

Well, if Henry's like that, Duffy thought, Angela will certainly be the right girl to know how to help him, by all accounts. He coughed. 'Do you think that Basil Berk's a good writer about restaurants?'

'He's not bad.'

'It looks a bloody easy job to me.'

'Just say there's saffron in everything.'

'That's right. Well . . . goodnight.'

Lucretia waved an arm in dismissal. If you could wave an arm in dismissal and not seem unfriendly, she managed it. Or maybe Duffy was fooling himself. He wondered what the joke about the nun with big tits was. He'd have to ask Taffy.

He lay on his bed thinking over the events of the last twenty-four hours. It didn't make sense, except on the psychopath theory. This was a very common phenomenon in American detective series on television, but less frequently encountered in real life. It was useful because it explained everything: Jimmy, for instance, left a dead bird on Angela's doorstep, killed her dog, planted some spoons on Mrs Colin, stashed four cases of wine in the Hardcastles' shed, hid the dog, found the dog, kidnapped Angela, tied her up, wanked over her, and when the police came ran off into the lake. He also let down Duffy's tyres, and Sally's confession was bogus. Why did old Jimmy do all these things? Because he's a psychopath. What's the definition of a psychopath? Someone who does all these things. Perfect.

There were times, of course, in police work, when you longed for the odd psychopath – especially one with a willingness to confess to any old crime you shoved in front of him. Compliant psychopaths would certainly help tidy up the crime figures. Though there were simpler ways of cooking the books if that's what you were after.

The next morning, while they were still in theory housebound and awaiting the return of D/S Vine, Duffy decided it was time to make a very small start. He was pretending without much sincerity to examine a bit of wiring in the alarm system when he saw Nikki coming along the corridor. She stopped, looked up at him, and before she could open her mouth, he said, 'I'd love to see your dance, Nikki.'

'I thought you didn't. Taffy doesn't want to. Taffy always says he's got things to do.'

'I'd love to see it. Can you do it anywhere?' She looked dubious. 'Can I choose where I'd like you to do it for me?'

'All right.'

'The summerhouse. Now I've chosen that, you can have the second choice: either I can sit on the verandah and you can dance on the grass, or you can dance on the verandah and I'll sit on the grass.'

She thought it over as they crossed the lawn to the pagoda-like building that had been painted white in the days of the not-quite Lord Mayor psychedelic stripes under the tenancy of Izzy Dunn, but had now been toned down under the Crowthers to a mere bright Chinese red. Nikki took to this as a location and walked the length of the verandah as if pacing out her jumps. While Duffy lolled on the grass, she explained rather sombrely that she didn't yet go to ballet class, so what he was about to see wasn't a 'proper' dance, but rather something she'd invented. The music was also something she'd invented; at least, Duffy hoped no one had ever been paid for writing down the whoops and wails and little tra-la-las with which she accompanied her dance. As for the ballet itself, it didn't look bad to Duffy, who admitted he knew absolutely nothing at all about dance. She seemed to hop and twirl rather gracefully, he thought; even if he couldn't be said to be concentrating.

When silence and stillness from the verandah indicated that Nikki had finished her performance, he got off his haunches and gave her a standing ovation. She did the prima ballerina bit, bowing and all that; whereupon Duffy quickly pulled a few dandelions and daisies out of the grass, shuffled them together into a bouquet, and shyly edged forward to present them. Mademoiselle gave him a curtsey of thanks. He stepped up on to the verandah.

'Very nice, Nikki, very nice. I don't think you'll have any trouble with your ballet classes.'

As he was talking he crossed behind her to the window. He leaned back and pressed his palm against the glass. Then he stood away and acted the big surprise. 'Hey, look at this

651

Nikki.' She turned round and, at his bidding, examined the full set of fingerprints left on the dirty glass. 'I wonder who left them there?' Nikki shrugged, then laughed as Duffy took her hand and pretended to match it to the broad spread of the marks.

'I used to be a policeman, you know,' he said. 'If someone had broken into this summerhouse we'd have come along and a fellow with a brush and some special sort of dust would have gone over all the door-frames and window-frames. Now, say those weren't here' – he rubbed away his own prints with a wetted corner of handkerchief – 'they'd still be able to catch the fellow.'

'How?'

'Well, you leave prints even if you can't see them. You leave prints all the time, on everything you touch. Your knife and fork, that sort of thing. You may not see them but they're there right enough.'

'How long do they last?'

'Weeks,' said Duffy. 'Weeks and weeks.' There was a silence. Nikki held her bouquet of dandelions and daisies. Duffy timed the next bit carefully. 'Mrs Colin's very upset. She's very fond of you, Nikki. She won't be cross. Just tell your Dad.'

He could see the child's lips push forward, then came a bit of a frown. 'She shouldn't have stopped me watching video. It's not her house.'

'No, it's not her house. But would your mum have done any different if she'd found you in there?'

She didn't reply. They set off across the lawn. After a dozen or so paces, Nikki, still carefully holding her bouquet, slipped her hand up and into Duffy's. 'Next time I'll wear gloves,' she said crossly. In spite of himself, Duffy burst out laughing. He was still smiling when the explosion occurred.

The estate agents acting for Izzy Dunn had not gone into much detail about the construction of the stable block. In fact, it was an architectural hotch-potch. The two stables themselves dated back to the time of the not-quite Lord Mayor; the Hardcastles' cottage, at the other end of the block, had been put up ten years later with no particular regard for stylistic harmony; and the central section, which not surprisingly had given its designer a number of problems, had been completed only a few years before Izzy Dunn moved in. As it was modern, and flimsily built – merely a horizontal and vertical skin designed to protect three cars from the rain – the force of the explosion did not initially damage either the Hardcastles' cottage or the stabling proper. The danger to them was from fire, not blast.

When Duffy arrived people just seemed to be staring: at the blown-out garage door, the hole in the roof, the blazing car. Mrs Hardcastle, who had telephoned the fire brigade, stood on the gravel clutching her handbag and her wedding album. Vic, who had also called the fire brigade after a long wrangle with Damian who wouldn't get off the phone, was shaking his head. Taffy and Damian looked as if they were waiting for someone to start setting off the fireworks. Only Belinda, trying to calm two hysterical horses, was actually doing anything.

'Anyone in there?' asked Duffy. They nodded a negative. The middle car of the three was still burning hard. If the Range Rover on the left caught fire, then the stable proper would go; if the MG caught, then the Hardcastles would join the list of the nation's homeless. Duffy ran to his van and backed it across twenty yards of gravel towards the fire. He stopped about fifteen feet away, got out, opened the back and took out his towrope.

'Taffy,' he shouted as he started crawling under the Sherpa to fix one end of the rope. 'Taffy,' he shouted again. There was a pause, then the sound of feet sprinting across gravel. From under his van, Duffy thrust the clamp on the other end of the rope out towards his tardy helper. 'The axle, not the bumper,' he shouted. 'I know,' came the testy reply. Perhaps Taffy's voice had broken slightly with the excitement; and perhaps he'd also slipped into a pair of velvet trousers which hadn't previously been on display; but this seemed unlikely. Duffy jumped into the van, pulled the protesting Range Rover clear, backed up hard to the MG, saw Damian clamp the axle, and towed that to safety. Then they all watched the purply Datsun Cherry burn. After ten minutes or so, when the flames were beginning to die down, the fire brigade, clanging a needless bell, tanked up the drive and swirled to a stop in front of the porch. Vic shook his head. 'Look what they've done to my bloody gravel.'

6 • BEDROOMS

The last person out of the house to see the fire brigade douse the wreckage of the purply Datsun was its owner, Sally. She looked from Duffy to Vic, from Vic to Taffy, as if seeking permission to giggle. It wasn't forthcoming. Finally, Damian, brushing at some singe marks on his velvet jacket, murmured, 'Frightfully unstable, these foreign motors,' and that did the trick. Sally was back to her usual irritating self, and Damian, his surprise moment of heroism over, was also reverting as fast as possible.

'I'll have to buy a new set of maps,' giggled Sally, the funniest thing she'd said since the last funniest thing she'd said.

'It's my bloody garage,' said Vic, who wasn't at all entertained, 'and it nearly took my bloody stables.'

'Sorry,' said Sally. 'Sorry. It's just . . . it's just . . .' she wasn't even sure she could contain herself long enough to get the sentence out, 'It's just that these foreign motors are so frightfully unstable.'

'Well done,' said Duffy to Damian.

'I didn't need to be told about the axle,' he replied huffily. 'I've seen enough films where the bumper just gets pulled off.'

'Check. I thought you were going to be Taffy.'

There was a pause which invited the ex-con to explain himself. 'Always had this fear of fire, see. Two-bar electric fell on me when I was just out of my pram. Had this phobia ever since.'

And Moscow's the capital of America, thought Duffy. Strange how everyone had phobias these days. Nobody had phobias where he came from. Nowadays, if there was anything you didn't want to do you had a phobia which stopped you doing it. I've got a phobia about sitting on the top deck of a bus. I've got a phobia about cigarette smoke. I've got a phobia about wearing a seat belt. What they meant was they didn't like it. Duffy didn't care for aeroplanes, but he wouldn't say he had a phobia about them. He'd just say they made him bloody frightened; he just knew that if one of them took off with him on board he'd be shitting himself all the time until it crashed, which it inevitably would. That didn't seem to be a grand enough feeling to call a phobia. Maybe Taffy also had a phobia which led to him thieving and hitting people with iron bars. Oh, it's not that my client is a criminal, your honour; it's just that he has this phobia about going straight. Oh well, in that case, three months' probation. And then there was this new posh word Duffy had seen around called homophobia. In the old days there had been people who were prejudiced against homosexuals, or gays, or queers, or whatever people who were prejudiced against them called them. Nowadays these people didn't have prejudice, they had homophobia. Duffy disapproved. It sounded too much like a clinical condition, too much like something you couldn't help. So after kicking him in the groin and stealing his wallet you also stamped on his spectacles? Yes, officer, you see I got this attack of my homophobia. Shocking, it always comes on at this time of year, nuffink I can do about it, must be the east wind or something. Oh, I've also got this phobia about being arrested and charged and sent to prison. Well, in that case, on your bike, son, and watch the weather forecast more carefully next time.

'I suppose this means the boys in blue crawling all over the place again,' said Vic, who clearly suffered from an advanced case of copperphobia. 'What about a spot of lunch while we're waiting?'

That's another thing about posh people, thought Duffy as they moved inside. They eat a lot. Even someone like old Vic, who had only acquired the trappings of poshness recently, while remaining awesomely unposh in his own person, went on about his dinners. They drank a lot, and they ate a lot. What's more, they thought about it before they did it. They didn't just go out for meals, they read up in magazines first about where to go out for a meal. They didn't merely eat when they were hungry, or when it fitted in, they had thumping great dinner-hours which were always observed. If you wanted to torture any of this lot, all you'd have to say was, 'We don't know what time lunch is,' and they'd blab anything you needed to find out.

For the first ten minutes or so, Duffy looked rather hard across the table at Nikki. It was probably a psychological tactic which the European Court of Human Rights would have deemed illegal, but at least it worked. She slid from her chair, went and sat on Vic's knee, and whispered in his ear. Vic frowned at first, then nodded, muttered 'Good girl,' and pushed her off towards the kitchen, presumably to find Mrs Colin.

Since this tactic had worked so well on Nikki, he transferred it now to Sally, frowning at her across the table in a way that might look vaguely menacing. After a while she noticed this and said, 'You all right?'

'Fine,' said Duffy.

'Only you've got a funny expression on your face.'

'What do you think happened?'

'Happened?'

'To your car.'

'Dunno. Expect I left the ignition on or something,' she said rather airily. Then she caught Damian's eye and they chorused through giggles, 'It's just that these foreign motors are so frightfully unstable.'

'Knock it off, kids,' said Vic.

'Electrical fault?' Taffy suggested. Well at least he wasn't blaming the car's combustion on society's malice.

'When it isn't running?' said Duffy.

'Could happen.' Taffy was determined to back up his hypothesis, even if only because it had been attacked. 'F'rinstance, something like a squirrel could have got inside and chewed through a cable, you never know.'

'Round up all the usual squirrels,' bellowed Damian.

'Gypsies?' suggested Belinda.

'Could it have been . . . summer lightning?' This from Lucretia.

Christ, thought Duffy. Talk about another world. Or maybe they didn't want to think about it until they'd finished lunch. Well, he'd had enough to eat already. 'Christ,' he said forcefully. 'Squirrels? Summer lightning? Gypsies? If it was squirrels, why aren't cars blowing up all over the place? I mean, it took the roof off, didn't it?'

'So what do you think happened?' Lucretia didn't seem too dismayed by the rejection of her thesis.

'I think someone put a bomb under it.'

'Hang on, this isn't Northern Ireland,' said Vic.

'Or someone set light to it, which isn't all that easy unless you know what you're doing, and the explosion was the petrol tank going up. The coppers are quite good at finding out. They get a lot of practice nowadays.'

Duffy's suggestion was not very well received. He wondered why Sally wasn't asking more questions. He tried his questing look on her again.

'Who'd do something like that to my car?' she said, rather as if prompted, which indeed she had been.

'You tell us?'

'No idea. Maybe someone's in love with me,' she laughed. There was a tricky silence. Yeah, like Jimmy was in love with Angela, most people were thinking.

The fire brigade went away, and the police arrived. Perhaps we'll get the ambulance as well before the day's out, Duffy thought. Actually, the padded van would be more like it as far as some of those around here are concerned. They could take Taffy away and see if they could do something for his phobia about two-bar electric fires and anything upwards. They could take off Damian and find out why such a lazy, irritating prat didn't mind singeing his velvets when he hadn't even been asked. They could certainly put Sally under the lens and see if all her grey matter had dribbled out of her ears while she was asleep one night; perhaps a squirrel had climbed up her nose and chewed through a few cables inside her head – that might be the reason. And while they were about it, Duffy thought, they could examine Lucretia and tell him if she would by any chance be willing to go to bed with him.

They were told to stay within hailing distance of the house and await Detective-Sergeant Vine's summons. After turning down Damian's offer of some blindfold snooker, Duffy wandered out into the garden, vaguely hoping to find Lucretia. All he turned up was Taffy sitting on a bench with a thick volume over his knee. Duffy coughed a lot as he approached, knowing that cons – even incredibly reformed ex-cons who wouldn't steal the dandruff from your collar – don't like being crept up on. It makes them jumpy, and where they jump can end up being painful.

Taffy glanced up from his book like an Oxford don disturbed by a window cleaner. Hey, Duffy thought, don't *you* try putting me down as well. You haven't come up the slimy ladder that fast. Pointedly, he sat down on the bench beside Taffy; pointedly, Taffy carried on with his book. Duffy squinted across at the running title. Taffy was reading *Theories of Social Revolt*. He was doing it, Duffy also noted, without moving his lips or tracking his forefinger along each line like a wriggling salamander.

'Good, is it?' he asked, after a tactful wait until Taffy got to the end of the chapter.

'Bit simplistic. You wouldn't think he'd ever looked at Laing.'

'Surprising the gaps in some people's reading. By the way, what's the one about the nun with big tits?'

'Eh?' Taffy turned towards him for the first time, shifting his hulky shoulders all the way round as he did. They made the head look laughably small, but you didn't grin because of the still way the eyes rested on you.

'Lucretia said you like to tell it with the port and nuts.'

'Sounds like she's having you on.' Taffy started to swivel his torso back towards his book, as if he could only read when chest-on to the page.

'You still keep in shape?' Taffy arrested his movement. 'Got some weights myself,' Duffy went on, referring to the dusty bar-bells which skulked in his fitted cupboard. 'They sort of wear you out, though, don't they?'

'Not if you're fit. Got to go through the pain barrier, that's all.'

'I guess I never came out the other side. I'm a goalkeeper myself.'

'You look a bit small for a goalkeeper.'

Duffy rattled on. He kept throwing out hooks, but none of them would catch. 'I suppose I'd get more exercise if I moved upfield. Snooker doesn't exactly keep the muscles in trim, either. Not even if you play it the way Damian and Sally do.' Taffy didn't respond. 'Have you seen the way they do it?'

'No.'

'She takes her knickers off and sits in a corner pocket and he tries to pot the balls you know where.'

'Well, as long as it doesn't frighten the horses, eh?' Taffy went back to *Theories of Social Revolt*. Duffy wondered what it took to get a rise out of him. Quite a lot, obviously. That was another thing about ex-cons. After years of being cooped up you either came out with a hair-trigger temper, in which case you found yourself back inside again pretty soon; or else you learned to keep the lid on it. Taffy kept the lid on it so securely that you didn't even see a puff of steam. This took a lot of practice. Duffy imagined him in Maidstone or wherever: pull-ups and push-ups every day in the cell, thoughtful visits to the chapel and the library, a new line in politeness to the screws – all to make the parole board believe he'd really calmed down and got all that pus out of his system. Sometimes it was for real, of course, but mostly the cons would just be faking their new-found serenity.

One of the things that helped them fake it was fancy tobacco. Every so often, when there wasn't a royal wedding or garrulous star-fucker to fill the front page, the tabloids would wheel out the old story about drug-pushing in Her Majesty's prisons; how shocking it was that criminals were still able to go on committing crimes even when locked up, how the heroic Police Sniffer Dog Freddie (photo above) had located a milligram of hash in some lifer's bum, how if there wasn't law and order in our jails what hope was there for society, and by the way if you're exhausted by all these words just turn the page and you'll find this week's descendant of Belinda Blessing with her tits snouting out of the paper at you. Every such investigation would duly conclude with a stern statement from the Home Office that it was fully committed to stamping out the use of illegal substances in Britain's jails. What Duffy knew, and what the Home Office was thick if it didn't, was that the drug searches in Her Majesty's prisons could often get a bit perfunctory. The screws were well aware that if a con was smoking a nice fat home-made roll-up, then the chances of him getting off his bunk and teeing off with an iron bed-post weren't very great. In the old days they used to put things in the prisoners' tea to calm them down. Now, if the prisoners chose to put things in their own tea, or in their own cigarettes for that matter, who would bust a gut to restrain them? The habit was hardly surprising, what with all the overcrowding and the boredom. The screws could also work out that if they pretended not to notice that the tobacco smelt a bit funny, and the cons realized that the screws knew but did nothing, then this could turn into a handy extra means of control. I'm on to your little game, my son, but the Big Boss doesn't get to hear of it as long as you don't give me any trouble. Any naughtiness and before you know where you are I'll have Sniffer Dog Freddie so far up you that only his back paws and the tip of his tail will be showing. Do you read me, my son?

'So you're out on licence?' Duffy asked quietly. Taffy closed *Theories of Social Revolt* and turned to him. 'You know, you may drive that poxy van and put in alarm systems that don't work, but you still stink of copper.'

'Normal, isn't it?' said Duffy, getting up. 'And what makes you think I can't smell the con on you?'

D/S Barry Vine, who couldn't have cared a monkey's whether or not he stank of copper, hadn't expected to return to Braunscombe Hall until later in the afternoon, but he didn't mind arriving early. At least it meant a break from going round in circles with Jimmy Beckford. Most of it had been easy – except for the difficult part. Yes, that was his camp in the woods. Yes, everything in it did belong to him. Yes, he had known the woman in question for some time. Yes, he did have feelings for her. No, those feelings weren't reciprocated. Would it be an exaggeration, sir, to suggest that you were in love with her and she did not care for your attentions? No, that wouldn't be too much of an exaggeration. It was just, he said, that he hadn't done it. Where had he been between lunch and dinner? Well, he'd been around the grounds, but not up near his camp; in fact in the woods and the fields on the other side of the house. He'd been playing Army games. I see, sir, and while you were playing these Army games did you see anyone? Oh yes, he'd seen Taffy and Vic and Belinda and Lucretia. They could vouch for these meetings, could they? Oh no, they weren't meetings, I saw them. But they didn't see you? That's right, that's the point of Army games. Stealth, concealment, that sort of thing.

Look, put it this way, sir, if you were me, would you believe what I'm hearing? Jimmy Beckford, who had been arrested but not yet charged, thought for a long time over this question, and his reply, when it came, had rather impressed D/S Vine. If you believed how I loved Angela, he said, you'd know I couldn't have done it. Barry Vine was a family man of some years' standing, and he was also a copper; but he found himself curiously affected by Jimmy's words.

'It's just a thought,' said Duffy.

'Yes?' Detective-Sergeant Vine wasn't prejudiced against ex-coppers, though he was well-aware that some of the means by which they acquired that 'ex–' were a bit naughty. He hadn't properly talked to this chap who'd directed him to Jimmy Beckford's camp; but that action put him in credit so far.

'You'll have looked in Jimmy's tins. You'll have found that newspaper photo with bits burnt out of it.'

'When did you see it?'

'Oh, I was poking around. I came to mend the alarm system.'

'What, has Jimmy got a bell on his camp?'

'Not exactly. Look, I thought you ought to know Jimmy doesn't smoke.'

'I know. I asked him.'

'Ah.'

'But he admits burning the photo. With a piece of stick from his fire, he said. So it's not what you think.'

'Right.'

'I'll talk to you in a bit.'

Duffy went out on to the terrace with Vic. A clean, fresh breeze, lightly scented with roses, made them both cough.

'Wish I smoked,' said Vic.

'It keeps the wasps away as well.'

'Yeah. Right.'

'You miss the old days, Vic?' He didn't just mean the old days: also the old places, the old smells, the old rackets, the old racketeers. Duffy had known quite a few villains, and most of them, even when they'd made it to the big house and had the cabin cruiser moored down at the marina, even when they were big enough to bribe a junior cabinet minister and develop a taste for vintage claret, still felt attached to some particular square mile of territory. Some anonymous patch of a sprawling city sparkled in their memory like a little village – with its friendly vicar (sent down for his friendliness with juveniles), its beaming butcher (caught with his thumb on the scales) and its picturesque green (where the grass was carpet-bombed with dog turds). But this 'village' was where they first grew up, where they first learned to nick things and it made them tearfully sentimental. Perhaps their mum still lived in the same street, and some of their mates, whose careers hadn't prospered quite so well, could still be found in the council flats, except for when they were doing spells with Her Majesty. Vic's particular patch had been a little corner of Catford backing on to the railway line and the dog stadium. Of course, this was going back all the way: before he'd finally made the big jump to the Buckinghamshire/Bedfordshire borders he'd had a few years in Lewisham; and by the time he met Belinda he was up in ritzy Blackheath, which apart from anything else was handier for the offices of Laski & Lejeune.

'Thing about the old days,' said Vic philosophically, 'is that at the time they didn't seem like the old days.'

'They wouldn't, would they?'

'But you don't think that at the time, do you? You don't think, one day these are gonna be the old days. I mean, today for instance, you'll look back on today at some point in the future and say that was the old days. It gives the brain a bit of a spin, doesn't it?'

'You're a deep one and no mistake,' said Duffy. He gazed across at Vic: a stocky, red-faced man settling into late middle-age who didn't dress as if he'd ever been to the country, let alone lived there. Duffy wondered if Belinda had had a go at him about his clothes. You'd still take him for a mildly sucessful street trader, a barrow boy who'd made it big and could now afford to pay someone to run his stall on Saturday afternoons while he went down the football. 'See much of the first Mrs Crowther?'

'I keep in touch. Don't let on to Bel, though.' Duffy nodded

665

a promise. 'Well, you can't just tear up your life like that, can you? And she's got these legs now, you know.'

'Sorry to hear that, Vic.' Didn't she have legs before? Duffy remembered Bessie Crowther as having pretty vigorous legs, with one of which she'd attempted to separate his wedding tackle from the rest of his body one evening in the old days when he'd popped round and tried to arrest Vic.

'Something to do with the circulation, they say. Anyway, she has to have these check-ups. She's back in that little house we had when we were first married. I sort of never got rid of it, you know, and when we broke up I said she could live in it if she wanted to.'

'Bel doesn't know that either?'

'That I've still got the house? No, she'd hit the roof if she knew. See, it's a bit complicated. I mean, Bel's always believed that when we met my marriage was on the rocks. Well it was, but only because the rocks, if you get my drift, was Bel. Otherwise I suppose Bessie and me would still be together now. I was gone potty on Bel from the moment I clapped eyes on her. But I'm only flesh and blood; I couldn't just throw Bessie over like that. Every so often, when I'm down in London, I take her out like in the old days. Schooner of sherry, scampi and chips, that's what she likes, that's what she gets.'

Must make a nice change from all the posh scoff he gets around here, Duffy thought. And it all sounded just like Vic: walking both sides of the street, even in his marriages. Perhaps it gave him a funny sort of thrill, to kiss his second wife goodbye and go off for an illicit night out with his first wife. Made him feel like a salamander walking through fire or something.

Apart from how he juggled his marriages, how did he juggle his finances? Two establishments, the horses, all those house guests, the servants. 'Do you still have the launderettes?' Duffy asked suddenly.

'Why? You got any complaints?'

'No. Well, now you mention it . . . No, forget it.' That was hardly central to the current business. 'And the video shops?'

'I'm on social security, Duffy, what do you think?'

'What about the others, do they have jobs?'

'You mean, do they pay rent here or are they squatters?' Vic was beginning to get testy.

'No, just curiosity. That Sally, for instance, what does she do for a living? She an estate agent as well?'

'Those are real copper's questions, you know. Or maybe they're just London questions. We don't ask things like that down in the country. Do you want to marry her or something?'

'Maybe,' said Duffy. Then she wouldn't have so far to go whenever she wanted to have a whole load of fun and let his van tyres down.

'Her dad's got a spot of cash. She was married when she was about twenty and picked up something from that. She does some of that art. She sells the odd drawing, if you must know. Don't ask me how much she gets, I haven't bought one.'

'I'm surprised she can draw straight.' Surprised she can find the crayons to start with.

'Well, she doesn't as a matter of fact. It's got a name.'

'What has?'

'Not drawing straight. You know, paint a dog and it comes out looking like a monkey. It's got a posh name in the right circles, that has.'

'Check. And what about Bel?'

'What about her? You want to see her bank statements?'

'No. Just wondering if she missed the old days as well.'

'Oh. What, the modelling? Don't think so. She's all horsey nowadays. And mumsy as well, of course, with little Nikki. By the way, Duffy, congratulations.'

'Come again.'

'You did good with the spoons. Real good. Nothing like hiring a minder to look after one of your house guests and after she's got kidnapped and nearly raped he manages to screw a confession out of your own daughter that she's planted a few worthless spoons on one of your servants. I mean, how did you manage it, Duffy? Rubber hoses, water treatment, sensory deprivation?'

'See what you mean. Told her that her dabs were all over them.'

'That old lie?'

'It still works.'

'It never worked with me.'

Duffy thought back to the days of threatening calls from Laski & Lejeune. 'No, it didn't. By the way, if Nikki starts asking for a pair of gloves, I should lock your stuff away.'

'So what have we got now, Duffy? Moving up a league or two from Toytown crime.'

'Well, the car proves we haven't just got Jimmy, doesn't it?'

'Assuming it wasn't a squirrel.'

'Which we assume. So if we go along with Jimmy being rightly locked up, we've got one other something. If we don't go along with the Jimmy line, we might still have one other something. Or we could, of course, have two different somethings which happen to have coincided.'

'I like a bit of clear thinking,' said Vic ironically. 'You could put that in writing and start charging guineas.'

'With headed notepaper. I've thought of it, but I couldn't handle the VAT. The point is, who's being naughty around here? Are we dealing with strangers or are we dealing with your distinguished house guests? For instance, what about Angela and Taffy as a number?'

'Eh? I shouldn't think so. Poor old Taff. All these aspersions.'

'For instance, it was you who threw Ricky in the lake, wasn't it?'

This was perfectly timed. Vic was starting to say 'No' when he realized that only the person who'd thrown him in and the person who'd fished him out would know Ricky had spent some time under water, so he stopped, changed gear, and said, 'What, you mean they've found Ricky?'

Duffy laughed. 'I think you're about as unconvinced by yourself as I am, Vic.'

'Why on earth should I want to do a thing like that?' Vic demanded, all honest-citizen, all get-me-Laski-&-Lejeune.

'The dog's one of the main problems in this whole business.

I think I've worked out a bit of the dog, but I haven't worked out the whole dog.'

'Where is Ricky?'

'Up in London with his guts on a slab.'

'So Jimmy found him?'

'Jimmy found him. The problem was, who killed him and who threw him in the water. Why should anyone want to do first one and then the other? Why not just throw him in the water to start off with if that's what you wanted? So, the only sensible conclusion is, it was two different people, not connected with one another. Someone who we presume wanted to fuck up Angela, and then you.'

'Me.' It wasn't a question, or a protestation of innocence; it was more of a prompt.

'No body, no crime. No crime, no coppers. Sensible, really. The other side of it goes: no body, no criminal; no criminal, no justice. But it's all a matter of priorities.'

'So if I'm number two, who's number one?'

'I don't know. I really don't know.'

'Telephone, Mr Duffy.' It was Mrs Colin, beaming at him. She continued beaming as he followed her into the house and along a corridor. She didn't say a word, but then she didn't need to.

When Duffy emerged again into the unhealthy air, he was shaking his head. 'I think I've had enough for the moment,' he said to Vic. 'The old brain's racing. I'm going to have a snooker lesson. Give my regards to the Detective-Sergeant if he needs me.'

'Who was the call from?'

'And can I borrow a tie? Preferably without too much heraldry on it.'

Duffy took the five miles to Winterton House at a conservative speed. Off the M1 things were just as dangerous. There was a lot of inbreeding in the countryside, he knew, and everyone drove like lunatics whether they were or not. Carefully, he turned into the driveway of Winterton House, past some entrance pillars of genuinely weathered stone. He made the gentlest of rustles on the gravel, in case Henry's mother was taking an afternoon nap. As he got out of his van, Duffy adjusted the brown kipper tie Vic had lent him. This sartorial touch wasn't just a matter of courtesy; it was also to help with his cueing. Brush the knot lightly as you slide through on the shot: that was one of the things he had to remember.

A woman of indeterminate age and status answered the door, and after a brief discussion agreed not to send him round to the back despite his appearance. Henry seemed pleased to see him, and offered a large hand.

'Glad you telephoned. Mother says we are both to join her after our lesson. Tea is at four-thirty in the conservatory.'

'Did you hear about Sally's car?'

'Mmm. Ange telephoned. Dreadful. Didn't come over as Mother had a slight turn and . . . anyway, I wouldn't have been any help.'

Winterton House went back to 1730; it had been inhabited at one time by a fully paid-up, long-lasting Lord Mayor of London; it had a wine-cellar with properly dusty bottles; it had never been lived in by a rock musician who played with a feather up his bum; and its billiard room, though post-dating 1730 by at least a century, remained as it had been originally designed – a quiet enclave of mahogany and old leather, with a tang of yesterday's cigar smoke in the air. Duffy sniffed, and pretended to be reminded of something.

'Henry, tell me, is there a lot of drugging over at the Hall?'

'Drugging?'

'Yes. Taking drugs. You know what I mean.'

'Yes, I know what you mean. I'm just not sure that I . . . I . . . how can one tell? I don't think I'd be very good at telling. Who are you thinking of?'

'Well, I don't know them very well.'

'I don't think Ange would do anything like that,' said Henry. He drew the heavy plum curtains, pulled the cover off the table and while folding it, pointed to the cue rack. Duffy put a white on the table and played it firmly round the cushions. Then he did so again, in the opposite direction. Compared to this, the table at Braunscombe Hall was like a ploughed field.

'Lovely and true, Henry.'

'It's an 1866 Thurston. Looked after by them ever since.

Can't get slate like that nowadays. There's a real chunk of Wales under there.'

'New cloth?'

'Five years ago, actually. Mother thought the old one was quite good enough because it was still green, so I had it done on the sly. Bit of a row and all that. Didn't tell her I had new cushions at the same time.'

Henry was a fine player; indeed, he looked much more relaxed leaning over a snooker table than he did standing up and being normal. He was also a good teacher, patient yet firm. It was a revision course as much as anything; Duffy in theory knew all about not coming up on the shot, about follow-through, about matching your tactics to your capabilities; he just had to be constantly reminded about them. Henry was particularly keen on getting Duffy's stance right. 'If you don't stand right, you don't cue right, and if you don't cue right, you can't control the ball.' He demonstrated; Duffy tried to copy. 'Doesn't matter about the feet not being parallel as long as you're comfortable. What makes the difference is locking the hips.' Duffy was slow to get this bit. 'Look, get in position, and, excuse me, keep your feet exactly where they are, now, sorry about this bit.' In the crepuscular atmosphere of this Victorian gentlemen's room, Henry put his hands on Duffy's hips and tugged at him gently, like a sweet-palmed osteopath. Duffy's hips swivelled and locked. Henry took his hands away. Be my guest, murmured Duffy under his breath.

At four twenty-five the lesson stopped, and Henry went away to brush his hair before tea with Mother. Duffy didn't need to brush his hair. Instead, he adjusted Vic's kipper tie.

'How do you do, young man. What a very unattractive tie,' said Henry's mother. She was sitting on a wicker chair in the conservatory, surrounded by plants which Duffy might just have been able to identify if he'd done a ten-year course at Kew Gardens.

'It's not mine, actually.'

'Then why on earth do you wear it?' She was about eighty, an erect, bony figure, with sharp blue eyes and white hair cut short; she wore a pale green silk dress which Duffy reckoned had been very expensive about ten years before he was born, and pink running-shoes. 'So you're my son's new billiards partner?'

'He's giving me lessons. It's very useful.'

'I'm glad to hear he's good at something. He's always seemed to me singularly useless at most things.' Duffy glanced up at Henry, who wasn't reacting. He'd obviously had this for years. 'And you're staying over at the Hall with that crook, what's his name?'

'Vic Crowther. It's his tie, actually.'

'That doesn't surprise me in the least. The only interesting question is whether he paid for it with his own money.'

'Mother!'

'Well, of course he's a crook. Someone like him doesn't end up owning the Hall unless he's a crook, stands to reason.'

Duffy couldn't work out whether Henry's mother was as rude as this because she was posh, or because she was old, or a combination of both. Or maybe it wasn't to do with either: she was just rude, and that's all there was to it.

'So you will have examined the gel who is shortly to make Henry the happiest man in the world?'

'Angela. Yes.'

'And what do you make of her?'

What did Duffy make of her? 'I haven't really seen much of her.'

'How very diplomatic of you, particularly in front of your billiards tutor. She's obviously neurotic.'

'Mother!'

'The only thing I couldn't make out, because she was wearing such extraordinary clothes on the occasion I was permitted to meet her, was whether or not she has good child-bearing hips. Have you examined her hips?'

Duffy tried to remember. 'I think they'll do the business,' he suggested cautiously.

'Do the business? Do the business? I see what you mean. But will Henry be able to do the business?'

'Mother, really.'

'Perhaps it would be best if the line were just allowed to die out. Oh well,' she said, re-crossing her pink running-shoes, 'perhaps the gel will have her menopause before she gets to the altar. You definitely want another cup of tea.'

'I need one,' said Duffy.

'I hear she had some kind of bad turn the other day?'

Look, what's going on, Duffy thought. He couldn't follow this mixture of over-statement and under-statement. 'That's right, she had a bit of a turn. Someone tried to rape her.'

'Tried? What are the men coming to nowadays? When I was a gel they would have succeeded. It's just another name for marriage, anyway, isn't it?'

'I don't know. I've never tried it.'

'What, rape or marriage?'

'Either.'

'Mmm. Does that mean you're a bachelor boy like my Henry?'

'Uh-huh.'

'You're not one of those homosexuals, are you?' She pronounced the word with no apparent distaste, though using the old-fashioned long *o* on the first syllable.

Duffy thought it was too complicated to explain, so he nodded and said, 'That's right.'

'How fascinating. You know I've never met one who said he was. You must come to tea again and tell me what it is you do. I've always wondered what went where. Of course, that is, if you survive.'

'Oh, I'll survive.'

'But you're all dropping like flies, aren't you? They tell me there's this new disease which is going to purge the world of shirt-lifters, as my late husband used to refer to them. I hope you don't find the term offensive.'

'I think it's a bit of an exaggeration.'

'That's what it says in the newspaper.'

'The newspapers are full of homophobia,' said Duffy. Well, why not? She thinks I'm just a common shirt-lifter in a nasty tie. Why not show her I know a few long words as well?

'Never heard that term before,' said Henry's mum. 'I suppose it's a polite way of saying you don't like fairies.' Henry stood up and put his cup on the tray. 'You will bring your friend back again, won't you?' was the parting line from the wicker chair. 'I'm so looking forward to finding out what goes where after all these years.'

The gravel outside Winterton House seemed ever so slightly posher than the gravel over at the Hall. Perhaps you could even get upper-class gravel. Perhaps Vic's had fallen off the back of a lorry. 'She's a real character, your mum.'

'I don't know how to apologize . . .' Henry seemed to be almost blushing.

'Forget it. She's like a breath of fresh air compared to some I could mention. But if you want to apologize, you can give me another lesson. I don't think I'm confident of thumping Damian yet.'

'It'd be a pleasure.'

●

Back at the Hall D/S Vine had left for the day. He either had to charge Jimmy or release him in the next twelve hours or so – not that the fellow seemed particularly interested in his rights – and he might as well get on with it. The remains of Sally's Datsun Cherry were cordoned off with a rope which wouldn't have deterred a squirrel. As Duffy opened the front door he ran into Damian, who shook a finger at him. 'Naughty boy. Naughty boy.'

'Eh?'

'The rozzers. Not very content, the rozzers. A policeman's lot is not a happy one. Skipping off and leaving the scene of the crime. Had to tell them about rescuing the cars all by myself. Pulled them free with my bare teeth while thousands quailed.'

'I bet he believed you.'

'That was the trouble. He didn't even believe me when I told him the truth. Just because I'm pretty that beastly Detective-Sergeant thought I didn't know what an axle was. Said I'd get you to corroborate my deeds of heroism. And where were you? Skipped the country for all we knew.'

'I was having . . .' Duffy stopped. 'Actually, I was having tea with Henry's mum.'

'And you survived? You must have been wearing asbestos close to the skin.'

'No, I liked her. Not sure I could be married to her.'
Damian peered at Duffy as if to say, But who would have you
anyway? 'Incidentally, what happened to Henry's dad?'

'Keeled over from a punctured eardrum, I should imagine.
No idea – it was all long before Damian's time.'

Duffy chuckled. Thinking of Henry's mum made him
understand a bit more why posh people's architects set aside
certain parts of the house for gentlemen only. They were running away, that's what the men were doing. And the Henry's
mums of this world were all kitted out in pink running-shoes
so that they could chase after them and find out what goes
where. 'She seemed to be putting Henry down quite a bit.'

'I don't think he notices any more. Just gives that look of
his – you know, like a fairly intelligent Aberdeen Angus – and
occasionally a little smile, but he's probably leagues away.'

'You're not a writer, by any chance, are you, Damian?'

'Why do you ask?'

'Well, you use these words nobody else uses.'

'I do a bit of this and that,' said Damian, in a manner worthy
of his host. 'I have . . . ambitions.'

'Glad to hear it. No, cheers, mate.' Duffy was almost not
being ironic; it was a nice change for someone in this place to
mention, however vaguely, that they might want to, well,
have a job or something at some time in the future. 'What
does she think about Henry? About him getting married?'

'*His* getting married. Well, she's changed, of course. Spent
at least forty years telling Henry it was his duty as an only son
to keep the flag flying, and then as soon, or as late, as he brings
a girl home and says this is the one for me, she starts taking
the opposite line.'

'Doesn't she like Angela?'

'Nothing much to do with Ange, I don't think. She just
likes keeping Henry on the run. I suppose the fact that Ange
isn't a teenager gives her something to go on about though.
Says what's the point of marrying someone you can't breed
from. Says Henry might as well shack up with some ewe in a
stone barn.'

'She said that?'

'So Henry reported. Mind you, he seemed almost amused by it.'

'Can't Angela have children?'

'No reason why not. Not as far as anyone knows. She'll probably get a couple in before the old drawbridge comes up.'

'I'm surprised Henry hasn't killed his mum,' said Duffy. 'Or at least left home.'

'They tried that once, apparently. Shipped him out to Argentina, or "the Argentine" as they tend to refer to it. Some family connection with corned beef, I should think. He lasted three weeks. Took the next plane home.'

'Things must be bad in Argentina.'

'Couple of frames before dinner?' suggested Damian.

'Got a few things to do,' Duffy replied. 'Perhaps in a day or two.'

'I'll be waiting for you.'

Damian went off towards the ploughed-field snooker table. Duffy wandered into the family room, where he found Belinda reading *Horse and Hound*; beside her, Vic was bent over a copy of *Exchange and Mart*. 'Just looking up a good breakers' for the Datsun.'

'Breakers'? Is there anything left to break?'

'There's always something. Anyway, Sally says she's a bit strapped for cash at the moment, so I said I'd see what I could do.'

'She doesn't behave as if she's strapped for cash.'

'No, she doesn't.'

'There are those funny old-fashioned things called jobs,' said Duffy.

'You know, it's odd. Those kids don't seem to have heard of them.'

Belinda laughed. 'You two sound like you've got big grey beards.'

'Come on, Bel, you say it yourself. About when you were working. How it changed in the few years you were in it.'

'Sure,' said Belinda cautiously, not sure if the analogy was fair.

'How d'you mean?' asked Duffy.

'When I went into modelling, back in the Seventies' –

Belinda made it sound as if Queen Victoria had been on the throne at the time – 'I did all the training. Paid out a lot of cash. How to walk, how to hold yourself, how to show the clothes to the best advantage.' And how best to show the bits of you that burst out of the clothes like trains from a tunnel, thought Duffy. 'You know, the whole bit. Model school. Even taught you how to speak proper. *Ly*,' she added with a grin. 'Anyway, you went along to your first job, you knew more or less what you were in for, what was expected. And even then you sometimes got treated like a pushy tart.'

'Really?' Duffy tried to sound as straight-voiced as possible.

'Christ, yes. I mean, I was one of the new wave of models. I was sort of real. There were one or two others around at the same time, sure, I don't take any credit away from them, but it was mainly me. Before, the glamour models were sort of artificial, like packet custard. Wanting to have it both ways – taking off their clothes and pretending they weren't. And then they tried putting me down. Used to look down their nose-jobs at me and say I didn't have the "classic chassis". That was their phrase. All cause they had little ones. Bitches.' Her tone was friendly, though, as if she'd won by ending up in the big house.

'I quite like packet custard,' said Vic. Belinda slapped him playfully.

'And now?'

'Now? Christ, you get everyone thinking they can do it now. Girls of sixteen off the train from Leeds and Bradford, all squidgy with puppy-fat, dropping their blouses as soon as their foot touches the platform. They don't think it takes work. They think anyone can do it.'

'Maybe the country's going to the dogs,' suggested Duffy.

There was a ruminative silence. Belinda put down *Horse and Hound* with a sigh and headed off towards the kitchen. Vic turned confidingly to Duffy. 'By the way, our Detective-Sergeant is cross with you.'

'I heard. Still, he's bound to be back, isn't he?'

'Yeah, I think he went off to charge Jimmy.'

'Well, I'll wash behind my ears for him tomorrow.'

'I suppose,' said Vic musingly, 'I suppose it's just possible that Ricky died a natural death and that some yobbo who happened to be passing chucked him through the window.'

'You get many yobbos around here?'

'There are yobbos everywhere, Duffy. State of the country.' Of course, if they were around, your yobbos could mix with your Vics who were cuddling up with your Damians who were brown-nosing your Hugos, and everyone could join hands and sing 'Auld Lang Syne'.

'Bit of an outside runner, I'd say, Vic.'

Duffy could see Vic's line of thought, and it was natural in someone with Vic's background. Close down as much of this business as possible, that was his instinct. We've got a near-rape and we've got an exploding car and the coppers are crawling all over the place, why throw them a dead dog as well? Natural causes, a passing yobbo, and no body to show for it, that would sort things out. Vic was ever so quietly suggesting that Duffy didn't mention the dog business to the coppers when it came to his turn with the thumbscrews. Perhaps he was also fishing a bit, and wondering about the phone-call Duffy had had that afternoon.

But if Vic had kept quiet about dumping Ricky in the lake, Duffy felt he could reply with a bit of hush on his own account; even if Vic was paying him. So he merely repeated, 'Bit of an outside runner, I'd say,' and let Vic go back to his *Exchange and Mart*. The phone-call had changed things; had changed things quite a bit, and Duffy had to think carefully. He liked old Vic, but he wasn't sure he'd be able to go on confiding in him. If you showed Vic a knife with blood on it, he'd put it in the dishwasher and turn the knob. If you showed Vic a dismembered corpse left in brown-paper parcels in six different luggage lockers, he'd say it was shocking how people kept thinking up new ways to kill themselves. Duffy understood this instinct, but it wasn't always entirely helpful, except in giving Vic a quiet time. So he thought that for the moment he'd keep a few things to himself; especially the thing Jim Pringle had told him on the telephone.

It had all begun with the dog. The dog was in two parts (well, it was probably in even more parts now after featuring on Jim Pringle's slab). Duffy had solved the second part of the dog; solving the first part of the dog might be the key to the whole business. And just as there were two parts to the dog, there might turn out to be two parts to the business. One domestic, say, and one professional. Or two domestics that didn't know about one another. Or two professionals . . . The riddling combinations made Duffy realize how far he currently was from solving anything. He needed help. Of two kinds, in fact: domestic and professional.

The domestic help might be obtained from . . . well, the domestic help. Mrs Colin attributed her recent salvation in the matter of the missing cutlery to two causes: the power of prayer and the intervention of the man from London in the white van. It was, indeed, the power of prayer which had brought the man in the white van down to the Buckinghamshire/Bedfordshire borders to help her. If someone had pointed out to Mrs Colin that Nikki had in fact planted the spoons on her only after Duffy's arrival, this would have disturbed neither her faith nor her sense of logic. The Lord knew in advance the wickedness in little Nikki's mind, and Duffy was the temporal answer to it; the fact that he got to Braunscombe Hall before the sin was perpetrated was neither here nor there. This did not cast doubt on the efficacy of prayer; all it cast doubt on was the reliability of the man in the white van.

Mrs Colin's room was as bare as it had been on Duffy's previous visit. The process of packing, and soon afterwards unpacking again, hadn't affected the look of the place; not that these operations could have taken much time. Mrs Colin smiled broadly as Duffy knocked on the half-open door, came in, and sat down on the bed. There had been opportunities for Mrs Colin to thank Duffy verbally for her salvation, but she had not yet mentioned the matter, and she didn't do so now; she merely beamed at him. Perhaps she thought that a gesture, a smile, a series of smiles, was a truer way of showing gratitude than a few words in a foreign and untrustworthy language; or perhaps she thought that Duffy was merely an agent of help: spoken words of gratitude should all be divided between Our Lord and the holy sisters at the Church of Our

Lady of Penitence, who prayed for the moral safety of those in service overseas.

'Mrs Colin,' Duffy began, 'we're in a spot of trouble.'

'We?' Mrs Colin, sitting erect on a hard chair in front of one of Belinda's cast-off dressing-tables, was alarmed. Not more trouble already?

'No, not *us*. Not you, not me.'

'Ah.' But if it wasn't him and her, why had he said 'we'? Mrs Colin was confirmed in her belief that most of the time the face can speak more truly than the tongue.

'No, I mean the trouble at the Hall, here.'

'Trouble here?' More trouble, did he mean?

'The trouble about the dog, Mrs Colin. The trouble about Miss Angela in the woods. The trouble about Miss Sally's car.' Mrs Colin nodded. She knew all about *that* trouble. Why was he telling her what she knew already? Why did he come to her room, sit on her bed, smile at her, and tell her things that were familiar to both of them? An interesting thought crossed Mrs Colin's mind, and she smiled back at Duffy, though a little more shyly this time. He was short with darkish hair and quite powerfully built. He was much more the physical type she was used to in her own country; here this strange damp climate sprouted tall blond men with pot-bellies and dripping noses. That, at any rate, was Mrs Colin's generalized impression of the race she worked amongst. Perhaps this man in the white van . . .

'The point is, Mrs Colin, that Mr Crowther has asked me to help him. To help him find out what happened.'

'The policeman . . .'

'Mr Crowther is very grateful for the help the policemen are giving, and he is of course co-operating in every way with them, but he feels that any help I might be able to give them, with, well, the specialist knowledge I might be able to bring . . .' Duffy was waffling, and he knew it.

'Mr Crowther, he pays you for this?' It was not the question that Duffy had expected. Mrs Colin was looking sharply at him. One of the side-mirrors of Belinda's cast-off dressing-table gave Duffy a simultaneous view of her profile. She was looking just as sharply at him in profile.

'Well, sort of, I suppose.'

'And you want me to help you, to tell you things?'

'Mmm. Well, I was hoping . . .'

'So you will pay me, then.'

'Sorry?'

Mrs Colin suddenly laughed. She pulled open the bottom left-hand drawer of her dressing-table and fished out a small buff envelope, which she handed to Duffy. 'This is a manilla envelope,' she said, repeating one of Mr Colin's old jokes, 'It is for sending to the Philippines.' Then she turned her back on him.

Duffy looked at the address printed in red; it was that of a church, presumably in Mrs Colin's home town. He took out his wallet, stuffed a tenner into the envelope, paused, wondered if bribing Vic's domestic staff could be claimed back from Vic as legitimate expenses, and put in another tenner. As he licked the gum on the envelope, he realized that Mrs Colin, with an oblique glance in the side-mirror, had monitored the extent of Duffy's charitable impulse. She seemed to approve, and smiled shyly as she returned the envelope to her bottom drawer.

'Mrs Colin, you've been with Mr and Mrs Crowther for . . .'

'Five years. Two in London, three in the country.'

'And you're happy working for them?'

'Very happy.'

'No trouble?'

'No. No trouble.' This was just like talking to the policeman. Perhaps she should also have invited the Detective-Sergeant to assist the holy sisters at the Church of Our Lady of Penitence.

'Mr Crowther said to tell you that he wants you to answer my questions as truthfully as possible.' Mrs Colin nodded. Who did they think she was, these English policemen? She laid her hand gently against the bump of Our Saviour at her throat. Unlike the Detective-Sergeant, the stocky fellow with the white van didn't have a notebook. Perhaps he remembered all the answers. 'Did you see anyone near Miss Sally's car at any time before it caught fire?'

'No.'

'Have there been any quarrels?'

'Quarrels?'

'In the house. Anyone been cross with anyone?'

'Miss Blessing, she's cross.'

'Who with?'

'No, I mean, she's cross. That's what she's like. She's often cross.' Well, Mr Crowther had asked her to tell the truth. 'And Mr Damian, he's often cheeky. Very cheeky.'

'But no quarrels.'

'No quarrels.'

'And while you've been down here, in the country, have you seen anything . . . naughty. I mean, anything wrong?'

'Mr Hardcastle steals Mr Crowther's wine.' She said it as if it were a perfectly normal and regular occurrence, which perhaps it was.

'How does he do that?' Duffy felt slightly disappointed that he wasn't alone in having made this discovery.

'Oh, he waits until everybody is out and then he goes and takes it from the cellar.'

Subtle ploy, that, thought Duffy. The touch of a master criminal. 'You mean, a whole box of it?'

'Sometimes. Sometimes just a few bottles. Depends whether Mr and Mrs Hardcastle are running short or not.'

'Do they say anything to you about it?'

'Yes, they say do I want a bottle? But I do not drink.'

'Did they say anything else?'

'Yes, they say it is an old British custom in the big houses.'

'And you didn't tell anyone about this?'

'Who am I to question the old British customs?' said Mrs Colin. She gave one of those smiles that were handy for all occasions.

'And what about some of the newer British customs, Mrs Colin?'

'Which you mean?'

'Well, like, Look who's sleeping in my bed.'

'Who's sleeping in your bed?' Mrs Colin looked alarmed, as if something had gone wrong with the domestic arrangements at Braunscombe Hall and it might be her fault. At the same time, she wondered if this rather nice . . .

'I.o, I mean, you're delivering the breakfast trays, for instance, or you go in to turn the beds down, or to open a window. Or you just . . . notice things.' Monogrammed knickers, for instance; lingerie with a giveaway salamander or a tell-tale phoenix.

'You mean what Mr Damian calls fucky-fuck?' Mrs Colin wasn't to know that Mr Damian only used this expression when he knew that she was within earshot. He had several dozen other expressions for normal wear.

'What Mr Damian calls fucky-fuck, yes.'

Sally, it seemed, was the principal fucky-fuck artiste in the house; a fact which didn't greatly surprise Duffy, given the view he'd had the other night in the billiard room. Damian liked fucky-fuck too, though it had apparently struck Mrs Colin that Damian often seemed to prefer staying up late talking about fucky-fuck to actually doing fucky-fuck. Lucretia liked a certain amount of fucky-fuck, though not as much as Sally. Taffy had asked Mrs Colin for fucky-fuck on a couple of occasions; though he had been very polite about it, and completely understood when she had declined.

'Jimmy?'

Mrs Colin giggled. 'He likes fucky-fuck with girls in magazines,' she said, remembering an occasion when she had gone to change the flowers in Jimmy's room. She didn't think Duffy would need to know the details of what she had seen.

'Miss Angela?'

'Miss Angela's getting married. We're all going to the wedding.'

'So . . . Miss Angela and Mr Henry?'

Suddenly, Mrs Colin giggled. Duffy repeated his question and Mrs Colin silently shook her head, though whether in ignorance or denial of the engaged couple's sexual habits Duffy could not tell.

'So . . . Miss Angela.'

Mrs Colin shook her head again, more violently this time. Duffy noted this reaction. Then he dutifully checked the marital fidelity of Vic and Belinda with Mrs Colin, and moved on.

'What about drugs?'

'There are many drugs.' That was the thing about the British. Their bars looked like chemists' shops, and so did their bathroom cabinets. They were very worried about their health, the British. Perhaps they did not believe in God enough.

'But . . . naughty drugs.'

'You mean like the Beecham's?'

Duffy just about managed to look puzzled. 'What's the Beecham's?'

'The Beecham's. You put it up your nose for the hay fever.'

'Ah. And who has the hay fever?'

Damian had the hay fever; he also, Duffy realized, had a teasing vocabulary with which he had infected Mrs Colin. The other person to have the hay fever was Sally. In fact Sally had the hay fever all the year round, even when there was snow on the ground, and she needed a lot of Beecham's to cure it. Damian's hay fever wasn't half as bad as Sally's. Mrs Colin wasn't sure if there were any other sufferers in the household. Perhaps Lucretia, or Taffy? Perhaps; but she couldn't tell. She hadn't seen. Angela? No, she really couldn't tell.

The other thing that had to be kept at bay was the wasps. Damian had a special tobacco which he smoked to ward them off. It also worked, he said, for gnats, mosquitoes, midges, bees, tsetse flies and ladybirds. Unsurprisingly, Sally liked shooing away the wasps; Lucretia and Taffy didn't mind distracting them, either. There had even been an occasion, Mrs Colin revealed, when they persuaded Jimmy to try. It had been on the terrace, after dinner, when Mr and Mrs Crowther had been out. Jimmy had coughed a lot, and the others had laughed. Miss Angela had laughed as well. Miss Angela also seemed to enjoy special tobacco.

'Anything else?'

'Like what?'

'Like the Beecham's or the wasp tobacco?' Mrs Colin looked doubtful. Duffy wondered what Damian's euphemism for shooting up might be. 'Has anyone got anything like diabetes?'

'What's that?'

'It's a sort of illness. What you have to do if you've got it is take a little syringe and inject something into your arm. You have to do that for lots of other illnesses as well,' Duffy added hopefully.

'Maybe you look in the medicine cabinets,' said Mrs Colin. Really, the British were an odd people. Injecting themselves for all sorts of illnesses. In Davao only the doctor did that to you. Perhaps the doctors over here weren't as good as everyone said. That was why everybody drank so much – 'What's your medicine?' – and had to inject themselves.

Duffy didn't think he'd bother with the medicine cabinets; though it might be worth pulling open a few bottom drawers. Or rather – on the principle that people hide things not in the most obvious place but the next most obvious place – a few drawers up. He wondered whether Mrs Colin was quite as naïve as she made out. Perhaps she understood everything; perhaps she was finding a way to obey Mr Crowther's instruction (which Duffy in any case had invented) while seeming not to betray his guests.

'What about the dog?'

'What do you mean?'

'Did anyone . . . not like the dog?'

'Everyone liked the dog. No, that's not true.' Mrs Colin paused. She had been instructed to tell the truth, and so she would. Duffy was expectant. 'Everyone liked the dog except for one person. Me. I didn't like the dog. I was bitten by a dog in Davao when I was a girl. It was a dog that looked like Ricky.'

It seemed unnecessary to check with Mrs Colin whether Ricky's death was indeed a long-term Filipino canine revenge killing. He thanked her and left. He'd got . . . what? Confirmation rather than anything else. Bed-hopping, drugging – he'd more or less had that from Vic to start off with; Mrs Colin had just brought it more into focus, filled in who and what, relayed Damian's jaunty euphemisms. There'd been something about Angela and fucky-fuck – some hesitation on Mrs Colin's part – which might be worth pursuing. And he had, of course, received confirmation of Ron Hardcastle's enthusiasm for the Vinho Verde and the pink champagne. Would Vic be pleased with the news? Look, Vic, I bribed one of your servants with twenty quid I'd like you to refund me, and she said that one of your other servants was nicking from you. How would Vic react? Perhaps he might suggest that Duffy wasn't exactly concentrating on essentials.

One of the essentials was the dog, even though Vic had tried to dispose of all the evidence. Duffy sat on an uncomfortable rustic bench looking back at the terrace and the french windows, which still had a papered hole in them. A bumblebee droned slowly past, and Duffy clamped his lips together in case the insect flew into his mouth and stung him on his windpipe which would immediately swell up and stop him breathing and kill him unless he had a swift tracheotomy which could of course be an amateur job performed with a penknife but probably the only person around Braunscombe Hall who knew that sort of stuff was Jimmy because he'd been in the Army and probably received emergency medical training but Jimmy was all locked up so Duffy would simply have to die a horrible suffocating death on the bench. Oooff. The bumblebee passed on, and Duffy, who had been using his teeth as well to clamp his lips shut, briefly relaxed. Perhaps he needed some of that special tobacco which drove the insects away. And what if you kept your mouth shut but the bumblebee flew up your nose?

The dog, Duffy, the dog. What did the dog mean? Who was the dog aimed at? It was Angela's dog, so the obvious deduction was that Ricky's death was aimed at Angela. Someone, it seemed, had been trying to get at Angela, drive her potty, or whatever, and killing her dog was an intermediate stage between throwing a stone through her cottage window and kidnapping her in the wood. Was the same person responsible for all these actions? And was that person Jimmy? The police, who were looking as if they'd charge him quite soon, presumably thought so. Duffy was dubious. For a start, he instinctively distrusted the psycho theory – the one put forward by Henry and much loved by television script-writers. And what finally knocked it on the head for Duffy was the thing Jim Pringle had told him on the telephone. He hadn't heard of that being done to a dog before. Not the chucking through the window – anyone might come up with that – but the thing they'd done before, the way Ricky had actually died. To Duffy's mind, this ruled out Jimmy – poor old Jimmy, who in Mrs Colin's account was so unfamiliar even with ordinary funny tobacco that he'd spluttered and coughed on the terrace one night. No, Jimmy might still have done that thing to Angela in the wood; but he wouldn't have done the dog.

And was it, in any case, aimed at Angela? That was another loose aspect to the case. Perhaps the target was someone else. Vic, for instance: a warning over some contract or other. Or even a warning to the whole house? The whole house – apart from Mrs Colin – had liked Ricky; and the whole house – apart from Damian – had taken him for walks. Sally used to exercise him a lot, apparently. Hmmm. It was time, he decided, for a bit of professional help.

'I've never heard of that before,' said Detective-Sergeant Vine.

'Nor have I. Nasty.'

'Very nasty. Sick, in fact. London?'

'Could be.' Duffy was non-committal.

'London, definitely.' D/S Vine didn't have a whisper of evidence for this statement apart from somehow wanting it to be true. Country policemen tended to see the big cities as the source of all corruption. This wasn't sentimentality about their own patch – they knew vice could flourish just as well among the bluebells as among the council flats – but observation. The criminal psyche always did seem to spawn its sickest novelties up in London or Glasgow or wherever. D/S Vine had a wife and kids – a dog, too, for that matter; and when you heard about some nasty new trick you always imagined it invading your own village. It tended to make you a little conservative; which was only normal.

'You realize . . .' he began, but Duffy cut him off with a nod and a grunt before he got going. He was about to mention freelancing, and cowboys, and the illegal removing of evidence in a criminal case. But on the other hand it had been this ex-copper who had led him to the camp in the woods, and if this ex-copper had removed evidence from the scene of the crime and taken it to London for examination, he had also found that evidence after it had disappeared in the first place. Or rather, caused it to be found. Jimmy in his frogman suit had done the diving. Jimmy, who had only been charged with assault to be going on with, just to hold him. They were taking advice on the merits of gross indecency versus attempted rape versus something even tastier; and there would be a kidnapping charge as well in due course.

But for the moment Vine saw there was too much going on around Braunscombe Hall for him not to need all the inside help he could get. When the case had merely been a question of a disappearing female he had not been struck by the helpfulness of the Hall's inhabitants and house guests. Some of them were unconcerned, some of them downright cheeky. And when that car had gone up, they didn't seem much more bothered. When he'd asked the owner to describe what had happened, she'd giggled and replied, 'I'm afraid these foreign motors are frightfully unstable.' Now there was the dog as well.

'I shall have to ask you . . .'

'Sure. I'll go down and fetch it. Probably tomorrow, if that's all right.' One thing about being an ex-copper was that it made you guess what coppers were going to ask.

D/S Vine was a fair man; and feeling a touch unhappy about a case made you perhaps even fairer. 'Look, I'm grateful . . .'

'Sure,' said Duffy. 'But this is a police investigation into a serious offence and you're not going to start trading information with a freelance, and on the other hand it is of course my duty to turn over to you immediately anything I do discover.'

'Something like that.' Vine grinned. 'Don't know why you ever left the Force.' Duffy didn't return the smile. 'But what I will say is I'm not going to tell you to keep your nose out of things. That's strictly off the record, of course.'

'Of course,' said Duffy. 'And when I bring you the dog back I'm sure I wouldn't like to overhear you talking to yourself about what made that car explode. I mean, some of the locals have this theory that a squirrel might have bitten through an electric cable or something.'

'Strictly off the record,' said Vine, 'I think I can let you know that there was a shortage of electrocuted squirrel bodies found at the scene of the incident. And I have been known to start talking to myself occasionally. But only when I'm under stress.'

'This looks a pretty stressful case to me,' said Duffy.

'Could be. By the way, I can't work out why Vic Crowther doesn't have a record.'

Duffy grinned. 'Nor could we. We did our best when he was down in our manor. Still, Taffy more than makes up for it.'

'He told me. Not that I didn't know already. Sometimes I think I'd rather talk to a straightforward villain who's lying through his teeth than to a reformed ex-con with a degree in sociology or whatever he's got.'

'Did he tell you the one about getting nicked being a symbolic reintegration into society?'

'Sounds a laugh a minute,' said Vine. 'Perhaps I could pay him not to tell me.'

'First you'd have to listen to him thinking aloud about whether or not to take the money. He's got this phobia about not boring you.'

D/S Vine nodded at Duffy. 'I'll be in touch.'

'Ditto.'

It felt like a reasonable arrangement to Duffy. In fact, it felt like the best arrangement he could hope for. Vine was using him as a sniffer dog. Nothing wrong in that, as long as the collar wasn't too tight and the choke-chain wasn't pulled on him whenever he found something naughty going on under his nose. At the same time, Duffy hadn't made any promises to Vine. The detective-sergeant hadn't overtly rebuked him for his freelance treatment of Ricky's body, and Duffy took this as a wink of permission in case he wanted to forget about the small print of legality on a similar occasion. Provided things worked out right, of course. If they didn't . . . well, he'd only come to mend the burglar alarm, Chief Inspector, honest.

It was plain to Duffy that the case needed a bit of forcing. The coppers were concentrating on Jimmy at the moment – quite right, too, it was the most serious part of the business so far – and were waiting for the report on the car and then the delivery of Ricky. It gave Duffy a day or two in which to press. The obvious place to press was Angela. She was where it all started.

He was supposed to have been minding her, of course, but somehow that bit of the job had got blown off course. Well, maybe he'd better go and mind her for a while. Only earning his money, after all. He didn't actually like Angela, which was one reason why he probably hadn't minded her as much as he should have done. Another reason was the size of Braunscombe Hall: maybe he should have tied a bleeper to her at the start of the job. Yet another reason was that she obviously didn't much care for Duffy. It wasn't that she was frosty with him – which he could have handled, or reacted to; it was just that he seemed not to exist for her. He was a sort of delivery boy who had strayed into the house and somehow kept turning up to meals, a consequence of Vic's puzzlingly generous open-door policy. Duffy remembered that at no point had she thanked him for finding her up at Jimmy's camp.

He tried saying poor kid to himself as he hitchhiked round the Hall looking for her; but he wasn't really convinced. Poor kid for what happened up in the woods, sure. Poor kid for the life she led, sorry, nothing doing. Duffy didn't soften at the sufferings of the rich. He'd heard about them often enough, he'd seen them all the time in American soap operas on the telly; but he didn't buy the package. People with money didn't have the right to whinge, that's what Duffy thought. He'd known a lot of people with no money, most of whom frequently imagined that the solution to everything would be to have some; so it was up to rich people not to disillusion them. They had what everyone else wanted: shut up and enjoy it, that was Duffy's line. Vic Crowther would probably have called it chippy, but Duffy didn't care.

'Do you mind if I show you something?' He had found her in the family room, looking out of the picture window up towards the wood. A couple of upturned magazines lay on the floor; a cigarette busily smoked itself in the ashtray. She turned. Duffy could tell that when she was looking at you, when she dropped her lethargic profile and gave you the big brown eyes and the shiny red hair, she was in theory attractive; but he didn't fancy her. No doubt that was chippy, too; he probably suffered from physical chippiness as well as social chippiness. Still, if he were to be tempted by upward sexual mobility, Lucretia would be the one to get the nod.

'What?'

'Do you mind if I show you something? It's not far.'

'Can't you tell me what it is?'

'I'd rather show you.'

Reluctantly, she accompanied him through the kitchen, out across the lawn and into the long grass at the edge of the lake.

'We've found Ricky.'

'Oh yes.' Her expression, as she stared over his shoulder and took another puff of her cigarette, didn't change. What had Vic said? *She's a sweet kid underneath it all*. So why was there all that stuff on top?

'Don't you want to know where we found him?' Don't you want to know who I mean by 'we' anyway?

'You're going to tell me, aren't you?'

'I thought you might be pleased that we found him, so that you can bury him properly now.'

'Is that why you found him, because you thought I'd be pleased? I don't remember you asking. Did you ask me if I'd be pleased?' Her tone was neutral and unimpressed; as if she couldn't even get around to faking irritation.

'Jimmy found him.'

'Jimmy's always good for useless things.'

'Jimmy found him in the lake.'

'Do you want to bury him now? Is that why you've brought me out here? Put flowers on his grave?'

'Ricky had a rope round his neck when he was found. It was attached to a brick or something. Jimmy had to cut it away.'

'I don't think it matters what happens to people after they die. I only think it matters what happens to them while they're alive. I don't know why you didn't just leave him in the lake.'

Right, my girl, thought Duffy, and grabbed her by the elbow. She tried to shake him free but her movements were as listless as her speech, and in any case Duffy had marched her several yards before she appreciated what was happening. He took her over to a bench and shoved her down on it. He remained standing, and faced her, leaning over.

'Right,' he said. 'You don't think it matters what happened to your dog after it died. So I'll tell you. Jimmy fished it out of the lake, I took it to London and a bloke I know cut it up. He cut it up because I asked him to find out how it had died. Are you any more interested in knowing what happened to your dog before it died than after it died?' Duffy's tone was deliberately insulting, but she avoided his eye and let him go on. 'Your dog died of an overdose of heroin. A huge overdose. Enough to kill a cow.'

Duffy watched her face as she took another draw on her cigarette. She showed no anger, either at the event or at the bringer of the news. He put one foot up on the bench and leaned over. He became sarcastic as well as aggressive. 'Now I think we can rule out the possibility that Ricky was an addict who got his sums wrong. I don't think his paw slipped on the plunger. I don't think he suddenly started using with pure stuff because he forgot to cut it with something else. I don't think that happened. Someone took your dog,' he leaned more closely towards her, 'and shot enough heroin into it to kill a cow.'

'I'd have had to get rid of Ricky anyway,' she finally said. 'Henry's mother drew the line at him. Perhaps it was providential.'

'Jesus,' said Duffy, and slumped down on the bench beside her. 'Jesus. You mean you're tabbing Henry's mum for this job? Came creeping round in her pink running-shoes and snaffled Ricky? Got some other old age pensioner to help her chuck him through the window.'

'It'll never happen,' said Angela. Her voice wasn't lethargic now, but sharply sad. 'It'll never happen.' She threw her half-smoked cigarette out into the grass and immediately lit another.

'What'll never happen?' asked Duffy, as gently as he could.

'I'll never get married,' she said. 'I'm going to come to a bad end, I know it.'

'Course you're getting married. I'll see you up the aisle myself, if you like.'

'Hah.' Angela laughed, the first sign of animation since Duffy had taken her outside. 'Why do they always say that, up the *aisle*. You don't go up the *aisle*. You go up the bloody nave. The aisle's the bloody side thing. Do you see,' she turned to Duffy and was shouting now, 'it's up the nave not up the bloody aisle.'

Duffy, who had got the point fairly early on in this outburst, said, 'I'm not married myself.'

'It's not going to happen,' Angela repeated. 'I'm going to come to a bad end.'

'No you're not,' said Duffy quietly. He was suddenly sorry for her. He didn't like her, but he was sorry for her. He knew terror when he heard it.

'Anyway I haven't been a user for ages.'

'But you were?'

'Who wasn't?' she said, her voice regaining its original apathy. 'They sent me away a couple of times. I beat it, I really did. I haven't used for about five years. I sometimes think it's the only thing I've done in my life, stopping, I mean. But then again, I sometimes think I might as well have gone on, because I'm going to come to a bad end anyway.'

'But you take . . . other stuff.'

'Not really. It's pills mainly. They keep you going.'

'What about the tobacco that keeps the wasps away?'

'You've been talking to Mrs Colin,' she said suddenly. Damn, thought Duffy, damn. But her neutral tone was swiftly resumed. 'Well, who doesn't? Anyway, it's only a puff. But I haven't used for years. I really, really haven't.'

'I believe you,' said Duffy. 'And I'll get you up the nave or whatever you like to call it.' Even if Henry's mum was lurking behind a pillar in her pink running-shoes with a syringeful of smack in her handbag.

'It's not that I didn't care about Ricky when he was alive. It's just that caring about him seems pointless after he's dead.

I don't want people caring for me after I'm dead. It wouldn't be worth it.'

Christ, thought Duffy, she really could be on the edge. She needs minding not just because of what someone else might do to her. There was a silence as they both gazed across towards the lake for a minute or two. Finally, Duffy said, 'Do you know who it is that's blackmailing you?'

'Some foreigner,' she replied wearily. It seemed not to matter any more, now that she wasn't going to get married anyway.

'Anyone you know?'

'No.'

'How much?'

'Two thousand quid a couple of weeks ago. Two thousand quid last week.'

Christ, thought Duffy. He must really have got something on her.

'Where do you pay?'

'Oh, it's not far. Very considerate, really. End of the drive, turn left, and it's only half a mile or so.'

'Same place each time?'

'Yes.'

Amateurs, thought Duffy, amateurs. Greedy amateurs, mind. 'What's it about?'

'The usual thing.'

'What's the usual thing?'

'Sex,' said Angela. 'That's what everybody means by the usual thing, isn't it?'

'I don't know. I didn't think anyone cared about it so much. I mean, I didn't think anyone paid out for it any more.'

'You don't live in the country,' she said, turning and looking him in the eye. 'You aren't marrying a man who is saving himself for marriage. You aren't having to get through a whole year without sex and finding it difficult. You aren't expected to know how to behave because you're going to give that old baggage up at the House a grandchild. You didn't find it hard to take and you didn't do something bloody silly and stupid just four months before your wedding.'

It was quickly told. Henry had been going through a patch

of keeping away from her. There'd been this nice boy, just down for a week from London, she'd been a bit drunk, well, why not, who's to find out? Yes, at her cottage, and then once again, here at the Hall, it had seemed safer here, and she'd got away with it, she really thought she had. The boy had gone back to London, he'd understood, he hadn't made a fuss, and then three months later, out of the blue, a telephone call from some foreigner. How he was sure she wouldn't want him to spoil the lovely wedding and all that. How he needed some money to go back to his own country.

'Did he have any proof?'

'What, like polaroid photos? He didn't need them, did he?'

'Did you tell anyone?'

'Not about the boy. I sort of told Vic about paying out.'

'Do you think this foreigner sounds like the boy?'

'No. Anyway, he's not that type.'

'Why did you pay?'

'Because I could afford it. Because it was only a few weeks to the wedding. It seemed easier.'

It always did. That was blackmail's false sweetness to the victim. Duffy used to have a dentist who'd say to him, when drilling a cavity, 'Once more and that'll be the end of it.' This was the blackmailer's promise. Once more and that'll be the end of it. But then the drill came back again and again, and there was never an end to it.

'It's getting cold,' she said. They rose and started back towards the house. Halfway across the lawn, she went on casually, 'He asked for another payment tomorrow. But I thought I wouldn't this time. Not if I'm not getting married. Not if I'm coming to a bad end.'

'Have you told him you've changed your mind?'

'Haven't got his telephone number, have I?'

'Pity about that,' said Duffy. Though good in another way, of course.

●

At dinner everyone was a bit subdued. Even Sally wasn't giggling so much; perhaps she hadn't got a good enough offer for the burnt-out bits of her Datsun Cherry. Angela was quiet;

perhaps the fate of Ricky was getting to her at last. Jimmy's absence was also having an effect. It wasn't that Jimmy was good company; he was pretty slow, and all his jokes had mould on them. But he made everyone else feel good company, made them feel bright and witty and sophisticated and successful. They didn't do much, this crowd, thought Duffy, and they really needed the presence of this hopeless estate agent who hadn't knowingly sold a single bungalow.

'Cheer up, you laughing girls and boys.' Damian, of course, was the first to react against the general mood. 'How about getting out the old modelling albums, Belinda?'

But Belinda didn't think this a smart idea. She reacted as if he'd said, 'Belinda, why don't you show us your tits?' – which in a way, of course, he had. Damian tried again.

'My dear Taffy, there must be a really violent gangster film on the box.'

'I don't like that stuff,' said Taffy. 'It's not . . . realistic enough.'

'Not enough blood for you, Taff?'

'No, not that. There's too much for me, usually. It's just, things aren't like that. Not enough goes wrong. Or it may go wrong for one side but not the other. Out in the real world it goes wrong for everyone. It's just a question of making less mistakes than the other side.' Duffy was yawning already. And the other thing the films get wrong is that they don't show villains with phobias. Very delicate, some of our finest criminal minds, they are; got phobias about fire, or dogs, or being locked up, or whatever.

'Was that a yawn I espied?' Uh-uh. Damian didn't miss too much. 'How about a clatter round the green baize, Duffy? Touch of the old in—off and six away?'

'I don't think I'm ready for you yet, to be honest. Give me another couple of days.'

'Well, I can't say I've caught you putting in much practice. Sneaking down in your shortie dressing-gown in the middle of the night, are we?'

'No,' said Duffy. He half-expected Sally to giggle, but she was silent.

'Well if you don't all perk up a bit,' said Damian, 'I shall sing you "The Dogs".'

'Oh, not "The Dogs".' Even Sally, who clearly went along with everything, registered a protest.

'Yes, "The Dogs", "The Dogs".' In a creamy baritone, with the swanky over-emphasis of an opera singer on television, he began:

'The dogs they had a meeting,
They came from near and far;
And some dogs came by aeroplane,
And some dogs came by car.'

Damian paused. Duffy half-recognized the tune. It was one of those hymns. He didn't have many hymns at his beck and call, to be honest, and he didn't know if he'd ever sung this one. The tune sounded a bit posh for him. Perhaps he'd heard someone else singing it. He was waiting for the second verse, when Lucretia said, 'Damian, you can be a real berk, you know,' and nodded towards Angela.

'God, what long memories people have,' said Damian wearily.

'Actually, I don't mind.' Angela didn't seem to. 'I'm sort of over it now. It doesn't matter.'

Lucretia looked across at Damian as if to tell him Angela didn't mean it. Sally said, 'Go on, Dame, what's next?' even though she had heard the song dozens of times.

'Won't,' he replied. 'You're so *boring* this evening. Damian's going to sulk in the snooker room.' He did a stage pout, and left the room. The evening broke up. Duffy tried to catch Lucretia's eye, but she failed to catch his back. Instead, he found himself in the kitchen with Vic. Perhaps Vic had been a bit quiet at dinner because he was wondering how long he'd have the coppers inviting themselves round for a rummage whenever they felt like it.

'Couple of things, Vic.'

'Sure.'

'The dog business. Anything to do with you?'

'How do you mean?'

'Well, any . . . troubles lately? Could it have been meant for you?'

'Me?'

'A warning or something.'

Vic did his honest-citizen chuckle. 'You don't let go, Duffy, do you? I mean, only another twenty years and I might convince you I'm legit.'

'You and Taffy should stand for Parliament,' said Duffy.

'And the other thing?'

'When Angela told you about being blackmailed, did she say anything else?'

'No, I said.'

'But . . . how did it come up?'

'Well, things don't really come up with Angela, do they? I mean, you may have noticed, she doesn't exactly follow the normal rules of conversation.' Duffy nodded. 'So, we were just talking about something else and out of the blue she said she was being blackmailed. No who, no why, no anything. Shut up at once. Told me not to tell anybody.'

'Guesses?'

Vic shook his head. 'Have you tried asking her?'

'Mmm. She wouldn't tell me a thing.'

In bed that night, Duffy found himself re-reading Basil Berk's restaurant column in the *Tatler*. He'd have to put up his daily rates if he was ever going to afford the Poison d'Or. Half asleep, he found his brain idling over two things: the location of tomorrow's drop, and the location of Lucretia's bedroom.

One of these sites was more easily identified than the other. Duffy was fairly sure they were dealing with amateurs: the time, the place, and the amount of money hadn't changed over three successive weeks. The drop was ordered for three o'clock that afternoon; so he reckoned it was probably safe for Angela and him, quite by coincidence of course, to run into one another at the top of the drive during their morning constitutionals.

Left at the gates, and half a mile took them to a T-junction. Well, maybe not so amateur: that made three directions in which to escape if necessary. On the opposite verge was a large County Council grit-bin, painted green. The sort of object the eye didn't notice for eleven months of the year; only in the twelfth, when snow fell and motorists got panicky, did you suddenly spot it. You might even go across to it out of curiosity, pull up the heavy lid, and wonder why it was empty.

'In there,' said Angela, with a spectacularly stagey nod of the head.

'Keep walking.'

It wasn't a bad place for a pick-up. Nor was it a bad place for hiding in the trees and jumping the postman. On their way back to the Hall they had the argument about whether Angela should be allowed to watch with Duffy. It sounded a terrible idea to Duffy, but Angela, who only yesterday had seemed apathetic about the idea of being blackmailed now started insisting that as it was her money, she should see where it was going. Duffy gave in.

By one-thirty Duffy was squatting in some bracken about twenty yards from the grit-bin. He had excused himself from lunch, driven off for a pub sandwich, found a hiding-place for the van, and worked his way through some woods to his present uncomfortable niche. With an hour to kill he tried plaiting himself a camouflage hat out of ferns, like the one Jimmy had worn when he'd caught Duffy poking in Mr Hardcastle's shed; but he couldn't get it to stick together, not without sellotape or something. No doubt there was an art to it.

At two-thirty he heard footsteps from the direction of the drive, then saw Angela, unsuitably dressed for a country walk, come into view. She headed straight for the bin, dropped a brown envelope into it, didn't look round (as he had instructed) and started off up the road to the right. Five minutes later, after only a certain amount of crackling undergrowth and shouts of 'Oh, shit,' she was by his side.

'I don't really like the country,' she said, as she patted the ground testingly before sitting down. 'Bloody prickly.'

Duffy grunted, and kept his gaze on the road. Five minutes later, she said, 'It's quite exciting, this, isn't it?' She gave him the eyes, and a half-smile too.

'Shh.' Mum's the word, he'd said to Jimmy, and Jimmy

had replied, 'My mum talked *all the bloody time.*' Angela went quiet.

At six minutes to three, by which time two cars and a motor-caravan had gone past, a bicycle came into view. It was an old-fashioned machine with stand-up handlebars and a basket on the front. The rider looked pretty old-fashioned, too, pedalling along with his knees and elbows out. On his head he wore a deerstalker. If this is anything to do with it, thought Duffy, if this is the postman, or even just a lookout, they're definitely amateur. Probably want the money to pay for new bicycles. The figure got nearer, and was about fifteen yards from the grit-bin when Angela suddenly got to her feet, started waving and shouting, 'Henry, Henry.' She ran down the bank towards the road, crashing through the undergrowth and shouting 'Henry' in an increasingly hysterical voice. The cyclist, now five yards short of the grit-bin, looked up, saw her, cycled straight on and pulled up by the side of the road. Angela started hugging him, which was not easy given the presence of the handlebars.

Duffy swore, got up, kicked away his feeble attempt at a fern hat, and trotted down the slope to the road.

'What are you doing in the woods with my fiancée?' Henry bellowed, and then burst out laughing, as if he was sure there was a reasonable explanation. Duffy laughed back, and tried to think of one. He saw Angela about to open her mouth and quickly got in before she could screw things up further.

'We were looking for Ricky's body, actually. What happened to your car? Broke down or something?' Henry had two cars, and his mother had one, and there was always the Land Rover in emergency.

'Felt like the exercise. Nice day. Thought I'd pop over and see my gel.'

'You are romantic, Henry,' said Angela. She took his arm, and started leading him and the bike up the drive to Braunscombe Hall. Romantic, grumbled Duffy to himself as he followed them at ten paces or so. Romantic! Just because he won't go to bed with you and rides a funny old bike and has a stupid hat on his head. If that was romantic, it wasn't a difficult trick to pull, provided you didn't mind behaving like a prat and a wally all the time.

Of course she'd screwed up the drop deliberately. She'd seen Henry coming and couldn't bear to watch him delving in the grit-bin. She'd rather marry someone she thought was probably blackmailing her than not marry someone because she definitely knew he was blackmailing her. She must be really lost, thought Duffy, nothing but panic and terror gurgling through her all the time. He wondered if Henry knew the ins and outs of this girl who came over all story-book lovey-dovey whenever he hove into sight.

It must *be* Henry, mustn't it? It looked like an amateur, it had to be someone who knew Angela or could find out about her, it must be someone local; and Henry had turned up at the drop at precisely six minutes to three. What did it look like?

Duffy didn't know why he was following them back to the house. He didn't know why he sat with them in the family room, occasionally picking pieces of bracken off his trousers, for half an hour or more. Maybe he was expecting Angela to apologize; maybe he was expecting Henry to confess. The atmosphere during that half-hour was hardly relaxed. Angela was ignoring Duffy, as if to say, you bloody suspect Henry, don't you, you've got the nerve to suspect Henry, haven't you, why don't you piss off. Duffy was ignoring Angela in return, as if to say, you knew, didn't you, you suspected, I bet you recognized his voice, perhaps he didn't even put on a fancy foreign accent, that's why you insisted on coming with me, that's why you screwed up the drop, you bloody guessed, didn't you? Henry sat making polite remarks in both directions, but with a slight frown, as if to say, what were these two doing in the bracken in the middle of the afternoon, and if you really were looking for a dead dog, shouldn't you have had a stick or something so that you could bash down the brambles?

'Got to see to the van,' said Duffy, and left without anyone saying goodbye to him. He stamped across the gravel and up the drive. He marched past the pre-weathered salamander clinging to its pre-weathered globe. For once he was too cross even to notice the smell of the countryside. He got to the grit-bin and wrenched open the lid to retrieve Angela's envelope. There was nothing in the grit-bin apart from grit. 'Bugger,' said Duffy.

It was a half-hour walk to fetch the van, which didn't improve Duffy's temper. He drove carelessly back to Braunscombe Hall and as he turned in at the gates he had to pull sharply over on to the grass to avoid Henry, who was pedalling down the middle of the drive, back erect and knees pointing out sharply like a frog's.

'Sorry,' said Duffy, even though it was a 50–50 case.

'Maybe you *are* after my fiancée,' said Henry cheerfully, then turned round in the saddle, without wobbling, and added, 'Don't forget your lesson.'

'Right.'

When Duffy got back to the family room, Angela didn't wait for him to sit down. 'You bloody think he did it, don't you, you nasty common little person. You bloody think he did it, don't you?'

'If you were so sure it wasn't him, why didn't you wait till he got past the grit-bin? Another ten yards and everything would have been clear.'

'There, you bloody do think he did it, you common little person.' Duffy didn't answer. 'Anyway, I was pleased to see him. Fiancée's prerogative,' she added rather smugly.

Duffy was glad he didn't have to handle these mood-swings in more than a business capacity. One moment she was coming to a bad end and wouldn't get up the bloody aisle, let alone the bloody nave, and the next moment it was all sweet Henry and 'Here Comes the Bride' stuff. Was it pills, or was that just what she was like? Or was she even worse without the pills?

'Henry didn't stay long,' he said as neutrally as he could.

'What the fuck's that got to do with you?' There was a hostile silence. 'If you must know, he didn't have any lights on his bike.'

It was a good two hours before dusk, and Henry's ride couldn't have been longer than forty minutes, but Duffy thought he would let that pass. 'I think you could have let him go the extra ten yards,' he said. 'You see, I went back and checked the grit-bin. The envelope's gone. So it couldn't have been Henry.'

'You incompetent little man,' she shouted. 'Why didn't you stay in the wood? Then you could have seen who took it.' Duffy thought this hadn't seemed a plausible option at the time. 'Anyway,' she went on, suddenly cheerful, 'what's another two thousand?'

'Hang on,' said Duffy. 'You don't mean you put real money in the envelope?'

'Of course I did.'

'Christ. You weren't meant to.'

'What do you mean? You told me we were doing the drop. So we did the drop. And you were meant to hang about in the trees and catch them. Wasn't that the idea?'

'You said you'd decided not to pay. You were meant to put newspaper or something in the envelope. I thought that was obvious. Haven't you ever seen any films or anything?'

'You screwed up properly, didn't you?' But her tone was still cheerful, as if the fact that Henry wasn't the blackmailer had made everything all right again.

'*You* screwed up. Well, we both screwed up. This is hopeless.' Not just hopeless, amateurish. An amateur blackmailer, an amateur blackmailee; and he hadn't exactly been quick off the mark himself, had he?

Before dinner he ran into Sally at the foot of the stairs. As she was brushing past him he said, 'Oh, er, I understand you do the drawing.'

She turned. With her big black eyes and lolloping curls she could be a good-looking girl if she wanted to, Duffy thought; all she needed was to get some focus into her eyes, like now. 'So?'

'Well, just wondered if I could see them.'

'Who's your favourite painter?'

'Have you got any of them around?'

'Who do you prefer? Picasso or Braque?'

'I understand they're very nice.'

'Matisse or Renoir?'

'It must take a lot of skill to make a dog look like a monkey.'

'Jackson Pollock or Pele?'

'Pele's a footballer.'

'That's right,' said Sally as she walked off. Half-incredulous, she muttered to herself, '*He*'s asking to see *my* etchings.'

●

Dinner that evening was no more lively an affair than the previous day. Duffy sat well away from Angela, and diagonally across from Lucretia. It looked as if she'd washed her hair. Duffy persuaded himself that she didn't really look posh; no, posh wasn't the word for her, she was more . . . sort of . . . classy. Those clear-cut, slightly carved features, the half-smile, yes, she was doing it again. Once or twice he would catch her eye and she would look back at him. What did that glance mean? Did it mean, frankly you haven't got a prayer, or did it mean, why not give it a go? Mrs Colin had said that Lucretia did less fucky-fuck than Sally; but that could still mean a healthy and democratic amount of fucky-fuck.

When the coffee had been handed round and Mrs Hardcastle had retired, there was the scrape of a chair. Damian was on his feet, a glass of wine held in front of him as if he were preparing to toast someone. 'Gentlemen,' he said, 'I give you "The Dogs".' Sally clapped; Taffy looked perplexed; Duffy glanced across at Lucretia, whose eyes were elsewhere. He looked back and up to Damian, who was addressing him. 'The tune, for strangers to the house and lower-class persons generally, is "The Church's One Foundation".' Damian cleared his throat and began:

'The dogs they had a meeting,
They came from near and far;
And some dogs came by aeroplane,
And some dogs came by car.

'They came into the courtroom
And signed the visitors' book,
And each dog took his arsehole
And hung it on a hook.'

Damian's creamy baritone was briefly lubricated with a sip of wine. Sally was looking up at the singer expectantly; Taffy seemed to be examining his cutlery.

'The dogs they were well-seated,
Each mother's son and sire,
When a naughty little mongrel
Got up and shouted "Fire!"

'The dogs they were in panic,
They had no time to look,
So each one grabbed an arsehole
From off the nearest hook.'

The tune was growing on him, thought Duffy. He wasn't sure about the song.

'The dogs they were so angry,
For it is very sore,
To wear another's arsehole
You've never worn before.

'And that is then the reason,
The dog will leave his bone,
To sniff another's arsehole,
In hope it is his own.'

Damian drew out the last line, with lots of wobble on the final vowel, closed his eyes in a mock excess of emotion, drained his glass and bowed. His face glowed and the end of his nose twitched slightly. Sally clapped again, and Taffy, like an old clubman, tapped the edge of the table with the flat of his fingers and murmured, 'Very amusing.'

'Glad you liked it. My old school song.'

'Where was that, then?'

'The Kennel Club, O Taffy.'

Damian's performance seemed to put everyone into a good mood. If it worked that well, Duffy thought, maybe they should play it instead of 'Here Comes the Bride' when Angela went trotting up the nave. But no one talked about the chances of that event taking place, or about Angela's ordeal in the woods, or Ricky's death, or the spontaneous combustion of Sally's car. For at least an hour, everyone seemed keen to pretend that this was just another jolly evening on the Buckinghamshire/Bedfordshire borders. How did they manage it? All this cheerfulness was starting to make Duffy feel depressed.

The whisky got taken seriously for a while, and then people began to sidle off to bed. Duffy, without knowing how much was his cunning and how much was her complicity, ended up in the family room with Lucretia. They seemed to be alone.

'What did you think of the song?' she asked.

'I thought it could have done with a bit more saffron in it.'

'You're funny, you know.'

'Right.' Had that been a compliment? He could scarcely check with her, could he? Instead, for no reason except that it came into his head, he told her about the football team he played in, the Western Sunday Reliables. He told her about what it was like to be a goalkeeper, the sort of opponents they came up against, the speed of their young striker Karl French, and his hopes for the forthcoming season. He went on about all this with some enthusiasm, then found himself stopping and feeling awkward. 'I suppose I should have asked if you're interested in football.'

'I suppose you should,' she said, with a half-smile. 'I'm afraid I'm not.'

'Why not?'

'Boring, I suppose. All that putting the boot in. I mean, just not interesting enough.'

'Right. Well, tell me about some restaurants then.'

'You don't want to know about restaurants.'

'Why not? Perhaps I could take you to one. In London. You know, up the West End.'

She didn't answer. He got up from his chair and started slowly walking across towards her. Boy, she looked classy, all cool and blonde and wreathed in cigarette smoke. 'Did you wash your hair today?' he asked.

Lucretia burst into laughter. 'I can afford to have it done, you know.' Her response froze Duffy halfway across the carpet, one foot hovering in the air, as if he might put it down on a pressure plate and set off the whole alarm system. She gave him a more or less friendly gaze, compared that is to her fashion-page fuck-off glance.

'Look, I may as well say it, so there aren't any misunderstandings. You're quite funny, but I don't find you at all sexy.'

Duffy's foot did not descend. Instead, he shuffled round through 180 degrees before placing it back on the carpet. Then he walked slowly to the door. As he grasped the handle, he turned and said, 'Is that funny as in funny ha-ha or as in funny peculiar?'

'I'll let you know, Duffy. I'll let you know.'

As he crossed the hall he thought he heard a chuckle, a creamy baritone chuckle. He lay in bed and reflected that in a single day Angela had called him common and incompetent, Damian had called him lower-class, and Lucretia had called him not sexy. He slept badly and six hours later, before any-one else had risen, he was trundling south on the M1 through the morning mist.

When he got back to the flat he felt he needed a bath. No, he needed more than that: he wouldn't mind strapping himself to the top of his Sherpa van and putting himself through a carwash. All those lovely big brushes scratching away at the muck he felt encrusted with, and lots of water squirting, and then big floppy mops polishing him back to normal. He had breakfast and lunch on one plate at Sam Widges, then collected the remains of Ricky from Jim Pringle (who was disappointed that Duffy didn't want him stuffed and mounted). At three o'clock Carol found him bent over the end pages of the *Stan-dard*. He got up, kissed her, patted her bum, smiled and trotted back to his chair.

'Bad as that, was it?' After all these years Carol did not deceive herself that Duffy's behaviour was the result of her new hemline, or that touch of scent behind the ears.

'Romford, Walthamstow or Wimbledon?'

'What?'

'I'm taking you out.'

'Really that bad? You all right?'

'You ever been beaten up with words? It seems to last a lot longer, somehow.'

A few hours later, in the van, Carol finally asked, 'Where are we going?'

'Walthamstow. To the dogs.'

'The *dogs*?'

'We'll have a nice meal. Bottle of wine.'

'Why are we going to the dogs?' Carol was mystified.

'Because *they* wouldn't go there.' Duffy gripped the steering wheel. 'Because *they* wouldn't go there.'

'Sure,' said Carol, not asking, not wanting to know. 'But Duffy, you don't like the dogs, do you?' She looked across at his profile, lower lip jutting and a frown that wasn't caused by the traffic.

'I'm going to learn to like them,' said Duffy. 'I'm sure there's a lot to be said for dogs.'

They parked up the street from the stadium and joined a crowd that was peaceful and anticipatory. A pair of coppers stood on the pavement outside, but they were strictly for decoration: doing the stadium was an easy option. You didn't get football yobbos here; there was even the odd East End family outing complete with permed gran and a couple of kids. Duffy began to relax. No chance of running into Damian or Lucretia here; no chance of catching Henry on his antique bicycle, Jimmy doing his Army crawl around the track, Taffy trying to poach the hare.

Inside, they walked down a dim corridor with heavy glass doors at intervals. They climbed up to a sharply tiered restaurant and looked down through large windows at a track lit half by the evening sun and half by floodlights. Jolly signs dotted here and there said WELCOME TO THE STOW. Beneath them a corpulent man in jodhpurs and a bowler hat led the parade for the first race: he was followed by six men in white coats, like off-duty chemists, proudly showing six dogs of varied colour and elegance. Away to their left the tote board flickered constantly as the odds changed. Duffy caught the arm of a motherly waitress in a tight black skirt and frilly white blouse. As the traps sprang up and the six dogs leapt into the bright lights in vain pursuit of a hare they would never catch and which wasn't a hare in the first place anyway, Duffy popped the cork on the Veuve du Vernay, filled their glasses, put his arm proprietorially round Carol, and murmured, 'Welcome to the Stow.'

'You are a scream, Duffy.' Still, he was taking her out, that was something; and Carol knew not to examine the reasons for it too closely. They ordered the prawn cocktail – Duffy asking for extra sauce as if he were a gastronome who knew that the bottled stuff they served here was especially fine – followed by the rump steak and chips. They looked at their programme, a cyclostyled single sheet of paper with the following Thursday's details on the other side. Nine more races to come, three big ones over 640 metres, the other six over 475. 'Billy's Flyer,' Duffy read out, 'Philomena's Ark, Rockfield Rover, Bernie's Gamble, Ding Along Dell and Desert Dancer. Fancy any of them?'

Carol couldn't decide. Duffy squinted at previous form and announced knowingly, 'It must be between Bernie's Gamble and Ding Along Dell.'

'I'll have Desert Dancer then.'

He grinned and pushed down a switch on the bet-summoner, swiftly bringing a waitress with a large tray to their table.

'A fiver for the lady on number two.'

'Duffy, that's a lot of money. And by the way, you're beginning to sound a bit posh. *A fiver for the lady on number two*,' she mimicked.

He grinned. He still grinned when Desert Dancer was pipped on the line by Ding Along Dell. They ate their prawn cocktails and drank their Veuve du Vernay and backed another loser.

'You know,' said Carol, 'you could have quite a nice time if you let yourself.'

Duffy grunted. He wasn't sure if that was what it was about. Those people up on the Buckinghamshire/Bedfordshire borders – they were all out to have a nice time, weren't they? And look at them. Duffy shook the vision from his head, wolfed a few chips, and tried to concentrate on more important matters. Should he have gone for Rhincrew Doc or Chiming Valley? He hadn't been able to make up his mind, and it was too late now as the stadium lights were dimmed and several thousand faces pointed towards a little row of stalls where six dogs yelped quietly in anticipation. Thirty seconds later the electric hare was being covered up again with a cloth, the six dogs had been recaptured, and Duffy was a bit relieved as neither Rhincrew Doc nor Chiming Valley had got a nose near the hindquarters of Art Grass. At the table behind, a permed gran celebrated noisily.

They walked out through a slurry of discarded tote tickets into the warm night air. The two coppers were rocking on their heels and bidding some of the punters goodnight. There hadn't been a sniff of trouble all evening. The winners were happy; the losers were pretty sure they'd be winners next time round. As they climbed into the van, Duffy said, 'It's really nice there. I could do that again.'

'It's rather a long way.' And she had to get up for the early shift.

'But it's really nice. Nice people, nice dogs, no trouble. Nice food.'

'Duffy,' said Carol, with a teasing sharpness in her voice, 'are you going soggy or something?'

'What?'

'Duffy, what makes you think there weren't as many villains in that crowd as there are in any other crowd?'

'Well, there were whole families and stuff.'

'Yeah, sure, villains taking their families out. Probably a few nice deals going on over the prawn cocktails. I mean, it's a handy sort of place to go, isn't it?'

But Duffy wasn't to be deterred. 'Nah. It's really nice. And you can tell they love those dogs, can't you? Always patting them, stroking them. Probably give them lumps of sugar when they get back to the kennels.'

'I think you ought to see a specialist,' said Carol. 'Do you think it's cleaner than any other sport?'

'Must be,' said Duffy, smiling at the traffic in the Seven Sisters Road.

'I knew a Detective-Constable once, he was on a case with the dogs. Somewhere out Romford way I think it was. Said it was awful the things he found out they did to the dogs to make them run faster. He wouldn't tell me some of them. But it stands to reason. Think what those athletes get up to – and they're doing it to *themselves*. If it was only a dog, you wouldn't think twice, would you?'

'You can tell they love those dogs,' said Duffy warmly.

'But it's about money, isn't it? There was a lot of money

changing hands tonight, I don't know if you noticed. Well, you should have done, quite a lot of it was yours.'

'Do you know what the top prize was tonight? Seventy-five quid plus a trophy, with twenty-five quid to the second. That's peanuts.'

'It's the betting. Same as the horses. It's all about betting. And if there's only six dogs in each race, it's easier to predict than with the horses, isn't it?'

'Nah. If you gave your dog something special to make it go faster, they'd catch you, wouldn't they? They must test the winners.'

'You don't have to do it that way round, Duffy. Say there are two class dogs in a race and one of them's yours. You can't make yours go faster without being caught, so what do you do? You make yours go slower.'

'How do you do that?'

'I don't know. Feed it prawn cocktail and steak and chips the night before. Cut its toenails so that it hurts or something. Then you bet on the other dog.'

'So you bet against yourself?'

'Sure.'

Duffy continued to look a bit disbelieving, as if he declined to let this sour burst of scepticism invade the pleasure of the evening. They drove along in silence for a bit, then Duffy nodded, swerved towards the kerb, braked sharply causing a protest of horns from behind, pulled on the handbrake and turned to Carol. 'Has anyone ever told you, you might be a genius?' he asked.

She reached across and patted him on the thigh. 'You really are soggy tonight, aren't you?'

7 ● NEIGHBOURHOOD

Did he have a runner? Had Carol given him a tip and did he have a runner? This was the question Duffy debated as he headed back up the M1 with nothing but a ragout of dog in a plastic bag for company. And if he did have a runner, the next problem was, which race was it in? The trouble with this case was that the runners kept on turning out not to be in the races you thought they'd been entered for. For instance, Angela's dog gets knocked off, but does this have anything to do with Angela? It ought to, and it ought to connect up with the blackmail, but it didn't seem to: the blackmail was a nice regular weekly transaction. What happened to Ricky wasn't being used to raise the stakes.

Then there was the blackmail itself. When Henry had toddled up on his bicycle, it looked as if that put him in the frame, but it didn't. Or take Jimmy and the business up at his camp: that had looked a pretty reliable runner, but it too had gone lame. The coppers had charged him, but even they knew a bit more was needed to make things stick. The only aspect of the case with no obvious runners so far was the car. Well, perhaps it would be the responsibility of a delinquent squirrel after all.

At his meeting with Detective-Sergeant Vine he traded his plastic bag for the information that there was still no information on the Datsun Cherry: they hadn't found any bits of timer, or traces of familiar explosive. It might turn out to be something simple like a bit of rope dipped in tar; one of your good old-fashioned country ways of setting fire to things, none of your city tricks. D/S Vine had interviewed the Datsun's owner, but hadn't got anything out of her, which he suspected was because there wasn't much inside her anyway. Duffy forgot to tell Vine about the encounter by the grit-bin – well, nothing had really happened, had it? – but did venture the opinion that some of the folk at Braunscombe Hall got on his tits. Vine chuckled.

'By the way, anything new out of old Jimmy?'

'Remanded for a week. Sits in his cell and says he didn't do it. He seems a bit potty to me. Might have to get in the headshrinker to take a squint at him.'

'Get him to give the rest of the Hall the once-over while

he's about it,' said Duffy. 'By the way, talking of something completely different, do you get much drugs around here?'

'No, not really. If we do, it comes down from London. We've got a drugs squad, of course, but that's mainly because the local paper thinks we ought to have one. They're on other duties most of the time.'

'So no big local suppliers?'

'Not that we know of. And I think we would know, even if we couldn't make a case. You want me to get the Hall raided by any chance?'

'That's jumping the gun a bit. Just something I'm working on.'

'I'm sure the squad'd like it. They spend most of their time dressing up like hippies and waiting to get approached in pubs. The most that happens is the publican throws them out because he doesn't like smelly hippies in his bar.'

'Well, keep them on hold.'

'Will do.'

When Duffy got back to Braunscombe Hall he didn't give the salamander a glance and he wasn't too careful with Vic's gravel as he pulled up. He was pissed off with being patronized. He'd taken against these people at first, that was only normal, then one after the other – Belinda, Lucretia, Angela, Damian – they'd half-made him quarter-like them. It hadn't been much of a shift, but it had made him uncertain how he saw things. That was bad. It was also unprofessional.

He started by calling Henry and asking if he could come over for a snooker lesson on his 1866 Thurston that afternoon. Good, and sure, he'd be happy to have tea with Henry's mum afterwards. Then he rounded up Damian and Sally, who were loitering over a late breakfast in the kitchen. He took them into the billiard room. The curtains were drawn back, and the morning light made the baize a fainter colour than the spotlights did; the room seemed unfamiliar, colder somehow. Duffy told them to sit on the chintz sofa. Then he stood facing them, his bottom half-perched on the rail.

'I always find,' Damian remarked to Sally, 'that attacks of masterfulness in men are directly related to disappointment in love.'

So he had been listening. Or maybe he'd just been told. Duffy didn't care. That was a day and a half ago. He'd been greyhound racing since then. He wasn't so certain any more that he'd taken to the sport, but he thought he'd keep it in reserve, for those times when he felt tempted to like the wrong sort of people. Come and sit on my lap, Duffy? No, I'm off down the Stow. Listen to my old school song? Sorry, I'm going to the dogs.

'You could get yourselves killed,' he said.

'Oh, God, here we go again.' Sally's tone was sarcastically bored. 'Old spoilsport sticking his nose in. Don't put your heels on the cloth you might rip it. Don't do this, don't do that. Don't have a little fun or you might kill yourself. One drink leads to another, one roll-up and next day you're making with the syringe. Government health warning number twenty-three.'

'I didn't say that,' Duffy replied. He felt Damian's eyes on him, while Sally was looking angrily away. 'I didn't say you'd kill yourselves. As far as I'm concerned you can stick what you like up your nose and you can stick what you like in your arm. I didn't say you could kill yourselves. I said you could get yourselves killed.'

'Speak on, O wise man from the East End,' said Damian.

'I don't think you're making connections. I'm not sure they're all obvious to me, but they ought to be to you.' Damian uttered a stagey sigh – the schoolboy irritated by the pedantic master.

'Did Angela tell you how Ricky died?' They shook their heads. 'Ricky didn't die from being thrown through the french windows.' He paused, and Damian gave him a get-on-with-it twitch of the head. 'Ricky died from being injected with enough heroin to kill a cow.' Actually Duffy didn't know how much more heroin this took than was required to dispose of a dog, but the phrase sounded tasty.

'Poor old Ricky,' Sally wailed, and turned her head into Damian's shoulder on the sofa.

'So you found the body?' Damian, at least, seemed to be taking things a little more usefully than Sally. Duffy nodded. 'But why did they get rid of it in the first place?'

'Someone else did. Someone with a tidy mind that happened along.'

'Someone whose name you're not going to tell us.'

'That's right.'

'So why should anyone do that to Angela's dog?'

'You're not making the connection, are you?'

'What connection?'

'The dog and the car. The dog and the car.'

'What are you talking about?' Sally took her head out of Damian's shoulder. 'Ricky was Angela's dog. And the thing about these foreign motors' – Sally started to grin in a hysterical manner – 'is that they're so frightfully . . .'

'Shut up, Sal. Listen.'

'You walked the dog a lot, didn't you, Sally? You walked the dog as much as Angela did?' She nodded silently. 'They thought the dog was yours. Well, they got that wrong. But they knew the car was yours so they got that right. But you should have made the connection. The third time they won't be after dogs and cars. They'll be after bits of you that break easily. And the time after that you could get yourselves killed. I've seen it all before. Lots of times, and I can assure you it's a lot nastier than when you don't keep up the hire-purchase on the spin-drier.'

Damian looked as if he was going to smirk at Duffy's analogy, but the expression never got going. He turned to Sally and said, 'Maybe we'll have to go to your pater on our bendeds.' When she didn't reply, he turned to Duffy and said, 'Any suggestions?'

'How much do you owe?'

'About eight.'

'Christ. How much did you start off owing?'

'Fifteen.'

'Christ. So,' Duffy went on pedantically, 'you've paid off seven.'

'About that.'

Seven. Six plus one. Three twos are six, went Duffy. Gotcha. 'And who's using?' Damian and Sally looked at one another. 'OK, you're both using. Is it fifty–fifty?'

'No,' said Sally. 'It's nearly all me.'

'I only use it for snooker, more or less,' said Damian ingratiatingly. 'Find it settles the nerves wonderfully. Stops that sort of cue-twitch I see you've still got, my dear Duffy. Makes you see shots you didn't know were on. That plant across the table into the middle pocket – you'd never even spot it without a little help.'

It was Damian's last attempt at a flourish. Duffy went remorselessly on. 'So she uses almost all of it, gives you a little gratuity to help with the snooker. But you're the one who does the shopping?'

'Mmm.'

'Well, if I were them I'd go to work on you first, and probably make quite a mess of you, and if they decided they couldn't get any more out of you, they'd move on to her.'

'I had thought of selling the Datsun,' said Sally. 'Until they blew it up. That's cutting off their nose to spite their face.'

'They're more likely to cut off your nose,' said Duffy brutally.

'Oh God,' said Damian, 'Oh God, oh God, oh God.'

'What are we actually talking about?' said Duffy. 'A variety of substances or just the one?'

'Only coke, for Christ's sake.' Damian sounded angry. 'I wouldn't touch the other stuff. And anyway,' he added with needless disloyalty, '*she*'s the user, not me.'

Sure, thought Duffy. She's the user, you're just the shopper. She's the one who climbs up on the snooker table and takes off her knickers, you're just the innocent fellow with the cue. She's the one who lets down my van tyres, you're the one who suggests it and then bottles out at the last minute in case someone's coming. She's going to be the casualty, you're going to be the survivor; but without people like you she'd never have been a casualty in the first place. Have a taste of this, go on, no I'm not feeling hungry myself. Bed? You're not on the pill? Come on, let's risk it, be a sport. Have another drink, why not have a double, actually I won't, I'm driving myself. Then the Damians of this world would skedaddle away leaving the Sallies addicted, pregnant, drunk, wrecked. If there was anything to be said for the rough justice administered by the pushers, it was that it treated the Damians and the Sallies with even-handedness.

'So you started off with a bill of fifteen. How did you let it get that big?'

'They have this wonderful system of credit,' said Damian enthusiastically, then stopped. It was obviously a phrase from before the trouble started.

'And you had about a thousand, but that left you owing fourteen, so you had this idea of getting it out of Angela.' He said it as a statement of the obvious. When they didn't reply, he went on. 'I'm not a copper. On the other hand, I'm not stupid. I just don't see why you didn't ask her for a loan.'

'People are funny about money,' said Sally, as if he ought to know. 'Well, she's got it, she doesn't know what to do with it, she's going to get more when she marries Henry. Anyway, it was more fun this way.'

Of course, thought Duffy, I keep forgetting about the fun factor, it's more fun to blackmail one of your friends than just ask her for money which you might later have to repay. That's the big difference between the two ways of doing it: the fun.

'It was a sort of joke, really,' said Damian, almost apologetically. 'To start off with. We tried to think of who wouldn't miss a chunk of cash, and we thought of Angela, and then we wondered what we might have on her. And then we remembered her sneaking off upstairs with some boy here. I mean, we didn't catch them at it or anything, she may have been showing him the view from the roof for all we knew, but we just thought we'd give it a run.'

'So you went to a phone-box and put on your funny foreign accent.'

'Foreign? Oi put on moi Oirish accent, that's all. Tells you how much Angela notices things.'

'And she paid?'

'We couldn't believe it. I kept the folks entertained with some tittle-tattle, Sally pretended to go and lie down with girls' trouble, and sneaked off up the drive. It was all so ridiculously easy. We didn't really believe it, so we just kept going back to the same place.'

'I don't see why you didn't ask her for a loan,' Duffy repeated.

'People are funny about money,' said Sally again, as if pronouncing a rare truth.

'Where do you do your shopping. Up in London?'

'No, no, no. They come to us. It's all very well-organized.'

'What, here?' Duffy imagined a van with a fancy name on the side and a royal 'By Appointment' crest on the front. 'Messrs Smack, Coke & Hash: Purveyors of Narcotics to the Gentry. Deliveries Thursday and Saturday. Credit Allowances.'

'Course not. We do it at the motorway caff.'

Fair enough. One of the usual places. Duffy sometimes wondered what would happen if they cracked down on all the naughtiness – from adulterous hand-holding to criminal meets – that took place in motorway caffs. Would the restaurants survive?

They all looked at one another for a minute or so. 'What's going to happen now?' asked Damian.

'I don't know.' Duffy had no particular reason – or desire – to be soft on them. 'It's up to D/S Vine from here on. Obviously I'll pass on what you've told me. He'll probably want to go over the same ground again. Then it's up to him. He might think it would be a good idea for you to make another payment under laboratory conditions. Or he might just throw you in a cell, of course. It all depends on whether he takes a light-hearted view of blackmail and hard drugs or not.'

'Oh God,' said Damian, 'you're making it sound so *serious*.'

'It was only fun,' Sally repeated. 'Don't you ever have fun?' Duffy didn't answer that. He wasn't altogether sure about fun. Take the dogs at Walthamstow: that had felt like fun, but maybe it was only fun because he'd just been having such a shitty time on the Buckinghamshire/Bedfordshire borders. Sally had another question. 'Are you going to tell Ange?'

'Perhaps it would be better coming from you.' Sally seemed to be one of those girls people always did things for. Well, she could get on with this by herself.

Duffy straightened up. As he turned to go, Damian said,

'Assuming I'm not in the slammer, you won't forget our little grudge match on the green baize?'

'Assuming,' said Duffy. Most people didn't have any sense of priorities, he reflected.

'And I'll do my best to stay off the infamous marching powder beforehand.'

'I can't think why you use it,' said Duffy.

'I can't think why you don't, given the wretched little prod-and-poke game you seem to be managing with at the moment. Gives you flow, that's what it does, gives you flow.'

Duffy agreed that his game required a bit of flow, as well as a few other things – like skill, accuracy, reliability, nerve – but he was committed to getting them in the old-fashioned way. When he turned up for his lesson at Winterton House the gravel made the same posh sound, like some breakfast cereal whispering back to him as he poured on the milk. Henry, in a typical mixture of large-checked jacket, floppy handkerchief, foulard and cavalry twill trousers, greeted him with a punch on the shoulder. 'Who's been going into the woods with me gel, eh?'

'I told you . . .' Duffy hoped that Angela hadn't blabbed to Henry after he'd gone off to look for the drop.

'So you did.' Henry put his large, square, red face closer to Duffy's. 'How much is that doggie in the woodshed, and all that. Eh?'

'Sure.'

'Mother's expecting us for tea at four-thirty, so why don't we get down to it.'

Once again, they went through the house to the gentlemen's quarters, to the darkened billiard room with its smell of old leather and yesterday's cigar smoke. On the sideboard Duffy noticed one of those Victorian decanter units with a lock to stop the servants from sneaking a drink; though, if Braunscombe Hall was anything to go by, the servants wouldn't bother with half-full decanters of whisky. They'd just unload a case of the stuff straight from the wine merchant's van into their own back kitchen. 'An old British custom in the big houses,' as Mrs Colin had put it.

'You rack the balls,' said Henry, who was picking out his

cue. Duffy gathered the reds together and began to corral them into the heavy mahogany triangle. Was it an illusion, or did they sound a bit solider as they clanked gently together? And weren't some of the colours marginally different from those at Braunscombe Hall? The blue ball seemed a little darker, the brown a little redder. Of course: Henry had the authentic ivory balls, Vic the new super-crystallate jobs. Over the last few years they'd fiddled with some of the colours to make them show up better on television. Duffy wasn't sure he approved. He was no traditionalist, but he preferred the feel of the old-fashioned set. He also preferred Henry's immaculate 1866 Thurston to Vic's table, which had more runkles than an unmade bed.

In the cloister calm of the billiard room, with its old smells, its quietly clicking ivory, and its fierce burst of colour in the midst of darkness, Henry became subtly altered. Duffy had seen fat men put on ice skates and acquire a sudden elegance as the blade bit its frozen trail; and something of the sort happened to Henry. A large, rigid fellow who bicycled with knees and elbows out became smoother and neater; even smaller, if that was possible. As Damian would have put it, he had flow. He wasn't flash – he didn't start moving on to the next shot before the pot had gone down – but he had a certainty of purpose about him. He looked at ease.

Duffy was much less relaxed. Henry's confidence made him edgy, and Henry's game made him edgier still. He found himself charging at risky long pots, then ruthlessly pinned back into baulk, then humiliatingly snookered. He had a little run on the colours towards the end, but still had to chew on the wrong end of a 72–28 scoreline.

Then they had the lesson. Henry was very keen on getting Duffy's stance right. He made him take up position and promptly started adjusting him, like a photographer with a model. He fiddled with the splaying fingers of Duffy's bridge hand. He pushed the head down further over the cue. He knelt and shifted Duffy's legs around until his feet were a bit more parallel. He pushed the right hand a few inches down the cue and tried to make the forearm hang vertically from the elbow. Finally, he made Duffy practise locking his hips. This part involved Henry taking him by the waist, slipping his hands down a couple of inches, and tugging gently in a clockwise direction.

Duffy's hips locked, and he found himself in a perfect cueing position; but something seemed to be preventing him from playing the shot. For a start, Henry was half-resting on his back; more noticeably, Henry's large palms, which had been glued to Duffy's hip-bones, had contrived to ease themselves into his trouser pockets. Duffy didn't move. He let Henry rummage around for a while before coughing gently and lining up a brown.

Henry withdrew his hands. 'Just checking the balls were in the right pockets,' he said cheerily.

The lesson continued, with Henry occasionally laying hands on Duffy, who didn't shrug him off but didn't exactly reciprocate. Then they played another frame, which Henry won less easily, though whether this was because Duffy's game had improved or Henry was thinking of other things was impossible to tell. With twenty minutes left before they were expected for tea by Henry's mother, he suggested another lesson. Duffy claimed to have had enough, so they sat down on the creaky leather settle from which men with mutton-chops and big cigars and glasses of port would once have presided over some after-dinner billiards.

'How's Angela?'

'Top-notch. Taken all this stuff like a trooper.'

'I expect you can't wait to get married?' Duffy couldn't resist the question, even if it might be a little cruel, given Henry's recently declared fondness for pocket billiards.

'Rather.'

'Terrible thing to happen to her, though, so soon before the wedding.'

'Fancy old Jimmy turning out to be a psycho.' Henry shook his head sadly.

'You wouldn't have thought him capable, then?'

'Well, that's the point, you can't tell with psychos, can you?'

'Anyway,' said Duffy, 'they'll soon prove whether it was him or not.'

'What do you mean?'

'Well, tests and things.'

'Fingerprints?'

'That sort of thing . . .' Duffy was deliberately drawing it out. 'Not exactly . . .'

'Look, just spit it out. She's my gal, I think I ought to know.'

'Sorry, Henry, it's just a bit . . . embarrassing, really.' Duffy appeared to be broaching a tricky subject with reluctance. 'I was talking to D/S Vine about it. He's very interested in all the latest technology, that sort of stuff. Well, you know what happened to Angela . . . after she was tied up.' Henry looked away and nodded. 'According to Vine, what they can do now is examine it. They've found a way of analysing it. Under a microscope. Sperm,' he said abruptly. 'It's like fingerprints. They can find out where it came from.'

'I've never heard of that,' said Henry.

'Nor had I,' said Duffy. 'Apparently it's pretty new and pretty expensive, so they can only use it in special cases. I mean, someone does a rape in London, they couldn't possibly go round collecting samples from everybody. But in the present case . . . well, Jimmy's denying it, isn't he? It may have happened up at his camp but no one saw him there. Angela didn't recognize him. So obviously they'll make him give a sample and that will clinch it one way or the other.' Duffy paused, waiting for Henry to ask the obvious question. He didn't. 'And of course, if they don't get a match, then that would put Jimmy pretty much in the clear.' Again, no question came. 'And as there can't be that many males who are regular frequenters of Braunscombe Hall, I should think the obvious course would be to come round and collect a few more samples. Eliminate all the obvious candidates, as it were. I'm only guessing. It'd be up to Vine to make the decision.'

Henry nodded and didn't say anything. 'What about tea?' Duffy suggested.

Henry's mother was in the conservatory, surrounded by Kew Gardens. She still had on her pink running-shoes but was now in a cream linen suit with lots of beads round her neck. Except that they wouldn't be just beads, any more than Henry's snooker balls would be made of super-crystallate.

'Still wearing that nasty tie you borrowed from the crook.'

'He doesn't have a criminal record, if you must know.' Suddenly, Duffy felt defensive about old Vic, even if he was a bit of a chancer.

'That's a very narrow definition of a crook. If you had to have a criminal record to be a crook . . . Take Henry, for instance.'

'Mother!'

'Well, you're a crook, aren't you, dear?' Duffy noted that the first time Henry's mother had used a term of endearment to her son was in the same breath as accusing him of being a criminal. Henry opened his mouth, but his mother went on. 'That diseased veal you sold, remember?'

'We didn't know for sure it was diseased.'

'You mean they hadn't actually died?'

'But you can't obey all the Min. of Ag.'s regulations, otherwise you'd go mad. I only did what any other farmer . . .'

'Exactly. All the other farmers are crooks, too. Are you a crook, by the way?'

'Me?' said Duffy.

'You're certainly wearing a crook's tie. You don't mind my asking?'

'No, sure. I'm a crook, too. You can tell by looking.' Duffy was less charmed on this visit by Henry's mum. He took a bite of fruit cake. That tasted posh as well. Where he came from it was cake with bits of fruit in; here it was fruit with bits of cake in. Easy on the flour, you could hear them shouting.

Henry wasn't saying much, and after a single cup of tea Duffy got up to leave. 'So sorry you have to go,' said Henry's mum brightly. 'Do come again. I still want to be told what goes where.'

By the time Duffy got back to Braunscombe Hall, Detective-Sergeant Vine was installed for another session. The analysis on the Datsun had come through but had proved inconclusive: no bomb, no commercial explosives, on the other hand no carbonized squirrel with sharp teeth, and no reports of summer lightning striking at random across the county. A bit of string stuck down the petrol tank, something like that seemed the most likely. An efficient piece of destruction, but less than hi-tech.

D/S Vine had talked to the Datsun's owners again, and Sally had had a small confession to make. Damian had come along, and offered a small confession of his own. But the morning story and the afternoon story – as Duffy discovered when D/S Vine relayed the latter version to him – were about as similar as a video nasty and a kid's pop-up book. There had been some thinking done while Duffy had been away, and it was pretty clear that Damian had been doing it. There had been some thinking, and also some closing of ranks. Angela, for a start, had been squared.

The new account – the one some expensive lawyers might in the future be hired to defend – went like this. Damian and Sally had, they admitted, been a little naughty in the past. They had, because it was part of the life-style of their generation, dabbled in drugs; well, go to London nowadays and you practically get a free sample as you buy your return ticket, you know what it's like, Mr Vine, sir, don't you? They'd done a little coke in their time, and they were prepared to pay for this sin whatever price society demanded. But they hadn't used for a while, in fact they'd given up going to London. They lived quietly in the country with their friends now. The trouble was, London had come to them. They were being blackmailed by someone they had once bought drugs from, someone who had sought them out and demanded money. They'd paid him three times so far, but he was still greedy. The terrible thing was, they didn't have much money between the two of them, and when they'd mentioned their plight to Angela she had insisted on footing the bill. She was incredibly generous, Angela, and said she had lots of money, but it was all getting out of hand. The blackmailers must have seen Sally taking Ricky for a walk and then killed him; they'd set fire to her car; and they probably had worse things up their sleeve. Could Mr Vine help them, please? Perhaps when Damian made their next payment, which Angela was kindly putting up, and which was due to be handed over at the motorway caff the following day?

Duffy whistled when he heard Vine's version. Not bad for

a couple of hours. The best quick-change artists outside the music hall: from blackmailer to blackmailee in the twinkling of an eye. Angela changed from victim to sterling friend as soon as you turned your back. Roll up, roll up, and watch posh people closing ranks! Duffy supplied the earlier account of events and it was Vine's turn to whistle. 'It makes you just want to let them all get on with it, doesn't it?' he said.

'But you won't.'

'Not if they're blowing up cars, et cetera.'

'Sure.'

'After all, we're still after the same person or persons. Then, when we catch them, we'll decide whether to do them for blackmail or pushing.'

'You're going to have to alert London.'

'I know.'

'Pity we couldn't have had that raid on the Hall.' Duffy wished he'd been able to watch Damian being held upside-down by a muscular police sergeant while all sorts of pills and powders and funny tobacco fell out of his trouser pockets. But what hadn't been destroyed before Detective-Sergeant Vine's first visit would certainly have been flushed away by now.

Vine didn't need any help from Duffy in planning things for the next day. He would alert London, get the local drugs squad back off traffic duty, arrange the tail, fix for a takeover vehicle half-way to London, and so on. But perhaps Duffy might like to sit in on the drop; just in case the messenger turned out to be local. Wouldn't do to scare him away with a familiar face. Duffy accepted.

●

He stayed away from the Hall that evening. He didn't want to meet Lucretia in the family room and be told whether he was funny ha-ha or funny peculiar. He didn't want to sit opposite Damian at dinner and find him shiny with self-confidence again, all plumped up with how cleverly he'd snookered D/S Vine and how he and Sally might be looking at not much more than a suspended sentence, max. He didn't want to run into Angela and start wondering how she woozily

728

sorted out what she thought of her charming friends; nor did he much want to look at her and remember Henry's big red hands sliding into his trousers. 'Just checking if the balls are in the right pockets.' Duffy sat in the motorway caff pushing a lukewarm shepherd's pie round his plate, and sipping at the alcohol-free lager he'd chosen to counteract the effects of the shovelful of chips with which he'd anointed his pie. After a slice of fruit tart and a plain yoghurt he returned to the Hall and went to bed early, taking care not to disturb the others.

'Any advice?' said Damian the next morning when they ran into one another on the terrace. Duffy, keen to get out of the house, had gone for an uncharacteristic walk: an hour or so of plodding head-down through the woods, watching out for nettles and bear-traps, trying not to OD on the country air.

'You mean generally?' Duffy could have got quite enthusiastic when it came to giving general advice to Damian.

'About this evening. My big night. PC Plod has told you, I assume.'

'Right. Don't play to the audience, that's all.'

'What audience?'

'Well, me for a start.'

'You? I am touched. Maybe we should meet for a gourmet Colonel Sanders beforehand or something.'

'You don't amuse me I'm afraid.'

'Oh.' Damian's face fell theatrically. 'Come on. You used to like me. A bit, anyway. Didn't you? Didn't you think I was brave about the cars?'

'By the way, if there's any trouble . . .'

'Trouble?'

'If there's any trouble, if, say, for instance, they decide to rough you up a little, don't worry. The coppers, who have been thoroughly informed of the esteem in which you hold them, will come running almost as fast as they're able.' That seemed to dispose of the confident expression on Damian's face.

A van prominently marked DUFFY SECURITY probably wouldn't look too clever in the motorway caff car-park, so Duffy drove to the police station and took a lift with one of the tails. He was in position at a table by the door well in advance. At a quarter to seven Damian arrived, to be greeted like an old friend by one of the girls at the self-service counter. After a little ostentatious flirting he took a cup of coffee across to a table overlooking the car-park.

Duffy played with his food and tried to guess from the backs of customers coming past him which was Damian's meet. After about eight wrong guesses he picked right: a short fellow, mid-twenties, in a jeans jacket, who stood rather impatiently in the queue, tapping his foot as he waited to buy a cup of tea and a pork pie. The caff was by no means full, and Duffy noted with amusement how Damian and his meet played an elaborate game of dumb show before they ended up sharing a table. Damian did well: Duffy scarcely noted the envelope change hands. After a while, the runner got up. Duffy rose at the same moment, and spent some time scrabbling in his pockets looking for a tip to leave on the table. His head was down as he did this, but his eyes were not. Five five, he said to himself, dark brown hair over the collar, black eyes, broad face, bump in the nose, thin lips, ring in the left ear, jeans jacket, green T-shirt, black trousers, running-shoes, brand uncertain, but basic colour maroon. Do you see the man you observed on that occasion in court today? Would you point him out, please? Thank you.

Duffy didn't look at Damian, who had been instructed to wait at least ten minutes, and followed the man outside. He didn't need to keep close, because he wasn't tailing him: if Damian's table overlooked the car-park, the car-park equally overlooked Damian's table, and the officers who were to take the first stretch had already examined Damian's meet. Duffy got into D/S Vine's unmarked Cortina and watched the tail begin.

'I hate this bit.'

'Right,' said Vine. 'You set it up and then it just runs away from you. Those buggers in London either screw it all up or they claim all the credit. How did the boy do?'

'All right. I mean he didn't drop the envelope or anything. Looked a bit nervous, but that was what he was meant to be. I don't think the runner had a degree in psychology.'

'Right. Well, it's back to the station, then.'

They left the radio channel open, without expecting to hear much. The runner had climbed into a brown Fiesta and headed off south down the motorway. The coppers, who were under instruction to use as few words as possible, probably wouldn't break radio silence until the first change-over at the Watford Gap, or perhaps even beyond that. Vine and Duffy chatted about the case. Vine confirmed that Jimmy's condition, and Jimmy's story, both remained the same. Duffy asked Vine about the semen test he'd outlined to Henry that afternoon.

'Never heard of it,' said Vine. 'Hasn't reached the sticks yet.' He chuckled. 'Shouldn't think it'll be too popular with the medical fellows. Bad enough taking all that blood and pee. Now they'll be giving out test-tubes with big wide ends or something.'

'What if someone refused to give a sample?' Duffy chuckled. 'Do you think they'd have to . . .'

'Shh.' Vine cocked an ear towards the radio. 'That's funny.'

The brown Fiesta, heading south from intersection 13, had turned off at intersection 11. But it hadn't gone east, and it hadn't gone west. It had rejoined the motorway and was now heading back north again. Vine pulled over and they waited in silence for the next report.

They looked at one another when they heard that the Fiesta had turned off at intersection 13, and was heading straight back into Vine's manor. At first its direction seemed to be Talworth, then Illingham, then, after a bit of circling around, it seemed to settle on Fen Burton as a destination. Vine drove fast enough to get to the Seven Bells free house within five minutes of the brown Fiesta's arrival. He got out and talked to the policeman in the tailing car, then came back to Duffy.

'One of them's gone in after him. Should be another car along in a couple of minutes.'

'I suppose,' said Duffy, 'that as I'm not on duty, there wouldn't be any objection to a citizen having a drink himself.'

'As long as you're not planning to drive afterwards, sir.'

Duffy strolled across the road to the Seven Bells. It was a normal village pub with all the traditional country entertainments like a juke box, a Space Invader machine and a one-armed bandit. To the background of this quiet popping and bleeping and blaring a couple of dozen locals were sinking a choice of eight different beers. Duffy ordered half a pint of something he'd never heard of, found a secluded table, nodded to the nearest drinkers, and looked around. He could almost not quite pick out the plain-clothes copper, who was sitting up at the bar. The driver of the brown Fiesta was in the far corner, pretending to watch a darts game, but scuttling a glance towards the door whenever he heard a noise. After a while he looked up and then didn't look down immediately. Here he comes, thought Duffy, and squinted sideways without raising his head as a man walked past. He wasn't big, but he was strongly built; either that or he had shoulder-pads in his raincoat. He bought a drink and went to sit by his runner. Duffy could see him in profile now and immediately ruled out the possibility of shoulder-pads.

There was always something faintly pleasant about watching a suspect who didn't know he was being watched. And in the present case, the pleasure was more than faint. Duffy watched the figures as they nodded and sipped their drinks; he noticed the envelope being transferred quite openly from one pocket to another; he smiled as the runner got up, hunched his shoulders in his jeans jacket, ducked his head as a farewell, and headed towards the door.

Duffy continued to smile as he got slowly to his feet, a near-empty half-pint mug in his hand. Slowly he walked along the bar, deliberately nudging the copper as he went past. When he reached the corner near the darts players, he said quietly, 'Can I buy you the other half, Taffy?'

At this point things got a bit messy. Taffy half-stood up, a little bit of beer-foam glistening on his jazz-man's beard, and said with an answering smile, 'Why don't I get it?'

Duffy backed off a little but was firm. 'No, it's my turn.'

Taffy, now fully on his feet, politely declined. 'Oh, but I insist.'

Duffy remained untouched by such generosity. 'I really can't let you pay, I'm afraid.'

The conversation stalemated, Taffy resorted to non-verbal communication. Perhaps it was a tactic he'd picked up from *Theories of Social Revolt*. He shoulder-charged Duffy, who might have been knocked flat if he hadn't half-turned and shoved his beer-glass at Taffy's head. The unplanned angle of Duffy's attack meant that the glass skidded off the side of the jazz-man's face but did not break. A long red mark on Taffy's cheek began to pop blood. Both men were half off-balance. In Duffy's philosophy of fighting, if you had a small weapon and your opponent, though unarmed, had a reputation for thumping people with iron bars, then you got your retaliation in first. He pulled back his arm and prepared to mug Taffy more seriously this time, when his fist got stuck up in the air and a rural voice, belonging to someone who thought hooligans should fight in their own pubs, not other people's, said, 'You bloody yob.' The voice's owner bent Duffy's forearm slowly behind his back; Taffy, surprised by such impartial intervention, thumped Duffy once more as he ran past.

The plain-clothes man at the bar obviously thought that showing Taffy his warrant card wouldn't cut much ice, so he tripped him up as he ran and watched unsentimentally as Taffy's fall took him into a glass table full of drinks. Then he sat on his head, shouted 'Police', ordered two of the heftiest locals to hold down Taffy's legs, and waved his warrant card when they hesitated. Everyone panted heavily for a while, then Duffy was frog-marched across the bar by his unseen assailant, who said proudly to the plain-clothes man, 'I got the other one for you.'

'Well, well, well,' said Vine as Duffy, still puffing, settled himself in the front seat of the Cortina a few minutes later. 'Now that is what I call an abuse of hospitality.'

'Poor old Vic.' Not that Duffy really meant it. It was nice to catch someone like Vic being naïve for once.

'Where do you think Taffy got his supplies?' Duffy asked.

'London, probably. We'll have a go, but I shouldn't think we'll get anywhere. He looks a tough nut.'

'It pisses me off that you never find out.'

'Well, if you want someone to blame,' said Vine, 'it goes like this. Taffy bought it in London from someone else, who bought it from an importer, who got it from somewhere tacky in Spain, who had it flown in from the West Indies, who had it flown in from probably Colombia, where it was grown by

733

a peasant who you can't blame because he can't live off any crop apart from that because his land is so poor, and then does that make it the Government's fault, well no because the Government's only a puppet Government, so who's paying the bills and you end up with Washington, and so you blame the American President. Why not?'

'Are you political by any chance?'

'No, I'm just saying you go daft if you start thinking about it. We got two tonight. They may not be big, but we got two, and that's a good night's shopping.'

'Check. You might have a problem with the charges, though.'

'How do you mean?'

'Well, Damian's story, which you're acting on, was that he was being blackmailed. So it depends on how Taffy reacts to that. If he knows he's going down, would he rather go down for blackmail or for drugs? He'd have to weigh up the sentencing, wouldn't he? And if it seemed six of one and half a dozen of the other, he might just want to take Damian down with him.'

'He might.'

'Do you get more for blackmail or for drugs around here?'

'Bit of a toss-up. Depends on the drugs. Depends on which judge you draw. Depends what he had for breakfast.'

'Sounds like a good pay-day for the lawyers.'

Vine nodded. 'I don't think I'd like to be that Damian fellow over the next few months,' he said.

'I'll pass it on.'

Vine dropped him at the station and Duffy picked up the van. It had been a good evening. Something had got solved, and he'd hardly been beaten up. He reckoned the local force should consider recruiting that fellow who had held back his arm. Except he was probably earning more dragging double-decker buses along by his teeth at local fairs.

Duffy returned to Braunscombe Hall with the cheerfulness of someone bearing interesting news. He might just put Damian through it a bit as well. But when he got there, he didn't have the chance. A late-night parliamentary session consisting of Vic, Belinda, Lucretia and a depleted whisky bottle was gathered at the kitchen table. They looked up at Duffy when he came in, but didn't greet him. OK, so he wasn't popular, well, stuff that, thought Duffy. They can bloody well hear the latest about two of their esteemed house-guests.

He had just shuffled his chair into position when Vic said, 'Henry shot himself.'

'Christ. Dead?'

'Oh yes, dead. He wouldn't miss from that range. Gave himself both barrels.'

'I don't want to hear this again,' said Belinda. 'I'll go and see how Ange is sleeping.'

'About six o'clock this evening,' said Vic, answering the unasked question. 'He did it in the snooker room. Didn't leave a note or anything.'

'Billiard room,' said Duffy. 'They called it the billiard room there.'

'His mum found him, apparently. Said there was blood all over the cloth.'

'How's Angela taking it?'

'She just wanted some pills. So we called the doctor and he told us what to let her have, and she's been out ever since.'

'Christ,' said Duffy. 'I didn't think he'd do that.' He coughed, and instead of explaining his heroic role in the capture of a criminal house-guest, found himself explaining his unheroic role in the suicide of a neighbour. He told them about his first snooker lesson, his second snooker lesson, and the conversation that followed it. He told them it all as accurately as he could remember, in preparation for repeating it to D/S Vine. He missed out the bit about Vine never having heard of semen typing.

'You killed him,' said Lucretia at the end.

'No, he killed himself,' said Duffy. 'That's what suicide means. You kill yourself.' It was a point people often preferred to evade.

'You killed him.'

'He did that thing to your friend Angela in the woods,' said Duffy. 'He was quite happy to see your friend Jimmy go down for ten years. And when he thought he might get found

735

out he didn't make it easier for either of them, did he? Or his mum for that matter.'

'His mother's an old cow,' said Lucretia.

'So he did all that other stuff, then?' Vic asked.

'He did all the harassing to start off with. Maybe he thought he'd drive her a bit nutty, then he wouldn't have to marry her. She came to you for protection, and he decided to up the ante. Use more forceful methods.'

'Why didn't he just break off the engagement?' Lucretia was still asking the obvious, and therefore difficult, questions.

'Dunno. Maybe he reckoned people would start looking at him if he did that, start wondering if he was queer or something. Maybe he thought if Angela pulled out or went potty, he wouldn't ever have to marry. Could play the tragic lover with the broken engagement and that would last until his mum died and then the pressure would be off. Look, maybe it's a bit like at the greyhound racing, people betting against their own dogs. It doesn't make sense to you, but it makes sense to them.'

'Oh, spare us your working-class analogies,' said Lucretia.

'Talking of dogs,' said Vic. 'Did he do Ricky?'

'No, someone else did Ricky. That wasn't Henry.'

'Are you queer as well?' The question did not come from Vic.

Duffy looked at Lucretia. 'It depends,' he replied. 'Sometimes I don't think you'd notice the difference.'

'You're queer. You killed Henry and you're queer.' It came with sudden violence, as if she really had fancied Duffy all along and was now relieved to have found a belated excuse for having turned him down. Duffy registered her tone of voice, as you would register a belt round the ear; its possible implications only came to him later.

'Kids,' said Vic wearily, 'that's enough for tonight.'

Duffy woke up feeling depressed. It was a beautiful autumn morning, with a crisp sun and the sky a super-crystallate blue; there was a crust of russet on the woods to the south. He had solved a case, and Mrs Colin had brought him breakfast in bed with a smile that seemed to exceed the call of duty. But Duffy felt depressed. He longed to be back in London where, on the whole, blokes didn't half-rape their fiancées and then top themselves because they felt a stir at tight-trousered bums bent over snooker tables. He remembered Vic's sentimental homage to social mobility and rearranged it while he shaved. England is a place where your Rons can steal from your Vics, where your Damians can blackmail your Angelas, where your Taffies can strongarm your Sallies, and where your Henries will let your Jimmies go to the stake for them.

Most of the morning was spent with D/S Vine. Taffy was still dishing out the expected line about the two thousand quid in the brown envelope being a gambling debt; but the runner wasn't so smart, and Vine thought they'd break through quite soon. Whether they could pin the dog and the car directly on Taffy was the only problem area. He might well have contracted out for these two jobs.

'He claims to have this phobia about fire,' said Duffy, 'so he may have got someone else in. On the other hand, he could just have been lying.'

'Odd how they can't tell the truth, isn't it? It's a sort of habit, I suppose. And the trouble is, it gets infectious. I mean, us coppers sometimes find ourselves telling a few fibs as well, just to see how they react.'

'You might find yourself fibbing about the dog and the car?'

'Always possible. Finding dog-hairs in his trouser pockets, that sort of thing. Course I wouldn't have to do it if he told the truth. By the way, why do you reckon he did the dog? Given that it wasn't Sally's.'

'I thought about that,' said Duffy. 'I guess it was just handy. It didn't have to be Sally's, and it was a bonus that she was fond of Ricky. She was obviously meant to find out what they'd done to it, and then a nasty phone-call. Your turn next, darling, or whatever. Except Vic got tidy-minded and the dog did a runner.'

Two things happened after lunch. As they rose from the table, Damian reminded Duffy about their return snooker match.

'I was thinking of getting back quite soon, actually.'

'You can't let me down. Not now. After all, they might not have a table in the slammer.'

They went along to the billiard room and shut the curtains against the bright autumn sun. Before he broke, Damian melodramatically pulled apart the lids of his right eye with two fingers and put his face up close to Duffy's. 'Look, no marching powder,' he declared. Then, without the help of anything illegal, he beat Duffy by two frames to none. Duffy's heart wasn't in it; besides, Vic's table felt like corrugated iron after Henry's Thurston. He wondered why Henry had topped himself where he had. Was it to do with the lessons, or that argument he'd had with his mum about replacing the cloth? Was it because that part of the house was originally intended only for men? Perhaps it was mere chance – he just happened to be there when the terrible decision made itself for him. Damian set up a third frame and blasted the reds apart. To Duffy they looked like a glistening scatter of blood on an 1866 Thurston. It was time to go. He racked his cue and left Damian to it.

The second thing happened just as Duffy was about to depart. There was a scream from upstairs; a woman's scream, and quite loud. Then there was some banging of doors. Duffy told himself firmly that it was probably nothing more than Sally making up her mind who to do fucky-fuck with. This reminded him to say goodbye to Mrs Colin. He found her in the kitchen. They nodded and smiled at one another for a minute or so, as if neither of them was fluent in English.

He explained to Vic that he'd have to come back to the Buckinghamshire/Bedfordshire borders to give evidence, first at the inquest – though somehow he felt he mightn't be called – and later at the trial. But he thought he wouldn't stay at the Hall if that was all right. On the other hand, Vic might like to take out a regular maintenance contract for the alarm system.

'Oh, I don't think I'll bother,' said Vic. 'It seems to be working pretty well. And I'm sure you'll knock me out a decent price if anything goes wrong. Just for old times' sake.'

Duffy nodded. 'I'll think it over. By the way, what was all that screaming?'

'That was Angela, I'm afraid. They let Jimmy out, he came straight round here. Only natural, I suppose. Wanted to see Angela, well, that was natural, too, wasn't it? She's still in bed, in this little cot in our room, like we told you.' Duffy imagined the scene. 'Soon as old Jimmy sees her, what does he do? Gets down on his knees and asks her to marry him.'

Duffy shook his head sadly and climbed into his white Sherpa van. 'He'll never get anything right, will he?' Then he slid the door shut and did a racing turn in front of the porch which fucked up Vic's gravel properly. He drove fast until he got to the bright brick entrance pillars bearing aloft the family arms of the Blessing-Crowther dynasty: Two Tits Rampant with a weathered ferret crawling all over them. Perhaps they should stick another animal on the unoccupied stone globe, for balance. Like a drowned dog.

●

A few days later, Duffy was carrying his bright yellow laundry-bag up Goldsmith Avenue, Acton W3. It was a dull Sunday morning, and there was a spatter of rain about, but Duffy felt content. He'd had a good breakfast at Sam Widges, and for once it had been his lucky day: the laundromat had disgorged exactly the same number of socks as he'd fed into it. He sucked in the acrid, dusty, fumey air, still loaded with Saturday night's smells, and it tasted good to him. He thought of young Karl French, lean as a whippet, pounding the roads in preparation for the football season. Well, he was a striker, after all. Walking to the launderette with a heavy bag of clothes and walking all the way back again on a full stomach was quite enough exercise to keep a goalie in trim.

Three hours later he and Carol sat over the fish in low-calorie sauce which had survived Duffy's absence uneaten. He was still brooding about his stay at Braunscombe Hall.

'Does it ever strike you that the country's going to the dogs?'

'I think it's always been like this, Duffy.'

'I'm beginning to wonder if it's such a good idea for your

Vics to mingle with your Damians and your Damians to go camping with your Henries.' Carol wisely let this inscrutable utterance pass. 'I mean, down at that place, they were all doing something naughty. They should all have been arrested, all of them.'

'Even that one you fancied?'

'Lucretia? I didn't say I fancied her.'

'You didn't have to.'

Hmm. Carol knew him well and no mistake. Not that it was always too bad, being known well. 'Lucretia,' he said forcefully, 'Lucretia should have been arrested just for being Lucretia.'

'Duffy, you are a scream. But it's all right, you know. Anyway, what do.you think of the fish?'

Duffy took a gourmet's tiny forkful and ingested it with a careful frown. 'I think it needs a little more saffron,' he announced.

Carol giggled. 'Do you know what saffron tastes like?'

'Actually,' he replied, with as severe a face as he could manage, 'I haven't the slightest idea.'

FOR THE BEST IN PAPERBACKS, LOOK FOR THE 🐧

In every corner of the world, on every subject under the sun, Penguin represents quality and variety – the very best in publishing today.

For complete information about books available from Penguin – including Puffins, Penguin Classics and Arkana – and how to order them, write to us at the appropriate address below. Please note that for copyright reasons the selection of books varies from country to country.

A CHOICE OF PENGUIN FICTION

The Woman in Black Susan Hill

Young Arthur Kipps had no suspicion that Eel Marsh House guarded the memories of a pitiful secret – nor did he understand that the black-robed woman who inhabited its shuttered rooms exacted a terrible revenge. 'Authentically chilling' – *Sunday Times*

A Handful of Dust Evelyn Waugh

From a decaying country estate to the decadent savagery of thirties London society, and finally to a living hell in the Brazilian jungle ... With cold comedy and lacerating irony, Waugh's masterpiece traces the break-up of a marriage.

Animal Farm George Orwell

'The creatures outside looked from pig to man, and from man to pig, and from pig to man again; but already it was impossible to say which was which.' Orwell's fable of a revolution that went wrong has become the classic satire of the twentieth century.

The Old Devils Kingsley Amis

This Booker Prize-winning novel about Alun Weaver's and his wife's return to their Celtic roots is 'vintage Kingsley Amis, 50 per cent pure alcohol with splashes of sad savagery' – *The Times*. 'Crackling with marvellous Taff comedy ... this is probably Mr Amis's best book since *Lucky Jim*' – *Guardian*

Him with His Foot in His Mouth Saul Bellow

A collection of first-class short stories. 'If there is a better living writer of fiction, I'd very much like to know who he or she is' – *The Times*

A CHOICE OF PENGUIN FICTION

Stars and Bars William Boyd

Well-dressed, quite handsome, unfailingly polite and charming, who would guess that Henderson Dores, the innocent Englishman abroad in wicked America, has a guilty secret? 'Without doubt his best book so far … made me laugh out loud' – *The Times*

Difficulties With Girls Kingsley Amis

Last seen in *Take a Girl Like You*, Patrick Standish and Jenny, née Bunn, are now married and up-and-coming south of the Thames. Unfortunately, like his neighbours, Patrick continues to have difficulties with girls... 'Very funny … vintage Amis' – *Guardian*

The Levant Trilogy Olivia Manning

The concluding trilogy of *Fortunes of War*. 'The finest fictional record of the war produced by a British writer. Her gallery of personages is huge, her scene painting superb, her pathos controlled, her humour quiet and civilized' – *Sunday Times*

July's People Nadine Gordimer

'So flawlessly written that every one of its events seems chillingly, ominously possible' – *The New York Times Book Review*. 'This is the best novel that Miss Gordimer has ever written' – Alan Paton

The Vivisector Patrick White

In this prodigious novel about the life and death of a great painter, Patrick White, winner of the Nobel Prize for Literature, illuminates creative experience with unique truthfulness.